PENGUIN BOOKS

# THE PORTABLE CONRAD

Each volume in The Viking Portable Library either presents a representative selection from the works of a single outstanding writer or offers a comprehensive anthology on a special subject. Averaging 700 pages in length and designed for compactness and readability, these books fill a need not met by other compilations. All are edited by distinguished authorities, who have written introductory essays and included much other helpful material.

"The Viking Portables have done more for good reading and good writers than anything that has come along since I can remember."
—Arthur Mizener

Morton Dauwen Zabel was Professor of English at the University of Chicago. He is the author of *Craft and Character in Modern Fiction, Literary Opinion in America, The Masters of American Literature;* and co-author of *Literary History of the United States* and *Forms of Modern Fiction.* Professor Zabel also edited the works of Henry James and Charles Dickens.

*The Portable*

# CONRAD

EDITED, AND WITH AN INTRODUCTION AND NOTES, BY

MORTON DAUWEN ZABEL

Revised by Frederick R. Karl
The City College, City University of New York

PENGUIN BOOKS

PENGUIN BOOKS
Published by the Penguin Group
Viking Penguin Inc., 40 West 23rd Street, New York, New York 10010, U.S.A.
Penguin Books Ltd, 27 Wrights Lane, London W8 5TZ, England
Penguin Books Australia Ltd, Ringwood, Victoria, Australia
Penguin Books Canada Ltd, 2801 John Street,
Markham, Ontario, Canada L3R 1B4
Penguin Books (N.Z.) Ltd, 182–190 Wairau Road,
Auckland 10, New Zealand

Penguin Books Ltd, Registered Offices:
Harmondsworth, Middlesex, England

First published in the United States of America by The Viking Press 1947
Revised edition published 1969
Reprinted 1972, 1973, 1974, 1975
Published in Penguin Books 1976

10 9

LIBRARY OF CONGRESS CATALOGING IN PUBLICATION DATA
Conrad, Joseph, 1857–1924.
The portable Conrad.
Reprint of the 1969 ed. published by The Viking Press, New York, which was
issued as P33 of the Viking portable library. Originally published in 1947.
I. Title
PZ3.C764PS9     [PR6005.04]     823'.9'12     76-48272
ISBN 0 14 015. 033 1

Printed in the United States of America
by Kingsport Press, Inc., Kingsport, Tennessee
Set in Linotype Caledonia

Thanks are due to Doubleday & Company, Inc., New York, for permission to
reprint the Conrad text in this volume. All the selections are copyright and may
not be reproduced without their permission. Acknowledgment is made also to
Yale University Press, New Haven, for excerpts from *Letters of Joseph Conrad
to Marguerite Poradowska*. Thanks are due in addition to J. M. Dent & Sons
Ltd., Methuen & Co., Ltd., William Heinemann Ltd., Ernest Benn Limited, and
William Blackwood & Sons Ltd., London.

# Contents

v

EUROPE, ASIA, AND THE EAST

ON LIFE AND LETTERS

# Editor's Introduction

ON AUGUST 3, 1924, Joseph Conrad died at his last English home, Oswalds, Bishopsbourne, near Canterbury, in the sixty-seventh year of his life. On the title-page of his last completed novel, *The Rover*, in 1923, he had set two lines from Spenser:

Sleep after toyle, port after stormie seas,
Ease after warre, death after life, does greatly please.

The same words were later cut in the stone that was raised on his grave in the cemetery at Canterbury.

The man who reached his final port in a quiet English country graveyard had weathered, before he reached it, stormier seas than figure in the careers of most literary artists. They were not only the perils of the oceans he had sailed for almost twenty years of his life; they were the storms of a spirit whose toil and warfare had been harsh and unrelenting. They had begun in another land, the Poland of his boyhood where, as Jozef Teodor Konrad Nałęcz Korzeniowski, he was born in 1857, and where his people had fought and suffered in the cause of rebellion against a hated occupation. Fifty years before his death he had left that country to turn westward, leaving behind him a family decimated by death and exile, and boarding the Vienna express in Cracow for France "as a man might get into a dream." The dream took him to the ends of the earth: to Marseilles,

1

to the coasts of Spain as a gun-runner for the Carlists, to the West Indies, to England, to Asia and the East, across seas he sailed as a common seaman, mate, and master for nearly twenty years. In 1894 he left his last ship in London to enter on a voyage even more hazardous to a man of his tense, unconfident nature. "Alone in the world," and armed only with the unfinished manuscript of a story he had been writing for five years in the ports and ships of his travels, he had dared to become a writer in a language foreign to him. From that moment his life was to be a long uncompromising labor on the books that slowly, after another twenty years of severe endurances and discouragements, brought him to a position of pre-eminence in the English-speaking world and beyond it. And at the height of that fame he died.

Only Conrad himself, and those closest to him, knew the full irony of that tardy recognition. When the value and lesson of his books might have been most useful to the literature of his era, they were—except by a band of faithful admirers and fellow-artists—largely ignored in favor of the slacker fiction and dull prose preferred by the popular taste of late-Victorian and Edwardian England. An apotheosis—romantic, fabulous, always uneasy and somehow incredible to him—attended his last years and lingered for some time beyond his death. Then a reaction, the inevitable probationary reaction of literary reputation, set in as the violence and cynicism of contemporary events and attitudes in a disrupted time—the two decades *entre deux guerres:* 1918-39—disputed the note of heroic idealism Conrad has sounded. Today, almost a quarter-century after his death, when the world in which his tales are set has receded to historic distance and become, with its standards of honor and fidelity, a dimming memory in men's minds, his work may appear to take on the quality of an elegiac memorial to a vanished and simpler order of life. So it would be in fact had Conrad been nothing more than the romantic fabulist, the yarn-spinner of maritime tradition, his belated public too glibly credited him with being.

But he was more than that—more by his own intention and harassed protestation; more by the achieved insight and artistry of his finest work; more by the recognition that came to him early and late from his greatest contemporaries in England and Europe—Henry James, H. G. Wells, Thomas Mann, André Gide, Paul Valéry; more by comparison with the greater part of the English literature of an era whose hazards he, as much as any man of his time, helped to define and to redeem. Historically considered alone, he now appears an English writer of European and world stature in an age too readily given to the easy rewards of sentimental provincialism and complacent nationalisms. There will probably always adhere to his name some of the distinction that comes from contemporary comparison; but the fact now reappears that a distinction belongs to him which confines him to no given period but demands a larger reference, bringing him into the highest company the English, and the European, novel provides. It is a distinction that entails certain firm discriminations in his own production, but it also reveals an honor in craftsmanship and purpose which only a few novelists of his age can as justly claim.

II

Conrad's first book, *Almayer's Folly*, was published in 1895, the year in which Hardy retired from fiction under the blast of censure directed against *Jude the Obscure*. The Victorian masters of the novel were gone or aging; it was a low point in the fortunes of English fiction, and a sense of crisis possessed the survivors in that art. Hardy's retreat was symptomatic of the situation. Meredith had driven the new values of intellection and sensibility to the desperate brink of what Henley rightly called "spiritual suicide." The great claims for the novel that had been advanced in France and elsewhere in Europe were met—at that moment even by Henry James, their greatest defender in the English-speaking world—with uneasiness and doubt. The Victorian novel had expanded, explored, digressed, moralized, and conquered. It had created, like the age that fathered it, a new world of matter and experience. But then, as recurrently in the history of fiction, the vagaries and instability of the art seemed bent on confounding its privileges. No other art is so treacherously empirical in its conditions, so insecure in tradition, so much the vehicle and the victim of specialized and limiting principles. It becomes alternately obsessed by documentation and reform, or recklessly indulgent of wayward impulses and the selective techniques of innovation—naturalism, impressionism, psychological method, symbolic impulse. Whatever the reason, the novel appears to exhaust its larger force and energy and to arrive at an impasse of demoralization every quarter-century or so. We have seen such crises in our own century. Another was apparent fifty years ago when Conrad began to write.

Such moments redeem themselves by the challenge and test they offer, and their heroes are the men capable of surviving these. It was the fortune of English literature at that final hour of the nineteenth century that it was not, despite the prevalent abdication from artistic authority of many gifted talents, lacking in defenders. Of the verse of that decade T. S. Eliot has remarked:

"Whatever may be said of the poetry of the nineties, it cannot be accused of inbreeding." The same plea may be argued for the fiction of the nineties. What the example of France was giving to the poetry of the moment through the services of Symons, Dowson, and the Rhymers, what Ireland was giving it through Yeats, and what the classics were giving it through Lionel Johnson, a new growth in curiosity and invention was giving to fiction in its gropings toward renovation and a reviving discipline. The ferment of a new spirit was in the air. Kipling burst upon the scene with the lore of Empire and Orient. George Moore advanced the claims of French naturalism. Wells offered the zest of the scientific fable and a new social comedy. French and Russian masters appeared in multiplying translations. Stephen Crane—it is notable how much of the genuine talent of the decade came from outside England—presently came from America to contribute his accurate eye and phrase to story-telling. Another American, Henry James, was continuing his labors, not only by carrying the art of fiction to constantly greater refinements and insights, but by defending their necessity in his critical writings. Ford Madox Hueffer mingled the foreign sympathies of Germany and Pre-Raphaelism in his promising talent. All, or almost all, of these men considered innovations in subject matter suspect without an accompanying discipline in form and technique. It was the moment for curiosity, novelty, exoticism, but it was the moment of aestheticism too; of form, style, and the *mot juste;* and Flaubert, Stendhal, and Turgenev had as much to say to English novelists as Symbolism and Parnassianism had to give to poets. Only one thing was lacking in the English scene of 1895 to make these stirrings of the anti-provincial conscience complete and that was someone to bring into English writing the tragic vision, the tenacious endurances, and the fathoming probity that seemed at that moment to belong to Eastern and Slavic Europe, out of which the great books of Turgenev, Tolstoy, and Dostoevsky had come. *Almayer's Folly*, which combined exotic material with a passionate emotion unlike anything else then perceptible in English story-telling, announced an arresting talent. Men concerned with watching the weather of art were soon conscious of a new force in the air.

Conrad thus entered the scene at a crucial and—in spite of the neglect he suffered for almost twenty years— a strategic moment. It is difficult to think of him in an earlier phase of Victorian literature. His talent was joined with a historic opportunity, one whose advantages he is now seen to share with James, Crane, and only a few other men of that hour. He already had behind him a fair lifetime of ordeal and adventure: he was thirty-eight when his first book was published. He offers the rare example of a man who was middle-aged before he took up the profession of literature. He presents, of course, an even rarer case, something George Gissing early announced as "one of the miracles of literature" and for which Thomas Mann was later to find a single European comparison in Chamisso—a novelist who challenged the public and its critics, and arrived at mastery, in a language not natively his own. Conrad was to convert both these liabilities into assets. His distinction originates as much in the maturity of vision he brought to his task as in the tests a mastered language imposed on his conscience and sensibility. It attaches also— doubtless by reason of his being beyond the age for youthful partisanships and literary politics—to the non-sectarian, unspecialized, untactical view he took of the aesthetic vogues and tactics around him.

The assertive dignity—solitary, willful, askance—of

his nature was soon apparent. In a preface he wrote for his first book in 1895, he wryly rejected a lady critic's description of his tale and characters as "decivilized." "A judgment that has nothing to do with justice," he called it. "I am speaking here of men and women—not of the charming and graceful phantoms that move about in our mud and smoke and are softly luminous with the radiance of all our virtues; that are possessed of all refinements, of all sensibilities, of all wisdom—but, being only phantoms, possess no heart . . . I am content to sympathize with common mortals, no matter where they live." Amateur in literature though he was, he sensed the predicament of his art at the outset, and his instinct soon became articulate. Though early enlisted by his first literary friends—James, Crane, and others— in the search for "form" and the *mot juste,* he had an extreme aversion to the specialized theories that were encouraging the novel of arbitrary limits and schematized content. His youthful devotion to Marryat, Cooper, and the Dickens of *Bleak House,* whom he had read as a boy in Poland, now balanced his admiration of Flaubert, Turgenev, and James. He considered aestheticism as much "a treacherous ideal" as James did. He disliked Stendhal's conception of the novel as *"un miroir qu'on promène le long d'un chemin"* ("a mirror dawdling down a lane") as much as Yeats did. The great problem of modern art he saw unmistakably. Having revolted against the older conventions of omniscience, dramatic artifice, and moral didacticism, its makers were now falling prey to new formulations— aesthetic, scientific, sociological, technical. They were satisfied with fragments. They objectified their problems in arguments ungrounded in character or action. They evaded their responsibilities by specialized and arbitrary techniques. They were failing, in a new way, to unify principle with substance. They wrote, most of them, under the infirmity of an ideal.

Conrad, as much as Ibsen, more austerely than Butler or Shaw, was by instinct and conviction—and despite his declared purpose "to get at, to bring forth *les valeurs idéales*"—a critic of the ideal in matters of art or morality. He joined the attack—it extends from Blake to Yeats, Proust, and Eliot among modern writers—upon the nineteenth century's seduction by abstractions, by the resounding appeal of moral terms or shibboleths that had lost their basis in conduct or sincerity. Out of his struggle with "illusion," that persistent term of his prose which usually means with him the illusion of untested and self-flattering hopes or impostures, he made the basic principle of his craft. He wrote it down in a few pages of "Preface" when he finished *The Nigger of the "Narcissus"* in 1897, a manifesto whose consciously noble accents and appeals should not disguise its importance as a document in the aesthetics of modern fiction. To the genuine artist "the temporary formulas of his craft" must always appear deceptive. "The enduring part of them—the truth which each only imperfectly veils—should abide with him as the most precious of his possessions, but they all—Realism, Romanticism, Naturalism, even the unofficial Sentimentalism . . .— all these gods must, after a short period of fellowship, abandon him—even on the very threshold of the temple —to the stammerings of his conscience and to the outspoken consciousness of the difficulties of his work." "A work that aspires, however humbly, to the condition of art should carry its justification in very line." "The artist descends within himself, and in that lonely region of stress and strife, if he be deserving and fortunate, he finds the terms of his appeal." "Temperament, whether individual or collective, is not amenable to persuasion." The artist must reveal "the stress and passion within the core of each convincing moment." He must stir in men a "feeling of unavoidable solidarity." "Fiction . . . must be, like painting, like music, like all art, the appeal of one temperament to all the other innumerable temperaments whose subtle and resistless power endows passing events with their true meaning, and creates the moral, the emotional atmosphere of the place and time. Such an appeal, to be effective, must be an impression conveyed through the senses." All art "appeals primarily to the senses . . . if its high desire is to reach the secret spring of responsive emotions." By thus assuming a "complete, unswerving devotion to the perfect blending of form and substance," and by dedicating his talent to achieving the "plasticity" which arrives when form is animated by the living reality of experience and intelligence, Conrad arrived at his declaration of aims: "My task which I am trying to achieve is, by the power of the written word, to make you hear, to make you feel—it is, before all, to make you *see*. That —and no more, and it is everything."

These sentences have become familiar through repetition; they obviously belong to a well-defined line of modern aesthetics. But their bearing on Conrad's own work, and on the whole craft of words in our time, is easily misjudged. They have caused him to be set down as an "impressionist," some kind of literary equivalent of Monet or Renoir, perhaps a forerunner of Virginia Woolf's art of subjective reverie, a classification which some of his slacker or more exotic prose, early and late, encourages. They may appear to connect with the moral ambiguity of Conrad's ideas which caused E. M. Forster to assert that "he is misty at the center as well as at the edges, that the secret casket of his genius contains a vapour rather than a jewel, and that we needn't try to write him down philosophically, because there is, in this direction, nothing to write. No creed, in fact. Only opinions, and the right to throw them overboard when facts make them look absurd. Opinions held under the semblance of eternity, girt with the sea, crowned with stars, and therefore easily mistaken for a creed."

This criticism is radical; and it is not without its partial justice. (It should be said for Forster that it was made of Conrad's essays rather than of his novels.) There is little reason to suppose that, had Conrad expounded his ideas as a moralist, they would not have retained the enigmatic stoicism, somber, suspicious, inscrutable, that appears in his personal writings and beyond which his stubbornly defensive, abruptly secretive nature did not, there, permit him to go. His critical sense of both heroic and personal values in his essays and autobiographical books is constrained and masked. It assumes the diffidence of a moral confessor who offers a flattering brand of the muscular stoicism that has been capitalized by Conrad's more conventional admirers and that has promoted him, in their hands, to the rank of a somber yea-sayer for the stolider manly virtues and moral complacency that readily pass as substitutes for serious thought, tragic insight, and humane virtue in modern writing. But Conrad, though consciously moral in his utterances and standards, was hardly an explicit moralist. He was a novelist, a dramatic artist in human character. His best work is always more than the sum of his conscious motives and critical faculties. He never (apart from his private letters) spoke with his full voice except as an imaginative writer. And even there his voice broke through his scruples, his severe self-scrutiny, and his language with no smooth facility or self-assurance. It was checked by the doubts, uncertainties, and exactions of a brutally rigorous sincerity. He committed himself to his task with none of the excitement and exhilaration of more freely inspired artists.

His creative impulse, declaring itself comparatively late in life, was resolved for him during the years of crisis that followed his return from the desperate journey to Africa and the Congo in 1890—a crisis that tested to the utmost the latent irresolution, excitement, and self-absorption of his temper. His veerings between indolence and despair, his indecision, his lurking sense of guilt in having abandoned the sacred trust of his family's Polish allegiances, his fretting suspicions and trussed-up sense of honor, his tranced compulsion to write in the face of stupendous handicaps of scruple, language, and mental insecurity—these define the state of soul out of which, by an appalling exertion of will power, his books were shaped, their style determined, their characters and method wrought, their actual themes and substance evoked. His tales, with their repeated patterns of conduct, ordeal, and conscience, their tenacious fixity of purpose, their deviously incremental sincerity and exhaustive analysis of static or trance-bound situations, their centripetal mode of moral and dramatic analysis, had their source in a creative necessity of a peculiar kind. Conrad's talent was not instinctively dramatic, not natively inventive, not naturally precocious or boldly inspired. When he said that "the sustained invention of a really telling lie demands a talent which I do not possess," he was indicating one of the hardest conditions of his art.

Writing is, of course, done in many ways. It is done by some happy writers in a state of sustained excitement, those who, like Gustave von Aschenbach, are possessed by "the onward sweep of the productive mechanism . . . that *motus animi continuus* in which, according to Cicero, eloquence resides." Some, like the

Abbé Morellet, find "the quill dashing over the paper with a heavenly speed." Still others, like Flaubert, may wrestle for days on end to find a single exact word or turn over the pages of four weighty volumes from the Colonial Ministry to locate the right name of an African mineral for a sentence in *Salammbô*. The happiest are probably those who coolly dominate and control their material. For Conrad none of these privileges was possible. Neither the daily requirements of bread-winning nor the nature of his imagination permitted them. He was condemned to a compulsion that drove and baffled him. He consciously likened himself to a criminal dragging "the ball and chain of one's selfhood to the end . . . the price one pays for the devilish and divine privilege of thought." He was never free from Baudelaire's "'stérilités des écrivains nerveux' . . . that anguished suspension of all power of thought that comes to one often in the midst of a very revel of production, like the slave with his *memento mori* at a feast." The unwritten page never lost for him its terrifying blankness. "Inspiration comes to me in looking at the paper," he wrote in 1894. "Then there are soaring flights; my thought goes wandering through vast spaces filled with shadowy forms. All is yet chaos, but, slowly, the apparitions change into living flesh, the shimmering mists take shape, and—who knows?—something may be born of the clash of nebulous ideas." He was repeatedly tortured by exhausted energy and morbid crises. Every new book was likely to be begun as if he had never written a book before. When he had finished *Typhoon* and not yet begun *Nostromo* he felt that "there was nothing more in the world to write about," and could only do again what he had done already: "Once the general idea is settled on, you must let yourself be led by the inspiration of the moment." Yet it was out of these crises of desperation

that Conrad made powerful fiction, dramatizing the
*idées fixes* of the obsessed conscience, devising a personal method and style out of a condition of profound
introversion, draining the classic moral situations and
the pathos of modern skepticism of the last drop of their
blood, and so adding to English fiction, during a period
of triumphant journalism and commercialized banalities,
an exotic force of language and a passion of moral insight that now appear as two of its few redeeming assets.

He did something more. He corrected the failure of his
contemporaries to become morally implicated in what
they were doing. The facts of human action and conscience which most of them were content to record passively, detachedly, critically, theoretically, he brought
all his forces to the task of *penetrating*. He himself became involved in his story. So, when we read it, do we.
The action, the emotion, the state of mind of the characters, enclose and surround us. We enter a reality of
three dimensions. We begin, as Conrad intended, to
hear, to feel, to see. We also begin to understand why
Conrad held theory at arm's length—scientific theory
no less than aesthetic—and why he always held the
visionary or philosophic tendencies of fiction under suspicion. His dislike of Dostoevsky, whom he considered
inferior to Turgenev, has often been taken as a symptom
of his Polish hostility to Russia or as a refusal to recognize his true father in art. It may have another import,
one on which we get some light in a report of the French
dramatist Lenormand, who tells that once when he lent
Conrad two books of Freud's, Conrad regarded them
*"avec une ironie méprisante,"* took them to his room,
and later returned them unopened. The tendency of
Dostoevsky toward mystical illuminism seems to have
been for him as great a danger to the creative will and
responsibility as the scientific or rational objectification

of the artist's material. Even the ideal of consciousness
espoused by James and Mann he considered inimical to
aesthetic vitality. For an artist, the retreat of the creative intelligence into science or aestheticism was as
great a presumption on the moral imperatives of his art
as the mystic's refuge in vision. "All these gods must,
after a short period of fellowship, abandon him—even
on the very threshold of the temple—to the stammerings
of his conscience and to the outspoken consciousness of
the difficulties of his work." The snatching of the hurrying moment, the scrutiny of the selected fragment of
life, is "only the beginning of the task." To suspend existence in sensation or in idealism is to invite moral im-
potence and the nihilism of temperament. Conrad knew
these evils because they haunted him all his life; he made
his art the battleground of his resistance to them. In his
greater work he exonerates the tormenting ambivalence
of his temperament by a dynamic drama of forces: of
sensibility against action, of analysis against plot, of the
isolated self with its illusions and fixations against the
imperatives of human honor and sacrifice. In this ten-
sion of elements exists the secret of his power. He found
a dramatic equivalent for the law that operates in both
society and psyche—that "supreme law" by which the
soul is compelled out of isolation and personal illusion
into the whole organism of life, into a "solidarity with
mankind," into that moral teleology of humanity which
must be the novel's supreme theme and problem. "Without mankind," he wrote at the end of his life, "my art,
an infinitesimal thing, could not exist."

## III

It was inevitable, especially in England, that Conrad
should have become celebrated as a sea-writer, and

there can be little question that he brought the sea-tale to its finest point of artistry in English literature. But his relegation by public and critics to that category came more and more to distress him. As late as 1923 he hoped "to get freed from that infernal tail of ships and that obsession of my sea life. . . . I may have been a seaman, but I am a writer of prose. Indeed, the nature of my writing runs the risk of being obscured by the nature of my material. I admit it is natural; but only the appreciation of a special personal intelligence can counteract the superficial appreciation of the inferior intelligence of the mass of readers and critics." The general public still, however, tends to associate him with Marryat (whom, incidentally, he admired); if another classification is wanted, it is likely to be that of oriental exoticism. That the sea was Conrad's most deeply felt poetic element, and that the enchantment of the East left its permanent mark on his imagination, is testified to by the recurrence of these scenes in his fiction, all the way from *The Nigger of the "Narcissus"* to *The Rover,* and from *Almayer's Folly* to *The Rescue;* but that the poetry and mystery they afforded his imagination were corrected by a realistic instinct is unmistakable. It becomes more unmistakable when we turn to the books in which both sea-life and Orient disappear from the page and we find ourselves in an element that resists the indulgences of heroic or exotic mystery.

Critical terminology has applied another adjective to Conrad's talent; he is invariably classified in some way as a romantic. And that his temperament, as well as his style and concepts, have a romantic cast was not to be denied, even by himself. "The romantic feeling of reality was in me an inborn faculty," he admitted. "This in itself may be a curse, but, when disciplined by a sense of personal responsibility and a recognition of the hard facts of existence shared with the rest of mankind, becomes but a point of view from which the very shadows of life appear endowed with an internal glow. And such romanticism is not a sin. It is none the worse for the knowledge of truth. It only tries to make the best of it, hard as it may be; and in this hardness discovers a certain aspect of beauty."

Romanticism and reality; beauty and hardness—he was capable of both, yet the pitch at which he held their opposing claims always threatened and sometimes betrayed him. As in all artists of a certain intensity, he felt the conflict of his members, the collision of the elements that formed his nature. He was never at his best when writing too close to himself—his private history, his secret emotions, the self behind the mask. To write his best he needed the distance of irony, as in *The Secret Agent;* of history, as in *Nostromo;* of dramatic structure and objectification, as in *Victory;* or of that intermediary voice—Marlow's or another's—which seems to have set his sensibility responding to its rhythm and persuasion during his days at sea, and which he had to hear sounding in the ear of his imagination before he could fall under the spell of narrative and allow the words and the events to flow from his pen. No modern writer has used the voice of a narrator as often or as complexly as Conrad, but the usage—in "Heart of Darkness," *Under Western Eyes,* or *Chance*—becomes more than a device of oral verisimilitude or a means of virtuosity in wielding the "point of view." It becomes an instrument of consciousness, a mode of sympathy, a means —especially in *Chance,* where the narrator is sometimes five times removed from the event he is detailing—of presenting experience and intelligence in their fullest possible complex of handicaps, prejudices, distortion, and human obstacles.

That he needed such modes of objectifying and forming his material is seen especially in *The Arrow of Gold,* based directly on his youthful years in Marseilles and among the Carlists; it is the poorest of his books, collapsing into a worried, over-insistent abstraction of an idea too much a part of himself to admit its necessary projection as drama. So also the memory preserved in "Youth" shows the strain of a cloying lyric verbalism, and even in "Heart of Darkness" there appears what F. R. Leavis has called an "adjectival insistence upon inexpressible and incomprehensible mystery," a "thrilled sense of the unspeakable potentialities of the human soul," which betrays the effort Conrad exerted on inducing the required excitement into his tale, leading him to employ the excessive emphasis that fatigues the style of Poe. His treatment of the sea, of life, of chance, and of woman as inscrutable entities can pall with an insistence that is a prevalent threat to his realism, his sincerity, and his truth. The struggle of twenty years he put into completing *The Rescue* shows in the lassitude that overtook that noble narrative and leaves it marked, like other work of his final years, with the scars of a labor too protracted. But these are defects that come from an intense and passionate siege of the citadel of human vanity and delusion, and Conrad knew where that sinister fortress exists in the make-up of man.

His clues thread the pages of his dramas, but they also appear on his title pages, in those epigraphs which, as Mrs. Conrad has said, "had always a close and direct relation to the contents of the book itself," expressing "the mood in which the work was written." The quotation below the title of *Lord Jim* hints not only of the narrative method which, in his long recitatives and monologues, Conrad made his special instrument of realism and form, but of the psychological compulsion under which his characters, caught in the moral or circumstantial prisons of their lives, are forced to speak and by which Conrad himself was compelled toward his special kind of art and revelation: "It is certain my Conviction gains infinitely, the moment another soul will believe in it." Novalis' sentence is the key to the method and necessity that are the source both of Conrad's originality and of his appeal to psychological realists. Sometimes the complex of fate requires solution by something more violent than an ordeal of individual sublimation. Shakespeare's "So foul a sky clears not without a storm" at the head of *Nostromo* suggests a prevailing symbol. A phrase from Boethius—". . . for this míracle or this wonder troubleth me right gretly"—stands at the head of *The Mirror of the Sea*. The quotation on *Almayer's Folly* is from Amiel: *"Qui de nous n'a eu sa terre promise, son jour d'extase, et sa fin en exil?"* Baudelaire's *"D'autres fois, calme plat, grand miroir/De mon désespoir"* serves as motto to *The Shadow Line*. An aphorism from La Bruyère acts as a clue to *The Arrow of Gold: "Celui qui n'a vu que des hommes polis et raisonnables, ou ne connaît pas l'homme, ou ne le connaît qu'à demi."* The motto for *The Rescue* is from Chaucer's *Frankeleyn's Tale:*

> "Alas!" quod she, "that ever this sholde happe!
> For wende I never, by possibilitee,
> That swich a monstre or merveille mighte be!"

Most specific of all, the quotation below the title of *Chance* is from Sir Thomas Browne: "Those that hold that all things are governed by Fortune had not erred, had they not persisted there."

The meaning of these passages is clear; they give what is perhaps the basic theme of Conrad's fiction. His work dramatizes a hostility of forces that exists both in the conditions of practical life and in the constitution of man himself. Men who show any fundamental vitality of nature, will, or imagination are not initially men of caution, tact, or prudence, "*polis et raisonnables.*" They are possessed by an enthusiasm that makes them approach life as an adventure. They attack the struggle with all the impulsive force of their illusion, their pride, their idealism, their desire for fame and power, their confidence that Chance is a friend and Fortune a guide who will lead them to a promised goal of happiness or success, wealth or authority. Chance, under this aspect of youthful illusion, is the ideal of expectation and generosity. She takes the color of her benevolence from youth's impetuosity and ardor before those qualities have revealed their full cost in experience and disillusionment. Sometimes the illusion we impose on our lives is not enthusiastic but cynical or pessimistic. The cost then proves all the greater. The hero of "Youth," *Lord Jim, The Shadow Line,* and *The Arrow of Gold* is at times supplanted by a man like Heyst in *Victory* or Razumov in *Under Western Eyes,* whose untested misanthropy is as fatally romantic a presumption on the conditions of the responsible life or the obligations of character as an untested optimism ("Woe to the man whose heart has not learned while young to hope, to love—and to put its trust in life!"). An equal enemy lies in wait for both—"our common enemy," leaping from unknown coverts, sometimes from the hiding places that fate has prepared, but more often and seriously, like James's beast in the jungle, from the unfathomed depths of our secret natures, our ignorance, our unconscious and untested selves.

When the moment comes, the victim must commit himself to it. It is the signal of his destiny, and there is no escape for the man who meets it unprepared. The terms of life are reversed by it. It is the stroke by which fate compels recognition—of one's self, of reality, of error or mistaken expectation or defeat. At that moment, if he can measure up to it, a man's conscious moral existence begins: "We begin to live when we have conceived life as tragedy." Such living may destroy, but it is a certainty that only such living can save; and those capable of salvation are those who can say, in another sentence of Yeats's which is an explicit phrasing of Conrad's idea: "When I think of life as a struggle with the Daemon who would ever set us to the hardest work among those not impossible, I understand why there is a deep enmity between a man and his destiny, and why a man loves nothing but his destiny." There are other men who never meet the test, men who sail "over the surface of the oceans as some men go skimming over the years of existence to sink gently into a placid grave, ignorant of life to the last, without ever having been made to see all it may contain of perfidy, of violence, and of terror." Yes, says Conrad of Captain MacWhirr in *Typhoon,* "there are on sea and land such men thus fortunate—or thus disdained by destiny or by the sea."

The sentence expresses the severest judgment he ever uttered—his judgment on a world evasive of personal responsibility and so committed to a morality of casuistry and opportunism. It was not only in political and commercial society that he saw the results of such cynicism, depicted in varying degrees of brutality in *The Secret Agent, Under Western Eyes,* and *Chance*—novels whose wholly European settings gave little occasion for an occluding exoticism and so brought out the full force of Conrad's critical powers. He saw it in the crisis of civilization he witnessed in Europe, and he saw it there in terms of a question whose import he felt with personal intensity and even with guilt—the question of Poland.

Conrad's temperament, like that of his characteristic heroes, was rooted in an impulse, an impetuosity, that involves the poet, as much as the man of action, in a presumption on the laws of moral responsibility. He was initially an idealist whose passions were early set at a pitch of heroic resolution, committed to a struggle that called on the utmost determination of will and spirit. The fiery hopes of Polish nationalism and the cause of Polish freedom had exacted the fullest share of bravery, suffering, and ignominy from Conrad's people. His father was a nationalist of Shelleyan vision, translator of Shakespeare, Vigny, and Hugo, whose own poetry was passionate in its defiance of misfortune.

> May cowards tremble at lofty waves,
> To you they bring good fortune!
> You know the hidden reefs,
> And are familiar with the tempests!

Conrad once protested that his father should not be called a revolutionist, since "no epithet could be more inapplicable to a man with such a strong sense of responsibility in the region of ideas and action and so indifferent to the promptings of personal ambition"; rather he was "simply a patriot in the sense of a man who, believing in the spirituality of a national existence, could not bear to see that spirit enslaved." But Danilowski, the Polish historian, described this father as "an honorable but too ardent patriot" who was known to the Czarist police as an "agitator" and author of the seditious mandate which caused his arrest in October, 1861, his imprisonment in Warsaw, and his subsequent deportation to Russia for a four-year exile, his wife and son accompanying him, which brought on the death of his wife and eventually his own death as well. This "Korzeniowski strain," as his wife's relatives called it, with its devotion to Utopian ideals and revolutionary hazards—im-

pulsive, sarcastic, impatient—made him appear to the
Bobrowski family "an undesirable pretender" when he
courted their daughter. The Bobrowskis were, like the
Korzeniowskis, of the land-tilling gentry, with a brilliant
record as soldiers and patriots, but they were of more
conservative, reformist leanings: agricultural, closely devoted as a family, apparently more realistic and cautious
in their attitude toward the nationalist cause than the
young poet whom they knew as a "Red" and who, despite his sensitive character, was famed for his recklessness and scurrilous impatience with temporizers. The
hazardous conditions of Conrad's youth (he was only
five when his father was deported), the unsettled fortunes of the family, and his knowledge of his father's
courage, must have fostered his early ambitions about
his own career. When, at seventeen, with both parents
dead, he turned from the East which he always feared
and disliked, since it represented the national enemy
Russia, he looked toward countries that promised a career of greater opportunity and security. He looked toward France, where, at Marseilles, he found his first
adventures in love, maritime service, and gun-running
for the Carlists. Conrad's celebrations of the hope and
illusion of youth, of innocence, courage, and the bravery
they support in the untest nature of the immature man,
and of the sincerity which blesses this primitive kind of
emotion—these cannot be doubted as revivals, in his
later memory, of the excitement with which he launched
himself on life when he left Poland in 1874.

Once Conrad had embarked on that adventure, however, a rival strain of his inheritance asserted itself. After three years in France, his affairs there arrived at a
crisis. His friendships in the conservative *légitimiste*
circle of the banker Delestang disintegrated; his romantic episode of gun-running for the Carlists on the

tartane *Tremolino* was short-lived; his love affair with the prototype of Rita de Lastaola and his duel with the American adventurer Blunt (later to be told in *The Arrow of Gold*) ended in fiasco and caused so much alarm among his relatives in Poland that his guardian uncle Tadeusz Bobrowski threatened to stop his allowance and compel him to come home.* Wounded in the duel, Conrad was barely on his legs when his alarmed uncle arrived from Kiev to find his nephew deserted by his Carlist friends, embittered, ready to throw up all adventurous escapades in favor of a job on an English freighter, the *Mavis,* carrying coal and linseed-oil cargoes between Lowestoft and Constantinople. When Conrad arrived at Lowestoft on June 18, 1878, he stepped on English soil for the first time, practically without money, without acquaintances in England, "alone in the world." The moment was decisive for him. Poland, Marseilles, Carlism, and youth were behind him. Poverty and the rigorous routine of a merchant vessel descended on him and fixed his life for the next seventeen years.

What now rose in Conrad's personality was a force more familiar to us in his books than the ecstatic emotion of youth. Troubled, in the early eighties, by the growing melancholy and introspection induced by long sea-watches, by solitary duties, by a lonely life, and by the racking boredom he confessed in later life to be the one sensation he remembered from his sailing days, he found confirmed in his nature the tragic inheritance of his race and family. His life had begun in disturbance, danger, and a great ascendant hope. It had become vividly adventurous in France, Spain, and the West Indies. Now, abruptly, it became confined, vigilant, curtailed to the most tyrannous necessities. His voyages to the Atlantic and Pacific, the Americas, and the coasts

* See Addendum, p. 47.—F. R. K.

and seas of the East brought contrasts of novelty and exotic discovery; but by the time Conrad took his harrowing journey to the Congo in 1890, reality had become unconditional. The African venture figured as his descent into Hell. He returned ravaged by the illness and mental disruption which undermined his health for the remaining years of his life.* Back home—and homeless—in London, ill with fever and dysentery, he had only his distant cousin-by-marriage, the Belgian novelist Marguerite Poradowska, as his confidante in western Europe. His uncle Tadeusz, now growing old in Poland, remained his last link with his immediate family there, and he was to die in 1894. In 1891 Conrad received a letter from him from Poland, sagely counseling him in fortitude and realism. "I cannot say that I am pleased by your state of mind," he wrote his "dear pessimist": "or that I am without apprehension about your future . . . Thinking over the causes of your melancholy most carefully I cannot attribute it either to youth or to age." No, it came from ill-health, from the wretched sufferings in Africa, but also from something more: "the habit of reverie which I have observed to be part of your character. It is inherited; it has always been there, in spite of your active life." He counseled his nephew to "avoid all meditations, which lead to pessimistic conclusions" and "to lead a more active life than ever and to cultivate cheerful habits." "Our country," he added, "is the 'pan' of the nations, which, in plain prose, means that we are a nation who consider ourselves great and misunderstood, the possessors of a greatness which others do not recognize and will never recognize. If individuals and nations would set duty before themselves as an aim, instead of grandiose ideals, the world would be a happier

* Dr. Bernard Meyer "diagnoses" Conrad's physical ailment as an incurable disease of the joints (*Joseph Conrad: A Psychoanalytic Biography*; Princeton, N.J.; 1967, p. 100).—F. R. K.

place. . . . Perhaps you will reply that these are the sentiments of one who has always had 'a place in the sun.' Not at all. I have endured many ups and downs; I have suffered in my private life, in my family life, and as a Pole; and it is thanks to these mortifications that I have arrived at a calm and modest estimate of life and its duties, and that I have taken as my motto *usque ad finem';* as my guide, the love of the duty which circumstances define."

Conrad's sense of the crisis of moral isolation and recognition in which the individual meets his first full test of character is repeatedly emphasized in his novels. Even by 1891 that sense—implied in his uncle's letter—had become inescapable to him. For three more years he worked on ships. In 1894 his last vessel, the *Adowa,* docked at London, and Conrad—though he did not yet know it; indeed he tried for another six years to return to the sea, even after his first five books were published—had finished his career in the Merchant Service. Then it was that he took up the manuscript he had begun impulsively in 1889, the story of a defeated Dutchman, Almayer, living lost to the world of his futile dreams on a jungle river in Borneo. He had worked on the manuscript desultorily on land and sea during the following five years. Now, in dismal London lodgings, he set himself to finish it. It was his sole stake in a new life. Thus began the long, lonely, agonized labor of writing, an "imprisonment" that was to last for thirty years. By brutal application he sweated out its last pages. To his own astonishment *Almayer's Folly* was published in 1895 in London, and the die was cast. The stone of Sisyphus became his acknowledged burden. His commitment became irrevocable in 1896 when he married an English wife. To his old fears and uncertainties was now added a career of maddening risk and uncertainty in art, with the world of literary professionalism to conquer and a public to court that promised even less security than the berths and ships of his seafaring days.

The plight of the man on whom life closes down inexorably, divesting him of the supports and illusory protection of friendship, social privilege, or love, now emerged as the characteristic theme of his books. It is a subject that has become familiar to us in modern literature. Ibsen, James, Mann, Gide, and Kafka have successively employed it. It appears in Joyce, in Hemingway, in Dos Passos, and other novelists of our time. Its latest appearance is among the French Existentialists, who have given heroism a new setting in the absurdity of society and the universe. But it is doubtful if any of these writers, possibly excepting Kafka, has achieved a more successful *dramatic* version of the problem than Conrad did—a more complete coincidence of the processes of psychic recognition and recovery with the dramatic necessities of the plot; and this for the reason which distinguishes Conrad's contribution to modern fictional method: his imposition of the processes and structures of the moral experience (particularly the experience of recognition) on the form of the plot. Obviously this theme has a classic ancestry; it is the oldest mode of tragedy. Conrad was taxed with giving it its fullest possible analysis, for it virtually constitutes the whole and central matter of his work. Even in James, whose genius also took this direction—and who was an artist of so much greater resource and invention, as of a freer imaginative range—the ratiocinative element and structural manipulation of the drama did not permit an equal coincidence of sensibility with form or an equal immersion in "the destructive element" of reality—that element into which a man that is born falls "like a man who falls into the sea," and of which Stein, in *Lord Jim*, was to say: "The way is to the destructive element submit yourself, and with the exertions of your hands and feet in the water make the deep, deep sea keep you up."

The conditions that mark the plight of a Conrad character who is caught in the grip of circumstances that enforce self-discovery and its cognate, the discovery of reality or truth, are consistent throughout his books. The condition of moral isolation is the first of them—the isolation of Razumov in *Under Western Eyes,* of Heyst in *Victory,* of Flora de Barral in *Chance,* of Lord Jim in his disgrace, and of a long series of other outcasts, exiles, or estranged souls—Willems, Mrs. Travers, Mrs. Verloc, Peyrol; even men whom age or fame has suddenly bereft of the solid ground of security or confidence: Captain Whalley, Captain MacWhirr, the young captain on his first command in *The Shadow Line,* or Kurtz of "Heart of Darkness" in his last abandonment of soul. A man may be alone because he is a banished wastrel who has made life a law to himself, like Willems; because he is young and irresponsible, like Mr. George; because fate has estranged him from the ties of a normal life, like Lingard and Captain Whalley; because he has become disgraced in the eyes of society or betrayed by a false confidence or idealism, like Jim and Flora; because he has betrayed a trust, like Razumov; because he fosters the intolerance and arrogance of self-willed pride, like Nostromo; or because, like Heyst, a fatal vein of skepticism in his nature had induced a nihilism of all values. Conrad leaves no doubt of the extreme to which he pushed this condition. Of Heyst we hear that "Not a single soul belonging to him lived anywhere on earth . . . he was alone on the bank of the stream. In his pride he determined not to enter it." And of Razumov: "He was as lonely in the world as a man swimming in the deep sea . . . He had nothing. He had not even a moral refuge—the refuge of confidence."

But nature abhors that solitude as much as its victims (depending on their characters) woo or dread it.
"Who knows what true loneliness is—not the conventional word but the naked terror? To the lonely themselves it wears a mask. The most miserable outcast hugs
some memory or some illusion . . . No human being
could bear a steady view of moral solitude without going mad." "I am being crushed—and I can't even run
away," cries Razumov. The solitary may take to self-law
like Willems: even that does not permit him to escape.
He may rise to power or fame like Kurtz: that permits
escape least of all. He may believe he has formed a
world of his own like Heyst: "It was the essence of his
life to be a solitary achievement . . . In this scheme he
had perceived the means of passing through life without suffering and almost without care in the world—invulnerable because elusive!" But life permits no such
independence. The man who is alone in the world can
never escape, for he is always with himself. Unless he is
morally abandoned beyond the point of significance, he
lives in the company of a ruthless inquisitor, a watcher
who never sleeps, an eternally vigilant judge. The *alter
ego* of the conscience demands its justice; the *Doppel-
gänger* becomes part of the drama of character and self-
determination. "No decent feeling was ever scorned by
Heyst," and that fact proves his undoing and finally his
salvation. When Jim delivers his long monologues to
Marlow; when Flora bares her soul to Marlow, Mrs.
Fyne, or Captain Anthony; when Razumov disburdens
his heart in his diary, to the old professor, or finally to
Nathalie Haldin herself; when Decoud or Mrs. Gould
ruminate their secret selves, these people are really
carrying out the drama of their divided natures, objectifying under a compulsion which psychologists accept as

a therapeutic necessity their souls' dilemmas, and thus saving themselves from the madness or violence that afflict men when they refuse to face such recognition. The divided man—the face and its mask, the soul and its shadow—is never, in Conrad, an individual and nothing more. He becomes—especially in novels of historical scope or parabolic implications like *Nostromo, Under Western Eyes,* and *Victory*—a metaphor of society and of humanity.

Thus love, or the sense of honor, or the obligation of duty, or even the social instinct itself, enters the novels as a means whereby the individual is forced out of his isolation and morbid surrender. The inward-driving, center-fathoming obsession of the tale becomes reversed toward external standards of value. It is finally the world that saves us—the world of human necessities and duty. It may be the world of a ship and its crew, as in *The Nigger of the "Narcissus"* or *The Shadow Line;* it may be the world of an island and a single fellow-soul, as in *Victory;* it may be that wider world of social and political facts which appears in solid form in *Nostromo, The Secret Agent, Under Western Eyes,* and *Chance.* In one of his most perfect tales, "The Secret Sharer," we have, as Miss M. C. Bradbrook has recently observed, the microcosm of Conrad's fiction. Leggatt, the swimmer, has committed murder and so, by a moment's action, has ruined his life. He escapes, but finds refuge under cover of night on a strange ship—"a fugitive and a vagabond on the earth, with no brand of the curse on his sane forehead to stay a slaying hand." The captain hides him, guesses his guilt, and so becomes allied to that guilt, the refugee's secret becoming a projection of the captain's own secret and unacknowledged life. The hidden self of the captain is " 'exactly the same' as the other, but guilty, and always of necessity concealed from the eyes of the world; dressed in a sleeping suit, the garb of the unconscious life, appearing and disappearing out of, and into, the infinite sea." But before Leggatt disappears at last, the captain has come to know the secret soul he lives with. His life is changed. A new vision of humanity has broken in upon the masked and impersonal regimen of his days. His existence, like every man's, has come to include the larger workings of the moral law, of society, of justice. "A train of thought is never false," said Conrad. "The falsehood lies deep in the necessities of existence, in secret fears and half-formed ambitions, in the secret confidence combined with a secret mistrust of ourselves, in the love of hope and the dread of uncertain days." And Razumov, faced by the first horror of his self-betrayal, knows another truth: "All a man can betray is his conscience."

IV

It was Henry James, one of Conrad's first admirers and a novelist whom Conrad took as an almost solitary master in the England of his literary beginnings, who gave the classic description of Conrad's way of writing. It is, he said in one of the last essays of his life, "The New Novel" in 1914, "an extraordinary exhibition of method by the fact that the method is, we venture to say, without a precedent in any like work. It places Mr. Conrad absolutely alone as a votary of the way to do a thing that shall make it undergo most doing. The way to do it that shall make it undergo least is the line on which we are mostly now used to see prizes carried off; so that the author of *Chance* gathers up on this showing all sorts of comparative distinction."

The attraction of Conrad's novels for students of craftsmanship is strong; and the art he perfected remains permanently stamped by the impress not only of his aesthetic principles but of the temperament that conceived and shaped his dramas. He belongs with Flaubert, James, Joyce, and Gide, among his contemporaries, in the conscious share he took in the renovation of the form and craft of fiction. What he gave the modern novel may be seen in any of his major works. *Under Western Eyes* presents his method in archetype.

When Conrad first began the writing of this book, he called it *Razumov* and described its plot in a letter to Galsworthy on January 6, 1908. (See page 741.) "Listen to the theme," he said. "The Student Razumov (a natural son of a Prince K.) gives up secretly to the police his fellow student, Haldin, who seeks refuge in his rooms after committing a political crime (supposed to be the murder of de Plehve). First movement in St. Petersburg. (Haldin is hanged, of course.) Second in Genève. The Student Razumov meeting abroad the mother and sister of Haldin falls in love with that last, marries her and, after a time, confesses to her the part he played in the arrest of her brother. The psychological developments leading to Razumov's betrayal of Haldin, to the confession of the fact to his wife and to the death of these people (brought about mainly by the resemblance of their child to the late Haldin), form the real subject of the story."

It was almost four years before the novel was completed and published on October 5, 1911; but when it appeared, it was not only its title that had been changed. The plot was also transformed. Razumov and Natalie Haldin never marry; they never have a child who resembles her dead brother and thus "brings about" the deaths of these people. The book had become radically altered in composition. Its new title indicates a shift in the post of observation from the hero to a disinterested spectator (the old English teacher of languages in Geneva who tells the story) through whom, and through Razumov's diary which he transcribes, the story comes to us. Conrad, if we follow the word of friends like Ford Madox Ford and Richard Curle or of his own letters, seldom outlined or schematized a book in advance. He pondered, brooded, lived and slept with it, immersed himself in its mood and movement, began writing, and so moved, sensibly, forcibly, almost physically, into the impulse and element of the tale word by word. The devices he employed—the time-shift, the plot-inversion and dislocation, the repetition of motifs, the use of interlocutors and other agencies for realistic and analytical observation, his highly specialized use of indirection—originated in something different from the conscious reform and manipulation of fictional method among experimental writers from Flaubert and James onward. They seem to have originated in profoundly habitual, deeply ingrained, almost incurably obsessional tendences of his character. His letter to Galsworthy shows that he conceived the story of *Under Western Eyes* in strongly dramatic terms. But the more he pondered it, the more he came to grips with the writing of it, the less he was able to adhere to an objective dramatization of his idea. His ponderous imagination was forced from its inertia by a haphazard, precipitous mode of composition. We sense the prolonged ordeal of immersion in a story's theme and mood that preceded the setting of words to paper, and the almost frenzied compulsion he found necessary to transfer that modal saturation to the sheet before him. He was obliged to submit to an almost purely empirical mode of imaginative realization. When he took up a new theme, he often did so because he hit upon it accidentally—found it in a suggestion of apparently minute inadequacy as compared with the complex book that finally resulted, yet illustrating what James called "that odd law which somehow always makes the minimum of valid suggestion serve the man of imagination better than the maximum."

To that suggestion he submitted himself for long periods of gestation that seem, from his own accounts of them, to have been of an almost will-less and trance-like passivity. He made himself the registering medium of what, in *Chance,* he calls "the irresistible pressure of imaginary griefs, crushing conscience, scruples, prudence, under their ever expanding volume," and of "the somber and venomous irony in the obsession." He gave himself up to "that complete mastery of one fixed idea, not a reasonable but an emotional mastery, a sort of concentrated exaltation. Under its empire men rush blindly through fire and water and opposing violence, and nothing can stop them—unless, sometimes, a grain of sand." At one point in *Chance* Marlow pauses to ask his listener: "You understand?" and the listener says: "Perfectly. . . . You are the expert in the psychological wilderness. This is like one of those Redskin stories where the noble savages carry off a girl and the honest backwoodsman with his incomparable knowledge follows the track and reads the signs of her fate in a footprint here, a broken twig there, a trinket dropped by the way. I have always liked such stories. Go on!"

So the tale began. It might, when it lacked a sufficiently strong impulse, show the marks of the struggle that went to make it. In a good many of Conrad's tales, from *Almayer's Folly* to *The Rescue,* one senses a huddled, torpid, sluggishly regressive quality in the action for chapters on end. The narrative motion is struggling to emerge and free itself from its roots and hindrances; it may not be until late that the movement leaps free

and carries the plot forward to its climax. The act of
creation in Conrad apparently took place between two
contradictory impulses—the one instinctive, casual, tentative, unmethodical, and yet intensely and passionately
absorbed; the other analytical, cautious, scrupulously
calculating, with checkings and delayings of action, re-
gressions of impulse, retracing and testing of motives,
and with a complicated exercise of the mode of averted
suspense which the Renaissance rhetoricians called *oc-
cupatio*. Elizabeth Bowen has said that Conrad's way
of projecting a dramatic concept was not through a
development but by means of a soaking. No attentive
reader can overlook the verbal, modal, and atmospheric
saturation to which he subjected his themes, or the
equally exhaustive wringing out or draining out of them
of their whole content of motive and consciousness.
Conrad's state of mind seems to have combined the inexhaustible impressionability of his seamen with their
canny disillusionment. "A turn of mind composed of
innocence and skepticism is common to them all," he
once said, "with the addition of an unexpected insight
into motives, as of disinterested lookers-on at a game."

As a novelist he submitted to the passive fascination
of his conjurings at the same moment that he was tormented by the labor of reconciling them to the reality
of words. He repeatedly shared with young Powell
(again in *Chance*) that "moment of incredulity as to
the truth of his own conviction because it had failed to
affect the safe aspect of familiar things. He doubted
his eyes too. He must have dreamt it all! 'I am dream-
ing now,' he said. And very likely for a few seconds he
must have looked like a man in a trance or profoundly
asleep on his feet, and with a glass of brandy-and-water
in his hand." Conrad was constantly fascinated by the
dreamlike unreality of experience, by the terror of the

awakenings which personal crises bring about in a man's life, by the power of the dream to appall and defeat a man's conscious efforts to control or understand it. His nature was poised between the world of fantasies and impossible desires and the world of brutal facts. Three proverbs haunted him all his life. One was "Life is a dream"; another, "All things belong to the young"; a third, *"Tout passe, tout lasse."*

As fantasy was challenged by reality, so the devious, peripheral, inquisitive exploration of a situation in Conrad was challenged by his sense of form. But unlike many modern innovators, he would not permit the form to falsify the situation or the psychic and moral conditions it entailed. As he himself, in his letters and personal writings, presents an unmistakable case of introverted sensibility impelled toward manic-depressive tendencies from which only an appalling exercise of will power could rescue him for the writing of his books, so it is the obedience of his characters to some law of action or honor that saves them from the nihilism of their private worlds of solitude or negation. He detested the crude chronological machinery of the conventional novel; his friend Galsworthy's books, which he admired and praised on occasion, always left him unsatisfied. His prodigious curiosity about the sources of action in the moral nature, the buried psychic forces, and the expiatory or recriminative processes of the human conscience, demanded satisfaction in a form of fiction that should dissect and analyze as well as narrate or entertain. Conrad has told us too much about himself in his letters to keep us from ascribing this curiosity to the agonized ordeal of his own conscience—a conscience profoundly susceptible, intensified and made luminous by the events of his own history. His congenital impulsiveness and enthusiasm was repeatedly and brutally checked by acute principles of honor and sincerity. We may not wholly agree with Gustav Morf when he credits the motif of guilt, exile, and expiation in the novels to Conrad's sense of guilt in deserting Poland and his family's part in the revolutionary cause there. By the time those novels were written more than personal history had gone into their making. But that some such instinct of guilt and moral recrimination operates continuously in his work, from *An Outcast of the Islands* through *Lord Jim, Nostromo, Under Western Eyes,* and *Chance* to *Victory,* is clear. It is the deepest animus of their pages; and the heroism—expressed in acts of expiation, self-vindication, or secret moral victory—which he confers on his heroes gives them their distinguishing mark in modern fiction.

They are, all of them, men who enact Conrad's central faith: that the personal illusion of values in men must be compelled out of vanity, negation, or despair by the human necessity of action and sacrifice. By that law they meet the crisis of their lives. Once the crisis is established there are certain conditions necessary to render it dramatic, so bringing a man to the abrupt realization of his destiny, his responsibility, his conscious selfhood. These may vary from the taking of one's first command on a ship to the falling upon life of a mortal blow to security or reputation; from the making of an unpremeditated but inescapable mistake to the secret or public violation of one's good name. And there must exist in that character and in the world in which he lives a recognized principle of honor. It is the principle of honor—Conrad is one of its most persistent defenders among modern writers—that binds the private agony of a Conrad hero to the outer world of values and proofs. It brings into the unity of a single life and of an individual focus the ramifications of truth and ethical justice in a world of treachery and violence. The idea of honor, operating within the acute confines of a morbid conflict, a psychic trance or a trapped sensibility, thus provides the moral and dramatic leverage of Conrad's plots. And what it illuminates widens as his stories succeed one another: the history of a ship, of a Malay tribe, of an island, of South American politics, of modern commerce and finance, of Russia, of Europe, of "international evil" and the crisis in the modern world itself.

James M. Cline, a modern student of John Donne, has said of certain of his elaborately rhetorical sermons: "There is no advance in thought, only a refinement of it, a deepening and gathering intensity of realization; until finally the great period crashes to a close, still reiterating, still sustaining an incremental movement of passion and of mind." This admirable remark may be applied to Conrad's art and the principles on which it is founded. Once the rationale of his method is seized and its relevance to his personal history is reasonably allowed, the famous technical devices in his books take on a fresh importance, as do also his defects and mannerisms. We see how the time-shift, the use of narrators, the repeated motif or incident, the exhaustive analysis of events, became in his hands instruments of consciousness, a mode of sympathy, a method of exploring sensibility and instinct. The recurring incident (Jim's jump from the boat, Flora's suicidal appearance at the cliff's edge, Mrs. Schomberg's shawl) goes beyond the ordinary uses of the *leit-motif* by making each of its repetitions serve to mark an expanding realization, an advancing penetration, of the event. The event thus becomes deepened in our consciousness and vision. The fact has gained a wider periphery of relevance. What seems to be a tied plot, gyrating aimlessly around a static point of obsession, is actually growing in meaning and moral import, taking on a wider increment of value. Conrad worked at a time when musical devices were appealing to novelists; I think we must agree with Edward Crankshaw that Conrad's reference to music as the "art of arts" in his artistic credo indicates his belief in the musical possibilities of the novel and thus anticipates the experiments of Proust and Mann; and that his exhaustive treatment of themes and motifs is comparable to the principle of nuclear analysis that appears in such high examples of the variation form as the last piano sonata and the Diabelli Variations of Beethoven.

We are, in any case, concerned in Conrad with a novelist in whom the devices of arrested action, thematic repetition, and incremental veracity were driven to the limits of their utility. By the analysis thus induced the nature of illusion is probed, the residue of truth is sublimated, the operations of intelligence and consciousness are tested, until finally, out of that vaporous haze of skepticism and desperate imposture of values which were threats to Conrad's personal and artistic security, a hard irreducible center of moral certitude and human conviction is arrived at. When Conrad, through Stein in *Lord Jim*, counsels men to submit to the destructive element, "and with the exertions of your hands and feet in the water make the deep, deep sea keep you up," he was not talking about the loss or surrender of personality, as some of his modern readers seem to think. He was talking about the salvation of personality by the test of experience and the recognition of selfhood. He was perhaps talking also about the rescue of his own character from its defeats and confusions by the ordeal of his art; and he was certainly making unmistakable the means of redemption allowed to modern man as he finds it necessary to rescue himself from the willing impersonality, the irresponsibly abstract faiths, and the moral nihilism to which the modern world encourages him to surrender himself. Like Baudelaire, whom he salutes in the epigraph to *The Shadow Line,* Conrad believed it is as impossible as it is futile for a man to know or save mankind before he has first learned to know and save himself. "Those who read me," he said, "know my conviction that the world, the temporal world, rests on a few very simple ideas; so simple that they must be as old as the hills. It rests notably, amongst others, on the idea of Fidelity. At a time when nothing which is not revolutionary in some way or other can expect to attract much attention, I have not been revolutionary in my writings. The revolutionary spirit is mighty convenient in this, that it frees one from all scruples as regards ideas. Its hard, absolute optimism is repulsive to my mind by the menace of fanaticism and intolerance it contains. No doubt one should smile at these things; but, imperfect Esthete, I am no better Philosopher. All claim to special righteousness awakens in me that scorn and anger from which a philosophical mind should be free . . ."

v

It was a strange destiny that brought the Polish exile into English literature to leave on it the mark of his tragic history, his proud and troubled vision, his long conquest of the art in which he worked. But it was not merely English fiction that Conrad enriched. It was the moral stamina of his craft in the twentieth century.

Scott Fitzgerald, in whom Conrad's influence worked, once wrote in a letter: "So many writers, Conrad for instance, have been aided by being brought up in a *métier* utterly unrelated to literature. It gives an abundance of material and, more important, an attitude from which to view the world. So much writing nowadays suffers both from lack of an attitude and from sheer lack of any material, save what is accumulated in a purely social life. The world, as a rule, does not live on beaches and in country clubs." And Thomas Mann noted in Conrad the "refusal of a very much engaged intelligence to hang miserably in the air between contraries." Something stronger than division worked in him: "a passion for freedom" which knew what freedom cost its defender. Once it was possible to look for literary masters in men who had the security of a stable tradition behind them. Today, with that stability broken and the whole human condition in crisis, we are more likely to find masters in artists who are put to the test of recovering certitude and courage in their own persons. The hero of modern fiction—in James, Mann, Joyce, Kafka, but no less in Conrad—is the man marked by apartness and alienation. It is he who must serve as a focus of worth and honor when the world forgets what these things mean.

It will be argued: what of Conrad's aristocratic temper, his intemperate self-regard, his reverence for ceremony, his respect for rank, his respect above all—vexing to iconoclastic admirers like Wells, Norman Douglas, and Liam O'Flaherty—for "the God of the British Empire as something that must not be surpassed" and that keeps his heroes "standing on tiptoe striving to be like that God, who is a good honest trader, a man brave in adversity, a home-lover, a man who keeps his word to his friend and robs those who are not of his kin"? These too were part of his make-up. They made themselves felt in those men of strength in his novels—Lingard, Captain Anthony, Captain Vincent—whose touch of inscrutable sanctimony makes them at times the bores of his pages. But it should be remembered that many men irreverent of authority would never risk their lives to defy it; that iconoclasts can be bigots; and that the most facile rebel is he who sits secure in the protection of law and order. A man who never knew such authority, whose life was a matter of risk and uncertainty from youth to old age, had learned from his own history how easy it is to lose what we once possess and how hard the regaining of it can be. "The unequivocal, the even tendentious Western bias" which Mann first saw in Conrad betrayed the craving of a deracinated Pole for the tribal impregnability, the warm domestic comforts, and the mental ease from which he was excluded. But any reader who takes servility to prestige as the essential quality of Conrad had best look to the art he produced. There the essential Conrad is found—one who knew the humiliations of the spirit at their cruelest and who spared neither himself nor his heroes the humility of standing alone with fate, in mortal enmity and embrace with the Self that commits us to the one destiny that is inescapable.

When Paul Claudel first introduced the name of Conrad to André Gide, Gide asked him what books of Conrad's he should read. "All of them," answered Claudel. The advice is still valuable, if only to disprove that futile kind of criticism which argues that we can have the virtues of an artist without having also his defects. The world is too poor, at the present moment, in writers who show us how it takes the whole strength and dedication of a lifetime to achieve literary endurance, to permit us to minimize Conrad's example. This is not to say that his achievement is consistent. It was rightly said by Galsworthy—perhaps it must be said of every serious artist—that "it does disservice to Conrad to be indiscriminate in praise of his work" and "imperils a just estimate of his greatness." When he is weak it can be, in the writer of *Under Western Eyes* and *Victory,* a weakness of astonishing ineptitude. Some of the stories in *A Set of Six* or *Within the Tides* are as incredible, with their lip-service to popular standards in romance, as the bad plays in James's *Theatricals.* His early work—*Almayer's Folly, An Outcast of the Islands,* three of the *Tales of Unrest*—is, for all its virtuosity, heavily shackled by sensuous luxuriance and spasmodic contrivance. He never completely freed himself of such handicaps. Even some of his serious works—*Lord Jim, Nostromo,* the long-delayed *Rescue*—show the strain, attenuation, the all-but-baffled jugglery of their elements, that Conrad, given his laboriously inductive, trial-and-error workmanship, met in their making. *The Arrow of Gold* is a significant failure. But it is *Nostromo* that remains the distinct test case for critics.

Conrad called it "the most anxiously meditated" of his longer novels, "an intense creative effort on what, I suppose, will always remain my largest canvas." None of his books has elicited a greater division of opinion. Two recent judgments, Leavis' and Miss Bradbrook's, place it among his highest achievements, "one of the great novels of the language," in which "Conrad is openly and triumphantly the artist by *métier,*" and which, despite "something hollow about it," shows an Elizabethan richness and reverberation. Another critic, J. W. Beach, finds that its excessive complexity and congested impressionism produce "very dubious results," with no real center of interest to guide the reader "through the tangled underbrush of this well-nigh pathless forest." It is a book incomparably rich among English novels in conception and material, but equally incomparable in dramatic impenetrability. For the present writer, the reading of it has been a matter of years, never found genuinely sympathetic until he too came to know something of the riddled scene of South American history it explores and by whose confusions it is almost defeated. Yet seen as a matrix and medium of Conrad's historical sensibility, the book grows in fascination, rings with the resonance of a profound if elusive drama of moralities, races, and creeds of conduct.

Only when, however, that drama becomes genuinely focused in an individual destiny is Conrad in his fullest powers. *Lord Jim,* paradigm of his central theme, is too dilated to be a masterpiece. It is when its subject comes under the full control of his irony, his racial and social insights, or his superb skill in parabolic drama, that he wrote with his surest hand and produced *The Secret Agent, Under Western Eyes, Chance, Victory.* Within fifteen years he wrote seven novels and five tales that are second to nothing in English fiction, a rare example of powers in concentrated fruition.

The end was epilogue. He turned to memories—of his first command in *The Shadow Line,* of his French adventure in youth in *The Arrow of Gold,* of what the East had taught him in *The Rescue,* finished now after having been started twenty years earlier, and showing the noble fatigue and resigned fortitude of age. He began working up Napoleonic history for *Suspense* and talked of writing a novel about a modern politician. *The Rover,* also below his best work, came in 1923 as a by-product of *Suspense,* yet it shows better than any of these last books the final release of his spirit into reconciliation. Gustav Morf calls it "the first of his books in which the outcast gets back to his own country, and, what is still more significant, in which he proves that he is, in spite of everything, a good patriot." In the old French seaman Peyrol we have, as Miss Bradbrook rightly observes, "the supreme case of the simple coming to the rescue of the complex." Peyrol has come home to France as Conrad's memory returned to Poland. He is alone and old, but seeing the tragic plight of those time-caught lovers, orphans of the Revolution, Réal and Arlette ("she, whose little feet had run ankle deep through the terror of death, had brought to him the sense of triumphant life"), he can still sacrifice his life to their happiness and to what it promises for the future of their homeland. "Doesn't it seem funny to you," Peyrol asks his old boatman Michel, "to think that you have left nothing and nobody behind?" And Michel, who like his master has a "sense of his own insignificant position at the tail of mankind," says "in the fundamental axiom of his philosophy: 'Somebody must be last in this world.' "

It was not only the novel itself which Conrad charged with a new energy; it was the language in which he wrote. He protested that English had always been the language of his imagination. He repudiated the notion that he might have become a French writer. "I began to think in English long before I mastered, I won't say the style (I haven't done that yet), but the mere uttered speech," he wrote in a letter in 1918. "Is it thinkable that anybody possessed of some effective inspiration should contemplate for a moment such a frantic thing as translating it into another tongue? . . . You may take it from me that if I had not known English I wouldn't have written a line for print, in my life." It was "the sheer appeal of the language, my quickly awakened love for its prose cadences, a subtle and unforeseen accord of my emotional nature with its genius," that impelled him to it. But a foreigner can never use a speech with the tacit familiarity of a native. Whatever

we may believe about the genius of language—whether
it comes most profoundly from unconscious instinct or
takes its strength from some creative ordeal of utterance—we know that it assumes, like any medium of
art, its force through the resistance or obduracy by
which it challenges its wielder. Such obduracy Conrad's
language offered him no less than his subject-matter.
His mastery of the one coincided with his conquest of
the other. T. S. Eliot once grouped Conrad's work with
Joyce's in speaking of a language that is important to
us because it "is struggling to digest and express new
objects, new groups of objects, new feelings, new aspects" in art. That struggle gave Conrad's words, as
they advanced out of their earlier opulence, their keen-
ness, their firmness in specification and aphorism. His
words, like his plots, fell short of the conscious control
of James's, but at their best they breathe with immedi-
acy, strike with a physical impact. His mastery of sensibility was coeval with the personal and structural
growth his books required. He had no choice in the
matter. What he had to say was indissociable from his
way of learning to say it. The conventional division of
form and content could not exist for him. Words themselves—and in no arbitrary aesthetic sense—made the
artist and the man.

So we come to know him in his books: not as a man
who merely tells a tale but as a poet in fiction. The man
who suffers and the mind which creates may be, ideally,
separate and apart. But after their ordeal is finished,
they merge once more. The mind has created more than
a book. It has created the man who wrote the book, in
the only sense in which we can genuinely know him.
It is not the Conrad who left Poland, sailed seas, saw
strange men and places, who finally concerns us. It is
the man who used those experiences as an artist, and

who re-created himself in his mastery of them. When
Conrad takes us on occasion into what Forster calls
"the severe little apartment that must, for want of a
better word, be called his confidence," and from which
he can so curtly dismiss us, he is virtually a stranger to
us. Terse, courtly, or embarrassed, he soon bows us out
and shuts the door. But when he comes to us as Singleton, Jim, Decoud, Razumov, or Heyst, we know a man
who has escaped the confines of his single person and
perpetuated his mind and emotion in the human spirit.

On none of his truest work can the current literary
judgment be passed: "It isn't written." Conrad's pages
are so deeply scored, so passionately inscribed, that
he can become for us a classic instance of the reality—
single, wholly absorbed, all-consuming—of the life in
art. Few writers take us so deeply into the agony of the
creative process as he does; few illustrate so clearly
what the artist's quarrel with himself and his destiny
can give to literature. He tried to be other things but
his fate claimed him. He pushed the stone. He dragged
"the ball and chain of one's selfhood to the end." It
was the price of "the devilish and divine privilege of
thought; so that in this life it is only the elect who
are convicts—a glorious band which comprehends and
groans but which treads the earth amidst a multitude
of phantoms with maniacal gestures, with idiotic grimaces. Which would you be: idiot or convict?" His mind
broke free only in the things it created. He was compelled to his bondage and he was liberated by it too,
but not before he had descended "within himself, and
in that lonely region of stress and strife" found "the
terms of his appeal."

Of the work of the artist in words Henry Adams once
said that it "may be a stimulant more exhausting than
alcohol, and as morbid as morphine. The fascination of

the silent midnight, the veiled lamp, the smoldering fire, the white paper asking to be covered with elusive words, the thoughts grouping themselves into architectural forms, and slowly rising into dreamy structures, constantly changing, shifting, beautifying their outlines —this is the subtlest of solitary temptations, and the loftiest of the intoxications of genius." For Conrad the fascination was less alluring than brutal, but it was a fascination none the less. He put comfort and peace away to pursue it. It made him a stranger to his family and friends for months on end. The black fit besieged him; disgust and desperation shattered him. But he knew in his deepest need that only one liberty was permitted him—the liberation that would come when the page was written, the book finished, the story told. No novelist has ever known harsher conditions in his art, and few a more eloquent triumph. It enabled him to become—like the man he saw in the East: "appealing —significant—under a cloud"—permanently and securely "one of us."

MORTON DAUWEN ZABEL

### ADDENDUM, 1968

Recent discoveries indicate that the so-called duel with the American adventurer Blunt (see page 23) was more likely a suicide attempt on Conrad's part. The first indication comes in the "Document" compiled by Conrad's maternal uncle, Tadeusz Bobrowski. The entry for February 1878 reads, in part: ". . . I got news from Mr. Fecht that you [Conrad] had shot yourself." Later, in a letter to Conrad (for 26 June/8 July 1878), Uncle Tadeusz reproaches his nephew: "You were idling for nearly a whole year—you fell into debt, you deliberately shot yourself. . . ." Even more conclusively, Tadeusz Bobrowski wrote to his friend Stefan Buszczyński (12/24 March 1879): ". . . wishing to improve his finances, [Conrad] tries his luck in Monte Carlo and loses the 800 fr. he had borrowed. Having managed his affairs so excellently he returns to Marseilles and one fine evening invites his friend the creditor to tea, and before his arrival attempts to take his life with a revolver. (Let this detail remain between us, as I have been telling everyone that he was wounded in a duel. From you I neither wish to nor should keep it a secret.) The bullet goes durch [through] and durch near his heart without damaging any vital organ." (The documents above are translated by Zdzisław Najder in his *Conrad's Polish Background;* London, 1964.)

—F. R. K.

# Note and Acknowledgments

The present collection of Conrad's work attempts to show the range of his art early and late. It includes one of his novels, *The Nigger of the "Narcissus,"* written in 1896-97 (revised in 1914), described by him as "the tale by which I am willing to stand or fall as a writer"; a shorter novel, *Typhoon,* of 1900-1901; three of his finest long stories, "Youth" (1898), "Heart of Darkness" (1898-99), and "The Secret Sharer" (1909); and six shorter stories ranging from "The Lagoon" of 1896 to "The Warrior's Soul" of 1916. A selection is also given of passages by Conrad on "The Condition of Art," extending from the "Preface" to *The Nigger of the "Narcissus"* in 1897 to the end of his life; a similar short anthology of passages on "The Condition of Life"; and finally a selection from Conrad's letters, his most intimate personal record, dating from 1891 to 1923. All together, tales and passages from twenty-three of Conrad's books are here printed, including excerpts from his long novels—not only the better-known *Lord Jim* and *Victory,* but such masterpieces of non-maritime fiction as *Nostromo, Under Western Eyes,* and *Chance*—which, impossible to present here in uncut form, are perhaps indicated in their essential themes and motives, and will reveal Conrad to the reader on his largest scale and in his fullest powers.

For permission to use the texts of Conrad, acknowledgment is gratefully made to his American publishers, Doubleday & Co., and to the administrators of the author's estate. The texts from editions published by Doubleday are: "The Lagoon" and "An Outpost of Progress" from *Tales of Unrest; The Nigger of the "Narcissus"* from the volume so titled; "Youth" and "Heart of Darkness" from *Youth: A Narrative and Two Other Stories;* "Typhoon" and "Amy Foster" from *Typhoon and Other Stories* ("Amy Foster" also appearing in some editions in the volume titled *Falk and Other Stories*); "Il Conde" from *A Set of Six;* "The Secret Sharer" from *'Twixt Land and Sea;* "Prince Roman" and "The Warrior's Soul" from *Tales of Hearsay;* the letters, with the exception of the three to Mme. Poradowska, from *Joseph Conrad: Life and Letters* by G. Jean-Aubry; and the shorter passages in the final sections of this volume from the books by Conrad named at the end of individual passages.

Permission to quote the three letters to Mme. Poradowska has been generously given by the Yale University Press, publishers of *Letters of Joseph Conrad to Marguerite Poradowska: 1890-1920,* translated from the French and edited by John A. Gee and Paul J. Sturm (1940).

Certain portions of the material in the editor's "Introduction" have appeared in another form in *The New Republic, The Nation,* and *The Sewanee Review.* A Conrad Chronology, including his principal works with the dates of their book appearance, follows this page, and a bibliographical note will be found at the end of the volume.

M.D.Z.

# A Conrad Chronology

1857.   December 3. Jozef Teodor Konrad Nałęcz Korzeniowski· born at Berdyczew in Poland (under Russian rule) to Apollo Nałecz Korzeniowski (born 1820) and his wife Ewelina Bobrowska, aged 26.

1862.   Parents move to Warsaw. Father condemned to exile in Russia for his part in the secret Polish National Committee, his wife and son accompanying him.

1865.   April 6. Conrad's mother dies as a result of hardships in exile.

1866.   Conrad sent to his uncle, Tadeusz Bobrowski, at Nowofastow, Polish Ukraine. Then to Kiev.

1868.   Father permitted to live in Lemberg, Galicia. Conrad in high school there.

1869.   They move to Cracow. Conrad in preparatory school there. Father dies, May 23. Conrad at St. Anne High School, Cracow. In summer to Wartenberg, Bohemia, with grandmother.

1870-74. Studies under tutor, Mr. Pulman, a student in the University of Cracow.

1872.   Conrad given freedom of Cracow, exempt from tax, in honor of his father. Fails to secure Austrian citizenship. Tells uncle Thaddeus of his desire to be a seaman.

1873.   On vacation with Mr. Pulman in Germany, Switzerland, Italy. Sees the sea for the first time at Venice.

**1874-75.** October 14, to Marseilles. Employed by Delestang and Sons, bankers and shippers. Enters French marine service. Apprenticeship on *Mont-Blanc* on voyage from Marseilles to Martinique to Le Havre (June-December 1875).

**1876-77.** In Marseilles in the *légitimiste* circle of the banker Delestang. Then on schooner *St.-Antoine* to West Indies (July 1876-February 1877).

**1877.** Buys share in the tartane *Tremolino* carrying arms illegally from Marseilles to Spain for the Carlist rising in support of the Spanish pretender Don Carlos.

**1878.** After unhappy ending of love affair (cf. *The Arrow of Gold*) and duel with the American J. M. K. Blunt,* leaves Marseilles, April 24, on British steamer *Mavis* for Constantinople. On June 18 reaches England for the first time, on the *Mavis* at Lowestoft.

**1878-79.** Sails as ordinary seaman on *The Skimmer of the Seas*, English east coast; *Duke of Sutherland*, London-Australia; *Europa*, London-Mediterranean.

**1880-90.** Career as Merchant Service officer (third mate papers, 1880; first mate, 1883; master, 1886) on ships *Loch-Etive*, London-Australia; *Anna Frost; Palestine*, London-Indian Ocean; *Riversdale*, London-Madras; *Narcissus*, Bombay-Dunkirk; *Tilkhurst*, Hull-Cardiff-Singapore; *Highland Forest*, Amsterdam-Java; *Vidar*, Singapore-Borneo; *Melita*, Singapore-Bangkok; *Otago*, Bangkok-Sydney-Mauritius-Port Adelaide (first command, 1888-89). Etc.

**1886.** August 19. Naturalized as British subject.

**1890.** On the *Ville de Maceio*, in the employ of the Société Anonyme Belge pour le Commeroe du Haut-Congo, from France to the Belgian Congo. On the SS *Roi des Belges* up the Congo River. Ill with dysentery, fever, and gout.

**1891.** Manages Thames-side warehouses of Barr, Moering and Co., London.

* See Addendum, p. 47.—F. R. K.

1891-93. First mate on *Torrens,* Plymouth-Adelaide-Cape Town-St. Helena-London.

1893-94. Second mate on *Adowa,* London-Rouen-London. Ends seaman's career January 14, 1894.

1895. *Almayer's Folly* published in London (begun in London, 1889, and written on voyages and in ports, 1889-95). Lives in London, 17 Gillingham St., S. W.

1896. *An Outcast of the Islands.* Marries Jessie George, March 24. Honeymoon in Brittany. Begin housekeeping at Ivy Walls, Stanford-le-Hope, Essex.

1897. *The Nigger of the "Narcissus."*

1898. *Tales of Unrest* ("Karain: A Memory," "The Idiots," "An Outpost of Progress," "The Return," "The Lagoon"). Son Borys born. Moves to Pent Farm, Kent.

1899. Shares *The Academy* prize of 150 guineas for *Tales of Unrest* (with Maurice Hewlett and Sydney Lee).

1900. *Lord Jim.*

1901. *The Inheritors* (written with Ford Madox Hueffer [Ford]).

1902. *Typhoon.*

1902. *Youth: A Narrative, and Two Other Stories* ("Heart of Darkness," "The End of the Tether").

1903. *Typhoon and Other Stories* ("Amy Foster," "Falk," "Tomorrow").

1903. *Romance* (with Ford Madox Hueffer [Ford]).

1904. *Nostromo.*

1905. Granted a Civil List pension, at instigation of William Rothenstein and Edmund Gosse. Travels on continent for 4 months.

1906. *The Mirror of the Sea.* Spends two months in Montpellier, France. Son John Alexander born.

1907. *The Secret Agent.* Moves to Someries, near Luton, Bedfordshire.

1908. *A Set of Six* ("The Informer," "Gaspar Ruiz," "The Brute," "An Anarchist," "The Duel," "Il Conde").

1909. Moves to Aldington, near Hythe, Kent.

1910. Moves to Capel House, Orlestone, near Ashford, Kent.

1911. *Under Western Eyes.*

1912. *Some Reminiscences* (*A Personal Record*).

1912. *'Twixt Land and Sea* ("A Smile of Fortune," "The Secret Sharer," "Freya of the Seven Isles").

1914. *Chance* (first issues dated 1913). Revisits Poland with his family; caught there by the war in August; their escape aided by Frederic Courtland Penfield, American ambassador to Austria; return to England in November.

1915. *Within the Tides* ("The Planter of Malata," "The Partner," "The Inn of the Two Witches," "Because of the Dollars"). *Victory.*

1916. Visits naval stations in North Sea on invitation of Admiralty.

1917. *The Shadow-Line.* Writes prefaces for collected edition of works, 1917-20.

1919. *The Arrow of Gold.* Moves to Oswalds, Bishopsbourne, near Canterbury.

1920. *The Rescue.* Writes dramatization of *The Secret Agent.*

1921. *Notes on Life and Letters.* Visits Corsica with Mrs. Conrad.

1922. *The Secret Agent* presented as play for short run in London, November 3.

1923. *The Rover.* Visits the United States, April-June. Last sea voyage. Gives one reading from his books (*Victory*) at house of Mrs. Arthur Curtiss James, New York, May 10.

1924. Declines knighthood. Dies suddenly of heart attack on August 3, at Oswalds. Buried at Canterbury.

1925. *Suspense* (unfinished).

1925. *Tales of Hearsay* ("The Warrior's Soul," "Prince Roman," "The Tale," "The Black Mate").

1926. *Last Essays.*

# Poland and the Past

~~~~~~~~~~~~~~~~~~~~~~~~~~~~~~~~~~~~~~~~~~~~~~~

## PRINCE ROMAN

## THE WARRIOR'S SOUL

Qui de nous n'a eu sa terre promise, son jour d'extase, et sa fin en exil.
>
> —Amiel [on the title-page of *Almayer's Folly*]

"I would take liberty from any hand as a hungry man would snatch a piece of bread."
>
> —Miss Haldin [on the title-page of *Under Western Eyes*]

That country which demands to be loved as no other country has ever been loved, with the mournful affection one bears to the unforgotten dead and with the unextinguishable fire of a hopeless passion which only a living, breathing, warm ideal can kindle in our breasts for our pride, for our weariness, for our exultation, for our undoing.
>
> —Conrad: *Tales of Hearsay*

One's literary life must turn frequently for sustenance to memories and seek discourse with the shades. . . . I would not like to be left standing as a mere spectator on the bank of the great stream carrying onward so many lives. I would fain claim for myself the faculty of so much insight as can be expressed in a voice of sympathy and compassion.
>
> —Conrad: *A Personal Record*

Conrad was born in Berdyczew, Poland, then under Russian rule, on December 3, 1857. The two families of his parents—the Korzeniowskis and the Bobrowskis—were Poles of the "land-tilling gentry" with connections in the Almanach de Gotha, and they were also zealous patriots. His uncle Stefan Bobrowski was in the Provisional Polish Government and died in a duel with a political enemy in 1862. His uncle Robert Korzeniowski was killed in the Polish rising against Russia in 1863. Another uncle, Hilary Korzeniowski, was exiled to Siberia in 1863 and died there ten years later. Conrad's father, Apollo Nałęcz Korzeniowski, an ardent patriot and rebel as well as a gifted poet and translator, was deported to the Government Vologda in Russia for his part in the secret Polish National Committee in 1862, his wife and young son accompanying him. Both parents died as a result of the hardships of exile, the mother in 1865 and the father in 1869. Conrad remained in Poland with his mother's people until he was almost seventeen years old. By that time his inclination toward western Europe and a career as seaman had asserted itself, and he took the Vienna express that brought him to Marseilles in October 1874. Then followed his four years in Marseilles and in the French merchant marine service; his trips in 1875 and 1876-77 on French ships to the West Indies; his adventure in 1877 carrying illegal arms on the tartane *Tremolino* to the Carlists in Spain; his first trip on an English boat, the *Mavis,* and his landing on English soil for the first time at Lowestoft on June 18, 1878; his sixteen years of service as seaman and marine officer that took him over the oceans of the world, to Asia, the Pacific, and the Congo; and eventually his career as a writer which began with the publication of *Almayer's Folly* in 1895. He visited his guardian uncle Tadeusz Bobrowski in Poland in 1890 and in 1893, but did not return again until he went there with his wife and sons in the summer of 1914, when they were caught by the mobilization and aided in their return to England by the American ambassador in Vienna, Frederic Courtland Penfield, to whom *The Rescue* was dedicated in gratitude in 1920. Before leaving on that journey Conrad wrote to Galsworthy: "In 1874 I got into a train in Cracow (Vienna Express) on my way to the sea, as a man might get into a dream. And here is the dream going on still. Only now it is peopled by ghosts and the moment of awakening draws near."

Polish loyalty and feeling remained deep in Conrad. One interpreter of his work, Gustav Morf, has gone so far as to charge the essential animus and motivation of Conrad's art to the Polish heritage of his family and to his own sense of deserting a sacred patriotic trust. His return in 1914 awakened memories and ties that had lain dormant over forty years. His story "Amy Foster" of 1901 had already told the tale of a Pole exiled in England, and both *The Secret Agent* (1907) and *Under Western Eyes* (1911) dealt with characters of the enemy country of Russia. *A Personal Record* (1912) revived the scenes of his childhood and youth. Conrad returned to Slavic themes in "Prince Roman" (1911), based on the career in Polish patriotism and Siberian exile of his grandfather Korzeniowski's old comrade-in-arms Prince Roman Sanguszko, and in "The Warrior's Soul" (1916), both of which were included in the posthumous *Tales of Hearsay* (1925). During these years Conrad also wrote the five Polish and political essays included in *Notes on Life and Letters* (1921), in one of which, "Poland Revisited" (1915), he gave a moving account of his return to Poland in 1914: "this journey of ours, which for me was essentially not a progress, but a retracing of footsteps on the road of life It seemed to me that if I remained longer there . . . I should become the helpless prey of the shadows I had called up. They were crowding upon me, enigmatic and insistent, in their clinging air of the grave that tasted of dust and of the bitter vanity of old hopes."

# Prince Roman

~~~~~~~~~~~~~~~~~~~~~~~~~~~~~~~~~~~~~~~~

"EVENTS which happened seventy years ago are perhaps rather too far off to be dragged aptly into a mere conversation. Of course the year 1831 is for us an historical date, one of these fatal years when in the presence of the world's passive indignation and eloquent sympathies we had once more to murmur 'Væ Victis' and count the cost in sorrow. Not that we were ever very good at calculating, either, in prosperity or in adversity. That's a lesson we could never learn, to the great exasperation of our enemies who have bestowed upon us the epithet of Incorrigible. . . ."

The speaker was of Polish nationality, that nationality not so much alive as surviving, which persists in thinking, breathing, speaking, hoping, and suffering in its grave, railed in by a million bayonets and triple-sealed with the seals of three great empires.

The conversation was about aristocracy. How did this, nowadays discredited, subject come up? It is some years ago now and the precise recollection has faded. But I remember that it was not considered practically as an ingredient in the social mixture; and I truly believed that we arrived at that subject through some exchange of ideas about patriotism—a somewhat discredited sentiment, because the delicacy of our humanitarians regards it as a relic of barbarism. Yet neither the great Florentine painter who closed his eyes in death

thinking of his city, nor St. Francis blessing with his last
breath the town of Assisi, were barbarians. It requires
a certain greatness of soul to interpret patriotism
worthily—or else a sincerity of feeling denied to the
vulgar refinement of modern thought which cannot understand the august simplicity of a sentiment proceeding from the very nature of things and men.

The aristocracy we were talking about was the very
highest, the great families of Europe, not impoverished,
not converted, not liberalized, the most distinctive and
specialized class of all classes, for which even ambition
itself does not exist among the usual incentives to activity and regulators of conduct.

The undisputed right of leadership having passed
away from them, we judged that their great fortunes,
their cosmopolitanism brought about by wide alliances,
their elevated station, in which there is so little to gain
and so much to lose, must make their position difficult
in times of political commotion or national upheaval.
No longer born to command—which is the very essence
of aristocracy—it becomes difficult for them to do anything else but hold aloof from the great movements of
popular passion.

We had reached that conclusion when the remark
about far-off events was made and the date of 1831
mentioned. And the speaker continued:

"I don't mean to say that I knew Prince Roman at
that remote time. I begin to feel pretty ancient, but I
am not so ancient as that. In fact Prince Roman was
married the very year my father was born. It was in
1828; the nineteenth century was young yet and the
Prince was even younger than the century, but I don't
know exactly by how much. In any case his was an early
marriage. It was an ideal alliance from every point of
view. The girl was young and beautiful, an orphan heir-

ess of a great name and of a great fortune. The Prince,
then an officer in the Guards and distinguished amongst
his fellows by something reserved and reflective in his
character, had fallen headlong in love with her beauty,
her charm, and the serious qualities of her mind and
heart. He was a rather silent young man; but his glances,
his bearing, his whole person expressed his absolute devotion to the woman of his choice, a devotion which she
returned in her own frank and fascinating manner.

"The flame of this pure young passion promised to
burn for ever; and for a season it lit up the dry, cynical
atmosphere of the great world of St. Petersburg. The
Emperor Nicholas himself, the grandfather of the present man, the one who died from the Crimean War, the
last perhaps of the autocrats with a mystical belief in the
divine character of his mission, showed some interest
in this pair of married lovers. It is true that Nicholas
kept a watchful eye on all the doings of the great Polish
nobles. The young people leading a life appropriate to
their station were obviously wrapped up in each other;
and society, fascinated by the sincerity of a feeling moving serenely among the artificialities of its anxious and
fastidious agitation, watched them with benevolent indulgence and an amused tenderness.

"The marriage was the social event of 1828, in the
capital. Just forty years afterwards I was staying in the
country house of my mother's brother in our southern
provinces.

"It was the dead of winter. The great lawn in front
was as pure and smooth as an alpine snowfield, a white
and feathery level sparkling under the sun as if sprinkled
with diamond-dust, declining gently to the lake—a long,
sinuous piece of frozen water looking bluish and more
solid than the earth. A cold brilliant sun glided low
above an undulating horizon of great folds of snow in

which the villages of Ukrainian peasants remained out of sight, like clusters of boats hidden in the hollows of a running sea. And everything was very still.

"I don't know now how I had managed to escape at eleven o'clock in the morning from the schoolroom. I was a boy of eight, the little girl, my cousin, a few months younger than myself, though hereditarily more quick-tempered, was less adventurous. So I had escaped alone; and presently I found myself in the great stone-paved hall, warmed by a monumental stove of white tiles, a much more pleasant locality than the school-room, which for some reason or other, perhaps hygienic, was always kept at a low temperature.

"We children were aware that there was a guest stay-ing in the house. He had arrived the night before just as we were being driven off to bed. We broke back through the line of beaters to rush and flatten our noses against the dark windowpanes; but we were too late to see him alight. We had only watched in a ruddy glare the big traveling carriage on sleigh-runners harnessed with six horses, a black mass against the snow, going off to the stables, preceded by a horseman carrying a blazing ball of tow and resin in an iron basket at the end of a long stick swung from his saddle bow. Two stable boys had been sent out early in the afternoon along the snow-tracks to meet the expected guest at dusk and light his way with these road torches. At that time, you must remember, there was not a single mile of railways in our southern provinces. My little cousin and I had no knowledge of trains and engines, except from picture books, as of things rather vague, extremely remote, and not particularly interesting unless to grownups who traveled abroad.

"Our notion of princes, perhaps a little more precise, was mainly literary and had a glamor reflected from the light of fairy tales, in which princes always appear young, charming, heroic, and fortunate. Yet, as well as any other children, we could draw a firm line between the real and the ideal. We knew that princes were historical personages. And there was some glamor in that fact, too. But what had driven me to roam cautiously over the house like an escaped prisoner was the hope of snatching an interview with a special friend of mine, the head forester, who generally came to make his report at that time of the day. I yearned for news of a certain wolf. You know, in a country where wolves are to be found, every winter almost brings forward an individual eminent by the audacity of his misdeeds, by his more perfect wolfishness—so to speak. I wanted to hear some new thrilling tale of that wolf—perhaps the dramatic story of his death. . . .

"But there was no one in the hall.

"Deceived in my hopes, I became suddenly very much depressed. Unable to slip back in triumph to my studies I elected to stroll spiritlessly into the billiard room where certainly I had no business. There was no one there either, and I felt very lost and desolate under its high ceiling, all alone with the massive English billiard table which seemed, in heavy, rectilinear silence, to disapprove of that small boy's intrusion.

"As I began to think of retreat I heard footsteps in the adjoining drawing room; and, before I could turn tail and flee, my uncle and his guest appeared in the doorway. To run away after having been seen would have been highly improper, so I stood my ground. My uncle looked surprised to see me; the guest by his side was a spare man, of average stature, buttoned up in a black frock coat and holding himself very erect with a stiffly soldier-like carriage. From the folds of a soft white

cambric neck-cloth peeped the points of a collar close
against each shaven cheek. A few wisps of thin gray hair
were brushed smoothly across the top of his bald head.
His face, which must have been beautiful in its day,
had preserved in age the harmonious simplicity of its
lines. What amazed me was its even, almost deathlike
pallor. He seemed to me to be prodigiously old. A faint
smile, a mere momentary alteration in the set of his thin
lips acknowledged my blushing confusion; and I became greatly interested to see him reach into the inside
breastpocket of his coat. He extracted therefrom a lead
pencil and a block of detachable pages, which he
handed to my uncle with an almost imperceptible bow.

"I was very much astonished, but my uncle received
it as a matter of course. He wrote something at which
the other glanced and nodded slightly. A thin wrinkled
hand—the hand was older than the face—patted my
cheek and then rested on my head lightly. An unringing
voice, a voice as colorless as the face itself, issued from
his sunken lips, while the eyes, dark and still, looked
down at me kindly.

" 'And how old is this shy little boy?' "

"Before I could answer my uncle wrote down my age
on the pad. I was deeply impressed. What was this
ceremony? Was this personage too great to be spoken
to? Again he glanced at the pad, and again gave a nod,
and again that impersonal, mechanical voice was heard:
'He resembles his grandfather.'

"I remembered my paternal grandfather. He had died
not long before. He, too, was prodigiously old. And to
me it seemed perfectly natural that two such ancient
and venerable persons should have known each other in
the dim ages of creation before my birth. But my uncle
obviously had not been aware of the fact. So obviously

that the mechanical voice explained: 'Yes, yes. Comrades in '31. He was one of those who knew. Old times, my dear sir, old times. . . .'

"He made a gesture as if to put aside an importunate ghost. And now they were both looking down at me. I wondered whether anything was expected from me. To my round, questioning eyes my uncle remarked: 'He's completely deaf.' And the unrelated, inexpressive voice said: 'Give me your hand.'

"Acutely conscious of inky fingers I put it out timidly. I had never seen a deaf person before and was rather startled. He pressed it firmly and then gave me a final pat on the head.

"My uncle addressed me weightily: 'You have shaken hands with Prince Roman S——. It's something for you to remember when you grow up.'

"I was impressed by his tone. I had enough historical information to know vaguely that the Princes S—— counted amongst the sovereign Princes of Ruthenia till the union of all Ruthenian lands to the kingdom of Poland, when they became great Polish magnates, some time at the beginning of the fifteenth century. But what concerned me most was the failure of the fairy-tale glamor. It was shocking to discover a prince who was deaf, bald, meager, and so prodigiously old. It never occurred to me that this imposing and disappointing man had been young, rich, beautiful; I could not know that he had been happy in the felicity of an ideal marriage uniting two young hearts, two great names and two great fortunes; happy with a happiness which, as in fairy tales, seemed destined to last forever. . . .

"But it did not last forever. It was fated not to last very long even by the measure of the days allotted to men's passage on this earth where enduring happiness is only found in the conclusion of fairy tales. A daughter was born to them and shortly afterwards, the health of the young princess began to fail. For a time she bore up with smiling intrepidity, sustained by the feeling that now her existence was necessary for the happiness of two lives. But at last the husband, thoroughly alarmed by the rapid changes in her appearance, obtained an unlimited leave and took her away from the capital to his parents in the country.

"The old prince and princess were extremely frightened at the state of their beloved daughter-in-law. Preparations were at once made for a journey abroad. But it seemed as if it were already too late; and the invalid herself opposed the project with gentle obstinacy. Thin and pale in the great armchair, where the insidious and obscure nervous malady made her appear smaller and more frail every day without effacing the smile of her eyes or the charming grace of her wasted face, she clung to her native land and wished to breathe her native air. Nowhere else could she expect to get well so quickly, nowhere else would it be so easy for her to die.

"She died before her little girl was two years old. The grief of the husband was terrible and the more alarming to his parents because perfectly silent and dry-eyed. After the funeral, while the immense bareheaded crowd of peasants surrounding the private chapel on the grounds was dispersing, the Prince, waving away his friends and relations, remained alone to watch the masons of the estate closing the family vault. When the last stone was in position he uttered a groan, the first sound of pain which had escaped from him for days, and walking away with lowered head shut himself up again in his apartments.

"His father and mother feared for his reason. His out-

ward tranquillity was appalling to them. They had nothing to trust to but that very youth which made his
despair so self-absorbed and so intense. Old Prince John,
fretful and anxious, repeated: 'Poor Roman should be
roused somehow. He's so young.' But they could find
nothing to rouse him with. And the old princess, wiping
her eyes, wished in her heart he were young enough to
come and cry at her knee.

"In time Prince Roman, making an effort, would join
now and again the family circle. But it was as if his
heart and his mind had been buried in the family vault
with the wife he had lost. He took to wandering in the
woods with a gun, watched over secretly by one of the
keepers, who would report in the evening that 'His
Serenity has never fired a shot all day.' Sometimes walking to the stables in the morning he would order in subdued tones a horse to be saddled, wait switching his
boot till it was led up to him, then mount without a
word and ride out of the gates at a walking pace. He
would be gone all day. People saw him on the roads
looking neither to the right nor to the left, white-faced,
sitting rigidly in the saddle like a horseman of stone on
a living mount.

"The peasants working in the fields, the great un-
hedged fields, looked after him from the distance; and
sometimes some sympathetic old woman on the threshold of a low, thatched hut was moved to make the sign
of the cross in the air behind his back; as though he
were one of themselves, a simple village soul struck by
a sore affliction.

"He rode looking straight ahead, seeing no one, as if
the earth were empty and all mankind buried in that
grave which had opened so suddenly in his path to
swallow up his happiness. What were men to him with
their sorrows, joys, labors and passions from which she

who had been all the world to him had been cut off so early?

"They did not exist; and he would have felt as completely lonely and abandoned as a man in the toils of a cruel nightmare if it had not been for this countryside where he had been born and had spent his happy boyish years. He knew it well—every slight rise crowned with trees amongst the plowed fields, every dell concealing a village. The dammed streams made a chain of lakes set in the green meadows. Far away to the north the great Lithuanian forest faced the sun, no higher than a hedge; and to the south, the way to the plains, the vast brown spaces of the earth touched the blue sky.

"And this familiar landscape associated with the days without thought and without sorrow, this land the charm of which he felt without even looking at it soothed his pain, like the presence of an old friend who sits silent and disregarded by one in some dark hour of life.

"One afternoon, it happened that the Prince after turning his horse's head for home remarked a low dense cloud of dark dust cutting off slantwise a part of the view. He reined in on a knoll and peered. There were slender gleams of steel here and there in that cloud, and it contained moving forms which revealed themselves at last as a long line of peasant carts full of soldiers, moving slowly in double file under the escort of mounted Cossacks.

"It was like an immense reptile creeping over the fields; its head dipped out of sight in a slight hollow and its tail went on writhing and growing shorter as though the monster were eating its way slowly into the very heart of the land.

"The Prince directed his way through a village lying a little off the track. The roadside inn with its stable, byre, and barn under one enormous thatched roof resembled a deformed, hunchbacked, ragged giant, sprawling amongst the small huts of the peasants. The innkeeper, a portly, dignified Jew, clad in a black satin coat reaching down to his heels and girt with a red sash, stood at the door stroking his long silvery beard.

"He watched the Prince approach and bowed gravely from the waist, not expecting to be noticed even, since it was well known that their young lord had no eyes for anything or anybody in his grief. It was quite a shock for him when the Prince pulled up and asked:

" 'What's all this, Yankel?'

" 'That is, please your Serenity, that is a convoy of foot soldiers. They are hurrying down to the south.'

"He glanced right and left cautiously, but as there was no one near but some children playing in the dust of the village street, he came up close to the stirrup.

" 'Doesn't your Serenity know? It has begun already down there. All the landowners great and small are out in arms and even the common people have risen. Only yesterday the saddler from Grodek (it was a tiny market town near by) went through here with his two apprentices on his way to join. He left even his cart with me. I gave him a guide through our neighborhood. You know, your Serenity, our people they travel a lot and they see all that's going on, and they know all the roads.'

"He tried to keep down his excitement, for the Jew Yankel, innkeeper and tenant of all the mills on the estate, was a Polish patriot. And in a still lower voice:

" 'I was already a married man when the French and all the other nations passed this way with Napoleon. Tse! Tse! That was a great harvest for death, *nu!* Perhaps this time God will help.'

"The Prince nodded. 'Perhaps'—and falling into deep meditation he let his horse take him home.

"That night he wrote a letter, and early in the morning sent a mounted express to the post town. During the day he came out of his taciturnity, to the great joy of the family circle, and conversed with his father of recent events—the revolt in Warsaw, the flight of the Grand Duke Constantine, the first slight successes of the Polish army (at that time there was a Polish army); the risings in the provinces. Old Prince John, moved and uneasy, speaking from a purely aristocratic point of view, mistrusted the popular origins of the movement, regretted its democratic tendencies, and did not believe in the possibility of success. He was sad, inwardly agitated.

" 'I am judging all this calmly. There are secular principles of legitimacy and order which have been violated in this reckless enterprise for the sake of most subversive illusions. Though of course the patriotic impulses of the heart. . . .'

"Prince Roman had listened in a thoughtful attitude. He took advantage of the pause to tell his father quietly that he had sent that morning a letter to St. Petersburg resigning his commission in the Guards.

"The old prince remained silent. He thought that he ought to have been consulted. His son was also ordnance officer to the Emperor and he knew that the Tsar would never forget this appearance of defection in a Polish noble. In a discontented tone he pointed out to his son that as it was he had an unlimited leave. The right thing would have been to keep quiet. They had too much tact at Court to recall a man of his name. Or at worst some distant mission might have been asked for—to the Caucasus for instance—away from this unhappy struggle which was wrong in principle and therefore destined to fail.

" 'Presently you shall find yourself without any interest in life and with no occupation. And you shall need something to occupy you, my poor boy. You have acted rashly, I fear.'

"Prince Roman murmured.

" 'I thought it better.'

"His father faltered under his steady gaze.

" 'Well, well—perhaps! But as ordnance officer to the Emperor and in favor with all the Imperial family. . . .'

" 'Those people had never been heard of when our house was already illustrious,' the young man let fall disdainfully.

"This was the sort of remark to which the old prince was sensible.

" 'Well—perhaps it is better,' he conceded at last.

"The father and son parted affectionately for the night. The next day Prince Roman seemed to have fallen back into the depths of his indifference. He rode out as usual. He remembered that the day before he had seen a reptile-like convoy of soldiery, bristling with bayonets, crawling over the face of that land which was his. The woman he loved had been his, too. Death had robbed him of her. Her loss had been to him a moral shock. It had opened his heart to a greater sorrow, his mind to a vaster thought, his eyes to all the past and to the existence of another love fraught with pain but as mysteriously imperative as that lost one to which he had entrusted his happiness.

"That evening he retired earlier than usual and rang for his personal servant.

" 'Go and see if there is light yet in the quarters of the Master-of-the-Horse. If he is still up ask him to come and speak to me.'

"While the servant was absent on this errand the Prince tore up hastily some papers, locked the drawers of his desk, and hung a medallion, containing the miniature of his wife, round his neck against his breast.

"The man the Prince was expecting belonged to that past which the death of his love had called to life. He was of a family of small nobles who for generations had been adherents, servants, and friends of the Princes S——. He remembered the times before the last partition and had taken part in the struggles of the last hour. He was a typical old Pole of that class, with a great capacity for emotion, for blind enthusiasm; with martial instincts and simple beliefs; and even with the old-time habit of larding his speech with Latin words. And his kindly shrewd eyes, his ruddy face, his lofty brow and his thick, gray, pendent mustache were also very typical of his kind.

" 'Listen, Master Francis,' the Prince said familiarly and without preliminaries. 'Listen, old friend. I am going to vanish from here quietly. I go where something louder than my grief and yet something with a voice very like it calls me. I confide in you alone. You will say what's necessary when the time comes.'

"The old man understood. His extended hands trembled exceedingly. But as soon as he found his voice he thanked God aloud for letting him live long enough to see the descendant of the illustrious family in its youngest generation give an example *coram Gentibus* of the love of his country and of valor in the field. He doubted not of his dear Prince attaining a place in council and in war worthy of his high birth; he saw already that *in fulgore* of family glory *affulget patride serenitas*. At the end of the speech he burst into tears and fell into the Prince's arms.

"The Prince quieted the old man and when he had him seated in an armchair and comparatively composed he said:

" 'Don't misunderstand me, Master Francis. You

know how I loved my wife. A loss like that opens one's eyes to unsuspected truths. There is no question here of leadership and glory. I mean to go alone and to fight obscurely in the ranks. I am going to offer my country what is mine to offer, that is my life, as simply as the saddler from Grodek who went through yesterday with his apprentices.'

"The old man cried out at this. That could never be. He could not allow it. But he had to give way before the arguments and the express will of the Prince.

"'Ha! If you say that it is a matter of feeling and conscience—so be it. But you cannot go utterly alone. Alas! that I am too old to be of any use. *Cripit verba dolor,* my dear Prince, at the thought that I am over seventy and of no more account in the world than a cripple in the church porch. It seems that to sit at home and pray to God for the nation and for you is all I am fit for. But there is my son, my youngest son, Peter. He will make a worthy companion for you. And as it happens he's staying with me here. There has not been for ages a Prince S—— hazarding his life without a companion of our name to ride by his side. You must have by you somebody who knows who you are if only to let your parents and your old servant hear what is happening to you. And when does your Princely Mightiness mean to start?'

"'In an hour,' said the Prince; and the old man hurried off to warn his son.

"Prince Roman took up a candlestick and walked quietly along a dark corridor in the silent house. The head nurse said afterwards that waking up suddenly she saw the Prince looking at his child, one hand shading the light from its eyes. He stood and gazed at her for some time, and then putting the candlestick on the floor bent over the cot and kissed lightly the little girl who did not wake. He went out noiselessly, taking the light away with him. She saw his face perfectly well, but she could read nothing of his purpose in it. It was pale but perfectly calm and after he turned away from the cot he never looked back at it once.

"The only other trusted person, besides the old man and his son Peter, was the Jew Yankel. When he asked the Prince where precisely he wanted to be guided the Prince answered: 'To the nearest party.' A grandson of the Jew, a lanky youth, conducted the two young men by little-known paths across woods and morasses, and led them in sight of the few fires of a small detachment camped in a hollow. Some invisible horses neighed, a voice in the dark cried: 'Who goes there?' . . . and the young Jew departed hurriedly, explaining that he must make haste home to be in time for keeping the Sabbath.

"Thus humbly and in accord with the simplicity of the vision of duty he saw when death had removed the brilliant bandage of happiness from his eyes, did Prince Roman bring his offering to his country. His companion made himself known as the son of the Master-of-the-Horse to the Princes S—— and declared him to be a relation, a distant cousin from the same parts as himself and, as people presumed, of the same name. In truth no one inquired much. Two more young men clearly of the right sort had joined. Nothing more natural.

"Prince Roman did not remain long in the south. One day while scouting with several others, they were ambushed near the entrance of a village by some Russian infantry. The first discharge laid low a good many and the rest scattered in all directions. The Russians, too, did not stay, being afraid of a return in force. After some time, the peasants coming to view the scene extricated Prince Roman from under his dead horse. He was unhurt but his faithful companion had been one of the first to fall. The Prince helped the peasants to bury him and the other dead.

"Then alone, not certain where to find the body of partisans which was constantly moving about in all directions, he resolved to try and join the main Polish army facing the Russians on the borders of Lithuania. Disguised in peasant clothes, in case of meeting some marauding Cossacks, he wandered a couple of weeks before he came upon a village occupied by a regiment of Polish cavalry on outpost duty.

"On a bench, before a peasant hut of a better sort, sat an elderly officer whom he took for the colonel. The Prince approached respectfully, told his story shortly and stated his desire to enlist; and when asked his name by the officer, who had been looking him over carefully, he gave on the spur of the moment the name of his dead companion.

"The elderly officer thought to himself: Here's the son of some peasant proprietor of the liberated class. He liked his appearance.

" 'And can you read and write, my good fellow?' he asked.

" 'Yes, your honor, I can,' said the Prince.

" 'Good. Come along inside the hut; the regimental adjutant is there. He will enter your name and administer the oath to you.'

"The adjutant stared very hard at the newcomer but said nothing. When all the forms had been gone through and the recruit gone out, he turned to his superior officer.

" 'Do you know who that is?'

" 'Who? That Peter? A likely chap.'

" 'That's Prince Roman S——.'

" 'Nonsense.'

"But the adjutant was positive. He had seen the Prince several times, about two years before, in the Castle in Warsaw. He had even spoken to him once at a reception of officers held by the Grand Duke.

" 'He's changed. He seems much older, but I am certain of my man. I have a good memory for faces.'

"The two officers looked at each other in silence.

" 'He's sure to be recognized sooner or later,' murmured the adjutant. The colonel shrugged his shoulders.

" 'It's no affair of ours—if he has a fancy to serve in the ranks. As to being recognized it's not so likely. All our officers and men come from the other end of Poland.'

"He meditated gravely for a while, then smiled. 'He told me he could read and write. There's nothing to prevent me making him a sergeant at the first opportunity. He's sure to shape all right.'

"Prince Roman as a noncommissioned officer surpassed the colonel's expectations. Before long Sergeant Peter became famous for his resourcefulness and courage. It was not the reckless courage of a desperate man; it was a self-possessed, as if conscientious, valor which nothing could dismay; a boundless but equable devotion, unaffected by time, by reverses, by the discouragement of endless retreats, by the bitterness of waning hopes and the horrors of pestilence added to the toils and perils of war. It was in this year that the cholera made its first appearance in Europe. It devastated the camps of both armies, affecting the firmest minds with the terror of a mysterious death stalking silently between the piled-up arms and around the bivouac fires.

"A sudden shriek would wake up the harassed soldiers and they would see in the glow of embers one of themselves writhe on the ground like a worm trodden on by an invisible foot. And before the dawn broke he would be stiff and cold. Parties so visited have been known to rise like one man, abandon the fire and run off into the night in mute panic. Or a comrade talking to you on the march would stammer suddenly in the middle of a sentence, roll affrighted eyes, and fall down with distorted face and blue lips, breaking the ranks with the convulsions of his agony. Men were struck in the saddle, on sentry duty, in the firing line, carrying orders, serving the guns. I have been told that in a battalion forming under fire with perfect steadiness for the assault of a village, three cases occurred within five minutes at the head of the column; and the attack could not be delivered because the leading companies scattered all over the fields like chaff before the wind.

"Sergeant Peter, young as he was, had a great influence over his men. It was said that the number of desertions in the squadron in which he served was less than in any other in the whole of that cavalry division. Such was supposed to be the compelling example of one man's quiet intrepidity in facing every form of danger and terror.

"However that may be, he was liked and trusted generally. When the end came and the remnants of that army corps, hard pressed on all sides, were preparing to cross the Prussian frontier, Sergeant Peter had enough influence to rally round him a score of troopers. He managed to escape with them at night, from the hemmed-in army. He led this band through two hundred miles of country covered by numerous Russian detachments and ravaged by the cholera. But this was not to avoid captivity, to go into hiding and try to save themselves. No. He led them into a fortress which was still occupied by the Poles, and where the last stand of the vanquished revolution was to be made.

"This looks like mere fanaticism. But fanaticism is

human. Man has adored ferocious divinities. There is
ferocity in every passion, even in love itself. The religion
of undying hope resembles the mad cult of despair, of
death, of annihilation. The difference lies in the moral
motive springing from the secret needs and the unexpressed aspiration of the believers. It is only to vain men
that all is vanity; and all is deception only to those who
have never been sincere with themselves.

"It was in the fortress that my grandfather found himself together with Sergeant Peter. My grandfather was
a neighbor of the S—— family in the country but he did
not know Prince Roman, who however knew his name
perfectly well. The Prince introduced himself one night
as they both sat on the ramparts, leaning against a gun
carriage.

"The service he wished to ask for was, in case of his
being killed, to have the intelligence conveyed to his
parents.

"They talked in low tones, the other servants of the
piece lying about near them. My grandfather gave the
required promise, and then asked frankly—for he was
greatly interested by the disclosure so unexpectedly
made:

" 'But tell me, Prince, why this request? Have you
any evil forebodings as to yourself?'

" 'Not in the least; I was thinking of my people. They
have no idea where I am,' answered Prince Roman. 'I'll
engage to do as much for you, if you like. It's certain
that half of us at least shall be killed before the end, so
there's an even chance of one of us surviving the other.'

"My grandfather told him where, as he supposed,
his wife and children were then. From that moment
till the end of the siege the two were much together.
On the day of the great assault my grandfather received
a severe wound. The town was taken. Next day the

citadel itself, its hospital full of dead and dying, its magazines empty, its defenders having burnt their last cartridge, opened its gates.

"During all the campaign the Prince, exposing his person conscientiously on every occasion, had not received a scratch. No one had recognized him or at any rate had betrayed his identity. Till then, as long as he did his duty, it had mattered nothing who he was.

"Now, however, the position was changed. As ex-guardsman and as late ordnance officer to the Emperor, this rebel ran a serious risk of being given special attention in the shape of a firing squad at ten paces. For more than a month he remained lost in the miserable crowd of prisoners packed in the casemates of the citadel, with just enough food to keep body and soul together but otherwise allowed to die from wounds, privation, and disease at the rate of forty or so a day.

"The position of the fortress being central, new parties, captured in the open in the course of a thorough pacification, were being sent in frequently. Amongst such newcomers there happened to be a young man, a personal friend of the Prince from his school days. He recognized him, and in the extremity of his dismay cried aloud: 'My God! Roman, you here!'

"It is said that years of life embittered by remorse paid for this momentary lack of self-control. All this happened in the main quadrangle of the citadel. The warning gesture of the Prince came too late. An officer of the gendarmes on guard had heard the exclamation. The incident appeared to him worth inquiring into. The investigation which followed was not very arduous because the Prince, asked categorically for his real name, owned up at once.

"The intelligence of the Prince S—— being found amongst the prisoners was sent to St. Petersburg. His parents were already there living in sorrow, incertitude, and apprehension. The capital of the Empire was the safest place to reside in for a noble whose son had disappeared so mysteriously from home in a time of rebellion. The old people had not heard from him, or of him, for months. They took care not to contradict the rumors of suicide from despair circulating in the great world, which remembered the interesting love-match, the charming and frank happiness brought to an end by death. But they hoped secretly that their son survived, and that he had been able to cross the frontier with that part of the army which had surrendered to the Prussians.

"The news of his captivity was a crushing blow. Directly, nothing could be done for him. But the greatness of their name, of their position, their wide relations and connections in the highest spheres, enabled his parents to act indirectly and they moved heaven and earth, as the saying is, to save their son from the 'consequences of his madness,' as poor Prince John did not hesitate to express himself. Great personages were approached by society leaders, high dignitaries were interviewed, powerful officials were induced to take an interest in that affair. The help of every possible secret influence was enlisted. Some private secretaries got heavy bribes. The mistress of a certain senator obtained a large sum of money.

"But, as I have said, in such a glaring case no direct appeal could be made and no open steps taken. All that could be done was to incline by private representation the mind of the President of the Military Commission to the side of clemency. He ended by being impressed by the hints and suggestions, some of them from very high quarters, which he received from St. Petersburg. And, after all, the gratitude of such great nobles as the

Princes S—— was something worth having from a worldly point of view. He was a good Russian but he was also a good-natured man. Moreover, the hate of Poles was not at that time a cardinal article of patriotic creed as it became some thirty years later. He felt well disposed at first sight towards that young man, bronzed, thin-faced, worn out by months of hard campaigning, the hardships of the siege and the rigors of captivity.

"The Commission was composed of three officers. It sat in the citadel in a bare vaulted room behind a long black table. Some clerks occupied the two ends, and besides the gendarmes who brought in the Prince there was no one else there.

"Within those four sinister walls shutting out from him all the sights and sounds of liberty, all hopes of the future, all consoling illusions—alone in the face of his enemies erected for judges, who can tell how much love of life there was in Prince Roman? How much remained in that sense of duty, revealed to him in sorrow? How much of his awakened love for his native country? That country which demands to be loved as no other country has ever been loved, with the mournful affection one bears to the unforgotten dead and with the unextinguishable fire of a hopeless passion which only a living, breathing, warm ideal can kindle in our breasts for our pride, for our weariness, for our exultation, for our undoing.

"There is something monstrous in the thought of such an exaction till it stands before us embodied in the shape of a fidelity without fear and without reproach. Nearing the supreme moment of his life the Prince could only have had the feeling that it was about to end. He answered the questions put to him clearly, concisely— with the most profound indifference. After all those tense months of action, to talk was a weariness to him.

But he concealed it, lest his foes should suspect in his manner the apathy of discouragement or the numbness of a crushed spirit. The details of his conduct could have no importance one way or another; with his thoughts these men had nothing to do. He preserved a scrupulously courteous tone. He had refused the permission to sit down.

"What happened at this preliminary examination is only known from the presiding officer. Pursuing the only possible course in that glaringly bad case he tried from the first to bring to the Prince's mind the line of defense he wished him to take. He absolutely framed his questions so as to put the right answers in the culprit's mouth, going so far as to suggest the very words: how, distracted by excessive grief after his young wife's death, rendered irresponsible for his conduct by his despair, in a moment of blind recklessness, without realizing the highly reprehensible nature of the act, nor yet its danger and its dishonor, he went off to join the nearest rebels on a sudden impulse. And that now, penitently. . . .

"But Prince Roman was silent. The military judges looked at him hopefully. In silence he reached for a pen and wrote on a sheet of paper he found under his hand: 'I joined the national rising from conviction.'

"He pushed the paper across the table. The president took it up, showed it in turn to his two colleagues sitting to the right and left, then looking fixedly at Prince Roman let it fall from his hand. And the silence remained unbroken till he spoke to the gendarmes ordering them to remove the prisoner.

"Such was the written testimony of Prince Roman in the supreme moment of his life. I have heard that the Princes of the S—— family, in all its branches, adopted the last two words: 'From conviction' for the device un-

der the armorial bearings of their house. I don't know
whether the report is true. My uncle could not tell me.
He remarked only, that naturally, it was not to be seen
on Prince Roman's own seal.

"He was condemned for life to Siberian mines. Emperor Nicholas, who always took personal cognizance
of all sentences on Polish nobility, wrote with his own
hand in the margin: 'The authorities are severely
warned to take care that this convict walks in chains
like any other criminal every step of the way.'

"It was a sentence of deferred death. Very few survived entombment in these mines for more than three
years. Yet as he was reported as still alive at the end of
that time he was allowed, on a petition of his parents
and by way of exceptional grace, to serve as common
soldier in the Caucasus. All communication with him
was forbidden. He had no civil rights. For all practical
purposes except that of suffering he was a dead man.
The little child he had been so careful not to wake up
when he kissed her in her cot, inherited all the fortune
after Prince John's death. Her existence saved those
immense estates from confiscation.

"It was twenty-five years before Prince Roman, stone
deaf, his health broken, was permitted to return to
Poland. His daughter married splendidly to a Polish-
Austrian *grand seigneur* and, moving in the cosmopolitan sphere of the highest European aristocracy, lived
mostly abroad in Nice and Vienna. He, settling down
on one of her estates, not the one with the palatial
residence but another where there was a modest little
house, saw very little of her.

"But Prince Roman did not shut himself up as if his
work were done. There was hardly anything done in
the private and public life of the neighborhood, in

which Prince Roman's advice and assistance were not called upon, and never in vain. It was well said that his days did not belong to himself but to his fellow citizens. And especially he was the particular friend of all returned exiles, helping them with purse and advice, arranging their affairs and finding them means of livelihood.

"I heard from my uncle many tales of his devoted activity, in which he was always guided by a simple wisdom, a high sense of honor, and the most scrupulous conception of private and public probity. He remains a living figure for me because of that meeting in a billiard room, when, in my anxiety to hear about a particularly wolfish wolf, I came in momentary contact with a man who was pre-eminently a man amongst all men capable of feeling deeply, of believing steadily, of loving ardently.

"I remember to this day the grasp of Prince Roman's bony, wrinkled hand closing on my small inky paw, and my uncle's half-serious, half-amused way of looking down at his trespassing nephew.

"They moved on and forgot that little boy. But I did not move; I gazed after them, not so much disappointed as disconcerted by this prince so utterly unlike a prince in a fairy tale. They moved very slowly across the room. Before reaching the other door the Prince stopped, and I heard him—I seem to hear him now—saying: 'I wish you would write to Vienna about filling up that post. He's a most deserving fellow—and your recommendation would be decisive.'

"My uncle's face turned to him expressed genuine wonder. It said as plainly as any speech could say: What better recommendation than a father's can be needed? The Prince was quick at reading expressions.

Again he spoke with the toneless accent of a man who has not heard his own voice for years, for whom the soundless world is like an abode of silent shades.

"And to this day I remember the very words: 'I ask you because, you see, my daughter and my son-in-law don't believe me to be a good judge of men. They think that I let myself be guided too much by mere sentiment.'"

# The Warrior's Soul

THE old officer with long white mustaches gave rein to his indignation.

"Is it possible that you youngsters should have no more sense than that! Some of you had better wipe the milk off your upper lip before you start to pass judgment on the few poor stragglers of a generation which has done and suffered not a little in its time."

His hearers having expressed much compunction the ancient warrior became appeased. But he was not silenced.

"I am one of them—one of the stragglers, I mean," he went on patiently. "And what did we do? What have we achieved? He—the great Napoleon—started upon us to emulate the Macedonian Alexander, with a ruck of nations at his back. We opposed empty spaces to French impetuosity, then we offered them an interminable battle so that their army went at last to sleep in its positions lying down on the heaps of its own dead. Then came the wall of fire in Moscow. It toppled down on them.

"Then began the long rout of the Grand Army. I have seen it stream on, like the doomed flight of haggard, spectral sinners across the innermost frozen circle of Dante's Inferno, ever widening before their despairing eyes.

"They who escaped must have had their souls doubly

riveted inside their bodies to carry them out of Russia through that frost fit to split rocks. But to say that it was our fault that a single one of them got away is mere ignorance. Why! Our own men suffered nearly to the limit of their strength. Their Russian strength!

"Of course our spirit was not broken; and then our cause was good—it was holy. But that did not temper the wind much to men and horses.

"The flesh is weak. Good or evil purpose, Humanity has to pay the price. Why! In that very fight for that little village of which I have been telling you we were fighting for the shelter of those old houses as much as victory. And with the French it was the same.

"It wasn't for the sake of glory, or for the sake of strategy. The French knew that they would have to retreat before morning and we knew perfectly well that they would go. As far as the war was concerned there was nothing to fight about. Yet our infantry and theirs fought like wildcats, or like heroes if you like that better, amongst the houses—hot work enough—while the supports out in the open stood freezing in a tempestuous north wind which drove the snow on earth and the great masses of clouds in the sky at a terrific pace. The very air was inexpressibly somber by contrast with the white earth. I have never seen God's creation look more sinister than on that day.

"We, the cavalry (we were only a handful), had not much to do except turn our backs to the wind and receive some stray French round shot. This, I may tell you, was the last of the French guns and it was the last time they had their artillery in position. Those guns never went away from there either. We found them abandoned next morning. But that afternoon they were keeping up an infernal fire on our attacking column; the furious wind carried away the smoke and even the noise but we could see the constant flicker of the tongues of fire along the French front. Then a driving flurry of snow would hide everything except the dark red flashes in the white swirl.

"At intervals when the line cleared we could see away across the plain to the right a somber column moving endlessly; the great rout of the Grand Army creeping on and on all the time while the fight on our left went on with a great din and fury. The cruel whirlwind of snow swept over that scene of death and desolation. And then the wind fell as suddenly as it had arisen in the morning.

"Presently we got orders to charge the retreating column; I don't know why unless they wanted to prevent us from getting frozen in our saddles by giving us something to do. We changed front half right and got into motion at a walk to take that distant dark line in flank. It might have been half-past two in the afternoon.

"You must know that so far in this campaign my regiment had never been on the main line of Napoleon's advance. All these months since the invasion the army we belonged to had been wrestling with Oudinot in the north. We had only come down lately, driving him before us to the Beresina.

"This was the first occasion, then, that I and my comrades had a close view of Napoleon's Grand Army. It was an amazing and terrible sight. I had heard of it from others; I had seen the stragglers from it: small bands of marauders, parties of prisoners in the distance. But this was the very column itself! A crawling, stumbling, starved, half-demented mob. It issued from the forest a mile away and its head was lost in the murk of the fields. We rode into it at a trot, which was the most we could get out of our horses, and we stuck in that human mass as if in a moving bog. There was no resistance. I heard a few

shots, half a dozen perhaps. Their very senses seemed
frozen within them. I had time for a good look while
riding at the head of my squadron. Well, I assure you,
there were men walking on the outer edge so lost to
everything but their misery that they never turned their
heads to look at our charge. Soldiers!

"My horse pushed over one of them with his chest.
The poor wretch had a dragoon's blue cloak, all torn
and scorched, hanging from his shoulders and he didn't
even put his hand out to snatch at my bridle and save
himself. He just went down. Our troopers were pointing and slashing; well, and of course at first I myself
. . . What would you have! An enemy is an enemy. Yet
a sort of sickening awe crept into my heart. There was
no tumult—only a low deep murmur dwelt over them
interspersed with louder cries and groans while that
mob kept on pushing and surging past us, sightless and
without feeling. A smell of scorched rags and festering
wounds hung in the air. My horse staggered in the
eddies of swaying men. But it was like cutting down
galvanized corpses that didn't care. Invaders! Yes . . .
God was already dealing with them.

"I touched my horse with the spurs to get clear. There
was a sudden rush and a sort of angry moan when our
second squadron got into them on our right. My horse
plunged and somebody got hold of my leg. As I had no
mind to get pulled out of the saddle I gave a back-
handed slash without looking. I heard a cry and my leg
was let go suddenly.

"Just then I caught sight of the subaltern of my troop
at some little distance from me. His name was Tomassov. That multitude of resurrected bodies with glassy
eyes was seething round his horse as if blind, growling
crazily. He was sitting erect in his saddle, not looking
down at them and sheathing his sword deliberately.

"This Tomassov, well, he had a beard. Of course we all had beards then. Circumstances, lack of leisure, want of razors, too. No, seriously, we were a wild-looking lot in those unforgotten days which so many, so very many of us did not survive. You know our losses were awful, too. Yes, we looked wild. *Des Russes sauvages*—what!

"So he had a beard—this Tomassov I mean; but he did not look *sauvage*. He was the youngest of us all. And that meant real youth. At a distance he passed muster fairly well, what with the grime and the particular stamp of that campaign on our faces. But directly you were near enough to have a good look into his eyes, that was where his lack of age showed, though he was not exactly a boy.

"Those same eyes were blue, something like the blue of autumn skies, dreamy and gay, too—innocent, believing eyes. A topknot of fair hair decorated his brow like a gold diadem in what one would call normal times.

"You may think I am talking of him as if he were the hero of a novel. Why, that's nothing to what the adjutant discovered about him. He discovered that he had a 'lover's lips'—whatever that may be. If the adjutant meant a nice mouth, why, it was nice enough, but of course it was intended for a sneer. That adjutant of ours was not a very delicate fellow. 'Look at those lover's lips,' he would exclaim in a loud tone while Tomassov was talking.

"Tomassov didn't quite like that sort of thing. But to a certain extent he had laid himself open to banter by the lasting character of his impressions which were connected with the passion of love and, perhaps, were not of such a rare kind as he seemed to think them. What made his comrades tolerant of his rhapsodies was the fact that they were connected with France, with Paris!

"You of the present generation, you cannot conceive

how much prestige there was then in those names for
the whole world. Paris was the center of wonder for all
human beings gifted with imagination. There we were,
the majority of us young and well connected, but not
long out of our hereditary nests in the provinces; simple
servants of God; mere rustics, if I may say so. So we
were only too ready to listen to the tales of France from
our comrade Tomassov. He had been attached to our
mission in Paris the year before the war. High protections very likely—or maybe sheer luck.

"I don't think he could have been a very useful member of the mission because of his youth and complete
inexperience. And apparently all his time in Paris was
his own. The use he made of it was to fall in love, to remain in that state, to cultivate it, to exist only for it in a
manner of speaking.

"Thus it was something more than a mere memory
that he had brought with him from France. Memory
is a fugitive thing. It can be falsified, it can be effaced,
it can be even doubted. Why! I myself come to doubt
sometimes that I, too, have been in Paris in my turn.
And the long road there with battles for its stages would
appear still more incredible if it were not for a certain
musket ball which I have been carrying about my person ever since a little cavalry affair which happened in
Silesia at the very beginning of the Leipzig campaign.

"Passages of love, however, are more impressive perhaps than passages of danger. You don't go affronting
love in troops as it were. They are rarer, more personal
and more intimate. And remember that with Tomassov
all that was very fresh yet. He had not been home from
France three months when the war began.

"His heart, his mind were full of that experience. He
was really awed by it, and he was simple enough to let

it appear in his speeches. He considered himself a sort of privileged person, not because a woman had looked at him with favor, but simply because, how shall I say it, he had had the wonderful illumination of his worship for her, as if it were heaven itself that had done this for him.

"Oh yes, he was very simple. A nice youngster, yet no fool; and with that, utterly inexperienced, unsuspicious, and unthinking. You will find one like that here and there in the provinces. He had some poetry in him too. It could only be natural, something quite his own, not acquired. I suppose Father Adam had some poetry in him of that natural sort. For the rest *un Russe sauvage* as the French sometimes call us, but not of that kind which, they maintain, eats tallow candle for a delicacy. As to the woman, the French woman, well, though I have also been in France with a hundred thousand Russians, I have never seen her. Very likely she was not in Paris then. And in any case hers were not the doors that would fly open before simple fellows of my sort, you understand. Gilded salons were never in my way. I could not tell you how she looked, which is strange considering that I was, if I may say so, Tomassov's special confidant.

"He very soon got shy of talking before the others. I suppose the usual campfire comments jarred his fine feelings. But I was left to him and truly I had to submit. You can't very well expect a youngster in Tomassov's state to hold his tongue altogether; and I—I suppose you will hardly believe me—I am by nature a rather silent sort of person.

"Very likely my silence appeared to him sympathetic. All the month of September our regiment, quartered in villages, had come in for an easy time. It was then that I heard most of that—you can't call it a story. The story I have in my mind is not in that. Outpourings, let us call them.

"I would sit quite content to hold my peace, a whole hour perhaps, while Tomassov talked with exaltation. And when he was done I would still hold my peace. And then there would be produced a solemn effect of silence which, I imagine, pleased Tomassov in a way.

"She was of course not a woman in her first youth. A widow, maybe. At any rate I never heard Tomassov mention her husband. She had a salon, something very distinguished; a social center in which she queened it with great splendor.

"Somehow, I fancy her court was composed mostly of men. But Tomassov, I must say, kept such details out of his discourses wonderfully well. Upon my word I don't know whether her hair was dark or fair, her eyes brown or blue; what was her stature, her features, or her complexion. His love soared above mere physical impressions. He never described her to me in set terms; but he was ready to swear that in her presence everybody's thoughts and feelings were bound to circle round her. She was that sort of woman. Most wonderful conversations on all sorts of subjects went on in her salon: but through them all there flowed unheard like a mysterious strain of music the assertion, the power, the tyranny of sheer beauty. So apparently the woman was beautiful. She detached all these talking people from their life interests, and even from their vanities. She was a secret delight and a secret trouble. All the men when they looked at her fell to brooding as if struck by the thought that their lives had been wasted. She was the very joy and shudder of felicity and she brought only sadness and torment to the hearts of men.

"In short, she must have been an extraordinary woman,

or else Tomassov was an extraordinary young fellow to feel in that way and to talk like this about her. I told you the fellow had a lot of poetry in him and observed that all this sounded true enough. It would be just about the sorcery a woman very much out of the common would exercise, you know. Poets do get close to truth somehow—there is no denying that.

"There is no poetry in my composition, I know, but I have my share of common shrewdness, and I have no doubt that the lady was kind to the youngster, once he did find his way inside her salon. His getting in is the real marvel. However, he did get in, the innocent, and he found himself in distinguished company there, amongst men of considerable position. And you know what that means: thick waists, bald heads, teeth that are not—as some satirist puts it. Imagine amongst them a nice boy, fresh and simple, like an apple just off the tree; a modest, good-looking, impressionable, adoring young barbarian. My word! What a change! What a relief for jaded feelings! And with that, having in his nature that dose of poetry which saves even a simpleton from being a fool.

"He became an artlessly, unconditionally devoted slave. He was rewarded by being smiled on and in time admitted to the intimacy of the house. It may be that the unsophisticated young barbarian amused the exquisite lady. Perhaps—since he didn't feed on tallow candles—he satisfied some need of tenderness in the woman. You know, there are many kinds of tenderness highly civilized women are capable of. Women with heads and imagination, I mean, and no temperament to speak of, you understand. But who is going to fathom their needs or their fancies? Most of the time they themselves don't know much about their innermost moods, and blunder out of one into another, sometimes with catastrophic results. And then who is more surprised than they? However, Tomassov's case was in its nature quite idyllic. The fashionable world was amused. His devotion made for him a kind of social success. But he didn't care. There was his one divinity, and there was the shrine where he was permitted to go in and out without regard for official reception hours.

"He took advantage of that privilege freely. Well, he had no official duties, you know. The Military Mission was supposed to be more complimentary than anything else, the head of it being a personal friend of our Emperor Alexander; and he, too, was laying himself out for successes in fashionable life exclusively—as it seemed. As it seemed.

"One afternoon Tomassov called on the mistress of his thoughts earlier than usual. She was not alone. There was a man with her, not one of the thick-waisted, bald-headed personages, but a somebody all the same, a man over thirty, a French officer who to some extent was also a privileged intimate. Tomassov was not jealous of him. Such a sentiment would have appeared presumptuous to the simple fellow.

"On the contrary he admired that officer. You have no idea of the French military men's prestige in those days, even with us Russian soldiers who had managed to face them perhaps better than the rest. Victory had marked them on the forehead—it seemed forever. They would have been more human if they had not been conscious of it; but they were good comrades and had a sort of brotherly feeling for all who bore arms, even if it was against them.

"And this was quite a superior example, an officer of the major-general's staff, and a man of the best society besides. He was powerfully built, and thoroughly masculine, though he was as carefully groomed as a

woman. He had the courteous self-possession of a man
of the world. His forehead, white as alabaster, contrasted impressively with the healthy color of his face.

"I don't know whether he was jealous of Tomassov,
but I suspect that he might have been a little annoyed
at him as at a sort of walking absurdity of the sentimental order. But these men of the world are impenetrable, and outwardly he condescended to recognize
Tomassov's existence even more distinctly than was
strictly necessary. Once or twice he had offered him
some useful worldly advice with perfect tact and delicacy. Tomassov was completely conquered by that
evidence of kindness under the cold polish of the best
society.

"Tomassov, introduced into the *petit salon,* found
these two exquisite people sitting on a sofa together
and had the feeling of having interrupted some special
conversation. They looked at him strangely, he thought;
but he was not given to understand that he had in-
truded. After a time the lady said to the officer—his
name was De Castel—'I wish you would take the
trouble to ascertain the exact truth as to that rumor.'

" 'It's much more than a mere rumor,' remarked the
officer. But he got up submissively and went out. The
lady turned to Tomassov and said: 'You may stay with
me.'

"This express command made him supremely happy,
though as a matter of fact he had had no idea of going.

"She regarded him with her kindly glances, which
made something glow and expand within his chest.
It was a delicious feeling, even though it did cut one's
breath short now and then. Ecstatically he drank in the
sound of her tranquil, seductive talk full of innocent
gaiety and of spiritual quietude. His passion appeared
to him to flame up and envelop her in blue fiery tongues

from head to foot and over her head, while her soul reposed in the center like a big white rose. . . .

"H'm, good this. He told me many other things like that. But this is the one I remember. He himself remembered everything because these were the last memories of that woman. He was seeing her for the last time though he did not know it then.

"M. De Castel returned, breaking into that atmosphere of enchantment Tomassov had been drinking in even to complete unconsciousness of the external world. Tomassov could not help being struck by the distinction of his movements, the ease of his manner, his superiority to all the other men he knew, and he suffered from it. It occurred to him that these two brilliant beings on the sofa were made for each other.

"De Castel sitting down by the side of the lady murmured to her discreetly, 'There is not the slightest doubt that it's true,' and they both turned their eyes to Tomassov. Roused thoroughly from his enchantment he became self-conscious; a feeling of shyness came over him. He sat smiling faintly at them.

"The lady without taking her eyes off the blushing Tomassov said with a dreamy gravity quite unusual to her:

"'I should like to know that your generosity can be supreme—without a flaw. Love at its highest should be the origin of every perfection.'

"Tomassov opened his eyes wide with admiration at this, as though her lips had been dropping real pearls. The sentiment, however, was not uttered for the primitive Russian youth but for the exquisitely accomplished man of the world, De Castel.

"Tomassov could not see the effect it produced because the French officer lowered his head and sat there contemplating his admirably polished boots. The lady whispered in a sympathetic tone:

" 'You have scruples?'

"De Castel, without looking up, murmured: 'It could be turned into a nice point of honor.'

"She said vivaciously: 'That surely is artificial. I am all for natural feelings. I believe in nothing else. But perhaps your conscience. . . .'

"He interrupted her: 'Not at all. My conscience is not childish. The fate of those people is of no military importance to us. What can it matter? The fortune of France is invincible.'

" 'Well then . . . ,' she uttered, meaningly, and rose from the couch. The French officer stood up, too. Tomassov hastened to follow their example. He was pained by his state of utter mental darkness. While he was raising the lady's white hand to his lips he heard the French officer say with marked emphasis:

" 'If he has the soul of a warrior (at that time, you know, people really talked in that way), if he has the soul of a warrior he ought to fall at your feet in gratitude.'

"Tomassov felt himself plunged into even denser darkness than before. He followed the French officer out of the room and out of the house; for he had a notion that this was expected of him.

"It was getting dusk, the weather was very bad, and the street was quite deserted. The Frenchman lingered in it strangely. And Tomassov lingered, too, without impatience. He was never in a hurry to get away from the house in which she lived. And besides, something wonderful had happened to him. The hand he had reverently raised by the tips of its fingers had been pressed against his lips. He had received a secret favor! He was almost frightened. The world had reeled—and it had hardly steadied itself yet. De Castel stopped short at the corner of the quiet street.

"'I don't care to be seen too much with you in the lighted thoroughfares, M. Tomassov,' he said in a strangely grim tone.

"'Why?' asked the young man, too startled to be offended.

"'From prudence,' answered the other curtly. 'So we will have to part here; but before we part I'll disclose to you something of which you will see at once the importance.'

"This, please note, was an evening in late March of the year 1812. For a long time already there had been talk of a growing coolness between Russia and France. The word war was being whispered in drawing rooms louder and louder, and at last was heard in official circles. Thereupon the Parisian police discovered that our military envoy had corrupted some clerks at the Ministry of War and had obtained from them some very important confidential documents. The wretched men (there were two of them) had confessed their crime and were to be shot that night. Tomorrow all the town would be talking of the affair. But the worst was that the Emperor Napoleon was furiously angry at the discovery, and had made up his mind to have the Russian envoy arrested.

"Such was De Castel's disclosure; and though he had spoken in low tones Tomassov was stunned as by a great crash.

"'Arrested,' he murmured, desolately.

"'Yes, and kept as a state prisoner—with everybody belonging to him. . . .'

"The French officer seized Tomassov's arm above the elbow and pressed it hard.

"'And kept in France,' he repeated into Tomassov's very ear, and then letting him go stepped back a space and remained silent.

"'And it's you, you, who are telling me this!' cried Tomassov in an extremity of gratitude that was hardly greater than his admiration for the generosity of his future foe. Could a brother have done for him more! He sought to seize the hand of the French officer, but the latter remained wrapped up closely in his cloak. Possibly in the dark he had not noticed the attempt. He moved back a bit and in his self-possessed voice of a man of the world, as though he were speaking across a card table or something of the sort, he called Tomassov's attention to the fact that if he meant to make use of the warning the moments were precious.

"'Indeed they are,' agreed the awed Tomassov. 'Good-by then. I have no word of thanks to equal your generosity; but if ever I have an opportunity, I swear it, you may command my life. . . .'

"But the Frenchman retreated, had already vanished in the dark lonely street. Tomassov was alone, and then he did not waste any of the precious minutes of that night.

"See how people's mere gossip and idle talk pass into history. In all the memoirs of the time if you read them you will find it stated that our envoy had a warning from some highly placed woman who was in love with him. Of course it's known that he had successes with women, and in the highest spheres, too, but the truth is that the person who warned him was no other than our simple Tomassov—an altogether different sort of lover from himself.

"This then is the secret of our Emperor's representative's escape from arrest. He and all his official household got out of France all right—as history records.

"And amongst that household there was our Tomassov of course. He had, in the words of the French officer, the soul of a warrior. And what more desolate prospect for a man with such a soul than to be imprisoned on the eve of war; to be cut off from his country in danger, from his military family, from his duty, from honor, and —well—from glory, too.

"Tomassov used to shudder at the mere thought of the moral torture he had escaped; and he nursed in his heart a boundless gratitude to the two people who had saved him from that cruel ordeal. They were wonderful! For him love and friendship were but two aspects of exalted perfection. He had found these fine examples of it and he vowed them indeed a sort of cult. It affected his attitude towards Frenchmen in general, great patriot as he was. He was naturally indignant at the invasion of his country, but this indignation had no personal animosity in it. His was fundamentally a fine nature. He grieved at the appalling amount of human suffering he saw around him. Yes, he was full of compassion for all forms of mankind's misery in a manly way.

"Less fine natures than his own did not understand this very well. In the regiment they had nicknamed him the Humane Tomassov.

"He didn't take offense at it. There is nothing incompatible between humanity and a warrior's soul. People without compassion are the civilians, government officials, merchants and such like. As to the ferocious talk one hears from a lot of decent people in war time—well, the tongue is an unruly member at best, and when there is some excitement going on there is no curbing its furious activity.

"So I had not been very surprised to see our Tomassov sheathe deliberately his sword right in the middle of that charge, you may say. As we rode away after it he was very silent. He was not a chatterer as a rule, but it was evident that this close view of the Grand Army had affected him deeply, like some sight not of this earth. I had always been a pretty tough individual myself— well, even I . . . and there was that fellow with a lot of poetry in his nature! You may imagine what he made of it to himself. We rode side by side without opening our lips. It was simply beyond words.

"We established our bivouac along the edge of the forest so as to get some shelter for our horses. However, the boisterous north wind had dropped as quickly as it had sprung up, and the great winter stillness lay on the land from the Baltic to the Black Sea. One could almost feel its cold, lifeless immensity reaching up to the stars.

"Our men had lighted several fires for their officers and had cleared the snow around them. We had big logs of wood for seats; it was a very tolerable bivouac upon the whole, even without the exultation of victory. We were to feel that later, but at present we were oppressed by our stern and arduous task.

"There were three of us round my fire. The third one was that adjutant. He was perhaps a well-meaning chap but not so nice as he might have been had he been less rough in manner and less crude in his perceptions. He would reason about people's conduct as though a man were as simple a figure as, say, two sticks laid across each other; whereas a man is much more like the sea whose movements are too complicated to explain, and whose depths may bring up God only knows what at any moment.

"We talked a little about that charge. Not much. That sort of thing does not lend itself to conversation. Tomassov muttered a few words about a mere butchery. I had nothing to say. As I told you I had very soon let my sword hang idle at my wrist. That starving mob had not even *tried* to defend itself. Just a few shots. We had two men wounded. Two! . . . and we had charged the main column of Napoleon's Grand Army.

"Tomassov muttered wearily: 'What was the good of it?' I did not wish to argue, so I only just mumbled: 'Ah, well!' But the adjutant struck in unpleasantly:

" 'Why, it warmed the men a bit. It has made me warm. That's a good enough reason. But our Tomassov is so humane! And besides he has been in love with a French woman, and thick as thieves with a lot of Frenchmen, so he is sorry for them. Never mind, my boy, we are on the Paris road now and you shall soon see her!' This was one of his usual, as we believed them, foolish speeches. None of us but believed that the getting to Paris would be a matter of years—of years. And lo! less than eighteen months afterwards I was rooked of a lot of money in a gambling hell in the Palais Royal.

"Truth, being often the most senseless thing in the world, is sometimes revealed to fools. I don't think that adjutant of ours believed in his own words. He just wanted to tease Tomassov from habit. Purely from habit. We of course said nothing, and so he took his head in his hands and fell into a doze as he sat on a log in front of the fire.

"Our cavalry was on the extreme right wing of the army, and I must confess that we guarded it very badly. We had lost all sense of insecurity by this time; but still we did keep up a pretense of doing it in a way. Presently a trooper rode up leading a horse and Tomassov mounted stiffly and went off on a round of the outposts. Of the perfectly useless outposts.

"The night was still, except for the crackling of the fires. The raging wind had lifted far above the earth and not the faintest breath of it could be heard. Only the full moon swam out with a rush into the sky and suddenly hung high and motionless overhead. I remember raising my hairy face to it for a moment. Then, I truly believe, I dozed off, too, bent double on my log with my head towards the fierce blaze.

"You know what an impermanent thing such slumber is. One moment you drop into an abyss and the next you are back in the world that you would think too deep for any noise but the trumpet of the Last Judgment. And then off you go again. Your very soul seems to slip down into a bottomless black pit. Then up once more into a startled consciousness. A mere plaything of cruel sleep one is, then. Tormented both ways.

"However, when my orderly appeared before me, repeating: 'Won't your Honor be pleased to eat? . . . Won't your Honor be pleased to eat? . . .' I managed to keep my hold of it—I mean that gaping consciousness. He was offering me a sooty pot containing some grain boiled in water with a pinch of salt. A wooden spoon was stuck in it.

"At that time these were the only rations we were getting regularly. Mere chicken food, confound it! But the Russian soldier is wonderful. Well, my fellow waited till I had feasted and then went away carrying off the empty pot.

"I was no longer sleepy. Indeed, I had become awake with an exaggerated mental consciousness of existence extending beyond my immediate surroundings. Those are but exceptional moments with mankind, I am glad to say. I had the intimate sensation of the earth in all its enormous expanse wrapped in snow, with nothing showing on it but trees with their straight stalklike trunks and their funeral verdure; and in this aspect of general mourning I seemed to hear the sighs of mankind falling to die in the midst of a nature without life. They were Frenchmen. We didn't hate them; they did not hate us; we had existed far apart—and suddenly they had come rolling in with arms in their hands, without fear of God, carrying with them other nations, and all to perish together in a long, long trail of frozen corpses. I had an actual vision of that trail: a pathetic multitude of small dark mounds stretching away under the moonlight in a clear, still, and pitiless atmosphere—a sort of horrible peace.

"But what other peace could there be for them? What else did they deserve? I don't know by what connection of emotions there came into my head the thought that the earth was a pagan planet and not a fit abode for Christian virtues.

"You may be surprised that I should remember all this so well. What is a passing emotion or half-formed thought to last in so many years of a man's changing, inconsequential life? But what has fixed the emotion of that evening in my recollection so that the slightest shadows remain indelible was an event of strange finality, an event not likely to be forgotten in a lifetime—as you shall see.

"I don't suppose I had been entertaining those thoughts more than five minutes when something induced me to look over my shoulder. I can't think it was a noise; the snow deadened all the sounds. Something it must have been, some sort of signal reaching my consciousness. Anyway, I turned my head, and there was the event approaching me, not that I knew it or had the slightest premonition. All I saw in the distance were two figures approaching in the moonlight. One of them was our Tomassov. The dark mass behind him which moved across my sight were the horses which his orderly was leading away. Tomassov was a very familiar appearance, in long boots, a tall figure ending in a pointed hood. But by his side advanced another figure. I mistrusted my eyes at first. It was amazing! It had a shining crested helmet on its head and was muffled up in a white cloak. The cloak was not as white as snow. Nothing in the world is. It was white more like mist, with an aspect that was ghostly and martial to an extraordinary degree. It was as if Tomassov had got hold of the God of War himself. I could see at once that he was leading this resplendent vision by the arm. Then I saw that he was holding it up. While I stared and stared, they crept on—for indeed they were creeping—and at last they crept into the light of our bivouac fire and passed beyond the log I was sitting on. The blaze played on the helmet. It was extremely battered and the frostbitten face, full of sores, under it was framed in bits of mangy fur. No God of War this, but a French officer. The great white cuirassier's cloak was torn, burnt full of holes. His feet were wrapped up in old sheepskins over remnants of boots. They looked monstrous and he tottered on them, sustained by Tomassov who lowered him most carefully onto the log on which I sat.

"My amazement knew no bounds.

" 'You have brought in a prisoner,' I said to Tomassov, as if I could not believe my eyes.

"You must understand that unless they surrendered in large bodies we made no prisoners. What would have been the good? Our Cossacks either killed the stragglers or else let them alone, just as it happened. It came really to the same thing in the end.

"Tomassov turned to me with a very troubled look.

" 'He sprang up from the ground somewhere as I was leaving the outpost,' he said. 'I believe he was making for it, for he walked blindly into my horse. He got hold of my leg and of course none of our chaps dared touch him then.'

" 'He had a narrow escape,' I said.

" 'He didn't appreciate it,' said Tomassov, looking even more troubled than before. 'He came along holding to my stirrup leather. That's what made me so late. He told me he was a staff officer; and then talking in a voice such, I suppose, as the damned alone use, a croaking of rage and pain, he said he had a favor to beg of me. A supreme favor. Did I understand him, he asked in a sort of fiendish whisper?

" 'Of course I told him that I did. I said: *Oui, je vous comprends.*'

" 'Then,' said he, 'do it. Now! At once—in the pity of your heart.'

"Tomassov ceased and stared queerly at me above the head of the prisoner.

"I said, 'What did he mean?'

" 'That's what I asked him,' answered Tomassov in a dazed tone, 'and he said that he wanted me to do him the favor to blow his brains out. As a fellow soldier,' he said. 'As a man of feeling—as—as a humane man.'

"The prisoner sat between us like an awful gashed mummy as to the face, a martial scarecrow, a grotesque horror of rags and dirt, with awful living eyes, full of vitality, full of unquenchable fire, in a body of horrible affliction, a skeleton at the feast of glory. And suddenly those shining unextinguishable eyes of his became fixed upon Tomassov. He, poor fellow, fascinated, returned the ghastly stare of a suffering soul in that mere husk of a man. The prisoner croaked at him in French.

" 'I recognize, you know. You are her Russian youngster. You were very grateful. I call on you to pay the debt. Pay it, I say, with one liberating shot. You are a man of honor. I have not even a broken saber. All my being recoils from my own degradation. You know me.'

"Tomassov said nothing.

" 'Haven't you got the soul of a warrior?' the Frenchman asked in an angry whisper, but with something of
a mocking intention in it.

" 'I don't know,' said poor Tomassov.

"What a look of contempt that scarecrow gave him
out of his unquenchable eyes. He seemed to live only
by the force of infuriated and impotent despair. Suddenly he gave a gasp and fell forward writhing in the
agony of cramp in all his limbs; a not unusual effect of
the heat of a campfire. It resembled the application of
some horrible torture. But he tried to fight against the
pain at first. He only moaned low while we bent over
him so as to prevent him rolling into the fire, and muttered feverishly at intervals: *Tuez moi, tuez moi . . .*
till, vanquished by the pain, he screamed in agony, time
after time, each cry bursting out through his compressed
lips.

"The adjutant woke up on the other side of the fire
and started swearing awfully at the beastly row that
Frenchman was making.

" 'What's this? More of your infernal humanity, Tomassov?' he yelled at us. 'Why don't you have him
thrown out of this to the devil on the snow?'

"As we paid no attention to his shouts, he got up,
cursing shockingly, and went away to another fire. Presently the French officer became easier. We propped him
up against the log and sat silent on each side of him till
the bugles started their call at the first break of day. The
big flame, kept up all through the night, paled on the
livid sheet of snow, while the frozen air all round rang
with the brazen notes of cavalry trumpets. The Frenchman's eyes, fixed in a glassy stare, which for a moment
made us hope that he had died quietly sitting there between us two, stirred slowly to right and left, looking at
each of our faces in turn. Tomassov and I exchanged

glances of dismay. Then De Castel's voice, unexpected
in its renewed strength and ghastly self-possession,
made us shudder inwardly.

" *'Bonjour, Messieurs.'*

"His chin dropped on his breast. Tomassov addressed
me in Russian.

" 'It is he, the man himself . . .' I nodded and Tomassov went on in a tone of anguish: 'Yes, he! Brilliant,
accomplished, envied by men, loved by that woman—
this horror—this miserable thing that cannot die. Look
at his eyes. It's terrible.'

"I did not look, but I understood what Tomassov
meant. We could do nothing for him. This avenging
winter of fate held both the fugitives and the pursuers
in its iron grip. Compassion was but a vain word before
that unrelenting destiny. I tried to say something about
a convoy being no doubt collected in the village—but
I faltered at the mute glance Tomassov gave me. We
knew what those convoys were like: appalling mobs
of hopeless wretches driven on by the butts of Cossacks'
lances, back to the frozen inferno, with their faces set
away from their homes.

"Our two squadrons had been formed along the edge
of the forest. The minutes of anguish were passing. The
Frenchman suddenly struggled to his feet. We helped
him almost without knowing what we were doing.

" 'Come,' he said, in measured tones. 'This is the moment.' He paused for a long time, then with the same
distinctness went on: 'On my word of honor, all faith
is dead in me.'

"His voice lost suddenly its self-possession. After
waiting a little while he added in a murmur: 'And even
my courage. . . . Upon my honor.'

"Another long pause ensued before, with a great

effort, he whispered hoarsely: 'Isn't this enough to move a heart of stone? Am I to go on my knees to you?'

"Again a deep silence fell upon the three of us. Then the French officer flung his last word of anger at Tomassov.

" 'Milksop!'

"Not a feature of the poor fellow moved. I made up my mind to go and fetch a couple of our troopers to lead that miserable prisoner away to the village. There was nothing else for it. I had not moved six paces towards the group of horses and orderlies in front of our squadron when . . . but you have guessed it. Of course. And I, too, I guessed it, for I give you my word that the report of Tomassov's pistol was the most insignificant thing imaginable. The snow certainly does absorb sound. It was a mere feeble pop. Of the orderlies holding our horses I don't think one turned his head round.

"Yes. Tomassov had done it. Destiny had led that De Castel to the man who could understand him perfectly. But it was poor Tomassov's lot to be the predestined victim. You know what the world's justice and mankind's judgment are like. They fell heavily on him with a sort of inverted hypocrisy. Why! That brute of an adjutant, himself, was the first to set going horrified allusions to the shooting of a prisoner in cold blood! Tomassov was not dismissed from the service of course. But after the siege of Danzig he asked for permission to resign from the army, and went away to bury himself in the depths of his province, where a vague story of some dark deed clung to him for years.

"Yes. He had done it. And what was it? One warrior's soul paying its debt a hundredfold to another warrior's soul by releasing it from a fate worse than death—the loss of all faith and courage. You may look on it in that way. I don't know. And perhaps poor Tomassov did not know himself. But I was the first to approach that appalling dark group on the snow: the Frenchman extended rigidly on his back, Tomassov kneeling on one knee rather nearer to the feet than to the Frenchman's head. He had taken his cap off and his hair shone like gold in the light drift of flakes that had begun to fall. He was stooping over the dead in a tenderly contemplative attitude. And his young, ingenuous face, with lowered eyelids, expressed no grief, no sternness, no horror—but was set in the repose of a profound, as if endless and endlessly silent, meditation."

# *England and the World*

~~~~~~~~~~~~~~~~~~~~~~~~~~~~~~~~~~~~~~~~~~~~~~~~~

## YOUTH

## AMY FOSTER

## TYPHOON

". . . But the Dwarf answered: No, something human is
dearer to me than the wealth of all the world."
> —*Grimm's Tales* [on the title-page of *Youth*]

> Far as the mariner on highest mast
> Can see all around upon the calmed vast,
> So. wide was Neptune's hall. . . .
> > —Keats [on the title-page of *Typhoon*]

> —D'autres fois, calme plat, grand miroir
> De mon désespoir.
> > —Baudelaire [epigraph to *The Shadow Line*]

The sea . . . had never put itself out to startle the silent man,
who seldom looked up, and wandered innocently over the
waters with the only visible purpose of getting food, raiment,
and house-room for three people ashore. Dirty weather he had
known, of course . . . But he had never been given a glimpse
of immeasurable strength and immoderate wrath, the wrath that
passes exhausted but never appeased—the wrath and fury of
the passionate sea . . . Captain MacWhirr had sailed over the
surface of the oceans as some men go skimming over the years
of existence to sink gently into a placid grave, ignorant of life
to the last, without ever having been made to see all it may
contain of perfidy, of violence, and of terror. There are on sea
and on land such men thus fortunate—or thus disdained by
destiny or by the sea.

> —Conrad: *Typhoon*

Conrad was naturalized as a British subject on August 19, 1886. By that act he acknowledged his lifelong admiration of England and her history. He had already spent eight years in the British Merchant Service, and he was to spend another seven years chiefly on English ships before ending his seaman's career in 1894. Western Europe had attracted him from early youth, when his native Poland was the occupied country of the German-Austrian-Russian Partition. Like other Slavic "Westernizers" in that era of division between East and West, Conrad's people had looked toward France and England for their political and cultural alliances. France had drawn Conrad himself in his first days of youthful adventure, but it was England and her sea tradition that had held the stronger attraction to a maritime apprentice. He knew her language and books from boyhood. "I had read the whole of Shakespeare by 1880," he once said; and it was his father's translations of Shakespeare that had helped him know English literature, authors as different as Dickens and Mill becoming his companions in early days at school and sea. The idea that Conrad might, but for an accident of fortune, have turned to French as a literary language when he began to write, was a view he took frequent pains to correct. "The impression of my having exercised a choice between the two languages, French and English, both foreign to me, has got abroad somehow," he wrote in *A Personal Record*. "That impression is erroneous. . . . I have a strange and over-powering feeling that [English] had always been an inherent part of myself. English was for me neither a matter of choice nor adoption. The merest idea of choice had never entered my head. And as to adoption—well, yes, there was adoption; but it was I who was adopted by the genius of the language, which, directly I came out of the stammering stage, made me its own so completely that its very idioms, I truly believe, had a direct action on my temperament and fashioned my still plastic character." In 1918 he wrote to Hugh Walpole: "When I wrote the first words of *Almayer's Folly,* I had been already for years and years *thinking* in English. . . . And there are also other considerations: such as the sheer appeal of the language, my quickly awakened love for its prose cadences, a subtle and unforeseen accord of my emotional nature with its genius. . . . You may take it from me that if I had not known English I wouldn't have written a line for print, in my life." England, moreover, in that age of her great political and economic ascendancy, represented to Conrad the stability and security—"the sanity and method"—of Western life, and her Merchant Marine, then supreme in prestige, confirmed her appeal to a child of lost causes, a partitioned homeland, and a family disintegrated by sacrifices and heroic martyrdom. If anything further was needed to bring Conrad to England it was the fiasco of his adventure in France in the years 1874-78, when the disruption of his fortunes in Marseilles, his unhappy love affair there, and the wound he received in a duel with the American J. M. K. Blunt* (events later employed in *The Arrow of Gold*) caused his uncle Tadeusz Bobrowski to hasten from Kiev with the idea of rescuing his nephew and bringing him back home. Conrad recovered; he got a job on an English freighter, the *Mavis,* plying the Mediterranean with coal and linseed cargoes; he landed on English soil for the first time on June 18, 1878. The course of his future life was fixed. Seventeen years later his first novel was published in London. On March 24, 1896 he married an English wife. Except for several continental vacation trips, a visit to Poland in 1914, and a voyage to America in 1923, he never left England again. He lies buried at Canterbury.

Yet inevitably Conrad knew and loved England as a foreigner, and he never wholly lost his foreignness. In spite of his mastery of English, he spoke the tongue with a strong accent until he died. His very mastery of the language, advancing from early richness and exoticism to later idiomatic ease

* See Addendum, p. 47.—F. R. K.

and spareness, never lost the conscious dignity of an acquired speech. His devotion to British traditions and institutions also retained an idealizing reverence which Britons of less convinced allegiance—Wells, Norman Douglas, D. H. Lawrence, and E. M. Forster, as well as Irishmen like George Moore and Liam O'Flaherty—found exaggerated and romantically excessive. Perhaps Conrad's secret and deepest loyalties lay in another quarter, and, like the shipwrecked Pole Yanko in "Amy Foster," it was for another home that he kept his inmost longing.

"Youth" was written in 1898 and gave its name to a volume of three tales in 1902. "Amy Foster" was written in June 1901 and was collected in a volume headed by "Typhoon" in 1903. *Typhoon,* written in the winter of 1900-01, was published as a separate volume in 1902.

# *Youth*

~~~~~~~~~~~~~~~~~~~~~~~~~~~~~~~~~~~~~

THIS could have occurred nowhere but in England, where men and sea interpenetrate, so to speak—the sea entering into the life of most men, and the men knowing something or everything about the sea, in the way of amusement, of travel, or of breadwinning.

We were sitting round a mahogany table that reflected the bottle, the claret glasses, and our faces as we leaned on our elbows. There was a director of companies, an accountant, a lawyer, Marlow, and myself. The director had been a *Conway* boy, the accountant had served four years at sea, the lawyer—a fine crusted Tory, High Churchman, the best of old fellows, the soul of honor—had been chief officer in the P. & O. service in the good old days when mailboats were square-rigged at least on two masts, and used to come down the China Sea before a fair monsoon with stun'sails set alow and aloft. We all began life in the merchant service. Between the five of us there was the strong bond of the sea, and also the fellowship of the craft, which no amount of enthusiasm for yachting, cruising, and so on can give, since one is only the amusement of life and the other is life itself.

Marlow (at least I think that is how he spelt his name) told the story, or rather the chronicle, of a voyage:

"Yes, I have seen a little of the Eastern seas; but

what I remember best is my first voyage there. You fellows know there are those voyages that seem ordered for the illustration of life, that might stand for a symbol of existence. You fight, work, sweat, nearly kill yourself, sometimes do kill yourself, trying to accomplish something—and you can't. Not from any fault of yours. You simply can do nothing, neither great nor little—not a thing in the world—not even marry an old maid, or get a wretched 600-ton cargo of coal to its port of destination.

"It was altogether a memorable affair. It was my first voyage to the East, and my first voyage as second mate; it was also my skipper's first command. You'll admit it was time. He was sixty if a day; a little man, with a broad, not very straight back, with bowed shoulders and one leg more bandy than the other, he had that queer twisted-about appearance you see so often in men who work in the fields. He had a nutcracker face—chin and nose trying to come together over a sunken mouth—and it was framed in iron-gray fluffy hair, that looked like a chinstrap of cotton-wool sprinkled with coaldust. And he had blue eyes in that old face of his, which were amazingly like a boy's, with that candid expression some quite common men preserve to the end of their days by a rare internal gift of simplicity of heart and rectitude of soul. What induced him to accept me was a wonder. I had come out of a crack Australian clipper, where I had been third officer, and he seemed to have a prejudice against crack clippers as aristocratic and high-toned. He said to me, 'You know, in this ship you will have to work.' I said I had to work in every ship I had ever been in. 'Ah, but this is different, and you gentlemen out of them big ships; . . . but there! I dare say you will do. Join tomorrow.'

"I joined tomorrow. It was twenty-two years ago; and

I was just twenty. How time passes! It was one of the happiest days of my life. Fancy! Second mate for the first time—a really responsible officer! I wouldn't have thrown up my new billet for a fortune. The mate looked me over carefully. He was also an old chap, but of another stamp. He had a Roman nose, a snow-white, long beard, and his name was Mahon, but he insisted that it should be pronounced Mann. He was well connected; yet there was something wrong with his luck, and he had never got on.

"As to the captain, he had been for years in coasters, then in the Mediterranean, and last in the West Indian trade. He had never been round the Capes. He could just write a kind of sketchy hand, and didn't care for writing at all. Both were thorough good seamen of course, and between those two old chaps I felt like a small boy between two grandfathers.

"The ship also was old. Her name was the *Judea*. Queer name, isn't it? She belonged to a man Wilmer, Wilcox—some name like that; but he has been bankrupt and dead these twenty years or more, and his name don't matter. She had been laid up in Shadwell basin for ever so long. You may imagine her state. She was all rust, dust, grime—soot aloft, dirt on deck. To me it was like coming out of a palace into a ruined cottage. She was about 400 tons, had a primitive windlass, wooden latches to the doors, not a bit of brass about her, and a big square stern. There was on it, below her name in big letters, a lot of scrollwork, with the gilt off, and some sort of a coat of arms, with the motto 'Do or Die' underneath. I remember it took my fancy immensely. There was a touch of romance in it, something that made me love the old thing—something that appealed to my youth!

"We left London in ballast—sand ballast—to load a

cargo of coal in a northern port for Bangkok. Bangkok!
I thrilled. I had been six years at sea, but had only seen
Melbourne and Sydney, very good places, charming
places in their way—but Bangkok!

"We worked out of the Thames under canvas, with
a North Sea pilot on board. His name was Jermyn, and
he dodged all day long about the galley drying his handkerchief before the stove. Apparently he never slept.
He was a dismal man, with a perpetual tear sparkling
at the end of his nose, who either had been in trouble,
or was in trouble, or expected to be in trouble—couldn't
be happy unless something went wrong. He mistrusted
my youth, my common sense, and my seamanship, and
made a point of showing it in a hundred little ways. I
dare say he was right. It seems to me I knew very little
then, and I know not much more now; but I cherish a
hate for that Jermyn to this day.

"We were a week working up as far as Yarmouth
Roads, and then we got into a gale—the famous October gale of twenty-two years ago. It was wind, lightning,
sleet, snow, and a terrific sea. We were flying light, and
you may imagine how bad it was when I tell you we had
smashed bulwarks and a flooded deck. On the second
night she shifted her ballast into the lee bow, and by
that time we had been blown off somewhere on the
Dogger Bank. There was nothing for it but go below
with shovels and try to right her, and there we were in
that vast hold, gloomy like a cavern, the tallow dips
stuck and flickering on the beams, the gale howling
above, the ship tossing about like mad on her side; there
we all were, Jermyn, the captain, everyone, hardly able
to keep our feet, engaged on that gravedigger's work,
and trying to toss shovelfuls of wet sand up to windward. At every tumble of the ship you could see vaguely
in the dim light men falling down with a great flourish

of shovels. One of the ship's boys (we had two), impressed by the weirdness of the scene, wept as if his heart would break. We could hear him blubbering somewhere in the shadows.

"On the third day the gale died out, and by and by a north-country tug picked us up. We took sixteen days in all to get from London to the Tyne! When we got into dock we had lost our turn for loading, and they hauled us off to a pier where we remained for a month. Mrs. Beard (the captain's name was Beard) came from Colchester to see the old man. She lived on board. The crew of runners had left, and there remained only the officers, one boy and the steward, a mulatto who answered to the name of Abraham. Mrs. Beard was an old woman, with a face all wrinkled and ruddy like a winter apple, and the figure of a young girl. She caught sight of me once, sewing on a button, and insisted on having my shirts to repair. This was something different from the captains' wives I had known on board crack clippers. When I brought her the shirts, she said: 'And the socks? They want mending, I am sure, and John's—Captain Beard's—things are all in order now. I would be glad of something to do.' Bless the old woman. She overhauled my outfit for me, and meantime I read for the first time *Sartor Resartus* and Burnaby's *Ride to Khiva*. I didn't understand much of the first then; but I remember I preferred the soldier to the philosopher at the time; a preference which life has only confirmed. One was a man, and the other was either more—or less. However, they are both dead and Mrs. Beard is dead, and youth, strength, genius, thoughts, achievements, simple hearts—all dies. . . . No matter.

"They loaded us at last. We shipped a crew. Eight able seamen and two boys. We hauled off one evening to the buoys at the dock gates, ready to go out, and with

a fair prospect of beginning the voyage next day. Mrs.
Beard was to start for home by a late train. When the
ship was fast we went to tea. We sat rather silent
through the meal—Mahon, the old couple, and I. I finished first, and slipped away for a smoke, my cabin
being in a deckhouse just against the poop. It was high
water, blowing fresh with a drizzle; the double dock
gates were opened, and the steam colliers were going in
and out in the darkness with their lights burning bright,
a great plashing of propellers, rattling of winches, and
a lot of hailing on the pierheads. I watched the procession of headlights gliding high and of green lights gliding low in the night, when suddenly a red gleam flashed
at me, vanished, came into view again, and remained.
The fore end of a steamer loomed up close. I shouted
down the cabin, 'Come up, quick!' and then heard a
startled voice saying afar in the dark, 'Stop her, sir.' A
bell jingled. Another voice cried warningly, 'We are
going right into that bark, sir.' The answer to this was a
gruff 'All right,' and the next thing was a heavy crash as
the steamer struck a glancing blow with the bluff of her
bow about our forerigging. There was a moment of confusion, yelling, and running about. Steam roared. Then
somebody was heard saying, 'All clear, sir.' . . . 'Are
you all right?' asked the gruff voice. I had jumped forward to see the damage, and hailed back, 'I think so.'
'Easy astern,' said the gruff voice. A bell jingled. 'What
steamer is that?' screamed Mahon. By that time she was
no more to us than a bulky shadow maneuvering a little
way off. They shouted at us some name—a woman's
name, Miranda or Melissa—or some such thing. 'This
means another month in this beastly hole,' said Mahon
to me, as we peered with lamps about the splintered
bulwarks and broken braces. 'But where's the captain?'

"We had not heard or seen anything of him all that

time. We went aft to look. A doleful voice arose hailing somewhere in the middle of the dock, '*Judea* ahoy!' . . . How the devil did he get there? . . . 'Hallo!' we shouted. 'I am adrift in our boat without oars,' he cried. A belated water-man offered his services, and Mahon struck a bargain with him for a half crown to tow our skipper alongside; but it was Mrs. Beard that came up the ladder first. They had been floating about the dock in the mizzly cold rain for nearly an hour. I was never so surprised in my life.

"It appears that when he heard my shout 'Come up' he understood at once what was the matter, caught up his wife, ran on deck, and across, and down into our boat, which was fast to the ladder. Not bad for a sixty-year-old. Just imagine that old fellow saving heroically in his arms that old woman—the woman of his life. He set her down on a thwart, and was ready to climb back on board when the painter came adrift somehow, and away they went together. Of course in the confusion we did not hear him shouting. He looked abashed. She said cheerfully, 'I suppose it does not matter my losing the train now?' 'No, Jenny—you go below and get warm,' he growled. Then to us: 'A sailor has no business with a wife—I say. There I was, out of the ship. Well, no harm done this time. Let's go and look at what that fool of a steamer smashed.'

"It wasn't much, but it delayed us three weeks. At the end of that time, the captain being engaged with his agents, I carried Mrs. Beard's bag to the railway station and put her all comfy into a third-class carriage. She lowered the window to say, 'You are a good young man. If you see John—Captain Beard—without his muffler at night, just remind him from me to keep his throat well wrapped up.' 'Certainly, Mrs. Beard,' I said. 'You are a good young man; I noticed how attentive you are to John—to Captain——' The train pulled out suddenly; I took my cap off to the old woman: I never saw her again. . . . Pass the bottle.

"We went to sea next day. When we made that start for Bangkok we had been already three months out of London. We had expected to be a fortnight or so—at the outside.

"It was January, and the weather was beautiful—the beautiful sunny winter weather that has more charm than in the summertime, because it is unexpected, and crisp, and you know it won't, it can't, last long. It's like a windfall, like a godsend, like an unexpected piece of luck.

"It lasted all down the North Sea, all down Channel; and it lasted till we were three hundred miles or so to the westward of the Lizards; then the wind went round to the sou'west and began to pipe up. In two days it blew a gale. The *Judea*, hove to, wallowed on the Atlantic like an old candle-box. It blew day after day: it blew with spite, without interval, without mercy, without rest. The world was nothing but an immensity of great foaming waves rushing at us, under a sky low enough to touch with the hand and dirty like a smoked ceiling. In the stormy space surrounding us there was as much flying spray as air. Day after day and night after night there was nothing round the ship but the howl of the wind, the tumult of the sea, the noise of water pouring over her deck. There was no rest for her and no rest for us. She tossed, she pitched, she stood on her head, she sat on her tail, she rolled, she groaned, and we had to hold on while on deck and cling to our bunks when below, in a constant effort of body and worry of mind.

"One night Mahon spoke through the small window of my berth. It opened right into my very bed, and I was lying there sleepless, in my boots, feeling as though

I had not slept for years, and could not if I tried. He said excitedly:

" 'You got the sounding rod in here, Marlow? I can't get the pumps to suck. By God! It's no child's play.'

"I gave him the sounding rod and lay down again, trying to think of various things—but I thought only of the pumps. When I came on deck they were still at it, and my watch relieved at the pumps. By the light of the lantern brought on deck to examine the sounding rod I caught a glimpse of their weary, serious faces. We pumped all the four hours. We pumped all night, all day, all the week—watch and watch. She was working herself loose, and leaked badly—not enough to drown us at once, but enough to kill us with the work at the pumps. And while we pumped the ship was going from us piecemeal: the bulwarks went, the stanchions were torn out, the ventilators smashed, the cabin door burst in. There was not a dry spot in the ship. She was being gutted bit by bit. The longboat changed, as if by magic, into matchwood where she stood in her gripes. I had lashed her myself, and was rather proud of my handiwork, which had withstood so long the malice of the sea. And we pumped. And there was no break in the weather. The sea was white like a sheet of foam, like a caldron of boiling milk; there was not a break in the clouds, no—not the size of a man's hand—no, not for so much as ten seconds. There was for us no sky, there were for us no stars, no sun, no universe—nothing but angry clouds and an infuriated sea. We pumped watch and watch, for dear life; and it seemed to last for months, for years, for all eternity, as though we had been dead and gone to a hell for sailors. We forgot the day of the week, the name of the month, what year it was, and whether we had ever been ashore. The sails blew away, she lay broadside on under a weather cloth, the ocean poured over her, and we did not care. We turned those handles, and had the eyes of idiots. As soon as we had crawled on deck I used to take a round turn with a rope about the men, the pumps, and the mainmast, and we turned, we turned incessantly, with the water to our waists, to our necks, over our heads. It was all one. We had forgotten how it felt to be dry.

"And there was somewhere in me the thought: By Jove! This is the deuce of an adventure—something you read about; and it is my first voyage as second mate—and I am only twenty—and here I am lasting it out as well as any of these men, and keeping my chaps up to the mark. I was pleased. I would not have given up the experience for worlds. I had moments of exultation. Whenever the old dismantled craft pitched heavily with her counter high in the air, she seemed to me to throw up, like an appeal, like a defiance, like a cry to the clouds without mercy, the words written on her stern: 'Judea, London. Do or Die.'

"O youth! The strength of it, the faith of it, the imagination of it! To me she was not an old rattletrap carting about the world a lot of coal for a freight—to me she was the endeavor, the test, the trial of life. I think of her with pleasure, with affection, with regret—as you would think of someone dead you have loved. I shall never forget her. . . . Pass the bottle.

"One night when tied to the mast, as I explained, we were pumping on, deafened with the wind, and without spirit enough in us to wish ourselves dead, a heavy sea crashed aboard and swept clean over us. As soon as I got my breath I shouted, as in duty bound, 'Keep on, boys!' when suddenly I felt something hard floating on deck strike the calf of my leg. I made a grab at it and missed. It was so dark we could not see each other's faces within a foot—you understand.

"After that thump the ship kept quiet for a while, and the thing, whatever it was, struck my leg again. This time I caught it—and it was a saucepan. At first, being stupid with fatigue and thinking of nothing but the pumps, I did not understand what I had in my hand. Suddenly it dawned upon me, and I shouted, 'Boys, the house on deck is gone. Leave this, and let's look for the cook.'

"There was a deckhouse forward, which contained the galley, the cook's berth, and the quarters of the crew. As we had expected for days to see it swept away, the hands had been ordered to sleep in the cabin—the only safe place in the ship. The steward, Abraham, however, persisted in clinging to his berth, stupidly, like a mule—from sheer fright I believe, like an animal that won't leave a stable falling in an earthquake. So we went to look for him. It was chancing death, since once out of our lashings we were as exposed as if on a raft. But we went. The house was shattered as if a shell had exploded inside. Most of it had gone overboard—stove, men's quarters, and their property, all was gone; but two posts, holding a portion of the bulkhead to which Abraham's bunk was attached, remained as if by a miracle. We groped in the ruins and came upon this, and there he was, sitting in his bunk, surrounded by foam and wreckage, jabbering cheerfully to himself. He was out of his mind; completely and forever mad, with this sudden shock coming upon the fag-end of his endurance. We snatched him up, lugged him aft, and pitched him headfirst down the cabin companion. You understand there was no time to carry him down with infinite precautions and wait to see how he got on. Those below would pick him up at the bottom of the stairs all right. We were in a hurry to go back to the pumps. That business could not wait. A bad leak is an inhuman thing.

"One would think that the sole purpose of that fiendish gale had been to make a lunatic of that poor devil of a mulatto. It eased before morning, and next day the sky cleared, and as the sea went down the leak took up. When it came to bending a fresh set of sails the crew demanded to put back—and really there was nothing else to do. Boats gone, decks swept clean, cabin gutted, men without a stitch but what they stood in, stores spoiled, ship strained. We put her head for home, and—would you believe it? The wind came east right in our teeth. It blew fresh, it blew continuously. We had to beat up every inch of the way, but she did not leak so badly, the water keeping comparatively smooth. Two hours' pumping in every four is no joke—but it kept her afloat as far as Falmouth.

"The good people there live on casualties of the sea, and no doubt were glad to see us. A hungry crowd of shipwrights sharpened their chisels at the sight of that carcass of a ship. And, by Jove! they had pretty pickings off us before they were done. I fancy the owner was already in a tight place. There were delays. Then it was decided to take part of the cargo out and calk her topsides. This was done, the repairs finished, cargo reshipped; a new crew came on board, and we went out—for Bangkok. At the end of a week we were back again. The crew said they weren't going to Bangkok—a hundred and fifty days' passage—in a something hooker that wanted pumping eight hours out of the twentyfour; and the nautical papers inserted again the little paragraph: 'Judea. Bark. Tyne to Bangkok; coals; put back to Falmouth leaky and with crew refusing duty.'

"There were more delays—more tinkering. The owner came down for a day, and said she was as right as a little fiddle. Poor old Captain Beard looked like the ghost of a Geordie skipper—through the worry and

humiliation of it. Remember he was sixty, and it was his
first command. Mahon said it was a foolish business,
and would end bádly. I loved the ship more than ever,
and wanted awfully to get to Bangkok. To Bangkok!
Magic name, blessed name. Mesopotamia wasn't a patch
on it. Remember I was twenty, and it was my first
second-mate's billet, and the East was waiting for me.

"We went out and anchored in the outer roads with
a fresh crew—the third. She leaked worse than ever.
It was as if those confounded shipwrights had actually
made a hole in her. This time we did not even go outside. The crew simply refused to man the windlass.

"They towed us back to the inner harbor, and we became a fixture, a feature, an institution of the place.
People pointed us out to visitors as 'That 'ere bark that's
going to Bangkok—has been here six months—put
back three times.' On holidays the small boys pulling
about in boats would hail, '*Judea*, ahoy!' and if a head
showed above the rail shouted, 'Where you bound to?—
Bangkok?' and jeered. We were only three on board.
The poor old skipper mooned in the cabin. Mahon undertook the cooking, and unexpectedly developed all
a Frenchman's genius for preparing nice little messes.
I looked languidly after the rigging. We became citizens
of Falmouth. Every shopkeeper knew us. At the barber's
or tobacconist's they asked familiarly, 'Do you think you
will ever get to Bangkok?' Meantime the owner, the
underwriters, and the charterers squabbled amongst
themselves in London, and our pay went on. . . . Pass
the bottle.

"It was horrid. Morally it was worse than pumping
for life. It seemed as though we had been forgotten by
the world, belonged to nobody, would get nowhere; it
seemed that, as if bewitched, we would have to live for
ever and ever in that inner harbor, a derision and a by-

word to generations of longshore loafers and dishonest boatmen. I obtained three months' pay and a five days' leave, and made a rush for London. It took me a day to get there and pretty well another to come back—but three months' pay went all the same. I don't know what I did with it. I went to a music hall, I believe, lunched, dined, and supped in a swell place in Regent Street, and was back on time, with nothing but a complete set of Byron's works and a new railway rug to show for three months' work. The boatman who pulled me off to the ship said: 'Hallo! I thought you had left the old thing. *She* will never get to Bangkok.' 'That's all *you* know about it,' I said, scornfully—but I didn't like that prophecy at all.

"Suddenly a man, some kind of agent to somebody, appeared with full powers. He had grog-blossoms all over his face, an indomitable energy, and was a jolly soul. We leaped into life again. A hulk came alongside, took our cargo, and then we went into dry dock to get our copper stripped. No wonder she leaked. The poor thing, strained beyond endurance by the gale, had, as if in disgust, spat out all the oakum of her lower seams. She was recalked, new-coppered, and made as tight as a bottle. We went back to the hulk and reshipped our cargo.

"Then, on a fine moonlight night, all the rats left the ship.

"We had been infested with them. They had destroyed our sails, consumed more stores than the crew, affably shared our beds and our dangers, and now, when the ship was made seaworthy, concluded to clear out. I called Mahon to enjoy the spectacle. Rat after rat appeared on our rail, took a last look over his shoulder, and leaped with a hollow thud into the empty hulk. We tried to count them, but soon lost the tale. Mahon said:

'Well, well! don't talk to me about the intelligence of rats. They ought to have left before, when we had that narrow squeak from foundering. There you have the proof how silly is the superstition about them. They leave a good ship for an old rotten hulk, where there is nothing to eat, too, the fools! . . . I don't believe they know what is safe or what is good for them, any more than you or I.'

"And after some more talk we agreed that the wisdom of rats had been grossly overrated, being in fact no greater than that of men.

"The story of the ship was known, by this, all up the Channel from Land's End to the Forelands, and we could get no crew on the south coast. They sent us one all complete from Liverpool, and we left once more—for Bangkok.

"We had fair breezes, smooth water right into the tropics, and the old *Judea* lumbered along in the sunshine. When she went eight knots everything cracked aloft, and we tied our caps to our heads; but mostly she strolled on at the rate of three miles an hour. What could you expect? She was tired—that old ship. Her youth was where mine is—where yours is—you fellows who listen to this yarn; and what friend would throw your years and your weariness in your face? We didn't grumble at her. To us aft, at least, it seemed as though we had been born in her, reared in her, had lived in her for ages, had never known any other ship. I would just as soon have abused the old village church at home for not being a cathedral.

"And for me there was also my youth to make me patient. There was all the East before me, and all life, and the thought that I had been tried in that ship and had come out pretty well. And I thought of men of old who, centuries ago, went that road in ships that sailed

no better, to the land of palms, and spices, and yellow
sands, and of brown nations ruled by kings more cruel
than Nero the Roman, and more splendid than Solomon
the Jew. The old bark lumbered on, heavy with her age
and the burden of her cargo, while I lived the life of
youth in ignorance and hope. She lumbered on through
an interminable procession of days; and the fresh gild-
ing flashed back at the setting sun, seemed to cry out
over the darkening sea the words painted on her stern,
'*Judea*, London. Do or Die.'

"Then we entered the Indian Ocean and steered
northerly for Java Head. The winds were light. Weeks
slipped by. She crawled on, do or die, and people at
home began to think of posting us as overdue.

"One Saturday evening, I being off duty, the men
asked me to give them an extra bucket of water or so—
for washing clothes. As I did not wish to screw on the
fresh-water pump so late, I went forward whistling, and
with a key in my hand to unlock the forepeak scuttle,
intending to serve the water out of a spare tank we kept
there.

"The smell down below was as unexpected as it was
frightful. One would have thought hundreds of paraffin
lamps had been flaring and smoking in that hole for
days. I was glad to get out. The man with me coughed
and said, 'Funny smell, sir.' I answered negligently, 'It's
good for the health, they say,' and walked aft.

"The first thing I did was to put my head down the
square of the midship ventilator. As I lifted the lid a
visible breath, something like a thin fog, a puff of faint
haze, rose from the opening. The ascending air was hot,
and had a heavy, sooty, paraffiny smell. I gave one sniff,
and put down the lid gently. It was no use choking myself. The cargo was on fire.

"Next day she began to smoke in earnest. You see it

was to be expected, for though the coal was of a safe kind, that cargo had been so handled, so broken up with handling, that it looked more like smithy coal than anything else. Then it had been wetted—more than once. It rained all the time we were taking it back from the hulk, and now with this long passage it got heated, and there was another case of spontaneous combustion.

"The captain called us into the cabin. He had a chart spread on the table, and looked unhappy. He said, 'The coast of West Australia is near, but I mean to proceed to our destination. It is the hurricane month, too; but we will just keep her head for Bangkok, and fight the fire. No more putting back anywhere, if we all get roasted. We will try first to stifle this 'ere damned combustion by want of air.'

"We tried. We battened down everything, and still she smoked. The smoke kept coming out through imperceptible crevices; it forced itself through bulkheads and covers; it oozed here and there and everywhere in slender threads, in an invisible film, in an incomprehensible manner. It made its way into the cabin, into the forecastle; it poisoned the sheltered places on the deck; it could be sniffed as high as the mainyard. It was clear that if the smoke came out the air came in. This was disheartening. This combustion refused to be stifled.

"We resolved to try water, and took the hatches off. Enormous volumes of smoke, whitish, yellowish, thick, greasy, misty, choking, ascended as high as the trucks. All hands cleared out aft. Then the poisonous cloud blew away, and we went back to work in a smoke that was no thicker now than that of an ordinary factory chimney.

"We rigged the force pump, got the hose along, and by and by it burst. Well, it was as old as the ship—a prehistoric hose, and past repair. Then we pumped with the feeble head pump, drew water with buckets, and in this way managed in time to pour lots of Indian Ocean into the main hatch. The bright stream flashed in sunshine, fell into a layer of white crawling smoke, and vanished on the black surface of coal. Steam ascended mingling with the smoke. We poured salt water as into a barrel without a bottom. It was our fate to pump in that ship, to pump out of her, to pump into her; and after keeping water out of her to save ourselves from being drowned, we frantically poured water into her to save ourselves from being burnt.

"And she crawled on, do or die, in the serene weather. The sky was a miracle of purity, a miracle of azure. The sea was polished, was blue, was pellucid, was sparkling like a precious stone, extending on all sides, all round to the horizon—as if the whole terrestrial globe had been one jewel, one colossal sapphire, a single gem fashioned into a planet. And on the luster of the great calm waters the *Judea* glided imperceptibly, enveloped in languid and unclean vapors, in a lazy cloud that drifted to leeward, light and slow; a pestiferous cloud defiling the splendor of sea and sky.

"All this time of course we saw no fire. The cargo smoldered at the bottom somewhere. Once Mahon, as we were working side by side, said to me with a queer smile: 'Now, if she only would spring a tidy leak—like that time when we first left the Channel—it would put a stopper on this fire. Wouldn't it?' I remarked irrelevantly, 'Do you remember the rats?'

"We fought the fire and sailed the ship too as carefully as though nothing had been the matter. The steward cooked and attended on us. Of the other twelve men, eight worked while four rested. Everyone took his turn, captain included. There was equality, and if not exactly fraternity, then a deal of good feeling. Sometimes a man, as he dashed a bucketful of water down the hatchway, would yell out, 'Hurrah for Bangkok!' and the rest laughed. But generally we were taciturn and serious—and thirsty. Oh! how thirsty! And we had to be careful with the water. Strict allowance. The ship smoked, the sun blazed. . . . Pass the bottle.

"We tried everything. We even made an attempt to dig down to the fire. No good, of course. No man could remain more than a minute below. Mahon, who went first, fainted there, and the man who went to fetch him out did likewise. We lugged them out on deck. Then I leaped down to show how easily it could be done. They had learned wisdom by that time, and contented themselves by fishing for me with a chainhook tied to a broom handle, I believe. I did not offer to go and fetch up my shovel, which was left down below.

"Things began to look bad. We put the longboat into the water. The second boat was ready to swing out. We had also another, a fourteen-foot thing, on davits aft, where it was quite safe.

"Then, behold, the smoke suddenly decreased. We redoubled our efforts to flood the bottom of the ship. In two days there was no smoke at all. Everybody was on the broad grin. This was on a Friday. On Saturday no work, but sailing the ship of course, was done. The men washed their clothes and their faces for the first time in a fortnight, and had a special dinner given them. They spoke of spontaneous combustion with contempt, and implied *they* were the boys to put out combustions. Somehow we all felt as though we each had inherited a large fortune. But a beastly smell of burning hung about the ship. Captain Beard had hollow eyes and sunken cheeks. I had never noticed so much before how twisted and bowed he was. He and Mahon prowled soberly about hatches and ventilators, sniffing. It struck me suddenly poor Mahon was a very, very old chap. As to me, I was pleased and proud as though I had helped to win a great naval battle. O youth!

"The night was fine. In the morning a homeward-bound ship passed us hull down—the first we had seen for months; but we were nearing the land at last, Java Head being about 190 miles off, and nearly due north.

"Next day it was my watch on deck from eight to twelve. At breakfast the captain observed, 'It's wonderful how that smell hangs about the cabin.' About ten, the mate being on the poop, I stepped down on the main deck for a moment. The carpenter's bench stood abaft the mainmast: I leaned against it sucking at my pipe, and the carpenter, a young chap, came to talk to me. He remarked, 'I think we have done very well, haven't we?' and then I perceived with annoyance the fool was trying to tilt the bench. I said curtly, 'Don't, Chips,' and immediately became aware of a queer sensation, of an absurd delusion—I seemed somehow to be in the air. I heard all round me like a pent-up breath released—as if a thousand giants simultaneously had said Phoo!—and felt a dull concussion which made my ribs ache suddenly. No doubt about it—I was in the air, and my body was describing a short parabola. But short as it was, I had the time to think several thoughts in, as far as I can remember, the following order: 'This can't be the carpenter—What is it?—Some accident—Submarine volcano?—Coals, gas!—By Jove! We are being blown up—Everybody's dead—I am falling into the afterhatch—I see fire in it.'

"The coaldust suspended in the air of the hold had glowed dull-red at the moment of the explosion. In the twinkling of an eye, in an infinitesimal fraction of a second since the first tilt of the bench, I was sprawling full length on the cargo. I picked myself up and scrambled out. It was quick like a rebound. The deck was a wilderness of smashed timber, lying crosswise like trees in a wood after a hurricane; an immense curtain of solid rags waved gently before me—it was the mainsail blown to strips. I thought: the masts will be toppling over directly; and to get out of the way bolted on all fours towards the poop ladder. The first person I saw was Mahon, with eyes like saucers, his mouth open, and the long white hair standing straight on end round his head like a silver halo. He was just about to go down when the sight of the main deck stirring, heaving up, and changing into splinters before his eyes, petrified him on the top step. I stared at him in unbelief, and he stared at me with a queer kind of shocked curiosity. I did not know that I had no hair, no eyebrows, no eyelashes, that my young mustache was burnt off, that my face was black, one cheek laid open, my nose cut, and my chin bleeding. I had lost my cap, one of my slippers, and my shirt was torn to rags. Of all this I was not aware. I was amazed to see the ship still afloat, the poop deck whole —and, most of all, to see anybody alive. Also the peace of the sky and the serenity of the sea were distinctly surprising. I suppose I expected to see them convulsed with horror. . . . Pass the bottle.

"There was a voice hailing the ship from somewhere —in the air, in the sky—I couldn't tell. Presently I saw the captain—and he was mad. He asked me eagerly, 'Where's the cabin table?' and to hear such a question was a frightful shock. I had just been blown up, you understand, and vibrated with that experience—I wasn't quite sure whether I was alive. Mahon began to stamp with both feet and yelled at him, 'Good God! don't you see the deck's blown out of her?' I found my voice, and stammered out as if conscious of some gross neglect of duty, 'I don't know where the cabin table is.' It was like an absurd dream.

"Do you know what he wanted next? Well, he wanted to trim the yards. Very placidly, and as if lost in thought, he insisted on having the foreyard squared. 'I don't know if there's anybody alive,' said Mahon, almost tearfully. 'Surely,' he said, gently, 'there will be enough left to square the foreyard.'

"The old chap, it seems, was in his own berth winding up the chronometers, when the shock sent him spinning. Immediately it occurred to him—as he said afterwards —that the ship had struck something, and ran out into the cabin. There, he saw, the cabin table had vanished somewhere. The deck being blown up, it had fallen down into the lazarette of course. Where we had our breakfast that morning he saw only a great hole in the floor. This appeared to him so awfully mysterious, and impressed him so immensely, that what he saw and heard after he got on deck were mere trifles in comparison. And, mark, he noticed directly the wheel deserted and his bark off her course—and his only thought was to get that miserable, stripped, undecked, smoldering shell of a ship back again with her head pointing at her port of destination. Bangkok! That's what he was after. I tell you this quiet, bowed, bandy-legged, almost deformed little man was immense in the singleness of his idea and in his placid ignorance of our agitation. He motioned us forward with a commanding gesture, and went to take the wheel himself.

"Yes; that was the first thing we did—trim the yards of that wreck! No one was killed, or even disabled, but everyone was more or less hurt. You should have seen them! Some were in rags, with black faces, like coal heavers, like sweeps, and had bullet heads that seemed closely cropped, but were in fact singed to the skin. Others, of the watch below, awakened by being shot out from their collapsing bunks, shivered incessantly, and kept on groaning even as we went about our work. But they all worked. That crew of Liverpool hard cases had in them the right stuff. It's my experience they always have. It is the sea that gives it—the vastness, the loneliness surrounding their dark stolid souls. Ah! Well! We stumbled, we crept, we fell, we barked our shins on the wreckage, we hauled. The masts stood, but we did not know how much they might be charred down below. It was nearly calm, but a long swell ran from the west and made her roll. They might go at any moment. We looked at them with apprehension. One could not foresee which way they would fall.

"Then we retreated aft and looked about us. The deck was a tangle of planks on edge, of planks on end, of splinters, of ruined woodwork. The masts rose from that chaos like big trees above a matted undergrowth. The interstices of that mass of wreckage were full of something whitish, sluggish, stirring—of something that was like a greasy fog. The smoke of the invisible fire was coming up again, was trailing, like a poisonous thick mist in some valley choked with dead wood. Already lazy wisps were beginning to curl upwards amongst the mass of splinters. Here and there a piece of timber, stuck upright, resembled a post. Half of a fife rail had been shot through the foresail, and the sky made a patch of glorious blue in the ignobly soiled canvas. A portion of several boards holding together had fallen across the rail, and one end protruded overboard, like a gangway leading upon nothing, like a gangway leading over the deep sea, leading to death—as if inviting

us to walk the plank at once and be done with our
ridiculous troubles. And still the air, the sky—a ghost,
something invisible was hailing the ship.

"Someone had the sense to look over, and there was
the helmsman, who had impulsively jumped overboard,
anxious to come back. He yelled and swam lustily like
a merman, keeping up with the ship. We threw him a
rope, and presently he stood amongst us streaming with
water and very crestfallen. The captain had surrendered
the wheel, and apart, elbow on rail and chin in hand,
gazed at the sea wistfully. We asked ourselves, What
next? I thought, Now, this is something like. This is
great. I wonder what will happen. O youth!

"Suddenly Mahon sighted a steamer far astern. Captain Beard said, 'We may do something with her yet.'
We hoisted two flags, which said in the international
language of the sea, 'On fire. Want immediate assistance.' The steamer grew bigger rapidly, and by and by
spoke with two flags on her foremast, 'I am coming to
your assistance.'

"In half an hour she was abreast, to windward, within
hail, and rolling slightly, with her engines stopped. We
lost our composure, and yelled all together with excitement, 'We've been blown up.' A man in a white helmet,
on the bridge, cried, 'Yes! All right! all right!' and he
nodded his head, and smiled, and made soothing motions with his hand as though at a lot of frightened
children. One of the boats dropped in the water, and
walked towards us upon the sea with her long oars. Four
Calashes pulled a swinging stroke. This was my first
sight of Malay seamen. I've known them since, but
what struck me then was their unconcern: they came
alongside, and even the bowman standing up and holding to our main chains with the boathook did not deign

to lift his head for a glance. I thought people who had been blown up deserved more attention.

"A little man, dry like a chip and agile like a monkey, clambered up. It was the mate of the steamer. He gave one look, and cried, 'O boys—you had better quit!'

"We were silent. He talked apart with the captain for a time—seemed to argue with him. Then they went away together to the steamer.

"When our skipper came back we learned that the steamer was the *Somerville*, Captain Nash, from West Australia to Singapore via Batavia with mails, and that the agreement was she should tow us to Anjer or Batavia, if possible, where we could extinguish the fire by scuttling, and then proceed on our voyage—to Bangkok! The old man seemed excited. 'We will do it yet,' he said to Mahon, fiercely. He shook his fist at the sky. Nobody else said a word.

"At noon the steamer began to tow. She went ahead slim and high, and what was left of the *Judea* followed at the end of seventy fathom of towrope—followed her swiftly like a cloud of smoke with mastheads protruding above. We went aloft to furl the sails. We coughed on the yards, and were careful about the bunts. Do you see the lot of us there, putting a neat furl on the sails of that ship doomed to arrive nowhere? There was not a man who didn't think that at any moment the masts would topple over. From aloft we could not see the ship for smoke, and they worked carefully, passing the gaskets with even turns. 'Harbor furl—aloft there!' cried Mahon from below.

"You understand this? I don't think one of those chaps expected to get down in the usual way. When we did I heard them saying to each other, 'Well, I thought we would come down overboard, in a lump—sticks and all

—blame me if I didn't.' 'That's what I was thinking to myself,' would answer wearily another battered and bandaged scarecrow. And, mind, these were men without the drilled-in habit of obedience. To an onlooker they would be a lot of profane scallywags without a redeeming point. What made them do it—what made them obey me when I, thinking consciously how fine it was, made them drop the bunt of the foresail twice to try and do it better? What? They had no professional reputation—no examples, no praise. It wasn't a sense of duty; they all knew well enough how to shirk, and laze, and dodge—when they had a mind to it—and mostly they had. Was it the two pounds ten a month that sent them there? They didn't think their pay half good enough. No; it was something in them, something inborn and subtle and everlasting. I don't say positively that the crew of a French or German merchantman wouldn't have done it, but I doubt whether it would have been done in the same way. There was a completeness in it, something solid like a principle, and masterful like an instinct—a disclosure of something secret—of that hidden something, that gift of good or evil that makes racial difference, that shapes the fate of nations.

"It was that night at ten that, for the first time since we had been fighting it, we saw the fire. The speed of the towing had fanned the smoldering destruction. A blue gleam appeared forward, shining below the wreck of the deck. It wavered in patches, it seemed to stir and creep like the light of a glowworm. I saw it first, and told Mahon. 'Then the game's up,' he said. 'We had better stop this towing, or she will burst out suddenly fore and aft before we can clear out.' We set up a yell; rang bells to attract their attention; they towed on. At last Mahon and I had to crawl forward and cut the rope with an axe. There was no time to cast off the lashings.

Red tongues could be seen licking the wilderness of splinters under our feet as we made our way back to the poop.

"Of course they very soon found out in the steamer that the rope was gone. She gave a loud blast of her whistle, her lights were seen sweeping in a wide circle, she came up ranging close alongside, and stopped. We were all in a tight group on the poop looking at her. Every man had saved a little bundle or a bag. Suddenly a conical flame with a twisted top shot up forward and threw upon the black sea a circle of light, with the two vessels side by side and heaving gently in its center. Captain Beard had been sitting on the gratings still and mute for hours, but now he rose slowly and advanced in front of us, to the mizzen-shrouds. Captain Nash hailed: 'Come along! Look sharp. I have mailbags on board. I will take you and your boats to Singapore.'

" 'Thank you! No!' said our skipper. 'We must see the last of the ship.'

" 'I can't stand by any longer,' shouted the other. 'Mails—you know.'

" 'Ay! ay! We are all right.'

" 'Very well! I'll report you in Singapore. . . . Good-by!'

"He waved his hand. Our men dropped their bundles quietly. The steamer moved ahead, and passing out of the circle of light, vanished at once from our sight, dazzled by the fire which burned fiercely. And then I knew that I would see the East first as commander of a small boat. I thought it fine; and the fidelity to the old ship was fine. We should see the last of her. Oh, the glamor of youth! Oh, the fire of it, more dazzling than the flames of the burning ship, throwing a magic light on the wide earth, leaping audaciously to the sky, presently to be quenched by time, more cruel, more

pitiless, more bitter than the sea—and like the flames of
the burning ship surrounded by an impenetrable night.

"The old man warned us in his gentle and inflexible
way that it was part of our duty to save for the underwriters as much as we could of the ship's gear. Accordingly we went to work aft, while she blazed forward to
give us plenty of light. We lugged out a lot of rubbish.
What didn't we save? An old barometer fixed with an
absurd quantity of screws nearly cost me my life: a sudden rush of smoke came upon me, and I just got away
in time. There were various stores, bolts of canvas, coils
of rope; the poop looked like a marine bazaar, and the
boats were lumbered to the gunwales. One would have
thought the old man wanted to take as much as he could
of his first command with him. He was very, very quiet,
but off his balance evidently. Would you believe it? He
wanted to take a length of old stream-cable and a kedge
anchor with him in the longboat. We said, 'Ay, ay, sir,'
deferentially, and on the quiet let the things slip overboard. The heavy medicine chest went that way, two
bags of green coffee, tins of paint—fancy, paint!—a
whole lot of things. Then I was ordered with two hands
into the boats to make a stowage and get them ready
against the time it would be proper for us to leave the
ship.

"We put everything straight, stepped the longboat's
mast for our skipper, who was to take charge of her, and
I was not sorry to sit down for a moment. My face felt
raw, every limb ached as if broken, I was aware of all
my ribs, and would have sworn to a twist in the backbone. The boats, fast astern, lay in a deep shadow, and
all around I could see the circle of the sea lighted by the
fire. A gigantic flame arose forward straight and clear.
It flared fierce, with noises like the whirr of wings, with

rumbles as of thunder. There were cracks, detonations, and from the cone of flame the sparks flew upwards, as man is born to trouble, to leaky ships, and to ships that burn.

"What bothered me was that the ship, lying broadside to the swell and to such wind as there was—a mere breath—the boats would not keep astern where they were safe, but persisted, in a pigheaded way boats have, in getting under the counter and then swinging alongside. They were knocking about dangerously and coming near the flame, while the ship rolled on them, and, of course, there was always the danger of the masts going over the side at any moment. I and my two boatkeepers kept them off as best we could, with oars and boathooks; but to be constantly at it became exasperating, since there was no reason why we should not leave at once. We could not see those on board, nor could we imagine what caused the delay. The boatkeepers were swearing feebly, and I had not only my share of the work but also had to keep at it two men who showed a constant inclination to lay themselves down and let things slide.

"At last I hailed, 'On deck there,' and someone looked over. 'We're ready here,' I said. The head disappeared, and very soon popped up again. 'The captain says, All right, sir, and to keep the boats well clear of the ship.'

"Half an hour passed. Suddenly there was a frightful racket, rattle, clanking of chain, hiss of water, and millions of sparks flew up into the shivering column of smoke that stood leaning slightly above the ship. The catheads had burned away, and the two red-hot anchors had gone to the bottom, tearing out after them two hundred fathom of red-hot chain. The ship trembled, the mass of flame swayed as if ready to collapse, and the

fore-topgallant mast fell. It darted down like an arrow
of fire, shot under, and instantly leaping up within an
oar's length of the boats, floated quietly, very black on
the luminous sea. I hailed the deck again. After some
time a man in an unexpectedly cheerful but also muffled
tone, as though he had been trying to speak with his
mouth shut, informed me, 'Coming directly, sir,' and
vanished. For a long time I heard nothing but the whirr
and roar of the fire. There were also whistling sounds.
The boats jumped, tugged at the painters, ran at each
other playfully, knocked their sides together, or, do
what we would, swung in a bunch against the ship's
side. I couldn't stand it any longer, and swarming up a
rope, clambered aboard over the stern.

"It was as bright as day. Coming up like this, the
sheet of fire facing me was a terrifying sight, and the
heat seemed hardly bearable at first. On a settee cushion
dragged out of the cabin Captain Beard, his legs drawn
up and one arm under his head, slept with the light
playing on him. Do you know what the rest were busy
about? They were sitting on deck right aft, round an
open case, eating bread and cheese and drinking bottled
stout.

"On the background of flames twisting in fierce
tongues above their heads they seemed at home like
salamanders, and looked like a band of desperate
pirates. The fire sparkled in the whites of their eyes,
gleamed on patches of white skin seen through the torn
shirts. Each had the marks as of a battle about him—
bandaged heads, tied-up arms, a strip of dirty rag round
a knee—and each man had a bottle between his legs
and a chunk of cheese in his hand. Mahon got up. With
his handsome and disreputable head, his hooked profile,
his long white beard, and with an uncorked bottle in his
hand, he resembled one of those reckless sea robbers of

old making merry amidst violence and disaster. 'The last meal on board,' he explained solemnly. 'We had nothing to eat all day, and it was no use leaving all this.' He flourished the bottle and indicated the sleeping skipper. 'He said he couldn't swallow anything, so I got him to lie down,' he went on; and as I stared, 'I don't know whether you are aware, young fellow, the man had no sleep to speak of for days—and there will be dam' little sleep in the boats.' 'There will be no boats by and by if you fool about much longer,' I said, indignantly. I walked up to the skipper and shook him by the shoulder. At last he opened his eyes, but did not move. 'Time to leave her, sir,' I said quietly.

"He got up painfully, looked at the flames, at the sea sparkling round the ship, and black, black as ink farther away; he looked at the stars shining dim through a thin veil of smoke in a sky black, black as Erebus.

" 'Youngest first,' he said.

"And the ordinary seaman, wiping his mouth with the back of his hand, got up, clambered over the taffrail, and vanished. Others followed. One, on the point of going over, stopped short to drain his bottle, and with a great swing of his arm flung it at the fire. 'Take this!' he cried.

"The skipper lingered disconsolately, and we left him to commune alone for a while with his first command. Then I went up again and brought him away at last. It was time. The ironwork on the poop was hot to the touch.

"Then the painter of the longboat was cut, and the three boats, tied together, drifted clear of the ship. It was just sixteen hours after the explosion when we abandoned her. Mahon had charge of the second boat, and I had the smallest—the fourteen-foot thing. The longboat would have taken the lot of us; but the skipper said we must save as much property as we could—for the underwriters—and so I got my first command. I had two men with me, a bag of biscuits, a few tins of meat, and a breaker of water. I was ordered to keep close to the longboat, that in case of bad weather we might be taken into her.

"And do you know what I thought? I thought I would part company as soon as I could. I wanted to have my first command all to myself. I wasn't going to sail in a squadron if there were a chance for independent cruising. I would make land by myself. I would beat the other boats. Youth! All youth! The silly, charming, beautiful youth.

"But we did not make a start at once. We must see the last of the ship. And so the boats drifted about that night, heaving and setting on the swell. The men dozed, waked, sighed, groaned. I looked at the burning ship.

"Between the darkness of earth and heaven she was burning fiercely upon a disc of purple sea shot by the blood-red play of gleams; upon a disc of water glittering and sinister. A high, clear flame, an immense and lonely flame, ascended from the ocean, and from its summit the black smoke poured continuously at the sky. She burned furiously; mournful and imposing like a funeral pile kindled in the night, surrounded by the sea, watched over by the stars. A magnificent death had come like a grace, like a gift, like a reward to that old ship at the end of her laborious days. The surrender of her weary ghost to the keeping of stars and sea was stirring like the sight of a glorious triumph. The masts fell just before daybreak, and for a moment there was a burst and turmoil of sparks that seemed to fill with flying fire the night patient and watchful, the vast night lying silent upon the sea. At daylight she was only a charred shell, floating still under a cloud of smoke and bearing a glowing mass of coal within.

"Then the oars were got out, and the boats forming in a line moved round her remains as if in procession— the longboat leading. As we pulled across her stern a slim dart of fire shot out viciously at us, and suddenly she went down, head first, in a great hiss of steam. The unconsumed stern was the last to sink; but the paint had gone, had cracked, had peeled off, and there were no letters, there was no word, no stubborn device that was like her soul, to flash at the rising sun her creed and her name.

"We made our way north. A breeze sprang up, and about noon all the boats came together for the last time. I had no mast or sail in mine, but I made a mast out of a spare oar and hoisted a boat-awning for a sail, with a boathook for a yard. She was certainly over-masted, but I had the satisfaction of knowing that with the wind aft I could beat the other two. I had to wait for them. Then we all had a look at the captain's chart, and, after a sociable meal of hard bread and water, got our last instructions. These were simple: steer north, and keep together as much as possible. 'Be careful with that jury-rig, Marlow,' said the captain; and Mahon, as I sailed proudly past his boat, wrinkled his curved nose and hailed, 'You will sail that ship of yours under water, if you don't look out, young fellow.' He was a malicious old man—and may the deep sea where he sleeps now rock him gently, rock him tenderly to the end of time!

"Before sunset a thick rain-squall passed over the two boats, which were far astern, and that was the last I saw of them for a time. Next day I sat steering my cockle-shell—my first command—with nothing but water and sky round me. I did sight in the afternoon the upper sails of a ship far away, but said nothing, and my men did not notice her. You see I was afraid she might be homeward bound, and I had no mind to turn back from the portals of the East. I was steering for Java—another blessed name—like Bangkok, you know. I steered many days.

"I need not tell you what it is to be knocking about in an open boat. I remember nights and days of calm, when we pulled, we pulled, and the boat seemed to stand still, as if bewitched within the circle of the sea horizon. I remember the heat, the deluge of rain-squalls that kept us baling for dear life (but filled our water cask), and I remember sixteen hours on end with a mouth dry as a cinder and a steering oar over the stern to keep my first command head on to a breaking sea. I did not know how good a man I was till then. I remember the drawn faces, the dejected figures of my two men, and I remember my youth and the feeling that will never come back any more—the feeling that I could last forever, outlast the sea, the earth, and all men; the deceitful feeling that lures us on to joys, to perils, to love, to vain effort—to death; the triumphant conviction of strength, the heat of life in the handful of dust, the glow in the heart that with every year grows dim, grows cold, grows small, and expires—and expires, too soon, too soon—before life itself.

"And this is how I see the East. I have seen its secret places and have looked into its very soul; but now I see it always from a small boat, a high outline of mountains, blue and afar in the morning; like faint mist at noon; a jagged wall of purple at sunset. I have the feel of the oar in my hand, the vision of a scorching blue sea in my eyes. And I see a bay, a wide bay, smooth as glass and polished like ice, shimmering in the dark. A red light

burns far off upon the gloom of the land, and the night
is soft and warm. We drag at the oars with aching arms,
and suddenly a puff of wind, a puff faint and tepid and
laden with strange odors of blossoms, of aromatic wood,
comes out of the still night—the first sigh of the East
on my face. That I can never forget. It was impalpable
and enslaving, like a charm, like a whispered promise of
mysterious delight.

"We had been pulling this finishing spell for eleven
hours. Two pulled, and he whose turn it was to rest
sat at the tiller. We had made out the red light in that
bay and steered for it, guessing it must mark some small
coasting port. We passed two vessels, outlandish and
high-sterned, sleeping at anchor, and, approaching the
light, now very dim, ran the boat's nose against the end
of a jutting wharf. We were blind with fatigue. My
men dropped the oars and fell off the thwarts as if dead.
I made fast to a pile. A current rippled softly. The
scented obscurity of the shore was grouped into vast
masses, a density of colossal clumps of vegetation, probably—mute and fantastic shapes. And at their foot the
semicircle of a beach gleamed faintly, like an illusion.
There was not a light, not a stir, not a sound. The mysterious East faced me, perfumed like a flower, silent
like death, dark like a grave.

"And I sat weary beyond expression, exulting like
a conqueror, sleepless and entranced as if before a profound, a fateful enigma.

"A splashing of oars, a measured dip reverberating
on the level of water, intensified by the silence of the
shore into loud claps, made me jump up. A boat, a
European boat, was coming in. I invoked the name of
the dead; I hailed: 'Judea ahoy!' A thin shout answered.

"It was the captain. I had beaten the flagship by three

hours, and I was glad to hear the old man's voice again, tremulous and tired. 'Is it you, Marlow?' 'Mind the end of that jetty, sir,' I cried.

"He approached cautiously, and brought up with the deep-sea lead line which we had saved—for the underwriters. I eased my painter and fell alongside. He sat, a broken figure at the stern, wet with dew, his hands clasped in his lap. His men were asleep already. 'I had a terrible time of it,' he murmured. 'Mahon is behind—not very far.' We conversed in whispers, in low whispers, as if afraid to wake up the land. Guns, thunder, earthquakes would not have awakened the men just then.

"Looking round as we talked, I saw away at sea a bright light traveling in the night. 'There's a steamer passing the bay,' I said. She was not passing, she was entering, and she even came close and anchored. 'I wish,' said the old man, 'you would find out whether she is English. Perhaps they could give us a passage somewhere.' He seemed nervously anxious. So by dint of punching and kicking I started one of my men into a state of somnambulism, and giving him an oar, took another and pulled towards the lights of the steamer.

"There was a murmur of voices in her, metallic hollow clangs of the engine room, footsteps on the deck. Her ports shone, round like dilated eyes. Shapes moved about, and there was a shadowy man high up on the bridge. He heard my oars.

"And then, before I could open my lips, the East spoke to me, but it was in a Western voice. A torrent of words was poured into the enigmatical, the fateful silence; outlandish, angry words, mixed with words and even whole sentences of good English, less strange but even more surprising. The voice swore and cursed violently; it riddled the solemn peace of the bay by a volley of abuse. It began by calling me Pig, and from that went crescendo into unmentionable adjectives—in English. The man up there raged aloud in two languages, and with a sincerity in his fury that almost convinced me I had, in some way, sinned against the harmony of the universe. I could hardly see him, but began to think he would work himself into a fit.

"Suddenly he ceased, and I could hear him snorting and blowing like a porpoise. I said:

" 'What steamer is this, pray?'

" 'Eh? What's this? And who are you?'

" 'Castaway crew of an English bark burnt at sea. We came here tonight. I am the second mate. The captain is in the longboat, and wishes to know if you would give us a passage somewhere.'

" 'Oh, my goodness! I say. . . . This is the *Celestial* from Singapore on her return trip. I'll arrange with your captain in the morning, . . . and, . . . I say, . . . did you hear me just now?'

" 'I should think the whole bay heard you.'

" 'I thought you were a shoreboat. Now, look here—this infernal lazy scoundrel of a caretaker has gone to sleep again—curse him. The light is out, and I nearly ran foul of the end of this damned jetty. This is the third time he plays me this trick. Now, I ask you, can anybody stand this kind of thing? It's enough to drive a man out of his mind. I'll report him. . . . I'll get the Assistant Resident to give him the sack, by—! See—there's no light. It's out, isn't it? I take you to witness the light's out. There should be a light, you know. A red light on the—'

" 'There was a light,' I said, mildly.

" 'But it's out, man! What's the use of talking like this? You can see for yourself it's out—don't you? If you had to take a valuable steamer along this Godforsaken coast you would want a light, too. I'll kick him from end to end of his miserable wharf. You'll see if I don't. I will—'

" 'So I may tell my captain you'll take us?' I broke in.

" 'Yes, I'll take you. Good night,' he said, brusquely.

"I pulled back, made fast again to the jetty, and then went to sleep at last. I had faced the silence of the East. I had heard some of its language. But when I opened my eyes again the silence was as complete as though it had never been broken. I was lying in a flood of light, and the sky had never looked so far, so high, before. I opened my eyes and lay without moving.

"And then I saw the men of the East—they were looking at me. The whole length of the jetty was full of people. I saw brown, bronze, yellow faces, the black eyes, the glitter, the color of an Eastern crowd. And all these beings stared without a murmur, without a sigh, without a movement. They stared down at the boats, at the sleeping men who at night had come to them from the sea. Nothing moved. The fronds of palms stood still against the sky. Not a branch stirred along the shore, and the brown roofs of hidden houses peeped through the green foliage, through the big leaves that hung shining and still like leaves forged of heavy metal. This was the East of the ancient navigators, so old, so mysterious, resplendent and somber, living and unchanged, full of danger and promise. And these were the men. I sat up suddenly. A wave of movement passed through the crowd from end to end, passed along the heads, swayed the bodies, ran along the jetty like a ripple on the water, like a breath of wind on a field—and all was still again. I see it now—the wide sweep of the bay, the glittering sands, the wealth of green infinite and varied, the sea blue like the sea of a dream, the crowd of attentive faces, the blaze of vivid color—the water reflecting it all, the curve of the shore, the jetty, the high-sterned

outlandish craft floating still, and the three boats with
the tired men from the West sleeping, unconscious of
the land and the people and of the violence of sunshine.
They slept thrown across the thwarts, curled on bottom-
boards, in the careless attitudes of death. The head of
the old skipper, leaning back in the stern of the longboat, had fallen on his breast, and he looked as though
he would never wake. Farther out old Mahon's face was
upturned to the sky, with the long white beard spread
out on his breast, as though he had been shot where he
sat at the tiller; and a man, all in a heap in the bows of
the boat, slept with both arms embracing the stemhead
and with his cheek laid on the gunwale. The East looked
at them without a sound.

"I have known its fascination since; I have seen the
mysterious shores, the still water, the lands of brown
nations, where a stealthy Nemesis lies in wait, pursues,
overtakes so many of the conquering race, who are
proud of their wisdom, of their knowledge, of their
strength. But for me all the East is contained in that
vision of my youth. It is all in that moment when I
opened my young eyes on it. I came upon it from a
tussle with the sea—and I was young—and I saw it
looking at me. And this is all that is left of it! Only a
moment; a moment of strength, of romance, of glamor
—of youth! . . . A flick of sunshine upon a strange
shore, the time to remember, the time for a sigh, and—
good-by!—Night—Good-by . . . !"

He drank.

"Ah! The good old time—the good old time. Youth
and the sea  Glamor and the sea! The good, strong sea,
the salt, bitter sea, that could whisper to you and roar
at you and knock your breath out of you."

He drank again.

"By all that's wonderful it is the sea, I believe, the

sea itself—or is it youth alone? Who can tell? But you here—you all had something out of life: money, love—whatever one gets on shore—and, tell me, wasn't that the best time, that time when we were young at sea; young and had nothing, on the sea that gives nothing, except hard knocks—and sometimes a chance to feel your strength—that only—that you all regret?"

And we all nodded at him: the man of finance, the man of accounts, the man of law, we all nodded at him over the polished table that like a still sheet of brown water reflected our faces, lined, wrinkled; our faces marked by toil, by deceptions, by success, by love; our weary eyes looking still, looking always, looking anxiously for something out of life, that while it is expected is already gone—has passed unseen, in a sigh, in a flash —together with the youth, with the strength, with the romance of illusions.

# Amy Foster

KENNEDY is a country doctor, and lives in Colebrook, on the shores of Eastbay. The high ground
rising abruptly behind the red roofs of the little town
crowds the quaint High Street against the wall which
defends it from the sea. Beyond the sea wall there
curves for miles in a vast and regular sweep the barren
beach of shingle, with the village of Brenzett standing
out darkly across the water, a spire in a clump of trees;
and still farther out the perpendicular column of a lighthouse, looking in the distance no bigger than a lead
pencil, marks the vanishing point of the land. The country at the back of Brenzett is low and flat; but the bay
is fairly well sheltered from the seas, and occasionally
a big ship, windbound or through stress of weather,
makes use of the anchoring ground a mile and a half due
north from you as you stand at the back door of the
"Ship Inn" in Brenzett. A dilapidated windmill near by,
lifting its shattered arms from a mound no loftier than
a rubbish heap, and a Martello tower squatting at the
water's edge half a mile to the south of the Coastguard
cottages, are familiar to the skippers of small craft.
These are the official seamarks for the patch of trust-
worthy bottom represented on the Admiralty charts by
an irregular oval of dots enclosing several figure sixes,
with a tiny anchor engraved among them, and the
legend "mud and shells" over all.

155

The brow of the upland overtops the square tower of the Colebrook Church. The slope is green and looped by a white road. Ascending along this road, you open a valley broad and shallow, a wide green trough of pastures and hedges merging inland into a vista of purple tints and flowing lines closing the view.

In this valley down to Brenzett and Colebrook and up to Darnford, the market town fourteen miles away, lies the practice of my friend Kennedy. He had begun life as surgeon in the Navy, and afterwards had been the companion of a famous traveler, in the days when there were continents with unexplored interiors. His papers on the fauna and flora made him known to scientific societies. And now he had come to a country practice—from choice. The penetrating power of his mind, acting like a corrosive fluid, had destroyed his ambition, I fancy. His intelligence is of a scientific order, of an investigating habit, and of that unappeasable curiosity which believes that there is a particle of a general truth in every mystery.

A good many years ago now, on my return from abroad, he invited me to stay with him. I came readily enough, and as he could not neglect his patients to keep me company, he took me on his rounds—thirty miles or so of an afternoon, sometimes. I waited for him on the roads; the horse reached after the leafy twigs, and, sitting high in the dogcart, I could hear Kennedy's laugh through the half-open door of some cottage. He had a big, hearty laugh that would have fitted a man twice his size, a brisk manner, a bronzed face, and a pair of gray, profoundly attentive eyes. He had the talent of making people talk to him freely, and an inexhaustible patience in listening to their tales.

One day, as we trotted out of a large village into a shady bit of road, I saw on our left hand a low, black cottage, with diamond panes in the windows, a creeper on the end wall, a roof of shingle, and some roses climbing on the rickety trelliswork of the tiny porch. Kennedy pulled up to a walk. A woman, in full sunlight, was throwing a dripping blanket over a line stretched between two old apple trees. And as the bobtailed, long-necked chestnut, trying to get his head, jerked the left hand, covered by a thick dogskin glove, the doctor raised his voice over the hedge: "How's your child, Amy?"

I had time to see her dull face, red, not with a mantling blush, but as if her flat cheeks had been vigorously slapped, and to take in the squat figure, the scanty, dusty brown hair drawn into a tight knot at the back of the head. She looked quite young. With a distinct catch in her breath, her voice sounded low and timid.

"He's well, thank you."

We trotted again. "A young patient of yours," I said; and the doctor, flicking the chestnut absently, muttered, "Her husband used to be."

"She seems a dull creature," I remarked, listlessly.

"Precisely," said Kennedy. "She is very passive. It's enough to look at the red hands hanging at the end of those short arms, at those slow, prominent brown eyes, to know the inertness of her mind—an inertness that one would think made it everlastingly safe from all the surprises of imagination. And yet which of us is safe? At any rate, such as you see her, she had enough imagination to fall in love. She's the daughter of one Isaac Foster, who from a small farmer has sunk into a shepherd; the beginning of his misfortunes dating from his runaway marriage with the cook of his widowed father —a well-to-do, apoplectic grazier, who passionately struck his name off his will, and had been heard to utter threats against his life. But this old affair, scandalous

enough to serve as a motive for a Greek tragedy, arose
from the similarity of their characters. There are other
tragedies, less scandalous and of a subtler poignancy,
arising from irreconcilable differences and from that fear
of the Incomprehensible that hangs over all our heads—
over all our heads. . . ."

The tired chestnut dropped into a walk; and the rim
of the sun, all red in a speckless sky, touched familiarly
the smooth top of a plowed rise near the road as I had
seen it times innumerable touch the distant horizon of
the sea. The uniform brownness of the harrowed field
glowed with a rose tinge, as though the powdered clods
had sweated out in minute pearls of blood the toil of
uncounted plowmen. From the edge of a copse a wagon
with two horses was rolling gently along the ridge.
Raised above our heads upon the skyline, it loomed up
against the red sun, triumphantly big, enormous, like a
chariot of giants drawn by two slow-stepping steeds of
legendary proportions. And the clumsy figure of the man
plodding at the head of the leading horse projected itself
on the background of the Infinite with a heroic uncouth-
ness. The end of his carter's whip quivered high up in
the blue. Kennedy discoursed.

"She's the eldest of a large family. At the age of
fifteen they put her out to service at the New Barns
Farm. I attended Mrs. Smith, the tenant's wife, and saw
that girl there for the first time. Mrs. Smith, a genteel
person with a sharp nose, made her put on a black dress
every afternoon. I don't know what induced me to
notice her at all. There are faces that call your attention
by a curious want of definiteness in their whole aspect,
as, walking in a mist, you peer attentively at a vague
shape which, after all, may be nothing more curious or
strange than a signpost. The only peculiarity I perceived
in her was a slight hesitation in her utterance, a sort of

preliminary stammer which passes away with the first
word. When sharply spoken to, she was apt to lose her
head at once; but her heart was of the kindest. She had
never been heard to express a dislike for a single human
being, and she was tender to every living creature. She
was devoted to Mrs. Smith, to Mr. Smith, to their dogs,
cats, canaries; and as to Mrs. Smith's gray parrot, its
peculiarities exercised upon her a positive fascination.
Nevertheless, when that outlandish bird, attacked by
the cat, shrieked for help in human accents, she ran out
into the yard stopping her ears, and did not prevent the
crime. For Mrs. Smith this was another evidence of her
stupidity; on the other hand, her want of charm, in view
of Smith's well-known frivolousness, was a great recommendation. Her shortsighted eyes would swim with pity
for a poor mouse in a trap, and she had been seen once
by some boys on her knees in the wet grass helping a
toad in difficulties. If it's true, as some German fellow
has said, that without phosphorus there is no thought,
it is still more true that there is no kindness of heart
without a certain amount of imagination. She had some.
She had even more than is necessary to understand
suffering and to be moved by pity. She fell in love under
circumstances that leave no room for doubt in the
matter; for you need imagination to form a notion of
beauty at all, and still more to discover your ideal in an
unfamiliar shape.

"How this aptitude came to her, what it did feed
upon, is an inscrutable mystery. She was born in the
village, and had never been farther away from it than
Colebrook or perhaps Darnford. She lived for four years
with the Smiths. New Barns is an isolated farmhouse a
mile away from the road, and she was content to look
day after day at the same fields, hollows, rises; at the
trees and the hedgerows; at the faces of the four men

about the farm, always the same—day after day, month after month, year after year. She never showed a desire for conversation, and, as it seemed to me, she did not know how to smile. Sometimes of a fine Sunday afternoon she would put on her best dress, a pair of stout boots, a large gray hat trimmed with a black feather (I've seen her in that finery), seize an absurdly slender parasol, climb over two stiles, tramp over three fields and along two hundred yards of road—never farther. There stood Foster's cottage. She would help her mother to give their tea to the younger children, wash up the crockery, kiss the little ones, and go back to the farm. That was all. All the rest, all the change, all the relaxation. She never seemed to wish for anything more. And then she fell in love. She fell in love silently, obstinately —perhaps helplessly. It came slowly, but when it came it worked like a powerful spell; it was love as the ancients understood it: an irresistible and fateful impulse —a possession! Yes, it was in her to become haunted and possessed by a face, by a presence, fatally, as though she had been a pagan worshiper of form under a joyous sky—and to be awakened at last from that mysterious forgetfulness of self, from that enchantment, from that transport, by a fear resembling the unaccountable terror of a brute. . . ."

With the sun hanging low on its western limit, the expanse of the grasslands framed in the counterscarps of the rising ground took on a gorgeous and somber aspect. A sense of penetrating sadness, like that inspired by a grave strain of music, disengaged itself from the silence of the fields. The men we met walked past, slow, unsmiling, with downcast eyes, as if the melancholy of an overburdened earth had weighted their feet, bowed their shoulders, borne down their glances.

"Yes," said the doctor to my remark, "one would

think the earth is under a curse, since of all her children these that cling to her the closest are uncouth in body and as leaden of gait as if their very hearts were loaded with chains. But here on this same road you might have seen amongst these heavy men a being lithe, supple and long-limbed, straight like a pine, with something striving upwards in his appearance as though the heart within him had been buoyant. Perhaps it was only the force of the contrast, but when he was passing one of these villagers here, the soles of his feet did not seem to me to touch the dust of the road. He vaulted over the stiles, paced these slopes with a long elastic stride that made him noticeable at a great distance, and had lustrous black eyes. He was so different from the mankind around that, with his freedom of movement, his soft—a little startled—glance, his olive complexion and graceful bearing, his humanity suggested to me the nature of a woodland creature. He came from there."

The doctor pointed with his whip, and from the summit of the descent seen over the rolling tops of the trees in a park by the side of the road, appeared the level sea far below us, like the floor of an immense edifice inlaid with bands of dark ripple, with still trails of glitter, ending in a belt of glassy water at the foot of the sky. The light blur of smoke, from an invisible steamer, faded on the great clearness of the horizon like the mist of a breath on a mirror; and, inshore, the white sails of a coaster, with the appearance of disentangling themselves slowly from under the branches, floated clear of the foliage of the trees.

"Shipwrecked in the bay?" I said.

"Yes; he was a castaway. A poor emigrant from Central Europe bound to America and washed ashore here in a storm. And for him, who knew nothing of the earth, England was an undiscovered country. It was some time before he learned its name; and for all I know he might have expected to find wild beasts or wild men here, when, crawling in the dark over the sea wall, he rolled down the other side into a dyke, where it was another miracle he didn't get drowned. But he struggled instinctively like an animal under a net, and this blind struggle threw him out into a field. He must have been, indeed, of a tougher fiber than he looked to withstand without expiring such buffetings, the violence of his exertions, and so much fear. Later on, in his broken English that resembled curiously the speech of a young child, he told me himself that he put his trust in God, believing he was no longer in this world. And truly—he would add—how was he to know? He fought his way against the rain and the gale on all fours, and crawled at last among some sheep huddled close under the lee of a hedge. They ran off in all directions, bleating in the darkness, and he welcomed the first familiar sound he heard on these shores. It must have been two in the morning then. And this is all we know of the manner of his landing, though he did not arrive unattended by any means. Only his grisly company did not begin to come ashore till much later in the day. . . ."

The doctor gathered the reins, clicked his tongue; we trotted down the hill. Then turning, almost directly, a sharp corner into High Street, we rattled over the stones and were home.

Late in the evening Kennedy, breaking a spell of moodiness that had come over him, returned to the story. Smoking his pipe, he paced the long room from end to end. A reading lamp concentrated all its light upon the papers on his desk; and, sitting by the open window, I saw, after the windless, scorching day, the frigid splendor of a hazy sea lying motionless under the moon. Not a whisper, not a splash, not a stir of the shingle, not a footstep, not a sigh came up from the earth below—never a sign of life but the scent of climbing jasmine; and Kennedy's voice, speaking behind me, passed through the wide casement, to vanish outside in a chill and sumptuous stillness.

". . . The relations of shipwrecks in the olden times tell us of much suffering. Often the castaways were only saved from drowning to die miserably from starvation on a barren coast; others suffered violent death or else slavery, passing through years of precarious existence with people to whom their strangeness was an object of suspicion, dislike or fear. We read about these things, and they are very pitiful. It is indeed hard upon a man to find himself a lost stranger, helpless, incomprehensible, and of a mysterious origin, in some obscure corner of the earth. Yet amongst all the adventurers shipwrecked in all the wild parts of the world, there is not one, it seems to me, that ever had to suffer a fate so simply tragic as the man I am speaking of, the most innocent of adventurers cast out by the sea in the bight of this bay, almost within sight from this very window.

"He did not know the name of his ship. Indeed, in the course of time we discovered he did not even know that ships had names—'like Christian people'; and when, one day, from the top of Talfourd Hill, he beheld the sea lying open to his view, his eyes roamed afar, lost in an air of wild surprise, as though he had never seen such a sight before. And probably he had not. As far as I could make out, he had been hustled together with many others on board an emigrant ship at the mouth of the Elbe, too bewildered to take note of his surroundings, too weary to see anything, too anxious to care. They were driven below into the 'tween-deck and battened down from the very start. It was a low timber dwelling—he would say—with wooden beams overhead, like the houses in his country, but you went into it down a ladder. It was very large, very cold, damp and somber, with places in the manner of wooden boxes where people had to sleep one above another, and it kept on rocking all ways at once all the time. He crept into one of these boxes and lay down there in the clothes in which he had left his home many days before, keeping his bundle and his stick by his side. People groaned, children cried, water dripped, the lights went out, the walls of the place creaked, and everything was being shaken so that in one's little box one dared not lift one's head. He had lost touch with his only companion (a young man from the same valley, he said), and all the time a great noise of wind went on outside and heavy blows fell—boom! boom! An awful sickness overcame him, even to the point of making him neglect his prayers. Besides, one could not tell whether it was morning or evening. It seemed always to be night in that place.

"Before that he had been traveling a long, long time on the iron track. He looked out of the window, which had a wonderfully clear glass in it, and the trees, the houses, the fields, and the long roads seemed to fly round and round about him till his head swam. He gave me to understand that he had on his passage beheld uncounted multitudes of people—whole nations—all dressed in such clothes as the rich wear. Once he was made to get out of the carriage, and slept through a night on a bench in a house of bricks with his bundle under his head; and once for many hours he had to sit on a floor of flat stones, dozing, with his knees up and with his bundle between his feet. There was a roof over him, which seemed made of glass, and was so high that the tallest mountain pine he had ever seen would have had room to grow under it. Steam machines rolled in at one end and out at the other. People swarmed more than you can see on a feast day round the miraculous Holy Image in the yard of the Carmelite Convent down in the plains where, before he left his home, he drove his mother in a wooden cart—a pious old woman who wanted to offer prayers and make a vow for his safety. He could not give me an idea of how large and lofty and full of noise and smoke and gloom, and clang of iron, the place was, but someone had told him it was called Berlin. Then they rang a bell, and another steam machine came in, and again he was taken on and on through a land that wearied his eyes by its flatness without a single bit of a hill to be seen anywhere. One more night he spent shut up in a building like a good stable with a litter of straw on the floor, guarding his bundle amongst a lot of men, of whom not one could understand a single word he said. In the morning they were all led down to the stony shores of an extremely broad muddy river, flowing not between hills but between houses that seemed immense. There was a steam machine that went on the water, and they all stood upon it packed tight, only now there were with them many women and children who made much noise. A cold rain fell, the wind blew in his face; he was wet through, and his teeth chattered. He and the young man from the same valley took each other by the hand.

"They thought they were being taken to America straight away, but suddenly the steam machine bumped against the side of a thing like a great house on the water. The walls were smooth and black, and there uprose, growing from the roof as it were, bare trees in the shape of crosses, extremely high. That's how it appeared to him then, for he had never seen a ship before. This was the ship that was going to swim all the way to America. Voices shouted, everything swayed; there was a ladder dipping up and down. He went up on his hands and knees in mortal fear of falling into the water below, which made a great splashing. He got separated from his companion, and when he descended into the bottom of that ship his heart seemed to melt suddenly within him.

"It was then also, as he told me, that he lost contact for good and all with one of those three men who the summer before had been going about through all the little towns in the foothills of his country. They would arrive on market days driving in a peasant's cart, and would set up an office in an inn or some other Jew's house. There were three of them, of whom one with a long beard looked venerable; and they had red cloth collars round their necks and gold lace on their sleeves like Government officials. They sat proudly behind a long table; and in the next room, so that the common people shouldn't hear, they kept a cunning telegraph machine, through which they could talk to the Emperor of America. The fathers hung about the door, but the young men of the mountains would crowd up to the table asking many questions, for there was work to be got all the year round at three dollars a day in America, and no military service to do.

"But the American Kaiser would not take everybody. Oh, no! He himself had great difficulty in getting accepted, and the venerable man in uniform had to go out of the room several times to work the telegraph on his behalf. The American Kaiser engaged him at last at three dollars, he being young and strong. However, many able young men backed out, afraid of the great distance; besides, those only who had some money could be taken. There were some who sold their huts and their land because it cost a lot of money to get to America; but then, once there, you had three dollars a day, and if you were clever you could find places where true gold could be picked up on the ground. His father's house was getting over-full. Two of his brothers were married and had children. He promised to send money home from America by post twice a year. His father sold an old cow, a pair of piebald mountain ponies of his own raising, and a cleared plot of fair pasture land on the sunny slope of a pineclad pass to a Jew innkeeper, in order to pay the people of the ship that took men to America to get rich in a short time.

"He must have been a real adventurer at heart, for how many of the greatest enterprises in the conquest of the earth had for their beginning just such a bargaining away of the paternal cow for the mirage or true gold far away! I have been telling you more or less in my own words what I learned fragmentarily in the course of two or three years, during which I seldom missed an opportunity of a friendly chat with him. He told me this story of his adventure with many flashes of white teeth and lively glances of black eyes, at first in a sort of anxious baby-talk, then, as he acquired the language, with great fluency, but always with that singing, soft, and at the same time vibrating intonation that instilled a strangely penetrating power into the sound of the most familiar English words, as if they had been the words of an unearthly language. And he always would come to an end, with many emphatic shakes of his head, upon that awful sensation of his heart melting within him directly he set foot on board that ship. Afterwards there seemed to come for him a period of blank ignorance, at any rate as to facts. No doubt he must have been abominably seasick and abominably unhappy—this soft and passionate adventurer, taken thus out of his knowledge, and feeling bitterly as he lay in his emigrant bunk his utter loneliness; for his was a highly sensitive nature.

The next thing we know of him for certain is that he had been hiding in Hammond's pig-pound by the side of the road to Norton, six miles, as the crow flies, from the sea. Of these experiences he was unwilling to speak: they seemed to have seared into his soul a somber sort of wonder and indignation. Through the rumors of the countryside, which lasted for a good many days after his arrival, we know that the fishermen of West Colebrook had been disturbed and startled by heavy knocks against the walls of weatherboard cottages, and by a voice crying piercingly strange words in the night. Several of them turned out even, but, no doubt, he had fled in sudden alarm at their rough angry tones hailing each other in the darkness. A sort of frenzy must have helped him up the steep Norton hill. It was he, no doubt, who early the following morning had been seen lying (in a swoon, I should say) on the roadside grass by the Brenzett carrier, who actually got down to have a nearer look, but drew back, intimidated by the perfect immobility, and by something queer in the aspect of that tramp, sleeping so still under the showers. As the day advanced, some children came dashing into school at Norton in such a fright that the schoolmistress went out and spoke indignantly to a 'horrid-looking man' on the road. He edged away, hanging his head, for a few steps, and then suddenly ran off with extraordinary fleetness. The driver of Mr. Bradley's milk cart made no secret of it that he had lashed with his whip at a hairy sort of gypsy fellow who, jumping up at a turn of the road by the Vents, made a snatch at the pony's bridle. And he caught him a good one, too, right over the face, he said, that made him drop down in the mud a jolly sight quicker than he had jumped up; but it was a good half a mile before he could stop the pony. Maybe that in his desperate endeavors to get help, and in his need to get in touch with someone, the poor devil had tried to stop the cart. Also three boys confessed afterwards to throwing stones at a funny tramp, knocking about all wet and muddy, and, it seemed, very drunk, in the narrow deep lane by the limekilns. All this was the talk of three villages for days; but we have Mrs. Finn's (the wife of Smith's wagoner) unimpeachable testimony that she saw him get over the low wall of Hammond's pig-pound and lurch straight at her, babbling aloud in a voice that was enough to make one die of fright. Having the baby with her in a perambulator, Mrs. Finn called out to him to go away, and as he persisted in coming nearer, she hit him courageously with her umbrella over the head, and, without once looking back, ran like the wind with the perambulator as far as the first house in the village. She stopped then, out of breath, and spoke to old Lewis, hammering there at a heap of stones; and the old chap, taking off his immense black wire goggles, got up on his shaky legs to look where she pointed. Together they followed with their eyes the figure of the man running over a field; they saw him fall down, pick himself up, and run on again, staggering and waving his long arms above his head, in the direction of the New Barns Farm. From that moment he is plainly in the toils of his obscure and touching destiny. There is no doubt after this of what happened to him. All is certain now: Mrs. Smith's intense terror; Amy Foster's stolid conviction held against the other's nervous attack, that the man 'meant no harm'; Smith's exasperation (on his return from Darnford Market) at finding the dog barking himself into a fit, the back door locked, his wife in hysterics; and all for an unfortunate dirty tramp, supposed to be even then lurking in his stackyard. Was he? He would teach him to frighten women.

"Smith is notoriously hot-tempered, but the sight of

some nondescript and miry creature sitting cross-legged amongst a lot of loose straw, and swinging itself to and fro like a bear in a cage, made him pause. Then this tramp stood up silently before him, one mass of mud and filth from head to foot. Smith, alone amongst his stacks with this apparition, in the stormy twilight ringing with the infuriated barking of the dog, felt the dread of an inexplicable strangeness. But when that being, parting with his black hands the long matted locks that hung before his face, as you part the two halves of a curtain, looked out at him with glistening, wild, black-and-white eyes, the weirdness of this silent encounter fairly staggered him. He has admitted since (for the story has been a legitimate subject of conversation about here for years) that he made more than one step backwards. Then a sudden burst of rapid, senseless speech persuaded him at once that he had to do with an escaped lunatic. In fact, that impression never wore off completely. Smith has not in his heart given up his secret conviction of the man's essential insanity to this very day.

"As the creature approached him, jabbering in a most discomposing manner, Smith (unaware that he was being addressed as 'gracious lord,' and adjured in God's name to afford food and shelter) kept on speaking firmly but gently to it, and retreating all the time into the other yard. At last, watching his chance, by a sudden charge he bundled him headlong into the wood-lodge, and instantly shot the bolt. Thereupon he wiped his brow, though the day was cold. He had done his duty to the community by shutting up a wandering and probably dangerous maniac. Smith isn't a hard man at all, but he had room in his brain only for that one idea of lunacy. He was not imaginative enough to ask himself whether the man might not be perishing with cold

and hunger. Meantime, at first, the maniac made a great
deal of noise in the lodge. Mrs. Smith was screaming
upstairs, where she had locked herself in her bedroom;
but Amy Foster sobbed piteously at the kitchen door,
wringing her hands and muttering, 'Don't! don't!' I
daresay Smith had a rough time of it that evening with
one noise and another, and this insane, disturbing voice
crying obstinately through the door only added to his
irritation. He couldn't possibly have connected this trou-
blesome lunatic with the sinking of a ship in Eastbay, of
which there had been a rumor in the Darnford market
place. And I dare say the man inside had been very near
to insanity on that night. Before his excitement collapsed
and he became unconscious he was throwing himself
violently about in the dark, rolling on some dirty sacks,
and biting his fists with rage, cold, hunger, amazement,
and despair.

"He was a mountaineer of the eastern range of the
Carpathians, and the vessel sunk the night before in
Eastbay was the Hamburg emigrant ship *Herzogin
Sophia-Dorothea,* of appalling memory.

"A few months later we could read in the papers the
accounts of the bogus 'Emigration Agencies' among the
Slavic peasantry in the more remote provinces of Austria. The object of these scoundrels was to get hold of
the poor ignorant people's homesteads, and they were
in league with the local usurers. They exported their
victims through Hamburg mostly. As to the ship, I had
watched her out of this very window, reaching close-
hauled under short canvas into the bay on a dark,
threatening afternoon. She came to an anchor, correctly
by the chart, off the Brenzett Coastguard station. I remember before the night fell looking out again at the
outlines of her spars and rigging that stood out dark and
pointed on a background of ragged, slaty clouds like

another and a slighter spire to the left of the Brenzett churchtower. In the evening the wind rose. At midnight I could hear in my bed the terrific gusts and the sounds of a driving deluge.

"About that time the Coastguardmen thought they saw the lights of a steamer over the anchoring ground. In a moment they vanished; but it is clear that another vessel of some sort had tried for shelter in the bay on that awful, blind night, had rammed the German ship amidships ('a breach'—as one of the divers told me afterwards—'that you could sail a Thames barge through'), and then had gone out either scatheless or damaged, who shall say; but had gone out, unknown, unseen, and fatal, to perish mysteriously at sea. Of her nothing ever came to light, and yet the hue and cry that was raised all over the world would have found her out if she had been in existence anywhere on the face of the waters.

"A completeness without a clue, and a stealthy silence as of a neatly executed crime, characterize this murderous disaster, which, as you may remember, had its gruesome celebrity. The wind would have prevented the loudest outcries from reaching the shore; there had been evidently no time for signals of distress. It was death without any sort of fuss. The Hamburg ship, filling all at once, capsized as she sank, and at daylight there was not even the end of a spar to be seen above water. She was missed, of course, and at first the Coastguardmen surmised that she had either dragged her anchor or parted her cable sometime during the night, and had been blown out to sea. Then, after the tide turned, the wreck must have shifted a little and released some of the bodies, because a child—a little fair-haired child in a red frock—came ashore abreast of the Martello tower. By the afternoon you could see along three miles of beach dark figures with bare legs dashing in and out of the tumbling foam, and rough-looking men, women with hard faces, children, mostly fair-haired, were being carried, stiff and dripping, on stretchers, on wattles, on ladders, in a long procession past the door of the 'Ship Inn,' to be laid out in a row under the north wall of the Brenzett Church.

"Officially, the body of the little girl in the red frock is the first thing that came ashore from that ship. But I have patients amongst the seafaring population of West Colebrook, and, unofficially, I am informed that very early that morning two brothers, who went down to look after their cobble hauled up on the beach, found a good way from Brenzett, an ordinary ship's hencoop, lying high and dry on the shore, with eleven drowned ducks inside. Their families ate the birds, and the hencoop was split into firewood with a hatchet. It is possible that a man (supposing he happened to be on deck at the time of the accident) might have floated ashore on that hencoop. He might. I admit it is improbable, but there was the man—and for days. nay, for weeks— it didn't enter our heads that we had amongst us the only living soul that had escaped from that disaster. The man himself, even when he learned to speak intelligibly, could tell us very little. He remembered he had felt better (after the ship had anchored, I suppose), and that the darkness, the wind, and the rain took his breath away. This looks as if he had been on deck sometime during that night. But we mustn't forget he had been taken out of his knowledge, that he had been seasick and battened down below for four days, that he had no general notion of a ship or of the sea, and therefore could have no definite idea of what was happening to him. The rain, the wind, the darkness he knew; he understood the bleating of the sheep, and he remembered the pain of his wretchedness and misery, his heartbroken astonishment that it was neither seen nor understood, his dismay at finding all the men angry and all the women fierce. He had approached them as a beggar, it is true, he said; but in his country, even if they gave nothing, they spoke gently to beggars. The children in his country were not taught to throw stones at those who asked for compassion. Smith's strategy overcame him completely. The wood-lodge presented the horrible aspect of a dungeon. What would be done to him next? . . . No wonder that Amy Foster appeared to his eyes with the aureole of an angel of light. The girl had not been able to sleep for thinking of the poor man, and in the morning, before the Smiths were up, she slipped out across the back yard. Holding the door of the wood-lodge ajar, she looked in and extended to him half a loaf of white bread—'such bread as the rich eat in my country,' he used to say.

"At this he got up slowly from amongst all sorts of rubbish, stiff, hungry, trembling, miserable, and doubtful. 'Can you eat this?' she asked in her soft and timid voice. He must have taken her for a 'gracious lady.' He devoured ferociously, and tears were falling on the crust. Suddenly he dropped the bread, seized her wrist, and imprinted a kiss on her hand. She was not frightened. Through his forlorn condition she had observed that he was good-looking. She shut the door and walked back slowly to the kitchen. Much later on, she told Mrs. Smith, who shuddered at the bare idea of being touched by that creature.

"Through this act of impulsive pity he was brought back again within the pale of human relations with his new surroundings. He never forgot it—never.

"That very same morning old Mr. Swaffer (Smith's nearest neighbor) came over to give his advice, and ended by carrying him off. He stood, unsteady on his legs, meek, and caked over in half-dried mud, while the two men talked around him in an incomprehensible tongue. Mrs. Smith had refused to come downstairs till the madman was off the premises; Amy Foster, far from within the dark kitchen, watched through the open back door; and he obeyed the signs that were made to him to the best of his ability. But Smith was full of mistrust. 'Mind, sir! It may be all his cunning,' he cried repeatedly in a tone of warning. When Mr. Swaffer started the mare, the deplorable being sitting humbly by his side, through weakness, nearly fell out over the back of the high two-wheeled cart. Swaffer took him straight home. And it is then that I come upon the scene.

"I was called in by the simple process of the old man beckoning to me with his forefinger over the gate of his house as I happened to be driving past. I got down, of course.

" 'I've got something here,' he mumbled, leading the way to an outhouse at a little distance from his other farm buildings.

"It was there that I saw him first, in a long, low room taken upon the space of that sort of coach house. It was bare and whitewashed, with a small square aperture glazed with one cracked, dusty pane at its further end. He was lying on his back upon a straw pallet; they had given him a couple of horse blankets, and he seemed to have spent the remainder of his strength in the exertion of cleaning himself. He was almost speechless; his quick breathing under the blankets pulled up to his chin, his glittering, restless black eyes reminded me of a wild bird caught in a snare. While I was examining him, old Swaffer stood silently by the door, passing the tips of his fingers along his shaven upper lip. I gave some directions, promised to send a bottle of medicine, and naturally made some inquiries.

" 'Smith caught him in the stackyard at New Barns,'
said the old chap in his deliberate, unmoved manner,
and as if the other had been indeed a sort of wild animal. 'That's how I came by him. Quite a curiosity, isn't
he? Now tell me, doctor—you've been all over the world
—don't you think that's a bit of a Hindu we've got hold
of here?'

"I was greatly surprised. His long black hair scattered
over the straw bolster contrasted with the olive pallor
of his face. It occurred to me he might be a Basque. It
didn't necessarily follow that he should understand
Spanish; but I tried him with the few words I know,
and also with some French. The whispered sounds I
caught by bending my ear to his lips puzzled me utterly.
That afternoon the young ladies from the rectory (one
of them read Goethe with a dictionary, and the other
had struggled with Dante for years), coming to see Miss
Swaffer, tried their German and Italian on him from the
doorway. They retreated, just the least bit scared by the
flood of passionate speech which, turning on his pallet,
he let out at them. They admitted that the sound was
pleasant, soft, musical—but, in conjunction with his
looks perhaps, it was startling—so excitable, so utterly
unlike anything one had ever heard. The village boys
climbed up the bank to have a peep through the little
square aperture. Everybody was wondering what Mr.
Swaffer would do with him.

"He simply kept him.

"Swaffer would be called eccentric were he not so
much respected. They will tell you that Mr. Swaffer sits
up as late as ten o'clock at night to read books, and they
will tell you also that he can write a check for two hundred pounds without thinking twice about it. He himself would tell you that the Swaffers had owned land
between this and Darnford for these three hundred

years. He must be eighty-five today, but he does not look a bit older than when I first came here. He is a great breeder of sheep, and deals extensively in cattle. He attends market days for miles around in every sort of weather, and drives sitting bowed low over the reins, his lank gray hair curling over the collar of his warm coat, and with a green plaid rug round his legs. The calmness of advanced age gives a solemnity to his manner. He is clean-shaved; his lips are thin and sensitive; something rigid and monachal in the set of his features lends a certain elevation to the character of his face. He has been known to drive miles in the rain to see a new kind of rose in somebody's garden, or a monstrous cabbage grown by a cottager. He loves to hear tell of or to be shown something what he calls 'outlandish.' Perhaps it was just that outlandishness of the man which influenced old Swaffer. Perhaps it was only an inexplicable caprice. All I know is that at the end of three weeks I caught sight of Smith's lunatic digging in Swaffer's kitchen garden. They had found out he could use a spade. He dug barefooted.

"His black hair flowed over his shoulders. I suppose it was Swaffer who had given him the striped old cotton shirt; but he wore still the national brown cloth trousers (in which he had been washed ashore) fitting to the leg almost like tights; was belted with a broad leather belt studded with little brass discs; and had never yet ventured into the village. The land he looked upon seemed to him kept neatly, like the grounds round a landowner's house; the size of the cart horses struck him with astonishment; the roads resembled garden walks, and the aspect of the people, especially on Sundays, spoke of opulence. He wondered what made them so hardhearted and their children so bold. He got his food at the back door, carried it in both hands, carefully, to his outhouse, and, sitting alone on his pallet, would make the sign of the cross before he began. Beside the same pallet, kneeling in the early darkness of the short days, he recited aloud the Lord's Prayer before he slept. Whenever he saw old Swaffer he would bow with veneration from the waist, and stand erect while the old man, with his fingers over his upper lip, surveyed him silently. He bowed also to Miss Swaffer, who kept house frugally for her father—a broad-shouldered, big-boned woman of forty-five, with the pocket of her dress full of keys, and a gray, steady eye. She was Church—as people said (while her father was one of the trustees of the Baptist Chapel)—and wore a little steel cross at her waist. She dressed severely in black, in memory of one of the innumerable Bradleys of the neighborhood, to whom she had been engaged some twenty-five years ago—a young farmer who broke his neck out hunting on the eve of the wedding day. She had the unmoved countenance of the deaf, spoke very seldom, and her lips, thin like her father's, astonished one sometimes by a mysteriously ironic curl.

"These were the people to whom he owed allegiance, and an overwhelming loneliness seemed to fall from the leaden sky of that winter without sunshine. All the faces were sad. He could talk to no one, and had no hope of ever understanding anybody. It was as if these had been the faces of people from the other world—dead people —he used to tell me years afterwards. Upon my word, I wonder he did not go mad. He didn't know where he was. Somewhere very far from his mountains—somewhere over the water. Was this America, he wondered?

"If it hadn't been for the steel cross at Miss Swaffer's belt he would not, he confessed, have known whether he was in a Christian country at all. He used to cast stealthy glances at it, and feel comforted. There was nothing here the same as in his country! The earth and the water were different; there were no images of the Redeemer by the roadside. The very grass was different, and the trees. All the trees but the three old Norway pines on the bit of lawn before Swaffer's house, and these reminded him of his country. He had been detected once, after dusk, with his forehead against the trunk of one of them, sobbing, and talking to himself. They had been like brothers to him at that time, he affirmed. Everything else was strange. Conceive you the kind of an existence overshadowed, oppressed, by the everyday material appearances, as if by the visions of a nightmare. At night, when he could not sleep he kept on thinking of the girl who gave him the first piece of bread he had eaten in this foreign land. She had been neither fierce nor angry, nor frightened. Her face he remembered as the only comprehensible face amongst all these faces that were as closed, as mysterious, and as mute as the faces of the dead who are possessed of a knowledge beyond the comprehension of the living. I wonder whether the memory of her compassion prevented him from cutting his throat. But there! I suppose I am an old sentimentalist, and forget the instinctive love of life which it takes all the strength of an uncommon despair to overcome.

"He did the work which was given him with an intelligence which surprised old Swaffer. By and by it was discovered that he could help at the plowing, could milk the cows, feed the bullocks in the cattle-yard, and was of some use with the sheep. He began to pick up words, too, very fast; and suddenly, one fine morning in spring, he rescued from an untimely death a grandchild of old Swaffer.

"Swaffer's younger daughter is married to Willcox, a solicitor and the town clerk of Colebrook. Regularly twice a year they come to stay with the old man for a few days. Their only child, a little girl not three years old at the time, ran out of the house alone in her little white pinafore, and, toddling across the grass of a terraced garden, pitched herself over a low wall headfirst into the horsepond in the yard below.

"Our man was out with the wagoner and the plow in the field nearest to the house, and as he was leading the team round to begin a fresh furrow, he saw, through the gap of a gate, what for anybody else would have been a mere flutter of something white. But he had straight-glancing, quick, far-reaching eyes, that only seemed to flinch and lose their amazing power before the immensity of the sea. He was barefooted, and looking as outlandish as the heart of Swaffer could desire. Leaving the horses on the turn, to the inexpressible disgust of the wagoner he bounded off, going over the plowed ground in long leaps, and suddenly appeared before the mother, thrust the child into her arms, and strode away.

"The pond was not very deep; but still, if he had not had such good eyes, the child would have perished—miserably suffocated in the foot or so of sticky mud at the bottom. Old Swaffer walked out slowly into the field, waited till the plow came over to his side, had a good look at him, and without saying a word went back to the house. But from that time they laid out his meals on the kitchen table; and at first, Miss Swaffer, all in black and with an inscrutable face, would come and stand in the doorway of the living room to see him make a big sign of the cross before he fell to. I believe that from that day, too, Swaffer began to pay him regular wages.

"I can't follow step by step his development. He cut his hair short, was seen in the village and along the road going to and fro to his work like any other man. Children ceased to shout after him. He became aware of social differences, but remained for a long time surprised at the bare poverty of the churches among so much wealth. He couldn't understand either why they were kept shut up on weekdays. There was nothing to steal in them. Was it to keep people from praying too often? The rectory took much notice of him about that time, and I believe the young ladies attempted to prepare the ground for his conversion. They could not, however, break him of his habit of crossing himself, but he went so far as to take off the string with a couple of brass medals the size of a sixpence, a tiny metal cross, and a square sort of scapulary which he wore round his neck. He hung them on the wall by the side of his bed, and he was still to be heard every evening reciting the Lord's Prayer, in incomprehensible words and in a slow, fervent tone, as he had heard his old father do at the head of all the kneeling family, big and little, on every evening of his life. And though he wore corduroys at work, and a slop-made pepper-and-salt suit on Sundays, strangers would turn round to look after him on the road. His foreignness had a peculiar and indelible stamp. At last people became used to seeing him. But they never became used to him. His rapid, skimming walk; his swarthy complexion; his hat cocked on the left ear; his habit, on warm evenings, of wearing his coat over one shoulder, like a hussar's dolman; his manner of leaping over the stiles, not as a feat of agility, but in the ordinary course of progression—all these peculiarities were, as one may say, so many causes of scorn and offense to the inhabitants of the village. *They* wouldn't in their dinner hour lie flat on their backs on the grass to stare at the sky. Neither did they go about the fields screaming dismal tunes. Many times have I heard his

high-pitched voice from behind the ridge of some sloping sheepwalk, a voice light and soaring, like a lark's,
but with a melancholy human note, over our fields that
hear only the song of birds. And I would be startled
myself. Ah! He was different; innocent of heart, and full
of good will, which nobody wanted, this castaway, that,
like a man transplanted into another planet, was separated by an immense space from his past and by an immense ignorance from his future. His quick, fervent
utterance positively shocked everybody. 'An excitable
devil,' they called him. One evening, in the taproom of
the Coach and Horses (having drunk some whisky), he
upset them all by singing a love song of his country.
They hooted him down, and he was pained; but Preble,
the lame wheelwright, and Vincent, the fat blacksmith,
and the other notables, too, wanted to drink their evening beer in peace. On another occasion he tried to
show them how to dance. The dust rose in clouds from
the sanded floor; he leaped straight up amongst the
deal tables, struck his heels together, squatted on one
heel in front of old Preble, shooting out the other leg,
uttered wild and exulting cries, jumped up to whirl on
one foot, snapping his fingers above his head—and a
strange carter who was having a drink in there began
to swear, and cleared out with his half-pint in his hand
into the bar. But when suddenly he sprang upon a table
and continued to dance among the glasses, the landlord
interfered. He didn't want any 'acrobat tricks in the
taproom.' They laid their hands on him. Having had a
glass or two, Mr. Swaffer's foreigner tried to expostu-
late: was ejected forcibly: got a black eye.

"I believe he felt the hostility of his human surroundings. But he was tough—tough in spirit, too, as well as
in body. Only the memory of the sea frightened him,
with that vague terror that is left by a bad dream. His

home was far away; and he did not want now to go to America. I had often explained to him that there is no place on earth where true gold can be found lying ready and to be got for the trouble of the picking up. How, then, he asked, could he ever return home with empty hands when there had been sold a cow, two ponies, and a bit of land to pay for his going? His eyes would fill with tears, and, averting them from the immense shimmer of the sea, he would throw himself face down on the grass. But sometimes, cocking his hat with a little conquering air, he would defy my wisdom. He had found his bit of true gold. That was Amy Foster's heart; which was 'a golden heart, and soft to people's misery,' he would say in the accents of overwhelming conviction.

"He was called Yanko. He had explained that this meant Little John; but as he would also repeat very often that he was a mountaineer (some word sounding in the dialect of his country like Goorall) he got it for his surname. And this is the only trace of him that the succeeding ages may find in the marriage register of the parish. There it stands—Yanko Goorall—in the rector's handwriting. The crooked cross made by the castaway, a cross whose tracing no doubt seemed to him the most solemn part of the whole ceremony, is all that remains now to perpetuate the memory of his name.

"His courtship had lasted some time—ever since he got his precarious footing in the community. It began by his buying for Amy Foster a green satin ribbon in Darnford. This was what you did in his country. You bought a ribbon at a Jew's stall on a fair-day. I don't suppose the girl knew what to do with it, but he seemed to think that his honorable intentions could not be mistaken.

"It was only when he declared his purpose to get married that I fully understood how, for a hundred futile and inappreciable reasons, how—shall I say odious?—he was to all the countryside. Every old woman in the village was up in arms. Smith, coming upon him near the farm, promised to break his head for him if he found him about again. But he twisted his little black mustache with such a bellicose air and rolled such big, black fierce eyes at Smith that this promise came to nothing. Smith, however, told the girl that she must be mad to take up with a man who was surely wrong in his head. All the same, when she heard him in the gloaming whistle from beyond the orchard a couple of bars of a weird and mournful tune, she would drop whatever she had in her hand—she would leave Mrs. Smith in the middle of a sentence—and she would run out to his call. Mrs. Smith called her a shameless hussy. She answered nothing. She said nothing at all to anybody, and went on her way as if she had been deaf. She and I alone in all the land, I fancy, could see his very real beauty. He was very good-looking, and most graceful in his bearing, with that something wild as of a woodland creature in his aspect. Her mother moaned over her dismally whenever the girl came to see her on her day out. The father was surly, but pretended not to know; and Mrs. Finn once told her plainly that 'this man, my dear, will do you some harm some day yet.' And so it went on. They could be seen on the roads, she tramping stolidly in her finery —gray dress, black feather, stout boots, prominent white cotton gloves that caught your eye a hundred yards away; and he, his coat slung picturesquely over one shoulder, pacing by her side, gallant of bearing and casting tender glances upon the girl with the golden heart. I wonder whether he saw how plain she was. Perhaps among types so different from what he had ever seen, he had not the power to judge; or perhaps he was seduced by the divine quality of her pity.

"Yanko was in great trouble meantime. In his country you get an old man for an ambassador in marriage affairs. He did not know how to proceed. However, one day in the midst of sheep in a field (he was now Swaffer's under-shepherd with Foster) he took off his hat to the father and declared himself humbly. 'I daresay she's fool enough to marry you,' was all Foster said. 'And then,' he used to relate, 'he puts his hat on his head, looks black at me as if he wanted to cut my throat, whistles the dog, and off he goes, leaving me to do the work.' The Fosters, of course, didn't like to lose the wages the girl earned: Amy used to give all her money to her mother. But there was in Foster a very genuine aversion to that match. He contended that the fellow was very good with sheep, but was not fit for any girl to marry. For one thing, he used to go along the hedges muttering to himself like a dam' fool; and then, these foreigners behave very queerly to women sometimes. And perhaps he would want to carry her off somewhere —or run off himself. It was not safe. He preached it to his daughter that the fellow might ill-use her in some way. She made no answer. It was, they said in the village, as if the man had done something to her. People discussed the matter. It was quite an excitement, and the two went on 'walking out' together in the face of opposition. Then something unexpected happened.

"I don't know whether old Swaffer ever understood how much he was regarded in the light of a father by his foreign retainer. Anyway the relation was curiously feudal. So when Yanko asked formally for an interview —'and the Miss, too' (he called the severe, deaf Miss Swaffer simply *Miss*)—it was to obtain their permission to marry. Swaffer heard him unmoved, dismissed him by a nod, and then shouted the intelligence into Miss Swaffer's best ear. She showed no surprise, and only remarked grimly, in a veiled blank voice, 'He certainly won't get any other girl to marry him.'

"It is Miss Swaffer who has all the credit for the munificence: but in a very few days it came out that Mr. Swaffer had presented Yanko with a cottage (the cottage you've seen this morning) and something like an acre of ground—had made it over to him in absolute property. Willcox expedited the deed, and I remember him telling me he had a great pleasure in making it ready. It recited: 'In consideration of saving the life of my beloved grandchild, Bertha Willcox.'

"Of course, after that no power on earth could prevent them from getting married.

"Her infatuation endured. People saw her going out to meet him in the evening. She stared with unblinking, fascinated eyes up the road where he was expected to appear, walking freely, with a swing from the hip, and humming one of the love tunes of his country. When the boy was born, he got elevated at the 'Coach and Horses,' essayed again a song and a dance, and was again ejected. People expressed their commiseration for a woman married to that jack-in-the-box. He didn't care. There was a man now (he told me boastfully) to whom he could sing and talk in the language of his country, and show how to dance by and by.

"But I don't know. To me he appeared to have grown less springy of step, heavier in body, less keen of eye. Imagination, no doubt; but it seems to me now as if the net of fate had been drawn closer round him already.

"One day I met him on the footpath over the Talfourd Hill. He told me that 'women were funny.' I had heard already of domestic differences. People were saying that Amy Foster was beginning to find out what sort of man she had married. He looked upon the sea with indifferent, unseeing eyes. His wife had snatched the child

out of his arms one day as he sat on the doorstep croon-
ing to it a song such as the mothers sing to babies in his
mountains. She seemed to think he was doing it some
harm. Women are funny. And she had objected to him
praying aloud in the evening. Why? He expected the
boy to repeat the prayer aloud after him by and by, as
he used to do after his old father when he was a child
—in his own country. And I discovered he longed for
their boy to grow up so that he could have a man to talk
with in that language that to our ears sounded so disturbing, so passionate, and so bizarre. Why his wife
should dislike the idea he couldn't tell. But that would
pass, he said. And tilting his head knowingly, he tapped
his breastbone to indicate that she had a good heart: not
hard, not fierce, open to compassion, charitable to the
poor!

"I walked away thoughtfully; I wondered whether
his difference, his strangeness, were not penetrating with
repulsion that dull nature they had begun by irresistibly
attracting. I wondered. . . ."

The doctor came to the window and looked out at
the frigid splendor of the sea, immense in the haze, as
if enclosing all the earth with all the hearts lost among
the passions of love and fear.

"Physiologically, now," he said, turning away
abruptly, "it was possible. It was possible."

He remained silent. Then went on—

"At all events, the next time I saw him he was ill—
lung trouble. He was tough, but I dare say he was not
acclimatized as well as I had supposed. It was a bad
winter; and, of course, these mountaineers do get fits
of homesickness; and a state of depression would make
him vulnerable. He was lying half dressed on a couch
downstairs.

"A table covered with a dark oilcloth took up all the

middle of the little room. There was a wicker cradle on the floor, a kettle spouting steam on the hob, and some child's linen lay drying on the fender. The room was warm, but the door opens right into the garden, as you noticed perhaps.

"He was very feverish, and kept on muttering to himself. She sat on a chair and looked at him fixedly across the table with her brown, blurred eyes. 'Why don't you have him upstairs?' I asked. With a start and a confused stammer she said, 'Oh! ah! I couldn't sit with him upstairs, sir.'

"I gave her certain directions; and going outside, I said again that he ought to be in bed upstairs. She wrung her hands. 'I couldn't. I couldn't. He keeps on saying something—I don't know what.' With the memory of all the talk against the man that had been dinned into her ears, I looked at her narrowly. I looked into her shortsighted eyes, at her dumb eyes that once in her life had seen an enticing shape, but seemed, staring at me, to see nothing at all now. But I saw she was uneasy.

" 'What's the matter with him?' she asked in a sort of vacant trepidation. 'He doesn't look very ill. I never did see anybody look like this before. . . .'

" 'Do you think,' I asked indignantly, 'he is shamming?'

" 'I can't help it, sir,' she said, stolidly. And suddenly she clapped her hands and looked right and left. 'And there's the baby. I am so frightened. He wanted me just now to give him the baby. I can't understand what he says to it.'

" 'Can't you ask a neighbor to come in tonight?' I asked.

" 'Please, sir, nobody seems to care to come,' she muttered, dully resigned all at once.

"I impressed upon her the necessity of the greatest

care, and then had to go. There was a good deal of sickness that winter. 'Oh, I hope he won't talk!' she exclaimed softly just as I was going away.

"I don't know how it is I did not see—but I didn't. And yet, turning in my trap, I saw her lingering before the door, very still, and as if meditating a flight up the miry road.

"Towards the night his fever increased.

"He tossed, moaned, and now and then muttered a complaint. And she sat with the table between her and the couch, watching every movement and every sound, with the terror, the unreasonable terror, of that man she could not understand creeping over her. She had drawn the wicker cradle close to her feet. There was nothing in her now but the maternal instinct and that unaccountable fear.

"Suddenly coming to himself, parched, he demanded a drink of water. She did not move. She had not understood, though he may have thought he was speaking in English. He waited, looking at her, burning with fever, amazed at her silence and immobility, and then he shouted impatiently, 'Water! Give me water!'

"She jumped to her feet, snatched up the child, and stood still. He spoke to her, and his passionate remonstrances only increased her fear of that strange man. I believe he spoke to her for a long time, entreating, wondering, pleading, ordering, I suppose. She says she bore it as long as she could. And then a gust of rage came over him.

"He sat up and called out terribly one word—some word. Then he got up as though he hadn't been ill at all, she says. And as in fevered dismay, indignation, and wonder he tried to get to her round the table, she simply opened the door and ran out with the child in her arms. She heard him call twice after her down the road in a terrible voice—and fled. . . . Ah! but you should have seen stirring behind the dull, blurred glance of those eyes that the specter of the fear which had haunted her on that night three miles and a half to the door of Foster's cottage! I did the next day.

"And it was I who found him lying face down and his body in a puddle, just outside the little wicker gate.

"I had been called out that night to an urgent case in the village, and on my way home at daybreak passed by the cottage. The door stood open. My man helped me to carry him in. We laid him on the couch. The lamp smoked, the fire was out, the chill of the stormy night oozed from the cheerless yellow paper on the wall. 'Amy!' I called aloud, and my voice seemed to lose itself in the emptiness of this tiny house as if I had cried in a desert. He opened his eyes. 'Gone!' he said, distinctly. 'I had only asked for water—only for a little water. . . .'

"He was muddy. I covered him up and stood waiting in silence, catching a painfully gasped word now and then. They were no longer in his own language. The fever had left him, taking with it the heat of life. And with his panting breast and lustrous eyes he reminded me again of a wild creature under the net; of a bird caught in a snare. She had left him. She had left him—sick—helpless—thirsty. The spear of the hunter had entered his very soul. 'Why?' he cried, in the penetrating and indignant voice of a man calling to a responsible Maker. A gust of wind and a swish of rain answered.

"And as I turned away to shut the door he pronounced the word 'Merciful!' and expired.

"Eventually I certified heart failure as the immediate cause of death. His heart must have indeed failed him, or else he might have stood this night of storm and exposure, too. I closed his eyes and drove away. Not very far from the cottage I met Foster walking sturdily between the dripping hedges with his collie at his heels.

" 'Do you know where your daughter is?' I asked.

" 'Don't I!' he cried. 'I am going to talk to him a bit. Frightening a poor woman like this.'

" 'He won't frighten her any more,' I said. 'He is dead.'

"He struck with his stick at the mud.

" 'And there's the child.'

"Then, after thinking deeply for a while—

" 'I don't know that it isn't for the best.'

"That's what he said. And she says nothing at all now. Not a word of him. Never. Is his image as utterly gone from her mind as his lithe and striding figure, his caroling voice are gone from our fields? He is no longer before her eyes to excite her imagination into a passion of love or fear; and his memory seems to have vanished from her dull brain as a shadow passes away upon a white screen. She lives in the cottage and works for Miss Swaffer. She is Amy Foster for everybody, and the child is 'Amy Foster's boy.' She calls him Johnny— which means Little John.

"It is impossible to say whether this name recalls anything to her. Does she ever think of the past? I have seen her hanging over the boy's cot in a very passion of maternal tenderness. The little fellow was lying on his back, a little frightened at me, but very still, with his big black eyes, with his fluttered air of a bird in a snare. And looking at him I seemed to see again the other one the father, cast out mysteriously by the sea to perish in the supreme disaster of loneliness and despair."

# Typhoon

CAPTAIN MACWHIRR, of the steamer *Nan-Shan*, had a physiognomy that, in the order of material appearances, was the exact counterpart of his mind: it presented no marked characteristics of firmness or stupidity; it had no pronounced characteristics whatever; it was simply ordinary, irresponsive, and unruffled.

The only thing his aspect might have been said to suggest, at times, was bashfulness; because he would sit, in business offices ashore, sunburnt and smiling faintly, with downcast eyes. When he raised them, they were perceived to be direct in their glance and of blue color. His hair was fair and extremely fine, clasping from temple to temple the bald dome of his skull in a clamp as of fluffy silk. The hair of his face, on the contrary, carroty and flaming, resembled a growth of copper wire clipped short to the line of the lip; while, no matter how close he shaved, fiery metallic gleams passed, when he moved his head, over the surface of his cheeks. He was rather below the medium height, a bit round-shouldered, and so sturdy of limb that his clothes always looked a shade too tight for his arms and legs. As if unable to grasp what is due to the difference of latitudes, he wore a brown bowler hat, a complete suit of a brownish hue, and clumsy black boots. These harbor togs gave to his thick figure an air of stiff and uncouth smartness. A thin silver watchchain looped his waistcoat, and he never left his ship for the shore without clutching in his powerful, hairy fist an elegant umbrella of the very best quality, but generally unrolled. Young Jukes, the chief mate, attending his commander to the gangway, would sometimes venture to say, with the greatest gentleness, "Allow me, sir"—and possessing himself of the umbrella deferentially, would elevate the ferule, shake the folds, twirl a neat furl in a jiffy, and hand it back; going through the performance with a face of such portentous gravity, that Mr. Solomon Rout, the chief engineer, smoking his morning cigar over the skylight, would turn away his head in order to hide a smile. "Oh! aye! The blessed gamp. . . . Thank 'ee, Jukes, thank 'ee," would mutter Captain MacWhirr, heartily, without looking up.

Having just enough imagination to carry him through each successive day, and no more, he was tranquilly sure of himself; and from the very same cause he was not in the least conceited. It is your imaginative superior who is touchy, overbearing, and difficult to please; but every ship Captain MacWhirr commanded was the floating abode of harmony and peace. It was, in truth, as impossible for him to take a flight of fancy as it would be for a watchmaker to put together a chronometer with nothing except a two-pound hammer and a whipsaw in the way of tools. Yet the uninteresting lives of men so entirely given to the actuality of the bare existence have their mysterious side. It was impossible in Captain Mac-Whirr's case, for instance, to understand what under heaven could have induced that perfectly satisfactory son of a petty grocer in Belfast to run away to sea. And yet he had done that very thing at the age of fifteen. It was enough, when you thought it over, to give you the idea of an immense, potent, and invisible hand thrust into the ant-heap of the earth, laying hold of

shoulders, knocking heads together, and setting the unconscious faces of the multitude towards inconceivable
goals and in undreamt-of directions.

His father never really forgave him for this undutiful
stupidity. "We could have got on without him," he used
to say later on, "but there's the business. And he an
only son, too!" His mother wept very much after his
disappearance. As it had never occurred to him to
leave word behind, he was mourned over for dead till,
after eight months, his first letter arrived from Tal-
cahuano. It was short, and contained the statement:
"We had very fine weather on our passage out." But
evidently, in the writer's mind, the only important intelligence was to the effect that his captain had, on the
very day of writing, entered him regularly on the ship's
articles as Ordinary Seaman. "Because I can do the
work," he explained. The mother again wept copiously,
while the remark, "Tom's an ass," expressed the emotions of the father. He was a corpulent man, with a gift
for sly chaffing, which to the end of his life he exercised
in his intercourse with his son, a little pityingly, as if
upon a half-witted person.

MacWhirr's visits to his home were necessarily rare,
and in the course of years he dispatched other letters
to his parents, informing them of his successive promo-
tions and of his movements upon the vast earth. In
these missives could be found sentences like this: "The
heat here is very great." Or: "On Christmas day at
4 P.M. we fell in with some icebergs." The old people
ultimately became acquainted with a good many names
of ships, and with the names of the skippers who commanded them—with the names of Scots and English
shipowners—with the names of seas, oceans, straits,
promontories—with outlandish names of lumber ports,
of rice ports, of cotton ports—with the names of islands

—with the name of their son's young woman. She was called Lucy. It did not suggest itself to him to mention whether he thought the name pretty. And then they died.

The great day of MacWhirr's marriage came in due course, following shortly upon the great day when he got his first command.

All these events had taken place many years before the morning when, in the chart room of the steamer *Nan-Shan,* he stood confronted by the fall of a barometer he had no reason to distrust. The fall—taking into account the excellence of the instrument, the time of the year, and the ship's position on the terrestrial globe— was of a nature ominously prophetic; but the red face of the man betrayed no sort of inward disturbance. Omens were as nothing to him, and he was unable to discover the message of a prophecy till the fulfillment had brought it home to his very door. "That's a fall, and no mistake," he thought. "There must be some uncommonly dirty weather knocking about."

The *Nan-Shan* was on her way from the southward to the treaty port of Fu-chau, with some cargo in her lower holds, and two hundred Chinese coolies returning to their village homes in the province of Fo-kien, after a few years of work in various tropical colonies. The morning was fine, the oily sea heaved without a sparkle, and there was a queer white misty patch in the sky like a halo of the sun. The foredeck, packed with China-men, was full of somber clothing, yellow faces, and pig-tails, sprinkled over with a good many naked shoulders, for there was no wind, and the heat was close. The coolies lounged, talked, smoked, or stared over the rail; some, drawing water over the side, sluiced each other; a few slept on hatches, while several small parties of six sat on their heels surrounding iron trays with plates

of rice and tiny teacups; and every single Celestial of
them was carrying with him all he had in the world—a
wooden chest with a ringing lock and brass on the corners, containing the savings of his labors: some clothes
of ceremony, sticks of incense, a little opium maybe, bits
of nameless rubbish of conventional value, and a small
hoard of silver dollars, toiled for in coal lighters, won in
gambling houses or in petty trading, grubbed out of
earth, sweated out in mines, on railway lines, in deadly
jungle, under heavy burdens—amassed patiently,
guarded with care, cherished fiercely.

A cross swell had set in from the direction of Formosa
Channel about ten o'clock, without disturbing these
passengers much, because the *Nan-Shan*, with her flat
bottom, rolling chocks on bilges, and great breadth of
beam, had the reputation of an exceptionally steady
ship in a seaway. Mr. Jukes, in moments of expansion
on shore, would proclaim loudly that the "old girl was
as good as she was pretty." It would never have occurred to Captain MacWhirr to express his favorable
opinion so loud or in terms so fanciful.

She was a good ship, undoubtedly, and not old either.
She had been built in Dumbarton less than three years
before, to the order of a firm of merchants in Siam—
Messrs. Sigg and Son. When she lay afloat, finished in
every detail and ready to take up the work of her life,
the builders contemplated her with pride.

"Sigg has asked us for a reliable skipper to take her
out," remarked one of the partners; and the other, after
reflecting for a while, said: "I think MacWhirr is ashore
just at present." "Is he? Then wire him at once. He's the
very man," declared the senior, without a moment's hesitation.

Next morning MacWhirr stood before them unper-
turbed, having traveled from London by the midnight

express after a sudden but undemonstrative parting with his wife. She was the daughter of a superior couple who had seen better days.

"We had better be going together over the ship, Captain," said the senior partner; and the three men started to view the perfections of the *Nan-Shan* from stem to stern, and from her keelson to the trucks of her two stumpy pole-masts.

Captain MacWhirr had begun by taking off his coat, which he hung on the end of a steam windlass embodying all the latest improvements.

"My uncle wrote of you favorably by yesterday's mail to our good friends—Messrs. Sigg, you know—and doubtless they'll continue you out there in command," said the junior partner. "You'll be able to boast of being in charge of the handiest boat of her size on the coast of China, Captain," he added.

"Have you? Thank 'ee," mumbled vaguely MacWhirr, to whom the view of a distant eventuality could appeal no more than the beauty of a wide landscape to a purblind tourist; and his eyes happening at the moment to be at rest upon the lock of the cabin door, he walked up to it, full of purpose, and began to rattle the handle vigorously, while he observed, in his low, earnest voice, "You can't trust the workmen nowadays. A brand-new lock, and it won't act at all. Stuck fast. See? See?"

As soon as they found themselves alone in their office across the yard: "You praised that fellow up to Sigg. What is it you see in him?" asked the nephew, with faint contempt.

"I admit he has nothing of your fancy skipper about him, if that's what you mean," said the elder man, curtly. "Is the foreman of the joiners on the *Nan-Shan* outside? . . . Come in, Bates. How is it that you let Tait's people put us off with a defective lock on the cabin door? The captain could see directly he set eyes on it. Have it replaced at once. The little straws, Bates . . . the little straws. . . ."

The lock was replaced accordingly, and a few days afterwards the *Nan-Shan* steamed out to the East, without MacWhirr having offered any further remark as to her fittings, or having been heard to utter a single word hinting at pride in his ship, gratitude for his appointment, or satisfaction at his prospects.

With a temperament neither loquacious nor taciturn he found very little occasion to talk. There were matters of duty, of course—directions, orders, and so on; but the past being to his mind done with, and the future not there yet, the more general actualities of the day required no comment—because facts can speak for themselves with overwhelming precision.

Old Mr. Sigg liked a man of few words, and one that "you could be sure would not try to improve upon his instructions." MacWhirr satisfying these requirements, was continued in command of the *Nan-Shan*, and applied himself to the careful navigation of his ship in the China seas. She had come out on a British register, but after some time Messrs. Sigg judged it expedient to transfer her to the Siamese flag.

At the news of the contemplated transfer Jukes grew restless, as if under a sense of personal affront. He went about grumbling to himself, and uttering short scornful laughs. "Fancy having a ridiculous Noah's Ark elephant in the ensign of one's ship," he said once at the engine-room door. "Dash me if I can stand it; I'll throw up the billet. Don't it make *you* sick, Mr. Rout?" The chief engineer only cleared his throat with the air of a man who knows the value of a good billet.

The first morning the new flag floated over the stern of the *Nan-Shan* Jukes stood looking at it bitterly from the bridge. He struggled with his feelings for a while, and then remarked, "Queer flag for a man to sail under, sir."

"What's the matter with the flag?" inquired Captain MacWhirr. "Seems all right to me." And he walked across to the end of the bridge to have a good look.

"Well, it looks queer to me," burst out Jukes, greatly exasperated, and flung off the bridge.

Captain MacWhirr was amazed at these manners. After a while he stepped quietly into the chart room, and opened his International Signal Code Book at the plate where the flags of all the nations are correctly figured in gaudy rows. He ran his finger over them, and when he came to Siam he contemplated with great attention the red field and the white elephant. Nothing could be more simple; but to make sure he brought the book out on the bridge for the purpose of comparing the colored drawing with the real thing at the flagstaff astern. When next Jukes, who was carrying on the duty that day with a sort of suppressed fierceness, happened on the bridge, his commander observed:

"There's nothing amiss with that flag."

"Isn't there?" mumbled Jukes, falling on his knees before a deck locker and perking therefrom viciously a spare lead line.

"No. I looked up the book. Length twice the breadth and the elephant exactly in the middle. I thought the people ashore would know how to make the local flag. Stands to reason. You were wrong, Jukes. . . ."

"Well, sir," began Jukes, getting up excitedly, "all I can say—" He fumbled for the end of the coil of line with trembling hands.

"That's all right." Captain MacWhirr soothed him, sitting heavily on a little canvas folding stool he greatly affected. "All you have to do is to take care they don't hoist the elephant upside-down before they get quite used to it."

Jukes flung the new lead line over on the foredeck with a loud "Here you are, bosun—don't forget to wet it thoroughly," and turned with immense resolution towards his commander; but Captain MacWhirr spread his elbows on the bridge rail comfortably.

"Because it would be, I suppose, understood as a signal of distress," he went on. "What do you think? That elephant there, I take it, stands for something in the nature of the Union Jack in the flag. . . ."

"Does it!" yelled Jukes, so that every head on the *Nan-Shan's* decks looked towards the bridge. Then he sighed, and with sudden resignation: "It would certainly be a dam' distressful sight," he said, meekly.

Later in the day he accosted the chief engineer with a confidential, "Here, let me tell you the old man's latest."

Mr. Solomon Rout (frequently alluded to as Long Sol, Old Sol, or Father Rout), from finding himself almost invariably the tallest man on board every ship he joined, had acquired the habit of a stooping, leisurely condescension. His hair was scant and sandy, his flat cheeks were pale, his bony wrists and long scholarly hands were pale, too, as though he had lived all his life in the shade.

He smiled from on high at Jukes, and went on smoking and glancing about quietly, in the manner of a kind uncle lending an ear to the tale of an excited schoolboy. Then, greatly amused but impassive, he asked:

"And did you throw up the billet?"

"No," cried Jukes, raising a weary, discouraged voice above the harsh buzz of the *Nan-Shan's* friction winches. All of them were hard at work, snatching slings of cargo, high up, to the end of long derricks, only, as it seemed, to let them rip down recklessly by the run. The cargo chains groaned in the gins, clinked on coamings, rattled over the side; and the whole ship quivered, with her long gray flanks smoking in wreaths of steam. "No," cried Jukes, "I didn't. What's the good? I might just as well fling my resignation at this bulkhead. I don't believe you can make a man like that understand anything. He simply knocks me over."

At that moment Captain MacWhirr, back from the shore, crossed the deck, umbrella in hand, escorted by a mournful, self-possessed Chinaman, walking behind in paper-soled silk shoes, and who also carried an umbrella.

The master of the *Nan-Shan*, speaking just audibly and gazing at his boots as his manner was, remarked that it would be necessary to call at Fu-chau this trip, and desired Mr. Rout to have steam up tomorrow afternoon at one o'clock sharp. He pushed back his hat to wipe his forehead, observing at the same time that he hated going ashore anyhow; while overtopping him Mr. Rout, without deigning a word, smoked austerely, nursing his right elbow in the palm of his left hand. Then Jukes was directed in the same subdued voice to keep the forward 'tween-deck clear of cargo. Two hundred coolies were going to be put down there. The Bun Hin Company were sending that lot home. Twenty-five bags of rice would be coming off in a sampan directly, for stores. All seven-years'-men they were, said Captain MacWhirr, with a camphor-wood chest to every man. The carpenter should be set to work nailing three-inch battens along the deck below, fore and aft, to keep these boxes from shifting in a seaway. Jukes had better look to it at once. "D'ye hear, Jukes?" This Chinaman here was coming with the ship as far as Fu-chau—a sort of interpreter he would be. Bun Hin's clerk he was, and wanted to have a look at the space. Jukes had better take him forward. "D'ye hear, Jukes?"

Jukes took care to punctuate these instructions in proper places with the obligatory "Yes, sir," ejaculated without enthusiasm. His brusque "Come along, John; make look see" set the Chinaman in motion at his heels.

"Wanchee look see, all same look see can do," said Jukes, who having no talent for foreign languages mangled the very pidgin-English cruelly. He pointed at the open hatch. "Catchee number one piecie place to sleep in. Eh?"

He was gruff, as became his racial superiority, but not unfriendly. The Chinaman, gazing sad and speechless into the darkness of the hatchway, seemed to stand at the head of a yawning grave.

"No catchee rain down there—savee?" pointed out Jukes. "Suppose all'ee same fine weather, one piecie coolie-man come topside," he pursued, warming up imaginatively. "Make so—Phooooo!" He expanded his chest and blew out his cheeks. "Savee, John? Breathe—fresh air. Good. Eh? Washee him piecie pants, chow-chow topside—see, John?"

With his mouth and hands he made exuberant motions of eating rice and washing clothes; and the Chinaman, who concealed his distrust of this pantomime under a collected demeanor tinged by a gentle and refined melancholy, glanced out of his almond eyes from Jukes to the hatch and back again. "Velly good," he murmured, in a disconsolate undertone, and hastened smoothly along the decks, dodging obstacles in his course. He disappeared, ducking low under a sling of ten dirty gunny bags full of some costly merchandise and exhaling a repulsive smell.

Captain MacWhirr meantime had gone on the bridge,

and into the chart room, where a letter, commenced two days before, awaited termination. These long letters began with the words, "My darling wife," and the steward, between the scrubbing of the floors and the dusting of chronometer boxes, snatched at every opportunity to read them. They interested him much more than they possibly could the woman for whose eye they were intended; and this for the reason that they related in minute detail each successive trip of the *Nan-Shan.*

Her master, faithful to facts, which alone his consciousness reflected, would set them down with painstaking care upon many pages. The house in a northern suburb to which these pages were addressed had a bit of garden before the bow-windows, a deep porch of good appearance, colored glass with imitation lead frame in the front door. He paid five-and-forty pounds a year for it, and did not think the rent too high, because Mrs. MacWhirr (a pretentious person with a scraggy neck and a disdainful manner) was admittedly ladylike, and in the neighborhood considered as "quite superior." The only secret of her life was her abject terror of the time when her husband would come home to stay for good. Under the same roof there dwelt also a daughter called Lydia and a son, Tom. These two were but slightly acquainted with their father. Mainly, they knew him as a rare but privileged visitor, who of an evening smoked his pipe in the dining room and slept in the house. The lanky girl, upon the whole, was rather ashamed of him; the boy was frankly and utterly indifferent in a straightforward, delightful, unaffected way manly boys have.

And Captain MacWhirr wrote home from the coast of China twelve times every year, desiring quaintly to be "remembered to the children," and subscribing himself "your loving husband," as calmly as if the words so long used by so many men were, apart from their shape, worn-out things, and of a faded meaning.

The China seas north and south are narrow seas. They are seas full of everyday, eloquent facts, such as islands, sand banks, reefs, swift and changeable currents—tangled facts that nevertheless speak to a seaman in clear and definite language. Their speech appealed to Captain MacWhirr's sense of realities so forcibly that he had given up his stateroom below and practically lived all his days on the bridge of his ship, often having his meals sent up, and sleeping at night in the chart room. And he indited there his home letters. Each of them, without exception, contained the phrase, "The weather has been very fine this trip," or some other form of a statement to that effect. And this statement, too, in its wonderful persistence, was of the same perfect accuracy as all the others they contained.

Mr. Rout likewise wrote letters; only no one on board knew how chatty he could be pen in hand, because the chief engineer had enough imagination to keep his desk locked. His wife relished his style greatly. They were a childless couple, and Mrs. Rout, a big, high-bosomed, jolly woman of forty, shared with Mr. Rout's toothless and venerable mother a little cottage near Teddington. She would run over her correspondence, at breakfast, with lively eyes, and scream out interesting passages in a joyous voice at the deaf old lady, prefacing each extract by the warning shout, "Solomon says!" She had the trick of firing off Solomon's utterances also upon strangers, astonishing them easily by the unfamiliar text and the unexpectedly jocular vein of these quotations. On the day the new curate called for the first time at the cottage, she found occasion to remark, "As Solomon says: 'the engineers that go down to the sea in ships behold the wonders of sailor nature' "; when a change in the visitor's countenance made her stop and stare.

"Solomon. . . . Oh! . . . Mrs. Rout," stuttered the young man, very red in the face, "I must say . . . I don't. . . ."

"He's my husband," she announced in a great shout, throwing herself back in the chair. Perceiving the joke, she laughed immoderately with a handkerchief to her eyes, while he sat wearing a forced smile, and, from his inexperience of jolly women, fully persuaded that she must be deplorably insane. They were excellent friends afterwards; for, absolving her from irreverent intention, he came to think she was a very worthy person indeed; and he learned in time to receive without flinching other scraps of Solomon's wisdom.

"For my part," Solomon was reported by his wife to have said once, "give me the dullest ass for a skipper before a rogue. There is a way to take a fool; but a rogue is smart and slippery." This was an airy generalization drawn from the particular case of Captain Mac-Whirr's honesty, which, in itself, had the heavy obviousness of a lump of clay. On the other hand, Mr. Jukes, unable to generalize, unmarried, and unengaged, was in the habit of opening his heart after another fashion to an old chum and former shipmate, actually serving as second officer on board an Atlantic liner.

First of all he would insist upon the advantages of the Eastern trade, hinting at its superiority to the Western ocean service. He extolled the sky, the seas, the ships, and the easy life of the Far East. The Nan-Shan, he affirmed, was second to none as a sea boat.

"We have no brass-bound uniforms, but then we are like brothers here," he wrote. "We all mess together and live like fighting cocks. . . . All the chaps of the black-squad are as decent as they make that kind, and old Sol,

the Chief, is a dry stick. We are good friends. As to our
old man, you could not find a quieter skipper. Sometimes you would think he hadn't sense enough to see
anything wrong. And yet it isn't that. Can't be. He has
been in command for a good few years now. He doesn't
do anything actually foolish, and gets his ship along all
right without worrying anybody. I believe he hasn't
brains enough to enjoy kicking up a row. I don't take
advantage of him. I would scorn it. Outside the routine
of duty he doesn't seem to understand more than half of
what you tell him. We get a laugh out of this at times;
but it is dull, too, to be with a man like this—in the long
run. Old Sol says he hasn't much conversation. Conversation! O Lord! He never talks. The other day I had
been yarning under the bridge with one of the engineers, and he must have heard us. When I came up to
take my watch, he steps out of the chart room and has
a good look all round, peeps over at the sidelights,
glances at the compass, squints upwards at the stars.
That's his regular performance. By and by he says: 'Was
that you talking just now in the port alleyway?' 'Yes, sir.'
'With the third engineer?' 'Yes, sir.' He walks off to starboard, and sits under the dodger on a little campstool
of his, and for half an hour perhaps he makes no sound,
except that I heard him sneeze once. Then after a while
I hear him getting up over there, and he strolls across to
port, where I was. 'I can't understand what you can find
to talk about,' says he. "Two solid hours. I am not blam-
ing you. I see people ashore at it all day long, and then
in the evening they sit down and keep at it over the
drinks. Must be saying the same things over and over
again. I can't understand.'

"Did you ever hear anything like that? And he was
so patient about it. It made me quite sorry for him. But
he is exasperating, too, sometimes. Of course one would

not do anything to vex him even if it were worth while. But it isn't. He's so jolly innocent that if you were to put your thumb to your nose and wave your fingers at him he would only wonder gravely to himself what got into you. He told me once quite simply that he found it very difficult to make out what made people always act so queerly. He's too dense to trouble about, and that's the truth."

Thus wrote Mr. Jukes to his chum in the Western ocean trade, out of the fullness of his heart and the liveliness of his fancy.

He had expressed his honest opinion. It was not worth while trying to impress a man of that sort. If the world had been full of such men, life would have probably appeared to Jukes an unentertaining and unprofitable business. He was not alone in his opinion. The sea itself, as if sharing Mr. Jukes' good-natured forbearance, had never put itself out to startle the silent man, who seldom looked up, and wandered innocently over the waters with the only visible purpose of getting food, raiment, and house-room for three people ashore. Dirty weather he had known, of course. He had been made wet, uncomfortable, tired in the usual way, felt at the time and presently forgotten. So that upon the whole he had been justified in reporting fine weather at home. But he had never been given a glimpse of immeasurable strength and of immoderate wrath, the wrath that passes exhausted but never appeased—the wrath and fury of the passionate sea. He knew it existed, as we know that crime and abominations exist; he had heard of it as a peaceable citizen in a town that hears of battles, famines, and floods, and yet knows nothing of what these things mean—though, indeed, he may have been mixed up in a street row, have gone without his dinner once, or been soaked to the skin in a shower. Captain

MacWhirr had sailed over the surface of the oceans as some men go skimming over the years of existence to sink gently into a placid grave, ignorant of life to the last, without ever having been made to see all it may contain of perfidy, of violence, and of terror. There are on sea and land such men thus fortunate—or thus disdained by destiny or by the sea.


## II

Observing the steady fall of the barometer, Captain MacWhirr thought, "There's some dirty weather knocking about." This is precisely what he thought. He had had an experience of moderately dirty weather—the term dirty as applied to the weather implying only moderate discomfort to the seaman. Had he been informed by an indisputable authority that the end of the world was to be finally accomplished by a catastrophic disturbance of the atmosphere, he would have assimilated the information under the simple idea of dirty weather, and no other, because he had no experience of cataclysms, and belief does not necessarily imply comprehension. The wisdom of his country had pronounced by means of an Act of Parliament that before he could be considered as fit to take charge of a ship he should be able to answer certain simple questions on the subject of circular storms such as hurricanes, cyclones, typhoons; and apparently he had answered them, since he was now in command of the *Nan-Shan* in the China seas during the season of typhoons. But if he had answered he remembered nothing of it. He was, however, conscious of being made uncomfortable by the clammy heat. He came out on the bridge, and found no relief to this oppression. The air seemed thick. He gasped like a fish, and began to believe himself greatly out of sorts.

The *Nan-Shan* was plowing a vanishing furrow upon the circle of the sea that had the surface and the shimmer of an undulating piece of gray silk. The sun, pale and without rays, poured down leaden heat in a strangely indecisive light, and the Chinamen were lying prostrate about the decks. Their bloodless, pinched, yellow faces were like the faces of bilious invalids. Captain MacWhirr noticed two of them especially, stretched out on their backs below the bridge. As soon as they had closed their eyes they seemed dead. Three others, however, were quarreling barbarously away forward; and one big fellow, half naked, with herculean shoulders, was hanging limply over a winch; another, sitting on the deck, his knees up and his head drooping sideways in a girlish attitude, was plaiting his pigtail with infinite languor depicted in his whole person and in the very movement of his fingers. The smoke struggled with difficulty out of the funnel, and instead of streaming away spread itself out like an infernal sort of cloud, smelling of sulphur and raining soot all over the decks.

"What the devil are you doing there, Mr. Jukes?" asked Captain MacWhirr.

This unusual form of address, though mumbled rather than spoken, caused the body of Mr. Jukes to start as though it had been prodded under the fifth rib. He had had a low bench brought on the bridge, and sitting on it, with a length of rope curled about his feet and a piece of canvas stretched over his knees, was pushing a sail-needle vigorously. He looked up, and his surprise gave to his eyes an expression of innocence and candor.

"I am only roping some of that new set of bags we made last trip for whipping up coals," he remonstrated, gently. "We shall want them for the next coaling, sir."

"What became of the others?"

"Why, worn out of course, sir."

Captain MacWhirr, after glaring down irresolutely at his chief mate, disclosed the gloomy and cynical conviction that more than half of them had been lost overboard, "if only the truth was known," and retired to the other end of the bridge. Jukes, exasperated by this unprovoked attack, broke the needle at the second stitch, and dropping his work got up and cursed the heat in a violent undertone.

The propeller thumped, the three Chinamen forward had given up squabbling very suddenly, and the one who had been plaiting his tail clasped his legs and stared dejectedly over his knees. The lurid sunshine cast faint and sickly shadows. The swell ran higher and swifter every moment, and the ship lurched heavily in the smooth, deep hollows of the sea.

"I wonder where that beastly swell comes from," said Jukes aloud, recovering himself after a stagger.

"Northeast," grunted the literal MacWhirr, from his side of the bridge. "There's some dirty weather knocking about. Go and look at the glass."

When Jukes came out of the chart room, the cast of his countenance had changed to thoughtfulness and concern. He caught hold of the bridge rail and stared ahead.

The temperature in the engine room had gone up to a hundred and seventeen degrees. Irritated voices were ascending through the skylight and through the fiddle of the stokehold in a harsh and resonant uproar, mingled with angry clangs and scrapes of metal, as if men with limbs of iron and throats of bronze had been quarreling down there. The second engineer was falling foul of the stokers for letting the steam go down. He was a man with arms like a blacksmith, and generally feared; but that afternoon the stokers were answering him back reck-

lessly, and slammed the furnace doors with the fury of
despair. Then the noise ceased suddenly, and the second
engineer appeared, emerging out of the stokehold
streaked with grime and soaking wet like a chimney
sweep coming out of a well. As soon as his head was clear
of the fiddle he began to scold Jukes for not trimming
properly the stokehold ventilators; and in answer Jukes
made with his hands deprecatory soothing signs meaning: "No wind—can't be helped—you can see for yourself." But the other wouldn't hear reason. His teeth
flashed angrily in his dirty face. He didn't mind, he said,
the trouble of punching their blanked heads down there,
blank his soul, but did the condemned sailors think you
could keep steam up in the God-forsaken boilers simply
by knocking the blanked stokers about? No, by George!
You had to get some draught, too—may he be everlastingly blanked for a swab-headed deck hand if you
didn't! And the chief, too, rampaging before the steam
gauge and carrying on like a lunatic up and down the
engine room ever since noon. What did Jukes think he
was stuck up there for, if he couldn't get one of his
decayed, good-for-nothing deck-cripples to turn the
ventilators to the wind?

The relations of the "engine room" and the "deck" of
the *Nan-Shan* were, as is known, of a brotherly nature;
therefore Jukes leaned over and begged the other in a
restrained tone not to make a disgusting ass of himself;
the skipper was on the other side of the bridge. But the
second declared mutinously that he didn't care a rap
who was on the other side of the bridge, and Jukes,
passing in a flash from lofty disapproval into a state of
exaltation, invited him in unflattering terms to come up
and twist the beastly things to please himself, and catch
such wind as a donkey of his sort could find. The
second rushed up to the fray. He flung himself at the

port ventilator as though he meant to tear it out bodily and toss it overboard. All he did was to move the cowl round a few inches, with an enormous expenditure of force, and seemed spent in the effort. He leaned against the back of the wheelhouse, and Jukes walked up to him.

"Oh, Heavens!" ejaculated the engineer in a feeble voice. He lifted his eyes to the sky, and then let his glassy stare descend to meet the horizon that, tilting up to an angle of forty degrees, seemed to hang on a slant for a while and settled down slowly. "Heavens! Phew! What's up, anyhow?"

Jukes, straddling his long legs like a pair of compasses, put on an air of superiority. "We're going to catch it this time," he said. "The barometer is tumbling down like anything, Harry. And you trying to kick up that silly row. . . ."

The word "barometer" seemed to revive the second engineer's mad animosity. Collecting afresh all his energies, he directed Jukes in a low and brutal tone to shove the unmentionable instrument down his gory throat. Who cared for his crimson barometer? It was the steam—the steam—that was going down; and what between the firemen going faint and the chief going silly, it was worse than a dog's life for him; he didn't care a tinker's curse how soon the whole show was blown out of the water. He seemed on the point of having a cry, but after regaining his breath he muttered darkly, "I'll faint them," and dashed off. He stopped upon the fiddle long enough to shake his fist at the unnatural daylight, and dropped into the dark hole with a whoop.

When Jukes turned, his eyes fell upon the rounded back and the big red ears of Captain MacWhirr, who had come across. He did not look at his chief officer, but said at once, "That's a very violent man, that second engineer."

"Jolly good second, anyhow," grunted Jukes. "They can't keep up steam," he added, rapidly, and made a grab at the rail against the coming lurch.

Captain MacWhirr, unprepared, took a run and brought himself up with a jerk by an awning stanchion.

"A profane man," he said, obstinately. "If this goes on, I'll have to get rid of him the first chance."

"It's the heat," said Jukes. "The weather's awful. It would make a saint swear. Even up here I feel exactly as if I had my head tied up in a woolen blanket."

Captain MacWhirr looked up. "D'ye mean to say, Mr. Jukes, you ever had your head tied up in a blanket? What was that for?"

"It's a manner of speaking, sir," said Jukes, stolidly.

"Some of you fellows do go on! What's that about saints swearing? I wish you wouldn't talk so wild. What sort of saint would that be that would swear? No more saint than yourself, I expect. And what's a blanket got to do with it—or the weather either. . . . The heat does not make me swear—does it? It's filthy bad temper. That's what it is. And what's the good of your talking like this?"

Thus Captain MacWhirr expostulated against the use of images in speech, and at the end electrified Jukes by a contemptuous snort, followed by words of passion and resentment: "Damme! I'll fire him out of the ship if he don't look out."

And Jukes, incorrigible, thought: "Goodness me! Somebody's put a new inside to my old man. Here's temper, if you like. Of course it's the weather; what else? It would make an angel quarrelsome—let alone a saint."

All the Chinamen on deck appeared at their last gasp.

At its setting the sun had a diminished diameter and an expiring brown, rayless glow, as if millions of centuries elapsing since the morning had brought it near its end. A dense bank of cloud became visible to the northward; it had a sinister dark-olive tint, and lay low and motionless upon the sea, resembling a solid obstacle in the path of the ship. She went floundering towards it like an exhausted creature driven to its death. The coppery twilight retired slowly, and the darkness brought out overhead a swarm of unsteady, big stars, that, as if blown upon, flickered exceedingly and seemed to hang very near the earth. At eight o'clock Jukes went into the chart room to write up the ship's log.

He copied neatly out of the rough-book the number of miles, the course of the ship, and in the column for "wind" scrawled the word "calm" from top to bottom of the eight hours since noon. He was exasperated by the continuous, monotonous rolling of the ship. The heavy inkstand would slide away in a manner that suggested perverse intelligence in dodging the pen. Having written in the large space under the head of "Remarks" "Heat very oppressive," he stuck the end of the penholder in his teeth, pipe fashion, and mopped his face carefully.

"Ship rolling heavily in a high cross swell," he began again, and commented to himself, "Heavily is no word for it." Then he wrote: "Sunset threatening, with a low bank of clouds to N. and E. Sky clear overhead."

Sprawling over the table with arrested pen, he glanced out of the door, and in that frame of his vision he saw all the stars flying upwards between the teakwood jambs on a black sky. The whole lot took flight together and disappeared, leaving only a blackness flecked with white flashes, for the sea was as black as the sky and speckled with foam afar. The stars that had flown to the roll came back on the return swing of the ship, rushing downwards in their glittering multitude, not of fiery points, but enlarged to tiny discs brilliant with a clear wet sheen.

Jukes watched the flying big stars for a moment, and then wrote: "8 P.M. Swell increasing. Ship laboring and taking water on her decks. Battened down the coolies for the night. Barometer still falling." He paused, and thought to himself, "Perhaps nothing whatever'll come of it." And then he closed resolutely his entries: "Every appearance of a typhoon coming on."

On going out he had to stand aside, and Captain MacWhirr strode over the doorstep without saying a word or making a sign.

"Shut the door, Mr. Jukes, will you?" he cried from within.

Jukes turned back to do so, muttering ironically: "Afraid to catch cold, I suppose." It was his watch below, but he yearned for communion with his kind; and he remarked cheerily to the second mate: "Doesn't look so bad, after all—does it?"

The second mate was marching to and fro on the bridge, tripping down with small steps one moment, and the next climbing with difficulty the shifting slope of the deck. At the sound of Jukes' voice he stood still, facing forward, but made no reply.

"Hallo! That's a heavy one," said Jukes, swaying to meet the long roll till his lowered hand touched the planks. This time the second mate made in his throat a noise of an unfriendly nature.

He was an oldish, shabby little fellow, with bad teeth and no hair on his face. He had been shipped in a hurry in Shanghai, that trip when the second officer brought from home had delayed the ship three hours in port by contriving (in some manner Captain MacWhirr could never understand) to fall overboard into an empty coal lighter lying alongside, and had to be sent ashore to the hospital with concussion of the brain and a broken limb or two.

Jukes was not discouraged by the unsympathetic sound. "The Chinamen must be having a lovely time of it down there," he said. "It's lucky for them the old girl has the easiest roll of any ship I've ever been in. There now! This one wasn't so bad." ·

"You wait," snarled the second mate.

With his sharp nose, red at the tip, and his thin pinched lips, he always looked as though he were raging inwardly; and he was concise in his speech to the point of rudeness. All his time off duty he spent in his cabin with the door shut, keeping so still in there that he was supposed to fall asleep as soon as he had disappeared; but the man who came in to wake him for his watch on deck would invariably find him with his eyes wide open, flat on his back in the bunk, and glaring irritably from a soiled pillow. He never wrote any letters, did not seem to hope for news from anywhere; and though he had been heard once to mention West Hartlepool, it was with extreme bitterness, and only in connection with the extortionate charges of a boardinghouse. He was one of those men who are picked up at need in the ports of the world. They are competent enough, appear hopelessly hard up, show no evidence of any sort of vice, and carry about them all the signs of manifest failure. They come aboard on an emergency, care for no ship afloat, live in their own atmosphere of casual connection amongst their shipmates who know nothing of them, and make up their minds to leave at inconvenient times. They clear out with no words of leave-taking in some God-forsaken port other men would fear to be stranded in, and go ashore in company of a shabby sea chest, corded like a treasure box, and with an air of shaking the ship's dust off their feet.

"You wait," he repeated, balanced in great swings with his back to Jukes, motionless and implacable.

"Do you mean to say we are going to catch it hot?" asked Jukes with boyish interest.

"Say? . . . I say nothing. You don't catch me," snapped the little second mate, with a mixture of pride, scorn, and cunning, as if Jukes' question had been a trap cleverly detected. "Oh, no! None of you here shall make a fool of me if I know it," he mumbled to himself.

Jukes reflected rapidly that this second mate was a mean little beast, and in his heart he wished poor Jack Allen had never smashed himself up in the coal lighter. The far-off blackness ahead of the ship was like another night seen through the starry night of the earth—the starless night of the immensities beyond the created universe, revealed in its appalling stillness through a low fissure in the glittering sphere of which the earth is the kernel.

"Whatever there might be about," said Jukes, "we are steaming straight into it."

"*You've* said it," caught up the second mate, always with his back to Jukes. "You've said it, mind—not I."

"Oh, go to Jericho!" said Jukes, frankly; and the other emitted a triumphant little chuckle.

"You've said it," he repeated.

"And what of that?"

"I've known some real good men get into trouble with their skippers for saying a dam' sight less," answered the second mate feverishly. "Oh, no! You don't catch me."

"You seem deucedly anxious not to give yourself away," said Jukes, completely soured by such absurdity. "I wouldn't be afraid to say what I think."

"Aye, to me! That's no great trick. I am nobody, and well I know it."

The ship, after a pause of comparative steadiness, started upon a series of rolls, one worse than the other, and for a time Jukes, preserving his equilibrium, was too busy to open his mouth. As soon as the violent swinging had quieted down somewhat, he said: "This is a bit too much of a good thing. Whether anything is coming or not I think she ought to be put head on to that swell. The old man is just gone in to lie down. Hang me if I don't speak to him."

But when he opened the door of the chart room he saw his captain reading a book. Captain MacWhirr was not lying down: he was standing up with one hand grasping the edge of the bookshelf and the other holding open before his face a thick volume. The lamp wriggled in the gimbals, the loosened books toppled from side to side on the shelf, the long barometer swung in jerky circles, the table altered its slant every moment. In the midst of all this stir and movement Captain MacWhirr, holding on, showed his eyes above the upper edge, and asked, "What's the matter?"

"Swell getting worse, sir."

"Noticed that in here," muttered Captain MacWhirr. "Anything wrong?"

Jukes, inwardly disconcerted by the seriousness of the eyes looking at him over the top of the book, produced an embarrassed grin.

"Rolling like old boots," he said, sheepishly.

"Aye! Very heavy—very heavy. What do you want?"

At this Jukes lost his footing and began to flounder.

"I was thinking of our passengers," he said, in the manner of a man clutching at a straw.

"Passengers?" wondered the Captain, gravely. "What passengers?"

"Why, the Chinamen, sir," explained Jukes, very sick of this conversation.

"The Chinamen! Why don't you speak plainly? Couldn't tell what you meant. Never heard a lot of coolies spoken of as passengers before. Passengers, indeed! What's come to you?"

Captain MacWhirr, closing the book on his forefinger, lowered his arm and looked completely mystified. "Why are you thinking of the Chinamen, Mr. Jukes?" he inquired.

Jukes took a plunge, like a man driven to it. "She's rolling her decks full of water, sir. Thought you might put her head on perhaps—for a while. Till this goes down a bit—very soon, I dare say. Head to the eastward. I never knew a ship roll like this."

He held on in the doorway, and Captain MacWhirr, feeling his grip on the shelf inadequate, made up his mind to let go in a hurry, and fell heavily on the couch.

"Head to the eastward?" he said, struggling to sit up. "That's more than four points off her course."

"Yes, sir. Fifty degrees. . . . Would just bring her head far enough round to meet this. . . ."

Captain MacWhirr was now sitting up. He had not dropped the book, and he had not lost his place.

"To the eastward?" he repeated, with dawning astonishment. "To the . . . Where do you think we are bound to? You want me to haul a full-powered steamship four points off her course to make the Chinamen comfortable! Now, I've heard more than enough of mad things done in the world—but this. . . . If I didn't know you, Jukes, I would think you were in liquor. Steer four points off. . . . And what afterwards? Steer four points over the other way, I suppose, to make the course good. What put it into your head that I would start to tack a steamer as if she were a sailing ship?"

"Jolly good thing she isn't," threw in Jukes, with bitter readiness. "She would have rolled every blessed stick out of her this afternoon."

"Aye! And you just would have had to stand and see them go," said Captain MacWhirr, showing a certain animation. "It's a dead calm, isn't it?"

"It is, sir. But there's something out of the common coming, for sure."

"Maybe. I suppose you have a notion I should be getting out of the way of that dirt," said Captain Mac-Whirr, speaking with the utmost simplicity of manner and tone, and fixing the oilcloth on the floor with a heavy stare. Thus he noticed neither Jukes' discomfiture nor the mixture of vexation and astonished respect on his face.

"Now, here's this book," he continued with delibera-tion, slapping his thigh with the closed volume. "I've been reading the chapter on the storms there."

This was true. He had been reading the chapter on the storms. When he had entered the chart room, it was with no intention of taking the book down. Some influence in the air—the same influence, probably, that caused the steward to bring without orders the Cap-tain's sea boots and oilskin coat up to the chart room—had as it were guided his hand to the shelf; and without taking the time to sit down he had waded with a con-scious effort into the terminology of the subject. He lost himself amongst advancing semicircles, left- and right-hand quadrants, the curves of the tracks, the probable bearing of the center, the shifts of wind and the readings of barometer. He tried to bring all these things into a definite relation to himself, and ended by becoming contemptuously angry with such a lot of words and with so much advice, all headwork and supposition, without a glimmer of certitude.

"It's the damnedest thing, Jukes," he said. "If a fellow was to believe all that's in there, he would be running most of his time all over the sea trying to get behind the weather."

Again he slapped his leg with the book; and Jukes opened his mouth, but said nothing.

"Running to get behind the weather! Do you understand that, Mr. Jukes? It's the maddest thing!" ejaculated Captain MacWhirr, with pauses, gazing at the floor profoundly. "You would think an old woman had been writing this. It passes me. If that thing means anything useful, then it means that I should at once alter the course away, away to the devil somewhere, and come booming down on Fu-chau from the northward at the tail of this dirty weather that's supposed to be knocking about in our way. From the north! Do you understand, Mr. Jukes? Three hundred extra miles to the distance, and a pretty coal bill to show. I couldn't bring myself to do that if every word in there was gospel truth, Mr. Jukes. Don't you expect me. . . ."

And Jukes, silent, marveled at this display of feeling and loquacity.

"But the truth is that you don't know if the fellow is right, anyhow. How can you tell what a gale is made of till you get it? He isn't aboard here, is he? Very well. Here he says that the center of them things bears eight points off the wind; but we haven't got any wind, for all the barometer falling. Where's his center now?"

"We will get the wind presently," mumbled Jukes.

"Let it come, then," said Captain MacWhirr, with dignified indignation. "It's only to let you see, Mr. Jukes, that you don't find everything in books. All these rules for dodging breezes and circumventing the winds of heaven, Mr. Jukes, seem to me the maddest thing, when you come to look at it sensibly."

He raised his eyes, saw Jukes gazing at him dubiously, and tried to illustrate his meaning.

"About as queer as your extraordinary notion of dodging the ship head to sea, for I don't know how long, to make the Chinamen comfortable; whereas all we've got to do is to take them to Fu-chau, being timed to get there before noon on Friday. If the weather delays me—very well. There's your logbook to talk straight about the weather. But suppose I went swinging off my course and came in two days late, and they asked me: 'Where have you been all that time, Captain?' What could I say to that? 'Went around to dodge the bad weather,' I would say. 'It must've been dam' bad,' they would say. 'Don't know,' I would have to say; 'I've dodged clear of it.' See that, Jukes? I have been thinking it all out this afternoon."

He looked up again in his unseeing, unimaginative way. No one had ever heard him say so much at one time. Jukes, with his arms open in the doorway, was like a man invited to behold a miracle. Unbounded wonder was the intellectual meaning of his eye, while incredulity was seated in his whole countenance.

"A gale is a gale, Mr. Jukes," resumed the Captain, "and a full-powered steamship has got to face it. There's just so much dirty weather knocking about the world, and the proper thing is to go through it with none of what old Captain Wilson of the *Melita* calls 'storm strategy.' The other day ashore I heard him hold forth about it to a lot of shipmasters who came in and sat at a table next to mine. It seemed to me the greatest non-sense. He was telling them how he outmaneuvered, I think he said, a terrific gale, so that it never came nearer than fifty miles to him. A neat piece of headwork he called it. How he knew there was a terrific gale fifty miles off beats me altogether. It was like listening to a crazy man. I would have thought Captain Wilson was old enough to know better."

Captain MacWhirr ceased for a moment, then said, "It's your watch below, Mr. Jukes?"

Jukes came to himself with a start. "Yes, sir."

"Leave orders to call me at the slightest change," said the Captain. He reached up to put the book away, and tucked his legs upon the couch. "Shut the door so that it don't fly open, will you? I can't stand a door banging. They've put a lot of rubbishy locks into this ship, I must say."

Captain MacWhirr closed his eyes.

He did so to rest himself. He was tired, and he experienced that state of mental vacuity which comes at the end of an exhaustive discussion that has liberated some belief matured in the course of meditative years. He had indeed been making his confession of faith, had he only known it; and its effect was to make Jukes, on the other side of the door, stand scratching his head for a good while.

Captain MacWhirr opened his eyes.

He thought he must have been asleep. What was that loud noise? Wind? Why had he not been called? The lamp wriggled in its gimbals, the barometer swung in circles, the table altered its slant every moment; a pair of limp sea boots with collapsed tops went sliding past the couch. He put out his hand instantly, and captured one.

Jukes' face appeared in a crack of the door; only his

face, very red, with staring eyes. The flame of the lamp leaped, a piece of paper flew up, a rush of air enveloped Captain MacWhirr. Beginning to draw on the boot, he directed an expectant gaze at Jukes' swollen, excited features.

"Came on like this," shouted Jukes, "five minutes ago . . . all of a sudden."

The head disappeared with a bang, and a heavy splash and patter of drops swept past the closed door as if a pailful of melted lead had been flung against the house. A whistling could be heard now upon the deep vibrating noise outside. The stuffy chart room seemed as full of drafts as a shed. Captain MacWhirr collared the other sea boot on its violent passage along the floor. He was not flustered, but he could not find at once the opening for inserting his foot. The shoes he had flung off were scurrying from end to end of the cabin, gamboling playfully over each other like puppies. As soon as he stood up he kicked at them viciously, but without effect.

He threw himself into the attitude of a lunging fencer, to reach after his oilskin coat; and afterwards he staggered all over the confined space while he jerked himself into it. Very grave, straddling his legs far apart, and stretching his neck, he started to tie deliberately the strings of his sou'-wester under his chin, with thick fingers that trembled slightly. He went through all the movements of a woman putting on her bonnet before a glass, with a strained, listening attention, as though he had expected every moment to hear the shout of his name in the confused clamor that had suddenly beset his ship. Its increase filled his ears while he was getting ready to go out and confront whatever it might mean. It was tumultuous and very loud—made up of the rush of the wind, the crashes of the sea, with that prolonged deep vibration of the air, like the roll of an immense and remote drum beating the charge of the gale.

He stood for a moment in the light of the lamp, thick, clumsy, shapeless in his panoply of combat, vigilant and red-faced.

"There's a lot of weight in this," he muttered.

As soon as he attempted to open the door the wind caught it. Clinging to the handle, he was dragged out over the doorstep, and at once found himself engaged with the wind in a sort of personal scuffle whose object was the shutting of that door. At the last moment a tongue of air scurried in and licked out the flame of the lamp.

Ahead of the ship he perceived a great darkness lying upon a multitude of white flashes; on the starboard beam a few amazing stars drooped, dim and fitful, above an immense waste of broken seas, as if seen through a mad drift of smoke.

On the bridge a knot of men, indistinct and toiling, were making great efforts in the light of the wheelhouse windows that shone mistily on their heads and backs. Suddenly darkness closed upon one pane, then on another. The voices of the lost group reached him after the manner of men's voices in a gale, in shreds and fragments of forlorn shouting snatched past the ear. All at once Jukes appeared at his side, yelling, with his head down.

"Watch—put—in—wheelhouse—shutters—glass—afraid—blow in."

Jukes heard his commander upbraiding.

"This—come—anything—warning—call me."

He tried to explain, with the uproar pressing on his lips.

"Light air—remained—bridge—sudden—northeast—could turn—thought—you—sure—hear."

They had gained the shelter of the weather cloth, and could converse with raised voices, as people quarrel.

"I got the hands along to cover up all the ventilators. Good job I had remained on deck. I didn't think you would be asleep, and so . . . What did you say, sir? What?"

"Nothing," cried Captain MacWhirr. "I said—all right."

"By all the powers! We've got it this time," observed Jukes in a howl.

"You haven't altered her course?" inquired Captain MacWhirr, straining his voice.

"No, sir. Certainly not. Wind came out right ahead. And here comes the head sea."

A plunge of the ship ended in a shock as if she had landed her forefoot upon something solid. After a moment of stillness a lofty flight of sprays drove hard with the wind upon their faces.

"Keep her at it as long as we can," shouted Captain MacWhirr.

Before Jukes had squeezed the salt water out of his eyes all the stars had disappeared.

III

Jukes was as ready a man as any half-dozen young mates that may be caught by casting a net upon the waters; and though he had been somewhat taken aback by the startling viciousness of the first squall, he had pulled himself together on the instant, had called out the hands and had rushed them along to secure such openings about the deck as had not been already battened down earlier in the evening. Shouting in his fresh, stentorian voice, "Jump, boys, and bear a hand!"

he led in the work, telling himself the while that he had "just expected this."

But at the same time he was growing aware that this was rather more than he had expected. From the first stir of the air felt on his cheek the gale seemed to take upon itself the accumulated impetus of an avalanche. Heavy sprays enveloped the Nan-Shan from stem to stern, and instantly in the midst of her regular rolling she began to jerk and plunge as though she had gone mad with fright.

Jukes thought, "This is no joke." While he was exchanging explanatory yells with his captain, a sudden lowering of the darkness came upon the night, falling before their vision like something palpable. It was as if the masked lights of the world had been turned down. Jukes was uncritically glad to have his captain at hand. It relieved him as though that man had, by simply coming on deck, taken most of the gale's weight upon his shoulders. Such is the prestige, the privilege, and the burden of command.

Captain MacWhirr could expect no relief of that sort from anyone on earth. Such is the loneliness of command. He was trying to see, with that watchful manner of a seaman who stares into the wind's eye as if into the eye of an adversary, to penetrate the hidden intention and guess the aim and force of the thrust. The strong wind swept at him out of a vast obscurity; he felt under his feet the uneasiness of his ship, and he could not even discern the shadow of her shape. He wished it were not so; and very still he waited, feeling stricken by a blind man's helplessness.

To be silent was natural to him, dark or shine. Jukes, at his elbow, made himself heard yelling cheerily in the gusts, "We must have got the worst of it at once, sir." A faint burst of lightning quivered all round, as if

flashed into a cavern—into a black and secret chamber
of the sea, with a floor of foaming crests.

It unveiled for a sinister, fluttering moment a ragged
mass of clouds hanging low, the lurch of the long outlines of the ship, the black figures of men caught on
the bridge, heads forward, as if petrified in the act of
butting. The darkness palpitated down upon all this,
and then the real thing came at last.

It was something formidable and swift, like the sudden smashing of a vial of wrath. It seemed to explode
all round the ship with an overpowering concussion and
a rush of great waters, as if an immense dam had been
blown up to windward. In an instant the men lost touch
of each other. This is the disintegrating power of a great
wind: it isolates one from one's kind. An earthquake,
a landslip, an avalanche, overtake a man incidentally,
as it were—without passion. A furious gale attacks him
like a personal enemy, tries to grasp his limbs, fastens
upon his mind, seeks to rout his very spirit out of him.

Jukes was driven away from his commander. He
fancied himself whirled a great distance through the
air. Everything disappeared—even, for a moment, his
power of thinking; but his hand had found one of the
rail stanchions. His distress was by no means alleviated
by an inclination to disbelieve the reality of this experience. Though young, he had seen some bad weather,
and had never doubted his ability to imagine the worst;
but this was so much beyond his powers of fancy that
it appeared incompatible with the existence of any ship
whatever. He would have been incredulous about himself in the same way, perhaps, had he not been so
harassed by the necessity of exerting a wrestling effort
against a force trying to tear him away from his hold.
Moreover, the conviction of not being utterly destroyed

returned to him through the sensations of being half-drowned, bestially shaken, and partly choked.

It seemed to him he remained there precariously alone with the stanchion for a long, long time. The rain poured on him, flowed, drove in sheets. He breathed in gasps; and sometimes the water he swallowed was fresh and sometimes it was salt. For the most part he kept his eyes shut tight, as if suspecting his sight might be destroyed in the immense flurry of the elements. When he ventured to blink hastily, he derived some moral support from the green gleam of the starboard light shining feebly upon the flight of rain and sprays. He was actually looking at it when its ray fell upon the uprearing sea which put it out. He saw the head of the wave topple over, adding the mite of its crash to the tremendous uproar raging around him, and almost at the same instant the stanchion was wrenched away from his embracing arms. After a crushing thump on his back he found himself suddenly afloat and borne upwards. His first irresistible notion was that the whole China Sea had climbed on the bridge. Then, more sanely, he concluded himself gone overboard. All the time he was being tossed, flung, and rolled in great volumes of water, he kept on repeating mentally, with the utmost precipitation, the words: "My God! My God! My God! My God!"

All at once, in a revolt of misery and despair, he formed the crazy resolution to get out of that. And he began to thrash about with his arms and legs. But as soon as he commenced his wretched struggles he discovered that he had become somehow mixed up with a face, an oilskin coat, somebody's boots. He clawed ferociously all these things in turn, lost them, found them again, lost them once more, and finally was himself caught in the firm clasp of a pair of stout arms. He returned the embrace closely round a thick solid body. He had found his captain.

They tumbled over and over, tightening their hug. Suddenly the water let them down with a brutal bang; and, stranded against the side of the wheelhouse, out of breath and bruised, they were left to stagger up in the wind and hold on where they could.

Jukes came out of it rather horrified, as though he had escaped some unparalleled outrage directed at his feelings. It weakened his faith in himself. He started shouting aimlessly to the man he could feel near him in that fiendish blackness, "Is it you, sir? Is it you, sir?" till his temples seemed ready to burst. And he heard in answer a voice, as if crying far away, as if screaming to him fretfully from a very great distance, the one word "Yes!" Other seas swept again over the bridge. He received them defenselessly right over his bare head, with both his hands engaged in holding.

The motion of the ship was extravagant. Her lurches had an appalling helplessness: she pitched as if taking a header into a void, and seemed to find a wall to hit every time. When she rolled she fell on her side headlong, and she would be righted back by such a demolishing blow that Jukes felt her reeling as a clubbed man reels before he collapses. The gale howled and scuffled about gigantically in the darkness, as though the entire world were one black gully. At certain moments the air streamed against the ship as if sucked through a tunnel with a concentrated solid force of impact that seemed to lift her clean out of the water and keep her up for an instant with only a quiver running through her from end to end. And then she would begin her tumbling again as if dropped back into a boiling caldron. Jukes tried hard to compose his mind and judge things coolly.

The sea, flattened down in the heavier gusts, would

uprise and overwhelm both ends of the *Nan-Shan* in
snowy rushes of foam, expanding wide, beyond both
rails, into the night. And on this dazzling sheet, spread
under the blackness of the clouds and emitting a bluish
glow, Captain MacWhirr could catch a desolate glimpse
of a few tiny specks black as ebony, the tops of the
hatches, the battened companions, the heads of the
covered winches, the foot of a mast. This was all he
could see of his ship. Her middle structure, covered by
the bridge which bore him, his mate, the closed wheelhouse where a man was steering shut up with the fear
of being swept overboard together with the whole thing
in one great crash—her middle structure was like a half-
tide rock awash upon a coast. It was like an outlying
rock with the water boiling up, streaming over, pouring
off, beating round—like a rock in the surf to which
shipwrecked people cling before they let go—only it
rose, it sank, it rolled continuously, without respite and
rest, like a rock that should have miraculously struck
adrift from a coast and gone wallowing upon the sea.

The *Nan-Shan* was being looted by the storm with a
senseless, destructive fury: trysails torn out of the extra
gaskets, double-lashed awnings blown away, bridge
swept clean, weather cloths burst, rails twisted, light-
screens smashed—and two of the boats had gone already. They had gone unheard and unseen, melting, as
it were, in the shock and smother of the wave. It was
only later, when upon the white flash of another high
sea hurling itself amidships, Jukes had a vision of two
pairs of davits leaping black and empty out of the solid
blackness, with one overhauled fall flying and an iron-
bound block capering in the air, that he became aware
of what had happened within about three yards of his
back.

He poked his head forward, groping for the ear of

his commander. His lips touched it—big, fleshy, very wet. He cried in an agitated tone, "Our boats are going now, sir."

And again he heard that voice, forced and ringing feebly, but with a penetrating effect of quietness in the enormous discord of noises, as if sent out from some remote spot of peace beyond the black wastes of the gale; again he heard a man's voice—the frail and indomitable sound that can be made to carry an infinity of thought, resolution and purpose, that shall be pronouncing confident words on the last day, when heavens fall, and justice is done—again he heard it, and it was crying to him, as if from very, very far—"All right."

He thought he had not managed to make himself understood. "Our boats—I say boats—the boats, sir! Two gone!"

The same voice, within a foot of him and yet so remote, yelled sensibly, "Can't be helped."

Captain MacWhirr had never turned his face, but Jukes caught some more words on the wind.

"What can—expect—when hammering through— such—— Bound to leave—something behind—stands to reason."

Watchfully Jukes listened for more. No more came. This was all Captain MacWhirr had to say; and Jukes could picture to himself rather than see the broad squat back before him. An impenetrable obscurity pressed down upon the ghostly glimmers of the sea. A dull conviction seized upon Jukes that there was nothing to be done.

If the steering gear did not give way, if the immense volumes of water did not burst the deck in or smash one of the hatches, if the engines did not give up, if way could be kept on the ship against this terrific wind, and she did not bury herself in one of these awful seas, of whose white crests alone, topping high above her bows, he could now and then get a sickening glimpse— then there was a chance of her coming out of it. Something within him seemed to turn over, bringing uppermost the feeling that the *Nan-Shan* was lost.

"She's done for," he said to himself, with a surprising mental agitation, as though he had discovered an unexpected meaning in this thought. One of these things was bound to happen. Nothing could be prevented now, and nothing could be remedied. The men on board did not count, and the ship could not last. This weather was too impossible.

Jukes felt an arm thrown heavily over his shoulders; and to this overture he responded with great intelligence by catching hold of his captain round the waist.

They stood clasped thus in the blind night, bracing each other against the wind, cheek to cheek and lip to ear, in the manner of two hulks lashed stem to stern together.

And Jukes heard the voice of his commander hardly any louder than before, but nearer, as though, starting to march athwart the prodigious rush of the hurricane, it had approached him, bearing that strange effect of quietness like the serene glow of a halo.

"D'ye know where the hands got to?" it asked, vigorous and evanescent at the same time, overcoming the strength of the wind, and swept away from Jukes instantly.

Jukes didn't know. They were all on the bridge when the real force of the hurricane struck the ship. He had no idea where they had crawled to. Under the circumstances they were nowhere, for all the use that could be made of them. Somehow the Captain's wish to know distressed Jukes.

"Want the hands, sir?" he cried, apprehensively.

"Ought to know," asserted Captain MacWhirr. "Hold hard."

They held hard. An outburst of unchained fury, a vicious rush of the wind absolutely steadied the ship; she rocked only, quick and light like a child's cradle, for a terrific moment of suspense, while the whole atmosphere, as it seemed, streamed furiously past her, roaring away from the tenebrous earth.

It suffocated them, and with eyes shut they tightened their grasp. What from the magnitude of the shock might have been a column of water running upright in the dark, butted against the ship, broke short, and fell on her bridge, crushingly, from on high, with a dead burying weight.

A flying fragment of that collapse, a mere splash, enveloped them in one swirl from their feet over their heads, filling violently their ears, mouths and nostrils with salt water. It knocked out their legs, wrenched in haste at their arms, seethed away swiftly under their chins; and opening their eyes, they saw the piled-up masses of foam dashing to and fro amongst what looked like the fragments of a ship. She had given way as if driven straight in. Their panting hearts yielded, too, before the tremendous blow; and all at once she sprang up again to her desperate plunging, as if trying to scramble out from under the ruins.

The seas in the dark seemed to rush from all sides to keep her back where she might perish. There was hate in the way she was handled, and a ferocity in the blows that fell. She was like a living creature thrown to the rage of a mob: hustled terribly, struck at, borne up, flung down, leaped upon. Captain MacWhirr and Jukes kept hold of each other, deafened by the noise, gagged by the wind; and the great physical tumult beating about their bodies, brought, like an unbridled display of passion, a profound trouble to their souls. One of those wild and appalling shrieks that are heard at times passing mysteriously overhead in the steady roar of a hurricane, swooped, as if borne on wings, upon the ship, and Jukes tried to outscream it.

"Will she live through this?"

The cry was wrenched out of his breast. It was as unintentional as the birth of a thought in the head, and he heard nothing of it himself. It all became extinct at once—thought, intention, effort—and of his cry the inaudible vibration added to the tempest waves of the air.

He expected nothing from it. Nothing at all. For indeed what answer could be made? But after a while he heard with amazement the frail and resisting voice in his ear, the dwarf sound, unconquered in the giant tumult.

"She may!"

It was a dull yell, more difficult to seize than a whisper. And presently the voice returned again, half submerged in the vast crashes, like a ship battling against the waves of an ocean.

"Let's hope so!" it cried—small, lonely and unmoved, a stranger to the visions of hope or fear; and it flickered into disconnected words: "Ship. . . . This. . . . Never —Anyhow . . . for the best." Jukes gave it up.

Then, as if it had come suddenly upon the one thing fit to withstand the power of a storm, it seemed to gain force and firmness for the last broken shouts:

"Keep on hammering . . . builders . . . good men. . . . And chance it     engines. . . . Rout . . . good man."

Captain MacWhirr removed his arm from Jukes' shoulders, and thereby ceased to exist for his mate, so dark it was; Jukes, after a tense stiffening of every muscle, would let himself go limp all over. The gnawing of profound discomfort existed side by side with an incredible disposition to somnolence, as though he had been buffeted and worried into drowsiness. The wind would get hold of his head and try to shake it off his shoulders; his clothes, full of water, were as heavy as lead, cold and dripping like an armor of melting ice: he shivered—it lasted a long time; and with his hands closed hard on his hold, he was letting himself sink slowly into the depths of bodily misery. His mind became concentrated upon himself in an aimless, idle way, and when something pushed lightly at the back of his knees he nearly, as the saying is, jumped out of his skin.

In the start forward he bumped the back of Captain MacWhirr, who didn't move; and then a hand gripped his thigh. A lull had come, a menacing lull of the wind, the holding of a stormy breath—and he felt himself pawed all over. It was the boatswain. Jukes recognized these hands, so thick and enormous that they seemed to belong to some new species of man.

The boatswain had arrived on the bridge, crawling on all fours against the wind, and had found the chief mate's legs with the top of his head. Immediately he crouched and began to explore Jukes' person upwards with prudent, apologetic touches, as became an inferior.

He was an ill-favored, undersized, gruff sailor of fifty, coarsely hairy, short-legged, long-armed, resembling an elderly ape. His strength was immense; and in his great lumpy paws, bulging like brown boxing gloves on the end of furry forearms, the heaviest objects were handled like playthings. Apart from the grizzled pelt on his chest, the menacing demeanor and the hoarse voice, he had none of the classical attributes of his rating. His good nature almost amounted to imbecility: the men did what they liked with him, and he had not an ounce of initiative in his character, which was easygoing and talkative. For these reasons Jukes disliked him; but Captain MacWhirr, to Jukes' scornful disgust, seemed to regard him as a first-rate petty officer.

He pulled himself up by Jukes' coat, taking that liberty with the greatest moderation, and only so far as it was forced upon him by the hurricane.

"What is it, bosun,. what is it?" yelled Jukes, impatiently. What could that fraud of a bosun want on the bridge? The typhoon had got on Jukes' nerves. The husky bellowings of the other, though unintelligible, seemed to suggest a state of lively satisfaction. There could be no mistake. The old fool was pleased with something.

The boatswain's other hand had found some other body, for in a changed tone he began to inquire: "Is it you, sir? Is it you, sir?" The wind strangled his howls.

"Yes!" cried Captain MacWhirr.

IV

All that the boatswain, out of a superabundance of yells, could make clear to Captain MacWhirr was the bizarre intelligence that "All them Chinamen in the fore 'tween-deck have fetched away, sir."

Jukes to leeward could hear these two shouting within six inches of his face, as you may hear on a still night half a mile away two men conversing across a field. He heard Captain MacWhirr's exasperated "What? What?" and the strained pitch of the other's hoarseness. "In a lump . . . seen them myself. . . . Awful sight, sir . . . thought . . . tell you."

Jukes remained indifferent, as if rendered irresponsible by the force of the hurricane, which made the very thought of action utterly vain. Besides, being very young, he had found the occupation of keeping his heart completely steeled against the worst so engrossing that he had come to feel an overpowering dislike towards any other form of activity whatever. He was not scared; he knew this because, firmly believing he would never see another sunrise, he remained calm in that belief.

These are the moments of do-nothing heroics to which even good men surrender at times. Many officers of ships can no doubt recall a case in their experience when just such a trance of confounded stoicism would come all at once over a whole ship's company. Jukes, however, had no wide experience of men or storms. He conceived himself to be calm—inexorably calm; but as a matter of fact he was daunted; not abjectly, but only so far as a decent man may, without becoming loathsome to himself.

It was rather like a forced-on numbness of spirit. The long, long stress of a gale does it; the suspense of the interminably culminating catastrophe; and there is a bodily fatigue in the mere holding on to existence within the excessive tumult; a searching and insidious fatigue that penetrates deep into a man's breast to cast down and sadden his heart, which is incorrigible, and of all the gifts of the earth—even before life itself—aspires to peace.

Jukes was benumbed much more than he supposed. He held on—very wet, very cold, stiff in every limb; and in a momentary hallucination of swift visions (it is said that a drowning man thus reviews all his life) he beheld all sorts of memories altogether unconnected with his present situation. He remembered his father, for instance: a worthy businessman, who at an unfortunate crisis in his affairs went quietly to bed and died forthwith in a state of resignation. Jukes did not recall these circumstances, of course, but remaining otherwise unconcerned he seemed to see distinctly the poor man's face; a certain game of nap played when quite a boy in Table Bay on board a ship, since lost with all hands; the thick eyebrows of his first skipper; and without any emotion, as he might years ago have walked listlessly into her room and found her sitting there with a book, he remembered his mother—dead, too, now—the resolute woman, left badly off, who had been very firm in his bringing up.

It could not have lasted more than a second, perhaps not so much. A heavy arm had fallen about his shoulders; Captain MacWhirr's voice was speaking his name into his ear.

"Jukes! Jukes!"

He detected the tone of deep concern. The wind had thrown its weight on the ship, trying to pin her down amongst the seas. They made a clean breach over her, as over a deep-swimming log; and the gathered weight of crashes menaced monstrously from afar. The breakers flung out of the night with a ghostly light on their crests —the light of sea foam that in a ferocious, boiling-up pale flash showed upon the slender body of the ship the toppling rush, the downfall, and the seething mad scurry of each wave. Never for a moment could she shake herself clear of the water; Jukes, rigid, perceived in her motion the ominous sign of haphazard floundering. She was no longer struggling intelligently. It was the beginning of the end; and the note of busy concern in Captain MacWhirr's voice sickened him like an exhibition of blind and pernicious folly

The spell of the storm had fallen upon Jukes. He was penetrated by it, absorbed by it; he was rooted in it with a rigor of dumb attention. Captain MacWhirr persisted in his cries, but the wind got between them like a solid wedge. He hung round Jukes' neck as heavy as a millstone, and suddenly the sides of their heads knocked together.

"Jukes! Mr. Jukes, I say!"

He had to answer that voice that would not be silenced. He answered in the customary manner: ". . . Yes, sir."

And directly, his heart, corrupted by the storm that breeds a craving for peace, rebelled against the tyranny of training and command.

Captain MacWhirr had his mate's head fixed firm in the crook of his elbow, and pressed it to his yelling lips mysteriously. Sometimes Jukes would break in, admonishing hastily: "Look out, sir!" or Captain MacWhirr would bawl an earnest exhortation to "Hold hard, there!" and the whole black universe seemed to reel together with the ship. They paused. She floated yet. And Captain MacWhirr would resume his shouts. ". . . Says . . . whole lot . . . fetched away. . . . Ought to see . . . what's the matter."

Directly the full force of the hurricane had struck the ship, every part of her deck became untenable; and the sailors, dazed and dismayed, took shelter in the port alleyway under the bridge. It had a door aft, which they shut; it was very black, cold, and dismal. At each heavy fling of the ship they would groan all together in the dark, and tons of water could be heard scuttling about as if trying to get at them from above. The boatswain had been keeping up a gruff talk, but a more unreasonable lot of men, he said afterwards, he had never been with. They were snug enough there, out of harm's way, and not wanted to do anything, either; and yet they did nothing but grumble and complain peevishly like so many sick kids. Finally, one of them said that if there had been at least some light to see each other's noses by, it wouldn't be so bad. It was making him crazy, he declared, to lie there in the dark waiting for the blamed hooker to sink.

"Why don't you step outside, then, and be done with it at once?" the boatswain turned on him.

This called up a shout of execration. The boatswain found himself overwhelmed with reproaches of all sorts. They seemed to take it ill that a lamp was not instantly created for them out of nothing. They would whine after a light to get drowned by—anyhow! And though the unreason of their revilings was patent—since no one could hope to reach the lamp room, which was forward—he became greatly distressed. He did not think it was decent of them to be nagging at him like this. He told them so, and was met by general contumely. He sought refuge, therefore, in an embittered silence. At the same time their grumbling and sighing and muttering worried him greatly, but by and by it occurred to him that there were six globe lamps hung in the 'tween-deck, and that there could be no harm in depriving the coolies of one of them.

The *Nan-Shan* had an athwartship coal bunker, which, being at times used as cargo space, communicated by an iron door with the fore 'tween-deck. It was empty then, and its manhole was the foremost one in the alleyway. The boatswain could get in, therefore, without coming out on deck at all; but to his great surprise he found he could induce no one to help him in taking off the manhole cover. He groped for it all the same, but one of the crew lying in his way refused to budge.

"Why, I only want to get you that blamed light you are crying for," he expostulated, almost pitifully.

Somebody told him to go and put his head in a bag. He regretted he could not recognize the voice, and that it was too dark to see, otherwise, as he said, he would have put a head on *that* son of a sea cook, anyway, sink or swim. Nevertheless, he had made up his mind to show them he could get a light, if he were to die for it.

Through the violence of the ship's rolling, every movement was dangerous. To be lying down seemed labor enough. He nearly broke his neck dropping into the bunker. He fell on his back, and was sent shooting helplessly from side to side in the dangerous company of a heavy iron bar—a coal-trimmer's slice probably— left down there by somebody. This thing made him as nervous as though it had been a wild beast. He could not see it, the inside of the bunker coated with coal-dust being perfectly and impenetrably black; but he heard it sliding and clattering, and striking here and there, always in the neighborhood of his head. It seemed to make an extraordinary noise, too—to give heavy thumps as though it had been as big as a bridge girder. This was remarkable enough for him to notice while he was flung from port to starboard and back again, and clawing desperately the smooth sides of the bunker in the endeavor to stop himself. The door into the 'tween-deck not fitting quite true, he saw a thread of dim light at the bottom.

Being a sailor, and a still active man, he did not want much of a chance to regain his feet; and as luck would have it, in scrambling up he put his hand on the iron slice, picking it up as he rose. Otherwise he would have been afraid of the thing breaking his legs, or at least knocking him down again. At first he stood still. He felt unsafe in this darkness that seemed to make the ship's motion unfamiliar, unforeseen, and difficult to counteract. He felt so much shaken for a moment that he dared not move for fear of "taking charge again." He had no mind to get battered to pieces in that bunker.

He had struck his head twice; he was dazed a little. He seemed to hear yet so plainly the clatter and bangs of the iron slice flying about his ears that he tightened his grip to prove to himself he had it there safely in his hand. He was vaguely amazed at the plainness with which down there he could hear the gale raging. Its howls and shrieks seemed to take on, in the emptiness of the bunker, something of the human character, of human rage and pain—being not vast but infinitely poignant. And there were, with every roll, thumps, too —profound, ponderous thumps, as if a bulky object of five-ton weight or so had got play in the hold. But there was no such thing in the cargo. Something on deck? Impossible. Or alongside? Couldn't be.

He thought all this quickly, clearly, competently, like a seaman, and in the end remained puzzled. This noise, though, came deadened from outside, together with the washing and pouring of water on deck above his head. Was it the wind? Must be. It made down there a row like the shouting of a big lot of crazed men. And he discovered in himself a desire for a light, too—if only to get drowned by—and a nervous anxiety to get out of that bunker as quickly as possible.

He pulled back the bolt: the heavy iron plate turned on its hinges; and it was though he had opened the door to the sounds of the tempest. A gust of hoarse yelling met him: the air was still; and the rushing of water overhead was covered by a tumult of strangled, throaty shrieks that produced an effect of desperate confusion. He straddled his legs the whole width of the doorway and stretched his neck. And at first he perceived only what he had come to seek: six small yellow flames swinging violently on the great body of the dusk.

It was stayed like the gallery of a mine, with a row of stanchions in the middle, and crossbeams overhead, penetrating into the gloom ahead—indefinitely. And to port there loomed, like the caving in of one of the sides, a bulky mass with a slanting outline. The whole place, with the shadows and the shapes, moved all the time. The boatswain glared: the ship lurched to starboard, and a great howl came from that mass that had the slant of fallen earth.

Pieces of wood whizzed past. Planks, he thought, inexpressibly startled, and flinging back his head. At his feet a man went sliding over, open-eyed, on his back, straining with uplifted arms for nothing: and another came bounding like a detached stone with his head between his legs and his hands clenched. His pigtail whipped in the air; he made a grab at the boatswain's legs, and from his opened hand a bright white disc rolled against the boatswain's foot. He recognized a silver dollar, and yelled at it with astonishment. With a precipitated sound of trampling and shuffling of bare feet, and with guttural cries, the mound of writhing bodies piled up to port detached itself from the ship's side and sliding, inert and struggling, shifted to starboard, with a dull, brutal thump. The cries ceased. The boatswain heard a long moan through the roar and whistling of the wind; he saw an inextricable confusion of heads and shoulders, naked soles kicking upwards, fists raised, tumbling backs, legs, pigtails, faces.

"Good Lord!" he cried, horrified, and banged-to the iron door upon this vision.

This was what he had come on the bridge to tell. He could not keep it to himself; and on board ship there is only one man to whom it is worth while to unburden yourself. On his passage back the hands in the alleyway swore at him for a fool. Why didn't he bring that lamp? What the devil did the coolies matter to anybody? And

when he came out, the extremity of the ship made what
went on inside of her appear of little moment.

At first he thought he had left the alleyway in the
very moment of her sinking. The bridge ladders had
been washed away, but an enormous sea filling the
afterdeck floated him up. After that he had to lie on his
stomach for some time, holding to a ring bolt, getting
his breath now and then, and swallowing salt water.
He struggled farther on his hands and knees, too frightened and distracted to turn back. In this way he reached
the after-part of the wheelhouse. In that comparatively
sheltered spot he found the second mate. The boatswain
was pleasantly surprised—his impression being that
everybody on deck must have been washed away a long
time ago. He asked eagerly where the Captain was.

The second mate was lying low, like a malignant little
animal under a hedge.

"Captain? Gone overboard, after getting us into this
mess." The mate, too, for all he knew or cared. Another
fool. Didn't matter. Everybody was going by and by.

The boatswain crawled out again into the strength
of the wind; not because he much expected to find anybody, he said, but just to get away from "that man."
He crawled out as outcasts go to face an inclement
world. Hence his great joy at finding Jukes and the Captain. But what was going on in the 'tween-deck was to
him a minor matter by that time. Besides, it was difficult
to make yourself heard. But he managed to convey the
idea that the Chinamen had broken adrift together with
their boxes, and that he had come up on purpose to report this. As to the hands, they were all right. Then,
appeased, he subsided on the deck in a sitting posture,
hugging with his arms and legs the stand of the engine-
room telegraph—an iron casting as thick as a post.

When that went, why, he expected he would go, too. He gave no more thought to the coolies.

Captain MacWhirr had made Jukes understand that he wanted him to go down below—to see.

"What am I to do then, sir?" And the trembling of his whole wet body caused Jukes' voice to sound like bleating.

"See first . . . Bosun . . . says . . . adrift."

"That bosun is a confounded fool," howled Jukes, shakily.

The absurdity of the demand made upon him revolted Jukes. He was as unwilling to go as if the moment he had left the deck the ship were sure to sink.

"I must know . . . can't leave. . . ."

"They'll settle, sir."

"Fight . . . bosun says they fight. . . . Why? Can't have . . . fighting . . . board ship. . . . Much rather keep you here . . . case . . . I should . . . washed overboard myself. . . . Stop it . . . some way. You see and tell me . . . through engine-room tube. Don't want you . . . come up here . . . too often. Dangerous . . . moving about . . . deck."

Jukes, held with his head in chancery, had to listen to what seemed horrible suggestions.

"Don't want . . . you get lost . . . so long . . . ship isn't. . . . Rout . . . Good man. . . . Ship . . . may . . . through this . . . all right yet."

All at once Jukes understood he would have to go.

"Do you think she may?" he screamed.

But the wind devoured the reply, out of which Jukes heard only the one word, pronounced with great energy ". . . Always. . . ."

Captain MacWhirr released Jukes, and bending over the boatswain, yelled, "Get back with the mate." Jukes only knew that the arm was gone off his shoulders. He was dismissed with his orders—to do what? He was exasperated into letting go his hold carelessly, and on the instant was blown away. It seemed to him that nothing could stop him from being blown right over the stern. He flung himself down hastily, and the boatswain, who was following, fell on him.

"Don't you get up yet, sir," cried the boatswain. "No hurry!"

A sea swept over. Jukes understood the boatswain to splutter that the bridge ladders were gone. "I'll lower you down, sir, by your hands," he screamed. He shouted also something about the smokestack being as likely to go overboard as not. Jukes thought it very possible, and imagined the fires out, the ship helpless. . . . The boatswain by his side kept on yelling. "What? What is it?" Jukes cried distressfully; and the other repeated, "What would my old woman say if she saw me now?"

In the alleyway, where a lot of water had got in and splashed in the dark, the men were still as death, till Jukes stumbled against one of them and cursed him savagely for being in the way. Two or three voices then asked, eager and weak, "Any chance for us, sir?"

"What's the matter with you fools?" he said brutally. He felt as though he could throw himself down amongst them and never move any more. But they seemed cheered; and in the midst of obsequious warnings, "Look out! Mind that manhole lid, sir," they lowered him into the bunker. The boatswain tumbled down after him, and as soon as he had picked himself up he remarked, "She would say, 'Serve you right, you old fool, for going to sea.'"

The boatswain had some means, and made a point of alluding to them frequently. His wife—a fat woman

—and two grown-up daughters kept a greengrocer's shop in the East End of London.

In the dark, Jukes, unsteady on his legs, listened to a faint thunderous patter. A deadened screaming went on steadily at his elbow, as it were; and from above the louder tumult of the storm descended upon these near sounds. His head swam. To him, too, in that bunker, the motion of the ship seemed novel and menacing, sapping his resolution as though he had never been afloat before.

He had half a mind to scramble out again; but the remembrance of Captain MacWhirr's voice made this impossible. His orders were to go and see. What was the good of it, he wanted to know. Enraged, he told himself he would see—of course. But the boatswain, staggering clumsily, warned him to be careful how he opened that door; there was a blamed fight going on. And Jukes, as if in great bodily pain, desired irritably to know what the devil they were fighting for.

"Dollars! Dollars, sir. All their rotten chests got burst open. Blamed money skipping all over the place, and they are tumbling after it head over heels—tearing and biting like anything. A regular little hell in there."

Jukes convulsively opened the door. The short boatswain peered under his arm.

One of the lamps had gone out, broken perhaps. Rancorous, guttural cries burst out loudly on their ears, and a strange panting sound, the working of all these straining breasts. A hard blow hit the side of the ship: water fell above with a stunning shock, and in the forefront of the gloom, where the air was reddish and thick, Jukes saw a head bang the deck violently, two thick calves waving on high, muscular arms twined round a naked body, a yellow face, openmouthed and with a set wild stare, look up and slide away. An empty chest clattered turning over; a man fell headfirst with a jump, as if lifted by a kick; and farther off, indistinct, others streamed like a mass of rolling stones down a bank, thumping the deck with their feet and flourishing their arms wildly. The hatchway ladder was loaded with coolies swarming on it like bees on a branch. They hung on the steps in a crawling, stirring cluster, beating madly with their fists the underside of the battened hatch, and the headlong rush of the water above was heard in the intervals of their yelling. The ship heeled over once more, and they began to drop off: first one, then two, then all the rest went away together, falling straight off with a great cry.

Jukes was confounded. The boatswain, with gruff anxiety, begged him, "Don't you go in there, sir."

The whole place seemed to twist upon itself, jumping incessantly the while; and when the ship rose to a sea Jukes fancied that all these men would be shot upon him in a body. He backed out, swung the door to, and with trembling hands pushed at the bolt. . . .

As soon as his mate had gone Captain MacWhirr, left alone on the bridge, sidled and staggered as far as the wheelhouse. Its door being hinged forward, he had to fight the gale for admittance, and when at last he managed to enter, it was with an instantaneous clatter and a bang, as though he had been fired through the wood. He stood within, holding on to the handle.

The steering gear leaked steam, and in the confined space the glass of the binnacle made a shiny oval of light in a thin white fog. The wind howled, hummed, whistled, with sudden booming gusts that rattled the doors and shutters in the vicious patter of sprays. Two coils of lead line and a small canvas bag hung on a long lanyard, swung wide off, and came back clinging to the bulkheads. The gratings underfoot were nearly afloat;

with every sweeping blow of a sea, water squirted violently through the cracks all round the door, and the
man at the helm had flung down his cap, his coat, and
stood propped against the gear casing in a striped cotton
shirt open on his breast. The little brass wheel in his
hands had the appearance of a bright and fragile toy.
The cords of his neck stood hard and lean, a dark patch
lay in the hollow of his throat, and his face was still and
sunken as in death.

Captain MacWhirr wiped his eyes. The sea that had
nearly taken him overboard had, to his great annoyance,
washed his sou'wester hat off his bald head. The fluffy,
fair hair, soaked and darkened, resembled a mean skein
of cotton threads festooned round his bare skull. His
face, glistening with sea water, had been made crimson
with the wind, with the sting of sprays. He looked as
though he had come off sweating from before a furnace.

"You here?" he muttered, heavily.

The second mate had found his way into the wheelhouse some time before. He had fixed himself in a corner
with his knees up, a fist pressed against each temple;
and this attitude suggested rage, sorrow, resignation,
surrender, with a sort of concentrated unforgiveness. He
said mournfully and defiantly, "Well, it's my watch below now; ain't it?"

The steam gear clattered, stopped, clattered again;
and the helmsman's eyeballs seemed to project out of a
hungry face as if the compass card behind the binnacle
glass had been meat. God knows how long he had been
left there to steer, as if forgotten by all his shipmates.
The bells had not been struck; there had been no reliefs;
the ship's routine had gone down wind; but he was trying to keep her head north-northeast. The rudder might
have been gone for all he knew, the fires out, the engines
broken down, the ship ready to roll over like a corpse,

He was anxious not to get muddled and lose control of her head, because the compass card swung far both ways, wriggling on the pivot, and sometimes seemed to whirl right round. He suffered from mental stress. He was horribly afraid, also, of the wheelhouse going. Mountains of water kept on tumbling against it. When the ship took one of her desperate dives the corners of his lips twitched.

Captain MacWhirr looked up at the wheelhouse clock. Screwed to the bulkhead, it had a white face on which the black hands appeared to stand quite still. It was half-past one in the morning.

"Another day," he muttered to himself.

The second mate heard him, and lifting his head as one grieving amongst ruins, "You won't see it break," he exclaimed. His wrists and his knees could be seen to shake violently. "No, by God! You won't. . . ."

He took his face again between his fists.

The body of the helmsman had moved slightly, but his head didn't budge on his neck—like a stone head fixed to look one way from a column. During a roll that all but took his booted legs from under him, and in the very stagger to save himself, Captain MacWhirr said austerely, "Don't you pay any attention to what that man says." And then, with an indefinable change of tone, very grave, he added, "He isn't on duty."

The sailor said nothing.

The hurricane boomed, shaking the little place, which seemed air-tight; and the light of the binnacle flickered all the time.

"You haven't been relieved," Captain MacWhirr went on, looking down. "I want you to stick to the helm, though, as long as you can. You've got the hang of her. Another man coming here might make a mess of it. Wouldn't do. No child's play. And the hands are probably busy with a job down below. . . . Think you can?".

The steering gear leaped into an abrupt short clatter, stopped smoldering like an ember; and the still man, with a motionless gaze, burst out, as if all the passion in him had gone into his lips: "By Heavens, sir! I can steer forever if nobody talks to me."

"Oh! aye! All right. . . ." The Captain lifted his eyes for the first time to the man, ". . . Hackett."

And he seemed to dismiss this matter from his mind. He stooped to the engine-room speaking tube, blew in, and bent his head. Mr. Rout below answered, and at once Captain MacWhirr put his lips to the mouthpiece.

With the uproar of the gale around him he applied alternately his lips and his ear, and the engineer's voice mounted to him, harsh and as if out of the heat of an engagement. One of the stokers was disabled, the others had given in, the second engineer and the donkeyman were firing-up. The third engineer was standing by the steam valve. The engines were being tended by hand. How was it above?

"Bad enough. It mostly rests with you," said Captain MacWhirr. Was the mate down there yet? No? Well, he would be presently. Would Mr. Rout let him talk through the speaking tube?—through the deck speaking tube, because he—the Captain—was going out again on the bridge directly. There was some trouble amongst the Chinamen. They were fighting, it seemed. Couldn't allow fighting anyhow. . . .

Mr. Rout had gone away, and Captain MacWhirr could feel against his ear the pulsation of the engines, like the beat of the ship's heart. Mr. Rout's voice down there shouted something distantly. The ship pitched headlong, the pulsation leaped with a hissing tumult, and stopped dead. Captain MacWhirr's face was im-

passive, and his eyes were fixed aimlessly on the crouching shape of the second mate. Again Mr. Rout's voice
cried out in the depths, and the pulsating beats recom-
menced, with slow strokes—growing swifter.

Mr. Rout had returned to the tube. "It don't matter
much what they do," he said, hastily; and then, with
irritation, "She takes these dives as if she never meant
to come up again."

"Awful sea," said the Captain's voice from above.

"Don't let me drive her under," barked Solomon Rout
up the pipe.

"Dark and rain. Can't see what's coming," uttered
the voice. "Must—keep—her—moving—enough to
steer—and chance it," it went on to state distinctly.

"I am doing as much as I dare."

"We are—getting—smashed up—a good deal up
here," proceeded the voice mildly. "Doing—fairly well
—though. Of course, if the wheelhouse should go. . . ."

Mr. Rout, bending an attentive ear, muttered peevishly something under his breath.

But the deliberate voice up there became animated
to ask: "Jukes turned up yet?" Then, after a short wait,
"I wish he would bear a hand. I want him to be done
and come up here in case of anything. To look after the
ship. I am all alone. The second mate's lost. . . ."

"What?" shouted Mr. Rout into the engine room,
taking his head away. Then up the tube he cried, "Gone
overboard?" and clapped his ear to.

"Lost his nerve," the voice from above continued in
a matter-of-fact tone. "Damned awkward circumstance."

Mr. Rout, listening with bowed neck, opened his eyes
wide at this. However, he heard something like the
sounds of a scuffle and broken exclamations coming
down to him. He strained his hearing; and all the time
Beale, the third engineer, with his arms uplifted, held

between the palms of his hands the rim of a little black
wheel projecting at the side of a big copper pipe. He
seemed to be poising it above his head, as though it
were a correct attitude in some sort of game.

To steady himself, he pressed his shoulder against
the white bulkhead, one knee bent, and a sweat-rag
tucked in his belt hanging on his hip. His smooth cheek
was begrimed and flushed, and the coaldust on his
eyelids, like the black penciling of a make-up, enhanced
the liquid brilliance of the whites, giving to his youthful
face something of a feminine, exotic and fascinating
aspect. When the ship pitched he would with hasty
movements of his hands screw hard at the little wheel.

"Gone crazy," began the Captain's voice suddenly in
the tube. "Rushed at me. . . . Just now. Had to knock
him down. . . . This minute. You heard, Mr. Rout?"

"The devil!" muttered Mr. Rout. "Look out, Beale!"

His shout rang out like the blast of a warning trumpet, between the iron walls of the engine room. Painted
white, they rose high into the dusk of the skylight, sloping like a roof; and the whole lofty space resembled the
interior of a monument, divided by floors of iron grating,
with lights flickering at different levels, and a mass of
gloom lingering in the middle, within the columnar stir
of machinery under the motionless swelling of the cylinders. A loud and wild resonance, made up of all the
noises of the hurricane, dwelt in the still warmth of the
air. There was in it the smell of hot metal, of oil, and a
slight mist of steam. The blows of the sea seemed to
traverse it in an unringing, stunning shock, from side to
side.

Gleams, like pale long flames, trembled upon the
polish of metal; from the flooring below the enormous
crank-heads emerged in their turns with a flash of brass
and steel—going over; while the connecting rods, big-

jointed, like skeleton limbs, seemed to thrust them down and pull them up again with an irresistible precision. And deep in the half-light other rods dodged deliberately to and fro, crossheads nodded, discs of metal rubbed smoothly against each other, slow and gentle, in a commingling of shadows and gleams.

Sometimes all those powerful and unerring movements would slow down simultaneously, as if they had been the functions of a living organism, stricken suddenly by the blight of languor; and Mr. Rout's eyes would blaze darker in his long sallow face. He was fighting this fight in a pair of carpet slippers. A short shiny jacket barely covered his loins, and his white wrists protruded far out of the tight sleeves, as though the emergency had added to his stature, had lengthened his limbs, augmented his pallor, hollowed his eyes.

He moved, climbing high up, disappearing low down, with a restless, purposeful industry, and when he stood still, holding the guard rail in front of the starting gear, he would keep glancing to the right at the steam gauge, at the water gauge, fixed upon the white wall in the light of a swaying lamp. The mouths of two speaking tubes gaped stupidly at his elbow, and the dial of the engine-room telegraph resembled a clock of large diameter, bearing on its face curt words instead of figures. The grouped letters stood out heavily black, around the pivot-head of the indicator, emphatically symbolic of loud exclamations: AHEAD, ASTERN, SLOW, HALF, STAND BY; and the fat black hand pointed downwards to the word FULL, which, thus singled out, captured the eye as a sharp cry secures attention.

The wood-encased bulk of the low-pressure cylinder, frowning portly from above, emitted a faint wheeze at every thrust, and except for that low hiss the engines worked their steel limbs headlong or slow with a silent, determined smoothness. And all this, the white walls, the moving steel, the floor plates under Solomon Rout's feet, the floors of iron grating above his head, the dusk and the gleams, uprose and sank continuously, with one accord, upon the harsh wash of the waves against the ship's side. The whole loftiness of the place, booming hollow to the great voice of the wind, swayed at the top like a tree, would go over bodily, as if borne down this way and that by the tremendous blasts.

"You've got to hurry up," shouted Mr. Rout, as soon as he saw Jukes appear in the stokehold doorway.

Jukes' glance was wandering and tipsy; his red face was puffy, as though he had overslept himself. He had had an arduous road, and had traveled over it with immense vivacity, the agitation of his mind corresponding to the exertions of his body. He had rushed up out of the bunker, stumbling in the dark alleyway amongst a lot of bewildered men who, trod upon, asked "What's up, sir?" in awed mutters all round him; down the stokehold ladder, missing many iron rungs in his hurry, down into a place deep as a well, black as Tophet, tipping over back and forth like a seesaw. The water in the bilges thundered at each roll, and lumps of coal skipped to and fro, from end to end, rattling like an avalanche of pebbles on a slope of iron.

Somebody in there moaned with pain, and somebody else could be seen crouching over what seemed the prone body of a dead man; a lusty voice blasphemed; and the glow under each fire door was like a pool of flaming blood radiating quietly in a velvety blackness.

A gust of wind struck upon the nape of Jukes' neck and next moment he felt it streaming about his wet ankles. The stokehold ventilators hummed; in front of the six fire doors two wild figures, stripped to the waist, staggered and stooped, wrestling with two shovels.

"Hallo! Plenty of draft now," yelled the second engineer at once, as though he had been all the time looking out for Jukes. The donkeyman, a dapper little chap with a dazzling fair skin and a tiny, gingery mustache, worked in a sort of mute transport. They were keeping a full head of steam, and a profound rumbling, as of an empty furniture van trotting over a bridge, made a sustained bass to all the other noises of the place.

"Blowing off all the time," went on yelling the second. With a sound as of a hundred scoured saucepans, the orifice of a ventilator spat upon his shoulder a sudden gush of salt water, and he volleyed a stream of curses upon all things on earth including his own soul, ripping and raving, and all the time attending to his business. With a sharp clash of metal the ardent pale glare of the fire opened upon his bullet head, showing his spluttering lips, his insolent face, and with another clang closed like the white-hot wink of an iron eye.

"Where's the blooming ship? Can you tell me? Blast my eyes! Under water—or what? It's coming down here in tons. Are the condemned cowls gone to Hades? Hey? Don't you know anything—you jolly sailor-man you . . . ?"

Jukes, after a bewildered moment, had been helped by a roll to dart through; and as soon as his eyes took in the comparative vastness, peace and brilliance of the engine room, the ship, setting her stern heavily in the water, sent him charging head down upon Mr. Rout.

The chief's arm, long like a tentacle, and straightening as if worked by a spring, went out to meet him, and deflected his rush into a spin towards the speaking tubes. At the same time Mr. Rout repeated earnestly:

"You've got to hurry up, whatever it is."

Jukes yelled "Are you there, sir?" and listened. Nothing. Suddenly the roar of the wind fell straight into his

ear, but presently a small voice shoved aside the shouting hurricane quietly.

"You, Jukes?—Well?"

Jukes was ready to talk: it was only time that seemed
to be wanting. It was easy enough to account for everything. He could perfectly imagine the coolies battened
down in the reeking 'tween-deck, lying sick and scared
between the rows of chests. Then one of these chests
—or perhaps several at once—breaking loose in a roll,
knocking out others, sides splitting, lids flying open, and
all these clumsy Chinamen rising up in a body to save
their property. Afterwards every fling of the ship would
hurl that tramping, yelling mob here and there, from
side to side, in a whirl of smashed wood, torn clothing,
rolling dollars. A struggle once started, they would be
unable to stop themselves. Nothing could stop them
now except main force. It was a disaster. He had seen it,
and that was all he could say. Some of them must be
dead, he believed. The rest would go on fighting. . . .

He sent up his words, tripping over each other,
crowding the narrow tube. They mounted as if into a
silence of an enlightened comprehension dwelling alone
up there with a storm. And Jukes wanted to be dismissed from the face of that odious trouble intruding
on the great need of the ship.


## v


He waited. Before his eyes the engines turned with
slow labor, that in the moment of going off into a mad
fling would stop dead at Mr. Rout's shout, "Look out,
Beale!" They paused in an intelligent immobility, stilled
in mid-stroke, a heavy crank arrested on the cant, as if
conscious of danger and the passage of time. Then, with
a "Now, then!" from the chief, and the sound of a breath

expelled through clenched teeth, they would accomplish the interrupted revolution and begin another.

There was the prudent sagacity of wisdom and the deliberation of enormous strength in their movements. This was their work—this patient coaxing of a distracted ship over the fury of the waves and into the very eye of the wind. At times Mr. Rout's chin would sink on his breast, and he watched them with knitted eyebrows as if lost in thought.

The voice that kept the hurricane out of Jukes' ear began: "Take the hands with you . . . ," and left off unexpectedly.

"What could I do with them, sir?"

A harsh, abrupt, imperious clang exploded suddenly. The three pairs of eyes flew up to the telegraph dial to see the hand jump from FULL to STOP, as if snatched by a devil. And then these three men in the engine room had the intimate sensation of a check upon the ship, of a strange shrinking, as if she had gathered herself for a desperate leap.

"Stop her!" bellowed Mr. Rout.

Nobody—not even Captain MacWhirr, who alone on deck had caught sight of a white line of foam coming on at such a height that he couldn't believe his eyes— nobody was to know the steepness of that sea and the awful depth of the hollow the hurricane had scooped out behind the running wall of water.

It raced to meet the ship, and, with a pause, as of girding the loins, the *Nan-Shan* lifted her bows and leaped. The flames in all the lamps sank, darkening the engine room. One went out. With a tearing crash and a swirling, raving tumult, tons of water fell upon the deck, as though the ship had darted under the foot of a cataract.

Down there they looked at each other, stunned.

"Swept from end to end, by God!" bawled Jukes.

She dipped into the hollow straight down, as if going over the edge of the world. The engine room toppled forward menacingly, like the inside of a tower nodding in an earthquake. An awful racket, of iron things falling, came from the stokehold. She hung on this appalling slant long enough for Beale to drop on his hands and knees and begin to crawl as if he meant to fly on all fours out of the engine room, and for Mr. Rout to turn his head slowly, rigid, cavernous, with the lower jaw dropping. Jukes had shut his eyes, and his face in a moment became hopelessly blank and gentle, like the face of a blind man.

At last she rose slowly, staggering, as if she had to lift a mountain with her bows.

Mr. Rout shut his mouth; Jukes blinked; and little Beale stood up hastily.

"Another one like this, and that's the last of her," cried the chief.

He and Jukes looked at each other, and the same thought came into their heads. The Captain! Everything must have been swept away. Steering gear gone —ship like a log. All over directly.

"Rush!" ejaculated Mr. Rout thickly, glaring with enlarged, doubtful eyes at Jukes, who answered him by an irresolute glance.

The clang of the telegraph gong soothed them instantly. The black hand dropped in a flash from STOP to FULL.

"Now then, Beale!" cried Mr. Rout.

The steam hissed low. The piston rods slid in and out. Jukes put his ear to the tube. The voice was ready for him. It said: "Pick up all the money. Bear a hand now. I'll want you up here." And that was all.

"Sir?" called up Jukes. There was no answer.

He staggered away like a defeated man from the field of battle. He had got, in some way or other, a cut above his left eyebrow—a cut to the bone. He was not aware of it in the least: quantities of the China Sea, large enough to break his neck for him, had gone over his head, had cleaned, washed, and salted that wound. It did not bleed, but only gaped red; and this gash over the eye, his disheveled hair, the disorder of his clothes, gave him the aspect of a man worsted in a fight with fists.

"Got to pick up the dollars." He appealed to Mr. Rout, smiling pitifully at random.

"What's that?" asked Mr. Rout, wildly. "Pick up . . . ? I don't care. . . ." Then, quivering in every muscle, but with an exaggeration of paternal tone, "Go away now, for God's sake. You deck people'll drive me silly. There's that second mate been going for the old man. Don't you know? You fellows are going wrong for want of something to do. . . ."

At these words Jukes discovered in himself the beginnings of anger. Want of something to do—indeed. . . . Full of hot scorn against the chief, he turned to go the way he had come. In the stokehold the plump donkeyman toiled with his shovel mutely, as if his tongue had been cut out; but the second was carrying on like a noisy, undaunted maniac, who had preserved his skill in the art of stoking under a marine boiler.

"Hallo, you wandering officer? Hey! Can't you get some of your slush-slingers to wind up a few of them ashes? I am getting choked with them here. Curse it! Hallo! Hey! Remember the articles: *Sailors and firemen to assist each other*. Hey! D'ye hear?"

Jukes was climbing out frantically, and the other, lifting up his face after him, howled, "Can't you speak? What are you poking about here for? What's your game, anyhow?"

A frenzy possessed Jukes. By the time he was back amongst the men in the darkness of the alleyway, he felt ready to wring all their necks at the slightest sign of hanging back. The very thought of it exasperated him. *He* couldn't hang back. They shouldn't.

The impetuosity with which he came amongst them carried them along. They had already been excited and startled at all his comings and goings—by the fierceness and rapidity of his movements; and more felt than seen in his rushes, he appeared formidable—busied with matters of life and death that brooked no delay. At his first word he heard them drop into the bunker one after another obediently, with heavy thumps.

They were not clear as to what would have to be done. "What is it? What is it?" they were asking each other. The boatswain tried to explain; the sounds of a great scuffle surprised them; and the mighty shocks, reverberating awfully in the black bunker, kept them in mind of their danger. When the boatswain threw open the door it seemed that an eddy of the hurricane, stealing through the iron sides of the ship, had set all these bodies whirling like dust: there came to them a confused uproar, a tempestuous tumult, a fierce mutter, gusts of screams dying away, and the tramping of feet mingling with the blows of the sea.

For a moment they glared amazed, blocking the doorway. Jukes pushed through them brutally. He said nothing, and simply darted in. Another lot of coolies on the ladder, struggling suicidally to break through the battened hatch to a swamped deck, fell off as before, and he disappeared under them like a man overtaken by a landslide.

The boatswain yelled excitedly: "Come along. Get the mate out. He'll be trampled to death. Come on."

They charged in, stamping on breasts, on fingers, on faces, catching their feet in heaps of clothing, kicking broken wood; but before they could get hold of him Jukes emerged waist deep in a multitude of clawing hands. In the instant he had been lost to view, all the buttons of his jacket had gone, its back had got split up to the collar, his waistcoat had been torn open. The central struggling mass of Chinamen went over to the roll, dark, indistinct, helpless, with a wild gleam of many eyes in the dim light of the lamps.

"Leave me alone—damn you. I am all right," screeched Jukes. "Drive them forward. Watch your chance when she pitches. Forward with 'em. Drive them against the bulkhead. Jam 'em up."

The rush of the sailors into the seething 'tween-deck was like a splash of cold water into a boiling caldron. The commotion sank for a moment.

The bulk of Chinamen were locked in such a compact scrimmage that, linking their arms and aided by an appalling dive of the ship, the seamen sent it forward in one great shove, like a solid block. Behind their backs small clusters and loose bodies tumbled from side to side.

The boatswain performed prodigious feats of strength. With his long arms open, and each great paw clutching at a stanchion, he stopped the rush of seven entwined Chinamen rolling like a boulder. His joints cracked, he said, "Ha!" and they flew apart. But the carpenter showed the greater intelligence. Without saying a word to anybody he went back into the alleyway, to fetch several coils of cargo gear he had seen there—chain and rope. With these life lines were rigged.

There was really no resistance. The struggle, however

it began, had turned into a scramble of blind panic. If the coolies had started up after their scattered dollars they were by that time fighting only for their footing. They took each other by the throat merely to save themselves from being hurled about. Whoever got a hold anywhere would kick at the others who caught at his legs and hung on, till a roll sent them flying together across the deck.

The coming of the white devils was a terror. Had they come to kill? The individuals torn out of the ruck became very limp in the seamen's hands: some, dragged aside by the heels, were passive, like dead bodies, with open, fixed eyes. Here and there a coolie would fall on his knees as if begging for mercy; several, whom the excess of fear made unruly, were hit with hard fists between the eyes, and cowered; while those who were hurt submitted to rough handling, blinking rapidly without a plaint. Faces streamed with blood; there were raw places on the shaven heads, scratches, bruises, torn wounds, gashes. The broken porcelain out of the chests was mostly responsible for the latter. Here and there a Chinaman, wild-eyed, with his tail unplaited, nursed a bleeding sole.

They had been ranged closely, after having been shaken into submission, cuffed a little to allay excitement, addressed in gruff words of encouragement that sounded like promises of evil. They sat on the deck in ghastly, drooping rows, and at the end the carpenter, with two hands to help him, moved busily from place to place, setting taut and hitching the life lines. The boatswain, with one leg and one arm embracing a stanchion, struggled with a lamp pressed to his breast, trying to get a light, and growling all the time like an industrious gorilla. The figures of seamen stooped repeatedly, with the movements of gleaners, and everything was being flung into the bunker: clothing, smashed wood, broken china, and the dollars, too, gathered up in men's jackets. Now and then a sailor would stagger towards the doorway with his arms full of rubbish; and dolorous, slanting eyes followed his movements.

With every roll of the ship the long rows of sitting Celestials would sway forward brokenly, and her headlong dives knocked together the line of shaven polls from end to end. When the wash of water rolling on the deck died away for a moment, it seemed to Jukes, yet quivering from his exertions, that in his mad struggle down there he had overcome the wind somehow: that a silence had fallen upon the ship, a silence in which the sea struck thunderously at her sides.

Everything had been cleared out of the 'tween-deck —all the wreckage, as the men said. They stood erect and tottering above the level of heads and drooping shoulders. Here and there a coolie sobbed for his breath. Where the high light fell, Jukes could see the salient ribs of one, the yellow, wistful face of another; bowed necks; or would meet a dull stare directed at his face. He was amazed that there had been no corpses; but the lot of them seemed at their last gasp, and they appeared to him more pitiful than if they had been all dead.

Suddenly one of the coolies began to speak. The light came and went on his lean, straining face; he threw his head up like a baying hound. From the bunker came the sounds of knocking and the tinkle of some dollars rolling loose; he stretched out his arm, his mouth yawned black, and the incomprehensible guttural hooting sounds, that did not seem to belong to a human language, penetrated Jukes with a strange emotion as if a brute had tried to be eloquent.

Two more started mouthing what seemed to Jukes fierce denunciations; the others stirred with grunts and growls. Jukes ordered the hands out of the 'tween-decks hurriedly. He left last himself, backing through the door, while the grunts rose to a loud murmur and hands were extended after him as after a malefactor. The boatswain shot the bolt, and remarked uneasily, "Seems as if the wind had dropped, sir."

The seamen were glad to get back into the alleyway. Secretly each of them thought that at the last moment he could rush out on deck—and that was a comfort. There is something horribly repugnant in the idea of being drowned under a deck. Now they had done with the Chinamen, they again became conscious of the ship's position.

Jukes on coming out of the alleyway found himself up to the neck in the noisy water. He gained the bridge, and discovered he could detect obscure shapes as if his sight had become preternaturally acute. He saw faint outlines. They recalled not the familiar aspect of the *Nan-Shan*, but something remembered—an old dismantled steamer he had seen years ago rotting on a mudbank. She recalled that wreck.

There was no wind, not a breath, except the faint currents created by the lurches of the ship. The smoke tossed out of the funnel was settling down upon her deck. He breathed it as he passed forward. He felt the deliberate throb of the engines, and heard small sounds that seemed to have survived the great uproar: the knocking of broken fittings, the rapid tumbling of some piece of wreckage on the bridge. He perceived dimly the squat shape of his captain holding on to a twisted bridge rail, motionless and swaying as if rooted to the planks. The unexpected stillness of the air oppressed Jukes.

"We have done it, sir," he gasped.

"Thought you would," said Captain MacWhirr.

"Did you?" murmured Jukes to himself.

"Wind fell all at once," went on the Captain.

Jukes burst out: "If you think it was an easy job—"

But his captain, clinging to the rail, paid no attention. "According to the books the worst is not over yet."

"If most of them hadn't been half dead with sea-sickness and fright, not one of us would have come out of that 'tween-deck alive," said Jukes.

"Had to do what's fair by them," mumbled Mac-Whirr, stolidly. "You don't find everything in books."

"Why, I believe they would have risen on us if I hadn't ordered the hands out of that pretty quick," continued Jukes with warmth.

After the whisper of their shouts, their ordinary tones, so distinct, rang out very loud to their ears in the amazing stillness of the air. It seemed to them they were talking in a dark and echoing vault.

Through a jagged aperture in the dome of clouds the light of a few stars fell upon the black sea, rising and falling confusedly. Sometimes the head of a watery cone would topple on board and mingle with the rolling flurry of foam on the swamped deck; and the *Nan-Shan* wallowed heavily at the bottom of a circular cistern of clouds. This ring of dense vapors, gyrating madly round the calm of the center, encompassed the ship like a motionless and unbroken wall of an aspect inconceivably sinister. Within, the sea, as if agitated by an internal commotion, leaped in peaked mounds that jostled each other, slapping heavily against her sides; and a low moaning sound, the infinite plaint of the storm's fury, came from beyond the limits of the menacing calm. Captain MacWhirr remained silent, and Jukes' ready ear caught suddenly the faint, long-drawn roar of some immense wave rushing unseen under that thick blackness, which made the appalling boundary of his vision.

"Of course," he started resentfully, "they thought we had caught at the chance to plunder them. Of course! You said—pick up the money. Easier said than done. They couldn't tell what was in our heads. We came in, smash—right into the middle of them. Had to do it by a rush."

"As long as it's done . . . ," mumbled the Captain, without attempting to look at Jukes. "Had to do what's fair."

"We shall find yet there's the devil to pay when this is over," said Jukes, feeling very sore. "Let them only recover a bit, and you'll see. They will fly at our throats, sir. Don't forget, sir, she isn't a British ship now. These brutes know it well, too. The damned Siamese flag."

"We are on board, all the same," remarked Captain MacWhirr.

"The trouble's not over yet," insisted Jukes, prophetically, reeling and catching on. "She's a wreck," he added, faintly.

"The trouble's not over yet," assented Captain Mac-Whirr, half aloud. . . . "Look out for her a minute."

"Are you going off the deck, sir?" asked Jukes, hurriedly, as if the storm were sure to pounce upon him as soon as he had been left alone with the ship.

He watched her, battered and solitary, laboring heavily in a wild scene of mountainous black waters lit by the gleams of distant worlds. She moved slowly, breathing into the still core of the hurricane the excess of her strength in a white cloud of steam—and the deep-toned vibration of the escape was like the defiant trumpeting of a living creature of the sea impatient for the renewal of the contest. It ceased suddenly. The still air moaned. Above Jukes' head a few stars shone into a pit of black vapors. The inky edge of the cloud-disc frowned upon the ship under the patch of glittering sky. The stars, too, seemed to look at her intently, as if for the last time, and the cluster of their splendor sat like a diadem on a lowering brow.

Captain MacWhirr had gone into the chart room. There was no light there; but he could feel the disorder of that place where he used to live tidily. His armchair was upset. The books had tumbled out on the floor: he scrunched a piece of glass under his boot. He groped for the matches, and found a box on a shelf with a deep ledge. He struck one, and puckering the corners of his eyes, held out the little flame towards the barometer whose glittering top of glass and metals nodded at him continuously.

It stood very low—incredibly low, so low that Captain MacWhirr grunted. The match went out, and hurriedly he extracted another, with thick, stiff fingers.

Again a little flame flared up before the nodding glass and metal of the top. His eyes looked at it, narrowed with attention, as if expecting an imperceptible sign. With his grave face he resembled a booted and misshapen pagan burning incense before the oracle of a joss. There was no mistake. It was the lowest reading he had ever seen in his life.

Captain MacWhirr emitted a low whistle. He forgot himself till the flame diminished to a blue spark, burnt his fingers and vanished. Perhaps something had gone wrong with the thing!

There was an aneroid glass screwed above the couch. He turned that way, struck another match, and discovered the white face of the other instrument looking at him from the bulkhead, meaningly, not to be gainsaid, as though the wisdom of men were made unerring by the indifference of matter. There was no room for doubt now. Captain MacWhirr pshawed at it, and threw the match down.

The worst was to come, then—and if the books were right this worst would be very bad. The experience of the last six hours had enlarged his conception of what heavy weather could be like. "It'll be terrific," he pronounced, mentally. He had not consciously looked at anything by the light of the matches except at the barometer; and yet somehow he had seen that his water bottle and the two tumblers had been flung out of their stand. It seemed to give him a more intimate knowledge of the tossing the ship had gone through. "I wouldn't have believed it," he thought. And his table had been cleared, too; his rulers, his pencils, the inkstand—all the things that had their safe appointed places—they were gone, as if a mischievous hand had plucked them out one by one and flung them on the wet floor. The hurricane had broken in upon the orderly arrangements of his privacy. This had never happened before, and the feeling of dismay reached the very seat of his composure. And the worst was to come yet! He was glad the trouble in the 'tween-deck had been discovered in time. If the ship had to go after all, then, at least, she wouldn't be going to the bottom with a lot of people in her fighting teeth and claw. That would have been odious. And in that feeling there was a humane intention and a vague sense of the fitness of things.

These instantaneous thoughts were yet in their essence heavy and slow, partaking of the nature of the man. He extended his hand to put back the matchbox in its corner of the shelf. There were always matches there—by his order. The steward had his instructions impressed upon him long before. "A box . . . just there, see? Not so very full . . . where I can put my hand on it, steward. Might want a light in a hurry. Can't tell on board ship *what* you might want in a hurry. Mind, now."

And of course on his side he would be careful to put it back in its place scrupulously. He did so now, but before he removed his hand it occurred to him that per-haps he would never have occasion to use that box any more. The vividness of the thought checked him and for an infinitesimal fraction of a second his fingers closed again on the small object as though it had been the symbol of all these little habits that chain us to the weary round of life. He released it at last, and letting himself fall on the settee, listened for the first sounds of return-ing wind.

Not yet. He heard only the wash of water, the heavy splashes, the dull shocks of the confused seas boarding his ship from all sides. She would never have a chance to clear her decks.

But the quietude of the air was startlingly tense and unsafe, like a slender hair holding a sword suspended over his head. By this awful pause the storm penetrated the defenses of the man and unsealed his lips. He spoke out in the solitude and the pitch darkness of the cabin, as if addressing another being awakened within his breast.

"I shouldn't like to lose her," he said half aloud.

He sat unseen, apart from the sea, from his ship, isolated, as if withdrawn from the very current of his own existence, where such freaks as talking to himself surely had no place. His palms reposed on his knees, he bowed his short neck and puffed heavily, surrendering to a strange sensation of weariness he was not enlight-ened enough to recognize for the fatigue of mental stress.

From where he sat he could reach the door of a wash-

stand locker. There should have been a towel there.
There was. Good. . . . He took it out, wiped his face,
and afterwards went on rubbing his wet head. He
toweled himself with energy in the dark, and then remained motionless with the towel on his knees. A moment passed, of a stillness so profound that no one could
have guessed there was a man sitting in that cabin. Then
a murmur arose.

"She may come out of it yet."

When Captain MacWhirr came out on deck, which
he did brusquely, as though he had suddenly become
conscious of having stayed away too long, the calm had
lasted already more than fifteen minutes—long enough
to make itself intolerable even to his imagination. Jukes,
motionless on the forepart of the bridge, began to speak
at once. His voice, blank and forced as though he were
talking through hard-set teeth, seemed to flow away on
all sides into the darkness, deepening again upon the
sea.

"I had the wheel relieved. Hackett began to sing out
that he was done. He's lying in there alongside the steering gear with a face like death. At first I couldn't get
anybody to crawl out and relieve the poor devil. That
bosun's worse than no good, I always said. Thought I
would have had to go myself and haul out one of them
by the neck."

"Ah, well," muttered the Captain. He stood watchful
by Jukes' side.

"The second mate's in there, too, holding his head. Is
he hurt, sir?"

"No—crazy," said Captain MacWhirr, curtly.

"Looks as if he had a tumble, though."

"I had to give him a push," explained the Captain.

Jukes gave an impatient sigh.

"It will come very sudden," said Captain MacWhirr,

"and from over there, I fancy. Gód only knows though. These books are only good to muddle your head and make you jumpy. It will be bad, and there's an end. If we only can steam her round in time to meet it. . . ."

A minute passed. Some of the stars winked rapidly and vanished.

"You left them pretty safe?" began the Captain abruptly, as though the silence were unbearable.

"Are you thinking of the coolies, sir? I rigged life lines all ways across that 'tween-deck."

"Did you? Good idea, Mr. Jukes."

"I didn't . . . think you cared to . . . know," said Jukes—the lurching of the ship cut his speech as though somebody had been jerking him around while he talked —"how I got on with . . . that infernal job. We did it. And it may not matter in the end."

"Had to do what's fair, for all—they are only China-men. Give them the same chance with ourselves—hang it all. She isn't lost yet. Bad enough to be shut up below in a gale—"

"That's what I thought when you gave me the job, sir," interjected Jukes, moodily.

"—without being battered to pieces," pursued Captain MacWhirr with rising vehemence. "Couldn't let that go on in my ship, if I knew she hadn't five minutes to live. Couldn't bear it, Mr. Jukes."

A hollow echoing noise, like that of a shout rolling in a rocky chasm, approached the ship and went away again. The last star, blurred, enlarged, as if returning to the fiery mist of its beginning, struggled with the colossal depth of blackness hanging over the ship—and went out.

"Now for it!" muttered Captain MacWhirr. "Mr. Jukes."

"Here, sir."

The two men were growing indistinct to each other.

"We must trust her to go through it and come out on the other side. That's plain and straight. There's no room for Captain Wilson's storm-strategy here."

"No, sir."

"She will be smothered and swept again for hours," mumbled the Captain. "There's not much left by this time above deck for the sea to take away—unless you or me."

"Both, sir," whispered Jukes, breathlessly.

"You are always meeting trouble halfway, Jukes," Captain MacWhirr remonstrated quaintly. "Though it's a fact that the second mate is no good. D'ye hear, Mr. Jukes? You would be left alone if . . ."

Captain MacWhirr interrupted himself, and Jukes, glancing on all sides, remained silent.

"Don't you be put out by anything," the Captain continued, mumbling rather fast. "Keep her facing it. They may say what they like, but the heaviest seas run with the wind. Facing it—always facing it—that's the way to get through. You are a young sailor. Face it. That's enough for any man. Keep a cool head."

"Yes, sir," said Jukes, with a flutter of the heart.

In the next few seconds the Captain spoke to the engine room and got an answer.

For some reason Jukes experienced an access of confidence, a sensation that came from outside like a warm breath, and made him feel equal to every demand. The distant muttering of the darkness stole into his ears. He noted it unmoved, out of that sudden belief in himself, as a man safe in a shirt of mail would watch a point.

The ship labored without intermission amongst the black hills of water, paying with this hard tumbling the price of her life. She rumbled in her depths, shaking a white plummet of steam into the night, and Jukes' thought skimmed like a bird through the engine room, where Mr. Rout—good man—was ready. When the rumbling ceased it seemed to him that there was a pause of every sound, a dead pause in which Captain Mac-Whirr's voice rang out startlingly.

"What's that? A puff of wind?"—it spoke much louder than Jukes had ever heard it before—"On the bow. That's right. She may come out of it yet."

The mutter of the winds drew near apace. In the forefront could be distinguished a drowsy waking plaint passing on, and far off the growth of a multiple clamor, marching and expanding. There was the throb as of many drums in it, a vicious rushing note, and like the chant of a tramping multitude.

Jukes could no longer see his captain distinctly. The darkness was absolutely piling itself upon the ship. At most he made out movements, a hint of elbows spread out, of a head thrown up.

Captain MacWhirr was trying to do up the top button of his oilskin coat with unwonted haste. The hurricane, with its power to madden the seas, to sink ships, to uproot trees, to overturn strong walls and dash the very birds of the air to the ground, had found this taciturn man in its path, and, doing its utmost, had managed to wring out a few words. Before the renewed wrath of winds swooped on his ship, Captain MacWhirr was moved to declare, in a tone of vexation, as it were: "I wouldn't like to lose her."

He was spared that annoyance.

## VI

On a bright sunshiny day, with the breeze chasing her smoke far ahead, the *Nan-Shan* came into Fu-chau. Her arrival was at once noticed on shore, and the seamen in harbor said: "Look! Look at that steamer. What's that? Siamese—isn't she? Just look at her!"

She seemed, indeed, to have been used as a running target for the secondary batteries of a cruiser. A hail of minor shells could not have given her upper works a more broken, torn, and devastated aspect; and she had about her the worn, weary air of ships coming from the far ends of the world—and indeed with truth, for in her short passage she had been very far; sighting, truly, even the coast of the Great Beyond, whence no ship ever returns to give up her crew to the dust of the earth. She was incrusted and gray with salt to the trucks of her masts and to the top of her funnel; as though (as some facetious seaman said) "the crowd on board had fished her out somewhere from the bottom of the sea and brought her in here for salvage." And further, excited by the felicity of his own wit, he offered to give five pounds for her—"as she stands."

Before she had been quite an hour at rest, a meager little man, with a red-tipped nose and a face cast in an angry mold, landed from a sampan on the quay of the Foreign Concession, and incontinently turned to shake his fist at her.

A tall individual, with legs much too thin for a rotund stomach, and with watery eyes, strolled up and remarked, "Just left her—eh? Quick work."

He wore a soiled suit of blue flannel with a pair of dirty cricketing shoes; a dingy gray mustache drooped from his lip, and daylight could be seen in two places between the rim and the crown of his hat.

"Hallo! what are you doing here?" asked the ex-second mate of the *Nan-Shan*, shaking hands hurriedly.

"Standing by for a job—chance worth taking—got a quiet hint," explained the man with the broken hat, in jerky, apathetic wheezes.

The second shook his fist again at the *Nan-Shan*. "There's a fellow there that ain't fit to have the command of a scow," he declared, quivering with passion, while the other looked about listlessly.

"Is there?"

But he caught sight on the quay of a heavy seaman's chest, painted brown under a fringed sailcloth cover, and lashed with new manila line. He eyed it with awakened interest.

"I would talk and raise trouble if it wasn't for that damned Siamese flag. Nobody to go to—or I would make it hot for him. The fraud! Told his chief engineer —that's another fraud for you—I had lost my nerve. The greatest lot of ignorant fools that ever sailed the seas. No! You can't think. . . ."

"Got your money all right?" inquired his seedy acquaintance suddenly.

"Yes. Paid me off on board," raged the second mate. " 'Get your breakfast on shore,' says he."

"Mean skunk!" commented the tall man, vaguely, and passed his tongue on his lips. "What about having a drink of some sort?"

"He struck me," hissed the second mate.

"No! Struck! You don't say?" The man in blue began to bustle about sympathetically. "Can't possibly talk here. I want to know all about it. Struck—eh? Let's get a fellow to carry your chest. I know a quiet place where they have some bottled beer. . . ."

Mr. Jukes, who had been scanning the shore through a pair of glasses, informed the chief engineer afterwards that "our late second mate hasn't been long in finding a friend. A chap looking uncommonly like a bummer. I saw them walk away together from the quay."

The hammering and banging of the needful repairs did not disturb Captain MacWhirr. The steward found in the letter he wrote, in a tidy chart room, passages of such absorbing interest that twice he was nearly caught in the act. But Mrs. MacWhirr, in the drawing room of the forty-pound house, stifled a yawn—perhaps out of self-respect—for she was alone.

She reclined in a plush-bottomed and gilt hammock-chair near a tiled fireplace, with Japanese fans on the mantel and a glow of coals in the grate. Lifting her hands, she glanced wearily here and there into the many pages. It was not her fault they were so prosy, so completely uninteresting—from "My darling wife" at the beginning, to "Your loving husband" at the end. She couldn't be really expected to understand all these ship affairs. She was glad, of course, to hear from him, but she had never asked herself why, precisely.

". . . They are called typhoons. . . . The mate did not seem to like it. . . . Not in books. . . . Couldn't think of letting it go on. . . ."

The paper rustled sharply. ". . . A calm that lasted more than twenty minutes," she read perfunctorily; and the next words her thoughtless eyes caught, on the top of another page, were: "see you and the children again. . . ." She had a movement of impatience. He was always thinking of coming home. He had never had such a good salary before. What was the matter now?

It did not occur to her to turn back overleaf to look. She would have found it recorded there that between 4 and 6 A.M. on December 25th, Captain MacWhirr did actually think that his ship could not possibly live another hour in such a sea, and that he would never see his wife and children again. Nobody was to know this (his letters got mislaid so quickly)—nobody whatever but the steward, who had been greatly impressed by that disclosure. So much so, that he tried to give the cook some idea of the "narrow squeak we all had" by saying solemnly, "The old man himself had a dam' poor opinion of our chance."

"How do you know?" asked, contemptuously, the cook, an old soldier. "He hasn't told you, maybe?"

"Well, he did give me a hint to that effect," the steward brazened it out.

"Get along with you! He will be coming to tell *me* next," jeered the old cook, over his shoulder.

Mrs. MacWhirr glanced farther, on the alert. ". . . Do what's fair. . . . Miserable objects. . . . Only three, with a broken leg each, and one. . . . Thought had better keep the matter quiet . . . hope to have done the fair thing. . . ."

She let fall her hands. No: there was nothing more about coming home. Must have been merely expressing a pious wish. Mrs. MacWhirr's mind was set at ease, and a black marble clock, priced by the local jeweler at £3 18s. 6d., had a discreet stealthy tick.

The door flew open, and a girl in the long-legged, short-frocked period of existence, flung into the room. A lot of colorless, rather lanky hair was scattered over her shoulders. Seeing her mother, she stood still, and directed her pale prying eyes upon the letter.

"From father," murmured Mrs. MacWhirr. "What have you done with your ribbon?"

The girl put her hands up to her head and pouted.

"He's well," continued Mrs. MacWhirr, languidly. "At least I think so. He never says." She had a little laugh. The girl's face expressed a wandering indifference, and Mrs. MacWhirr surveyed her with fond pride.

"Go and get your hat," she said after a while. "I am going out to do some shopping. There is a sale at Linom's."

"Oh, how jolly!" uttered the child, impressively, in unexpectedly grave vibrating tones, and bounded out of the room.

It was a fine afternoon, with a gray sky and dry sidewalks. Outside the draper's Mrs. MacWhirr smiled upon a woman in a black mantle of generous proportions armored in jet and crowned with flowers blooming falsely above a bilious matronly countenance. They broke into a swift little babble of greetings and exclamations both together, very hurried, as if the street were ready to yawn open and swallow all that pleasure before it could be expressed.

Behind them the high glass doors were kept on the swing. People couldn't pass, men stood aside waiting patiently, and Lydia was absorbed in poking the end of her parasol between the stone flags. Mrs. MacWhirr talked rapidly.

"Thank you very much. He's not coming home yet. Of course it's very sad to have him away, but it's such a comfort to know he keeps so well." Mrs. MacWhirr drew breath. "The climate there agrees with him," she added, beamingly, as if poor MacWhirr had been away touring in China for the sake of his health.

Neither was the chief engineer coming home yet. Mr. Rout knew too well the value of a good billet.

"Solomon says wonders will never cease," cried Mrs. Rout joyously at the old lady in her armchair by the fire. Mr. Rout's mother moved slightly, her withered hands lying in black half-mittens on her lap.

The eyes of the engineer's wife fairly danced on the paper. "That captain of the ship he is in—a rather simple man, you remember, mother?—has done something rather clever, Solomon says."

"Yes, my dear," said the old woman meekly, sitting with bowed silvery head, and that air of inward stillness characteristic of very old people who seem lost in watching the last flickers of life. "I think I remember."

Solomon Rout, Old Sol, Father Sol, the Chief, "Rout, good man"—Mr. Rout, the condescending and paternal friend of youth, had been the baby of her many children —all dead by this time. And she remembered him best as a boy of ten—long before he went away to serve his apprenticeship in some great engineering works in the North. She had seen so little of him since, she had gone through so many years, that she had now to retrace her steps very far back to recognize him plainly in the mist of time. Sometimes it seemed that her daughter-in-law was talking of some strange man.

Mrs. Rout, junior, was disappointed. "H'm. H'm." She turned the page. "How provoking! He doesn't say what it is. Says I couldn't understand how much there was in it. Fancy! What could it be so very clever? What a wretched man not to tell us!"

She read on without further remark soberly, and at last sat looking into the fire. The chief wrote just a word or two of the typhoon; but something had moved him to express an increased longing for the companionship of the jolly woman. "If it hadn't been that mother must be looked after, I would send you your passage money today. You could set up a small house out here. I would have a chance to see you sometimes then. We are not growing younger. . . ."

"He's well, mother," sighed Mrs. Rout, rousing herself.

"He always was a strong healthy boy," said the old woman, placidly.

But Mr. Jukes' account was really animated and very full. His friend in the Western Ocean trade imparted it freely to the other officers of his liner. "A chap I know writes to me about an extraordinary affair that hap-

pened on board his ship in that typhoon—you know—
that we read of in the papers two months ago. It's the
funniest thing! Just see for yourself what he says. I'll
show you his letter."

There were phrases in it calculated to give the impression of lighthearted, indomitable resolution. Jukes
had written them in good faith, for he felt thus when he
wrote. He described with lurid effect 'the scenes in the
'tween-deck. ". . . It struck me in a flash that those
confounded Chinamen couldn't tell we weren't a desperate kind of robbers. 'T isn't good to part the Chinaman from his money if he is the stronger party. We
need have been desperate indeed to go thieving in such
weather, but what could these beggars know of us? So,
without thinking of it twice, I got the hands away in a
jiffy. Our work was done—that the old man had set his
heart on. We cleared out without staying to inquire how
they felt. I am convinced that if they had not been so
unmercifully shaken, and afraid—each individual one
of them—to stand up, we would have been torn to
pieces. Oh! It was pretty complete, I can tell you; and
you may run to and fro across the Pond to the end of
time before you find yourself with such a job on your
hands."

After this he alluded professionally to the damage
done to the ship, and went on thus:

"It was when the weather quieted down that the
situation became confoundedly delicate. It wasn't made
any better by us having been lately transferred to the
Siamese flag; though the skipper can't see that it makes
any difference—'as long as *we* are on board'—he says.
There are feelings that this man simply hasn't got—and
there's an end of it. You might just as well try to make
a bedpost understand. But apart from this it is an in-
fernally lonely state for a ship to be going about the

China seas with no proper consuls, not even a gunboat of her own anywhere, nor a body to go to in case of some trouble.

"My notion was to keep these Johnnies under hatches for another fifteen hours or so; as we weren't much farther than that from Fu-chau. We would find there, most likely, some sort of a man-of-war, and once under her guns we were safe enough; for surely any skipper of a man-of-war—English, French, or Dutch—would see white men through as far as row on board goes. We could get rid of them and their money afterwards by delivering them to their Mandarin or Taotai, or whatever they call these chaps in goggles you see being carried about in sedan chairs through their stinking streets.

"The old man wouldn't see it somehow. He wanted to keep the matter quiet. He got that notion into his head, and a steam windlass couldn't drag it out of him. He wanted as little fuss made as possible, for the sake of the ship's name and for the sake of the owners—'for the sake of all concerned,' says he, looking at me very hard. It made me angry hot. Of course you couldn't keep a thing like that quiet; but the chests had been secured in the usual manner and were safe enough for any earthly gale, while this had been an altogether fiendish business I couldn't give you even an idea of.

"Meantime, I could hardly keep on my feet. None of us had a spell of any sort for nearly thirty hours, and there the old man sat rubbing his chin, rubbing the top of his head, and so bothered he didn't even think of pulling his long boots off.

"'I hope, sir,' says I, 'you won't be letting them out on deck before we make ready for them in some shape or other.' Not, mind you, that I felt very sanguine about controlling these beggars if they meant to take charge.

A trouble with a cargo of Chinamen is no child's play. I was dam' tired, too. 'I wish,' said I, 'you would let us throw the whole lot of these dollars down to them and leave them to fight it out amongst themselves, while we get a rest.'

"'Now you talk wild, Jukes,' says he, looking up in his slow way that makes you ache all over, somehow. 'We must plan out something that would be fair to all parties.'

"I had no end of work on hand, as you may imagine, so I set the hands going, and then I thought I would turn in a bit. I hadn't been asleep in my bunk ten minutes when in rushes the steward and begins to pull at my leg.

"'For God's sake, Mr. Jukes, come out! Come on deck quick, sir. Oh, do come out!'

"The fellow scared all the sense out of me. I didn't know what had happened: another hurricane—or what. Could hear no wind.

"'The Captain's letting them out. Oh, he is letting them out! Jump on deck, sir, and save us. The chief engineer has just run below for his revolver.'

"That's what I understood the fool to say. However, Father Rout swears he went in there only to get a clean pocket handkerchief. Anyhow, I made one jump into my trousers and flew on deck aft. There was certainly a good deal of noise going on forward of the bridge. Four of the hands with the bosun were at work abaft. I passed up to them some of the rifles all the ships on the China coast carry in the cabin, and led them on the bridge. On the way I ran against Old Sol, looking startled and sucking at an unlighted cigar.

"'Come along,' I shouted to him.

"We charged, the seven of us, up to the chart room. All was over. There stood the old man with his sea boots still drawn up to the hips and in shirtsleeves—got warm thinking it out, I suppose. Bun Hin's dandy clerk at his elbow, as dirty as a sweep, was still green in the face. I could see directly I was in for something.

" 'What the devil are these monkey tricks, Mr. Jukes?' asks the old man, as angry as ever he could be. I tell you frankly it made me lose my tongue. 'For God's sake, Mr. Jukes,' says he, 'do take away these rifles from the men. Somebody's sure to get hurt before long if you don't. Damme, if this ship isn't worse than Bedlam! Look sharp now. I want you up here to help me and Bun Hin's Chinaman to count that money. You wouldn't mind lending a hand, too, Mr. Rout, now you are here. The more of us the better.'

"He had settled it all in his mind while I was having a snooze. Had we been an English ship, or only going to land our cargo of coolies in an English port, like Hong Kong, for instance, there would have been no end of inquiries and bother, claims for damages and so on. But these Chinamen know their officials better than we do.

"The hatches had been taken off already, and they were all on deck after a night and a day down below. It made you feel queer to see so many gaunt, wild faces together. The beggars stared about at the sky, at the sea, at the ship, as though they had expected the whole thing to have been blown to pieces. And no wonder! They had had a doing that would have shaken the soul out of a white man. But then they say a Chinaman has no soul. He has, though, something about him that is deuced tough. There was a fellow (amongst others of the badly hurt) who had had his eye all but knocked out. It stood out of his head the size of half a hen's egg. This would have laid out a white man on his back for a month; and yet there was that chap elbowing here and there in the crowd and talking to the others as if nothing had been the matter. They made a great hubbub amongst themselves, and whenever the old man showed his bald head on the foreside of the bridge, they would all leave off jawing and look at him from below.

"It seems that after he had done his thinking he made that Bun Hin's fellow go down and explain to them the only way they could get their money back. He told me afterwards that, all the coolies having worked in the same place and for the same length of time, he reckoned he would be doing the fair thing by them as near as possible if he shared all the cash we had picked up equally among the lot. You couldn't tell one man's dollars from another's, he said, and if you asked each man how much money he brought on board he was afraid they would lie, and he would find himself a long way short. I think he was right there. As to giving up the money to any Chinese official he could scare up in Fuchau, he said he might just as well put the lot in his own pocket at once for all the good it would be to them. I suppose they thought so, too.

"We finished the distribution before dark. It was rather a sight: the sea running high, the ship a wreck to look at, these Chinamen staggering up on the bridge one by one for their share, and the old man still booted, and in his shirtsleeves, busy paying out at the chartroom door, perspiring like anything, and now and then coming down sharp on myself or Father Rout about one thing or another not quite to his mind. He took the share of those who were disabled himself to them on the No. 2 hatch. There were three dollars left over, and these went to the three most damaged coolies, one to each. We turned-to afterwards, and shoveled out on deck heaps of wet rags, all sorts of fragments of things without shape, and that you couldn't give a name to, and let them settle the ownership themselves.

"This certainly is coming as near as can be to keeping the thing quiet for the benefit of all concerned. What's your opinion, you pampered mailboat swell? The old chief says that this was plainly the only thing that could be done. The skipper remarked to me the other day, 'There are things you find nothing about in books.' I think that he got out of it very well for such a stupid man."

# A Tale of the Sea

~~~~~~~~~~~~~~~~~~~~~~~~~~~~~~~~~~~~~~~~~~~~~~~~~~~~~~

## THE NIGGER OF THE "NARCISSUS"

"My Lord in his discourse discovered a great deal of love to this ship."
<div style="text-align:right">—Diary of Samuel Pepys</div>

So foul a sky clears not without a storm.
<div style="text-align:right">—Shakespeare [on the title-page of <em>Nostromo</em>]</div>

There is such magnificent vagueness in the expectations that had driven each of us to sea, such a glorious indefiniteness, such a beautiful greed of adventures that are their own and only reward! What we get—well, we won't talk of that; but can one of us restrain a smile? In no other kind of life is the illusion more wide of reality—in no other is the beginning *all* illusion—the disenchantment more swift—the subjugation more complete. Hadn't we all commenced with the same desire, ended with the same knowledge, carried the memory of the same cherished glamour through the sordid days of imprecation?
<div style="text-align:right">—Conrad: <em>Lord Jim</em></div>

If you would know the age of the earth, look upon the sea in a storm.
<div style="text-align:right">—Conrad: <em>The Mirror of the Sea</em></div>

Both men and ships live in an unstable element.
<div style="text-align:right">—Conrad: <em>The Mirror of the Sea</em></div>

*The Nigger of the "Narcissus"* was Conrad's third book. His first, *Almayer's Folly* was begun in 1889 while he was still an officer in the Merchant Marine Service, was continued on voyages and in ports during the following five years, and was published by T. Fisher Unwin in London in 1895, on the recommendation of that firm's reader Edward Garnett. It won the notice of several discerning critics but no wide popularity, and Conrad, still at thirty-eight dubious about a career in literature, hesitated to begin another book. By his own later account it was Garnett who gave him the impetus to do so when he said, simply, "Why not write another?"

Conrad's second novel, *An Outcast of the Islands,* which dealt with the earlier history of certain characters in *Almayer's Folly,* appeared in 1896. Conrad next turned from the Eastern lands and waters of those two novels and revived a memory of his own days at sea—a voyage he made as second officer on the sailing ship *Narcissus* from Bombay, by way of the Cape of Good Hope, to Dunkirk, April 28-October 16, 1884. The men of the crew on that voyage, including a Negro who died at sea, served him as his characters, and his story became *The Nigger of the "Narcissus."* "After writing the last words of that book, in the revulsion of feeling before the accomplished task, I understood that I had done with the sea, and that henceforth I had to be a writer," he wrote in a later note to the novel. *The Nigger* was serialized in *The New Review,* edited by W. E. Henley, August-December 1897, and at the end of the last installment was printed the "Preface" in which Conrad stated his creed and conception of his art. (This appears in the present volume on pages 705-10.) The completed book was published on November 30, 1897, by Dodd, Mead and Co., in New York, under the title *The Children of the Sea: A Tale of the Forecastle,* and two days later by Heinemann in London—as eventually in 1914 by Doubleday, Page and Co. in New York—under its original and permanent title.

The book enlarged the number of Conrad's admirers, who now came to include Henry James, Stephen Crane, H. G. Wells, John Galsworthy, George Gissing, Harold Frederic, and R. B. Cunninghame Graham; and while it did not bring Conrad the public success or security he needed (these were not to come for another fifteen years), it convinced him of his vocation in literature and probably remained his own favorite among his works. In a "Note to My Readers in America," he later repeated what he had frequently said of it: "It is the book by which, not as a novelist perhaps, but as an artist striving for the utmost sincerity of expression, I am willing to stand or fall. Its pages are the tribute of my unalterable and profound affection for the ships, the seamen, the winds and the great sea—the moulders of my youth, the companions of the best years of my life." Henry James, in a letter to Edmund Gosse in 1902, said of it: "*The Nigger of the 'Narcissus'* is in my opinion the very finest and strongest picture of the sea and sea-life that our language possesses—the masterpiece in a whole great class; and *Lord Jim* runs it very close." The book remains, if not Conrad's greatest or most ambitious, one of his most perfectly realized and poetically conceived works; and if it invites a classification of Conrad's talent as that of a sea-writer, to which he came so strongly to object (a classification corrected by such masterly non-maritime novels as *Nostromo, The Secret Agent, Under Western Eyes,* and *Chance*), the reader will soon discover that it is something more than the tale of a ship at sea, and find in its narrative of human character and ordeal the clue to Conrad's reading of the lesson of human destiny, endurance, and survival.

The revised text of *The Nigger of the "Narcissus,"* published by Doubleday and Company in 1914, is used here.

From that evening when James Wait joined the ship —late for the muster of the crew—to the moment when he left us in the open sea, shrouded in sailcloth, through the open port, I had much to do with him. He was in my watch. A negro in a British forecastle is a lonely being. He has no chums. Yet James Wait, afraid of death and making her his accomplice, was an impostor of some character—mastering our compassion, scornful of our sentimentalism, triumphing over our suspicions.

But in the book he is nothing; he is merely the centre of the ship's collective psychology and the pivot of the action. Yet he, who in the family circle and amongst my friends is familiarly referred to as the Nigger, remains very precious to me. For the book written round him is not the sort of thing that can be attempted more than once in a lifetime. It is the book by which, not as a novelist perhaps, but as an artist striving for the utmost sincerity of expression, I am willing to stand or fall. Its pages are the tribute of my unalterable and profound affection for the ships, the seamen, the winds and the great sea—the moulders of my youth, the companions of the best years of my life.

After writing the last words of that book, in the revulsion of feeling before the accomplished task, I understood that I had done with the sea, and that henceforth I had to be a writer. And almost without laying down the pen I wrote a preface, trying to express the spirit in which I was entering on the task of my new life. That preface on advice (which I now think was wrong) was never published with the book. But the late W. E. Henley, who had the courage at that time (1897) to serialize my "Nigger" in the *New Review* judged it worthy to be printed as an afterword at the end of the last instalment of the tale.

I am glad that this book which means so much to me is coming out again, under its proper title of "The Nigger of the *Narcissus*" and under the auspices of my good friends and publishers Doubleday & Co., into the light of publicity.

Half the span of a generation has passed since W. E. Henley, after reading two chapters, sent me a verbal message: "Tell Conrad that if the rest is up to the sample it shall certainly come out in the *New Review*." The most gratifying recollection of my writer's life!

And here is the Suppressed Preface.*

*1914*

JOSEPH CONRAD

* See pp. 705-710, where the Preface appears as "The Condition of Art."—F. R. K.

# The Nigger of the "Narcissus"

*To EDWARD GARNETT, This Tale About My Friends of the Sea*

## I

MR. BAKER, chief mate of the ship *Narcissus*, stepped in one stride out of his lighted cabin into the darkness of the quarter-deck. Above his head, on the break of the poop, the night-watchman rang a double stroke. It was nine o'clock. Mr. Baker, speaking up to the man above him, asked:—"Are all the hands aboard, Knowles?"

The man limped down the ladder, then said reflectively:—"I think so, sir. All our old chaps are there, and a lot of new men has come. . . . They must be all there."

"Tell the boatswain to send all hands aft," went on Mr. Baker; "and tell one of the youngsters to bring a good lamp here. I want to muster our crowd."

The main deck was dark aft, but halfway from forward, through the open doors of the forecastle, two streaks of brilliant light cut the shadow of the quiet night that lay upon the ship. A hum of voices was heard there, while port and starboard, in the illuminated doorways, silhouettes of moving men appeared for a moment, very black, without relief, like figures cut out of sheet tin. The ship was ready for sea. The carpenter had driven in the last wedge of the main-hatch battens, and, throwing down his maul, had wiped his face with great deliberation, just on the stroke of five. The decks had been swept, the windlass oiled and made

294

ready to heave up the anchor; the big tow-rope lay in long bights along one side of the main deck, with one end carried up and hung over the bows, in readiness for the tug that would come paddling and hissing noisily, hot and smoky, in the limpid, cool quietness of the early morning. The captain was ashore, where he had been engaging some new hands to make up his full crew; and, the work of the day over, the ship's officers had kept out of the way, glad of a little breathing-time. Soon after dark the few liberty-men and the new hands began to arrive in shore-boats rowed by white-clad Asiatics, who clamoured fiercely for payment before coming alongside the gangway-ladder. The feverish and shrill babble of Eastern language struggled against the masterful tones of tipsy seamen, who argued against brazen claims and dishonest hopes by profane shouts. The resplendent and bestarred peace of the East was torn into squalid tatters by howls of rage and shrieks of lament raised over sums ranging from five annas to half a rupee; and every soul afloat in Bombay Harbour became aware that the new hands were joining the *Narcissus*.

Gradually the distracting noise had subsided. The boats came no longer in splashing clusters of three or four together, but dropped alongside singly, in a subdued buzz of expostulation cut short by a "Not a pice more! You go to the devil!" from some man staggering up the accommodation-ladder—a dark figure, with a long bag poised on the shoulder. In the forecastle the newcomers, upright and swaying amongst corded boxes and bundles of bedding, made friends with the old hands, who sat one above another in the two tiers of bunks, gazing at their future shipmates with glances critical but friendly. The two forecastle lamps were turned up high, and shed an intense hard glare; shore-going round hats were pushed far on the backs of heads, or rolled about on the deck amongst the chain cables; white collars, undone, stuck out on each side of red faces; big arms in white sleeves gesticulated; the growling voices hummed steady amongst bursts of laughter and hoarse calls. "Here, sonny, take that bunk! . . . Don't you do it! . . . What's your last ship? . . . I know her. . . . Three years ago, in Puget Sound. . . . This here berth leaks, I tell you! . . . Come on; give us a chance to swing that chest! . . . Did you bring a bottle, any of you shore toffs? . . . Give us a bit of 'baccy. . . . I know her; her skipper drank himself to death. . . . He was a dandy boy! . . . Liked his lotion inside, he did! . . . No! . . . Hold your row, you chaps! . . . I tell you, you came on board a hooker, where they get their money's worth out of poor Jack by——! . . ."

A little fellow, called Craik and nicknamed Belfast, abused the ship violently, romancing on principle, just to give the new hands something to think over. Archie, sitting aslant on his sea-chest, kept his knees out of the way, and pushed the needle steadily through a white patch in a pair of blue trousers. Men in black jackets and stand-up collars, mixed with men bare-footed, bare-armed, with coloured shirts open on hairy chests, pushed against one another in the middle of the forecastle. The group swayed, reeled, turning upon itself with the motion of a scrimmage, in a haze of tobacco smoke. All were speaking together, swearing at every second word. A Russian Finn, wearing a yellow shirt with pink stripes, stared upwards, dreamy-eyed, from under a mop of tumbled hair. Two young giants with smooth, baby faces—two Scandinavians—helped each other to spread their bedding, silent, and smiling placidly at the tempest of good-humoured and meaningless curses. Old Singleton, the oldest able seaman in the ship, sat apart on the deck right under the lamps, stripped to the waist, tattooed like a cannibal chief all over his powerful chest and enormous biceps. Between the blue and red patterns his white skin gleamed like satin; his bare back was propped against the heel of the bowsprit, and he held a book at arm's length before his big, sunburnt face. With his spectacles and a venerable white beard, he resembled a learned and savage patriarch, the incarnation of barbarian wisdom serene in the blasphemous turmoil of the world. He was intensely absorbed, and as he turned the pages an expression of grave surprise would pass over his rugged features. He was reading "Pelham." The popularity of Bulwer-Lytton in the forecastles of Southern-going ships is a wonderful and bizarre phenomenon. What ideas do his polished and so curiously insincere sentences awaken in the simple minds of the big children who people those dark and wandering places of the earth? What meaning can their rough, inexperienced souls find in the elegant verbiage of his pages? What excitement?— what forgetfulness?—what appeasement? Mystery! Is it the fascination of the incomprehensible?—is it the charm of the impossible? Or are those beings who exist beyond the pale of life stirred by his tales as by an enigmatical disclosure of a resplendent world that exists within the frontier of infamy and filth, within that border of dirt and hunger, of misery and dissipation, that comes down on all sides to the water's edge of the incorruptible ocean, and is the only thing they know of life, the only thing they see of surrounding land— those life long prisoners of the sea? Mystery!

Singleton, who had sailed to the southward since the age of twelve, who in the last forty-five years had lived (as we had calculated from his papers) no more than forty months ashore—old Singleton, who boasted, with the mild composure of long years well spent, that generally from the day he was paid off from one ship till the day he shipped in another he seldom was in a condition to distinguish daylight—old Singleton sat unmoved in the clash of voices and cries, spelling through "Pelham" with slow labour, and lost in an absorption profound enough to resemble a trance. He breathed regularly. Every time he turned the book in his enormous and blackened hands the muscles of his big white arms rolled slightly under the smooth skin. Hidden by the white moustache, his lips, stained with tobacco-juice that trickled down the long beard, moved in inward whisper. His bleared eyes gazed fixedly from behind the glitter of black-rimmed glasses. Opposite to him, and on a level with his face, the ship's cat sat on the barrel of the windlass in the pose of a crouching chimera, blinking its green eyes at its old friend. It seemed to meditate a leap on to the old man's lap over the bent back of the ordinary seaman who sat at Singleton's feet. Young Charley was lean and long-necked. The ridge of his backbone made a chain of small hills under the old shirt. His face of a street-boy—a face precocious, sagacious, and ironic, with deep downward folds on each side of the thin, wide mouth—hung low over his bony knees. He was learning to make a lanyard knot with a bit of an old rope. Small drops of perspiration stood out on his bulging forehead; he sniffed strongly from time to time, glancing out of the corners of his restless eyes at the old seaman, who took no notice of the puzzled youngster muttering at his work.

The noise increased. Little Belfast seemed, in the heavy heat of the forecastle, to boil with facetious fury. His eyes danced; in the crimson of his face, comical as a mask, the mouth yawned black, with strange grimaces. Facing him, a half-undressed man held his sides, and, throwing his head back, laughed with wet eyelashes. Others stared with amazed eyes. Men sitting doubled up in the upper bunks smoked short pipes, swinging bare brown feet above the heads of those who, sprawling below on sea-chests, listened, smiling stupidly or scornfully. Over the white rims of berths stuck out heads with blinking eyes; but the bodies were lost in the gloom of those places, that resembled narrow niches for coffins in a whitewashed and lighted mortuary. Voices buzzed louder. Archie, with compressed lips, drew himself in, seemed to shrink into a smaller space, and sewed steadily, industrious and dumb. Belfast shrieked like an inspired Dervish:—

". . . So I seez to him, boys, seez I, 'Beggin' yer pardon, sorr,' seez I to that second mate of that steamer—'beggin' your-r-r pardon, sorr, the Board of Trade must 'ave been drunk when they granted you your certificate!' 'What do you say, you—!' seez he, comin' at me like a mad bull . . . all in his white clothes; and I up with my tar-pot and capsizes it all over his blamed lovely face and his lovely jacket. . . . 'Take that!' seez I. 'I am a sailor, anyhow, you nosing, skipper-licking, useless, sooperfloos bridge-stanchion, you! That's the kind of man I am!' shouts I. . . . You should have seed him skip, boys! Drowned, blind with tar, he was! So . . ."

"Don't 'ee believe him! He never upset no tar; I was there!" shouted somebody. The two Norwegians sat on a chest side by side, alike and placid, resembling a pair of love-birds on a perch, and with round eyes stared innocently; but the Russian Finn, in the racket of explosive shouts and rolling laughter, remained motionless, limp and dull, like a deaf man without a backbone. Near him Archie smiled at his needle. A broad-chested, slow-eyed newcomer spoke deliberately to Belfast during an exhausted lull in the noise:—"I

wonder any of the mates here are alive yet with such
a chap as you on board! I concloode they ain't that bad
now, if you had the taming of them, sonny."

"Not bad! Not bad!" screamed Belfast. "If it wasn't
for us sticking together. . . . Not bad! They ain't
never bad when they ain't got a chawnce, blast their
black 'arts. . . ." He foamed, whirling his arms, then
suddenly grinned and, taking a tablet of black tobacco
out of his pocket, bit a piece off with a funny show of
ferocity. Another new hand—a man with shifty eyes
and a yellow hatchet face, who had been listening
open-mouthed in the shadow of the midship locker
—observed in a squeaky voice:—"Well, it's a 'ome-
ward trip, anyhow. Bad or good, I can do it on my 'ed
—s'long as I get 'ome. And I can look after my rights!
I will show 'em!" All the heads turned towards him.
Only the ordinary seaman and the cat took no notice.
He stood with arms akimbo, a little fellow with white
eyelashes. He looked as if he had known all the deg-
radations and all the furies. He looked as if he had
been cuffed, kicked, rolled in the mud; he looked as if
he had been scratched, spat upon, pelted with unmentionable filth . . . and he smiled with a sense of security at the faces around. His ears were bending down
under the weight of his battered felt hat. The torn tails
of his black coat flapped in fringes about the calves
of his legs. He unbuttoned the only two buttons that
remained and every one saw that he had no shirt under
it. It was his deserved misfortune that those rags which
nobody could possibly be supposed to own looked
on him as if they had been stolen. His neck was long
and thin; his eyelids were red; rare hairs hung about
his jaws; his shoulders were peaked and drooped like
the broken wings of a bird; all his left side was caked
with mud which showed that he had lately slept in a
wet ditch. He had saved his inefficient carcass from

violent destruction by running away from an American
ship where, in a moment of forgetful folly, he had
dared to engage himself; and he had knocked about
for a fortnight ashore in the native quarter, cadging
for drinks, starving, sleeping on rubbish-heaps, wandering in sunshine: a startling visitor from a world of
nightmares. He stood repulsive and smiling in the sudden silence. This clean white forecastle was his refuge;
the place where he could be lazy; where he could wallow, and lie and eat—and curse the food he ate; where
he could display his talents for shirking work, for
cheating, for cadging; where he could find surely some
one to wheedle and some one to bully—and where he
would be paid for doing all this. They all knew him. Is
there a spot on earth where such a man is unknown,
an ominous survival testifying to the eternal fitness of
lies and impudence? A taciturn long-armed shellback,
with hooked fingers, who had been lying on his back
smoking, turned in his bed to examine him dispassionately, then, over his head, sent a long jet of clear
saliva towards the door. They all knew him! He was
the man that cannot steer, that cannot splice, that
dodges the work on dark nights; that, aloft, holds on
frantically with both arms and legs, and swears at the
wind, the sleet, the darkness; the man who curses the
sea while others work. The man who is the last out and
the first in when all hands are called. The man who
can't do most things and won't do the rest. The pet of
philanthropists and self-seeking landlubbers. The sympathetic and deserving creature that knows all about
his rights, but knows nothing of courage, of endurance,
and of the unexpressed faith, of the unspoken loyalty
that knits together a ship's company. The independent
offspring of the ignoble freedom of the slums full of
disdain and hate for the austere servitude of the sea.

Some one cried at him: "What's your name?"—

"Donkin," he said, looking round with cheerful effron-
tery.—"What are you?" asked another voice.—"Why,
a sailor like you, old man," he replied, in a tone that
meant to be hearty but was impudent.—"Blamme if
you don't look a blamed sight worse than a broken-
down fireman," was the comment in a convinced mutter. Charley lifted his head and piped in a cheeky
voice: "He is a man and a sailor"—then wiping his nose
with the back of his hand bent down industriously over
his bit of rope. A few laughed. Others stared doubt-
fully. The ragged newcomer was indignant—"That's a
fine way to welcome a chap into a fo'c'sle," he snarled.
"Are you men or a lot of 'artless cannybals?"—"Don't
take your shirt off for a word, shipmate," called out
Belfast, jumping up in front, fiery, menacing, and
friendly at the same time.—"Is that 'ere bloke blind?"
asked the indomitable scarecrow, looking right and left
with affected surprise. "Can't 'ee see I 'aven't got no
shirt?"

He held both his arms out crosswise and shook the
rags that hung over his bones with dramatic effect.

"'Cos why?" he continued very loud. "The bloody
Yankees been tryin' to jump my guts out 'cos I stood
up for my rights like a good 'un. I am an Englishman,
I am. They set upon me an' I 'ad to run. That's why.
A'n't yer never seed a man 'ard up? Yah! What kind of
blamed ship is this? I'm dead broke. I 'aven't got
nothink. No bag, no bed, no blanket, no shirt—not a
bloomin' rag but what I stand in. But I 'ad the 'art to
stand up agin' them Yankees. 'As any of you 'art enough
to spare a pair of old pants for a chum?"

He knew how to conquer the naïve instincts of that
crowd. In a moment they gave him their compassion,
jocularly, contemptuously, or surlily; and at first it took
the shape of a blanket thrown at him as he stood there
with the white skin of his limbs showing his human kin-

ship through the black fantasy of his rags. Then a pair of old shoes fell at his muddy feet. With a cry:—"From under," a rolled-up pair of canvas trousers, heavy with tar stains, struck him on the shoulder. The gust of their benevolence sent a wave of sentimental pity through their doubting hearts. They were touched by their own readiness to alleviate a shipmate's misery. Voices cried:—"We will fit you out, old man." Murmurs: "Never seed seech a hard case. . . . Poor beggar. . . . I've got an old singlet. . . . Will that be of any use to you? . . . Take it, matey. . . ." Those friendly murmurs filled the forecastle. He pawed around with his naked foot, gathering the things in a heap and looked about for more. Unemotional Archie perfunctorily contributed to the pile an old cloth cap with the peak torn off. Old Singleton, lost in the serene regions of fiction, read on unheeding. Charley, pitiless with the wisdom of youth, squeaked:—"If you want brass buttons for your new unyforms I've got two for you." The filthy object of universal charity shook his fist at the youngster.—"I'll make you keep this 'ere fo'c'sle clean, young feller," he snarled viciously. "Never you fear. I will learn you to be civil to an able seaman, you ignerant ass." He glared harmfully, but saw Singleton shut his book, and his little beady eyes began to roam from berth to berth.—"Take that bunk by the door there—it's pretty fair," suggested Belfast. So advised, he gathered the gifts at his feet, pressed them in a bundle against his breast, then looked cautiously at the Russian Finn, who stood on one side with an unconscious gaze, contemplating, perhaps, one of those weird visions that haunt the men of his race.—"Get out of my road, Dutchy," said the victim of Yankee brutality. The Finn did not move—did not hear. "Get out, blast ye," shouted the other, shoving him aside with his elbow. "Get out, you blanked deaf and

dumb fool. Get out." The man staggered, recovered
himself, and gazed at the speaker in silence.—"Those
damned furriners should be kept under," opined the
amiable Donkin to the forecastle. "If you don't teach
'em their place they put on you like anythink." He
flung all his worldly possessions into the empty bed-
place, gauged with another shrewd look the risks of the
proceeding, then leaped up to the Finn, who stood pensive and dull.—"I'll teach you to swell around," he
yelled. "I'll plug your eyes for you, you blooming
squarehead." Most of the men were now in their bunks
and the two had the forecastle clear to themselves. The
development of the destitute Donkin aroused interest.
He danced all in tatters before the amazed Finn, squaring from a distance at the heavy, unmoved face. One
or two men cried encouragingly: "Go it, Whitechapel!"
settling themselves luxuriously in their beds to survey
the fight. Others shouted: "Shut yer row! . . . Go an'
put yer 'ed in a bag! . . ." The hubbub was recom-
mencing. Suddenly many heavy blows struck with a
handspike on the deck above boomed like discharges of
small cannon through the forecastle. Then the boatswain's voice rose outside the door with an authoritative note in its drawl:—"D'ye hear, below there? Lay
aft! Lay aft to muster all hands!"

There was a moment of surprised stillness. Then the
forecastle floor disappeared under men whose bare feet
flopped on the planks as they sprang clear out of their
berths. Caps were rooted for amongst tumbled blankets. Some, yawning, buttoned waistbands. Half-smoked
pipes were knocked hurriedly against woodwork and
stuffed under pillows. Voices growled:—"What's
up? . . . Is there no rest for us?" Donkin yelped:—
"If that's the way of this ship, we'll 'ave to change all
that. . . . You leave me alone. . . . I will soon. . . ."
None of the crowd noticed him. They were lurching in

twos and threes through the doors, after the manner of
merchant Jacks who cannot go out of a door fairly, like
mere landsmen. The votary of change followed them.
Singleton, struggling into his jacket, came last, tall and
fatherly, bearing high his head of a weather-beaten
sage on the body of an old athlete. Only Charley remained alone in the white glare of the empty place,
sitting between the two rows of iron links that stretched
into the narrow gloom forward. He pulled hard at the
strands in a hurried endeavour to finish his knot. Suddenly he started up, flung the rope at the cat, and
skipped after the black tom which went off leaping
sedately over chain compressors, with its tail carried
stiff and upright, like a small flagpole.

Outside the glare of the steaming forecastle the
serene purity of the night enveloped the seamen with
its soothing breath, with its tepid breath flowing under
the stars that hung countless above the mastheads in a
thin cloud of luminous dust. On the town side the blackness of the water was streaked with trails of light which
undulated gently on slight ripples, similar to filaments
that float rooted to the shore. Rows of other lights stood
away in straight lines as if drawn up on parade between
towering buildings; but on the other side of the harbour sombre hills arched high their black spines, on
which, here and there, the point of a star resembled a
spark fallen from the sky. Far off, Byculla way, the
electric lamps at the dock gates shone on the end of
lofty standards with a glow blinding and frigid like captive ghosts of some evil moons. Scattered all over the
dark polish of the roadstead, the ships at anchor floated
in perfect stillness under the feeble gleam of their
riding-lights, looming up, opaque and bulky, like
strange and monumental structures abandoned by men
to an everlasting repose.

Before the cabin door Mr. Baker was mustering the

crew. As they stumbled and lurched along past the mainmast, they could see aft his round, broad face with a white paper before it, and beside his shoulder the sleepy head, with dropped eyelids, of the boy, who held, suspended at the end of his raised arm, the luminous globe of a lamp. Even before the shuffle of naked soles had ceased along the decks, the mate began to call over the names. He called distinctly in a serious tone befitting this roll-call to unquiet loneliness, to inglorious and obscure struggle, or to the more trying endurance of small privations and wearisome duties. As the chief mate read out a name, one of the men would answer: "Yes, sir!" or "Here!" and, detaching himself from the shadowy mob of heads visible above the blackness of starboard bulwarks, would step barefooted into the circle of light, and in two noiseless strides pass into the shadows on the port side of the quarter-deck. They answered in divers tones: in thick mutters, in clear, ringing voices; and some, as if the whole thing had been an outrage on their feelings, used an injured intonation: for discipline is not ceremonious in merchant ships, where the sense of hierarchy is weak, and where all feel themselves equal before the unconcerned immensity of the sea and the exacting appeal of the work.

Mr. Baker read on steadily:—"Hanse—Campbell —Smith—Wamibo. Now, then, Wamibo. Why don't you answer? Always got to call your name twice." The Finn emitted at last an uncouth grunt, and, stepping out, passed through the patch of light, weird and gaudy, with the face of a man marching through a dream. The mate went on faster:—"Craik—Singleton—Donkin. . . . O Lord!" he involuntarily ejaculated as the incredibly dilapidated figure appeared in the light. It stopped; it uncovered pale gums and long, upper teeth in a malevolent grin.—"Is there anythink wrong with

me, Mister Mate?" it asked, with a flavour of insolence
in the forced simplicity of its tone. On both sides of the
deck subdued titters were heard.—"That'll do. Go
over," growled Mr. Baker, fixing the new hand with
steady blue eyes. And Donkin vanished suddenly out
of the light into the dark group of mustered men, to be
slapped on the back and to hear flattering whispers:—
"He ain't afeard, he'll give sport to 'em, see if he don't.
. . . Reg'lar Punch and Judy show. . . . Did ye see
the mate start at him? . . . Well! Damme, if I
ever! . . ."

The last man had gone over, and there was a moment
of silence while the mate peered at his list.—"Sixteen,
seventeen," he muttered. "I am one hand short, bo'sun,"
he said aloud. The big west-countryman at his elbow,
swarthy and bearded like a gigantic Spaniard, said in a
rumbling bass:—"There's no one left forward, sir. I had
a look round. He ain't aboard, but he may turn up before daylight."—"Ay. He may or he may not," commented the mate, "can't make out that last name. It's
all a smudge. . . . That will do, men. Go below."

The distinct and motionless group stirred, broke up,
began to move forward.

"Wait!" cried a deep, ringing voice.

All stood still. Mr. Baker, who had turned away
yawning, spun round open-mouthed. At last, furious,
he blurted out:—"What's this? Who said 'Wait'?
What . . ."

But he saw a tall figure standing on the rail. It came
down and pushed through the crowd, marching with a
heavy tread towards the light on the quarter-deck.
Then again the sonorous voice said with insistence:—
"Wait!" The lamplight lit up the man's body. He was
tall. His head was away up in the shadows of lifeboats
that stood on skids above the deck. The whites of his
eyes and his teeth gleamed distinctly, but the face was

indistinguishable. His hands were big and seemed gloved.

Mr. Baker advanced intrepidly. "Who are you? How dare you . . ." he began.

The boy, amazed like the rest, raised the light to the man's face. It was black. A surprised hum—a faint hum that sounded like the suppressed mutter of the word "Nigger"—ran along the deck and escaped out into the night. The nigger seemed not to hear. He balanced himself where he stood in a swagger that marked time. After a moment he said calmly:—"My name is Wait— James Wait."

"Oh!" said Mr. Baker. Then, after a few seconds of smouldering silence, his temper blazed out. "Ah! Your name is Wait. What of that? What do you want? What do you mean, coming shouting here?"

The nigger was calm, cool, towering, superb. The men had approached and stood behind him in a body. He overtopped the tallest by half a head. He said: "I belong to the ship." He enunciated distinctly, with soft precision. The deep, rolling tones of his voice filled the deck without effort. He was naturally scornful, unaffectedly condescending, as if from his height of six foot three he had surveyed all the vastness of human folly and had made up his mind not to be too hard on it. He went on:—"The captain shipped me this morning. I couldn't get aboard sooner. I saw you all aft as I came up the ladder, and could see directly you were mustering the crew. Naturally I called out my name. I thought you had it on your list, and would understand. You misapprehended." He stopped short. The folly around him was confounded. He was right as ever, and as ever ready to forgive. The disdainful tones had ceased, and, breathing heavily, he stood still, surrounded by all these white men. He held his head up in the glare of the lamp—a head vigorously modelled into deep shadows and shining lights—a head powerful and misshapen with a tormented and flattened face—a face pathetic and brutal: the tragic, the mysterious, the repulsive mask of a nigger's soul.

Mr. Baker, recovering his composure, looked at the paper close. "Oh, yes; that's so. All right, Wait. Take your gear forward," he said.

Suddenly the nigger's eyes rolled wildly, became all whites. He put his hand to his side and coughed twice, a cough metallic, hollow, and tremendously loud; it resounded like two explosions in a vault; the dome of the sky rang to it, and the iron plates of the ship's bulwarks seemed to vibrate in unison, then he marched off forward with the others. The officers lingering by the cabin door could hear him say: "Won't some of you chaps lend a hand with my dunnage? I've got a chest and a bag." The words, spoken sonorously, with an even intonation, were heard all over the ship, and the question was put in a manner that made refusal impossible. The short, quick shuffle of men carrying something heavy went away forward, but the tall figure of the nigger lingered by the main hatch in a knot of smaller shapes. Again he was heard asking: "Is your cook a coloured gentleman?" Then a disappointed and disapproving "Ah! h'm!" was his comment upon the information that the cook happened to be a mere white man. Yet, as they went all together towards the forecastle, he condescended to put his head through the galley door and boom out inside a magnificent "Good evening, doctor!" that made all the saucepans ring. In the dim light the cook dozed on the coal locker in front of the captain's supper. He jumped up as if he had been cut with a whip, and dashed wildly on deck to see the backs of several men going away laughing. Afterwards, when talking about that voyage, he used to say:—"The poor fellow had scared me. I thought I had seen the

devil." The cook had been seven years in the ship with
the same captain. He was a serious-minded man with a
wife and three children, whose society he enjoyed on
an average one month out of twelve. When on shore
he took his family to church twice every Sunday. At
sea he went to sleep every evening with his lamp
turned up full, a pipe in his mouth, and an open Bible
in his hand. Some one had always to go during the
night to put out the light, take the book from his hand,
and the pipe from between his teeth. "For"—Belfast
used to say, irritated and complaining—"some night,
you stupid cookie, you'll swallow your ould clay, and
we will have no cook."—"Ah! sonny, I am ready for
my Maker's call . . . wish you all were," the other
would answer with a benign serenity that was altogether imbecile and touching. Belfast outside the galley
door danced with vexation. "You holy fool! I don't
want you to die," he howled, looking up with furious,
quivering face and tender eyes. "What's the hurry?
You blessed wooden-headed ould heretic, the divvle
will have you soon enough. Think of Us . . . of Us
. . . of Us!" And he would go away, stamping, spitting
aside, disgusted and worried; while the other, stepping
out, saucepan in hand, hot, begrimed and placid,
watched with a superior, cocksure smile the back of
this "queer little man" reeling in a rage. They were
great friends.

Mr. Baker, lounging over the after-hatch, sniffed
the humid night in the company of the second mate.—
"Those West India niggers run fine and large—some
of them . . . Ough! . . . Don't they? A fine, big man
that, Mr. Creighton. Feel him on a rope. Hey? Ough!
I will take him into my watch, I think." The second
mate, a fair, gentlemanly young fellow, with a resolute
face and a splendid physique, observed quietly that it
was just about what he expected. There could be felt

in his tone some slight bitterness which Mr. Baker very kindly set himself to argue away. "Come, come, young man," he said, grunting between the words. "Come! Don't be too greedy. You had that big Finn in your watch all the voyage. I will do what's fair. You may have those two young Scandinavians and I . . . Ough! . . . I get the nigger, and will take that . . . Ough! that cheeky costermonger chap in a black frock-coat. I'll make him . . . Ough! . . . make him toe the mark, or my . . . Ough! . . . name isn't Baker. Ough! Ough! Ough!"

He grunted thrice—ferociously. He had that trick of grunting so between his words and at the end of sentences. It was a fine, effective grunt that went well with his menacing utterance, with his heavy, bull-necked frame, his jerky, rolling gait; with his big, seamed face, his steady eyes, and sardonic mouth. But its effect had been long ago discounted by the men. They liked him; Belfast—who was a favourite, and knew it—mimicked him, not quite behind his back. Charley—but with greater caution—imitated his rolling gait. Some of his sayings became established, daily quotations in the fore-castle. Popularity can go no farther! Besides, all hands were ready to admit that on a fitting occasion the mate could "jump down a fellow's throat in a reg'lar Western Ocean style."

Now he was giving his last orders. "Ough! . . . You, Knowles! Call all hands at four. I want . . . Ough! . . . to heave short before the tug comes. Look out for the captain. I am going to lie down in my clothes. . . . Ough! . . . Call me when you see the boat coming. Ough! Ough! . . . The old man is sure to have some-thing to say when he gets aboard," he remarked to Creighton. "Well, good-night. . . . Ough! A long day before us to-morrow. . . . Ough! . . . Better turn in now. Ough. Ough!"

Upon the dark deck a band of light flashed, then a door slammed, and Mr. Baker was gone into his neat cabin. Young Creighton stood leaning over the rail, and looked dreamily into the night of the East. And he saw in it a long country lane, a lane of waving leaves and dancing sunshine. He saw stirring boughs of old trees outspread, and framing in their arch the tender, the caressing blueness of an English sky. And through the arch a girl in a light dress, smiling under a sunshade, seemed to be stepping out of the tender sky.

At the other end of the ship the forecastle, with only one lamp burning now, was going to sleep in a dim emptiness traversed by loud breathings, by sudden short sighs. The double row of berths yawned black, like graves tenanted by uneasy corpses. Here and there a curtain of gaudy chintz, half drawn, marked the resting-place of a sybarite. A leg hung over the edge very white and lifeless. An arm stuck straight out with a dark palm turned up, and thick fingers half closed. Two light snores, that did not synchronise, quarrelled in funny dialogue. Singleton stripped again—the old man suffered much from prickly heat—stood cooling his back in the doorway, with his arms crossed on his bare and adorned chest. His head touched the beam of the deck above. The nigger, half undressed, was busy casting adrift the lashing of his box, and spreading his bedding in an upper berth. He moved about in his socks, tall and noiseless, with a pair of braces beating about his calves. Amongst the shadows of stanchions and bowsprit, Donkin munched a piece of hard ship's bread, sitting on the deck with upturned feet and restless eyes; he held the biscuit up before his mouth in the whole fist and snapped his jaws at it with a raging face. Crumbs fell between his outspread legs. Then he got up.

"Where's our water-cask?" he asked in a contained voice.

Singleton, without a word, pointed with a big hand that held a short smouldering pipe. Donkin bent over the cask, drank out of the tin, splashing the water, turned round and noticed the nigger looking at him over the shoulder with calm loftiness. He moved up sideways.

"There's a blooming supper for a man," he whispered bitterly. "My dorg at 'ome wouldn't 'ave it. It's fit enouf for you an' me. 'Ere's a big ship's fo'c'sle! . . . Not a blooming scrap of meat in the kids. I've looked in all the lockers. . . ."

The nigger stared like a man addressed unexpectedly in a foreign language. Donkin changed his tone:—"Giv' us a bit of 'baccy, mate," he breathed out confidentially, "I 'aven't 'ad smoke or chew for the last month. I am rampin' mad for it. Come on, old man!"

"Don't be familiar," said the nigger. Donkin started and sat down on a chest near by, out of sheer surprise. "We haven't kept pigs together," continued James Wait in a deep undertone. "Here's your tobacco." Then, after a pause, he inquired:—"What ship?"—"*Golden State,*" muttered Donkin indistinctly, biting the tobacco. The nigger whistled low.—"Ran?" he said curtly. Donkin nodded: one of his cheeks bulged out. "In course I ran," he mumbled. "They booted the life hout of one Dago chap on the passage 'ere, then started on me. I cleared hout 'ere."—"Left your dunnage behind?"—"Yes, dunnage and money," answered Donkin, raising his voice a little; "I got nothink. No clothes, no bed. A bandy legged little Hirish chap 'oro 'as givo mo a blan ket. . . . Think I'll go an' sleep in the fore topmast staysail to-night."

He went on deck trailing behind his back a corner of the blanket. Singleton, without a glance, moved slightly aside to let him pass. The nigger put away his shore togs and sat in clean working clothes on his box, one arm stretched over his knees. After staring at Singleton for some time he asked without emphasis:—"What kind of ship is this? Pretty fair? Eh?"

Singleton didn't stir. A long while after he said, with unmoved face:—"Ship! . . . Ships are all right. It is the men in them!"

He went on smoking in the profound silence. The wisdom of half a century spent in listening to the thunder of the waves had spoken unconsciously through his old lips. The cat purred on the windlass. Then James Wait had a fit of roaring, rattling cough, that shook him, tossed him like a hurricane, and flung him panting with staring eyes headlong on his sea-chest. Several men woke up. One said sleepily out of his bunk: "'Struth! what a blamed row!"—"I have a cold on my chest," gasped Wait.—"Cold! you call it," grumbled the man; "Should think 'twas something more. . . ."—"Oh! you think so," said the nigger upright and loftily scornful again. He climbed into his berth and began coughing persistently while he put his head out to glare all round the forecastle. There was no further protest. He fell back on the pillow, and could be heard there wheezing regularly like a man oppressed in his sleep.

Singleton stood at the door with his face to the light and his back to the darkness. And alone in the dim emptiness of the sleeping forecastle he appeared bigger, colossal, very old; old as Father Time himself, who should have come there into this place as quiet as a sepulchre to contemplate with patient eyes the short victory of sleep, the consoler. Yet he was only a child of time, a lonely relic of a devoured and forgotten generation. He stood, still strong, as ever unthinking; a ready man with a vast empty past and with no future, with his childlike impulses and his man's passions already dead within his tattooed breast. The men who could understand his silence were gone—those men who knew how to exist beyond the pale of life and within sight of eternity. They had been strong, as those are strong who know neither doubts nor hopes. They had been impatient and enduring, turbulent and devoted, unruly and faithful. Well-meaning people had tried to represent those men as whining over every mouthful of their food; as going about their work in fear of their lives. But in truth they had been men who knew toil, privation, violence, debauchery—but knew not fear, and had no desire of spite in their hearts. Men hard to manage, but easy to inspire; voiceless men—but men enough to scorn in their hearts the sentimental voices that bewailed the hardness of their fate. It was a fate unique and their own; the capacity to bear it appeared to them the privilege of the chosen! Their generation lived inarticulate and indispensable, without knowing the sweetness of affections or the refuge of a home— and died free from the dark menace of a narrow grave. Thy were the everlasting children of the mysterious sea. Their successors are the grown-up children of a discontented earth. They are less naughty, but less innocent; less profane, but perhaps also less believing; and if they have learned how to speak they have also learned how to whine. But the others were strong and mute; they were effaced, bowed and enduring, like stone caryatides that hold up in the night the lighted halls of a resplendent and glorious edifice. They are gone now—and it does not matter. The sea and the earth are unfaithful to their children: a truth, a faith, a generation of men goes—and is forgotten, and it does not matter! Except, perhaps, to the few of those who believed the truth, confessed the faith—or loved the men.

A breeze was coming. The ship that had been lying tide-rode swung to a heavier puff; and suddenly the slack of the chain cable between the windlass and the hawse-pipe clinked, slipped forward an inch, and rose gently off the deck with a startling suggestion as of unsuspected life that had been lurking stealthily in the iron. In the hawse-pipe the grinding links sent through the ship a sound like a low groan of a man sighing under a burden. The strain came on the windlass, the chain tautened like a string, vibrated—and the handle of the screw-brake moved in slight jerks. Singleton stepped forward.

Till then he had been standing meditative and unthinking, reposeful and hopeless, with a face grim and blank—a sixty-year-old child of the mysterious sea. The thoughts of all his lifetime could have been expressed in six words, but the stir of those things that were as much part of his existence as his beating heart called up a gleam of alert understanding upon the sternness of his aged face. The flame of the lamp swayed, and the old man, with knitted and bushy eyebrows, stood over the brake, watchful and motionless in the wild saraband of dancing shadows. Then the ship, obedient to the call of her anchor, forged ahead slightly and eased the strain. The cable relieved, hung down, and after swaying imperceptibly to and fro dropped with a loud tap on the hard wood planks. Singleton seized the high lever, and, by a violent throw forward of his body, wrung out another half-turn from the brake. He recovered himself, breathed largely, and remained for a while glaring down at the powerful and compact engine that squatted on the deck at his feet like some quiet monster—a creature amazing and tame.

"You . . . hold!" he growled at it masterfully, in the incult tangle of his white beard.

## II

Next morning, at daylight, the *Narcissus* went to sea. A slight haze blurred the horizon. Outside the har-

bour the measureless expanse of smooth water lay
sparkling like a floor of jewels, and as empty as the sky.
The short black tug gave a pluck to windward, in the
usual way, then let go the rope, and hovered for a moment on the quarter with her engines stopped; while
the slim, long hull of the ship moved ahead slowly under lower topsails. The loose upper canvas blew out in
the breeze with soft round contours, resembling small
white clouds snared in the maze of ropes. Then the
sheets were hauled home, the yards hoisted, and the
ship became a high and lonely pyramid, gliding, all
shining and white, through the sunlit mist. The tug
turned short round and went away towards the land.
Twenty-six pairs of eyes watched her low broad stern
crawling languidly over the smooth swell between the
two paddle-wheels that turned fast, beating the water
with fierce hurry. She resembled an enormous and
aquatic black beetle, surprised by the light, overwhelmed by the sunshine, trying to escape with ineffectual effort into the distant gloom of the land. She left
a lingering smudge of smoke on the sky, and two vanishing trails of foam on the water. On the place where
she had stopped a round black patch of soot remained,
undulating on the swell—an unclean mark of the creature's rest.

The *Narcissus* left alone, heading south, seemed to
stand resplendent and still upon the restless sea, under
the moving sun. Flakes of foam swept past her sides; the
water struck her with flashing blows; the land glided
away slowly fading; a few birds screamed on motionless wings over the swaying mastheads. But soon the
land disappeared, the birds went away; and to the west
the pointed sail of an Arab dhow running for Bombay
rose triangular and upright above the sharp edge of the
horizon, lingered, and vanished like an illusion. Then
the ship's wake, long and straight, stretched itself out

through a day of immense solitude. The setting sun, burning on the level of the water, flamed crimson below the blackness of heavy rain clouds. The sunset squall, coming up from behind, dissolved itself into the short deluge of a hissing shower. It left the ship glistening from trucks to waterline, and with darkened sails. She ran easily before a fair monsoon, with her decks cleared for the night; and, moving along with her, was heard the sustained and monotonous swishing of the waves, mingled with the low whispers of men mustered aft for the setting of watches; the short plaint of some block aloft; or, now and then, a loud sigh of wind.

Mr. Baker, coming out of his cabin, called out the first name sharply before closing the door behind him. He was going to take charge of the deck. On the homeward trip, according to an old custom of the sea, the chief officer takes the first night-watch—from eight till midnight. So Mr. Baker, after he had heard the last "Yes, sir!" said moodily, "Relieve the wheel and lookout"; and climbed with heavy feet the poop ladder to windward. Soon after Mr. Creighton came down, whistling softly, and went into the cabin. On the doorstep the steward lounged, in slippers, meditative, and with his shirt-sleeves rolled up to the armpits. On the main deck the cook, locking up the galley doors, had an altercation with young Charley about a pair of socks. He could be heard saying impressively, in the darkness amidships: "You don't deserve a kindness. I've been drying them for you, and now you complain about the holes—and you swear, too! Right in front of me! If I hadn't been a Christian—which you ain't, you young ruffian—I would give you a clout on the head. . . . Go away!" Men in couples or threes stood pensive or moved silently along the bulwarks in the waist. The first busy day of a homeward passage was sinking into the dull peace of resumed routine. Aft, on the high poop, Mr.

Baker walked shuffling and grunted to himself in the pauses of his thoughts. Forward, the look-out man, erect between the flukes of the two anchors, hummed an endless tune, keeping his eyes fixed dutifully ahead in a vacant stare. A multitude of stars coming out into the clear night peopled the emptiness of the sky. They glittered, as if alive above the sea; they surrounded the running ship on all sides; more intense than the eyes of a staring crowd, and as inscrutable as the souls of men.

The passage had begun, and the ship, a fragment detached from the earth, went on lonely and swift like a small planet. Round her the abysses of sky and sea met in an unattainable frontier. A great circular solitude moved with her, ever changing and ever the same, always monotonous and always imposing. Now and then another wandering white speck, burdened with life, appeared far off—disappeared; intent on its own destiny. The sun looked upon her all day, and every morning rose with a burning, round stare of undying curiosity. She had her own future; she was alive with the lives of those beings who trod her decks; like that earth which had given her up to the sea, she had an intolerable load of regrets and hopes. On her lived timid truth and audacious lies; and, like the earth, she was unconscious, fair to see—and condemned by men to an ignoble fate. The august loneliness of her path lent dignity to the sordid inspiration of her pilgrimage. She drove foaming to the southward, as if guided by the courage of a high endeavour. The smiling greatness of the sea dwarfed the extent of time. The days raced after one another, brilliant and quick like the flashes of a lighthouse, and the nights, eventful and short, resembled fleeting dreams.

The men had shaken into their places, and the half-hourly voice of the bells ruled their life of unceasing

care. Night and day the head and shoulders of a seaman could be seen aft by the wheel, outlined high
against sunshine or starlight, very steady above the stir
of revolving spokes. The faces changed, passing in rota-
tion. Youthful faces, bearded faces, dark faces: faces
serene, or faces moody, but all akin with the brother-
hood of the sea; all with the same attentive expression
of eyes, carefully watching the compass or the sails.
Captain Allistoun, serious, and with an old red muffler
round his throat, all day long pervaded the poop. At
night, many times he rose out of the darkness of the
companion, such as a phantom above a grave, and stood
watchful and mute under the stars, his night-shirt fluttering like a flag—then, without a sound, sank down
again. He was born on the shores of the Pentland Firth.
In his youth he attained the rank of harpooner in Peter-
head whalers. When he spoke of that time his restless
grey eyes became still and cold, like the loom of ice.
Afterwards he went into the East Indian trade for
the sake of change. He had commanded the *Narcissus*
since she was built. He loved his ship, and drove her
unmercifully; for his secret ambition was to make her
accomplish some day a brilliantly quick passage which
would be mentioned in nautical papers. He pronounced
his owner's name with a sardonic smile, spoke but seldom to his officers, and reproved errors in a gentle
voice, with words that cut to the quick. His hair was
iron-grey, his face hard and of the colour of pump-
leather. He shaved every morning of his life—at six—
but once (being caught in a fierce hurricane eighty
miles southwest of Mauritius) he had missed three con-
secutive days. He feared naught but an unforgiving
God, and wished to end his days in a little house, with a
plot of ground attached—far in the country—out of
sight of the sea.

He, the ruler of that minute world, seldom descended

from the Olympian heights of his poop. Below him—at his feet, so to speak—common mortals led their busy and insignificant lives. Along the main deck, Mr. Baker grunted in a manner bloodthirsty and innocuous; and kept all our noses to the grindstone, being—as he once remarked—paid for doing that very thing. The men working about the deck were healthy and contented —as most seamen are, when once well out to sea. The true peace of God begins at any spot a thousand miles from the nearest land; and when He sends there the messengers of His might it is not in terrible wrath against crime, presumption, and folly, but paternally, to chasten simple hearts—ignorant hearts that know nothing of life, and beat undisturbed by envy or greed.

In the evening the cleared decks had a reposeful aspect, resembling the autumn of the earth. The sun was sinking to rest, wrapped in a mantle of warm clouds. Forward, on the end of the spare spars, the boatswain and the carpenter sat together with crossed arms; two men friendly, powerful, and deep-chested. Beside them the short, dumpy sailmaker—who had been in the Navy—related, between the whiffs of his pipe, impossible stories about Admirals. Couples tramped backwards and forwards, keeping step and balance without effort, in a confined space. Pigs grunted in the big pigsty. Belfast, leaning thoughtfully on his elbow, above the bars, communed with them through the silence of his meditation. Fellows with shirts open wide on sunburnt breasts sat upon the mooring bits, and all up the steps of the forecastle ladders. By the foremast a few discussed in a circle the characteristics of a gentleman. One said:—"It's money as does it." Another maintained:—"No, it's the way they speak." Lame Knowles stumped up with an unwashed face (he had the distinction of being the dirty man of the forecastle),

and showing a few yellow fangs in a shrewd smile, explained craftily that he "had seen some of their pants."
The backsides of them—he had observed—were thinner than paper from constant sitting down in offices,
yet otherwise they looked first-rate and would last for
years. It was all appearance. "It was," he said, "bloomin' easy to be a gentleman when you had a clean job for
life." They disputed endlessly, obstinate and childish;
they repeated in shouts and with inflamed faces their
amazing arguments; while the soft breeze, eddying
down the enormous cavity of the foresail, distended
above their bare heads, stirred the tumbled hair with a
touch passing and light like an indulgent caress.

They were forgetting their toil, they were forgetting
themselves. The cook approached to hear, and stood
by, beaming with the inward consciousness of his faith,
like a conceited saint unable to forget his glorious reward; Donkin, solitary and brooding over his wrongs on
the forecastle-head, moved closer to catch the drift of
the discussion below him; he turned his sallow face to
the sea, and his thin nostrils moved, sniffing the breeze,
as he lounged negligently by the rail. In the glow of
sunset faces shone with interest, teeth flashed, eyes
sparkled. The walking couples stood still suddenly,
with broad grins; a man, bending over a washtub, sat
up, entranced, with the soapsuds flecking his wet arms.
Even the three petty officers listened leaning back,
comfortably propped, and with superior smiles. Belfast
left off scratching the ear of his favourite pig, and, open
mouthed, tried with eager eyes to have his say. He
lifted his arms, grimacing and baffled. From a distance
Charley screamed at the ring:—"I know about gentlemen more'n any of you. I've been intermit with 'em.
. . . I've blacked their boots." The cook, craning his
neck to hear better, was scandalised. "Keep your mouth
shut when your elders speak, you impudent young

heathen—you." "All right, old Hallelujah, I'm done," answered Charley, soothingly. At some opinion of dirty Knowles, delivered with an air of supernatural cunning, a ripple of laughter ran along, rose like a wave, burst with a startling roar. They stamped with both feet; they turned their shouting faces to the sky; many, spluttering, slapped their thighs; while one or two, bent double, gasped, hugging themselves with both arms like men in pain. The carpenter and the boatswain, without changing their attitude, shook with laughter where they sat; the sailmaker, charged with an anecdote about a Commodore, looked sulky; the cook was wiping his eyes with a greasy rag; and lame Knowles, astonished at his own success, stood in their midst showing a slow smile.

Suddenly the face of Donkin leaning high-shouldered over the after-rail became grave. Something like a weak rattle was heard through the forecastle door. It became a murmur; it ended in a sighing groan. The washerman plunged both his arms into the tub abruptly; the cook became more crestfallen than an exposed backslider; the boatswain moved his shoulders uneasily; the carpenter got up with a spring and walked away—while the sailmaker seemed mentally to give his story up, and began to puff at his pipe with sombre determination. In the blackness of the doorway a pair of eyes glimmered white, and big, and staring. Then James Wait's head protruding, became visible, as if suspended between the two hands that grasped a doorpost on each side of the face. The tassel of his blue woolen nightcap, cocked forward, danced gaily over his left eyelid. He stepped out in a tottering stride. He looked powerful as ever, but showed a strange and affected unsteadiness in his gait; his face was perhaps a trifle thinner, and his eyes appeared rather startlingly prominent. He seemed to hasten the retreat of departing light by his very presence; the setting sun dipped sharply, as though fleeing before our nigger; a black mist emanated from him; a subtle and dismal influence; a something cold and gloomy that floated out and settled on all the faces like a mourning veil. The circle broke up. The joy of laughter died on stiffened lips. There was not a smile left among all the ship's company. Not a word was spoken. Many turned their backs, trying to look unconcerned; others, with averted heads, sent half-reluctant glances out of the corners of their eyes. They resembled criminals conscious of misdeeds more than honest men distracted by doubt; only two or three stared frankly, but stupidly, with lips slightly open. All expected James Wait to say something, and, at the same time, had the air of knowing beforehand what he would say. He leaned his back against the doorpost, and with heavy eyes swept over them a glance domineering and pained, like a sick tyrant overawing a crowd of abject but untrustworthy slaves.

No one went away. They waited in fascinated dread. He said ironically, with gasps between the words:—

"Thank you . . . chaps. You . . . are nice . . . and . . . quiet . . . you are! Yelling so . . . before . . . the door. . . ."

He made a longer pause, during which he worked his ribs in an exaggerated labour of breathing. It was intolerable. Feet were shuffled. Belfast let out a groan; but Donkin above blinked his red eyelids with invisible eyelashes, and smiled bitterly over the nigger's head.

The nigger went on again with surprising ease. He gasped no more, and his voice rang, hollow and loud, as though he had been talking in an empty cavern. He was contemptuously angry.

"I tried to get a wink of sleep. You know I can't sleep o' nights. And you come jabbering near the door here like a blooming lot of old women. . . . You think your-

selves good shipmates. Do you? . . . Much you care
for a dying man!"

Belfast spun away from the pigsty. "Jimmy," he
cried tremulously, "if you hadn't been sick I would—"

He stopped. The nigger waited awhile, then said, in
a gloomy tone:—"You would. . . . What? Go an' fight
another such one as yourself. Leave me alone. It won't
be for long. I'll soon die. . . . It's coming right
enough!"

Men stood around very still and with exasperated
eyes. It was just what they had expected, and hated to
hear, that idea of a stalking death, thrust at them many
times a day like a boast and like a menace by this obnoxious nigger. He seemed to take a pride in that
death which, so far, had attended only upon the ease of
his life; he was overbearing about it, as if no one else
in the world had ever been intimate with such a companion; he paraded it unceasingly before us with an
affectionate persistence that made its presence indubita-
ble, and at the same time incredible. No man could
be suspected of such monstrous friendship! Was he a
reality—or was he a sham—this ever-expected visitor
of Jimmy's? We hesitated between pity and mistrust,
while, on the slightest provocation, he shook before
our eyes the bones of his bothersome and infamous
skeleton. He was for ever trotting him out. He would
talk of that coming death as though it had been already
there, as if it had been walking the deck outside, as if
it would presently come in to sleep in the only empty
bunk; as if it had sat by his side at every meal. It interfered daily with our occupations, with our leisure, with
our amusements. We had no songs and no music in the
evening, because Jimmy (we all lovingly called him
Jimmy, to conceal our hate of his accomplice) had managed, with that prospective decease of his, to disturb even Archie's mental balance. Archie was the

owner of the concertina; but after a couple of stinging
lectures from Jimmy he refused to play any more. He
said:—"Yon's an uncanny joker. I dinna ken what's
wrang wi' him, but there's something verra wrang, verra
wrang. It's nae manner of use asking me. I won't play."
Our singers became mute because Jimmy was a dying
man. For the same reason no chap—as Knowles remarked—could "drive in a nail to hang his few poor
rags upon," without being made aware of the enor-
mity he committed in disturbing Jimmy's interminable
last moments. At night, instead of the cheerful yell,
"One bell! Turn out! Do you hear there? Hey! hey! hey!
Show leg!" the watches were called man by man, in
whispers, so as not to interfere with Jimmy's, possibly,
last slumber on earth. True, he was always awake, and
managed, as we sneaked out on deck, to plant in our
backs some cutting remark that, for the moment, made
us feel as if we had been brutes, and afterwards made
us suspect ourselves of being fools. We spoke in low
tones within that fo'c'sle as though it had been a
church. We ate our meals in silence and dread, for
Jimmy was capricious with his food, and railed bitterly
at the salt meat, at the biscuits, at the tea, as at articles
unfit for human consumption—"let alone for a dying
man!" He would say:—"Can't you find a better slice of
meat for a sick man who's trying to get home to be
cured—or buried? But there! If I had a chance, you
fellows would do away with it. You would poison me.
Look at what you have given me!" We served him in
his bed with rage and humility, as though we had been
the base courtiers of a hated prince; and he rewarded
us by his unconciliating criticism. He had found the
secret of keeping for ever on the run the fundamental
imbecility of mankind; he had the secret of life, that
confounded dying man, and he made himself master of

every moment of our existence. We grew desperate, and remained submissive. Emotional little Belfast was for ever on the verge of assault or on the verge of tears. One evening he confided to Archie:—"For a ha'penny I would knock his ugly black head off—the skulking dodger!" And the straightforward Archie pretended to be shocked! Such was the infernal spell which that casual St. Kitt's nigger had cast upon our guileless manhood! But the same night Belfast stole from the galley the officers' Sunday fruit pie, to tempt the fastidious appetite of Jimmy. He endangered not only his long friendship with the cook but also—as it appeared—his eternal welfare. The cook was overwhelmed with grief; he did not know the culprit but he knew that wickedness flourished; he knew that Satan was aboard amongst those men, whom he looked upon as in some way under his spiritual care. Whenever he saw three or four of us standing together he would leave his stove, to run out and preach. We fled from him; and only Charley (who knew the thief) affronted the cook with a candid gaze which irritated the good man. "It's you, I believe," he groaned, sorrowful and with a patch of soot on his chin. "It's you. You are a brand for the burning! No more of YOUR socks in my galley." Soon, unofficially, the information was spread about that, should there be another case of stealing, our marmalade (an extra allowance: half a pound per man) would be stopped. Mr. Baker ceased to heap jocular abuse upon his favourites, and grunted suspiciously at all. The captain's cold eyes, high up on the poop, glittered mistrustful, as he surveyed us trooping in a small mob from halyards to braces for the usual evening pull at all the ropes. Such stealing in a merchant ship is difficult to check, and may be taken as a declaration by men of their dislike for their officers. It is a bad symptom. It may end in

God knows what trouble. The *Narcissus* was still a peaceful ship, but mutual confidence was shaken. Donkin did not conceal his delight. We were dismayed.

Then illogical Belfast reproached our nigger with great fury. James Wait, with his elbow on the pillow, choked, gasped out:—"Did I ask you to bone the dratted thing? Blow your blamed pie. It has made me worse—you little Irish lunatic, you!" Belfast, with scarlet face and trembling lips, made a dash at him. Every man in the forecastle rose with a shout. There was a moment of wild tumult. Some one shrieked piercingly: —"Easy, Belfast! Easy! . . ." We expected Belfast to strangle Wait without more ado. Dust flew. We heard through it the nigger's cough, metallic and explosive like a gong. Next moment we saw Belfast hanging over him. He was saying plaintively:—"Don't! Don't, Jimmy! Don't be like that. An angel couldn't put up with ye—sick as ye are." He looked round at us from Jimmy's bedside, his comical mouth twitching, and through tearful eyes; then he tried to put straight the disarranged blankets. The unceasing whisper of the sea filled the forecastle. Was James Wait frightened, or touched, or repentant? He lay on his back with a hand to his side, and as motionless as if his expected visitor had come at last. Belfast fumbled about his feet, repeating with emotion:—"Yes. We know. Ye are bad, but. . . . Just say what ye want done, and . . . We all know ye are bad—very bad. . . ." No! Decidedly James Wait was not touched or repentant. Truth to say, he seemed rather startled. He sat up with incredible suddenness and ease. "Ah! You think I am bad, do you?" he said gloomily, in his clearest baritone voice (to hear him speak sometimes you would never think there was anything wrong with that man). "Do you? . . . Well, act according! Some of you haven't sense enough to put a blanket shipshape over a sick man.

There! Leave it alone! I can die anyhow!" Belfast
turned away limply with a gesture of discouragement.
In the silence of the forecastle, full of interested men,
Donkin pronounced distinctly:—"Well, I'm blowed!"
and sniggered. Wait looked at him. He looked at him
in a quite friendly manner. Nobody could tell what
would please our incomprehensible invalid: but for us
the scorn of that snigger was hard to bear.

Donkin's position in the forecastle was distinguished
but unsafe. He stood on the bad eminence of a general dislike. He was left alone; and in his isolation he
could do nothing but think of the gales of the Cape
of Good Hope and envy us the possession of warm
clothing and waterproofs. Our sea-boots, our oilskin
coats, our well-filled sea-chests, were to him so many
causes for bitter meditation: he had none of those
things, and he felt instinctively that no man, when the
need arose, would offer to share them with him. He
was impudently cringing to us and systematically insolent to the officers. He anticipated the best results, for
himself, from such a line of conduct—and was mistaken. Such natures forget that under extreme provocation men will be just—whether they want to be so or
not. Donkin's insolence to long-suffering Mr. Baker became at last intolerable to us, and we rejoiced when the
mate, one dark night, tamed him for good. It was done
neatly, with great decency and decorum, and with little
noise. We had been called—just before midnight—to
trim the yards, and Donkin—as usual—made insulting
remarks. We stood sleepily in a row with the forebrace
in our hands waiting for the next order, and heard in
the darkness a scuffly trampling of feet, an exclamation of surprise, sounds of cuffs and slaps, suppressed,
hissing whispers:—"Ah! Will you!" . . . "Don't . . .
Don't" . . . "Then behave." . . . "Oh! Oh! . . ."
Afterwards there were soft thuds mixed with the rattle

of iron things as if a man's body had been tumbling helplessly amongst the main-pump rods. Before we could realise the situation, Mr. Baker's voice was heard very near and a little impatient:—"Haul away, men! Lay back on that rope!" And we did lay back on the rope with great alacrity. As if nothing had happened, the chief mate went on trimming the yards with his usual and exasperating fastidiousness. We didn't at the time see anything of Donkin, and did not care. Had the chief officer thrown him overboard, no man would have said as much as "Hallo! he's gone!" But, in truth, no great harm was done—even if Donkin did lose one of his front teeth. We perceived this in the morning, and preserved a ceremonious silence: the etiquette of the forecastle commanded us to be blind and dumb in such a case, and we cherished the decencies of our life more than ordinary landsmen respect theirs. Charley, with unpardonable want of *savoir vivre*, yelled out:— "'Ave you been to your dentyst? . . . Hurt ye, didn't it?" He got a box on the ear from one of his best friends. The boy was surprised, and remained plunged in grief for at least three hours. We were sorry for him, but youth requires even more discipline than age. Donkin grinned venomously. From that day he became pitiless; told Jimmy that he was a "black fraud"; hinted to us that we were an imbecile lot, daily taken in by a vulgar nigger. And Jimmy seemed to like the fellow!

Singleton lived untouched by human emotions. Taciturn and unsmiling, he breathed amongst us—in that alone resembling the rest of the crowd. We were trying to be decent chaps, and found it jolly difficult; we oscillated between the desire of virtue and the fear of ridicule; we wished to save ourselves from the pain of remorse, but did not want to be made the contemptible dupes of our sentiment. Jimmy's hateful accomplice seemed to have blown with his impure breath undreamt-of subtleties into our hearts. We were disturbed and cowardly. That we knew. Singleton seemed to know nothing, understand nothing. We had thought him till then as wise as he looked, but now we dared, at times, suspect him of being stupid—from old age. One day, however, at dinner, as we sat on our boxes round a tin dish that stood on the deck within the circle of our feet, Jimmy expressed his general disgust with men and things in words that were particularly disgusting. Singleton lifted his head. We became mute. The old man, addressing Jimmy, asked:—"Are you dying?" Thus interrogated, James Wait appeared horribly startled and confused. We all were startled. Mouths remained open; hearts thumped, eyes blinked; a dropped tin fork rattled in the dish; a man rose as if to go out, and stood still. In less than a minute Jimmy pulled himself together:—"Why? Can't you see I am?" he answered shakily. Singleton lifted a piece of soaked biscuit ("his teeth"—he declared—"had no edge on them now") to his lips.—"Well, get on with your dying," he said with venerable mildness; "don't raise a blamed fuss with us over that job. We can't help you." Jimmy fell back in his bunk, and for a long time lay very still wiping the perspiration off his chin. The dinner-tins were put away quickly. On deck we discussed the incident in whispers. Some showed a chuckling exultation. Many looked grave. Wamibo, after long periods of staring dreaminess, attempted abortive smiles; and one of the young Scandinavians, much tormented by doubt, ventured in the second dog-watch to approach Singleton (the old man did not encourage us much to speak to him) and ask sheepishly:—"You think he will die?" Singleton looked up.—"Why, of course he will die," he said deliberately. This seemed decisive. It was promptly imparted to every one by him who had consulted the oracle. Shy and eager, he would step up and with averted gaze recite his formula:—"Old Singleton says he will die." It was a relief! At last we knew that our compassion would not be misplaced, and we could again smile without misgivings—but we reckoned without Donkin. Donkin "didn't want to 'ave no truck with 'em dirty furriners." When Nilsen came to him with the news: "Singleton says he will die," he answered him by a spiteful "And so will you—you fat-headed Dutchman. Wish you Dutchmen were all dead—'stead comin' takin' our money inter your starvin' country." We were appalled. We perceived that after all Singleton's answer meant nothing. We began to hate him for making fun of us. All our certitudes were going; we were on doubtful terms with our officers; the cook had given us up for lost; we had overheard the boatswain's opinion that "we were a crowd of softies." We suspected Jimmy, one another, and even our very selves. We did not know what to do. At every insignificant turn of our humble life we met Jimmy overbearing and blocking the way, arm-in-arm with his awful and veiled familiar. It was a weird servitude.

It began a week after leaving Bombay and came on us stealthily like any other great misfortune. Every one had remarked that Jimmy from the first was very slack at his work; but we thought it simply the outcome of his philosophy of life. Donkin said:—"You put no more weight on a rope than a bloody sparrer." He disdained him. Belfast, ready for a fight, exclaimed provokingly: —"You don't kill yourself, old man!"—"Would you?" he retorted with extreme scorn—and Belfast retired. One morning, as we were washing decks, Mr. Baker called to him:—"Bring your broom over here, Wait." He strolled languidly. "Move yourself! Ough!" grunted Mr. Baker; "what's the matter with your hind legs?" He stopped dead short. He gazed slowly with eyes

that bulged out with an expression audacious and sad.
—"It isn't my legs," he said, "it's my lungs." Everybody listened.—"What's . . . Ough! . . . What's
wrong with them?" inquired Mr. Baker. All the watch
stood around on the wet deck, grinning, and with
brooms or buckets in their hands. He said mournfully:
—"Going—or gone. Can't you see I'm a dying man? I
know it!" Mr. Baker was disgusted.—"Then why the
devil did you ship aboard here?"—"I must live till I
die—mustn't I?" he replied. The grins became audible.
—"Go off the deck—get out of my sight," said Mr.
Baker. He was nonplussed. It was a unique experience.
James Wait, obedient, dropped his broom, and walked
slowly forward. A burst of laughter followed him. It
was too funny. All hands laughed. . . . They laughed!
. . . Alas!

He became the tormentor of all our moments; he was
worse than a nightmare. You couldn't see that there
was anything wrong with him: a nigger does not show.
He was not very fat—certainly—but then he was no
leaner than other niggers we had known. He coughed
often, but the most prejudiced person could perceive
that, mostly, he coughed when it suited his purpose.
He wouldn't, or couldn't, do his work—and he
wouldn't lie-up. One day he would skip aloft with the
best of them, and next time we would be obliged to
risk our lives to get his limp body down. He was reported, he was examined; he was remonstrated with,
threatened, cajoled, lectured. He was called into the
cabin to interview the captain. There were wild ru-
mours. It was said he had cheeked the old man; it was
said he had frightened him. Charley maintained that
the "skipper, weepin', 'as giv' 'im 'is blessin' an' a pot
of jam." Knowles had it from the steward that the unspeakable Jimmy had been reeling against the cabin
furniture; that he had groaned; that he had complained

of general brutality and disbelief and had ended by
coughing all over the old man's meteorological journals
which were then spread on the table. At any rate,
Wait returned forward supported by the steward,
who, in a pained and shocked voice, entreated us:—
"Here! Catch hold of him, one of you. He is to lie-up."
Jimmy drank a tin mugful of coffee, and, after bullying
first one and then another, went to bed. He remained
there most of the time, but when it suited him would
come on deck and appear amongst us. He was scornful
and brooding; he looked ahead upon the sea, and no
one could tell what was the meaning of that black man
sitting apart in a meditative attitude and as motionless
as a carving.

He refused steadily all medicine; he threw sago and
cornflour overboard till the steward got tired of bringing it to him. He asked for paregoric. They sent him a
big bottle; enough to poison a wilderness of babies.
He kept it between his mattress and the deal lining of
the ship's side; and nobody ever saw him take a dose.
Donkin abused him to his face, jeered at him while he
gasped; and the same day Wait would lend him a
warm jersey. Once Donkin reviled him for half an
hour; reproached him with the extra work his malingering gave to the watch; and ended by calling him
"a black-faced swine." Under the spell of our accursed
perversity we were horror-struck. But Jimmy positively
seemed to revel in that abuse. It made him look cheerful—and Donkin had a pair of old sea-boots thrown
at him. "Here, you East-end trash," boomed Wait,
"you may have that."

At last Mr. Baker had to tell the captain that James
Wait was disturbing the peace of the ship. "Knock
discipline on the head—he will, Ough," grunted Mr.
Baker. As a matter of fact, the starboard watch came as

near as possible to refusing duty, when ordered one
morning by the boatswain to wash out their forecastle.
It appears Jimmy objected to a wet floor—and that
morning we were in a compassionate mood. We
thought the boatswain a brute, and, practically, told
him so. Only Mr. Baker's delicate tact prevented an
all-fired row: he refused to take us seriously. He came
bustling forward, and called us many unpolite names
but in such a hearty and seamanlike manner that we
began to feel ashamed of ourselves. In truth, we
thought him much too good a sailor to annoy him will-
ingly: and after all Jimmy might have been a fraud—
probably was! The forecastle got a clean up that morning; but in the afternoon a sick-bay was fitted up in
the deck-house. It was a nice little cabin opening on
deck, and with two berths. Jimmy's belongings were
transported there, and then—notwithstanding his protests—Jimmy himself. He said he couldn't walk.
Four men carried him on a blanket. He complained
that he would have to die there alone, like a dog.
We grieved for him, and were delighted to have him
removed from the forecastle. We attended him as before. The galley was next door, and the cook looked
in many times a day. Wait became a little more cheerful. Knowles affirmed having heard him laugh to himself in peals one day. Others had seen him walking
about on deck at night. His little place, with the door
ajar on a long hook, was always full of tobacco smoke.
We spoke through the crack cheerfully, sometimes
abusively, as we passed by, intent on our work. He
fascinated us. He would never let doubt die. He overshadowed the ship. Invulnerable in his promise of
speedy corruption he trampled on our self-respect, he
demonstrated to us daily our want of moral courage;
he tainted our lives. Had we been a miserable gang of

wretched immortals, unhallowed alike by hope and fear, he could not have lorded it over us with a more pitiless assertion of his sublime privilege.

## III

Meantime the *Narcissus*, with square yards, ran out of the fair monsoon. She drifted slowly, swinging round and round the compass, through a few days of baffling light airs. Under the patter of short warm showers, grumbling men whirled the heavy yards from side to side; they caught hold of the soaked ropes with groans and sighs, while their officers, sulky and dripping with rain water, unceasingly ordered them about in wearied voices. During the short respites they looked with disgust into the smarting palms of their stiff hands, and asked one another bitterly:—"Who would be a sailor if he could be a farmer?" All the tempers were spoilt, and no man cared what he said. One black night, when the watch, panting in the heat and half-drowned with the rain, had been through four mortal hours hunted from brace to brace, Belfast declared that he would "chuck the sea for ever and go in a steamer." This was excessive, no doubt. Captain Allistoun, with great self-control, would mutter sadly to Mr. Baker:—"It is not so bad—not so bad," when he had managed to shove, and dodge, and manœuvre his smart ship through sixty miles in twenty-four hours. From the doorstep of the little cabin, Jimmy, chin in hand, watched our distasteful labours with insolent and melancholy eyes. We spoke to him gently—and out of his sight exchanged sour smiles.

Then, again, with a fair wind and under a clear sky, the ship went on piling up the South Latitude. She passed outside Madagascar and Mauritius without a glimpse of the land. Extra lashings were put on the spare spars. Hatches were looked to. The steward

in his leisure moments and with a worried air tried
to fit washboards to the cabin doors. Stout canvas was
bent with care. Anxious eyes looked to the westward,
towards the cape of storms. The ship began to dip into
a southwest swell, and the softly luminous sky of low
latitudes took on a harder sheen from day to day above
our heads: it arched high above the ship vibrating and
pale, like an immense dome of steel, resonant with the
deep voice of freshening gales. The sunshine gleamed
cold on the white curls of black waves. Before the
strong breath of westerly squalls the ship, with re-
duced sail, lay slowly over, obstinate and yielding. She
drove to and fro in the unceasing endeavour to fight
her way through the invisible violence of the winds:
she pitched headlong into dark smooth hollows; she
struggled upwards over the snowy ridges of great running seas; she rolled, restless, from side to side, like a
thing in pain. Enduring and valiant, she answered to
the call of men; and her slim spars waving for ever in
abrupt semicircles, seemed to beckon in vain for help
towards the stormy sky.

It was a bad winter off the Cape that year. The relieved helmsmen came off flapping their arms, or ran
stamping hard and blowing into swollen, red fingers.
The watch on deck dodged the sting of cold sprays or,
crouching in sheltered corners, watched dismally the
high and merciless seas boarding the ship time after
time in unappeasable fury. Water tumbled in cataracts
over the forecastle doors. You had to dash through a
waterfall to get into your damp bed. The men turned
in wet and turned out stiff to face the redeeming and
ruthless exactions of their glorious and obscure fate.
Far aft, and peering watchfully to windward, the officers could be seen through the mist of squalls. They
stood by the weather-rail, holding on grimly, straight
and glistening in their long coats; and in the disordered

plunges of the hard-driven ship, they appeared high up, attentive, tossing violently above the grey line of a clouded horizon in motionless attitudes.

They watched the weather and the ship as men on shore watch the momentous chances of fortune. Captain Allistoun never left the deck, as though he had been part of the ship's fittings. Now and then the steward, shivering, but always in shirt-sleeves, would struggle towards him with some hot coffee, half of which the gale blew out of the cup before it reached the master's lips. He drank what was left gravely in one long gulp, while heavy sprays pattered loudly on his oilskin coat, the seas swishing broke about his high boots; and he never took his eyes off the ship. He kept his gaze riveted upon her as a loving man watches the unselfish toil of a delicate woman upon the slender thread of whose existence is hung the whole meaning and joy of the world. We all watched her. She was beautiful and had a weakness. We loved her no less for that. We admired her qualities aloud, we boasted of them to one another, as though they had been our own, and the consciousness of her only fault we kept buried in the silence of our profound affection. She was born in the thundering peal of hammers beating upon iron, in black eddies of smoke, under a grey sky, on the banks of the Clyde. The clamorous and sombre stream gives birth to things of beauty that float away into the sunshine of the world to be loved by men. The *Narcissus* was one of that perfect brood. Less perfect than many perhaps, but she was ours, and, consequently, incomparable. We were proud of her. In Bombay, ignorant landlubbers alluded to her as that "pretty grey ship." Pretty! A scurvy meed of commendation! We knew she was the most magnificent sea-boat ever launched. We tried to forget that, like many good sea-boats, she was at times rather crank. She was exacting.

She wanted care in loading and handling, and no one knew exactly how much care would be enough. Such are the imperfections of mere men! The ship knew, and sometimes would correct the presumptuous human ignorance by the wholesome discipline of fear. We had heard ominous stories about past voyages. The cook (technically a seaman, but in reality no sailor)— the cook, when unstrung by some misfortune, such as the rolling over of a saucepan, would mutter gloomily while he wiped the floor:—"There! Look at what she has done! Some voy'ge she will drown all hands! You'll see if she won't." To which the steward, snatching in the galley a moment to draw breath in the hurry of his worried life, would remark philosophically:—"Those that see won't tell, anyhow. I don't want to see it." We derided those fears. Our hearts went out to the old man when he pressed her hard so as to make her hold her own, hold to every inch gained to windward; when he made her, under reefed sails, leap obliquely at enormous waves. The men, knitted together aft into a ready group by the first sharp order of an officer coming to take charge of the deck in bad weather:—"Keep handy the watch," stood admiring her valiance. Their eyes blinked in the wind; their dark faces were wet with drops of water more salty and bitter than human tears; beards and moustaches, soaked, hung straight and dripping like fine seaweed. They were fantastically misshapen; in high boots, in hats like helmets, and swaying clumsily, stiff and bulky in glistening oilskins, they resembled men strangely equipped for some fabulous adventure. Whenever she rose easily to a towering green sea, elbows dug ribs, faces brightened, lips murmured:—"Didn't she do it cleverly," and all the heads turning like one watched with sardonic grins the foiled wave go roaring to leeward, white with the foam of a monstrous rage. But when she had not been quick enough and, struck heavily, lay over trembling under the blow, we clutched at ropes, and looking up at the narrow bands of drenched and strained sails waving desperately aloft, we thought in our hearts: —"No wonder. Poor thing!"

The thirty-second day out of Bombay began inauspiciously. In the morning a sea smashed one of the galley doors. We dashed in through lots of steam and found the cook very wet and indignant with the ship:— "She's getting worse every day. She's trying to drown me in front of my own stove!" He was very angry. We pacified him, and the carpenter, though washed away twice from there, managed to repair the door. Through that accident our dinner was not ready till late, but it didn't matter in the end because Knowles, who went to fetch it, got knocked down by a sea and the dinner went over the side. Captain Allistoun, looking more hard and thin-lipped than ever, hung on to full topsails and foresail, and would not notice that the ship, asked to do too much, appeared to lose heart altogether for the first time since we knew her. She refused to rise, and bored her way sullenly through the seas. Twice running, as though she had been blind or weary of life, she put her nose deliberately into a big wave and swept the decks from end to end. As the boatswain observed with marked annoyance, while we were splashing about in a body to try and save a worthless washtub:—"Every blooming thing in the ship is going overboard this afternoon." Venerable Singleton broke his habitual silence and said with a glance aloft:—"The old man's in a temper with the weather, but it's no good bein' angry with the winds of heaven." Jimmy had shut his door, of course. We knew he was dry and comfortable within his little cabin, and in our absurd way were pleased one moment, exasperated the next, by that certitude. Donkin skulked shamelessly,

uneasy and miserable. He grumbled:—"I'm perishin'
with cold outside in bloomin' wet rags, an' that 'ere
black sojer sits dry on a blamed chest full of bloomin'
clothes; blank his black soul!" We took no notice of
him; we hardly gave a thought to Jimmy and his
bosom friend. There was no leisure for idle probing of
hearts. Sails blew adrift. Things broke loose. Cold and
wet, we were washed about the deck while trying to
repair damages. The ship tossed about, shaken furiously, like a toy in the hand of a lunatic. Just at sunset
there was a rush to shorten sail before the menace of a
sombre hail cloud. The hard gust of wind came brutal
like the blow of a fist. The ship relieved of her canvas
in time received it pluckily: she yielded reluctantly to
the violent onset; then, coming up with a stately and
irresistible motion, brought her spars to windward in
the teeth of the screeching squall. Out of the abysmal
darkness of the black cloud overhead white hail
streamed on her, rattled on the rigging, leaped in hand-
fuls off the yards, rebounded on the deck—round and
gleaming in the murky turmoil like a shower of peas.
It passed away. For a moment a livid sun shot horizon-
tally the last rays of sinister light between the hills of
steep, rolling waves. Then a wild night rushed in—
stamped out in a great howl that dismal remnant of a
stormy day.

There was no sleep on board that night. Most seamen remember in their life one or two such nights of a
culminating gale. Nothing seems left of the whole
univoroo but darkmooo, olamour, fury and the ehip.
And like the last vestige of a shattered creation she
drifts, bearing an anguished remnant of sinful mankind,
through the distress, tumult, and pain of an avenging
terror. No one slept in the forecastle. The tin oil-lamp
suspended on a long string, smoking, described wide
circles; wet clothing made dark heaps on the glisten-

ing floor; a thin layer of water rushed to and fro. In the
bed-places men lay booted, resting on elbows and with
open eyes. Hung-up suits of oilskin swung out and in,
lively and disquieting like reckless ghosts of decapi-
tated seamen dancing in a tempest. No one spoke and
all listened. Outside the night moaned and sobbed to
the accompaniment of a continuous loud tremor as of
innumerable drums beating far off. Shrieks passed
through the air. Tremendous dull blows made the ship
tremble while she rolled under the weight of the seas
toppling on her deck. At times she soared up swiftly
as if to leave this earth for ever, then during interminable moments fell through a void with all the hearts on
board of her standing still, till a frightful shock, expected and sudden, started them off again with a big
thump. After every dislocating jerk of the ship,
Wamibo, stretched full length, his face on the pillow,
groaned slightly with the pain of his tormented universe. Now and then, for the fraction of an intolerable
second, the ship, in the fiercer burst of a terrible uproar, remained on her side, vibrating and still, with a
stillness more appalling than the wildest motion. Then
upon all those prone bodies a stir would pass, a shiver
of suspense. A man would protrude his anxious head
and a pair of eyes glistened in the sway of light glaring
wildly. Some moved their legs a little as if making ready
to jump out. But several, motionless on their backs and
with one hand gripping hard the edge of the bunk,
smoked nervously with quick puffs, staring upwards;
immobilised in a great craving for peace.

At midnight, orders were given to furl the fore and
mizen topsails. With immense efforts men crawled
aloft through a merciless buffeting, saved the canvas
and crawled down almost exhausted, to bear in panting
silence the cruel battering of the seas. Perhaps for the
first time in the history of the merchant service the

watch, told to go below, did not leave the deck, as if compelled to remain there by the fascination of a venomous violence. At every heavy gust men, huddled together, whispered to one another:—"It can blow no harder"—and presently the gale would give them the lie with a piercing shriek, and drive their breath back into their throats. A fierce squall seemed to burst asunder the thick mass of sooty vapours; and above the wrack of torn clouds glimpses could be caught of the high moon rushing backwards with frightful speed over the sky, right into the wind's eye. Many hung their heads, muttering that it "turned their inwards out" to look at it. Soon the clouds closed up and the world again became a raging, blind darkness that howled, flinging at the lonely ship salt sprays and sleet.

About half-past seven the pitchy obscurity round us turned a ghastly grey, and we knew that the sun had risen. This unnatural and threatening daylight, in which we could see one another's wild eyes and drawn faces, was only an added tax on our endurance. The horizon seemed to have come on all sides within arm's length of the ship. Into that narrowed circle furious seas leaped in, struck, and leaped out. A rain of salt, heavy drops flew aslant like mist. The main-topsail had to be goose-winged, and with stolid resignation every one prepared to go aloft once more; but the officers yelled, pushed back, and at last we understood that no more men would be allowed to go on the yard than were absolutely necessary for the work. As at any moment the masts were likely to be jumped out of blown overboard, we concluded that the captain didn't want to see all his crowd go over the side at once. That was reasonable. The watch then on duty, led by Mr. Creighton, began to struggle up the rigging. The wind flattened them against the ratlines; then, easing a little, would let them ascend a couple of steps; and again, with a sudden gust, pin all up the shrouds the whole crawling line in attitudes of crucifixion. The other watch plunged down on the main deck to haul up the sail. Men's heads bobbed up as the water flung them irresistibly from side to side. Mr. Baker grunted encouragingly in our midst, spluttering and blowing amongst the tangled ropes like an energetic porpoise. Favoured by an ominous and untrustworthy lull, the work was done without any one being lost either off the deck or from the yard. For the moment the gale seemed to take off, and the ship, as if grateful for our efforts, plucked up heart and made better weather of it.

At eight the men off duty, watching their chance, ran forward over the flooded deck to get some rest. The other half of the crew remained aft for their turn of "seeing her through her trouble," as they expressed it. The two mates urged the master to go below. Mr. Baker grunted in his ear:—"Ough! surely now . . . Ough! . . . confidence in us . . . nothing more to do . . . she must lay it out or go. Ough! Ough!" Tall young Mr. Creighton smiled down at him cheerfully: —". . . She's as right as a trivet! Take a spell, sir." He looked at them stonily with bloodshot, sleepless eyes. The rims of his eyelids were scarlet, and he moved his jaws unceasingly with a slow effort, as though he had been masticating a lump of india-rubber. He shook his head. He repeated:—"Never mind me. I must see it out—I must see it out," but he consented to sit down for a moment on the skylight, with his hard face turned unflinchingly to windward. The sea spat at it—and stoical, it streamed with water as though he had been weeping. On the weather side of the poop the watch, hanging on to the mizen rigging and to one another, tried to exchange encouraging words. Singleton, at the wheel, yelled out:—

"Look out for yourselves!" His voice reached them in a warning whisper. They were startled.

A big, foaming sea came out of the mist; it made for the ship, roaring wildly, and in its rush it looked as mischievous and discomposing as a madman with an axe. One or two, shouting, scrambled up the rigging; most, with a convulsive catch of the breath, held on where they stood. Singleton dug his knees under the wheel-box, and carefully eased the helm to the head-long pitch of the ship, but without taking his eyes off the coming wave. It towered close-to and high, like a wall of green glass topped with snow. The ship rose to it as though she had soared on wings, and for a moment rested poised upon the foaming crest as if she had been a great sea-bird. Before we could draw breath a heavy gust struck her, another roller took her unfairly under the weather bow, she gave a toppling lurch, and filled her decks. Captain Allistoun leaped up, and fell; Archie rolled over him, screaming:—"She will rise!" She gave another lurch to leeward; the lower deadeyes dipped heavily; the men's feet flew from under them, and they hung kicking above the slanting poop. They could see the ship putting her side in the water, and shouted all together:—"She's going!" Forward the forecastle doors flew open, and the watch below were seen leaping out one after another, throwing their arms up; and, falling on hands and knees, scrambled aft on all fours along the high side of the deck, sloping more than the roof of a house. From leeward the seas rose, pursuing them, they looked wretched in a hopeless struggle, like vermin fleeing before a flood; they fought up the weather ladder of the poop one after another, half naked and staring wildly; and as soon as they got up they shot to leeward in clusters, with closed eyes, till they brought up heav-

ily with their ribs against the iron stanchions of the rail;
then, groaning, they rolled in a confused mass. The
immense volume of water thrown forward by the last
scend of the ship had burst the lee door of the forecastle. They could see their chests, pillows, blankets,
clothing, come out floating upon the sea. While they
struggled back to windward they looked in dismay. The
straw beds swam high, the blankets, spread out, undulated; while the chests, waterlogged and with a
heavy list, pitched heavily like dismasted hulks, before
they sank; Archie's big coat passed with outspread
arms, resembling a drowned seaman floating with his
head under water. Men were slipping down while trying to dig their fingers into the planks; others, jammed
in corners, rolled enormous eyes. They all yelled unceasingly:—"The masts! Cut! Cut! . . ." A black
squall howled low over the ship, that lay on her side
with the weather yard-arms pointing to the clouds;
while the tall masts, inclined nearly to the horizon,
seemed to be of an immeasurable length. The carpenter let go his hold, rolled against the skylight, and began to crawl to the cabin entrance, where a big axe
was kept ready for just such an emergency. At that
moment the topsail sheet parted, the end of the heavy
chain racketed aloft, and sparks of red fire streamed
down through the flying sprays. The sail flapped once
with a jerk that seemed to tear our hearts out
through our teeth, and instantly changed into a bunch
of fluttering narrow ribbons that tied themselves into
knots and became quiet along the yard. Captain Allistoun struggled, managed to stand up with his face
near the deck, upon which men swung on the ends of
ropes, like nest robbers upon a cliff. One of his feet was
on somebody's chest, his face was purple; his lips
moved. He yelled also; he yelled, bending down:—
"No! No!" Mr. Baker, one leg over the binnacle-

stand, roared out:—"Did you say no? Not cut?" He
shook his head madly. "No! No!" Between his legs the
crawling carpenter heard, collapsed at once, and lay
full length in the angle of the skylight. Voices took up
the shout—"No!" No!" then all became still. They
waited for the ship to turn over altogether, and shake
them out into the sea; and upon the terrific noise of
wind and sea not a murmur of remonstrance came out
from those men, who each would have given ever so
many years of life to see "them damned sticks go
overboard!" They all believed it their only chance; but
a little hard-faced man shook his grey head and
shouted "No!" without giving them as much as a
glance. They were silent, and gasped. They gripped
rails, they had wound ropes'-ends under their arms;
they clutched ringbolts, they crawled in heaps where
there was foothold; they held on with both arms,
hooked themselves to anything to windward with elbows, with chins, almost with their teeth: and some,
unable to crawl away from where they had been flung,
felt the sea leap up, striking against their backs as they
struggled upwards. Singleton had stuck to the wheel.
His hair flew out in the wind; the gale seemed to take
its life-long adversary by the beard and shake his old
head. He wouldn't let go, and, with his knees forced
between the spokes, flew up and down like a man on a
bough. As Death appeared unready, they began to
look about. Donkin, caught by one foot in a loop of
some rope, hung, head down, below us, and yelled,
with his face to the deck:—"Cut! Cut!" Two men
lowered themselves cautiously to him; others hauled
on the rope. They caught him up, shoved him into a
safer place, held him. He shouted curses at the master, shook his fist at him with horrible blasphemies,
called upon us in filthy words to "Cut! Don't mind that
murdering fool! Cut, some of you!" One of his rescuers

struck him a back-handed blow over the mouth; his head banged on the deck, and he became suddenly very quiet, with a white face, breathing hard, and with a few drops of blood trickling from his cut lip. On the lee side another man could be seen stretched out as if stunned; only the washboard prevented him from going over the side. It was the steward. We had to sling him up like a bale, for he was paralysed with fright. He had rushed up out of the pantry when he felt the ship go over, and had rolled down helplessly, clutching a china mug. It was not broken. With difficulty we tore it away from him, and when he saw it in our hands he was amazed. "Where did you get that thing?" he kept on asking us in a trembling voice. His shirt was blown to shreds; the ripped sleeves flapped like wings. Two men made him fast, and, doubled over the rope that held him, he resembled a bundle of wet rags. Mr. Baker crawled along the line of men, asking:—"Are you all there?" and looking them over. Some blinked vacantly, others shook convulsively; Wamibo's head hung over his breast; and in painful attitudes, cut by lashings, exhausted with clutching, screwed up in corners, they breathed heavily. Their lips twitched and at every sickening heave of the overturned ship they opened them wide as if to shout. The cook, embracing a wooden stanchion, unconsciously repeated a prayer. In every short interval of the fiendish noises around he could be heard there, without cap or slippers, imploring in that storm the Master of our lives not to lead him into temptation. Soon he also became silent. In all that crowd of cold and hungry men, waiting wearily for a violent death, not a voice was heard; they were mute, and in sombre thoughtfulness listened to the horrible imprecations of the gale.

Hours passed. They were sheltered by the heavy inclination of the ship from the wind that rushed in one

long unbroken moan above their heads, but cold rain
showers fell at times into the uneasy calm of their
refuge. Under the torment of that new infliction a pair
of shoulders would writhe a little. Teeth chattered. The
sky was clearing, and bright sunshine gleamed over the
ship. After every burst of battering seas, vivid and fleeting rainbows arched over the drifting hull in the flick
of sprays. The gale was ending in a clear blow, which
gleamed and cut like a knife. Between two bearded
shellbacks Charley, fastened with somebody's long
muffler to a deck ringbolt, wept quietly, with rare
tears wrung out by bewilderment, cold, hunger, and
general misery. One of his neighbours punched him
in the ribs asking roughly:—"What's the matter with
your cheek? In fine weather there's no holding you,
youngster." Turning about with prudence he worked
himself out of his coat and threw it over the boy. The
other man closed up, muttering:—"'Twill make a
bloomin' man of you, sonny." They flung their arms
over and pressed against him. Charley drew his feet
up and his eyelids dropped. Sighs were heard, as men,
perceiving that they were not to be "drowned in a
hurry," tried easier positions. Mr. Creighton, who had
hurt his leg, lay amongst us with compressed lips.
Some fellows belonging to his watch set about securing
him better. Without a word or a glance he lifted his
arms one after another to facilitate the operation, and
not a muscle moved in his stern, young face. They
asked him with solicitude:—"Easier now, sir?" He
answered with a curt:—"That'll do." He was a hard
young officer, but many of his watch used to say they
liked him well enough because he had "such a gentlemanly way of damning us up and down the deck."
Others unable to discern such fine shades of refinement
respected him for his smartness. For the first time since
the ship had gone on her beam ends Captain Allistoun

gave a short glance down at his men. He was almost upright—one foot against the side of the skylight, one
knee on the deck; and with the end of the vang round
his waist swung back and forth with his gaze fixed
ahead, watchful, like a man looking out for a sign. Before his eyes the ship, with half her deck below water,
rose and fell on heavy seas that rushed from under her
flashing in the cold sunshine. We began to think she
was wonderfully buoyant—considering. Confident
voices were heard shouting:—"She'll do, boys!" Belfast
exclaimed with fervour:—"I would giv' a month's
pay for a draw at a pipe!" One or two, passing dry
tongues on their salt lips, muttered something about a
"drink of water." The cook, as if inspired, scrambled
up with his breast against the poop water-cask and
looked in. There was a little at the bottom. He yelled,
waving his arms, and two men began to crawl backwards and forwards with the mug. We had a good
mouthful all round. The master shook his head impatiently, refusing. When it came to Charley one of his
neighbours shouted:—"That bloomin' boy's asleep."
He slept as though he had been dosed with narcotics.
They let him be. Singleton held to the wheel with
one hand while he drank, bending down to shelter his
lips from the wind. Wamibo had to be poked and
yelled at before he saw the mug held before his eyes.
Knowles said sagaciously:—"It's better'n a tot o'
rum." Mr. Baker grunted:—"Thank ye." Mr. Creighton drank and nodded. Donkin gulped greedily, glaring
over the rim. Belfast made us laugh when with grimacing mouth he shouted:—"Pass it this way. We're all
tay-tottlers here." The master, presented with the mug
again by a crouching man, who screamed up at him:—
"We all had a drink, captain," groped for it without
ceasing to look ahead, and handed it back stiffly as
though he could not spare half a glance away from the

ship. Faces brightened. We shouted to the cook:—
"Well done, doctor!" He sat to leeward, propped by
the water-cask and yelled back abundantly, but the
seas were breaking in thunder just then, and we only
caught snatches that sounded like: "Providence" and
"born again." He was at the old game of preaching. We
made friendly but derisive gestures at him, and from
below he lifted one arm, holding on with the other,
moved his lips; he beamed up to us, straining his voice
—earnest, and ducking his head before the sprays.

Suddenly some one cried:—"Where's Jimmy?" and
we were appalled once more. On the end of the row
the boatswain shouted hoarsely:—"Has any one seed
him come out?" Voices exclaimed dismally:—
"Drowned—is he? . . . No! In his cabin! . . . Good
Lord! . . . Caught like a bloomin' rat in a trap. . . .
Couldn't open his door . . . Aye! She went over too
quick and the water jammed it . . . Poor beggar!
. . . No help for 'im. . . . Let's go and see . . ."
"Damn him, who could go?" screamed Donkin.—"Nobody expects you to," growled the man next to him:
"you're only a thing."—"Is there half a chance to get
at 'im?" inquired two or three men together. Belfast
untied himself with blind impetuosity, and all at once
shot down to leeward quicker than a flash of lightning.
We shouted all together with dismay; but with his legs
overboard he held and yelled for a rope. In our extremity nothing could be terrible; so we judged him
funny kicking there, and with his scared face. Some one
began to laugh and, as if hysterically infected with
screaming merriment, all those haggard men went off
laughing, wild-eyed, like a lot of maniacs tied up on a
wall. Mr. Baker swung off the binnacle-stand and tend-
ered him one leg. He scrambled up rather scared,
and consigning us with abominable words to the "divvle." "You are. . . . Ough! You're a foul-mouthed

beggar, Craik," grunted Mr. Baker. He answered, stuttering with indignation:—"Look at 'em, sorr. The bloomin' dirty images! laughing at a chum going overboard. Call themselves men, too." But from the break of the poop the boatswain called out:—"Come along," and Belfast crawled away in a hurry to join him. The five men, poised and gazing over the edge of the poop, looked for the best way to get forward. They seemed to hesitate. The others, twisting in their lashings, turning painfully, stared with open lips. Captain Allistoun saw nothing; he seemed with his eyes to hold the ship up in a superhuman concentration of effort. The wind screamed loud in sunshine; columns of spray rose straight up; and in the glitter of rainbows bursting over the trembling hull the men went over cautiously, disappearing from sight with deliberate movements.

They went swinging from belaying pin to cleat above the seas that beat the half-submerged deck. Their toes scraped the planks. Lumps of green cold water toppled over the bulwark and on their heads. They hung for a moment on strained arms, with the breath knocked out of them, and with closed eyes— then, letting go with one hand, balanced with lolling heads, trying to grab some rope or stanchion further forward. The long-armed and athletic boatswain swung quickly, gripping things with a fist hard as iron, and remembering suddenly snatches of the last letter from his "old woman." Little Belfast scrambled in a rage spluttering "cursed nigger." Wamibo's tongue hung out with excitement; and Archie, intrepid and calm, watched his chance to move with intelligent coolness.

When above the side of the house, they let go one after another, and falling heavily, sprawled, pressing their palms to the smooth teak wood. Round them the backwash of waves seethed white and hissing. All the

doors had become trap-doors, of course. The first was
the galley door. The galley extended from side to side,
and they could hear the sea splashing with hollow
noises in there. The next door was that of the carpenter's shop. They lifted it, and looked down. The room
seemed to have been devastated by an earthquake.
Everything in it had tumbled on the bulkhead facing
the door, and on the other side of that bulkhead there
was Jimmy dead or alive. The bench, a half-finished
meat-safe, saws, chisels, wire rods, axes, crowbars,
lay in a heap besprinkled with loose nails. A sharp
adze stuck up with a shining edge that gleamed dangerously down there like a wicked smile. The men
clung to one another, peering. A sickening, sly
lurch of the ship nearly sent them overboard in a body.
Belfast howled "Here goes!" and leaped down. Archie
followed cannily, catching at shelves that gave way
with him, and eased himself in a great crash of ripped
wood. There was hardly room for three men to move.
And in the sunshiny blue square of the door, the boatswain's face, bearded and dark, Wamibo's face, wild
and pale, hung over—watching.

Together they shouted: "Jimmy! Jim!" From above
the boatswain contributed a deep growl: "You . . .
Wait!" In a pause, Belfast entreated: "Jimmy, darlin',
are ye aloive?" The boatswain said: "Again! All together, boys!" All yelled excitedly. Wamibo made
noises resembling loud barks. Belfast drummed on the
side of the bulkhead with a piece of iron. All ceased
suddenly. The sound of screaming and hammering
went on thin and distinct—like a solo after a chorus.
He was alive. He was screaming and knocking below
us with the hurry of a man prematurely shut up in a
coffin. We went to work. We attacked with desperation the abominable heap of things heavy, of things
sharp, of things clumsy to handle. The boatswain

crawled away to find somewhere a flying end of a rope;
and Wamibo, held back by shouts:— "Don't jump!
. . . Don't come in here, muddlehead!"—remained
glaring above us—all shining eyes, gleaming fangs,
tumbled hair; resembling an amazed and half-witted
fiend gloating over the extraordinary agitation of the
damned. The boatswain adjured us to "bear a hand,"
and a rope descended. We made things fast to it and
they went up spinning, never to be seen by man again.
A rage to fling things overboard possessed us. We
worked fiercely, cutting our hands and speaking
brutally to one another. Jimmy kept up a distracting
row; he screamed piercingly, without drawing breath,
like a tortured woman; he banged with hands and
feet. The agony of his fear wrung our hearts so terribly that we longed to abandon him, to get out of
that place deep as a well and swaying like a tree, to
get out of his hearing, back on the poop where we
could wait passively for death in incomparable repose.
We shouted to him to "shut up, for God's sake." He
redoubled his cries. He must have fancied we could
not hear him. Probably he heard his own clamour
but faintly. We could picture him crouching on the
edge of the upper berth, letting out with both fists
at the wood, in the dark, and with his mouth wide
open for that unceasing cry. Those were loathsome
moments. A cloud driving across the sun would darken
the doorway menacingly. Every movement of the ship
was pain. We scrambled about with no room to breathe,
and felt frightfully sick. The boatswain yelled down at
us:—"Bear a hand! Bear a hand! We two will be
washed away from here directly if you ain't quick!"
Three times a sea leaped over the high side and
flung bucketfuls of water on our heads. Then Jimmy,
startled by the shock, would stop his noise for a
moment—waiting for the ship to sink, perhaps—and

began again, distressingly loud, as if invigorated by the
gust of fear. At the bottom the nails lay in a layer several inches thick. It was ghastly. Every nail in the
world, not driven in firmly somewhere, seemed to have
found its way into that carpenter's shop. There they
were, of all kinds, the remnants of stores from seven
voyages. Tin-tacks, copper tacks (sharp as needles);
pump nails with big heads, like tiny iron mushrooms;
nails without any heads (horrible); French nails polished and slim. They lay in a solid mass more inabord-
able than a hedgehog. We hesitated, yearning for a
shovel, while Jimmy below us yelled as though he had
been flayed. Groaning, we dug our fingers in, and very
much hurt, shook our hands, scattering nails and drops
of blood. We passed up our hats full of assorted nails
to the boatswain, who, as if performing a mysterious
and appeasing rite, cast them wide upon a raging sea.

We got to the bulkhead at last. Those were stout
planks. She was a ship, well finished in every detail—
the *Narcissus* was. They were the stoutest planks ever
put into a ship's bulkhead—we thought—and then we
perceived that, in our hurry, we had sent all the tools
overboard. Absurd little Belfast wanted to break it
down with his own weight, and with both feet leaped
straight up like a springbok, cursing the Clyde shipwrights for not scamping their work. Incidentally
he reviled all North Britain, the rest of the earth, the sea
—and all his companions. He swore, as he alighted
heavily on his heels, that he would never, never any
more associate with any fool that "hadn't savee enough
to know his knee from his elbow." He managed by his
thumping to scare the last remnant of wits out of
Jimmy. We could hear the object of our exasperated
solicitude darting to and fro under the planks. He had
cracked his voice at last, and could only squeak miserably. His back or else his head rubbed the planks, now

here, now there, in a puzzling manner. He squeaked as he dodged the invisible blows. It was more heartrending even than his yells. Suddenly Archie produced a crowbar. He had kept it back; also a small hatchet. We howled with satisfaction. He struck a mighty blow and small chips flew at our eyes. The boatswain above shouted:—"Look out! Look out there. Don't kill the man. Easy does it!" Wamibo, maddened with excitement, hung head down and insanely urged us:—"Hoo! Strook 'im! Hoo! Hoo!" We were afraid he would fall in and kill one of us and, hurriedly, we entreated the boatswain to "shove the blamed Finn overboard." Then, all together, we yelled down at the planks:— "Stand from under! Get forward," and listened. We only heard the deep hum and moan of the wind above us, the mingled roar and hiss of the seas. The ship, as if overcome with despair, wallowed lifelessly, and our heads swam with that unnatural motion. Belfast clamoured:—"For the love of God, Jimmy, where are ye? . . . Knock! Jimmy darlint! . . . Knock! You bloody black beast! Knock!" He was as quiet as a dead man inside a grave; and, like men standing above a grave, we were on the verge of tears—but with vexation, the strain, the fatigue; with the great longing to be done with it, to get away, and lie down to rest somewhere where we could see our danger and breathe. Archie shouted:—"Gi'e me room!" We crouched behind him, guarding our heads, and he struck time after time in the joint of planks. They cracked. Suddenly the crowbar went halfway in through a splintered oblong hole. It must have missed Jimmy's head by less than an inch. Archie withdrew it quickly, and that infamous nigger rushed at the hole, put his lips to it, and whispered "Help," in an almost extinct voice; he pressed his head to it, trying madly to get out through that opening one inch wide and three inches long. In our disturbed state we were absolutely paralysed by his incredible action. It seemed impossible to drive him away. Even Archie at last lost his composure. "If ye don't clear oot I'll drive the crowbar thro' your head," he shouted in a determined voice. He meant what he said, and his earnestness seemed to make an impression on Jimmy. He disappeared suddenly, and we set to prising and tearing at the planks with the eagerness of men trying to get at a mortal enemy, and spurred by the desire to tear him limb from limb. The wood split, cracked, gave way. Belfast plunged in head and shoulders and groped viciously. "I've got 'im! Got 'im," he shouted. "Oh! There! . . . He's gone; I've got 'im! . . . Pull at my legs! . . . Pull!" Wamibo hooted unceasingly. The boatswain shouted directions:—"Catch hold of his hair, Belfast; pull straight up, you two! . . . Pull fair!" We pulled fair. We pulled Belfast out with a jerk, and dropped him with disgust. In a sitting posture, purple-faced, he sobbed despairingly:—"How can I hold on to 'is blooming short wool?" Suddenly Jimmy's head and shoulders appeared. He stuck half-way, and with rolling eyes foamed at our feet. We flew at him with brutal impatience, we tore the shirt off his back, we tugged at his ears, we panted over him; and all at once he came away in our hands as though somebody had let go his legs. With the same movement, without a pause, we swung him up. His breath whistled, he kicked our upturned faces, he grasped two pairs of arms above his head, and he squirmed up with such precipitation that he seemed positively to escape from our hands like a bladder full of gas. Streaming with perspiration, we swarmed up the rope, and, coming into the blast of cold wind, gasped like men plunged into icy water. With burning faces we shivered to the very marrow of our bones. Never before had the gale seemed to us more furious, the sea more mad, the sunshine more

merciless and mocking, and the position of the ship
more hopeless and appalling. Every movement of her
was ominous of the end of her agony and of the begin-
nir ; of ours. We staggered away from the door, and,
al .med by a sudden roll, fell down in a bunch. It appeared to us that the side of the house was more smooth
than glass and more slippery than ice. There was nothing to hang on to but a long brass hook used sometimes
to keep back an open door. Wamibo held on to it and
we held on to Wamibo, clutching our Jimmy. He had
completely collapsed now. He did not seem to have the
strength to close his hand. We stuck to him blindly in
our fear. We were not afraid of Wamibo letting go (we
remembered that the brute was stronger than any three
men in the ship), but we were afraid of the hook giving
way, and we also believed that the ship had made up
her mind to turn over at last. But she didn't. A sea swept
over us. The boatswain spluttered:—"Up and away.
There's a lull. Away aft with you, or we will all go to
the devil here." We stood up surrounding Jimmy. We
begged him to hold up, to hold on, at least. He glared
with his bulging eyes, mute as a fish, and with all the
stiffening knocked out of him. He wouldn't stand; he
wouldn't even as much as clutch at our necks; he was
only a cold black skin loosely stuffed with soft cotton
wool; his arms and legs swung jointless and pliable; his
head rolled about; the lower lip hung down, enormous
and heavy. We pressed round him, bothered and dismayed; sheltering him we swung here and there in a
body; and on the very brink of eternity we tottered all
together with concealing and absurd gestures, like a lot
of drunken men embarrassed with a stolen corpse.

Something had to be done. We had to get him aft. A
rope was tied slack under his armpits, and, reaching up
at the risk of our lives, we hung him on the foresheet
cleat. He emitted no sound; he looked as ridiculously

lamentable as a doll that had lost half its sawdust, and we started on our perilous journey over the main deck, dragging along with care that pitiful, that limp, that hateful burden. He was not very heavy, but had he weighed a ton he could not have been more awkward to handle. We literally passed him from hand to hand. Now and then we had to hang him up on a handy belaying-pin, to draw a breath and re-form the line. Had the pin broken he would have irretrievably gone into the Southern Ocean, but he had to take his chance of that; and after a little while, becoming apparently aware of it, he groaned slightly, and with a great effort whispered a few words. We listened eagerly. He was reproaching us with our carelessness in letting him run such risks: "Now, after I got myself out from there," he breathed out weakly. "There" was his cabin. And he got himself out. We had nothing to do with it apparently! . . . No matter. . . . We went on and let him take his chances, simply because we could not help it; for though at that time we hated him more than ever—more than anything under heaven—we did not want to lose him. We had so far saved him; and it had become a personal matter between us and the sea. We meant to stick to him. Had we (by an incredible hypothesis) undergone similar toil and trouble for an empty cask, that cask would have become as precious to us as Jimmy was. More precious, in fact, because we would have had no reason to hate the cask. And we hated James Wait. We could not get rid of the monstrous suspicion that this astounding black-man was shamming sick, had been malingering heartlessly in the face of our toil, of our scorn, of our patience—and now was malingering in the face of our devotion—in the face of death. Our vague and imperfect morality rose with disgust at his unmanly lie. But he stuck to it manfully—amazingly. No! It

couldn't be. He was at all extremity. His cantanker-
ous temper was only the result of the provoking in-
vincibleness of that death he felt by his side. Any
man may be angry with such a masterful chum. But,
then, what kind of men were we—with our thoughts!
Indignation and doubt grappled within us in a scuffle
that trampled upon the finest of our feelings. And we
hated him because of the suspicion; we detested him
because of the doubt. We could not scorn him safely
—neither could we pity him without risk to our dignity. So we hated him, and passed him carefully from
hand to hand. We cried, "Got him?"—"Yes. All right.
Let go." And he swung from one enemy to another,
showing about as much life as an old bolster would
do. His eyes made two narrow white slits in the black
face. The air escaped through his lips with a noise like
the sound of bellows. We reached the poop ladder at
last, and it being a comparatively safe place, we lay
for a moment in an exhausted heap to rest a little. He
began to mutter. We were always incurably anxious
to hear what he had to say. This time he mumbled
peevishly, "It took you some time to come. I began to
think the whole smart lot of you had been washed
overboard. What kept you back? Hey? Funk?" We said
nothing. With sighs we started again to drag him up.
The secret and ardent desire of our hearts was the desire to beat him viciously with our fists about the head;
and we handled him as tenderly as though he had
been made of glass. . . .

The return on the poop was like the return of wanderers after many years amongst people marked by the
desolation of time. Eyes were turned slowly in their
sockets, glancing at us. Faint murmurs were heard,
"Have you got 'im after all?" The well-known faces
looked strange and familiar; they seemed faded and
grimy; they had a mingled expression of fatigue and

eagerness. They seemed to have become much thinner
during our absence, as if all these men had been starving
for a long time in their abandoned attitudes. The captain, with a round turn of a rope on his wrist, and kneeling on one knee, swung with a face cold and stiff; but
with living eyes he was still holding the ship up, heed-
ing no one, as if lost in the unearthly effort of that endeavour. We fastened up James Wait in a safe place.
Mr. Baker scrambled along to lend a hand. Mr. Creighton, on his back, and very pale, muttered, "Well
done," and gave us, Jimmy and the sky, a scornful
glance, then closed his eyes slowly. Here and there a
man stirred a little, but most of them remained apathetic, in cramped positions, muttering between shivers.
The sun was setting. A sun enormous, unclouded and
red, declining low as if bending down to look into their
faces. The wind whistled across long sunbeams that,
resplendent and cold, struck full on the dilated pupils
of staring eyes without making them wink. The wisps
of hair and the tangled beards were grey with the salt
of the sea. The faces were earthy, and the dark patches
ur ler the eyes extended to the ears, smudged into the
hollows of sunken cheeks. The lips were livid and thin,
and when they moved it was with difficulty, as though
they had been glued to the teeth. Some grinned sadly
in the sunlight, shaking with cold. Others were sad
and still. Charley, subdued by the sudden disclosure of
the insignificance of his youth, darted fearful glances.
The two smooth-faced Norwegians resembled decrepit
children, staring stupidly. To leeward, on the edge of
the horizon, black seas leaped up towards the glowing
sun. It sank slowly, round and blazing, and the crests
of waves splashed on the edge of the luminous circle.
One of the Norwegians appeared to catch sight of it,
and. after giving a violent start, began to speak. His
voice, startling the others, made them stir. They

moved their heads stiffly, or turning with difficulty, looked at him with surprise, with fear, or in grave silence. He chattered at the setting sun, nodding his head, while the big seas began to roll across the crimson disc; and over miles of turbulent waters the shadows of high waves swept with a running darkness the faces of men. A crested roller broke with a loud hissing roar, and the sun, as if put out, disappeared. The chattering voice faltered, went out together with the light. There were sighs. In the sudden lull that follows the crash of a broken sea a man said wearily, "Here's that blooming Dutchman gone off his chump." A seaman, lashed by the middle, tapped the deck with his open hand with unceasing quick flaps. In the gathering greyness of twilight a bulky form was seen rising aft, and began marching on all fours with the movements of some big cautious beast. It was Mr. Baker passing along the line of men. He grunted encouragingly over every one, felt their fastenings. Some, with half-open eyes, puffed like men oppressed by heat; others mechanically and in dreamy voices answered him, "Aye! aye! sir!" He went from one to another grunting, "Ough! . . . See her through it yet"; and unexpectedly, with loud angry outbursts, blew up Knowles for cutting off a long piece from the fall of the relieving tackle. "Ough!—— Ashamed of yourself——Relieving tackle——Don't you know better!——Ough!——Able seaman! Ough!" The lame man was crushed. He muttered, "Get som'-think for a lashing for myself, sir."—"Ough! Lashing ——yourself. Are you a tinker or a sailor——What? Ough!——May want that tackle directly——Ough! ——More use to the ship than your lame carcass. Ough!——Keep it!——Keep it, now you've done it." He crawled away slowly, muttering to himself about some men being "worse than children." It had been a comforting row. Low exclamations were heard "Hallo

. . . Hallo." . . . Those who had been painfully dozing asked with convulsive starts, "What's up? . . .
What is it?" The answers came with unexpected cheer-
fulness: "The mate is going bald-headed for lame Jack
about something or other." "No!" . . . "What 'as he
done?" Some one even chuckled. It was like a whiff of
hope, like a reminder of safe days. Donkin, who had
been stupefied with fear, revived suddenly and began to
shout:—" 'Ear 'im; that's the way they tawlk to us. Vy
donch 'ee 'it 'im—one ov yer? 'It 'im. 'It 'im! Comin'
the mate over us. We are as good men as 'ee! We're
all goin' to 'ell now. We 'ave been starved in this rotten
ship, an' now we're goin' to be drowned for them black
'earted bullies! 'It 'im!" He shrieked in the deepening
gloom, he blubbered and sobbed, screaming:—" 'It
'im! 'It 'im!" The rage and fear of his disregarded right
to live tried the steadfastness of hearts more than the
menacing shadows of the night that advanced through
the unceasing clamour of the gale. From aft Mr. Baker
was heard:— "Is one of you men going to stop him—
must I come along?" "Shut up!" . . . "Keep quiet!"
cried various voices, exasperated, trembling with cold.
—"You'll get one across the mug from me directly,"
said an invisible seaman, in a weary tone, "I won't let
the mate have the trouble." He ceased and lay still
with the silence of despair. On the black sky the stars,
coming out, gleamed over an inky sea that, speckled
with foam, flashed back at them the evanescent and
pale light of a dazzling whiteness born from the black
turmoil of the waves. Remote in the eternal calm they
glittered hard and cold above the uproar of the earth;
they surrounded the vanquished and tormented ship
on all sides: more pitiless than the eyes of a triumphant
mob, and as unapproachable as the hearts of men.

The icy south wind howled exultingly under the
sombre splendour of the sky. The cold shook the men

with a resistless violence as though it had tried to shake them to pieces. Short moans were swept unheard off the stiff lips. Some complained in mutters of "not feeling themselves below the waist"; while those who had closed their eyes, imagined they had a block of ice on their chests. Others, alarmed at not feeling any pain in their fingers, beat the deck feebly with their hands— obstinate and exhausted. Wamibo stared vacant and dreamy. The Scandinavians kept on a meaningless mutter through chattering teeth. The spare Scotchmen, with determined efforts, kept their lower jaws still. The West-country men lay big and stolid in an invulnerable surliness. A man yawned and swore in turns. Another breathed with a rattle in his throat. Two elderly hard-weather shellbacks, fast side by side, whispered dismally to one another about the landlady of a boarding-house in Sunderland, whom they both knew. They extolled her motherliness and her liberality; they tried to talk about the joint of beef and the big fire in the downstairs kitchen. The words dying faintly on their lips ended in light sighs. A sudden voice cried into the cold night, "O Lord!" No one changed his position or took any notice of the cry. One or two passed, with a repeated and vague gesture, their hands over their faces, but most of them kept very still. In the benumbed immobility of their bodies they were excessively wearied by their thoughts, which rushed with the rapidity and vividness of dreams. Now and then, by an abrupt and startling exclamation, they answered the weird hail of some illusion; then, again, in silence contemplated the vision of known faces and familiar things. They recalled the aspect of forgotten shipmates and heard the voice of dead and gone skippers. They remembered the noise of gaslit streets, the steamy heat of tap-rooms or the scorching sunshine of calm days at sea.

Mr. Baker left his insecure place, and crawled, with

stoppages, along the poop. In the dark and on all fours
he resembled some carnivorous animal prowling amongst
corpses. At the break, propped to windward of a stanchion, he looked down on the main deck. It seemed to
him that the ship had a tendency to stand up a little
more. The wind had eased a little, he thought, but the
sea ran as high as ever. The waves foamed viciously,
and the lee side of the deck disappeared under a hissing
whiteness as of boiling milk, while the rigging sang
steadily with a deep vibrating note, and, at every upward swing of the ship, the wind rushed with a long-
drawn clamour amongst the spars. Mr. Baker watched
very still. A man near him began to make a blabbing
noise with his lips, all at once and very loud, as though
the cold had broken brutally through him. He went on:
—"Ba—ba—ba—brrr—brr—ba—ba."—"Stop    that!"
cried Mr. Baker, groping in the dark. "Stop it!" He
went on shaking the leg he found under his hand.—
"What is it, sir?" called out Belfast, in the tone of a man
awakened suddenly; "We are looking after that 'ere
Jimmy."—"Are you? Ough! Don't make that row then.
Who's that near you?"—"It's me—the boatswain,
sir," growled the West-country man; "we are trying to
keep life in that poor devil."—"Aye, aye!" said Mr.
Baker. "Do it quietly, can't you?"—"He wants us to
hold him up above the rail," went on the boatswain,
with irritation, "says he can't breathe here under our
jackets."—"If we lift 'im, we drop 'im overboard," said
another voice, "we can't feel our hands with cold."—
"I don't care. I am choking!" exclaimed James Wait
in a clear tone.—"Oh, no, my son," said the boatswain,
desperately, "you don't go till we all go on this fine
night."—"You will see yet many a worse," said Mr.
Baker, cheerfully.—"It's no child's play, sir!" answered
the boatswain. "Some of us further aft, here, are in a
pretty bad way."—"If the blamed sticks had been cut

out of her she would be running along on her bottom
now like any decent ship, an' giv' us all a chance," said
some one, with a sigh.—"The old man wouldn't have
it . . . much he cares for us," whispered another.—
"Care for you!" exclaimed Mr. Baker, angrily. "Why
should he care for you? Are you a lot of women passengers to be taken care of? We are here to take care of
the ship—and some of you ain't up to that. Ough! . . .
What have you done so very smart to be taken care
of? Ough! . . . Some of you can't stand a bit of a
breeze without crying over it."—"Come, sorr. We
ain't so bad," protested Belfast, in a voice shaken by
shivers; "we ain't . . . brr . . ."—"Again," shouted
the mate, grabbing at the shadowy form; "again! . . .
Why, you're in your shirt! What have you done?"
—"I've put my oilskin and jacket over that half-dead
nayggur—and he says he chokes," said Belfast, com-
plainingly.—"You wouldn't call me nigger if I wasn't
half dead, you Irish beggar!" boomed James Wait, vigorously.—"You . . . brr . . . You wouldn't be white
if you were ever so well . . . I will fight you . . .
brrr . . . in fine weather . . . brrr . . . with one
hand tied behind my back . . . brrrrr . . ."—"I don't
want your rags—I want air," gasped out the other
faintly, as if suddenly exhausted.

The sprays swept over whistling and pattering. Men
disturbed in their peaceful torpor by the pain of
quarrelsome shouts, moaned, muttering curses. Mr.
Baker crawled off a little way to leeward where a water-
cask boomed up big, with something white against it.
"Is it you, Podmore?" asked Mr. Baker. He had to repeat the question twice before the cook turned, coughing feebly.—"Yes, sir. I've been praying in my mind
for a quick deliverance; for I am prepared for any call.
. . . I——"—"Look here, cook," interrupted Mr. Baker, "the men are perishing with cold."—"Cold!" said

the cook, mournfully; "they will be warm enough before long."—"What?" asked Mr. Baker, looking along
the deck into the faint sheen of frothing water.—"They
are a wicked lot," continued the cook solemnly, but in
an unsteady voice, "about as wicked as any ship's company in this sinful world! Now, I"—he trembled so that
he could hardly speak; his was an exposed place, and
in a cotton shirt, a thin pair of trousers, and with his
knees under his nose, he received, quaking, the flicks of
stinging, salt drops; his voice sounded exhausted—
"now, I—any time . . . My eldest youngster, Mr.
Baker . . . a clever boy . . . last Sunday on shore
before this voyage he wouldn't go to church, sir. Says
I, 'You go and clean yourself, or I'll know the reason
why!' What does he do? . . . Pond, Mr. Baker—fell
into the pond in his best rig, sir! . . . Accident? . . .
'Nothing will save you, fine scholar though you are!'
says I. . . . Accident! . . . I whopped him, sir, till
I couldn't lift my arm. . . ." His voice faltered. "I
whopped 'im!" he repeated, rattling his teeth; then,
after a while, let out a mournful sound that was half a
groan, half a snore. Mr. Baker shook him by the shoulders. "Hey! Cook! Hold up, Podmore! Tell me—is there
any fresh water in the galley tank? The ship is lying
along less, I think; I would try to get forward. A little
water would do them good. Hallo! Look out! Look out!"
The cook struggled.—"Not you, sir—not you!" He began to scramble to windward. "Galley! . . . my business!" he shouted.—"Cook's going crazy now," said
several voices. He yelled:—"Crazy, am I? I am more
ready to die than any of you, officers incloosive—there!
As long as she swims I will cook! I will get you coffee."
—"Cook, ye are a gentleman!" cried Belfast. But the
cook was already going over the weather-ladder. He
stopped for a moment to shout back on the poop:—
"As long as she swims I will cook!" and disappeared as

though he had gone overboard. The men who had heard sent after him a cheer that sounded like a wail of sick children. An hour or more afterwards some one said distinctly: "He's gone for good."—"Very likely," assented the boatswain; "even in fine weather he was as smart about the deck as a milch-cow on her first voyage. We ought to go and see." Nobody moved. As the hours dragged slowly through the darkness Mr. Baker crawled back and forth along the poop several times. Some men fancied they had heard him exchange murmurs with the master, but at that time the memories were incomparably more vivid than anything actual, and they were not certain whether the murmurs were heard now or many years ago. They did not try to find out. A mutter more or less did not matter. It was too cold for curiosity, and almost for hope. They could not spare a moment or a thought from the great mental occupation of wishing to live. And the desire of life kept them alive, apathetic and enduring, under the cruel persistence of wind and cold; while the bestarred black dome of the sky revolved slowly above the ship, that drifted, bearing their patience and their suffering, through the stormy solitude of the sea.

Huddled close to one another, they fancied themselves utterly alone. They heard sustained loud noises, and again bore the pain of existence through long hours of profound silence. In the night they saw sunshine, felt warmth, and suddenly, with a start, thought that the sun would never rise upon a freezing world. Some heard laughter, listened to songs; others, near the end of the poop, could hear loud human shrieks, and opening their eyes, were surprised to hear them still, though very faint, and far away. The boatswain said:—"Why, it's the cook, hailing from forward, I think." He hardly believed his own words or recognised his own voice. It was a long time before the man next to him gave a sign of life. He punched hard his other neighbour and said:—"The cook's shouting!" Many did not understand, others did not care; the majority further aft did not believe. But the boatswain and another man had the pluck to crawl away forward to see. They seemed to have been gone for hours, and were very soon forgotten. Then suddenly men who had been plunged in a hopeless resignation became as if possessed with a desire to hurt. They belaboured one another with fists. In the darkness they struck persistently anything soft they could feel near, and with a greater effort than for a shout, whispered excitedly:—"They've got some hot coffee. . . . Boss'en got it. . . ." "No! . . . Where?" . . . "It's coming! Cook made it." James Wait moaned. Donkin scrambled viciously, caring not where he kicked, and anxious that the officers should have none of it. It came in a pot, and they drank in turns. It was hot, and while it blistered the greedy palates, it seemed incredible. The men sighed out parting with the mug:—"How 'as he done it?" Some cried weakly:—"Bully for you, doctor!"

He had done it somehow. Afterwards Archie declared that the thing was "meeraculous." For many days we wondered, and it was the one ever-interesting subject of conversation to the end of the voyage. We asked the cook, in fine weather, how he felt when he saw his stove "reared up on end." We inquired, in the north-east trade and on serene evenings, whether he had to stand on his head to put things right somewhat. We suggested he had used his bread-board for a raft, and from there comfortably had stoked his grate; and we did our best to conceal our admiration under the wit of fine irony. He affirmed not to know anything about it, rebuked our levity, declared himself, with solemn animation, to have been the object of a special mercy for the saving of our unholy lives. Fundamentally he was right, no doubt; but he need not have been so offensively positive about it—he need not have hinted so often that it would have gone hard with us had he not been there, meritorious and pure, to receive the inspiration and the strength for the work of grace. Had we been saved by his recklessness or his agility, we could have at length become reconciled to the fact; but to admit our obligation to anybody's virtue and holiness alone was as difficult for us as for any other handful of mankind. Like many benefactors of humanity, the cook took himself too seriously, and reaped the reward of irreverence. We were not ungrateful, however. He remained heroic. His saying—*the* saying of his life—became proverbial in the mouth of men as are the sayings of conquerors or sages. Later, whenever one of us was puzzled by a task and advised to relinquish it, he would express his determination to persevere and to succeed by the words: —"As long as she swims I will cook!"

The hot drink helped us through the bleak hours that precede the dawn. The sky low by the horizon took on the delicate tints of pink and yellow like the inside of a rare shell. And higher, where it glowed with a pearly sheen, a small black cloud appeared, like a forgotten fragment of the night set in a border of dazzling gold. The beams of light skipped on the crests of waves. The eyes of men turned to the eastward. The sunlight flooded their weary faces. They were giving themselves up to fatigue as though they had done for ever with their work. On Singleton's black oilskin coat the dried salt glistened like hoar frost. He hung on by the wheel, with open and lifeless eyes. Captain Allistoun, unblinking, faced the rising sun. His lips stirred, opened for the first time in twenty-four hours, and with a fresh firm voice he cried, "Wear ship!"

The commanding sharp tones made all these torpid men start like a sudden flick of a whip. Then again, motionless where they lay, the force of habit made some of them repeat the order in hardly audible murmurs. Captain Allistoun glanced down at his crew, and several, with fumbling fingers and hopeless movements, tried to cast themselves adrift. He repeated impatiently, "Wear ship. Now then, Mr. Baker, get the men along. What's the matter with them?"—"Wear ship. Do you hear there?—Wear ship!" thundered out the boatswain suddenly. His voice seemed to break through a deadly spell. Men began to stir and crawl.—"I want the fore-topmast staysail run up smartly," said the master, very loudly; "if you can't manage it standing up you must do it lying down—that's all. Bear a hand!"— "Come along! Let's give the old girl a chance," urged the boatswain.—"Aye! aye! Wear ship!" exclaimed quavering voices. The forecastle men, with reluctant faces, prepared to go forward. Mr. Baker pushed ahead, grunting, on all fours to show the way, and they followed him over the break. The others lay still with a vile hope in their hearts of not being required to move till they got saved or drowned in peace.

After some time they could be seen forward appearing on the forecastle head, one by one in unsafe attitudes; hanging on to the rails, clambering over the anchors; embracing the cross-head of the windlass or hugging the fore-capstan. They were restless with strange exertions, waved their arms, knelt, lay flat down, staggered up, seemed to strive their hardest to go overboard. Suddenly a small white piece of canvas fluttered amongst them, grew larger, beating. Its narrow head rose in jerks—and at last it stood distended and triangular in the sunshine.—"They have done it!" cried the voices aft. Captain Allistoun let go the rope he had round his wrist and rolled to leeward headlong. He could be seen casting the lee main braces off the pins while the backwash of waves splashed over him.

—"Square the main yard!" he shouted up to us—who stared at him in wonder. We hesitated to stir. "The main brace, men. Haul! haul anyhow! Lay on your backs and haul!" he screeched, half drowned down there. We did not believe we could move the main yard, but the strongest and the less discouraged tried to execute the order. Others assisted half-heartedly. Singleton's eyes blazed suddenly as he took a fresh grip of the spokes. Captain Allistoun fought his way up to windward.—"Haul, men! Try to move it! Haul, and help the ship." His hard face worked, suffused and furious. "Is she going off, Singleton?" he cried.—"Not a move yet, sir," croaked the old seaman in a horribly hoarse voice.—"Watch the helm, Singleton," spluttered the master. "Haul, men! Have you no more strength than rats? Haul, and earn your salt." Mr. Creighton, on his back, with a swollen leg and a face as white as a piece of paper, blinked his eyes; his bluish lips twitched. In the wild scramble men grabbed at him, crawled over his hurt leg, knelt on his chest. He kept perfectly still, setting his teeth without a moan, without a sigh. The master's ardour, the cries of that silent man inspired us. We hauled and hung in bunches on the rope. We heard him say with violence to Donkin, who sprawled abjectly on his stomach—"I will brain you with this belaying pin if you don't catch hold of the brace," and that victim of men's injustice, cowardly and cheeky, whimpered:—"Are you goin' to murder us now?" while with sudden desperation he gripped the rope. Men sighed, shouted, hissed meaningless words, groaned. The yards moved, came slowly square against the wind, that hummed loudly on the yard-arms.—"Going off, sir," shouted Singleton, "she's just started."—"Catch a turn with that brace. Catch a turn!" clamoured the master. Mr. Creighton, nearly suffocated and unable to move, made a mighty effort, and with his left hand managed to nip the rope—"All fast!" cried some one. He closed his eyes as if going off into a swoon, while huddled together about the brace we watched with scared looks what the ship would do now.

She went off slowly as though she had been weary and disheartened like the men she carried. She paid off very gradually, making us hold our breath till we choked, and as soon as she had brought the wind abaft the beam she started to move, and fluttered our hearts. It was awful to see her, nearly overturned, begin to gather way and drag her submerged side through the water. The dead-eyes of the rigging churned the breaking seas. The lower half of the deck was full of mad whirlpools and eddies; and the long line of the lee rail could be seen showing black now and then in the swirls of a field of foam as dazzling and white as a field of snow. The wind sang shrilly amongst the spars; and at every slight lurch we expected her to slip to the bottom sideways from under our backs. When dead before it she made the first distinct attempt to stand up, and we encouraged her with a feeble and discordant howl. A great sea came running up aft and hung for a moment over us with a curling top; then crashed down under the counter and spread out on both sides into a great sheet of bursting froth. Above its fierce hiss we heard Singleton's croak:—"She is steering!" He had both his feet now planted firmly on the grating, and the wheel spun fast as he eased the helm.—"Bring the wind on the port quarter and steady her!" called out the master, staggering to his feet, the first man up from amongst our prostrate heap. One or two screamed with excitement:—"She rises!" Far away forward, Mr. Baker and three others were seen erect and black on the clear sky, lifting their arms, and with open mouths as though they had been shouting all together. The ship trembled, trying to lift her side, lurched back, seemed to give up with a nerveless dip, and suddenly with an unexpected jerk swung violently to windward, as though she had torn herself out from a deadly grasp. The whole immense volume of water, lifted by her deck, was thrown bodily across to starboard. Loud cracks were heard. Iron ports breaking open thundered with ringing blows. The water topped over the starboard rail with the rush of a river falling over a dam. The sea on deck, and the seas on every side of her, mingled together in a deafening roar. She rolled violently. We got up and were helplessly run or flung about from side to side. Men, rolling over and over, yelled,—"The house will go!"—"She clears herself!" Lifted by a towering sea she ran along with it for a moment, spouting thick streams of water through every opening of her wounded sides. The lee braces having been carried away or washed off the pins, all the ponderous yards on the fore swung from side to side and with appalling rapidity at every roll. The men forward were seen crouching here and there with fearful glances upwards at the enormous spars that whirled about over their heads. The torn canvas and the ends of broken gear streamed in the wind like wisps of hair. Through the clear sunshine, over the flashing turmoil and uproar of the seas, the ship ran blindly, dishevelled and headlong, as if fleeing for her life; and on the poop we spun, we tottered about, distracted and noisy. We all spoke at once in a thin babble; we had the aspect of invalids and the gestures of maniacs. Eyes shone, large and haggard, in smiling, meagre faces that seemed to have been dusted over with powdered chalk. We stamped, clapped our hands, feeling ready to jump and do anything; but in reality hardly able to keep on our feet. Captain Allistoun, hard and slim, gesticulated

madly from the poop at Mr. Baker: "Steady these foreyards! Steady them the best you can!" On the main
deck, men excited by his cries, splashed, dashing aimlessly here and there with the foam swirling up to their
waists. Apart, far aft, and alone by the helm, old Singleton had deliberately tucked his white beard under the
top button of his glistening coat. Swaying upon the
din and tumult of the seas, with the whole battered
length of the ship launched forward in a rolling rush
before his steady old eyes, he stood rigidly still, forgotten by all, and with an attentive face. In front of his
erect figure only the two arms moved crosswise with a
swift and suddenly readiness, to check or urge again
the rapid stir of circling spokes. He steered with care.

## IV

On men reprieved by its disdainful mercy, the immortal sea confers in its justice the full privilege of desired unrest. Through the perfect wisdom of its grace
they are not permitted to meditate at ease upon the complicated and acrid savour of existence. They must without pause justify their life to the eternal pity that
commands toil to be hard and unceasing, from sunrise
to sunset, from sunset to sunrise; till the weary succession of nights and days tainted by the obstinate clamour of sages, demanding bliss and empty heaven, is
redeemed at last by the vast silence of pain and
labour, by the dumb fear and the dumb courage of
men obscure, forgetful, and enduring.

The master and Mr. Baker coming face to face stared
for a moment, with the intense and amazed looks of
men meeting unexpectedly after years of trouble.
Their voices were gone, and they whispered desperately at one another.—"Any one missing?" asked Captain Allistoun.—"No. All there."—"Anybody hurt?"

—"Only the second mate."—"I will look after him directly. We're lucky."—"Very," articulated Mr. Baker, faintly. He gripped the rail and rolled bloodshot eyes. The little grey man made an effort to raise his voice above a dull mutter, and fixed his chief mate with a cold gaze, piercing like a dart.—"Get sail on the ship," he said, speaking authoritatively and with an inflexible snap of his thin lips. "Get sail on her as soon as you can. This is a fair wind. At once, sir—Don't give the men time to feel themselves. They will get done up and stiff, and we will never . . . We must get her along now" . . . He reeled to a long heavy roll; the rail dipped into the glancing, hissing water. He caught a shroud, swung helplessly against the mate . . . "now we have a fair wind at last—Make—sail." His head rolled from shoulder to shoulder. His eyelids began to beat rapidly. "And the pumps—pumps, Mr. Baker." He peered as though the face within a foot of his eyes had been half a mile off." Keep the men on the move to—to get her along," he mumbled in a drowsy tone, like a man going off into a doze. He pulled himself together suddenly. "Mustn't stand. Won't do," he said with a painful attempt at a smile. He let go his hold, and, propelled by the dip of the ship, ran aft unwillingly, with small steps, till he brought up against the binnacle stand. Hanging on there he looked up in an aimless manner at Singleton, who, unheeding him, watched anxiously the end of the jib-boom—"Steering gear works all right?" he asked. There was a noise in the old seaman's throat, as though the words had been rattling together before they could come out.—"Steers . . . like a little boat," he said, at last, with hoarse tenderness, without giving the master as much as half a glance —then, watchfully, spun the wheel down, steadied, flung it back again. Captain Allistoun tore himself away from the delight of leaning against the binnacle,

and began to walk the poop, swaying and reeling to
preserve his balance. . . .

The pump-rods, clanking, stamped in short jumps
while the fly-wheels turned smoothly, with great speed,
at the foot of the mainmast, flinging back and forth
with a regular impetuosity two limp clusters of men
clinging to the handles. They abandoned themselves,
swaying from the hip with twitching faces and stony
eyes. The carpenter, sounding from time to time, exclaimed mechanically: "Shake her up! Keep her going!"
Mr. Baker could not speak, but found his voice to shout;
and under the goad of his objurgations, men looked to
the lashings, dragged out new sails; and thinking themselves unable to move, carried heavy blocks aloft—
overhauled the gear. They went up the rigging with
faltering and desperate efforts. Their heads swam as
they shifted their hold, stepped blindly on the yards
like men in the dark; or trusted themselves to the first
rope at hand with the negligence of exhausted
strength. The narrow escapes from falls did not disturb
the languid beat of their hearts; the roar of the seas
seething far below them sounded continuous and faint
like an indistinct noise from another world: the wind
filled their eyes with tears, and with heavy gusts tried
to push them off from where they swayed in insecure
positions. With streaming faces and blowing hair they
flew up and down between sky and water, bestriding
the ends of yard-arms, crouching on foot-ropes, embracing lifts to have their hands free, or standing up
against chain ties. Their thoughts floated vaguely between the desire of rest and the desire of life, while
their stiffened fingers cast off head-earrings, fumbled
for knives, or held with tenacious grip against the
violent shocks of beating canvas. They glared savagely
at one another, made frantic signs with one hand while
they held their life in the other, looked down on the

narrow strip of flooded deck, shouted along to leeward:
"Light-to!" . . . "Haul out!" . . . "Make fast!" Their
lips moved, their eyes started, furious and eager with
the desire to be understood, but the wind tossed their
words unheard upon the disturbed sea. In an unendurable and unending strain they worked like men driven
by a merciless dream to toil in an atmosphere of ice or
flame. They burnt and shivered in turns. Their eyeballs
smarted as if in the smoke of a conflagration; their heads
were ready to burst with every shout. Hard fingers
seemed to grip their throats. At every roll they thought:
Now I must let go. It will shake us all off—and thrown
about aloft they cried wildly: "Look out there—catch the
end." . . . "Reeve clear" . . . "Turn this block. . . ."
They nodded desperately; shook infuriated faces, "No!
No! From down up." They seemed to hate one another
with a deadly hate. The longing to be done with it all
gnawed their breasts, and the wish to do things well was
a burning pain. They cursed their fate, contemned
their life, and wasted their breath in deadly imprecations upon one another. The sailmaker, with his bald
head bared, worked feverishly, forgetting his intimacy
with so many admirals. The boatswain, climbing up
with marlin-spikes and bunches of spunyarn rovings,
or kneeling on the yard and ready to take a turn with
the midship-stop, had acute and fleeting visions of his
old woman and the youngsters in a moorland village.
Mr. Baker, feeling very weak, tottered here and there,
grunting and inflexible, like a man of iron. He waylaid
those who, coming from aloft, stood gasping for breath.
He ordered, encouraged, scolded. "Now then—to the
main topsail now! Tally on to that gantline. Don't stand
about there!"—"Is there no rest for us?" muttered
voices. He spun round fiercely, with a sinking heart.
—"No! No rest till the work is done. Work till you drop.
That's what you're here for." A bowed seaman at his

elbow gave a short laugh.—"Do or die," he croaked
bitterly, then spat into his broad palms, swung up his
long arms, and grasping the rope high above his head
sent out a mournful, wailing cry for a pull all together.
A sea boarded the quarter-deck and sent the whole lot
sprawling to leeward. Caps, handspikes floated.
Clenched hands, kicking legs, with here and there a
spluttering face, stuck out of the white hiss of foaming
water. Mr. Baker, knocked down with the rest,
screamed—"Don't let go that rope! Hold on to it!
Hold!" And sorely bruised by the brutal fling, they held
on to it, as though it had been the fortune of their life.
The ship ran, rolling heavily, and the topping crests
glanced past port and starboard flashing their white
heads. Pumps were freed. Braces were rove. The three
topsails and foresail were set. She spurted faster over
the water, outpacing the swift rush of waves. The
menacing thunder of distanced seas rose behind her
—filled the air with the tremendous vibrations of its
voice. And devastated, battered, and wounded she
drove foaming to the northward, as though inspired
by the courage of a high endeavour. . . .

The forecastle was a place of damp desolation. They
looked at their dwelling with dismay. It was slimy,
dripping; it hummed hollow with the wind, and was
strewn with shapeless wreckage, like a half-tide cavern
in a rocky and exposed coast. Many had lost all they
had in the world, but most of the starboard watch had
preserved their chests; thin streams of water trickled
out of them, however. The beds were soaked; the
blankets spread out and saved by some nails squashed
under foot. They dragged wet rags from evil-smelling
corners, and wringing the water out, recognised their
property. Some smiled stiffly. Others looked round
blank and mute. There were cries of joy over old waist-
coats, and groans of sorrow over shapeless things found

among the splinters of smashed bed boards. One lamp was discovered jammed under the bowsprit. Charley whimpered a little. Knowles stumped here and there, sniffing, examining dark places for salvage. He poured dirty water out of a boot, and was concerned to find the owner. Those who, overwhelmed by their losses, sat on the forepeak hatch, remained elbows on knees, and, with a fist against each cheek, disdained to look up. He pushed it under their noses. "Here's a good boot. Yours?" They snarled, "No—get out." One snapped at him, "Take it to hell out of this." He seemed surprised. "Why? It's a good boot," but remembering suddenly that he had lost every stitch of his clothing, he dropped his find and began to swear. In the dim light cursing voices clashed. A man came in and, dropping his arms, stood still, repeating from the doorstep, "Here's a bloomin' old go! Here's a bloomin' old go!" A few rooted anxiously in flooded chests for tobacco. They breathed hard, clamoured with heads down. "Look at that Jack!" . . . "Here! Sam! Here's my shore-going rig spoilt for ever." One blasphemed tearfully, holding up a pair of dripping trousers. No one looked at him. The cat came out from somewhere. He had an ovation. They snatched him from hand to hand, caressed him in a murmur of pet names. They wondered where he had "weathered it out"; disputed about it. A squabbling argument began. Two men brought in a bucket of fresh water, and all crowded round it; but Tom, lean and mewing, came up with every hair astir and had the first drink. A couple of hands went aft for oil and biscuits.

Then in the yellow light and in the intervals of mopping the deck they crunched hard bread, arranging to "worry through somehow." Men chummed as to beds. Turns were settled for wearing boots and having the use of oilskin coats. They called one another "old man" and "sonny" in cheery voices. Friendly slaps resounded. Jokes were shouted. One or two stretched on the wet deck, slept with heads pillowed on their bent arms, and several, sitting on the hatch, smoked. Their weary faces appeared through a thin blue haze, pacified and with sparkling eyes. The boatswain put his head through the door. "Relieve the wheel, one of you"—he shouted inside—"it's six. Blamme if that old Singleton hasn't been there more'n thirty hours. You are a fine lot." He slammed the door again. "Mate's watch on deck," said some one. "Hey, Donkin, it's your relief!" shouted three or four together. He had crawled into an empty bunk and on wet planks lay still. "Donkin, your wheel." He made no sound. "Donkin's dead," guffawed some one. "Sell 'is bloomin' clothes," shouted another. "Donkin, if ye don't go to the bloomin' wheel they will sell your clothes—d'ye hear?" jeered a third. He groaned from his dark hole. He complained about pains in all his bones, he whimpered pitifully. "He won't go,".. exclaimed a contemptuous voice, "your turn, Davis." The young seaman rose painfully, squaring his shoulders. Donkin stuck his head out, and it appeared in the yellow light, fragile and ghastly. "I will giv' yer a pound of tobaccer," he whined in a conciliating voice, "so soon as I draw it from aft. I will—s'elp me . . ." Davis swung his arm backhanded and the head vanished. "I'll go," he said, "but you will pay for it." He walked unsteady but resolute to the door. "So I will," yelped Donkin, popping out behind him. "So I will— s'elp me . . . a pound . . . three bob they chawrge." Davis flung the door open. "You will pay my price . . . in fine weather," he shouted over his shoulder. One of the men unbuttoned his wet coat rapidly, threw it at his head. "Here, Taffy—take that, you thief!" "Thank you!" he cried from the darkness above the swish of rolling water. He could be heard splashing; a sea came

on board with a thump. "He's got his bath already," remarked a grim shellback. "Aye, aye!" grunted others.
Then, after a long silence, Wamibo made strange noises.
"Hallo, what's up with you?" said some one grumpily. "He says he would have gone for Davy," explained
Archie, who was the Finn's interpreter generally. "I
believe him!" cried voices. . . . Never mind, Dutchy
. . . You'll do, muddle-head. . . . Your turn will
come soon enough . . . You don't know when ye're
well off." They ceased, and all together turned their
faces to the door. Singleton stepped in, advanced two
paces, and stood swaying slightly. The sea hissed,
flowed roaring past the bows, and the forecastle trembled, full of deep murmurs; the lamp flared, swinging
like a pendulum. He looked with a dreamy and puzzled
stare, as though he could not distinguish the still men
from their restless shadows. There were awestruck
exclamations:—"Hallo, hallo". . . "How does it look
outside now, Singleton?" Those who sat on the hatch
lifted their eyes in silence, and the next oldest seaman
in the ship (those two understood one another, though
they hardly exchanged three words in a day) gazed
up at his friend attentively for a moment, then taking a
short clay pipe out of his mouth, offered it without a
word. Singleton put out his arm towards it, missed, staggered, and suddenly fell forward, crashing down, stiff
and headlong like an uprooted tree. There was a swift
rush. Men pushed, crying:—"He's done!" . . . "Turn
him over!" . . . "Stand clear there!" Under a crowd
of startled faces bending over him he lay on his back,
staring upwards in a continuous and intolerable manner.
In the breathless silence of a general consternation, he
said in a grating murmur:—"I am all right," and
clutched with his hands. They helped him up. He mumbled despondently:—"I am getting old . . . old."—
"Not you," cried Belfast, with ready tact. Supported

on all sides, he hung his head.—"Are you better?" they asked. He glared at them from under his eyebrows with large black eyes, spreading over his chest the bushy whiteness of a beard long and thick.—"Old! old!" he repeated sternly. Helped along, he reached his bunk. There was in it a slimy soft heap of something that smelt, as does at dead low water a muddy foreshore. It was his soaked straw bed. With a convulsive effort he pitched himself on it, and in the darkness of the narrow place could be heard growling angrily, like an irritated and savage animal uneasy in its den:—"Bit of breeze . . . small thing . . . can't stand up . . . old!" He slept at last, high-booted, sou'wester on head, and his oilskin clothes rustled, when with a deep sighing groan he turned over. Men conversed about him in quiet concerned whispers. "This will break 'im up" . . . "Strong as a horse" . . . "Aye. But he ain't what he used to be." . . . In sad murmurs they gave him up. Yet at midnight he turned out to duty as if nothing had been the matter, and answered to his name with a mournful "Here!" He brooded alone more than ever, in an impenetrable silence and with a saddened face. For many years he had heard himself called "Old Singleton," and had serenely accepted the qualification, taking it as a tribute of respect due to a man who through half a century had measured his strength against the favours and the rages of the sea. He had never given a thought to his mortal self. He lived unscathed, as though he had been indestructible, surrendering to all the temptations, weathering many gales. He had panted in sunshine; shivered in the cold; suffered hunger, thirst, debauch; passed through many trials—known all the furies. Old! It seemed to him he was broken at last. And like a man bound treacherously while he sleeps, he woke up fettered by the long chain of disregarded years. He had to take up at once the burden of all his existence, and found it almost too heavy for his strength. Old! He moved his arms, shook his head, felt his limbs. Getting old . . . and then? He looked upon the immortal sea with the awakened and groping perception of its heartless might; he saw it unchanged, black and foaming under the eternal scrutiny of the stars; he heard its impatient voice calling for him out of a pitiless vastness full of unrest, of turmoil, and of terror. He looked afar upon it, and he saw an immensity tormented and blind, moaning and furious, that claimed all the days of his tenacious life, and, when life was over, would claim the worn-out body of its slave. . . .

This was the last of the breeze. It veered quickly, changed to a black south-easter, and blew itself out, giving the ship a famous shove to the northward into the joyous sunshine of the trade. Rapid and white she ran homewards in a straight path, under a blue sky and upon the plain of a blue sea. She carried Singleton's completed wisdom, Donkin's delicate susceptibilities, and the conceited folly of us all. The hours of ineffective turmoil were forgotten; the fear and anguish of these dark moments were never mentioned in the glowing peace of fine days. Yet from that time our life seemed to start afresh as though we had died and had been resuscitated. All the first part of the voyage, the Indian Ocean on the other side of the Cape, all that was lost in a haze, like an ineradicable suspicion of some previous existence. It had ended—then there were blank hours: a livid blur—and again we lived! Singleton was possessed of sinister truth; Mr. Creighton of a damaged leg; the cook of fame—and shamefully abused the opportunities of his distinction. Donkin had an added grievance. He went about repeating with insistence: " 'E said 'e would brain me—did yer 'ear? They are goin' to murder us now for the least little thing."

We began at last to think it was rather awful. And we were conceited! We boasted of our pluck, of our capacity for work, of our energy. We remembered honourable episodes: our devotion, our indomitable perseverance—and were proud of them as though they had been the outcome of our unaided impulses. We remembered our danger, our toil—and conveniently forgot our horrible scare. We decried our officers—who had done nothing—and listened to the fascinating Donkin. His care for our rights, his disinterested concern for our dignity, were not discouraged by the invariable contumely of our words, by the disdain of our looks. Our contempt for him was unbounded—and we could not but listen with interest to that consummate artist. He told us we were good men—a "bloomin' condemned lot of good men." Who thanked us? Who took any notice of our wrongs? Didn't we lead a "dorg's loife for two poun' ten a month?" Did we think that miserable pay enough to compensate us for the risk to our lives and for the loss of our clothes? "We've lost every rag!" he cried. He made us forget that he, at any rate, had lost nothing of his own. The younger men listened, thinking this 'ere Donkin's a long-headed chap, though no kind of man, anyhow. The Scandinavians were frightened at his audacities; Wamibo did not understand; and the older seamen thoughtfully nodded their heads making the thin gold earrings glitter in the fleshy lobes of hairy ears. Severe, sunburnt faces were propped meditatively on tattooed forearms. Veined, brown fists held in their knotted grip the dirty white clay of smouldering pipes. They listened, impenetrable, broad-backed, with bent shoulders, and in grim silence. He talked with ardour, despised and irrefutable. His picturesque and filthy loquacity flowed like a troubled stream from a poisoned source. His beady little eyes danced, glancing right and left, ever on the watch for the approach of an officer. Sometimes Mr. Baker going forward to take a look at the head sheets would roll with his uncouth gait through the sudden stillness of the men; or Mr. Creighton limped along, smooth-faced, youthful, and more stern than ever, piercing our short silence with a keen glance of his clear eyes. Behind his back Donkin would begin again darting stealthy, sidelong looks.—" 'Ere's one of 'em. Some of yer 'as made 'im fast that day. Much thanks yer got for it. Ain't 'ee a-drivin' yer wusse'n ever? . . . Let 'im slip overboard. . . . Vy not? It would 'ave been less trouble. Vy not?" He advanced confidentially, backed away with great effect; he whispered, he screamed, waved his miserable arms no thicker than pipestems—stretched his lean neck—spluttered—squinted. In the pauses of his impassioned orations the wind sighed quietly aloft, the calm sea unheeded murmured in a warning whisper along the ship's side. We abominated the creature and could not deny the luminous truth of his contentions. It was all so obvious. We were indubitably good men; our deserts were great and our pay small. Through our exertions we had saved the ship and the skipper would get the credit of it. What had he done? we wanted to know. Donkin asked:—"What 'ee could do without hus?" and we could not answer. We were oppressed by the injustice of the world, surprised to perceive how long we had lived under its burden without realising our unfortunate state, annoyed by the uneasy suspicion of our undiscerning stupidity. Donkin assured us it was all our "good 'eartedness," but we would not be consoled by such shallow sophistry. We were men enough to courageously admit to ourselves our intellectual shortcomings; though from that time we refrained from kicking him, tweaking his nose, or from accidentally knocking him about, which last, after we had weathered the Cape,

had been rather a popular amusement. Davis ceased
to talk at him provokingly about black eyes and flattened noses. Charley, much subdued since the gale,
did not jeer at him.. Knowles deferentially and with a
crafty air propounded questions such as:—"Could we
all have the same grub as the mates? Could we all stop
ashore till we got it? What would be the next thing to
try for if we got that?" He answered readily with contemptuous certitude; he strutted with assurance in
clothes that were much too big for him as though he
had tried to disguise himself. These were Jimmy's
clothes mostly—though he would accept anything from
anybody; but nobody, except Jimmy, had anything to
spare. His devotion to Jimmy was unbounded. He was
for ever dodging in the little cabin, ministering to
Jimmy's wants, humouring his whims, submitting to his
exacting peevishness, often laughing with him. Nothing
could keep him away from the pious work of visiting
the sick, especially when there was some heavy hauling
to be done on deck. Mr. Baker had on two occasions
jerked him out from there by the scruff of the neck to
our inexpressible scandal. Was a sick chap to be left
without attendance? Were we to be ill-used for attending a shipmate?—"What?" growled Mr. Baker, turning
menacingly at the mutter, and the whole half-circle like
one man stepped back a pace. "Set the topmast stun-
sail. Away aloft, Donkin, overhaul the gear," ordered
the mate inflexibly. "Fetch the sail along; bend the
down-haul clear. Bear a hand." Then, the sail set,
he would go slowly aft and stand looking at the compass
for a long time, careworn, pensive, and breathing hard
as if stifled by the taint of unaccountable ill-will that
pervaded the ship. "What's up amongst them?" he
thought. "Can't make out this hanging back and growling. A good crowd, too, as they go nowadays." On deck
the men exchanged bitter words, suggested by a silly

exasperation against something unjust and irremediable that would not be denied, and would whisper into their ears long after Donkin had ceased speaking. Our little world went on its curved and unswerving path carrying a discontented and aspiring population. They found comfort of a gloomy kind in an interminable and conscientious analysis of their unappreciated worth; and inspired by Donkin's hopeful doctrines they dreamed enthusiastically of the time when every lonely ship would travel over a serene sea, manned by a wealthy and well-fed crew of satisfied skippers.

It looked as if it would be a long passage. The southeast trades, light and unsteady, were left behind; and then, on the equator and under a low grey sky, the ship, in close heat, floated upon a smooth sea that resembled a sheet of ground glass. Thunder squalls hung on the horizon, circled round the ship, far off and growling angrily, like a troop of wild beasts afraid to charge home. The invisible sun, sweeping above the upright masts, made on the clouds a blurred stain of rayless light, and a similar patch of faded radiance kept pace with it from east to west over the unglittering level of the waters. At night, through the impenetrable darkness of earth and heaven, broad sheets of flame waved noiselessly; and for half a second the becalmed craft stood out with its masts and rigging, with every sail and every rope distinct and black in the centre of a fiery outburst, like a charred ship enclosed in a globe of fire. And, again, for long hours she remained lost in a vast universe of night and silence where gentle sighs, wandering here and there like forlorn souls, made the still sails flutter as in sudden fear, and the ripple of a beshrouded ocean whisper its compassion afar—in a voice mournful, immense, and faint. . . .

When the lamp was put out, and through the door thrown wide open, Jimmy, turning on his pillow, could see vanishing beyond the straight line of top-gallant rail, the quick, repeated visions of a fabulous world made up of leaping fire and sleeping water. The lightning gleamed in his big sad eyes that seemed in a red flicker to burn themselves out in his black face, and then he would lie blinded and invisible in the midst of an intense darkness. He could hear on the quiet deck soft footfalls, the breathing of some man lounging on the doorstep; the low creak of swaying masts; or the calm voice of the watch-officer reverberating aloft, hard and loud, amongst the unstirring sails. He listened with avidity, taking a rest in the attentive perception of the slightest sound from the fatiguing wanderings of his sleeplessness. He was cheered by the rattling of blocks, reassured by the stir and murmur of the watch, soothed by the slow yawn of some sleepy and weary seaman settling himself deliberately for a snooze on the planks. Life seemed an indestructible thing. It went on in darkness, in sunshine, in sleep; tireless, it hovered affectionately round the imposture of his ready death. It was bright, like the twisted flare of lightning, and more full of surprises than the dark night. It made him safe, and the calm of its overpowering darkness was as precious as its restless and dangerous light.

But in the evening, in the dog-watches, and even far into the first night-watch, a knot of men could always be seen congregated before Jimmy's cabin. They leaned on each side of the door peacefully interested and with crossed legs; they stood astride the doorstep discoursing, or sat in silent couples on his sea-chest; while against the bulwark along the spare topmast, three or four in a row stared meditatively; with their simple

faces lit up by the projected glare of Jimmy's lamp. The
little place, repainted white, had, in the night, the
brilliance of a silver shrine where a black idol, reclining
stiffly under a blanket, blinked its weary eyes and received our homage. Donkin officiated. He had the air
of a demonstrator showing a phenomenon, a manifestation bizarre, simple, and meritorious that, to the beholders, should be a profound and an everlasting lesson.
"Just look at 'im, 'ee knows what's what—never fear!"
he exclaimed now and then, flourishing a hand hard and
fleshless like the claw of a snipe. Jimmy, on his back,
smiled with reserve and without moving a limb. He
affected the languor of extreme weakness, so as to make
it manifest to us that our delay in hauling him out from
his horrible confinement, and then that night spent on
the poop among our selfish neglect of his needs, had
"done for him." He rather liked to talk about it, and of
course we were always interested. He spoke spasmodically, in fast rushes with long pauses between, as a
tipsy man walks. . . . "Cook had just given me a pan-
nikin of hot coffee. . . . Slapped it down there, on my
chest—banged the door to. . . . I felt a heavy roll
coming; tried to save my coffee, burnt my fingers . . .
and fell out of my bunk. . . . She went over so quick.
. . . Water came in through the ventilator. . . . I
couldn't move the door . . . dark as a grave . . .
tried to scramble up into the upper berth. . . . Rats
. . . a rat bit my finger as I got up. . . . I could hear
him swimming below me. . . . I thought you would
never come . . . I thought you were all gone overboard . . . of course . . . Could hear nothing but the
wind. . . . Then you came . . . to look for the
corpse, I suppose. A little more and . . ."

"Man! But ye made a rare lot of noise in here," observed Archie, thoughtfully.

"You chaps kicked up such a confounded row above.

. . . Enough to scare any one. . . . I didn't know what you were up to. . . . Bash in the blamed planks . . . my head. . . . Just what a silly, scary gang of fools would do. . . . Not much good to me anyhow. . . . Just as well . . . drown. . . . Pah."

He groaned, snapped his big white teeth, and gazed with scorn. Belfast lifted a pair of dolorous eyes, with a broken-hearted smile, clenched his fists stealthily; blue-eyed Archie caressed his red whiskers with a hesitating hand; the boatswain at the door stared a moment, and brusquely went away with a loud guffaw. Wamibo dreamed. . . . Donkin felt all over his sterile chin for the few rare hairs, and said, triumphantly, with a side-long glance at Jimmy:—"Look at 'im! Wish I was 'arf has 'ealthy as 'ee is—I do." He jerked a short thumb over his shoulder towards the after end of the ship. "That's the blooming way to do 'em!" he yelped, with forced heartiness. Jimmy said:—"Don't be a dam' fool," in a pleasant voice. Knowles, rubbing his shoulder against the doorpost, remarked shrewdly:—"We càn't all go an' be took sick—it would be mutiny."—"Mutiny —gawn!" jeered Donkin, "there's no bloomin' law against bein' sick."—"There's six weeks' hard work for refoosing dooty," argued Knowles, "I mind I once seed in Cardiff the crew of an overloaded ship—leastways she weren't overloaded, only a fatherly old gentleman with a white beard and an umbreller came along the quay and talked to the hands. Said as how it was crool hard to be drowned in winter just for the sake of a few pounds more for the owner—he said. Nearly cried over them—he did; and he had a square mainsail coat, and a gaff-topsail hat too—all proper. So they chaps they said they wouldn't go to be drownded in winter—depending upon that 'ere Plimsoll man to see 'em through the court. They thought to have a bloom-in' lark and two or three days' spree. And the beak giv' 'em six weeks—coss the ship warn't overloaded. Anyways they made it out in court that she wasn't. There wasn't one overloaded ship in Penarth Dock at all. 'Pears that old coon he was only on pay and allowance from some kind people, under orders to look for overloaded ships, and he couldn't see no further than the length of his umbreller. Some of us in the boardinghouse, where I live when I'm looking for a ship in Cardiff, stood by to duck that old weeping spunger in the dock. We kept a good look-out, too—but he topped his boom directly he was outside the court. . . . Yes. They got six weeks' hard. . . ."

They listened, full of curiosity, nodding in the pauses their rough pensive faces. Donkin opened his mouth once or twice, but restrained himself. Jimmy lay still with open eyes and not at all interested. A seaman emitted the opinion that after a verdict of atrocious partiality "the bloomin' beaks go an' drink at the skipper's expense." Others assented. It was clear, of course. Donkin said:—"Well, six weeks ain't much trouble. You sleep all night in, reg'lar, in chokey. Do it on my 'ead." "You are used to it ainch'ee, Donkin?" asked somebody. Jimmy condescended to laugh. It cheered up every one wonderfully. Knowles, with surprising mental agility, shifted his ground. "If we all went sick what would become of the ship? eh?" He posed the problem and grinned all round.—"Let 'er go to 'ell," sneered Donkin. "Damn 'er. She ain't yourn."—"What? Just let her drift?" insisted Knowles in a tone of unbelief.—"Aye! Drift, an' be blowed," affirmed Donkin with fine recklessness. The other did not see it—meditated.—"The stores would run out," he muttered, "and . . . never get anywhere . . . And what about pay-day?" he added with greater assurance.—"Jack likes a good pay-day," exclaimed a listener on the doorstep. "Aye, because then the girls put one arm round his neck an' t'other in his pocket, and call him ducky. Don't they, Jack?"—"Jack, you're a terror with the gals."—"He takes three of 'em in tow to once, like one of 'em Watkinses two-funnel tugs waddling away with three schooners behind."—"Jack, you're a lame scamp."—"Jack, tell us about that one with a blue eye and a black eye. Do."— "There's plenty of girls with one black eye along the Highway by . . ."—"No, that's a speshul one—come, Jack." Donkin looked severe and disgusted; Jimmy very bored; a grey-haired sea-dog shook his head slightly, smiling at the bowl of his pipe, discreetly amused. Knowles turned about bewildered; stammered first at one, then at another.— "No! . . . I never! . . . can't talk sensible sense midst you. . . . Always on the kid." He retired bashfully —muttering and pleased. They laughed, hooting in the crude light, around Jimmy's bed, when on a white pillow his hollowed black face moved to and fro restlessly. A puff of wind came, made the flame of the lamp leap, and outside, high up, the sails fluttered, while near by the block of the foresheet struck a ringing blow on the iron bulwark. A voice far off cried, "Helm up!" another, more faint, answered, "Hard-up, sir!" They became silent—waited expectantly. The grey-haired seaman knocked his pipe on the doorstep and stood up. The ship leaned over gently and the sea seemed to wake up, murmuring drowsily. "Here's a little wind comin'," said some one very low. Jimmy turned over slowly to face the breeze. The voice in the night cried loud and commanding:—"Haul the spanker out." The group before the door vanished out of the light. They could be heard tramping aft while they repeated with varied intonations:—"Spanker out!" . . . "Out spanker, sir!" Donkin remained alone with Jimmy.

There was a silence. Jimmy opened and shut his lips several times as if swallowing draughts of fresher air; Donkin moved the toes of his bare feet and looked at them thoughtfully.

"Ain't you going to give them a hand with the sail?" asked Jimmy.

"No. If six ov 'em ain't 'nough beef to set that blamed, rotten spanker, they ain't fit to live," answered Donkin in a bored, far-away voice, as though he had been talking from the bottom of a hole. Jimmy considered the conical, fowl-like profile with a queer kind of interest; he was leaning out of his bunk with the calculating, uncertain expression of a man who reflects how best to lay hold of some strange creature that looks as though it could sting or bite. But he said only:—"The mate will miss you—and there will be ructions."

Donkin got up to go. "I will do for 'im some dark night; see if I don't," he said over his shoulder.

Jimmy went on quickly:—"You're like a poll-parrot, like a screechin' poll-parrot." Donkin stopped and cocked his head attentively on one side. His big ears stood out, transparent and veined, resembling the thin wings of a bat.

"Yuss?" he said, with his back towards Jimmy.

"Yes! Chatter out all you know—like . . . like a dirty white cockatoo."

Donkin waited. He could hear the other's breathing, long and slow; the breathing of a man with a hundred-weight or so on the breastbone. Then he asked calmly:—"What do I know?"

"What? . . . What I tell you . . . not much. What do you want . . . to talk about my health so . . ."

"It's a blooming imposyshun. A bloomin', stinkin', first-class imposyshun—but it don't tyke me in. Not it."

Jimmy kept still. Donkin put his hands in his pockets, and in one slouching stride came up to the bunk.

"I talk—what's the odds. They ain't men 'ere—sheep they are. A driven lot of sheep. I 'old you up . . . Vy not? You're well orf."

"I am . . . I don't ;ay anything about that. . . ."

"Well. Let 'em see it. Let 'em larn what a man can do. I am a man, I know all about yer. . . ." Jimmy threw himself further away on the pillow; the other stretched out his skinny neck, jerked his bird face down at him as though pecking at the eyes. "I am a man. I've seen the inside of every chokey in the Colonies rather'n give up my rights. . . ."

"You are a jail-prop," said Jimmy, weakly.

"I am . . . an' proud of it, too. You! You 'aven't the bloomin' nerve—so you inventyd this 'ere dodge. . . ." He paused; then with marked after-thought accentuated slowly:—"Yer ain't sick—are yer?"

"No," said Jimmy, firmly. "Been out of sorts now and again this year," he mumbled with a sudden drop in his voice.

Donkin closed one eye, amicable and confidential. He whispered:—"Ye 'ave done this afore 'aven'tchee?" Jimmy smiled—then as if unable to hold back he let himself go:—"Last ship—yes. I was out of sorts on the passage. See? It was easy. They paid me off in Calcutta, and the skipper made no bones about it either. . . . I got my money all right. Laid up fifty-eight days! The fools! O Lord! The fools! Paid right off." He laughed spasmodically. Donkin chimed in giggling. Then Jimmy coughed violently. "I am as well as ever, he said, as soon as he could draw breath.

Donkin made a derisive gesture. "In course," he said, profoundly, "any one can see that."—"They don't," said Jimmy, gasping like a fish.—"They would swallow any yarn," affirmed Donkin.—"Don't you let on too much," admonished Jimmy in an exhausted voice.—

"Your little gyme? Eh?" commented Donkin, jovially. Then with sudden disgust: "Yer all for yerself, s'long as ye're right. . . ."

So charged with egoism James Wait pulled the blanket up to his chin and lay still for a while. His heavy lips protruded in an everlasting black pout. "Why are you so hot on making trouble?" he asked without much interest.

"'Cos it's a bloomin' shayme. We are put upon . . . bad food, bad pay . . . I want us to kick up a bloomin' row; a blamed 'owling row that would make 'em remember! Knocking people about . . . brain us . . . indeed! Ain't we men?" His altruistic indignation blazed. Then he said calmly:—"I've been airing yer clothes."—"All right," said Jimmy, languidly, "bring them in."—"Giv' us the key of your chest, I'll put 'em away for yer," said Donkin with friendly eagerness.— "Bring 'em in, I will put them away myself," answered James Wait with severity. Donkin looked down, muttering. . . . "What d'you say? What d'you say?" inquired Wait anxiously.—"Nothink. The night's dry, let 'em 'ang out till the morning," said Donkin, in a strangely trembling voice, as though restraining laughter or rage. Jimmy seemed satisfied.—"Give me a little water for the night in my mug—there," he said. Donkin took a stride over the doorstep.—"Git it yerself," he replied in a surly tone. "You can do it, unless you *are* sick."—"Of course I can do it," said Wait, "only . . ."—"Well, then, do it," said Donkin, viciously, "if yer can look after yer clothes, yer can look after yerself." He went on deck without a look back.

Jimmy reached out for the mug. Not a drop. He put it back gently with a faint sigh—and closed his eyes. He thought:—That lunatic Belfast will bring me some water if I ask. Fool. I am very thirsty. . . . It was very hot in the cabin, and it seemed to turn slowly round, detach itself from the ship, and swing out smoothly into a luminous, arid space where a black sun shone, spinning very fast. A place without any water! No water! A policeman with the face of Donkin drank a glass of beer by the side of an empty well, and flew away flapping vigorously. A ship whose mastheads protruded through the sky and could not be seen was discharging grain, and the wind whirled the dry husks in spirals along the quay of a dock with no water in it. He whirled along with the husks—very tired and light. All his inside was gone. He felt lighter than the husks— and more dry. He expanded his hollow chest. The air streamed in, carrying away in its rush a lot of strange things that resembled houses, trees, people, lamp-posts. . . . No more! There was no more air—and he had not finished drawing his long breath. But he was in jail! They were locking him up. A door slammed. They turned the key twice, flung a bucket of water over him—Phoo! What for?

He opened his eyes, thinking the fall had been very heavy for an empty man—empty—empty. He was in his cabin. Ah! All right! His face was streaming with perspiration, his arms heavier than lead. He saw the cook standing in the doorway, a brass key in one hand and a bright tin hook-pot in the other.

"I have locked up the galley for the night," said the cook, beaming benevolently. "Eight bells just gone. I brought you a pot of cold tea for your night's drinking, Jimmy. I sweetened it with some white cabin sugar, too. Well—it won't break the ship."

He came in, hung the pot on the edge of the bunk, asked perfunctorily, "How goes it?" and sat down on the box.—"H'm," grunted Wait, inhospitably. The cook wiped his face with a dirty cotton rag, which, afterwards, he tied round his neck.—"That's how them

firemen do in steamboats," he said, serenely, and much
pleased with himself. "My work is as heavy as theirs—
I'm thinking—and longer hours. Did you ever see them
down the stokehold? Like fiends they look—firing—
firing—firing—down there."

He pointed his forefinger at the deck. Some gloomy
thought darkened his shining face, fleeting, like the
shadow of a travelling cloud over the light of a peaceful
sea. The relieved watch tramped noisily forward, passing in a body across the sheen of the doorway. Some
one cried, "Good-night!" Belfast stopped for a moment
and looked at Jimmy, quivering and speechless with
repressed emotion. He gave the cook a glance charged
with dismal foreboding, and vanished. The cook cleared
his throat. Jimmy stared upwards and kept as still as a
man in hiding.

The night was clear, with a gentle breeze. Above
the mastheads the resplendent curve of the Milky
Way spanned the sky like a triumphal arch of eternal
light, thrown over the dark pathway of the earth. On
the forecastle head a man whistled with loud precision
a lively jig, while another could be heard faintly, shuffling and stamping in time. There came from forward
a confused murmur of voices, laughter—snatches of
song. The cook shook his head, glanced obliquely at
Jimmy, and began to mutter. "Aye. Dance and sing.
That's all they think of. I am surprised that Providence
don't get tired. . . . They forget the day that's sure
to come . . . but you. . . ."

Jimmy drank a gulp of tea, hurriedly, as though he
had stolen it, and shrank under his blanket, edging
away towards the bulkhead. The cook got up, closed
the door, then sat down again and said distinctly:—

"Whenever I poke my galley fire I think of you chaps
—swearing, stealing, lying, and worse—as if there was
no such thing as another world. . . . Not bad fellows,

either, in a way," he conceded, slowly; then, after a pause of regretful musing, he went on in a resigned tone:—"Well, well. They will have a hot time of it. Hot! Did I say? The furnaces of one of them White Star boats ain't nothing to it."

He kept very quiet for a while. There was a great stir in his brain; an addled vision of bright outlines; an exciting row of rousing songs and groans of pain. He suffered, enjoyed, admired, approved. He was delighted, frightened, exalted—as on that evening (the only time in his life—twenty-seven years ago; he loved to recall the number of years) when as a young man he had—through keeping bad company—become intoxicated in an East-end music-hall. A tide of sudden feeling swept him clean out of his body. He soared. He contemplated the secret of the hereafter. It commended itself to him. It was excellent; he loved it, himself, all hands, and Jimmy. His heart overflowed with tenderness, with comprehension, with the desire to meddle, with anxiety for the soul of that black man, with the pride of possessed eternity, with the feeling of might. Snatch him up in his arms and pitch him right into the middle of salvation. . . . The black soul—blacker—body—rot—Devil. No! Talk—strength—Samson. . . . There was a great din as of cymbals in his ears; he flashed through an ecstatic jumble of shining faces, lilies, prayer-books, unearthly joy, white skirts, gold harps, black coats, wings. He saw flowing garments, clean shaved faces, a sea of light—a lake of pitch. There were sweet scents, a smell of sulphur—red tongues of flame licking a white mist. An awesome voice thundered! . . . It lasted three seconds.

"Jimmy!" he cried in an inspired tone. Then he hesitated. A spark of human pity glimmered yet through the infernal fog of his supreme conceit.

"What?" said James Wait, unwillingly. There was a

silence. He turned his head just the least bit, and stole
a cautious glance. The cook's lips moved without a
sound; his face was rapt, his eyes turned up. He seemed
to be mentally imploring deck beams, the brass hook of
the lamp, two cockroaches.

"Look here," said Wait, "I want to go to sleep. I
think I could."

"This is no time for sleep!" exclaimed the cook, very
loud. He had prayerfully divested himself of the last
vestige of his humanity. He was a voice—a fleshless
and sublime thing, as on that memorable night—the
night when he went walking over the sea to make
coffee for perishing sinners. "This is no time for sleeping," he repeated with exaltation. "I can't sleep."

"Don't care a damn," said Wait, with factitious energy. "I can. Go an' turn in."

"Swear . . . in the very jaws! . . . In the very
jaws! Don't you see the everlasting fire . . . don't you
feel it? Blind, chockful of sin! Repent, repent! I can't
bear to think of you. I hear the call to save you. Night
and day. Jimmy, let me save you!" The words of en-
treaty and menace broke out of him in a roaring torrent. The cockroaches ran away. Jimmy perspired,
wriggling stealthily under his blanket. The cook yelled.
. . . "Your days are numbered! . . ."—"Get out of
this," boomed Wait, courageously.—"Pray with
me! . . ."—"I won't! . . ." The little cabin was as
hot as an oven. It contained an immensity of fear and
pain; an atmosphere of shrieks and moans; prayers
vociferated like blasphemies and whispered curses.
Outside, the men called by Charley, who informed
them in tones of delight that there was a holy row going
on in Jimmy's place, crowded before the closed door,
too startled to open it. All hands were there. The watch
below had jumped out on deck in their shirts, as after

a collision. Men running up asked:—"What is it?"
Others said:—"Listen!" The muffled screaming went
on:—"On your knees! On your knees!"—"Shut up!"
—"Never! You are delivered into my hands. . . .
Your life has been saved. . . . Purpose. . . . Mercy.
. . . Repent."—"You are a crazy fool! . . ."—"Account of you . . . you . . . Never sleep in this world,
if I . . ."—"Leave off."—"No! . . . stokehold . . .
only think! . . ." Then an impassioned screeching babble where words pattered like hail.—"No!" shouted
Wait.—"Yes. You are! . . . No help. . . . Everybody says so."—"You lie!"—"I see you dying this min-
nyt . . . before my eyes . . . as good as dead already."—"Help!" shouted Jimmy, piercingly.—"Not
in this valley. . . . look upwards," howled the other.
—"Go away! Murder! Help!" clamoured Jimmy. His
voice broke. There were moanings, low mutters, a few
sobs.

"What's the matter now?" said a seldom-heard voice.
—"Fall back, men! Fall back, there!" repeated Mr.
Creighton, sternly, pushing through.—"Here's the
old man," whispered some.—"The cook's in there, sir,"
exclaimed several, backing away. The door clattered
open; a broad stream of light darted out on wondering
faces: a warm whiff of vitiated air passed. The two
mates towered head and shoulders above the spare,
grey-haired man who stood revealed between them, in
shabby clothes, stiff and angular, like a small carved
figure, and with a thin, composed face. The cook got
up from his knees. Jimmy sat high in the bunk, clasping
his drawn-up legs. The tassel of the blue night-cap
almost imperceptibly trembled over his knees. They
gazed astonished at his long, curved back, while the
white corner of one eye gleamed blindly at them. He
was afraid to turn his head, he shrank within himself;

and there was an aspect astounding and animal-like in the perfection of his expectant immobility. A thing of instinct—the unthinking stillness of a scared brute.

"What are you doing here?" asked Mr. Baker, sharply. —"My duty," said the cook, with ardour.—"Your . . . what?" began the mate. Captain Allistoun touched his arm lightly.—"I know his caper," he said, in a low voice. "Come out of that, Podmore," he ordered, aloud. The cook wrung his hands, shook his fists above his head, and his arms dropped as if too heavy. For a moment he stood distracted and speechless.—"Never," he stammered, "I . . . he . . . I."—"What—do—you—say?" pronounced Captain Allistoun. "Come out at once—or . . ."—"I am going," said the cook, with a hasty and sombre resignation. He strode over the doorstep firmly—hesitated—made a few steps. They looked at him in silence.—"I make you responsible!" he cried, desperately, turning half round. "That man is dying. I make you . . ."—"You there yet?" called the master in a threatening tone.—"No, sir," he exclaimed, hurriedly, in a startled voice. The boatswain led him away by the arm; some one laughed; Jimmy lifted his head for a stealthy glance, and in one unexpected leap sprang out of his bunk; Mr. Baker made a clever catch and felt him very limp in his arms; the group at the door grunted with surprise.—"He lies," gasped Wait, "he talked about black devils—he is a devil—a white devil—I am all right." He stiffened himself, and Mr. Baker, experimentally, let him go. He staggered a pace or two; Captain Allistoun watched him with a quiet and penetrating gaze; Belfast ran to his support. He did not appear to be aware of any one near him; he stood silent for a moment, battling single-handed with a legion of nameless terrors, amidst the eager looks of excited men who watched him far off, utterly alone in the impenetrable solitude of his fear.

The sea gurgled through the scuppers as the ship heeled over to a short puff of wind.

"Keep him away from me," said James Wait at last in his fine baritone voice, and leaning with all his weight on Belfast's neck. "I've been better this last week . . . I am well . . . I was going back to duty . . . to-morrow—now if you like—Captain." Belfast hitched his shoulders to keep him upright.

"No," said the master, looking at him, fixedly.

Under Jimmy's armpit Belfast's red face moved uneasily. A row of eyes gleaming stared on the edge of light. They pushed one another with elbows, turned their heads, whispered. Wait let his chin fall on his breast and, with lowered eyelids, looked round in a suspicious manner.

"Why not?" cried a voice from the shadows, "the man's all right, sir."

"I am all right," said Wait, with eagerness. "Been sick . . . better . . . turn-to now." He sighed.—"Howly Mother!" exclaimed Belfast with a heave of the shoulders, "stand up, Jimmy."—"Keep away from me then," said Wait, giving Belfast a petulant push, and reeling fetched against the doorpost. His cheekbones glistened as though they had been varnished. He snatched off his night-cap, wiped his perspiring face with it, flung it on the deck. "I am coming out," he declared without stirring.

"No. You don't," said the master, curtly. Bare feet shuffled, disapproving voices murmured all round; he went on as if he had not heard:—"You have been skulking nearly all the passage and now you want to come out. You think you are near enough to the paytable now. Smell the shore, hey?"

"I've been sick . . . now—better," mumbled Wait, glaring in the light.—"You have been shamming sick," retorted Captain Allistoun with severity; "Why . . ."

he hesitated for less than half a second. "Why, anybody can see that. There's nothing the matter with you, but you choose to lie-up to please yourself—and now you shall lie-up to please me. Mr. Baker, my orders are that this man is not to be allowed on deck to the end of the passage."

There were exclamations of surprise, triumph, indignation. The dark group of men swung across the light. "What for?" "Told you so . . ." "Bloomin' shame . . ."—"We've got to say somethink about that," screeched Donkin from the rear.—"Never mind, Jim—we will see you righted," cried several together. An elderly seaman stepped to the front. "D'ye mean to say, sir," he asked, ominously, "that a sick chap ain't allowed to get well in this 'ere hooker?" Behind him Donkin whispered excitedly amongst a staring crowd where no one spared him a glance, but Captain Allistoun shook a forefinger at the angry bronzed face of the speaker.—"You—you hold your tongue," he said, warningly.—"This isn't the way," clamoured two or three younger men.—"Are we bloomin' masheens?" inquired Donkin in a piercing tone, and dived under the elbows of the front rank.—"Soon show 'im we ain't boys . . ."—"The man's a man if he is black."—"We ain't goin' to work this bloomin' ship shorthanded if Snowball's all right . . ."—"He says he is."—"Well then, strike, boys, strike!"—"That's the bloomin' ticket." Captain Allistoun said sharply to the second mate: "Keep quiet, Mr. Creighton," and stood composed in the tumult, listening with profound attention to mixed growls and screeches, to every exclamation and every curse of the sudden outbreak. Somebody slammed the cabin door to with a kick; the darkness full of menacing mutters leaped with a short clatter over the streak of light, and the men became gesticulating shadows that growled, hissed, laughed excitedly. Mr. Baker

whispered:—"Get away from them, sir." The big shape
of Mr. Creighton hovered silently about the slight
figure of the master.—"We have been hymposed upon
all this voyage," said a gruff voice, "but this 'ere fancy
takes the cake."—"That man is a shipmate."—"Are
we bloomin' kids?"—"The port watch will refuse duty."
Charley carried away by his feeling whistled shrilly,
then yelped:—"Giv' us our Jimmy!" This seemed to
cause a variation in the disturbance. There was a fresh
burst of squabbling uproar. A lot of quarrels were set
going at once.—"Yes."—"No."—"Never been sick."—
"Go for them to once."—"Shut yer mouth, youngster
—this is men's work."—"Is it?" muttered Captain Allistoun, bitterly. Mr. Baker grunted: "Ough! They're
gone silly. They've been simmering for the last month."
—"I did notice," said the master.—"They have started
a row amongst themselves now," said Mr. Creighton
with disdain, "better get aft, sir. We will soothe them."
"Keep your temper, Creighton," said the master. And
the three men began to move slowly towards the cabin
door.

In the shadows of the fore rigging a dark mass
stamped, eddied, advanced, retreated. There were
words of reproach, encouragement, unbelief, execration. The elder seamen, bewildered and angry, growled
their determination to go through with something or
other; but the younger school of advanced thought exposed their and Jimmy's wrongs with confused shouts
arguing amongst themselves. They clustered round that
moribund carcass, the fit emblem of their aspirations,
and encouraging one another they swayed, they
tramped on one spot, shouting that they would not be
"put upon." Inside the cabin, Belfast, helping Jimmy
into his bunk, twitched all over in his desire not to miss
all the row, and with difficulty restrained the tears of
his facile emotion. James Wait, flat on his back under

the blanket, gasped complaints.—"We will back you up, never fear," assured Belfast, busy about his feet.—"I'll come out to-morrow morning—take my chance—you fellows must—" mumbled Wait, "I come out to-morrow—skipper or no skipper." He lifted one arm with great difficulty, passed the hand over his face; "Don't you let that cook . . ." he breathed out.—"No, no," said Belfast, turning his back on the bunk, "I will put a head on him if he comes near you."—"I will smash his mug!" faintly Wait exclaimed, enraged and weak; "I don't want to kill a man, but . . ." He panted fast like a dog after a run in sunshine. Some one just outside the door shouted, "He's as fit as any ov us!" Belfast put his hand on the door-handle.—"Here!" called James Wait, hurriedly, and in such a clear voice that the other spun round with a start. James Wait, stretched out black and deathlike in the dazzling light, turned his head on the pillow. His eyes stared at Belfast, appealing and impudent. "I am rather weak from lying-up so long," he said, distinctly. Belfast nodded. "Getting quite well now," insisted Wait.—"Yes. I noticed you getting better this . . . last month," said Belfast, looking down. "Hallo! What's this?" he shouted and ran out.

He was flattened directly against the side of the house by two men who lurched against him. A lot of disputes seemed to be going on all round. He got clear and saw three indistinct figures standing along in the fainter darkness under the arched foot of the mainsail, that rose above their heads like a convex wall of a high edifice. Donkin hissed:—"Go for them . . . it's dark!" The crowd took a short run aft in a body—then there was check. Donkin, agile and thin, flitted past with his right arm going like a windmill—and then stood still suddenly with his arm pointing rigidly above his head. The hurtling flight of some heavy object was heard;

it passed between the heads of the two mates, bounded heavily along the deck, struck the after-hatch with a ponderous and deadened blow. The bulky shape of Mr. Baker grew distinct. "Come to your senses, men!" he cried, advancing at the arrested crowd. "Come back, Mr. Baker!" called the master's quiet voice. He obeyed unwillingly. There was a minute of silence, then a deafening hubbub arose. Above it Archie was heard energetically:—"If ye go oot ageen I wull tell!" There were shouts. "Don't!" "Drop it!"—"We ain't that kind!" The black cluster of human forms reeled against the bulwark, back again towards the house. Ringbolts rang under stumbling feet.—"Drop it!" "Let me!"—"No!" —"Curse you . . . hah!" Then sounds as of some one's face being slapped; a piece of iron fell on the deck; a short scuffle, and some one's shadowy body scuttled rapidly across the main hatch before the shadow of a kick. A raging voice sobbed out a torrent of filthy language . . .—"Throwing things—good God!" grunted Mr. Baker in dismay.—"That was meant for me," said the master, quietly; "I felt the wind of that thing; what was it—an iron belaying-pin?"—"By Jove!" muttered Mr. Creighton. The confused voices of men talking amidships mingled with the wash of the sea, ascended between the silent and distended sails— seemed to flow away into the night, further than the horizon, higher than the sky. The stars burned steadily over the inclined mastheads. Trails of light lay on the water, broke before the advancing hull, and, after she had passed, trembled for a long time as if in awe of the murmuring sea.

Meantime the helmsman, anxious to know what the row was about, had let go the wheel, and, bent double, ran with long, stealthy footsteps to the break of the poop. The *Narcissus*, left to herself, came up gently to the wind without any one being aware of it. She gave a slight roll, and the sleeping sails woke suddenly, coming all together with a mighty flap against the masts, then filled again one after another in a quick succession of loud reports that ran down the lofty spars, till the collapsed mainsail flew out last with a violent jerk. The ship trembled from trucks to keel; the sails kept on rattling like a discharge of musketry; the gin blocks groaned. It was as if an invisible hand had given the ship an angry shake to recall the men that peopled her decks to the sense of reality, vigilance, and duty.— "Helm up!" cried the master, sharply. "Run aft, Mr. Creighton, and see what that fool there is up to."— "Flatten in the head sheets. Stand by the weather forebraces," growled Mr. Baker. Startled men ran swiftly repeating the orders. The watch below, abandoned all at once by the watch on deck, drifted towards the forecastle in twos and three, arguing noisily as they went —"We shall see to-morrow!" cried a loud voice, as if to cover with a menacing hint an inglorious retreat. And then only orders were heard, the falling of heavy coils of rope, the rattling of blocks. Singleton's white head flitted here and there in the night, high above the deck, like the ghost of a bird.—"Going off, sir!" shouted Mr. Creighton from aft.—"Full again."—"All right . . ."—"Ease off the head sheets. That will do the braces. Coil the ropes up," grunted Mr. Baker, bustling about.

Gradually the tramping noises, the confused sound of voices, died out, and the officers, coming together on the poop, discussed the events. Mr. Baker was bewildered and grunted; Mr. Creighton was calmly furious; but Captain Allistoun was composed and thoughtful. He listened to Mr. Baker's growling argumentation, to Creighton's interjected and severe remarks, while looking down on the deck he weighed in his hand the iron belaying-pin—that a moment ago had just missed his head—as if it had been the only tangible fact of the whole transaction. He was one of those commanders who speak little, seem to hear nothing, look at no one—and know everything, hear every whisper, see every fleeting shadow of their ship's life. His two big officers towered above his lean, short figure; they talked over his head; they were dismayed, surprised, and angry, while between them the little quiet man seemed to have found his taciturn serenity in the profound depths of a larger experience. Lights were burning in the forecastle; now and then a loud gust of babbling chatter came from forward, swept over the decks, and became faint, as if the unconscious ship, gliding gently through the great peace of the sea, had left behind and for ever the foolish noise of turbulent mankind. But it was renewed again and again. Gesticulating arms, profiles of heads with open mouths appeared for a moment in the illuminated squares of doorways; black fists darted—withdrew . . . "Yes. It was most damnable to have such an unprovoked row sprung on one," assented the master. . . . A tumult of yells rose in the light, abruptly ceased. . . . He didn't think there would be any further trouble just then. . . . A bell was struck aft, another, forward, answered in a deeper tone, and the clamour of ringing metal spread round the ship in a circle of wide vibrations that ebbed away into the immeasurable night of an empty sea. . . . Didn't he know them! Didn't he! In past years. Better men, too. Real men to stand by one in a tight place. Worse than devils too sometimes—downright, horned devils. Pah! This—nothing. A miss as good as a mile. . . . The wheel was being relieved in the usual way.—"Full and by," said, very loud, the man going off.—"Full and by," repeated the other, catching hold of the spokes.—"This head wind is my trouble," exclaimed the master, stamping his foot in sudden anger; "head wind! all the rest is nothing." He was calm again in a moment. "Keep them on the move to-night, gentlemen; just to let them feel we've got hold all the time—quietly, you know. Mind you keep your hands off them, Creighton. To-morrow I will talk to them like a Dutch Uncle. A crazy crowd of tinkers! Yes, tinkers! I could count the real sailors amongst them on the fingers of one hand. Nothing will do but a row—if—you—please." He paused. "Did you think I had gone wrong there, Mr. Baker?" He tapped his forehead, laughed short. "When I saw him standing there, three parts dead and so scared—black amongst that gaping lot—no grit to face what's coming to us all—the notion came to me all at once, before I could think. Sorry for him—like you would be for a sick brute. If ever creature was in a mortal funk to die! . . . I thought I would let him go out in his own way. Kind of impulse. It never came into my head, those fools. . . . H'm! Stand to it now—of course." He stuck the belaying-pin in his pocket, seemed ashamed of himself, then sharply:— "If you see Podmore at his tricks again tell him I will have him put under the pump. Had to do it once before. The fellow breaks out like that now and then. Good cook tho'." He walked away quickly, came back to the companion. The two mates followed him through the starlight with amazed eyes. He went down three steps, and changing his tone, spoke with his head near the deck:—"I shan't turn in to-night, in case of any-thing; just call out if . . . Did you see the eyes of that sick nigger, Mr. Baker? I fancied he begged me for something. What? Past all help. One lone black beggar amongst the lot of us, and he seemed to look through me into the very hell. Fancy, this wretched Podmore! Well, let him die in peace. I am master here after all. Let him be. He might have been half a man once . . . Keep a good look-out." He disappeared down below, leaving his mates facing one another, and more impressed than if they had seen a stone image shed a miraculous tear of compassion over the incertitudes of life and death. . . .

In the blue mist spreading from twisted threads that stood upright in the bowls of pipes, the forecastle appeared as vast as a hall. Between the beams a heavy cloud stagnated; and the lamps surrounded by halos burned each at the core of a purple glow in two lifeless flames without rays. Wreaths drifted in denser wisps. Men sprawled about on the deck, sat in negligent poses, or, bending a knee, drooped with one shoulder against a bulkhead. Lips moved, eyes flashed, waving arms made sudden eddies in the smoke. The murmur of voices seemed to pile itself higher and higher as if unable to run out quick enough through the narrow doors. The watch below in their shirts, and striding on long white legs, resembled raving somnambulists; while now and then one of the watch on deck would rush in, looking strangely overdressed, listen a moment, fling a rapid sentence into the noise and run out again; but a few remained near the door, fascinated, and with one ear turned to the deck. "Stick together, boys," roared Davis. Belfast tried to make himself heard. Knowles grinned in a slow, dazed way. A short fellow with a thick clipped beard kept on yelling periodically:—"Who's afeard? Who's afeard?" Another one jumped up, excited, with glazing eyes, sent out a string of unattached curses and sat down quietly. Two men discussed familiarly, striking one another's breast in turn, to clinch arguments. Three others, with their heads in a bunch, spoke all together with a confidential air, and at the top of their voices. It was a stormy chaos of speech where intelligible fragments, tossing, struck the ear. One could hear:—"In the last ship"— "Who cares? Try it on any one of us if—." "Knock

under"—"Not a hand's turn"—"He says he is all right"
—"I always thought"—"Never mind. . . ." Donkin,
crouching all in a heap against the bowsprit, hunched
his shoulderblades as high as his ears, and hanging a
peaked nose, resembled a sick vulture with ruffled
plumes. Belfast, straddling his legs, had a face red with
yelling, and with arms thrown up, figured a Maltese
cross. The two Scandinavians, in a corner, had a dumb-
founded and distracted aspect of men gazing at a cat-
aclysm. And, beyond the light, Singleton stood in
the smoke, monumental, indistinct, with his head touching the beam; like a statue of heroic size in the gloom
of a crypt.

He stepped forward, impassive and big. The noise
subsided like a broken wave: but Belfast cried once
more with uplifted arms:—"The man is dying, I tell
ye!" then sat down suddenly on the hatch and took his
head between his hands. All looked at Singleton, gazing upwards from the deck, staring out of dark corners,
or turning their heads with curious glances. They were
expectant and appeased as if that old man, who looked
at no one, had possessed the secret of their uneasy indignations and desires, a sharper vision, a clearer
knowledge. And indeed standing there amongst them,
he had the uninterested appearance of one who had
seen multitudes of ships, had listened many times to
voices such as theirs, had already seen all that could
happen on the wide seas. They heard his voice rumble
in his broad chest as though the words had been rolling towards them out of a rugged past. "What do you
want to do?" he asked. No one answered. Only Knowles
muttered—"Aye, aye," and somebody said low:—"It's
a bloomin' shame." He waited, made a contemptuous
gesture.—"I have seen rows aboard ship before some
of you were born," he said, slowly, "for something or
nothing; but never for such a thing."—"The man is

dying, I tell ye," repeated Belfast, woefully, sitting at
Singleton's feet.—"And a black fellow, too," went on
the old seaman, "I have seen them die like flies." He
stopped, thoughtful, as if trying to recollect gruesome
things, details of horrors, hecatombs of niggers. They
looked at him fascinated. He was old enough to remember slavers, bloody mutinies, pirates perhaps; who
could tell through what violences and terrors he had
lived! What would he say? He said:—"You can't help
him; die he must." He made another pause. His
moustache and beard stirred. He chewed words, mumbled behind tangled white hairs; incomprehensible and
exciting, like an oracle behind a veil. . . .—"Stop
ashore—sick.—Instead—bringing all this head wind.
Afraid. The sea will have her own.—Die in sight of
land. Always so. They know it—long passage—more
days, more dollars.—You keep quiet.—What do you
want? Can't help him." He seemed to wake up from
a dream. "You can't help yourselves," he said,
austerely, "Skipper's no fool. He has something in
his mind. Look out—I say! I know 'em!" With eyes
fixed in front he turned his head from right to left,
from left to right, as if inspecting a long row of astute
skippers.—"'Ee said 'ee would brain me!" cried Donkin in a heartrending tone. Singleton peered downwards with puzzled attention, as though he couldn't
find him.—"Damn you!" he said, vaguely, giving it up.
He radiated unspeakable wisdom, hard unconcern, the
chilling air of resignation. Round him all the listeners
felt themselves somehow completely enlightened by
their disappointment, and mute, they lolled about with
the careless ease of men who can discern perfectly the
irremediable aspect of their existence. He, profound
and unconscious, waved his arm once, and strode out
on deck without another word.

Belfast was lost in a round-eyed meditation. One or

two vaulted heavily into upper berths, and, once there, sighed; others dived head first inside lower bunks— swift, and turning round instantly upon themselves, like animals going into lairs. The grating of a knife scraping burnt clay was heard. Knowles grinned no more. Davis said, in a tone of ardent conviction: "Then our skipper's looney." Archie muttered: "My faith! we haven't heard the last of it yet!" Four bells were struck. —"Half our watch below gone!" cried Knowles in alarm, then reflected. "Well, two hours' sleep is something towards a rest," he observed, consolingly. Some already pretended to slumber; and Charley, sound asleep, suddenly said a few slurred words in an arbitrary, blank voice.—"This blamed boy has worrums!" commented Knowles from under a blanket, in a learned manner. Belfast got up and approached Archie's berth. —"We pulled him out," he whispered, sadly.— "What?" said the other, with sleepy discontent.— "And now we will have to chuck him overboard," went on Belfast, whose lower lip trembled.—"Chuck what?" asked Archie.—"Poor Jimmy," breathed out Belfast.—"He be blowed!" said Archie with untruthful brutality, and sat up in his bunk; "It's all through him. If it hadn't been for me, there would have been murder on board this ship!"—" 'Tain't his fault, is it?" argued Belfast, in a murmur; "I've put him to bed . . . an' he ain't no heavier than an empty beef-cask," he added, with tears in his eyes. Archie looked at him steadily, then turned his nose to the ship's side with determination. Belfast wandered about as though he had lost his way in the dim forecastle, and nearly fell over Donkin. He contemplated him from on high for a while. "Ain't ye going to turn in?" he asked. Donkin looked up hopelessly.—"That black'earted Scotch son of a thief kicked me!" he whispered from the floor, in a tone of utter desolation.—"And a good job, too!"

said Belfast, still very depressed; "You were as near hanging as damn-it to-night, sonny. Don't you play any of your murthering games around my Jimmy! You haven't pulled him out. You just mind! 'Cos if I start to kick you"—he brightened up a bit—"if I start to kick you, it will be Yankee fashion—to break something!" He tapped lightly with his knuckles the top of the bowed head. "You moind that, my bhoy!" he concluded, cheerily. Donkin let it pass.—"Will they split on me?" he asked with pained anxiety.—"Who— split?" hissed Belfast, coming back a step. "I would split your nose this minyt if I hadn't Jimmy to look after! Who d'ye think we are?" Donkin rose and watched Belfast's back lurch through the doorway. On all sides invisible men slept, breathing calmly. He seemed to draw courage and fury from the peace around him. Venomous and thin-faced, he glared from the ample misfit of borrowed clothes as if looking for something he could smash. His heart leaped wildly in his narrow chest. They slept! He wanted to wring necks, gouge eyes, spit on faccs. He shook a dirty pair of meagre fists at the smoking lights. "Ye're no men!" he cried, in a deadened tone. No one moved. "Yer 'aven't the pluck of a mouse!" His voice rose to a husky screech. Wamibo darted out a dishevelled head, and looked at him wildly. "Ye're sweepings ov ships! I 'ope you will all rot before you die!" Wamibo blinked, uncomprehending but interested. Donkin sat down heavily; he blew with force through quivering nostrils, he ground and snapped his teeth, and, with the chin pressed hard against the breast, he seemed busy gnawing his way through it, as if to get at the heart within. . . .

In the morning the ship, beginning another day of her wandering life, had an aspect of sumptuous freshness, like the spring-time of the earth. The washed

decks glistened in a long clear stretch; the oblique
sunlight struck the yellow brasses in dazzling splashes,
darted over the polished rods in lines of gold, and the
single drops of salt water forgotten here and there
along the rail were as limpid as drops of dew, and
sparkled more than scattered diamonds. The sails slept,
hushed by a gentle breeze. The sun, rising lonely and
splendid in the blue sky, saw a solitary ship gliding
close-hauled on the blue sea.

The men pressed three deep abreast of the mainmast and opposite the cabin-door. They shuffled,
pushed, had an irresolute mien and stolid faces. At every slight movement Knowles lurched heavily on his
short leg. Donkin glided behind backs, restless and
anxious, like a man looking for an ambush. Captain Allistoun came out on the quarter-deck suddenly. He
walked to and fro before the front. He was grey, slight,
alert, shabby in the sunshine, and as hard as adamant.
He had his right hand in the side-pocket of his jacket,
and also something heavy in there that made folds all
down that side. One of the seamen cleared his throat
ominously.—"I haven't till now found fault with you
men," said the master, stopping short. He faced them
with his worn, steely gaze, that by a universal illusion
looked straight into every individual pair of the twenty
pairs of eyes before his face. At his back Mr. Baker,
gloomy and bull-necked, grunted low; Mr. Creighton,
fresh as paint, had rosy cheeks and a ready, resolute
bearing. "And I don't now," continued the master; "but
I am here to drive this ship and keep every man-jack
aboard of her up to the mark. If you knew your work
as well as I do mine, there would be no trouble. You've
been braying in the dark about 'See to-morrow morning!' Well, you see me now. What do you want?" He
waited, stepping quickly to and fro, giving them searching glances. What did they want? They shifted from

foot to foot, they balanced their bodies; some, pushing
back their caps, scratched their heads. What did they
want? Jimmy was forgotten; no one thought of him,
alone forward in his cabin, fighting great shadows,
clinging to brazen lies, chuckling painfully over his transparent deceptions. No, not Jimmy; he was more forgotten than if he had been dead. They wanted great things.
And suddenly all the simple words they knew seemed to
be lost for ever in the immensity of their vague and
burning desire. They knew what they wanted, but they
could not find anything worth saying. They stirred on
one spot, swinging, at the end of muscular arms, big tarry
hands with crooked fingers. A murmur died out.—"What
is it—food?" asked the master. "You know the stores have
been spoiled off the Cape."—"We know that sir," said a
bearded shell-back in the front rank.—"Work too hard
—eh? Too much for your strength?" he asked again.
There was an offended silence.—"We don't want to go
shorthanded, sir," began at last Davis in a wavering
voice, "and this 'ere black— . . ."—"Enough!" cried
the master. He stood scanning them for a moment, then
walking a few steps this way and that began to storm
at them coldly, in gusts violent and cutting like the gales
of those icy seas that had known his youth.—"Tell you
what's the matter? Too big for your boots. Think yourselves damn good men. Know half your work. Do half
your duty. Think it too much. If you did ten times as
much it wouldn't be enough."—"We did our best by
her, sir," cried some one with shaky exasperation.—
"Your best," stormed on the master; "You hear a lot on
shore, don't you? They don't tell you there your best
isn't much to boast of. I tell you—your best is no better
than bad. You can do no more? No, I know, and say
nothing. But you stop your caper or I will stop it for
you. I am ready for you! Stop it!" He shook a finger at
the crowd. "As to that man," he raised his voice very

much; "as to that man, if he puts his nose out on deck without my leave I will clap him in irons. There!" The cook heard him forward, ran out of the galley lifting his arms, horrified, unbelieving, amazed, and ran in again. There was a moment of profound silence during which a bow-legged seaman, stepping aside, expectorated decorously into the scupper. "There is another thing," said the master, calmly. He made a quick stride and with a swing took an iron belaying-pin out of his pocket. "This!" His movement was so unexpected and sudden that the crowd stepped back. He gazed fixedly at their faces, and some at once put on a surprised air as though they had never seen a belaying-pin before. He held it up. "This is my affair. I don't ask you any questions, but you all know it; it has got to go where it came from." His eyes became angry. The crowd stirred uneasily. They looked away from the piece of iron, they appeared shy, they were embarrassed and shocked as though it had been something horrid, scandalous, or indelicate, that in common decency should not have been flourished like this in broad daylight. The master watched them attentively. "Donkin," he called out in a short, sharp tone.

Donkin dodged behind one, then behind another, but they looked over their shoulders and moved aside. The ranks kept on opening before him, closing behind, till at last he appeared alone before the master as though he had come up through the deck. Captain Allistoun moved close to him. They were much of a size; and at short range the master exchanged a deadly glance with the beady eyes. They wavered.—"You know this?" asked the master.—"No, I don't," answered the other, with cheeky trepidation.—"You are a cur. Take it," ordered the master. Donkin's arms seemed glued to his thighs; he stood, eyes front, as if drawn on parade. "Take it," repeated the master, and stepped closer;

they breathed on one another. "Take it," said Captain
Allistoun again, making a menacing gesture. Donkin
tore away one arm from his side.—"Vy are yer down on
me?" he mumbled with effort and as if his mouth had
been full of dough.—"If you don't . . ." began the
master. Donkin snatched at the pin as though his intention had been to run away with it, and remained
stock still holding it like a candle. "Put it back where
you took it from," said Captain Allistoun, looking at
him fiercely. Donkin stepped back opening wide eyes.
"Go, you blackguard, or I will make you," cried the
master, driving him slowly backwards by a menacing
advance. He dodged, and with the dangerous iron tried
to guard his head from a threatening fist. Mr. Baker
ceased grunting for a moment.—"Good! By Jove,"
murmured appreciatively Mr. Creighton in the tone of
a connoisseur.—"Don't tech me," snarled Donkin,
backing away.—"Then go. Go faster."—"Don't yer 'it
me. . . . I will pull yer up afore the magistryt. . . .
I'll show yer up." Captain Allistoun made a long stride,
and Donkin, turning his back fairly, ran off a little, then stopped and over his shoulder showed yellow
teeth.—"Further on, fore-rigging," urged the master,
pointing with his arm.—"Are yer goin' to stand by and
see me bullied?" screamed Donkin at the silent crowd
that watched him. Captain Allistoun walked at him
smartly. He started off again with a leap, dashed at the
fore-rigging, rammed the pin into its hole violently.
"I'll be even with yer yet," he screamed at the ship
at large and vanished beyond the foremast. Captain
Allistoun spun round and walked back aft with a composed face, as though he had already forgotten the
scene. Men moved out of his way. He looked at no one.
—"That will do, Mr. Baker. Send the watch below,"
he said, quietly. "And you men try to walk straight for
the future," he added in a calm voice. He looked pen-

sively for a while at the backs of the impressed and retreating crowd. "Breakfast, steward," he called in a
tone of relief through the cabin door.—"I didn't like
to see you—Ough!—give that pin to that chap, sir,"
observed Mr. Baker; "he could have bust—Ough!—
bust your head like an eggshell with it."—"O! he!" muttered the master, absently. "Queer lot," he went on in
a low voice. "I suppose it's all right now. Can never tell
tho', nowadays, with such a . . . Years ago; I was a
young master then—one China voyage I had a mutiny; real mutiny, Baker. Different men tho'. I knew
what they wanted: they wanted to broach the cargo
and get at the liquor. Very simple. . . . We knocked
them about for two days, and when they had enough
—gentle as lambs. Good crew. And a smart trip I
made." He glanced aloft at the yards braced sharp up.
"Head wind day after day," he exclaimed, bitterly.
"Shall we never get a decent slant this passage?"—
"Ready, sir," said the steward, appearing before them
as if by magic and with a stained napkin in his hand.—
"Ah! All right. Come along, Mr. Baker—it's late—
with all this nonsense."

## V

A heavy atmosphere of oppressive quietude pervaded the ship. In the afternoon men went about washing clothes and hanging them out to dry in the un-
prosperous breeze with the meditative languor of disen-
chanted philosophers. Very little was said. The problem
of life seemed too voluminous for the narrow limits of
human speech, and by common consent it was abandoned to the great sea that had from the beginning enfolded it in its immense grip; to the sea that knew all,
and would in time infallibly unveil to each the wisdom
hidden in all the errors, the certitude that lurks in

doubts, the realm of safety and peace beyond the fron-
tiers of sorrow and fear. And in the confused current of
impotent thoughts that set unceasingly this way and
that through bodies of men, Jimmy bobbed up upon the
surface, compelling attention, like a black buoy chained
to the bottom of a muddy stream. Falsehood triumphed.
It triumphed through doubt, through stupidity, through
pity, through sentimentalism. We set ourselves to bolster
it up, from compassion, from recklessness, from a sense
of fun. Jimmy's steadfastness to his untruthful attitude
in the face of the inevitable truth had the proportions
of a colossal enigma—of a manifestation grand and incomprehensible that at times inspired a wondering awe;
and there was also, to many, something exquisitely droll
in fooling him thus to the top of his bent. The latent
egoism of tenderness to suffering appeared in the de-
veloping anxiety not to see him die. His obstinate non-
recognition of the only certitude whose approach we
could watch from day to day was as disquieting as the
failure of some law of nature. He was so utterly wrong
about himself that one could not but suspect him of
having access to some source of supernatural knowledge.
He was absurd to the point of inspiration. He was
unique, and as fascinating as only something inhuman
could be; he seemed to shout his denials already from
beyond the awful border. He was becoming immaterial
like an apparition; his cheekbones rose, the forehead
slanted more; the face was all hollows, patches of shade;
and the fleshless head resembled a disinterred black
skull, fitted with two restless globes of silver in the
sockets of eyes. He was demoralising. Through him we
were becoming highly humanised, tender, complex, excessively decadent: we understood the subtlety of his
fear, sympathised with all his repulsions, shrinkings,
evasions, delusions—as though we had been overcivil-
ised, and rotten, and without any knowledge of the

meaning of life. We had the air of being initiated in some infamous mysteries; we had the profound grimaces of conspirators, exchanged meaning glances, significant short words. We were inexpressibly vile and very much pleased with ourselves. We lied to him with gravity, with emotion, with unction, as if performing some moral trick with a view to an eternal reward. We made a chorus of affirmation to his wildest assertions, as though he had been a millionaire, a politician, or a reformer—and we a crowd of ambitious lubbers. When we ventured to question his statements we did it after the manner of obsequious sycophants, to the end that his glory should be augmented by the flattery of our dissent. He influenced the moral tone of our world as though he had it in his power to distribute honours, treasures, or pain; and he could give us nothing but his contempt. It was immense; it seemed to grow gradually larger, as his body day by day shrank a little more, while we looked. It was the only thing about him—of him—that gave the impression of durability and vigour. It lived within him with an unquenchable life. It spoke through the eternal pout of his black lips; it looked at us through the impertinent mournfulness of his languid and enormous stare. We watched him intently. He seemed unwilling to move, as if distrustful of his own solidity. The slightest gesture must have disclosed to him (it could not surely be otherwise) his bodily weakness, and caused a pang of mental suffering. He was chary of movements. He lay stretched out, chin on blanket, in a kind of sly, cautious immobility. Only his eyes roamed over faces: his eyes disdainful, penetrating and sad.

It was at that time that Belfast's devotion—and also his pugnacity—secured universal respect. He spent every moment of his spare time in Jimmy's cabin. He tended him, talked to him; was as gentle as a woman, as tenderly gay as an old philanthropist, as sentimentally careful of his nigger as a model slave-owner. But outside he was irritable, explosive as gunpowder, sombre, suspicious, and never more brutal than when most sorrowful. With him it was a tear and a blow: a tear for Jimmy, a blow for any one who did not seem to take a scrupulously orthodox view of Jimmy's case. We talked about nothing else. The two Scandinavians, even, discussed the situation—but it was impossible to know in what spirit, because they quarrelled in their own language. Belfast suspected one of them of irreverence, and in this incertitude thought that there was no option but to fight them both. They became very much terrified by his truculence, and henceforth lived amongst us, dejected, like a pair of mutes. Wamibo never spoke intelligibly, but he was as smileless as an animal— seemed to know much less about it all than the cat— and consequently was safe. Moreover, he had belonged to the chosen band of Jimmy's rescuers, and was above suspicion. Archie was silent generally, but often spent an hour or so talking to Jimmy quietly with an air of proprietorship. At any time of the day and often through the night some man could be seen sitting on Jimmy's box. In the evening, between six and eight, the cabin was crowded, and there was an interested group at the door. Every one stared at the nigger.

He basked in the warmth of our interest. His eyes gleamed ironically, and in a weak voice he reproached us with our cowardice. He would say, "If you fellows had stuck out for me I would be now on deck." We hung our heads. "Yes, but if you think I am going to let them put me in irons just to show you sport. . . . Well, no. . . . It ruins my health, this lying-up, it does. You don't care." We were as abashed as if it had been true. His superb impudence carried all before it. We would not have dared to revolt. We didn't want to, really.

We wanted to keep him alive till home—to the end of the voyage.

Singleton as usual held aloof, appearing to scorn the insignificant events of an ended life. Once only he came along, and unexpectedly stopped in the doorway. He peered at Jimmy in profound silence, as if desirous to add that black image to the crowd of Shades that peopled his old memory. We kept very quiet, and for a long time Singleton stood there as though he had come by appointment to call for some one, or to see some important event. James Wait lay perfectly still, and apparently not aware of the gaze scrutinising him with a steadiness full of expectation. There was a sense of a contest in the air. We felt the inward strain of men watching a wrestling bout. At last Jimmy with perceptible apprehension turned his head on the pillow.— "Good evening," he said in a conciliating tone.— "H'm," answered the old seaman, grumpily. For a moment longer he looked at Jimmy with severe fixity, then suddenly went away. It was a long time before any one spoke in the little cabin, though we all breathed more freely as men do after an escape from some dangerous situation. We all knew the old man's ideas about Jimmy, and nobody dared to combat them. They were unsettling, they caused pain; and, what was worse, they might have been true for all we knew. Only once did he condescend to explain them fully, but the impression was lasting. He said that Jimmy was the cause of head winds. Mortally sick men—he maintained—linger till the first sight of land, and then die; and Jimmy knew that the very first land would draw his life from him. It is so in every ship. Didn't we know it? He asked us with austere contempt: what did we know? What would we doubt next? Jimmy's desire encouraged by us and aided by Wamibo's (he was a Finn—wasn't he? Very well!) by Wamibo's spells de-

layed the ship in the open sea. Only lubberly fools
couldn't see it. Whoever heard of such a run of calms
and head winds? It wasn't natural. . . . We could not
deny that it was strange. We felt uneasy. The common
saying, "More days, more dollars," did not give the usual comfort because the stores were running short.
Much had been spoiled off the Cape, and we were on
half allowance of biscuit. Peas, sugar and tea had
been finished long ago. Salt meat was giving out. We
had plenty of coffee but very little water to make it
with. We took up another hole in our belts and went
on scraping, polishing, painting the ship from morning
to night. And soon she looked as though she had come
out of a band-box; but hunger lived on board of her.
Not dead starvation, but steady, living hunger that
stalked about the decks, slept in the forecastle; the
tormentor of waking moments, the disturber of dreams.
We looked to windward for signs of change. Every few
hours of night and day we put her round with the hope
that she would come up on that tack at last! She
didn't. She seemed to have forgotten the way home;
she rushed to and fro, heading northwest, heading
east; she ran backwards and forwards, distracted, like a
timid creature at the foot of a wall. Sometimes, as if
tired to death, she would wallow languidly for a day in
the smooth swell of an unruffled sea. All up the swinging masts the sails thrashed furiously through the hot
stillness of the calm. We were weary, hungry, thirsty;
we commenced to believe Singleton, but with un-
shaken fidelity dissembled to Jimmy. We spoke to him
with jocose allusiveness, like cheerful accomplices in
a clever plot; but we looked to the westward over the
rail with longing eyes for a sign of hope, for a sign of
fair wind; even if its first breath should bring death to
our reluctant Jimmy. In vain! The universe conspired
with James Wait. Light airs from the northward sprang

up again; the sky remained clear; and round our weariness the glittering sea, touched by the breeze, basked voluptuously in the great sunshine, as though it had forgotten our life and trouble.

Donkin looked out for a fair wind along with the rest. No one knew the venom of his thoughts now. He was silent, and appeared thinner, as if consumed slowly by an inward rage at the injustice of men and of fate. He was ignored by all and spoke to no one, but his hate for every man dwelt in his furtive eyes. He talked with the cook only, having somehow persuaded the good man that he—Donkin—was a much calumniated and persecuted person. Together they bewailed the immorality of the ship's company. There could be no greater criminals than we, who by our lies conspired to send the unprepared soul of a poor ignorant black man to everlasting perdition. Podmore cooked what there was to cook, remorsefully, and felt all the time that by preparing the food of such sinners he imperilled his own salvation. As to the Captain—he had sailed with him for seven years, now, he said, and would not have believed it possible that such a man . . . "Well. Well . . . There it was . . . Can't get out of it. Judgment capsized all in a minute . . . Struck in all his pride . . . More like a sudden visitation than anything else." Donkin, perched sullenly on the coal-locker, swung his legs and concurred. He paid in the coin of spurious assent for the privilege to sit in the galley; he was disheartened and scandalised; he agreed with the cook; could find no words severe enough to criticise our conduct; and when in the heat of reprobation he swore at us, Podmore, who would have liked to swear also if it hadn't been for his principles, pretended not to hear. So Donkin, unrebuked, cursed enough for two, cadged for matches, borrowed tobacco, and loafed for hours, very much at home, before the stove. From there he could hear us on the other side of the bulkhead, talking to Jimmy. The cook knocked the saucepans about, slammed the oven door, muttered prophesies of damnation for all the ship's company; and Donkin, who did not admit of any hereafter (except for purpose of blasphemy) listened, concentrated and angry, gloating fiercely over a called-up image of infinite torment—as men gloat over the accursed images of cruelty and revenge, of greed, and of power. . . .

On clear evenings the silent ship, under the cold sheen of the dead moon, took on a false aspect of passionless repose resembling the winter of the earth. Under her a long band of gold barred the black disc of the sea. Footsteps echoed on her quiet decks. The moonlight clung to her like a frosted mist, and the white sails stood out in dazzling cones as of stainless snow. In the magnificence of the phantom rays the ship appeared pure like a vision of ideal beauty, illusive like a tender dream of serene peace. And nothing in her was real, nothing was distinct and solid but the heavy shadows that filled her decks with their unceasing and noiseless stir: the shadows darker than the night and more restless than the thoughts of men.

Donkin prowled spiteful and alone amongst the shadows, thinking that Jimmy too long delayed to die. That evening land had been reported from aloft, and the master, while adjusting the tubes of the long glass, had observed with quiet bitterness to Mr. Baker that, after fighting our way inch by inch to the Western Islands, there was nothing to expect now but a spell of calm. The sky was clear and the barometer high. The light breeze dropped with the sun, and an enormous stillness, forerunner of a night without wind, descended upon the heated waters of the ocean. As long as daylight lasted, the hands collected on the fore-

castle-head watched on the eastern sky the island of
Flores, that rose above the level expanse of the sea
with irregular and broken outlines like a sombre ruin
upon a vast and deserted plain. It was the first land
seen for nearly four months. Charley was excited, and
in the midst of general indulgence took liberties with
his betters. Men strangely elated without knowing why
talked in groups, and pointed with bared arms. For the
first time that voyage Jimmy's sham existence seemed
for a moment forgotten in the face of a solid reality.
We had got so far anyhow. Belfast discoursed, quoting
imaginary examples of short homeward runs from the
Islands. "Them smart fruit schooners do it in five days,"
he affirmed. "What do you want?—only a good little
breeze." Archie maintained that seven days was the
record passage, and they disputed amicably with insulting words. Knowles declared he could already smell
home from there, and with a heavy list on his short leg
laughed fit to split his sides. A group of grizzled sea-
dogs looked out for a time in silence and with grim absorbed faces. One said suddenly—" 'Tain't far to London now."—"My first night ashore, blamme if I
haven't steak and onions for supper . . . and a pint of
bitter," said another.—"A barrel ye mean," shouted
someone.—"Ham an' eggs three times a day. That's
the way I live!" cried an excited voice. There was a
stir, appreciative murmurs; eyes began to shine; jaws
champed; short, nervous laughs were heard. Archie
smiled with reserve all to himself. Singleton came up,
gave a careless glance, and went down again without
saying a word, indifferent, like a man who had seen
Flores an incalculable number of times. The night
travelling from the East blotted out of the limpid sky
the purple stain of the high land. "Dead calm," said
somebody quietly. The murmur of lively talk suddenly

wavered, died out; the clusters broke up; men began
to drift away one by one, descending the ladders slowly
and with serious faces as if sobered by that reminder
of their dependence upon the invisible. And when the
big yellow moon ascended gently above the sharp rim
of the clear horizon it found the ship wrapped up in a
breathless silence; a fearless ship that seemed to sleep
profoundly, dreamlessly on the bosom of the sleeping
and terrible sea.

Donkin chafed at the peace—at the ship—at the sea
that stretching away on all sides merged into the illimitable silence of all creation. He felt himself pulled up
sharp by unrecognised grievances. He had been physically cowed, but his injured dignity remained indomitable, and nothing could heal his lacerated feelings.
Here was land already—home very soon—a bad pay-
day—no clothes—more hard work. How offensive all
this was. Land. The land that draws away life from sick
sailors. That nigger there had money—clothes—easy
times; and would not die. Land draws life away. . . .
He felt tempted to go and see whether it did. Perhaps
already . . . It would be a bit of luck. There was
money in the beggar's chest. He stepped briskly out
of the shadows into the moonlight, and instantly, his
craving, hungry face from sallow became livid. He
opened the door of the cabin and had a shock. Sure
enough, Jimmy was dead! He moved no more than a
recumbent figure with clasped hands, carved on the
lid of a stone coffin. Donkin glared with avidity. Then
Jimmy, without stirring, blinked his eyelids, and Donkin had another shock. Those eyes were rather startling. He shut the door behind his back with gentle
care, looking intently the while at James Wait as though
he had come in there at a great risk to tell some secret
of startling importance. Jimmy did not move but

glanced languidly out of the corners of his eyes.—
"Calm?" he asked.—"Yuss," said Donkin, very disappointed, and sat down on the box.

Jimmy was used to such visits at all times of night or
day. Men succeeded one another. They spoke in clear
voices, pronounced cheerful words, repeated old jokes,
listened to him; and each, going out, seemed to leave
behind a little of his own vitality, surrender some of his
own strength, renew the assurance of life—the indestructible thing! He did not like to be alone in his cabin,
because, when he was alone, it seemed to him as if he
hadn't been there at all. There was nothing. No pain.
Not now. Perfectly right—but he couldn't enjoy his
healthful repose unless some one was by to see it. This
man would do as well as anybody. Donkin watched
him stealthily:—"Soon home now," observed Wait.—
"Vy d'yer whisper?" asked Donkin with interest, "can't
yer speak up?" Jimmy looked annoyed and said nothing for a while; then in a lifeless, unringing voice:—
"Why should I shout? You ain't deaf that I know."—
"Oh! I can 'ear right enough," answered Donkin in a
low tone, and looked down. He was thinking sadly of
going out when Jimmy spoke again.—"Time we did get
home . . . to get something decent to eat . . . I am
always hungry." Donkin felt angry all of a sudden.—
"What about me," he hissed, "I am 'ungry too an' got
ter work. You, 'ungry!"—"Your work won't kill you,"
commented Wait, feebly; "there's a couple of biscuits
in the lower bunk there—you may have one. I can't
eat them." Donkin dived in, groped in the corner a¹ d
when he came up again his mouth was full. He
munched with ardour. Jimmy seemed to doze with
open eyes. Donkin finished his hard bread and got up.
—"You're not going?" asked Jimmy, staring at the ceiling.—"No," said Donkin, impulsively, and instead of
going out leaned his back against the closed door. He

looked at James Wait, and saw him long, lean, dried
up, as though all his flesh had shrivelled on his bones in
the heat of a white furnace; the meagre fingers of one
hand moved lightly upon the edge of the bunk playing
an endless tune. To look at him was irritating and fatiguing; he could last like this for days; he was outrageous—belonging wholly neither to death nor life,
and perfectly invulnerable in his apparent ignorance of
both. Donkin felt tempted to enlighten him.—"What
are yer thinkin' of?" he asked, surlily. James Wait had
a grimacing smile that passed over the deathlike im-
passiveness of his bony face, incredible and frightful as
would, in a dream, have been the sudden smile of a
corpse.

"There is a girl," whispered Wait. . . . "Canton
Street girl.—She chucked a third engineer of a Ren-
nie boat—for me. Cooks oysters just as I like . . .
She says—she would chuck—any toff—for a coloured
gentleman. . . . That's me. I am kind to wimmen," he
added, a shade louder.

Donkin could hardly believe his ears. He was scandalised—"Would she? Yer wouldn't be any good to
'er," he said with unrestrained disgust. Wait was not
there to hear him. He was swaggering up the East India Dock Road; saying kindly, "Come along for a
treat," pushing glass swing-doors, posing with superb
assurance in the gaslight above a mahogany counter.
—"D'yer think yer will ever get ashore?" asked Donkin, angrily. Wait came back with a start.—"Ten days,"
he said, promptly, and returned at once to the regions of memory that know nothing of time. He felt
untired, calm, and safely withdrawn within himself
beyond the reach of every grave incertitude. There
was something of the immutable quality of eternity in
the slow moments of his complete restfulness. He
was very quiet and easy amongst his vivid reminis-

cences which he mistook joyfully for images of an un-
doubted future. He cared for no one. Donkin felt this
vaguely like a blind man feeling in his darkness the
fatal antagonism of all the surrounding existences, that
to him shall for ever remain irrealisable, unseen and en-
viable. He had a desire to assert his importance, to
break, to crush; to be even with everybody for everything; to tear the veil, unmask, expose, leave no refuge—a perfidious desire of truthfulness! He laughed
in a mocking splutter and said:

"Ten days. Strike me blind if I ever! . . . You will
be dead by this time to-morrow p'r'aps. Ten days!"
He waited for a while. "D'ye 'ear me? Blamme if yer
don't look dead already."

Wait must have been collecting his strength, for he
said almost aloud—"You're a stinking, cadging liar.
Every one knows you." And sitting up, against all probability, startled his visitor horribly. But very soon Donkin recovered himself. He blustered, "What? What?
Who's a liar? You are—the crowd are—the skipper—
everybody. I ain't! Putting on airs! Who's yer?" He
nearly choked himself with indignation. "Who's yer
to put on airs," he repeated, trembling. "'Ave one—
'ave one, says 'ee—an' cawn't eat 'em 'isself. Now I'll
'ave both. By Gawd—I will! Yer nobody!"

He plunged into the lower bunk, rooted in there
and brought to light another dusty biscuit. He held it
up before Jimmy—then took a bite defiantly.

"What now?" he asked with feverish impudence.
"Yer may take one—says yer. Why not giv' me both?
No. I'm a mangy dorg. One fur a mangy dorg. I'll tyke
both. Can yer stop me? Try. Come on. Try."

Jimmy was clasping his legs and hiding his face on
the knees. His shirt clung to him. Every rib was visible. His emaciated back was shaken in repeated jerks
by the panting catches of his breath.

"Yer won't? Yer can't! What did I say?" went on Donkin, fiercely. He swallowed another dry mouthful with a hasty effort. The other's silent helplessness, his weakness, his shrinking attitude exasperated him. "Ye're done!" he cried. "Who's yer to be lied to; to be waited on 'and an' foot like a bloomin' ymperor. Yer nobody. Yer no one at all!" he spluttered with such a strength of unerring conviction that it shook him from head to foot in coming out, and left him vibrating like a released string.

James Wait rallied again. He lifted his head and turned bravely at Donkin, who saw a strange face, an unknown face, a fantastic and grimacing mask of despair and fury. Its lips moved rapidly; and hollow, moaning, whistling sounds filled the cabin with a vague mutter full of menace, complaint and desolation, like the far-off murmur of a rising wind. Wait shook his head; rolled his eyes; he denied, cursed, threatened —and not a word had the strength to pass beyond the sorrowful pout of those black lips. It was incomprehensible and disturbing; a gibberish of emotions, a frantic dumb show of speech pleading for impossible things, promising a shadowy vengeance. It sobered Donkin into a scrutinising watchfulness.

"Yer can't 'oller. See? What did I tell yer?" he said, slowly, after a moment of attentive examination. The other kept on headlong and unheard, nodding passionately, grinning with grotesque and appalling flashes of big white teeth. Donkin, as if fascinated by the dumb eloquence and anger of that black phantom, approached, stretching his neck out with distrustful curiosity; and it seemed to him suddenly that he was looking only at the shadow of a man crouching high in the bunk on the level with his eyes.—"What? What?" he said. He seemed to catch the shape of some words in the continuous panting hiss. "Yer will tell Belfast!

Will yer? Are ye a bloomin' kid?" He trembled with alarm and rage, "Tell yer gran'mother! Yer afeard! Who's yer ter be afeard more'n any one." His passionate sense of his own importance ran away with a last remnant of caution. "Tell an' be damned! Tell, if yer can!" he cried. "I've been treated worser'n a dorg by your blooming back-lickers. They 'as set me on, only to turn aginst me. I am the only man 'ere. They clouted me, kicked me—an' yer laffed—yer black, rotten incumbrance, you! You will pay fur it. They giv' yer their grub, their water—yer will pay fur it to me, by Gawd! Who axed me ter 'ave a drink of water? They put their bloomin' rags on yer that night, an' what did they giv' ter me—a clout on the bloomin' mouth—blast their . . . S'elp me! . . . Yer will pay fur it with yer money. I'm goin' ter 'ave it in a minyte; as soon has ye're dead, yer bloomin' useless fraud. That's the man I am. An' ye're a thing—a bloody thing. Yah—you corpse!"

He flung at Jimmy's head the biscuit he had been all the time clutching hard, but it only grazed, and striking with a loud crack the bulkhead beyond burst like a hand-grenade into flying pieces. James Wait, as if wounded mortally, fell back on the pillow. His lips ceased to move and the rolling eyes became quiet and stared upwards with an intense and steady persistence. Donkin was surprised; he sat suddenly on the chest, and looked down, exhausted and gloomy. After a moment, he began to mutter to himself, "Die, you beggar —die. Somebody'll come in . . . I wish I was drunk . . . Ten days . . . oysters . . ." He looked up and spoke louder. "No . . . No more for yer . . . no more bloomin' gals that cook oysters . . . Who's yer? It's my turn now . . . I wish I was drunk; I would soon giv' you a leg up. That's where yer bound to go.

Feet fust, through a port . . . Splash! Never see yer any more. Overboard! Good 'nuff fur yer."

Jimmy's head moved slightly and he turned his eyes to Donkin's face; a gaze unbelieving, desolated and appealing, of a child frightened by the menace of being shut up alone in the dark. Donkin observed him from the chest with hopeful eyes; then, without rising, tried the lid. Locked. "I wish I was drunk," he muttered and getting up listened anxiously to the distant sound of footsteps on the deck. They approached—ceased. Some one yawned interminably just outside the door, and the footsteps went away shuffling lazily. Donkin's fluttering heart eased its pace, and when he looked towards the bunk again Jimmy was staring as before at the white beam.—" 'Ow d'yer feel now?" he asked.—"Bad," breathed out Jimmy.

Donkin sat down patient and purposeful. Every half-hour the bells spoke to one another ringing along the whole length of the ship. Jimmy's respiration was so rapid that it couldn't be counted, so faint that it couldn't be heard. His eyes were terrified as though he had been looking at unspeakable horrors; and by his face one could see that he was thinking of abominable things. Suddenly with an incredibly strong and heart-breaking voice he sobbed out:

"Overboard! . . . I! . . . My God!"

Donkin writhed a little on the box. He looked unwillingly. James Wait was mute. His two long bony hands smoothed the blanket upwards, as though he had wished to gather it all up under his chin. A tear, a big solitary tear, escaped from the corner of his eye and, without touching the hollow cheek, fell on the pillow. His throat rattled faintly.

And Donkin, watching the end of that hateful nigger, felt the anguishing grasp of a great sorrow on his heart at the thought that he himself, some day, would have to go through it all—just like this—perhaps! His eyes became moist. "Poor beggar," he murmured. The night seemed to go by in a flash; it seemed to him he could hear the irremediable rush of precious minutes. How long would this blooming affair last? Too long surely. No luck. He could not restrain himself. He got up and approached the bunk. Wait did not stir. Only his eyes appeared alive and his hands continued their smoothing movement with a horrible and tireless industry. Donkin bent over.

"Jimmy," he called low. There was no answer, but the rattle stopped. "D'yer see me?" he asked, trembling. Jimmy's chest heaved. Donkin, looking away, bent his ear to Jimmy's lips, and heard a sound like the rustle of a single dry leaf driven along the smooth sand of a beach. It shaped itself.

"Light . . . the lamp . . . and . . . go," breathed out Wait.

Donkin, instinctively, glanced over his shoulder at the brilliant flame; then, still looking away, felt under the pillow for a key. He got it at once and for the next few minutes remained on his knees shakily but swiftly busy inside the box. When he got up, his face—for the first time in his life—had a pink flush—perhaps of triumph.

He slipped the key under the pillow again, avoiding to glance at Jimmy, who had not moved. He turned his back squarely from the bunk, and started to the door as though he were going to walk a mile. At his second stride he had his nose against it. He clutched the handle cautiously, but at that moment he received the irresistible impression of something happening behind his back. He spun round as though he had been tapped on the shoulder. He was just in time to see Wait's eyes blaze up and go out at once, like two lumps overturned together by a sweeping blow. Something resembling a scarlet thread hung down his chin out of the corner of his lips—and he had ceased to breathe.

Donkin closed the door behind him gently but firmly. Sleeping men, huddled under jackets, made on the lighted deck shapeless dark mounds that had the appearance of neglected graves. Nothing had been done all through the night and he hadn't been missed. He stood motionless and perfectly astounded to find the world outside as he had left it; there was the sea, the ship—sleeping men; and he wondered absurdly at it, as though he had expected to find the men dead, familiar things gone for ever: as though, like a wanderer returning after many years, he had expected to see bewildering changes. He shuddered a little in the penetrating freshness of the air, and hugged himself forlornly. The declining moon drooped sadly in the western board as if withered by the cold touch of a pale dawn. The ship slept. And the immortal sea stretched away, immense and hazy, like the image of life, with a glittering surface and lightless depths. Donkin gave it a defiant glance and slunk off noiselessly as if judged and cast out by the august silence of its might.

Jimmy's death, after all, came as a tremendous surprise. We did not know till then how much faith we had put in his delusions. We had taken his chances of life so much at his own valuation that his death, like the death of an old belief, shook the foundations of our society. A common bond was gone; the strong, effective and respectable bond of a sentimental lie. All that day we mooned at our work, with suspicious looks and a disabused air. In our hearts we thought that in the matter of his departure Jimmy had acted in a perverse and unfriendly manner. He didn't back us up, as a shipmate should. In going he took away with himself the gloomy and solemn shadow in which our folly had posed, with humane satisfaction, as a tender arbiter of fate. And now we saw it was no such thing. It was just common foolishness; a silly and ineffectual meddling with issues of majestic import—that is, if Podmore was right. Perhaps he was? Doubt survived Jimmy; and, like a community of banded criminals disintegrated by a touch of grace, we were profoundly scandalised with each other. Men spoke unkindly to their best chums. Others refused to speak at all. Singleton only was not surprised. "Dead—is he? Of course," he said, pointing at the island right abeam: for the calm still held the ship spell-bound within sight of Flores. Dead—of course. *He* wasn't surprised. Here was the land, and there, on the forehatch and waiting for the sailmaker—there was that corpse. Cause and effect. And for the first time that voyage, the old seaman became quite cheery and garrulous, explaining and illustrating from the stores of experience how, in sickness, the sight of an island (even a very small one) is generally more fatal than the view of a continent. But he couldn't explain why.

Jimmy was to be buried at five, and it was a long day till then—a day of mental disquiet and even of physical disturbance. We took no interest in our work and, very properly, were rebuked for it. This, in our constant state of hungry irritation, was exasperating. Donkin worked with his brow bound in a dirty rag, and looked so ghastly that Mr. Baker was touched with compassion at the sight of this plucky suffering.— "Ough! You, Donkin! Put down your work and go lay-up this watch. You look ill."—"I am bad, sir—in my 'ead," he said in a subdued voice, and vanished speedily. This annoyed many, and they thought the mate "bloomin' soft to-day." Captain Allistoun could be seen on the poop watching the sky to the southwest, and it soon got to be known about the decks that the barometer had begun to fall in the night, and that a breeze might be expected before long. This, by a subtle association of ideas, led to violent quarrelling as to the exact moment of Jimmy's death. Was it before or after "that 'ere glass started down"? It was impossible to know, and it caused much contemptuous growling at one another. All of a sudden there was a great tumult forward. Pacific Knowles and good-tempered Davis had come to blows over it. The watch below interfered with spirit, and for ten minutes there was a noisy scrimmage round the hatch, where, in the balancing shade of the sails, Jimmy's body, wrapped up in a white blanket, was watched over by the sorrowful Belfast, who, in his desolation, disdained the fray. When the noise had ceased, and the passions had calmed into surly silence, he stood up at the head of the swathed body, lifting both arms on high, cried with pained indignation:— "You ought to be ashamed of yourselves! . . ." We were.

Belfast took his bereavement very hard. He gave proofs of unextinguishable devotion. It was he, and no other man, who would help the sailmaker to prepare what was left of Jimmy for a solemn surrender to the insatiable sea. He arranged the weights carefully at the feet: two holystones, an old anchor-shackle without its pin, some broken links of a worn-out stream cable. He arranged them this way, then that. "Bless my soul! you aren't afraid he will chafe his heel?" said the sailmaker, who hated the job. He pushed the needle, puffing furiously, with his head in a cloud of tobacco smoke; he turned the flaps over, pulled at the stitches, stretched at the canvas. "Lift his shoulders. . . . Pull to you a bit. . . . So—o—o. Steady."

Belfast obeyed, pulled, lifted, overcome with sorrow, dropping tears on the tarred twine.—"Don't you drag the canvas too taut over his poor face, Sails," he entreated, tearfully.—"What are you fashing yourself for? He will be comfortable enough," assured the sail-maker, cutting the threat after the last stitch, which came about the middle of Jimmy's forehead. He rolled up the remaining canvas, put away the needles. "What makes you take on so?" he asked. Belfast looked down at the long package of grey sailcloth.—"I pulled him out, " he whispered, "and he did not want to go. If I had sat up with him last night he would have kept alive for me . . . but something made me tired." The sail-maker took vigorous draws at his pipe and mumbled: —"When I . . . West India Station . . . In the *Blanche* frigate . . . Yellow Jack . . . sewed in twenty men a week . . . Portsmouth-Devonport men —townies—knew their fathers, mothers, sisters—the whole boiling of 'em. Thought nothing of it. And these niggers like this one—you don't know where it comes from. Got nobody. No use to nobody. Who will miss him?"—"I do—I pulled him out," mourned Belfast dismally.

On two planks nailed together and apparently resigned and still under the folds of the Union Jack with a white border, James Wait, carried aft by four men, was deposited slowly, with his feet pointing at an open port. A swell had set in from the westward, and following on the roll of the ship, the red ensign, at half-mast, darted out and collapsed again on the grey sky, like a tongue of flickering fire; Charley tolled the bell; and at every swing to starboard the whole vast semicircle of steely waters visible on that side seemed to come up with a rush to the edge of the port, as if impatient to get at our Jimmy. Every one was there but Donkin, who was too ill to come; the Captain and Mr.

Creighton stood bareheaded on the break of the poop; Mr. Baker, directed by the master, who had said to him gravely:—"You know more about the prayer book than I do," came out of the cabin door quickly and a little embarrassed. All the caps went off. He began to read in a low tone, and with his usual harmlessly menacing utterance, as though he had been for the last time reproving confidentially that dead seaman at his feet. The men listened in scattered groups; they leaned on the fife rail, gazing on the deck; they held their chins in their hands thoughtfully, or, with crossed arms and one knee slightly bent, hung their heads in an attitude of upright meditation. Wamibo dreamed. Mr. Baker read on, grunting reverently at the turn of every page. The words, missing the unsteady hearts of men, rolled out to wander without a home upon the heartless sea; and James Wait, silenced for ever, lay uncritical and passive under the hoarse murmur of despair and hopes.

Two men made ready and waited for those words that send so many of our brothers to their last plunge. Mr. Baker began the passage. "Stand by," muttered the boatswain. Mr. Baker read out: "To the deep," and paused. The men lifted the inboard end of the planks, the boatswain snatched off the Union Jack, and James Wait did not move.—"Higher," muttered the boatswain angrily. All the heads were raised; every man stirred uneasily, but James Wait gave no sign of going. In death and swathed up for all eternity, he yet seemed to cling to the ship with the grip of an undying fear. "Higher! Lift!" whispered the boatswain, fiercely. —"He won't go," stammered one of the men, shakily, and both appeared ready to drop everything. Mr. Baker waited, burying his face in the book, and shuffling his feet nervously. All the men looked profoundly disturbed; from their midst a faint humming noise spread out—growling louder. . . . "Jimmy!" cried

Belfast in a wailing tone, and there was a second of shuddering dismay.

"Jimmy, be a man!" he shrieked, passionately. Every mouth was wide open, not an eyelid winked. He stared wildly, twitching all over; he bent his body forward like a man peering at a horror. "Go!" he shouted, and sprang out of the crowd with his arm extended. "Go, Jimmy!—Jimmy, go! Go!" His fingers touched the head of the body, and the grey package started reluctantly to whizz off the lifted planks all at once, with the suddenness of a flash of lightning. The crowd stepped forward like one man; a deep Ah—h—h! came out vibrating from the broad chests. The ship rolled as if relieved of an unfair burden; the sails flapped. Belfast, supported by Archie, gasped hysterically; and Charley, who, anxious to see Jimmy's last dive, leaped headlong on the rail, was too late to see anything but the faint circle of a vanishing ripple.

Mr. Baker, perspiring abundantly, read out the last prayer in a deep rumour of excited men and fluttering sails. "Amen!" he said in an unsteady growl, and closed the book.

"Square the yards!" thundered a voice above his head. All hands gave a jump; one or two dropped their caps; Mr. Baker looked up surprised. The master, standing on the break of the poop, pointed to the westward. "Breeze coming," he said, "Man the weather braces." Mr. Baker crammed the book hurriedly into his pocket. "Forward, there—let go the foretack!" he hailed joyfully, bareheaded and brisk; "Square the foreyard, you port-watch!"—"Fair wind—fair wind," muttered the men going to the braces.—"What did I tell you?" mumbled old Singleton, flinging down coil after coil with hasty energy; "I knowed it—he's gone, and here it comes."

It came with the sound of a lofty and powerful sigh.

The sails filled, the ship gathered way, and the waking sea began to murmur sleepily of home to the ears of men.

That night, while the ship rushed foaming to the Northward before a freshening gale, the boatswain unbosomed himself to the petty officers' berth:—"The chap was nothing but trouble," he said, "from the moment he came aboard—d'ye remember—that night in Bombay? Been bullying all that softy crowd—cheeked the old man—we had to go fooling all over a half-drowned ship to save him. Dam' nigh a mutiny all for him—and now the mate abused me like a pickpocket for forgetting to dab a lump of grease on them planks. So I did, but you ought to have known better, too, than to leave a nail sticking up—hey, Chips?"

"And you ought to have known better than to chuck all my tools overboard for 'im, like a skeary greenhorn," retorted the morose carpenter. "Well—he's gone after 'em now," he added in an unforgiving tone.—"On the China Station, I remember once, the Admiral he says to me . . ." began the sailmaker.

A week afterwards the *Narcissus* entered the chops of the Channel.

Under white wings she skimmed low over the blue sea like a great tired bird speeding to its nest. The clouds raced with her mastheads; they rose astern enormous and white, soared to the zenith, flew past, and falling down the wide curve of the sky seemed to dash headlong into the sea—the clouds swifter than the ship, more free, but without a home. The coast to welcome her stepped out of space into the sunshine. The lofty headlands trod masterfully into the sea; the wide bays smiled in the light; the shadows of homeless clouds ran along the sunny plains, leaped over valleys, without a check darted up the hills, rolled down the

slopes; and the sunshine pursued them with patches
of running brightness. On the brows of dark cliffs white
lighthouses shone in pillars of light. The Channel glittered like a blue mantle shot with gold and starred by
the silver of the capping seas. The *Narcissus* rushed
past the headlands and the bays. Outward-bound
vessels crossed her track, lying over, and with their
masts stripped for a slogging fight with the hard sou'-
wester. And, inshore, a string of smoking steamboats
waddled, hugging the coast, like migrating and amphibious monsters, distrustful of the restless waves.

At night the headlands retreated, the bays advanced
into one unbroken line of gloom. The lights of the earth
mingled with the lights of heaven; and above the tossing lanterns of a trawling fleet a great lighthouse shone
steadily, like an enormous riding light burning above a
vessel of fabulous dimensions. Below its steady glow,
the coast, stretching away straight and black, resembled the high side of an indestructible craft riding motionless upon the immortal and unresting sea. The dark
land lay alone in the midst of waters, like a mighty ship
bestarred with vigilant lights—a ship carrying the burden of millions of lives—a ship freighted with dross
and with jewels, with gold and with steel. She towered up immense and strong, guarding priceless traditions and untold suffering, sheltering glorious memories and base forgetfulness, ignoble virtues and splendid transgressions. A great ship! For ages had the ocean
battered in vain her enduring sides; she was there
when the world was vaster and darker, when the sea
was great and mysterious, and ready to surrender the
prize of fame to audacious men. A ship mother of fleets
and nations! The great flagship of the race; stronger
than the storms! and anchored in the open sea.

The *Narcissus*, heeling over to off-shore gusts,
rounded the South Foreland, passed through the

Downs, and, in tow, entered the river. Shorn of the
glory of her white wings, she wound obediently after
the tug through the maze of invisible channels. As she
passed them the red-painted light-vessels swung at
their moorings, seemed for an instant to sail with great
speed in the rush of tide, and the next moment were
left hopelessly behind. The big buoys on the tails of
banks slipped past her sides very low, and, dropping in
her wake, tugged at their chains like fierce watchdogs.
The reach narrowed; from both sides the land approached the ship. She went steadily up the river. On
the riverside slopes the houses appeared in groups—
seemed to stream down the declivities at a run to see
her pass, and, checked by the mud of the foreshore,
crowded on the banks. Further on, the tall factory
chimneys appeared in insolent bands and watched her
go by, like a straggling crowd of slim giants, swaggering
and upright under the black plummets of smoke, cav-
alierly aslant. She swept round the bends; an impure
breeze shrieked a welcome between her stripped spars;
and the land, closing in, stepped between the ship and
the sea.

A low cloud hung before her—a great opalescent and
tremulous cloud, that seemed to rise from the steaming brows of millions of men. Long drifts of smoky vapours soiled it with livid trails; it throbbed to the beat
of millions of hearts, and from it came an immense and
lamentable murmur—the murmur of millions of lips
praying, cursing, sighing, jeering—the undying murmur of folly, regret, and hope exhaled by the crowds
of the anxious earth. The *Narcissus* entered the cloud;
the shadows deepened; on all sides there was the clang
of iron, the sound of mighty blows, shrieks, yells. Black
barges drifted stealthily on the murky stream. A mad
jumble of begrimed walls loomed up vaguely in the
smoke, bewildering and mournful, like a vision of disas-

ter. The tugs backed and filled in the stream, to hold
the ship steady at the dock-gates; from her bows two
lines went through the air whistling, and struck at the
land viciously, like a pair of snakes. A bridge broke in
two before her, as if by enchantment; big hydraulic
capstans began to turn all by themselves, as though animated by a mysterious and unholy spell. She moved
through a narrow lane of water between two low walls
of granite, and men with check-ropes in their hands
kept pace with her, walking on the broad flagstones. A
group waited impatiently on each side of the vanished
bridge: rough heavy men in caps; sallow-faced men in
high hats; two bareheaded women; ragged children,
fascinated, and with wide eyes. A cart coming at a
jerky trot pulled up sharply. One of the women
screamed at the silent ship—"Hallo, Jack!" without
looking at any one in particular, and all hands looked at
her from the forecastle-head.—"Stand clear! Stand
clear of that rope!" cried the dockmen, bending over
stone posts. The crowd murmured, stamped where they
stood.—"Let go your quarter-checks! Let go!" sang out
a ruddy-faced old man on the quay. The ropes splashed
heavily falling in the water, and the *Narcissus* entered the dock.

The stony shores ran away right and left in straight
lines, enclosing a sombre and rectangular pool. Brick
walls rose high above the water—soulless walls, staring through hundreds of windows as troubled and dull
as the eyes of over-fed brutes. At their base monstrous
iron cranes crouched, with chains hanging from their
long necks, balancing cruel-looking hooks over the
decks of lifeless ships. A noise of wheels rolling over
stones, the thump of heavy things falling, the racket of
feverish winches, the grinding of strained chains,
floated on the air. Between high buildings the dust of
all the continents soared in short flights; and a pene-

trating smell of perfumes and dirt, of spices and hides, of things costly and of things filthy, pervaded the space, made for it an atmosphere precious and disgusting. The *Narcissus* came gently into her berth; the shadows of soulless walls fell upon her, the dust of all the continents leaped upon her deck, and a swarm of strange men, clambering up her sides, took possession of her in the name of the sordid earth. She had ceased to live.

A toff in a black coat and high hat scrambled with agility, came up to the second mate, shook hands, and said:—"Hallo, Herbert." It was his brother. A lady appeared suddenly. A real lady, in a black dress and with a parasol. She looked extremely elegant in the midst of us, and as strange as if she had fallen there from the sky. Mr. Baker touched his cap to her. It was the master's wife. And very soon the Captain, dressed very smartly and in a white shirt, went with her over the side. We didn't recognise him at all till, turning on the quay, he called to Mr. Baker:—"Don't forget to wind up the chronometers to-morrow morning." An underhand lot of seedy-looking chaps with shifty eyes wandered in and out of the forecastle looking for a job— they said.—"More likely for something to steal," commented Knowles, cheerfully. Poor beggars. Who cared? Weren't we home! But Mr. Baker went for one of them who had given him some cheek, and we were delighted. Everything was delightful.—"I've finished aft, sir," called out Mr. Creighton.—"No water in the well, sir," reported for the last time the carpenter, sounding-rod in hand. Mr. Baker glanced along the decks at the expectant group of sailors, glanced aloft at the yards.— "Ough! That will do, men," he grunted. The group broke up. The voyage was ended.

Rolled-up beds went flying over the rail; lashed chests went sliding down the gangway—mighty few of both at that. "The rest is having a cruise off the

Cape," explained Knowles enigmatically to a dock-loafer with whom he had struck a sudden friendship. Men ran, calling to one another, hailing utter strangers to "lend a hand with the dunnage," then with sudden decorum approached the mate to shake hands before going ashore.—"Good-bye, sir," they repeated in various tones. Mr. Baker grasped hard palms, grunted in a friendly manner at every one, his eyes twinkled.— "Take care of your money, Knowles. Ough! Soon get a nice wife if you do." The lame man was delighted.— "Good-bye, sir," said Belfast, with emotion, wringing the mate's hand, and looked up with swimming eyes. "I thought I would take 'im ashore with me," he went on, plaintively. Mr. Baker did not understand, but said kindly:—"Take care of yourself, Craik," and the bereaved Belfast went over the rail mourning and alone.

Mr. Baker, in the sudden peace of the ship, moved about solitary and grunting, trying door-handles, peering into dark places, never done—a model chief mate! No one waited for him ashore. Mother dead; father and two brothers, Yarmouth fishermen, drowned together on the Dogger Bank; sister married and unfriendly. Quite a lady. Married to the leading tailor of a little town, and its leading politician, who did not think his sailor brother-in-law quite respectable enough for him. Quite a lady, quite a lady, he thought, sitting down for a moment's rest on the quarter-hatch. Time enough to go ashore and get a bite and sup, and a bed somewhere. He didn't like to part with a ship. No one to think about then. The darkness of a misty evening fell, cold and damp, upon the deserted deck; and Mr. Baker sat smoking, thinking of all the successive ships to whom through many long years he had given the best of a seaman's care. And never a command in sight. Not once!—"I haven't somehow the cut of a skipper about me," he meditated, placidly, while the shipkeeper (who had taken possession of the galley), a wizened old man with bleared eyes, cursed him in whispers for "hanging about so."—"Now, Creighton," he pursued the unenvious train of thought, "quite a gentleman . . . swell friends . . . will get on. Fine young fellow . . . a little more experience." He got up and shook himself. "I'll be back first thing to-morrow morning for the hatches. Don't you let them touch anything before I come, shipkeeper," he called out. Then, at last, he also went ashore—a model chief mate!

The men scattered by the dissolving contact of the land came together once more in the shipping office.— "The *Narcissus* pays off," shouted outside a glazed door a brass-bound old fellow with a crown and the capitals B. T. on his cap. A lot trooped in at once but many were late. The room was large, white-washed, and bare; a counter surmounted by a brass-wire grating fenced off a third of the dusty space, and behind the grating a pasty-faced clerk, with his hair parted in the middle, had the quick, glittering eyes and the vivacious, jerky movements of a caged bird. Poor Captain Allistoun also in there, and sitting before a little table with piles of gold and notes on it, appeared subdued by his captivity. Another Board of Trade bird was perching on a high stool near the door: an old bird that did not mind the chaff of elated sailors. The crew of the *Narcissus*, broken up into knots, pushed in the corners. They had new shore togs, smart jackets that looked as if they had been shaped with an axe, glossy trousers that seemed made of crumpled sheet-iron, collarless flannel shirts, shiny new boots. They tapped on shoulders, button-holed one another, asked:—"Where did you sleep last night?" whispered gaily, slapped their thighs with bursts of subdued laughter. Most had clean, radiant faces; only one or two turned up dishevelled and sad; the two young Norwegians looked tidy, meek, and altogether of a promising material for the kind ladies who patronise the Scandinavian Home. Wamibo, still in his working clothes, dreamed, upright and burly in the middle of the room, and, when Archie came in, woke up for a smile. But the wide-awake clerk called out a name, and the paying-off business began.

One by one they came up to the pay-table to get the wages of their glorious and obscure toil. They swept the money with care into broad palms, rammed it trustfully into trousers' pockets, or, turning their backs on the table, reckoned with difficulty in the hollow of their stiff hands.—"Money right? Sign the release. There— there," repeated the clerk, impatiently. "How stupid those sailors are!" he thought. Singleton came up, ven- erable—and uncertain as to daylight; brown drops of tobacco juice hung in his white beard; his hands, that never hesitated in the great light of the open sea, could hardly find the small pile of gold in the profound dark- ness of the shore. "Can't write?" said the clerk, shocked. "Make a mark, then." Singleton painfully sketched in a heavy cross, blotted the page. "What a disgusting old brute," muttered the clerk. Somebody opened the door for him, and the patriarchal seaman passed through unsteadily, without as much as a glance at any of us.

Archie displayed a pocket-book. He was chaffed. Belfast, who looked wild, as though he had already luffed up through a public-house or two, gave signs of emotion and wanted to speak to the Captain privately. The master was surprised. They spoke through the wires, and we could hear the Captain saying:—"I've given it up to the Board of Trade." "I should've liked to get something of his," mumbled Belfast. "But you can't, my man. It's given up, locked and sealed, to the Marine Office," expostulated the master; and Belfast stood back, with drooping mouth and troubled eyes. In a pause of the business we heard the master and the clerk talking. We caught: "James Wait—deceased—found no papers of any kind—no relations—no trace —the Office must hold his wages then." Donkin entered. He seemed out of breath, was grave, full of business. He went straight to the desk, talked with animation to the clerk, who thought him an intelligent man. They discussed the account, dropping h's against one another as if for a wager—very friendly. Captain Allistoun paid. "I give you a bad discharge," he said, quietly. Donkin raised his voice:—"I don't want your bloomin' discharge—keep it. I'm goin' ter 'ave a job ashore." He turned to us. "No more bloomin' sea fur me," he said, aloud. All looked at him. He had better clothes, had an easy air, appeared more at home than any of us; he stared with assurance, enjoying the effect of his declaration. "Yuss. I 'ave friends well off. That's more'n you got. But I am a man. Yer shipmates for all that. Who's comin' fur a drink?"

No one moved. There was a silence; a silence of blank faces and stony looks. He waited a moment, smiled bitterly, and went to the door. There he faced round once more. "You won't? You bloomin' lot of yrpocrits. No? What 'ave I done to yer? Did I bully yer? Did I 'urt yer? Did I? . . . You won't drink? . . . No! . . . Then may ye die of thirst, every mother's son of yer! Not one of yer 'as the sperrit of a bug. Ye're the scum of the world. Work and starve!"

He went out, and slammed the door with such violence that the old Board of Trade bird nearly fell off his perch.

"He's mad," declared Archie. "No! No! He's drunk," insisted Belfast, lurching about, and in a maudlin tone. Captain Allistoun sat smiling thoughtfully at the cleared pay-table.

Outside, on Tower Hill, they blinked, hesitated
clumsily, as if blinded by the strange quality of the
hazy light, as if discomposed by the view of so many
men; and they who could hear one another in the howl
of gales seemed deafened and distracted by the dull
roar of the busy earth.—"To the Black Horse! To the
Black Horse!" cried some. "Let us have a drink together before we part." They crossed the road, clinging to one another. Only Charley and Belfast wandered
off alone. As I came up I saw a red-faced, blowsy
woman, in a grey shawl, and with dusty, fluffy hair,
fall on Charley's neck. It was his mother. She slobbered
over him:—"O, my boy! My boy!"—"Leggo of
me," said Charley, "Leggo, mother!" I was passing him
at the time, and over the untidy head of the blubbering woman he gave me a humorous smile and a glance
ironic, courageous, and profound, that seemed to put
all my knowledge of life to shame. I nodded and
passed on, but heard him say again, good-naturedly:
—"If you leggo of me this minyt—ye shall 'ave a bob
for a drink out of my pay." In the next few steps I came
upon 'Belfast. He caught my arm with tremulous enthusiasm.—"I couldn't go wi' 'em," he stammered, indicating by a nod our noisy crowd, that drifted slowly
along the other sidewalk. "When I think of Jimmy . . .
Poor Jim! When I think of him I have no heart for
drink. You were his chum, too . . . but I pulled him
out . . . didn't I? Short wool he had. . . . Yes. And I
stole the blooming pie. . . . He wouldn't go. . . . He
wouldn't go for nobody." He burst into tears. "I never
touched him—never—never!" he sobbed. "He went
for me like . . . like . . . a lamb."

I disengaged myself gently. Belfast's crying fits generally ended in a fight with some one, and I wasn't
anxious to stand the brunt of his inconsolable sor-

row. Moreover, two bulky policemen stood near by, looking at us with a disapproving and incorruptible gaze.—"So long!" I said, and went on my way.

But at the corner I stopped to take my last look at the crew of the *Narcissus*. They were swaying irresolute and noisy on the broad flagstones before the Mint. They were bound for the Black Horse, where men, in fur caps with brutal faces and in shirt sleeves, dispense out of varnished barrels the illusions of strength, mirth, happiness; the illusion of splendour and poetry of life, to the paid-off crews of southern-going ships. From afar I saw them discoursing, with jovial eyes and clumsy gestures, while the sea of life thundered into their ears ceaseless and unheeded. And swaying about there on the white stones, surrounded by the hurry and clamour of men, they appeared to be creatures of another kind—lost, alone, forgetful, and doomed; they were like castaways, like reckless and joyous castaways, like mad castaways making merry in the storm and upon an insecure ledge of a treacherous rock. The roar of the town resembled the roar of topping breakers, merciless and strong, with a loud voice and cruel purpose; but overhead the clouds broke; a flood of sunshine streamed down the walls of grimy houses. The dark knot of seamen drifted in sunshine. To the left of them the trees in Tower Gardens sighed, the stones of the Tower, gleaming, seemed to stir in the play of light, as if remembering suddenly all the great joys and sorrows of the past, the fighting prototypes of these men; press-gangs; mutinous cries; the wailing of women by the riverside, and the shouts of men welcoming victories. The sunshine of heaven fell like a gift of grace on the mud of the earth, on the remembering and mute stones, on greed, selfishness; on the anxious faces of forgetful men. And to the right of the dark group the stained front of the Mint, cleansed by the flood of light, stood out for a moment dazzling and white like a marble palace in a fairy tale. The crew of the *Narcissus* drifted out of sight.

I never saw them again. The sea took some, the steamers took others, the graveyards of the earth will account for the rest. Singleton has no doubt taken with him the long record of his faithful work into the peaceful depths of an hospitable sea. And Donkin, who never did a decent day's work in his life, no doubt earns his living by discoursing with filthy eloquence upon the right of labour to live. So be it! Let the earth and the sea each have its own.

A gone shipmate, like any other man, is gone for ever: and I never met one of them again. But at times the spring-flood of memory sets with force up the dark River of the Nine Bends. Then on the waters of the forlorn stream drifts a ship—a shadowy ship manned by a crew of Shades. They pass and make a sign, in a shadowy hail. Haven't we, together and upon the immortal sea, wrung out a meaning from our sinful lives? Good-bye, brothers! You were a good crowd. As good a crowd as ever fisted with wild cries the beating canvas of a heavy foresail; or tossing aloft, invisible in the night, gave back yell for yell to a westerly gale.

# *Africa and the Congo*

~~~~~~~~~~~~~~~~~~~~~~~~~~~~~~~~~~~~~~~~~~~~

## AN OUTPOST OF PROGRESS

## HEART OF DARKNESS

Those that hold that all things are governed by Fortune had
not erred, had they not persisted there.
>—Sir Thomas Browne [on the title-page of *Chance*]

'Alas!' quod she, 'that ever this sholde happe!
For wende I never, by possibilitee,
That swich a monstre or merveille mighte be!'
>—Chaucer: *The Frankeleyn's Tale*
>[on the title-page of *The Rescue*]

Celui qui n'a connu que des hommes polis et raisonnables, ou
ne connaît pas l'homme ou ne le connaît qu'à demi.
>—La Bruyère: *Caractères* [on the
>title-page of *The Arrow of Gold*]

It is certain my Conviction gains infinitely, the moment another soul will believe in it.
>—Novalis [on the title page of *Lord Jim*]

Africa exerted its spell on Conrad even in boyhood. "It was in 1868," he wrote in *A Personal Record,* "when I was nine years old or thereabouts, that while looking at a map of Africa of the time and putting my finger on the blank space then representing the unsolved mystery of that continent, I said to myself with absolute assurance and an amazing audacity which are no longer in my character now: 'When I grow up I shall go *there.*'" That time was to come in 1890, when he was in his thirty-third year.

Sometime in the early summer of 1889 Conrad returned to London from a long voyage as master of the barque *Otago* which had taken him from Bangkok to Singapore, Australia, the Torres Strait, Mauritius, and Port Adelaide. Letters from Poland indicated that his uncle Tadeusz Bobrowski was in ill health. Conrad accordingly resigned his command of the *Otago,* went to London to obtain the official Russian document that would permit him to visit his uncle, and while waiting there began, "by a sudden and incomprehensible impulse," to write the story of *Almayer's Folly,* which was to occupy him at intervals for the next five years. Obtaining the necessary travel papers, he arrived at his uncle's at Kazimierowka in Polish Ukraine for a stay of nearly two months —his next to last visit with that loved guardian who died January 29, 1894. Traveling thither he crossed Brussels where, on February 4, 1890, he saw his "aunt," the novelist Marguerite Gachet Poradowska, the talented wife of Alexandre Poradowski, Conrad's maternal grandmother's first cousin, and had an interview with the secretary of the Société Anonyme Belge pour le Commerce du Haut-Congo. He had, in his footloose condition, been hoping to secure a new command. None being forthcoming during his weeks in London, his old friend Adolph Krieger had put him in touch with a firm of Antwerp shippers, but an appointment to one of their

boats was also delayed. Conrad turned his thoughts toward
Africa and the Congo which, since Leopold II had founded
the International Association for the Civilization of Central
Africa in 1875, had been much in the world's news. Conrad's
relatives in Brussels revived his old hope that he too might
now go to the mysterious continent. Mme. Poradowska's connections in the Belgian colonial circles encouraged his desire;
his friend Krieger also acted again to help him to realize
it. The result was that, on arriving back in Brussels from
Poland in April 1890, he again saw the Belgian colonial officials and obtained the command of a small Congo steamboat. He hurried briefly to London, returned to Brussels on
May 7 to sign his contract, embarked at Bordeaux on a
French steamship, the *Ville de Maceio,* on the twelfth, and so
sailed by way of Sierra Leone to Boma, thence going by a
smaller boat to Matadi, a station on the Congo River, where
he had to wait fifteen days (June 13-27)—"an eternity!"—
before marching two hundred miles by caravan through the
jungle to Kinchassa above the rapids to take charge of his
own boat. Finding it laid up for repairs, Conrad then embarked as mate on another, the *Roi des Belges* on August 2,
advanced upriver to the Stanley Falls, there took on board a
Company agent, Klein, who was ill and died on the steamer,
and so returned to Kinchassa on September 24. Thus "the
only fresh-water voyage that Conrad ever accomplished was
at an end."

It was a journey that cost him dear. The fever and dysentery he suffered on it undermined the health of his body and
nerves for the remainder of his life. "Everything" became
repellent to him in the fetid jungle country: "men and things,
but especially men." The sordid dealings of the white traders
and exploiters caused as much revulsion as the wilderness of
jungle around him. When he reached Europe again the following January, he faced a long illness and never fully regained his old stamina. But the Congo did give him something. It gave him two stories, "An Outpost of Progress"
(1896) for the *Tales of Unrest* volume of 1898 and "Heart
of Darkness" (1898-99) for the *Youth* volume of 1902—"the

loot I carried off from Central Africa"—and it served to confirm the forces of his imagination and temperament. "Before the Congo," he once told Garnett, "I was just a mere animal." Henceforth he was to be a man tested by severer endurances than he had ever known before. M. Jean-Aubry believes that "it may be said that Africa killed Conrad the sailor and strengthened Conrad the novelist."

"An Outpost of Progress" is comparatively slight, though it is Conrad's first exercise in the dramatic and moral irony that was to develop into such later novels as *The Secret Agent* and *Chance;* but "Heart of Darkness" is indisputably one of Conrad's highest achievements. When T. S. Eliot used its haunting climactic phrase—"Mistah Kurtz, he dead"—as epigraph for his poem "The Hollow Men" in 1925, he acknowledged, as André Gide, Thomas Mann, and others have, that Conrad became, in such tales, a master of the tragedy of moral desolation and defeated egoism which is one of the salient themes of modern literature.

# An Outpost of Progress

THERE were two white men in charge of the trading station. Kayerts, the chief, was short and fat; Carlier, the assistant, was tall, with a large head and a very broad trunk perched upon a long pair of thin legs. The third man on the staff was a Sierra Leone nigger, who maintained that his name was Henry Price. However, for some reason or other, the natives down the river had given him the name of Makola, and it stuck to him through all his wanderings about the country. He spoke English and French with a warbling accent, wrote a beautiful hand, understood bookkeeping, and cherished in his innermost heart the worship of evil spirits. His wife was a negress from Loanda, very large and very noisy. Three children rolled about in sunshine before the door of his low, shed-like dwelling. Makola, taciturn and impenetrable, despised the two white men. He had charge of a small clay storehouse with a dried-grass roof, and pretended to keep a correct account of beads, cotton cloth, red kerchiefs, brass wire, and other trade goods it contained. Besides the storehouse and Makola's hut, there was only one large building in the cleared ground of the station. It was built neatly of reeds, with a veranda on all the four sides. There were three rooms in it. The one in the middle was the living room, and had two rough tables and a few stools in it. The other two were the bedrooms for the white men.

Each had a bedstead and a mosquito net for all furniture. The plank floor was littered with the belongings of the white men; open half-empty boxes, torn wearing apparel, old boots; all the things dirty, and all the things broken, that accumulate mysteriously round untidy men. There was also another dwelling place some distance away from the buildings. In it, under a tall cross much out of the perpendicular, slept the man who had seen the beginning of all this; who had planned and had watched the construction of this outpost of progress. He had been, at home, an unsuccessful painter who, weary of pursuing fame on an empty stomach, had gone out there through high protections. He had been the first chief of that station. Makola had watched the energetic artist die of fever in the just finished house with his usual kind of "I told you so" indifference. Then, for a time, he dwelt alone with his family, his account books, and the Evil Spirit that rules the lands under the equator. He got on very well with his god. Perhaps he had propitiated him by a promise of more white men to play with, by and by. At any rate the director of the Great Trading Company, coming up in a steamer that resembled an enormous sardine box with a flat-roofed shed erected on it, found the station in good order, and Makola as usual quietly diligent. The director had the cross put up over the first agent's grave, and appointed Kayerts to the post. Carlier was told off as second in charge. The director was a man ruthless and efficient, who at times, but very imperceptibly, indulged in grim humor. He made a speech to Kayerts and Carlier, pointing out to them the promising aspect of their station. The nearest trading post was about three hundred miles away. It was an exceptional opportunity for them to distinguish themselves and to earn percentages on the trade. This appointment was a favor done to beginners.

Kayerts was moved almost to tears by his director's kindness. He would, he said, by doing his best, try to justify the flattering confidence, etc., etc. Kayerts had been in the Administration of the Telegraphs, and knew how to express himself correctly. Carlier, an ex-noncommissioned officer of cavalry in an army guaranteed from harm by several European powers, was less impressed. If there were commissions to get, so much the better; and, trailing a sulky glance over the river, the forests, the impenetrable bush that seemed to cut off the station from the rest of the world, he muttered between his teeth, "We shall see, very soon."

Next day, some bales of cotton goods and a few cases of provisions having been thrown on shore, the sardine-box steamer went off, not to return for another six months. On the deck the director touched his cap to the two agents, who stood on the bank waving their hats, and turning to an old servant of the Company on his passage to headquarters, said, "Look at those two imbeciles. They must be mad at home to send me such specimens. I told those fellows to plant a vegetable garden, build new storehouses and fences, and construct a landing stage. I bet nothing will be done! They won't know how to begin. I always thought the station on this river useless, and they just fit the station!"

"They will form themselves there," said the old stager with a quiet smile.

"At any rate, I am rid of them for six months," retorted the director.

The two men watched the steamer round the bend, then, ascending arm in arm the slope of the bank, returned to the station. They had been in this vast and dark country only a very short time, and as yet always in the midst of other white men, under the eye and guidance of their superiors. And now, dull as they were to the subtle influences of surroundings, they felt themselves very much alone, when suddenly left unassisted to face the wilderness; a wilderness rendered more strange, more incomprehensible by the mysterious glimpses of the vigorous life it contained. They were two perfectly insignificant and incapable individuals, whose existence is only rendered possible through the high organization of civilized crowds. Few men realize that their life, the very essence of their character, their capabilities and their audacities, are only the expression of their belief in the safety of their surroundings. The courage, the composure, the confidence; the emotions and principles; every great and every insignificant thought belongs not to the individual but to the crowd: to the crowd that believes blindly in the irresistible force of its institutions and of its morals, in the power of its police and of its opinion. But the contact with pure unmitigated savagery, with primitive nature and primitive man, brings sudden and profound trouble into the heart. To the sentiment of being alone of one's kind, to the clear perception of the loneliness of one's thoughts, of one's sensations—to the negation of the habitual, which is safe, there is added the affirmation of the unusual, which is dangerous; a suggestion of things vague, uncontrollable, and repulsive, whose discomposing intrusion excites the imagination and tries the civilized nerves of the foolish and the wise alike.

Kayerts and Carlier walked arm in arm, drawing close to one another as children do in the dark; and they had the same, not altogether unpleasant, sense of danger which one half suspects to be imaginary. They chatted persistently in familiar tones. "Our station is prettily situated," said one. The other assented with enthusiasm, enlarging volubly on the beauties of the situation. Then they passed near the grave. "Poor devil!" said Kayerts.

"He died of fever, didn't he?" muttered Carlier, stopping short. "Why," retorted Kayerts, with indignation, "I've been told that the fellow exposed himself recklessly to the sun. The climate here, everybody says, is not at all worse than at home, as long as you keep out of the sun. Do you hear that, Carlier? I am chief here, and my orders are that you should not expose yourself to the sun!" He assumed his superiority jocularly, but his meaning was serious. The idea that he would, perhaps, have to bury Carlier and remain alone, gave him an inward shiver. He felt suddenly that this Carlier was more precious to him here, in the center of Africa, than a brother could be anywhere else. Carlier, entering into the spirit of the thing, made a military salute and answered in a brisk tone, "Your orders shall be attended to, chief!" Then he burst out laughing, slapped Kayerts on the back and shouted, "We shall let life run easily here! Just sit still and gather in the ivory those savages will bring. This country has its good points, after all!" They both laughed loudly while Carlier thought: "That poor Kayerts; he is so fat and unhealthy. It would be awful if I had to bury him here. He is a man I respect." . . . Before they reached the veranda of their house they called one another "my dear fellow."

The first day they were very active, pottering about with hammers and nails and red calico, to put up curtains, make their house habitable and pretty; resolved to settle down comfortably to their new life. For them an impossible task. To grapple effectually with even purely material problems requires more serenity of mind and more lofty courage than people generally imagine. No two beings could have been more unfitted for such a struggle. Society, not from any tenderness, but because of its strange needs, had taken care of those two men, forbidding them all independent thought, all initiative, all departure from routine; and forbidding it under pain of death. They could only live on condition of being machines. And now, released from the fostering care of men with pens behind the ears, or of men with gold lace on the sleeves, they were like those life-long prisoners who, liberated after many years, do not know what use to make of their freedom. They did not know what use to make of their faculties, being both, through want of practice, incapable of independent thought.

At the end of two months' Kayerts often would say, "If it was not for my Melie, you wouldn't catch me here." Melie was his daughter. He had thrown up his post in the Administration of the Telegraphs, though he had been for seventeen years perfectly happy there, to earn a dowry for his girl. His wife was dead, and the child was being brought up by his sisters. He regretted the streets, the pavements, the cafés, his friends of many years; all the things he used to see, day after day; all the thoughts suggested by familiar things—the thoughts effortless, monotonous, and soothing of a Government clerk; he regretted all the gossip, the small enmities, the mild venom, and the little jokes of Government offices. "If I had had a decent brother-in-law," Carlier would remark, "a fellow with a heart, I would not be here." He had left the army and had made himself so obnoxious to his family by his laziness and impudence, that an exasperated brother-in-law had made superhuman efforts to procure him an appointment in the Company as a second-class agent. Having not a penny in the world he was compelled to accept this means of livelihood as soon as it became quite clear to him that there was nothing more to squeeze out of his relations. He, like Kayerts, regretted his old life. He regretted the clink of saber and spurs on a fine afternoon, the barrack-room witticisms, the girls of garrison towns; but, besides, he had also a sense of grievance. He was evidently a much ill-used man. This made him moody, at times. But the two men got on well together in the fellowship of their stupidity and laziness. Together they did nothing, absolutely nothing, and enjoyed the sense of the idleness for which they were paid. And in time they came to feel something resembling affection for one another.

They lived like blind men in a large room, aware only of what came in contact with them (and of that only imperfectly), but unable to see the general aspect of things. The river, the forest, all the great land throbbing with life, were like a great emptiness. Even the brilliant sunshine disclosed nothing intelligible. Things appeared and disappeared before their eyes in an unconnected and aimless kind of way. The river seemed to come from nowhere and flow nowhither. It flowed through a void. Out of that void, at times, came canoes, and men with spears in their hands would suddenly crowd the yard of the station. They were naked, glossy black, ornamented with snowy shells and glistening brass wire, perfect of limb. They made an uncouth babbling noise when they spoke, moved in a stately manner, and sent quick, wild glances out of their startled, never-resting eyes. Those warriors would squat in long rows, four or more deep, before the veranda, while their chiefs bargained for hours with Makola over an elephant tusk. Kayerts sat on his chair and looked down on the proceedings, understanding nothing. He stared at them with his round blue eyes, called out to Carlier, "Here, look! look at that fellow there—and that other one, to the left. Did you ever see such a face? Oh, the funny brute!"

Carlier, smoking native tobacco in a short wooden pipe, would swagger up twirling his mustaches, and surveying the warriors with haughty indulgence, would say:

"Fine animals. Brought any bone? Yes? It's not any too soon. Look at the muscles of that fellow—third from the end. I wouldn't care to get a punch on the nose from him. Fine arms, but legs no good below the knee. Couldn't make cavalry men of them." And after glancing down complacently at his own shanks, he always concluded. "Pah! Don't they stink! You, Makola! Take that herd over to the fetish" (the storehouse was in every station called the fetish, perhaps because of the spirit of civilization it contained) "and give them up some of the rubbish you keep there. I'd rather see it full of bone than full of rags."

Kayerts approved.

"Yes, yes! Go and finish that palaver over there, Mr. Makola. I will come round when you are ready, to weigh the tusk. We must be careful." Then turning to his companion: "This is the tribe that lives down the river; they are rather aromatic. I remember, they had been once before here. D'ye hear that row? What a fellow has got to put up with in this dog of a country! My head is split."

Such profitable visits were rare. For days the two pioneers of trade and progress would look on their empty courtyard in the vibrating brilliance of vertical sunshine. Below the high bank, the silent river flowed on glittering and steady. On the sands in the middle of the stream, hippos and alligators sunned themselves side by side. And stretching away in all directions, surrounding the insignificant cleared spot of the trading post, immense forests, hiding fateful complications of fantastic life, lay in the eloquent silence of mute greatness. The two men understood nothing, cared for nothing but for the passage of days that separated them from the steamer's return. Their predecessor had left some torn books. They took up these wrecks of novels, and, as they had never read anything of the kind before, they were surprised and amused. Then during long days there were interminable and silly discussions about plots and personages. In the center of Africa they made acquaintance of Richelieu and of d'Artagnan, of Hawk's Eye and of Father Goriot, and of many other people. All these imaginary personages became subjects for gossip as if they had been living friends. They discounted their virtues, suspected their motives, decried their successes; were scandalized at their duplicity or were doubtful about their courage. The accounts of crimes filled them with indignation, while tender or pathetic passages moved them deeply. Carlier cleared his throat and said in a soldierly voice, "What nonsense!" Kayerts, his round eyes suffused with tears, his fat cheeks quivering, rubbed his bald head, and declared, "This is a splendid book. I had no idea there were such clever fellows in the world." They also found some old copies of a home paper. That print discussed what it was pleased to call "Our Colonial Expansion" in high-flown language. It spoke much of the rights and duties of civilization, of the sacredness of the civilizing work, and extolled the merits of those who went about bringing light, and faith and commerce to the dark places of the earth. Carlier and Kayerts read, wondered, and began to think better of themselves. Carlier said one evening, waving his hand about, "In a hundred years, there will be perhaps a town here. Quays, and warehouses, and barracks, and—and bil liard rooms. Civilization, my boy, and virtue—and all. And then, chaps will read that two good fellows, Kayerts and Carlier, were the first civilized men to live in this very spot!" Kayerts nodded, "Yes, it is a consolation to think of that." They seemed to forget their dead predecessor; but, early one day, Carlier went out and replanted the cross firmly. "It used to make me squint whenever I walked that way," he explained to Kayerts over the morning coffee. "It made me squint, leaning over so much. So I just planted it upright. And solid, I promise you! I suspended myself with both hands to the cross-piece. Not a move. Oh, I did that properly."

At times Gobila came to see them. Gobila was the chief of the neighboring villages. He was a gray-headed savage, thin and black, with a white cloth round his loins and a mangy panther skin hanging over his back. He came up with long strides of his skeleton legs, swinging a staff as tall as himself, and, entering the common room of the station, would squat on his heels to the left of the door. There he sat, watching Kayerts, and now and then making a speech which the other did not understand. Kayerts, without interrupting his occupation, would from time to time say in a friendly manner: "How goes it, you old image?" and they would smile at one another. The two whites had a liking for that old and incomprehensible creature, and called him Father Gobila. Gobila's manner was paternal, and he seemed really to love all white men. They all appeared to him very young, indistinguishably alike (except for stature), and he knew that they were all brothers, and also immortal. The death of the artist, who was the first white man whom he knew intimately, did not disturb this belief, because he was firmly convinced that the white stranger had pretended to die and got himself buried for some mysterious purpose of his own, into which it was useless to inquire. Perhaps it was his way of going home to his own country? At any rate, these were his brothers, and he transferred his absurd affection to them. They returned it in a way. Carlier slapped him on the back, and recklessly struck off matches for his amusement. Kayerts was always ready to let him have a sniff at the ammonia bottle. In short, they behaved just like that other white creature that had hidden itself in a hole in the ground. Gobila considered them attentively. Perhaps they were the same being with the other—or one of them was. He couldn't decide—clear up that mystery; but he remained always very friendly. In consequence of that friendship the women of Gobila's village walked in single file through the reedy grass, bringing every morning to the station, fowls, and sweet potatoes, and palm wine, and sometimes a goat. The Company never provisions the stations fully, and the agents required those local supplies to live. They had them through the good will of Gobila, and lived well. Now and then one of them had a bout of fever, and the other nursed him with gentle devotion. They did not think much of it. It left them weaker, and their appearance changed for the worse. Carlier was hollow-eyed and irritable. Kayerts showed a drawn, flabby face above the rotundity of his stomach, which gave him a weird aspect. But being constantly together, they did not notice the change that took place gradually in their appearance, and also in their dispositions.

Five months passed in that way.

Then, one morning, as Kayerts and Carlier, lounging in their chairs under the veranda, talked about the approaching visit of the steamer, a knot of armed men came out of the forest and advanced towards the station. They were strangers to that part of the country. They were tall, slight, draped classically from neck to heel in blue fringed cloths, and carried percussion muskets over their bare right shoulders. Makola showed signs of excitement, and ran out of the storehouse (where he spent all his days) to meet these visitors. They came into the courtyard and looked about them with steady, scornful glances. Their leader, a powerful and determined-looking Negro with bloodshot eyes, stood in front of the veranda and made a long speech. He gesticulated much, and ceased very suddenly.

There was something in his intonation, in the sounds of the long sentences he used, that startled the two whites. It was like a reminiscence of something not exactly familiar, and yet resembling the speech of civilized men. It sounded like one of those impossible languages which sometimes we hear in our dreams.

"What lingo is that?" said the amazed Carlier. "In the first moment I fancied the fellow was going to speak French. Anyway, it is a different kind of gibberish to what we ever heard."

"Yes," replied Kayerts. "Hey, Makola, what does he say? Where do they come from? Who are they?"

But Makola, who seemed to be standing on hot bricks, answered hurriedly, "I don't know. They come from very far. Perhaps Mrs. Price will understand. They are perhaps bad men."

The leader, after waiting for a while, said something sharply to Makola, who shook his head. Then the man, after looking round, noticed Makola's hut and walked over there. The next moment Mrs. Makola was heard speaking with great volubility. The other strangers— they were six in all—strolled about with an air of ease, put their heads through the door of the storeroom, congregated round the grave, pointed understandingly at the cross, and generally made themselves at home.

"I don't like those chaps—and, I say, Kayerts, they must be from the coast; they've got firearms," observed the sagacious Carlier.

Kayerts also did not like those chaps. They both, for the first time, became aware that they lived in conditions where the unusual may be dangerous, and that there was no power on earth outside of themselves to stand between them and the unusual. They became uneasy, went in and loaded their revolvers. Kayerts said, "We must order Makola to tell them to go away before dark."

The strangers left in the afternoon, after eating a meal prepared for them by Mrs. Makola. The immense woman was excited, and talked much with the visitors. She rattled away shrilly, pointing here and there at the forests and at the river. Makola sat apart and watched. At times he got up and whispered to his wife. He accompanied the strangers across the ravine at the back of the station-ground, and returned slowly looking very thoughtful. When questioned by the white men he was very strange, seemed not to understand, seemed to have forgotten French—seemed to have forgotten how to speak altogether. Kayerts and Carlier agreed that the nigger had had too much palm wine.

There was some talk about keeping a watch in turn, but in the evening everything seemed so quiet and peaceful that they retired as usual. All night they were disturbed by a lot of drumming in the villages. A deep, rapid roll near by would be followed by another far off —then all ceased. Soon short appeals would rattle out here and there, then all mingle together, increase, become vigorous and sustained, would spread out over the forest, roll through the night, unbroken and ceaseless, near and far, as if the whole land had been one immense drum booming out steadily an appeal to heaven. And through the deep and tremendous noise sudden yells that resembled snatches of songs from a madhouse darted shrill and high in discordant jets of sound which seemed to rush far above the earth and drive all peace from under the stars.

Carlier and Kayerts slept badly. They both thought

they had heard shots fired during the night—but they
could not agree as to the direction. In the morning
Makola was gone somewhere. He returned about noon
with one of yesterday's strangers, and eluded all Kayerts'
attempts to close with him: had become deaf apparently. Kayerts wondered. Carlier, who had been fishing
off the bank, came back and remarked while he showed
his catch, "The niggers seem to be in a deuce of a stir;
I wonder what's up. I saw about fifteen canoes cross the
river during the two hours I was there fishing." Kayerts,
worried, said, "Isn't this Makola very queer today?"
Carlier advised, "Keep all our men together in case of
some trouble."

## II

There were ten station men who had been left by the
Director. Those fellows, having engaged themselves to
the Company for six months (without having any idea
of a month in particular and only a very faint notion of
time in general), had been serving the cause of progress
for upwards of two years. Belonging to a tribe from a
very distant part of the land of darkness and sorrow,
they did not run away, naturally supposing that as wandering strangers they would be killed by the inhabitants
of the country; in which they were right. They lived in
straw huts on the slope of a ravine overgrown with
reedy grass, just behind the station buildings. They were
not happy, regretting the festive incantations, the sor-
ceries, the human sacrifices of their own land; where
they also had parents, brothers, sisters, admired chiefs,
respected magicians, loved friends, and other ties supposed generally to be human. Besides, the rice rations
served out by the Company did not agree with them,
being a food unknown to their land, and to which they
could not get used. Consequently they were unhealthy

and miserable. Had they been of any other tribe they would have made up their minds to die—for nothing is easier to certain savages than suicide—and so have escaped from the puzzling difficulties of existence. But belonging, as they did, to a warlike tribe with filed teeth, they had more grit, and went on stupidly living through disease and sorrow. They did very little work, and had lost their splendid physique. Carlier and Kayerts doctored them assiduously without being able to bring them back into condition again. They were mustered every morning and told off to different tasks—grass-cutting, fence-building, tree-felling, etc., etc., which no power on earth could induce them to execute efficiently. The two whites had practically very little control over them.

In the afternoon Makola came over to the big house and found Kayerts watching three heavy columns of smoke rising above the forests. "What is that?" asked Kayerts. "Some villages burn," answered Makola, who seemed to have regained his wits. Then he said abruptly: "We have got very little ivory; bad six months' trading. Do you like get a little more ivory?"

"Yes," said Kayerts, eagerly. He thought of percentages which were low.

"Those men who came yesterday are traders from Loanda who have got more ivory than they can carry home. Shall I buy? I know their camp."

"Certainly," said Kayerts. "What are those traders?"

"Bad fellows," said Makola, indifferently. "They fight with people, and catch women and children. They are bad men, and got guns. There is a great disturbance in the country. Do you want ivory?"

"Yes," said Kayerts. Makola said nothing for a while. Then: "Those workmen of ours are no good at all," he muttered, looking round. "Station in very bad order, sir.

Director will growl. Better get a fine lot of ivory, then he say nothing."

"I can't help it; the men won't work," said Kayerts. "When will you get that ivory?"

"Very soon," said Makola. "Perhaps tonight. You leave it to me, and keep indoors, sir. I think you had better give some palm wine to our men to make a dance this evening. Enjoy themselves. Work better tomorrow. There's plenty palm wine—gone a little sour."

Kayerts said "yes," and Makola, with his own hands carried big calabashes to the door of his hut. They stood there till the evening, and Mrs. Makola looked into every one. The men got them at sunset. When Kayerts and Carlier retired, a big bonfire was flaring before the men's huts. They could hear their shouts and drumming. Some men from Gobila's village had joined the station hands, and the entertainment was a great success.

In the middle of the night, Carlier waking suddenly, heard a man shout loudly; then a shot was fired. Only one. Carlier ran out and met Kayerts on the veranda. They were both startled. As they went across the yard to call Makola, they saw shadows moving in the night. One of them cried, "Don't shoot! It's me, Price." Then Makola appeared close to them. "Go back, go back, please," he urged, "you spoil all." "There are strange men about," said Carlier. "Never mind; I know," said Makola. Then he whispered, "All right. Bring ivory. Say nothing! I know my business." The two white men reluctantly went back to the house, but did not sleep. They heard footsteps, whispers, some groans. It seemed as if a lot of men came in, dumped heavy things on the ground, squabbled a long time, then went away. They lay on their hard beds and thought: "This Makola is invaluable." In the morning Carlier came out, very sleepy, and pulled at the cord of the big bell. The station hands mustered every morning to the sound of the bell. That morning nobody came. Kayerts turned out also, yawning. Across the yard they saw Makola come out of his hut, a tin basin of soapy water in his hand. Makola, a civilized nigger, was very neat in his person. He threw the soapsuds skillfully over a wretched little yellow cur he had, then turning his face to the agent's house, he shouted from the distance, "All the men gone last night!"

They heard him plainly, but in their surprise they both yelled out together: "What!" Then they stared at one another. "We are in a proper fix now," growled Carlier. "It's incredible!" muttered Kayerts. "I will go to the huts and see," said Carlier, striding off. Makola coming up found Kayerts standing alone.

"I can hardly believe it," said Kayerts, tearfully. "We took care of them as if they had been our children."

"They went with the coast people," said Makola after a moment of hesitation.

"What do I care with whom they went—the ungrateful brutes!" exclaimed the other. Then with sudden suspicion, and looking hard at Makola, he added: "What do you know about it?"

Makola moved his shoulders, looking down on the ground. "What do I know? I think only. Will you come and look at the ivory I've got there? It is a fine lot. You never saw such."

He moved towards the store. Kayerts followed him mechanically, thinking about the incredible desertion of the men. On the ground before the door of the fetish lay six splendid tusks.

"What did you give for it?" asked Kayerts, after surveying the lot with satisfaction.

"No regular trade," said Makola. "They brought the ivory and gave it to me. I told them to take what they most wanted in the station. It is a beautiful lot. No station can show such tusks. Those traders wanted carriers badly, and our men were no good here. No trade, no entry in books; all correct."

Kayerts nearly burst with indignation. "Why!" he shouted, "I believe you have sold our men for these tusks!" Makola stood impassive and silent. "I—I—will —I," stuttered Kayerts. "You fiend!" he yelled out.

"I did the best for you and the Company," said Makola, imperturbably. "Why you shout so much? Look at this tusk."

"I dismiss you! I will report you—I won't look at the tusk. I forbid you to touch them. I order you to throw them into the river. You—you!"

"You very red, Mr. Kayerts. If you are so irritable in the sun, you will get fever and die—like the first chief!" pronounced Makola impressively.

They stood still, contemplating one another with intense eyes, as if they had been looking with effort across immense distances. Kayerts shivered. Makola had meant no more than he said, but his words seemed to Kayerts full of ominous menace! He turned sharply and went away to the house. Makola retired into the bosom of his family; and the tusks, left lying before the store, looked very large and valuable in the sunshine.

Carlier came back on the veranda. "They're all gone, hey?" asked Kayerts from the far end of the common room in a muffled voice. "You did not find anybody?"

"Oh, yes," said Carlier, "I found one of Gobila's people lying dead before the huts—shot through the body. We heard that shot last night."

Kayerts came out quickly. He found his companion staring grimly over the yard at the tusks, away by the store. They both sat in silence for a while. Then Kayerts related his conversation with Makola. Carlier said nothing. At the midday meal they ate very little. They hardly exchanged a word that day. A great silence seemed to lie heavily over the station and press on their lips. Makola did not open the store; he spent the day playing with his children. He lay full-length on a mat outside his door, and the youngsters sat on his chest and clambered all over him. It was a touching picture. Mrs. Makola was busy cooking all day as usual. The white men made a somewhat better meal in the evening. Afterwards, Carlier smoking his pipe strolled over to the store; he stood for a long time over the tusks, touched one or two with his foot, even tried to lift the largest one by its small end. He came back to his chief, who had not stirred from the veranda, threw himself in the chair and said:

"I can see it! They were pounced upon while they slept heavily after drinking all that palm wine you've allowed Makola to give them. A put-up job! See? The worst is, some of Gobila's people were there, and got carried off too, no doubt. The least drunk woke up, and got shot for his sobriety. This is a funny country. What will you do now?"

"We can't touch it, of course," said Kayerts.

"Of course not," assented Carlier.

"Slavery is an awful thing," stammered out Kayerts in an unsteady voice.

"Frightful—the sufferings," grunted Carlier with conviction.

They believed their words. Everybody shows a respectful deference to certain sounds that he and his fellows can make. But about feelings people really know nothing. We talk with indignation or enthusiasm; we talk about oppression, cruelty, crime, devotion, self-sacrifice, virtue, and we know nothing real beyond the words. Nobody knows what suffering or sacrifice mean

—except, perhaps the victims of the mysterious purpose of these illusions.

Next morning they saw Makola very busy setting up in the yard the big scales used for weighing ivory. By and by Carlier said: "What's that filthy scoundrel up to?" and lounged out into the yard. Kayerts followed. They stood watching. Makola took no notice. When the balance was swung true, he tried to lift a tusk into the scale. It was too heavy. He looked up helplessly without a word, and for a minute they stood round that balance as mute and still as three statues. Suddenly Carlier said: "Catch hold of the other end, Makola—you beast!" and together they swung the tusk up. Kayerts trembled in every limb. He muttered, "I say! O! I say!" and putting his hand in his pocket found there a dirty bit of paper and the stump of a pencil. He turned his back on the others, as if about to do something tricky, and noted stealthily the weights which Carlier shouted out to him with unnecessary loudness. When all was over Makola whispered to himself: "The sun's very strong here for the tusks." Carlier said to Kayerts in a careless tone: "I say, chief, I might just as well give him a lift with this lot into the store."

As they were going back to the house Kayerts observed with a sigh: "It had to be done." And Carlier said: "It's deplorable, but, the men being Company's men the ivory is Company's ivory. We must look after it." "I will report to the Director, of course," said Kayerts. "Of course; let him decide," approved Carlier.

At midday they made a hearty meal. Kayerts sighed from time to time. Whenever they mentioned Makola's name they always added to it an opprobrious epithet. It eased their conscience. Makola gave himself a half-holiday, and bathed his children in the river. No one from Gobila's villages came near the station that day.

No one came the next day, and the next, nor for a whole week. Gobila's people might have been dead and buried for any sign of life they gave. But they were only mourning for those they had lost by the witchcraft of white men, who had brought wicked people into their country. The wicked people were gone, but fear remained. Fear always remains. A man may destroy everything within himself, love and hate and belief, and even doubt; but as long as he clings to life he cannot destroy fear: the fear, subtle, indestructible, and terrible, that pervades his being; that tinges his thoughts; that lurks in his heart; that watches on his lips the struggle of his last breath. In his fear, the mild old Gobila offered extra human sacrifices to all the Evil Spirits that had taken possession of his white friends. His heart was heavy. Some warriors spoke about burning and killing, but the cautious old savage dissuaded them. Who could foresee the woe those mysterious creatures, if irritated, might bring? They should be left alone. Perhaps in time they would disappear into the earth as the first one had disappeared. His people must keep away from them, and hope for the best.

Kayerts and Carlier did not disappear, but remained above on this earth, that, somehow, they fancied had become bigger and very empty. It was not the absolute and dumb solitude of the post that impressed them so much as an inarticulate feeling that something from within them was gone, something that worked for their safety, and had kept the wilderness from interfering with their hearts. The images of home, the memory of people like them, of men that thought and felt as they used to think and feel, receded into distances made indistinct by the glare of unclouded sunshine. And out of the great silence of the surrounding wilderness, its very hopelessness and savagery seemed to approach them nearer, to draw them gently, to look upon them, to envelop them with a solicitude irresistible, familiar, and disgusting.

Days lengthened into weeks, then into months. Gobila's people drummed and yelled to every new moon, as of yore, but kept away from the station. Makola and Carlier tried once in a canoe to open communications, but were received with a shower of arrows, and had to fly back to the station for dear life. That attempt set the country up and down the river into an uproar that could be very distinctly heard for days. The steamer was late. At first they spoke of delay jauntily, then anxiously, then gloomily. The matter was becoming serious. Stores were running short. Carlier cast his lines off the bank, but the river was low, and the fish kept out in the stream. They dared not stroll far away from the station to shoot. Moreover, there was no game in the impenetrable forest. Once Carlier shot a hippo in the river. They had no boat to secure it, and it sank. When it floated up it drifted away, and Gobila's people secured the carcass. It was the occasion for a national holiday, but Carlier had a fit of rage over it and talked about the necessity of exterminating all the niggers before the country could be made habitable. Kayerts mooned about silently; spent hours looking at the portrait of his Melie. It represented a little girl with long bleached tresses and a rather sour face. His legs were much swollen, and he could hardly walk. Carlier, undermined by fever, could not swagger any more, but kept tottering about, still with a devil-may-care air, as became a man who remembered his crack regiment. He had become hoarse, sarcastic, and inclined to say unpleasant things. He called it "being frank with you." They had long ago reckoned their percentages on trade, including in them that last deal of "this infamous

Makola." They had also concluded not to say anything about it. Kayerts hesitated at first—was afraid of the Director.

"He has seen worse things done on the quiet," maintained Carlier, with a hoarse laugh. "Trust him! He won't thank you if you blab. He is no better than you or me. Who will talk if we hold our tongues? There is nobody here."

That was the root of the trouble! There was nobody there; and being left there alone with their weakness, they became daily more like a pair of accomplices than like a couple of devoted friends. They had heard nothing from home for eight months. Every evening they said, "Tomorrow we shall see the steamer." But one of the Company's steamers had been wrecked, and the Director was busy with the other, relieving very distant and important stations on the main river. He thought that the useless station, and the useless men, could wait. Meantime Kayerts and Carlier lived on rice boiled without salt, and cursed the Company, all Africa, and the day they were born. One must have lived on such diet to discover what ghastly trouble the necessity of swallowing one's food may become. There was literally nothing else in the station but rice and coffee; they drank the coffee without sugar. The last fifteen lumps Kayerts had solemnly locked away in his box, together with a half-bottle of cognac, "in case of sickness," he explained. Carlier approved. "When one is sick," he said, "any little extra like that is cheering."

They waited. Rank grass began to sprout over the courtyard. The bell never rang now. Days passed, silent, exasperating, and slow. When the two men spoke, they snarled; and their silences were bitter, as if tinged by the bitterness of their thoughts.

One day after a lunch of boiled rice, Carlier put

down his cup untasted, and said: "Hang it all! Let's have a decent cup of coffee for once. Bring out that sugar, Kayerts!"

"For the sick," muttered Kayerts, without looking up.

"For the sick," mocked Carlier. "Bosh! . . . Well! I am sick."

"You are no more sick than I am, and I go without," said Kayerts in a peaceful tone.

"Come! Out with that sugar, you stingy old slave dealer."

Kayerts looked up quickly. Carlier was smiling with marked insolence. And suddenly it seemed to Kayerts that he had never seen that man before. Who was he? He knew nothing about him. What was he capable of? There was a surprising flash of violent emotion within him, as if in the presence of something undreamt-of, dangerous, and final. But he managed to pronounce with composure:

"That joke is in very bad taste. Don't repeat it."

"Joke!" said Carlier, hitching himself forward on his seat. "I am hungry—I am sick—I don't joke! I hate hypocrites. You are a hypocrite. You are a slave dealer. I am a slave dealer. There's nothing but slave dealers in this cursed country. I mean to have sugar in my coffee today, anyhow!"

"I forbid you to speak to me in that way," said Kayerts with a fair show of resolution.

"You!—What?" shouted Carlier, jumping up.

Kayerts stood up also. "I am your chief," he began, trying to master the shakiness of his voice.

"What?" yelled the other. "Who's chief? There's no chief here. There's nothing here: there's nothing but you and I. Fetch the sugar—you pot-bellied ass."

"Hold your tongue. Go out of this room," screamed Kayerts. "I dismiss you—you scoundrel!"

Carlier swung a stool. All at once he looked dangerously in earnest. "You flabby, good-for-nothing civilian
—take that!" he howled.

Kayerts dropped under the table, and the stool struck
the grass inner wall of the room. Then, as Carlier was
trying to upset the table, Kayerts in desperation made a
blind rush, head low, like a cornered pig would do, and
overturning his friend, bolted along the veranda, and
into his room. He locked the door, snatched his revolver,
and stood panting. In less than a minute Carlier was
kicking at the door furiously, howling, "If you don't
bring out that sugar, I will shoot you at sight, like a dog.
Now then—one—two—three. You won't? I will show
you who's the master."

Kayerts thought the door would fall in, and scrambled through the square hole that served for a window
in his room. There was then the whole breadth of the
house between them. But the other was apparently not
strong enough to break in the door, and Kayerts heard
him running round. Then he also began to run laboriously on his swollen legs. He ran as quickly as he could,
grasping the revolver, and unable yet to understand
what was happening to him. He saw in succession Makola's house, the store, the river, the ravine, and the low
bushes; and he saw all those things again as he ran for
the second time round the house. Then again they
flashed past him. That morning he could not have
walked a yard without a groan.

And now he ran. He ran fast enough to keep out of
sight of the other man.

Then as, weak and desperate, he thought, "Before I
finish the next round I shall die," he heard the other
man stumble heavily, then stop. He stopped also. He
had the back and Carlier the front of the house, as
before. He heard him drop into a chair cursing, and

suddenly his own legs gave way, and he slid down into a sitting posture with his back to the wall. His mouth was as dry as a cinder, and his face was wet with per-spiration—and tears. What was it all about? He thought it must be a horrible illusion; he thought he was dream-ing; he thought he was going mad! After a while he col-lected his senses. What did they quarrel about? That sugar! How absurd! He would give it to him—didn't want it himself. And he began scrambling to his feet with a sudden feeling of security. But before he had fairly stood upright, a common-sense reflection occurred to him and drove him back into despair. He thought: "If I give way now to that brute of a soldier, he will be-gin this horror again tomorrow—and the day after—every day—raise other pretensions, trample on me, torture me, make me his slave—and I will be lost! Lost! The steamer may not come for days—may never come." He shook so that he had to sit down on the floor again. He shivered forlornly. He felt he could not, would not move any more. He was completely distracted by the sudden perception that the position was without issue—that death and life had in a moment become equally difficult and terrible.

All at once he heard the other push his chair back; and he leaped to his feet with extreme facility. He lis-tened and got confused. Must run again! Right or left? He heard footsteps. He darted to the left, grasping his revolver, and at the very same instant, as it seemed to him, they came into violent collision. Both shouted with surprise. A loud explosion took place between them; a roar of red fire, thick smoke; and Kayerts, deafened and blinded, rushed back thinking: "I am hit—it's all over." He expected the other to come round—to gloat over his agony. He caught hold of an upright of the roof—"All over!" Then he heard a crashing fall on the other side of

the house, as if somebody had tumbled headlong over
a chair—then silence. Nothing more happened. He did
not die. Only his shoulder felt as if it had been badly
wrenched, and he had lost his revolver. He was dis-
armed and helpless! He waited for his fate. The other
man made no sound. It was a stratagem. He was stalking him now! Along what side? Perhaps he was taking
aim this very minute!

After a few moments of an agony frightful and absurd, he decided to go and meet his doom. He was prepared for every surrender. He turned the corner, steady-
ing himself with one hand on the wall; made a few
paces, and nearly swooned. He had seen on the floor,
protruding past the other corner, a pair of turned-up
feet. A pair of white naked feet in red slippers. He felt
deadly sick, and stood for a time in profound darkness.
Then Makola appeared before him, saying quietly:
"Come along, Mr. Kayerts. He is dead." He burst into
tears of gratitude; a loud, sobbing fit of crying. After
a time he found himself sitting in a chair and looking at
Carlier, who lay stretched on his back. Makola was
kneeling over the body.

"Is this your revolver?" asked Makola, getting up.

"Yes," said Kayerts; then he added very quickly, "He
ran after me to shoot me—you saw!"

"Yes, I saw," said Makola. "There is only one revolver; where's his?"

"Don't know," whispered Kayerts in a voice that had
become suddenly very faint.

"I will go and look for it," said the other, gently. He
made the round along the veranda, while Kayerts sat
still and looked at the corpse. Makola came back empty-
handed, stood in deep thought, then stepped quietly
into the dead man's room, and came out directly with
a revolver, which he held up before Kayerts. Kayerts

shut his eyes. Everything was going round. He found life more terrible and difficult than death. He had shot an unarmed man.

After meditating for a while, Makola said softly, pointing at the dead man who lay there with his right eye blown out:

"He died of fever." Kayerts looked at him with a stony stare. "Yes," repeated Makola, thoughtfully, stepping over the corpse, "I think he died of fever. Bury him tomorrow."

And he went away slowly to his expectant wife, leaving the two white men alone on the veranda.

Night came, and Kayerts sat unmoving on his chair. He sat quiet as if he had taken a dose of opium. The violence of the emotions he had passed through produced a feeling of exhausted serenity. He had plumbed in one short afternoon the depths of horror and despair, and now found repose in the conviction that life had no more secrets for him: neither had death! He sat by the corpse thinking; thinking very actively, thinking very new thoughts. He seemed to have broken loose from himself altogether. His old thoughts, convictions, likes and dislikes, things he respected and things he abhorred, appeared in their true light at last! Appeared contemptible and childish, false and ridiculous. He reveled in his new wisdom while he sat by the man he had killed. He argued with himself about all things under heaven with that kind of wrong-headed lucidity which may be observed in some lunatics. Incidentally he reflected that the fellow dead there had been a noxious beast anyway; that men died every day in thousands; perhaps in hundreds of thousands—who could tell?— and that in the number, that one death could not possibly make any difference; couldn't have any importance, at least to a thinking creature. He, Kayerts, was a thinking creature. He had been all his life, till that moment, a believer in a lot of nonsense like the rest of mankind—who are fools; but now he thought! IIe knew! He was at peace; he was familiar with the highest wisdom! Then he tried to imagine himself dead, and Carlier sitting in his chair watching him; and his attempt met with such unexpected success, that in a very few moments he became not at all sure who was dead and who was alive. This extraordinary achievement of his fancy startled him, however, and by a clever and timely effort of mind he saved himself just in time from becoming Carlier. His heart thumped, and he felt hot all over at the thought of that danger. Carlier! What a beastly thing! To compose his now disturbed nerves—and no wonder!—he tried to whistle a little. Then, suddenly, he fell asleep, or thought he had slept; but at any rate there was a fog, and somebody had whistled in the fog.

He stood up. The day had come, and a heavy mist had descended upon the land: the mist penetrating, enveloping, and silent; the morning mist of tropical lands; the mist that clings and kills; the mist white and deadly, immaculate and poisonous. He stood up, saw the body, and threw his arms above his head with a cry like that of a man who, waking from a trance, finds himself immured forever in a tomb. *"Help! . . . My God!"*

A shriek inhuman, vibrating and sudden, pierced like a sharp dart the white shroud of that land of sorrow. Three short, impatient screeches followed, and then, for a time, the fog-wreaths rolled on, undisturbed, through a formidable silence. Then many more shrieks, rapid and piercing, like the yells of some exasperated and ruthless creature, rent the air. Progress was calling to Kayerts from the river. Progress and civilization and all the virtues. Society was calling to its accomplished child to come, to be taken care of, to be instructed, to be judged, to be condemned; it called him to return to that rubbish heap from which he had wandered away, so that justice could be done.

Kayerts heard and understood. He stumbled out of the veranda, leaving the other man quite alone for the first time since they had been thrown there together. He groped his way through the fog, calling in his ignorance upon the invisible heaven to undo its work. Makola flitted by in the mist, shouting as he ran:

"Steamer! Steamer! They can't see. They whistle for the station. I go ring the bell. Go down to the landing, sir. I ring."

He disappeared. Kayerts stood still. He looked upwards; the fog rolled low over his head. He looked round like a man who has lost his way; and he saw a dark smudge, a cross-shaped stain, upon the shifting purity of the mist. As he began to stumble towards it, the station bell rang in a tumultuous peal its answer to the impatient clamor of the steamer.

The Managing Director of the Great Civilizing Company (since we know that civilization follows trade) landed first, and incontinently lost sight of the steamer. The fog down by the river was exceedingly dense; above, at the station, the bell rang unceasing and brazen.

The Director shouted loudly to the steamer:

"There is nobody down to meet us; there may be something wrong, though they are ringing. You had better come, too!"

And he began to toil up the steep bank. The captain and the engine-driver of the boat followed behind. As they scrambled up the fog thinned, and they could see their Director a good way ahead. Suddenly they saw him start forward, calling to them over his shoulder:

"Run! Run to the house! I've found one of them. Run, look for the other!"

He had found one of them! And even he, the man of varied and startling experience, was somewhat discomposed by the manner of this finding. He stood and fumbled in his pockets (for a knife) while he faced Kayerts, who was hanging by a leather strap from the cross. He had evidently climbed the grave, which was high and narrow, and after tying the end of the strap to the arm, had swung himself off. His toes were only a couple of inches above the ground; his arms hung stiffly down; he seemed to be standing rigidly at attention, but with one purple cheek playfully posed on the shoulder. And, irreverently, he was putting out a swollen tongue at his Managing Director.

# Heart of Darkness

~~~~~~~~~~~~~~~~~~~~~~~~~~~~~~~~~~~~~~~~~~~~~

THE *Nellie,* a cruising yawl, swung to her anchor without a flutter of the sails, and was at rest. The flood had made, the wind was nearly calm, and being bound down the river, the only thing for it was to come to and wait for the turn of the tide.

The sea-reach of the Thames stretched before us like the beginning of an interminable waterway. In the offing the sea and the sky were welded together without a joint, and in the luminous space the tanned sails of the barges drifting up with the tide seemed to stand still in red clusters of canvas sharply peaked, with gleams of varnished spirits. A haze rested on the low shores that ran out to sea in vanishing flatness. The air was dark above Gravesend, and farther back still seemed condensed into a mournful gloom, brooding motionless over the biggest, and the greatest, town on earth.

The Director of Companies was our captain and our host. We four affectionately watched his back as he stood in the bows looking to seaward. On the whole river there was nothing that looked half so nautical. He resembled a pilot, which to a seaman is trustworthiness personified. It was difficult to realize his work was not out there in the luminous estuary, but behind him, within the brooding gloom.

Between us there was, as I have already said somewhere, the bond of the sea. Besides holding our hearts together through long periods of separation, it had the effect of making us tolerant of each other's yarns—and even convictions. The lawyer—the best of old fellows—had, because of his many years and many virtues, the only cushion on deck, and was lying on the only rug. The accountant had brought out already a box of dominoes, and was toying architecturally with the bones. Marlow sat cross-legged right aft, leaning against the mizzenmast. He had sunken cheeks, a yellow complexion, a straight back, an ascetic aspect, and, with his arms dropped, the palms of hands outwards, resembled an idol. The director, satisfied the anchor had good hold, made his way aft and sat down amongst us. We exchanged a few words lazily. Afterwards there was silence on board the yacht. For some reason or other we did not begin that game of dominoes. We felt meditative, and fit for nothing but placid staring. The day was ending in a serenity of still and exquisite brilliance. The water shone pacifically; the sky, without a speck, was a benign immensity of unstained light; the very mist on the Essex marshes was like a gauzy and radiant fabric, hung from the wooded rises inland, and draping the low shores in diaphanous folds. Only the gloom to the west, brooding over the upper reaches, became more somber every minute, as if angered by the approach of the sun.

And at last, in its curved and imperceptible fall, the sun sank low, and from glowing white changed to a dull red without rays and without heat, as if about to go out suddenly, stricken to death by the touch of that gloom brooding over a crowd of men.

Forthwith a change came over the waters, and the serenity became less brilliant but more profound. The old river in its broad reach rested unruffled at the decline of day, after ages of good service done to the race that peopled its banks, spread out in the tranquil dignity of a waterway leading to the uttermost ends of the earth. We looked at the venerable stream not in the vivid flush of a short day that comes and departs forever, but in the august light of abiding memories. And indeed nothing is easier for a man who has. as the phrase goes, "followed the sea" with reverence and affection, than to evoke the great spirit of the past upon the lower reaches of the Thames. The tidal current runs to and fro in its unceasing service, crowded with memories of men and ships it had borne to the rest of home or to the battles of the sea. It had known and served all the men of whom the nation is proud, from Sir Francis Drake to Sir John Franklin, knights all, titled and untitled—the great knights-errant of the sea. It had borne all the ships whose names are like jewels flashing in the night of time, from the *Golden Hind* returning with her round flanks full of treasure, to be visited by the Queen's Highness and thus pass out of the gigantic tale, to the *Erebus* and *Terror,* bound on other conquests—and that never returned. It had known the ships and the men. They had sailed from Deptford, from Greenwich, from Erith—the adventurers and the settlers; kings' ships and the ships of men on 'Change; captains, admirals, the dark "interlopers" of the Eastern trade, and the commissioned "generals" of East India fleets. Hunters for gold or pursuers of fame, they all had gone out on that stream, bearing the sword, and often the torch, messengers of the might within the land, bearers of a spark from the sacred fire. What greatness. had not floated on the ebb of that river into the mystery of an unknown earth! . . . The dreams of men,. the seed of commonwealths, the germs of empires.

The sun set; the dusk fell on the stream, and lights began to appear along the shore. The Chapman lighthouse, a three-legged thing erect on a mud-flat, shone strongly. Lights of ships moved in the fairway—a great stir of lights going up and going down. And farther west on the upper reaches the place of the monstrous town was still marked ominously on the sky, a brooding gloom in sunshine, a lurid glare under the stars.

"And this also," said Marlow suddenly, "has been one of the dark places of the earth."

He was the only man of us who still "followed the sea." The worse that could be said of him was that he did not represent his class. He was a seaman, but he was a wanderer, too, while most seamen lead, if one may so express it, a sedentary life. Their minds are of the stay-at-home order, and their home is always with them —the ship; and so is their country—the sea. One ship is very much like another, and the sea is always the same. In the immutability of their surroundings the foreign shores, the foreign faces, the changing immensity of life, glide past, veiled not by a sense of mystery but by a slightly disdainful ignorance; for there is nothing mysterious to a seaman unless it be the sea itself, which is the mistress of his existence and as inscrutable as destiny. For the rest, after his hours of work, a casual stroll or a casual spree on shore suffices to unfold for him the secret of a whole continent, and generally he finds the secret not worth knowing. The yarns of seamen have a direct simplicity, the whole meaning of which lies within the shell of a cracked nut. But Marlow was not typical (if his propensity to spin yarns be excepted), and to him the meaning of an episode was not inside like a kernel but outside, enveloping the tale which brought it out only as a glow brings out a haze, in the likeness of one of these misty halos that sometimes are made visible by the spectral illumination of moonshine.

His remark did not seem at all surprising. It was just

like Marlow. It was accepted in silence. No one took the trouble to grunt even; and presently he said, very slow:

"I was thinking of very old times, when the Romans first came here, nineteen hundred years ago—the other day. . . . Light came out of this river since—you say knights? Yes; but it is like a running blaze on a plain, like a flash of lightning in the clouds. We live in the flicker—may it last as long as the old earth keeps rolling! But darkness was here yesterday. Imagine the feelings of a commander of a fine—what d'ye call 'em?—trireme in the Mediterranean, ordered suddenly to the north; run overland across the Gauls in a hurry; put in charge of one of these craft the legionaries—a wonderful lot of handy men they must have been, too—used to build, apparently by the hundred, in a month or two, if we may believe what we read. Imagine him here—the very end of the world, a sea the color of lead, a sky the color of smoke, a kind of ship about as rigid as a concertina—and going up this river with stores, or orders, or what you like. Sandbanks, marshes, forests, savages—precious little to eat fit for a civilized man, nothing but Thames water to drink. No Falernian wine here, no going ashore. Here and there a military camp lost in a wilderness, like a needle in a bundle of hay—cold, fog, tempests, disease, exile, and death—death skulking in the air, in the water, in the bush. They must have been dying like flies here. Oh, yes—he did it. Did it very well, too, no doubt, and without thinking much about it either, except afterwards to brag of what he had gone through in his time, perhaps. They were men enough to face the darkness. And perhaps he was cheered by keeping his eye on a chance of promotion to the fleet at Ravenna by and by, if he had good friends in Rome and survived the awful climate. Or think of a decent young citizen in a toga—perhaps too much dice, you know—

coming out here in the train of some prefect, or tax-gatherer, or trader even, to mend his fortunes. Land in a swamp, march through the woods, and in some inland post feel the savagery, the utter savagery, had closed round him—all that mysterious life of the wilderness that stirs in the forest, in the jungles, in the hearts of wild men. There's no initiation either into such mysteries. He has to live in the midst of the incomprehensible, which is also detestable. And it has a fascination, too, that goes to work upon him. The fascination of the abomination—you know, imagine the growing regrets, the longing to escape, the powerless disgust, the surrender, the hate."

He paused.

"Mind," he began again, lifting one arm from the elbow, the palm of the hand outwards, so that, with his legs folded before him, he had the pose of a Buddha preaching in European clothes and without a lotus flower—"Mind, none of us would feel exactly like this. What saves us is efficiency—the devotion to efficiency. But these chaps were not much account, really. They were no colonists; their administration was merely a squeeze, and nothing more, I suspect. They were conquerors, and for that you want only brute force—nothing to boast of, when you have it, since your strength is just an accident arising from the weakness of others. They grabbed what they could get for the sake of what was to be got. It was just robbery with violence, aggravated murder on a great scale, and men going at it blind—as is very proper for those who tackle a darkness. The conquest of the earth, which mostly means the taking it away from those who have a different complexion or slightly flatter noses than ourselves, is not a pretty thing when you look into it too much. What redeems it is the idea only. An idea at the back of it; not a sentimental

pretence but an idea; and an unselfish belief in the idea
—something you can set up, and bow down before, and
offer a sacrifice to. . . ."

He broke off. Flames glided in the river, small green
flames, red flames, white flames, pursuing, overtaking,
joining, crossing each other—then separating slowly or
hastily. The traffic of the great city went on in the deepening night upon the sleepless river. We looked on,
waiting patiently—there was nothing else to do till the
end of the flood; but it was only after a long silence,
when he said, in a hesitating voice, "I suppose you fellows remember I did once turn fresh-water sailor for a
bit," that we knew we were fated, before the ebb began
to run, to hear about one of Marlow's inconclusive experiences.

"I don't want to bother you much with what happened to me personally," he began, showing in this remark the weakness of many tellers of tales who seem so
often unaware of what their audience would best like
to hear; "yet to understand the effect of it on me you
ought to know how I got out there, what I saw, how I
went up that river to the place where I first met the poor
chap. It was the farthest point of navigation and the
culminating point of my experience. It seemed somehow to throw a kind of light on everything about me—
and into my thoughts. It was somber enough, too—
and pitiful—not extraordinary in any way—not very
clear either. No, not very clear. And yet it seemed to
throw a kind of light.

"I had then, as you remember, just returned to London after a lot of Indian Ocean, Pacific, China Seas—
a regular dose of the East—six years or so, and I was
loafing about, hindering you fellows in your work and
invading your homes, just as though I had got a heavenly mission to civilize you. It was very fine for a time,

but after a bit I did get tired of resting. Then I began to look for a ship—I should think the hardest work on earth. But the ships wouldn't even look at me. And I got tired of that game, too.

"Now when I was a little chap I had a passion for maps. I would look for hours at South America, or Africa, or Australia, and lose myself in all the glories of exploration. At that time there were many blank spaces on the earth, and when I saw one that looked particularly inviting on a map (but they all look that) I would put my finger on it and say, 'When I grow up I will go there.' The North Pole was one of these places, I remember. Well, I haven't been there yet, and shall not try now. The glamor's off. Other places were scattered about the Equator, and in every sort of latitude all over the two hemispheres. I have been in some of them, and . . . well, we won't talk about that. But there was one yet—the biggest, the most blank, so to speak—that I had a hankering after.

"True, by this time it was not a blank space any more. It had got filled since my boyhood with rivers and lakes and names. It had ceased to be a blank space of delightful mystery—a white patch for a boy to dream gloriously over. It had become a place of darkness. But there was in it one river especially, a mighty big river, that you could see on the map, resembling an immense snake uncoiled, with its head in the sea, its body at rest curving afar over a vast country, and its tail lost in the depths of the land. And as I looked at the map of it in a shop window, it fascinated me as a snake would a bird—a silly little bird. Then I remembered there was a big concern, a company for trade on that river. Dash it all! I thought to myself, they can't trade without using some kind of craft on that lot of fresh water—steamboats! Why shouldn't I try to get charge of one? I went on along Fleet Street, but could not shake off the idea. The snake had charmed me.

"You understand it was a continental concern, that trading society; but I have a lot of relations living on the continent, because it's cheap and not so nasty as it looks, they say.

"I am sorry to own I began to worry them. This was already a fresh departure for me. I was not used to get things that way, you know. I always went my own road and on my own legs where I had a mind to go. I wouldn't have believed it of myself; but, then—you see —I felt somehow I must get there by hook or by crook. So I worried them. The men said 'My dear fellow,' and did nothing. Then—would you believe it?—I tried the women. I, Charlie Marlow, set the women to work— to get a job. Heavens! Well, you see, the notion drove me. I had an aunt, a dear enthusiastic soul. She wrote: 'It will be delightful. I am ready to do anything, anything for you. It is a glorious idea. I know the wife of a very high personage in the administration, and also a man who has lots of influence with,' etc., etc. She was determined to make no end of fuss to get me appointed skipper of a river steamboat, if such was my fancy.

"I got my appointment—of course; and I got it very quick. It appears the company had received news that one of their captains had been killed in a scuffle with the natives. This was my chance, and it made me the more anxious to go. It was only months and months after-wards, when I made the attempt to recover what was left of the body, that I heard the original quarrel arose from a misunderstanding about some hens. Yes, two black hens. Fresleven—that was the fellow's name, a Dane—thought himself wronged somehow in the bar-gain, so he went ashore and started to hammer the chief of the village with a stick. Oh, it didn't surprise me in

the least to hear this, and at the same time to be told
that Fresleven was the gentlest, quietest creature that
ever walked on two legs. No doubt he was; but he had
been a couple of years already out there engaged in the
noble cause, you know, and he probably felt the need at
last of asserting his self-respect in some way. Therefore
he whacked the old nigger mercilessly, while a big
crowd of his people watched him, thunderstruck, till
some man—I was told the chief's son—in desperation at
hearing the old chap yell, made a tentative jab with a
spear at the white man—and of course it went quite
easy between the shoulder blades. Then the whole population cleared into the forest, expecting all kinds of
calamities to happen, while, on the other hand, the
steamer Fresleven commanded left also in a bad panic,
in charge of the engineer, I believe. Afterwards nobody
seemed to trouble much about Fresleven's remains, till
I got out and stepped into his shoes. I couldn't let it rest,
though; but when an opportunity offered at last to meet
my predecessor, the grass growing through his ribs
was tall enough to hide his bones. They were all there.
The supernatural being had not been touched after he
fell. And the village was deserted, the huts gaped black,
rotting, all askew within the fallen enclosures. A calamity had come to it, sure enough. The people had vanished. Mad terror had scattered them, men, women, and
children, through the bush, and they had never returned. What became of the hens I don't know either. I
should think the cause of progress got them, anyhow.
However, through this glorious affair I got my appointment, before I had fairly begun to hope for it.

"I flew around like mad to get ready, and before
forty-eight hours I was crossing the Channel to show
myself to my employers, and sign the contract. In a very
few hours I arrived in a city that always makes me

think of a whited sepulcher. Prejudice no doubt. I had no difficulty in finding the company's offices. It was the biggest thing in the town, and everybody I met was full of it. They were going to run an oversea empire, and make no end of coin by trade.

"A narrow and deserted street in deep shadow, high houses, innumerable windows with venetian blinds, a dead silence, grass sprouting between the stones, imposing carriage archways right and left, immense double doors standing ponderously ajar. I slipped through one of these cracks, went up a swept and ungarnished staircase, as arid as a desert, and opened the first door I came to. Two women, one fat and the other slim, sat on straw-bottomed chairs, knitting black wool. The slim one got up and walked straight at me—still knitting with downcast eyes—and only just as I began to think of getting out of her way, as you would for a somnambulist, stood still, and looked up. Her dress was as plain as an umbrella-cover, and she turned round without a word and preceded me into a waiting room. I gave my name, and looked about. Deal table in the middle, plain chairs all round the walls, on one end a large shining map, marked with all the colors of a rainbow. There was a vast amount of red—good to see at any time, because one knows that some real work is done in there, a deuce of a lot of blue, a little green, smears of orange, and, on the East Coast, a purple patch, to show where the jolly pioneers of progress drink the jolly lager beer. However, I wasn't going into any of these. I was going into the yellow. Dead in the center. And the river was there— fascinating—deadly—like a snake. Ough! A door opened, a white-haired secretarial head, but wearing a compassionate expression, appeared, and a skinny forefinger beckoned me into the sanctuary. Its light was dim, and a heavy writing desk squatted in the middle.

From behind that structure came out an impression of pale plumpness in a frock coat. The great man himself. He was five feet six, I should judge, and had his grip on the handle-end of ever so many millions. He shook hands, I fancy, murmured vaguely, was satisfied with my French. *Bon voyage.*

"In about forty-five seconds I found myself again in the waiting room with the compassionate secretary, who, full of desolation and sympathy, made me sign some document. I believe I undertook amongst other things not to disclose any trade secrets. Well, I am not going to.

"I began to feel slightly uneasy. You know I am not used to such ceremonies, and there was something ominous in the atmosphere. It was just as though I had been let into some conspiracy—I don't know—something not quite right; and I was glad to get out. In the outer room the two women knitted black wool feverishly. People were arriving, and the younger one was walking back and forth introducing them. The old one sat on her chair. Her flat cloth slippers were propped up on a foot-warmer, and a cat reposed on her lap. She wore a starched white affair on her head, had a wart on one cheek, and silver-rimmed spectacles hung on the tip of her nose. She glanced at me above the glasses. The swift and indifferent placidity of that look troubled me. Two youths with foolish and cheery countenances were being piloted over, and she threw at them the same quick glance of unconcerned wisdom. She seemed to know all about them and about me, too. An eerie feeling came over me. She seemed uncanny and fateful. Often far away there I thought of these two, guarding the door of darkness, knitting black wool as for a warm pall, one introducing, introducing continuously to the unknown, the other scrutinizing the cheery and foolish faces with unconcerned old eyes. *Ave!* Old knitter of black wool. *Morituri te salutant.* Not many of those she looked at ever saw her again—not half, by a long way.

"There was yet a visit to the doctor. 'A simple formality,' assured me the secretary, with an air of taking an immense part in all my sorrows. Accordingly a young chap wearing his hat over the left eyebrow, some clerk I suppose—there must have been clerks in the business, though the house was as still as a house in a city of the dead—came from somewhere upstairs, and led me forth. He was shabby and careless, with inkstains on the sleeves of his jacket, and his cravat was large and billowy, under a chin shaped like the toe of an old boot. It was a little too early for the doctor, so I proposed a drink, and thereupon he developed a vein of joviality. As we sat over our vermouths he glorified the company's business, and by and by I expressed casually my surprise at him not going out there. He became very cool and collected all at once. 'I am not such a fool as I look, quoth Plato to his disciples,' he said sententiously, emptied his glass with great resolution, and we rose.

"The old doctor felt my pulse, evidently thinking of something else the while. 'Good, good for there,' he mumbled, and then with a certain eagerness asked me whether I would let him measure my head. Rather surprised, I said 'yes,' when he produced a thing like calipers and got the dimensions back and front and every way, taking notes carefully. He was an unshaven little man in a threadbare coat like a gaberdine, with his feet in slippers, and I thought him a harmless fool. 'I always ask leave, in the interests of science, to measure the crania of those going out there,' he said. 'And when they come back, too?' I asked. 'Oh, I never see them,' he remarked; 'and, moreover, the changes take place inside,

you know.' He smiled, as if at some quiet joke. 'So you
are going out there. Famous. Interesting, too.' He gave
me a searching glance, and made another note. 'Ever
any madness in your family?' he asked, in a matter-of-
fact tone. I felt very annoyed. 'Is that question in the
interests of science, too?' 'It would be,' he said, without.
taking notice of my irritation, 'interesting for science to
watch the mental changes of individuals, on the spot,
but . . .' 'Are you an alienist?' I interrupted. 'Every
doctor should be—a little,' answered that original, imperturbably. 'I have a little theory which you messieurs
who go out there must help me to prove. This is my
share in the advantages my country shall reap from the
possession of such a magnificent dependency. The mere
wealth I leave to others. Pardon my questions, but you
are the first Englishman coming under my observation.
. . .' I hastened to assure him I was not in the least
typical. 'If I were,' said I, 'I wouldn't be talking like this
with you.' 'What you say is rather profound, and probably erroneous,' he said, with a laugh. 'Avoid irritation
more than exposure to the sun. Adieu. How do you English say, eh? Good-by. Ah! Good-by. Adieu. In the
tropics one must before everything keep calm.' . . . He
lifted a warning forefinger. . . . *'Du calme, du calme.
Adieu.'*

"One thing more remained to do—say good-by to my
excellent aunt. I found her triumphant. I had a cup of
tea—the last decent cup of tea for many days—and in
a room that most soothingly looked just as you would
expect a lady's drawing room to look, we had a long
quiet chat by the fireside. In the course of these con-
fidences it became quite plain to me I had been represented to the wife of the high dignitary, and goodness
knows to how many more people besides, as an exceptional and gifted creature—a piece of good fortune for

the company—a man you don't get hold of every day. Good heavens! and I was going to take charge of a two-penny-half-penny river steamboat with a penny whistle attached! It appeared, however, I was also one of the Workers, with a capital—you know. Something like an emissary of light, something like a lower sort of apostle. There had been a lot of such rot let loose in print and talk just about that time, and the excellent woman, living right in the rush of all that humbug, got carried off her feet. She talked about 'weaning those ignorant millions from their horrid ways,' till, upon my word, she made me quite uncomfortable. I ventured to hint that the company was run for profit.

" 'You forget, dear Charlie, that the laborer is worthy of his hire,' she said, brightly. It's queer how out of touch with truth women are. They live in a world of their own, and there had never been anything like it, and never can be. It is too beautiful altogether, and if they were to set it up it would go to pieces before the first sunset. Some confounded fact we men have been living contentedly with ever since the day of creation would start up and knock the whole thing over.

"After this I got embraced, told to wear flannel, be sure to write often, and so on—and I left. In the street —I don't know why—a queer feeling came to me that I was an impostor. Odd thing that I, who used to clear out for any part of the world at twenty-four hours' notice, with less thought than most men give to the crossing of a street, had a moment—I won't say of hesitation, but of startled pause, before this commonplace affair. The best way I can explain it to you is by saying that, for a second or two, I felt as though, instead of going to the center of a continent, I were about to set off for the center of the earth.

"I left in a French steamer, and she called in every

blamed port they have out there, for, as far as I could
see, the sole purpose of landing soldiers and customhouse officers. I watched the coast. Watching a coast as
it slips by the ship is like thinking about an enigma.
There it is before you—smiling, frowning, inviting,
grand, mean, insipid, or savage, and always mute with
an air of whispering, Come and find out. This one was
almost featureless, as if still in the making, with an
aspect of monotonous grimness. The edge of a colossal
jungle, so dark-green as to be almost black, fringed with
white surf, ran straight, like a ruled line, far, far away
along a blue sea whose glitter was blurred by a creeping
mist. The sun was fierce, the land seemed to glisten and
drip with steam. Here and there grayish-whitish specks
showed up clustered inside the white surf, with a flag
flying above them perhaps. Settlements some centuries
old, and still no bigger than pinheads on the untouched
expanse of their background. We pounded along,
stopped, landed soldiers; went on, landed customhouse
clerks to levy toll in what looked like a God-forsaken
wilderness, with a tin shed and a flagpole lost in it;
landed more soldiers—to take care of the customhouse clerks, presumably. Some, I heard, got drowned in
the surf; but whether they did or not, nobody seemed
particularly to care. They were just flung out there, and
on we went. Every day the coast looked the same, as
though we had not moved; but we passed various places
—trading places—with names like Gran' Bassam, Little
Popo; names that seemed to belong to some sordid farce
acted in front of a sinister back cloth. The idleness of
a passenger, my isolation amongst all these men with
whom I had no point of contact, the oily and languid
sea, the uniform somberness of the coast, seemed to
keep me away from the truth of things, within the toil
of a mournful and senseless delusion. The voice of the

surf heard now and then was a positive pleasure, like
the speech of a brother. It was something natural, that
had its reason, that had a meaning. Now and then a boat
from the shore gave one a momentary contact with
reality. It was paddled by black fellows. You could see
from afar the white of their eyeballs glistening. They
shouted, sang; their bodies streamed with perspiration;
they had faces like grotesque masks—these chaps; but
they had bone, muscle, a wild vitality, an intense energy
of movement, that was as natural and true as the surf
along their coast. They wanted no excuse for being
there. They were a great comfort to look at. For a time I
would feel I belonged still to a world of straightforward
facts; but the feeling would not last long. Something
would turn up to scare it away. Once, I remember, we
came upon a man-of-war anchored off the coast. There
wasn't even a shed there, and she was shelling the bush.
It appears the French had one of their wars going on
thereabouts. Her ensign dropped limp like a rag; the
muzzles of the long six-inch guns stuck out all over the
low hull; the greasy, slimy swell swung her up lazily
and let her down, swaying her thin masts. In the empty
immensity of earth, sky, and water, there she was, incomprehensible, firing into a continent. Pop, would go
one of the six-inch guns; a small flame would dart and
vanish, a little white smoke would disappear, a tiny
projectile would give a feeble screech—and nothing
happened. Nothing could happen. There was a touch of
insanity in the proceeding, a sense of lugubrious drollery
in the sight; and it was not dissipated by somebody on
board assuring me earnestly there was a camp of natives
—he called them enemies!—hidden out of sight somewhere.

"We gave her her letters (I heard the men in that
lonely ship were dying of fever at the rate of three a

day) and went on. We called at some more places with farcical names, where the merry dance of death and trade goes on in a still and earthly atmosphere as of an overheated catacomb; all along the formless coast bordered by dangerous surf, as if Nature herself had tried to ward off intruders; in and out of rivers, streams of death in life, whose banks were rotting into mud, whose waters, thickened into slime, invaded the contorted mangroves, that seemed to writhe at us in the extremity of an impotent despair. Nowhere did we stop long enough to get a particularized impression, but the general sense of vague and oppressive wonder grew upon me. It was like a weary pilgrimage amongst hints for nightmares.

"It was upward of thirty days before I saw the mouth of the big river. We anchored off the seat of the government. But my work would not begin till some two hundred miles farther on. So as soon as I could I made a start for a place thirty miles higher up.

"I had my passage on a little seagoing steamer. Her captain was a Swede, and knowing me for a seaman, invited me on the bridge. He was a young man, lean, fair, and morose, with lanky hair and a shuffling gait. As we left the miserable little wharf, he tossed his head contemptuously at the shore. 'Been living there?' he asked. I said, 'Yes.' 'Fine lot these government chaps— are they not?' he went on, speaking English with great precision and considerable bitterness. 'It is funny what some people will do for a few francs a month. I wonder what becomes of that kind when it goes up country?' I said to him I expected to see that soon. 'So-o-o!' he exclaimed. He shuffled athwart, keeping one eye ahead vigilantly. 'Don't be too sure,' he continued. 'The other day I took up a man who hanged himself on the road. He was a Swede, too.' 'Hanged himself! Why, in God's name?' I cried. He kept on looking out watchfully. 'Who knows? The sun too much for him, or the country perhaps.'

"At last we opened a reach. A rocky cliff appeared, mounds of turned-up earth by the shore, houses on a hill, others with iron roofs, amongst a waste of excavations, or hanging to the declivity. A continuous noise of the rapids above hovered over this scene of inhabited devastation. A lot of people, mostly black and naked, moved about like ants. A jetty projected into the river. A blinding sunlight drowned all this at times in a sudden recrudescence of glare. 'There's your company's station,' said the Swede, pointing to three wooden barrack-like structures on the rocky slope. 'I will send your things up. Four boxes did you say? So. Farewell.'

"I came upon a boiler wallowing in the grass, then found a path leading up the hill. It turned aside for the boulders, and also for an undersized railway truck lying there on its back with its wheels in the air. One was off. The thing looked as dead as the carcass of some animal. I came upon more pieces of decaying machinery, a stack of rusty rails. To the left a clump of trees made a shady spot, where dark things seemed to stir feebly. I blinked, the path was steep. A horn tooted to the right, and I saw the black people run. A heavy and dull detonation shook the ground, a puff of smoke came out of the cliff, and that was all. No change appeared on the face of the rock. They were building a railway. The cliff was not in the way or anything; but this objectless blasting was all the work going on.

"A slight clinking behind me made me turn my head. Six black men advanced in a file, toiling up the path. They walked erect and slow, balancing small baskets full of earth on their heads, and the clink kept time with their footsteps. Black rags were wound round their loins, and the short ends behind waggled to and fro like tails. I could see every rib, the joints of their limbs were like knots in a rope; each had an iron collar on his neck, and all were connected together with a chain whose bights swung between them, rhythmically clinking. Another report from the cliff made me think suddenly of that ship of war I had seen firing into a continent. It was the same kind of ominous voice; but these men could by no stretch of imagination be called enemies. They were called criminals, and the outraged law, like the bursting shells, had come to them, an insoluble mystery from the sea. All their meager breasts panted together, the violently dilated nostrils quivered, the eyes stared stonily uphill. They passed me within six inches, without a glance, with that complete, deathlike indifference of unhappy savages. Behind this raw matter one of the reclaimed, the product of the new forces at work, strolled despondently, carrying a rifle by its middle. He had a uniform jacket with one button off, and seeing a white man on the path, hoisted his weapon to his shoulder with alacrity. This was simple prudence, white men being so much alike at a distance that he could not tell who I might be. He was speedily reassured, and with a large, white, rascally grin, and a glance at his charge, seemed to take me into partnership in his exalted trust. After all, I also was a part of the great cause of these high and just proceedings.

"Instead of going up, I turned and descended to the left. My idea was to let that chain gang get out of sight before I climbed the hill. You know I am not particularly tender; I've had to strike and to fend off. I've had to resist and to attack sometimes—that's only one way of resisting—without counting the exact cost, according to the demands of such sort of life as I had blundered into. I've seen the devil of violence, and the devil of

greed, and the devil of hot desire; but, by all the stars!
these were strong, lusty, red-eyed devils, that swayed
and drove men—men, I tell you. But as I stood on this
hillside, I foresaw that in the blinding sunshine of that
land I would become acquainted with a flabby, pretending, weak-eyed devil of a rapacious and pitiless folly.
How insidious he could be, too, I was only to find out
several months later and a thousand miles farther. For
a moment I stood appalled, as though by a warning.
Finally I descended the hill, obliquely, towards the trees
I had seen.

"I avoided a vast artificial hole somebody had been
digging on the slope, the purpose of which I found it
impossible to divine. It wasn't a quarry or a sandpit,
anyhow. It was just a hole. It might have been connected with the philanthropic desire of giving the criminals something to do. I don't know. Then I nearly fell
into a very narrow ravine, almost no more than a scar
in the hillside. I discovered that a lot of imported drain-
age pipes for the settlement had been tumbled in there.
There wasn't one that was not broken. It was a wanton
smashup. At last I got under the trees. My purpose
was to stroll into the shade for a moment; but no
sooner within than it seemed to me I had stepped into
the gloomy circle of some inferno. The rapids were
near, and an uninterrupted, uniform, headlong, rushing
noise filled the mournful stillness of the grove, where
not a breath stirred, not a leaf moved, with a mysterious
sound—as though the tearing pace of the launched
earth had suddenly become audible.

"Black shapes crouched, lay, sat between the trees
leaning against the trunks, clinging to the earth, half
coming out, half effaced within the dim light, in all the
attitudes of pain, abandonment, and despair. Another
mine on the cliff went off, followed by a slight shudder

of the soil under my feet. The work was going on. The work! And this was the place where some of the helpers had withdrawn to die.

"They were dying slowly—it was very clear. They were not enemies, they were not criminals, they were nothing earthly now, nothing but black shadows of disease and starvation, lying confusedly in the greenish gloom. Brought from all the recesses of the coast in all the legality of time contracts, lost in uncongenial surroundings, fed on unfamiliar food, they sickened, became inefficient, and were then allowed to crawl away and rest. These moribund shapes were free as air—and nearly as thin. I began to distinguish the gleam of the eyes under the trees. Then, glancing down, I saw a face near my hand. The black bones reclined at full length with one shoulder against the tree, and slowly the eyelids rose and the sunken eyes looked up at me, enormous and vacant, a kind of blind, white flicker in the depths of the orbs, which died out slowly. The man seemed young—almost a boy—but you know with them it's hard to tell. I found nothing else to do but to offer him one of my good Swede's ship's biscuits I had in my pocket. The fingers closed slowly on it and held—there was no other movement and no other glance. He had tied a bit of white worsted round his neck—Why? Where did he get it? Was it a badge—an ornament—a charm—a propitiatory act? Was there any idea at all connected with it? It looked startling round his black neck, this bit of white thread from beyond the seas.

"Near the same tree two more bundles of acute angles sat with their legs drawn up. One, with his chin propped on his knees, stared at nothing, in an intolerable and appalling manner: his brother phantom rested its forehead, as if overcome with a great weariness; and all about others were scattered in every pose of contorted collapse, as in some picture of a massacre or a pestilence. While I stood horror-struck, one of these creatures rose to his hands and knees, and went off on all fours towards the river to drink. He lapped out of his hand, then sat up in the sunlight, crossing his shins in front of him, and after a time let his wooly head fall on his breastbone.

"I didn't want any more loitering in the shade, and I made haste towards the station. When near the buildings I met a white man, in such an unexpected elegance of getup that in the first moment I took him for a sort of vision. I saw a high starched collar, white cuffs, a light alpaca jacket, snowy trousers, a clear necktie, and varnished boots. No hat. Hair parted, brushed, oiled, under a green-lined parasol held in a big white hand. He was amazing, and had a penholder behind his ear.

"I shook hands with this miracle, and I learned he was the company's chief accountant, and that all the bookkeeping was done at this station. He had come out for a moment, he said, 'to get a breath of fresh air.' The expression sounded wonderfully odd, with its suggestion of sedentary desk life. I wouldn't have mentioned the fellow to you at all, only it was from his lips that I first heard the name of the man who is so indissolubly connected with the memories of that time. Moreover, I respected the fellow. Yes; I respected his collars, his vast cuffs, his brushed hair. His appearance was certainly that of a hairdresser's dummy; but in the great demoralization of the land he kept up his appearance. That's backbone. His starched collars and got-up shirt fronts were achievements of character. He had been out nearly three years; and, later, I could not help asking him how he managed to sport such linen. He had just the faintest blush, and said modestly, 'I've been teaching one of the native women about the sta-

tion. It was difficult. She had a distaste for the work.'
Thus this man had truly accomplished something. And
he was devoted to his books, which were in apple-pie
order.

"Everything else in the station was in a muddle—
heads, things, buildings. Strings of dusty niggers with
splay feet arrived and departed; a stream of manufac-
tured goods, rubbishy cottons, beads, and brass wire set
into the depths of darkness, and in return came a precious trickle of ivory.

"I had to wait in the station for ten days—an eternity.
I lived in a hut in the yard, but to be out of the chaos
I would sometimes get into the accountant's office. It
was built of horizontal planks, and so badly put together that, as he bent over his high desk, he was barred
from neck to heels with narrow strips of sunlight. There
was no need to open the big shutter to see. It was hot
there, too; big flies buzzed fiendishly, and did not sting,
but stabbed. I sat generally on the floor, while, of fault-
less appearance (and even slightly scented), perching
on a high stool, he wrote, he wrote. Sometimes he stood
up for exercise. When a truckle bed with a sick man
(some invalid agent from upcountry) was put in there,
he exhibited a gentle annoyance. 'The groans of this
sick person,' he said, 'distract my attention. And without
that it is extremely difficult to guard against clerical
errors in this climate.'

"One day he remarked, without lifting his head, 'In
the interior you will no doubt meet Mr. Kurtz.' On my
asking who Mr. Kurtz was, he said he was a first-class
agent; and seeing my disappointment at this information, he added slowly, laying down his pen, 'He is a
very remarkable person.' Further questions elicited from
him that Mr. Kurtz was at present in charge of a trading
post, a very important one, in the true ivory-country,

at 'the very bottom of there. Sends in as much ivory as all the others put together. . . .' He began to write again. The sick man was too ill to groan. The flies buzzed in a great peace.

"Suddenly there was a growing murmur of voices and a great tramping of feet. A caravan had come in. A violent babble of uncouth sounds burst out on the other side of the planks. All the carriers were speaking together, and in the midst of the uproar the lamentable voice of the chief agent was heard 'giving it up' tearfully for the twentieth time that day. . . . He rose slowly. 'What a frightful row,' he said. He crossed the room gently to look at the sick man, and returning, said to me, 'He does not hear.' 'What! Dead?' I asked, startled. 'No, not yet,' he answered, with great composure. Then, alluding with a toss of the head to the tumult in the station yard, 'When one has got to make correct entries, one comes to hate those savages—hate them to the death.' He remained thoughtful for a moment. 'When you see Mr. Kurtz,' he went on, 'tell him from me that everything here'—he glanced at the desk—'is very satisfactory. I don't like to write to him—with those messengers of ours you never know who may get hold of your letter—at that Central Station.' He stared at me for a moment with his mild, bulging eyes. 'Oh, he will go far, very far,' he began again. 'He will be a somebody in the administration before long. They, above—the council in Europe, you know—mean him to be.'

"He turned to his work. The noise outside had ceased, and presently in going out I stopped at the door. In the steady buzz of flies the homeward-bound agent was lying flushed and insensible; the other, bent over his books, was making correct entries of perfectly correct transactions; and fifty feet below the doorstep I could see the still treetops of the grove of death.

"Next day I left that station at last, with a caravan of sixty men, for a two-hundred-mile tramp.

"No use telling you much about that. Paths, paths, everywhere; a stamped-in network of paths spreading over the empty land, through long grass, through burnt grass, through thickets, down and up chilly ravines, up and down stony hills ablaze with heat; and a solitude, a solitude, nobody, not a hut. The population had cleared out a long time ago. Well, if a lot of mysterious niggers armed with all kinds of fearful weapons suddenly took to traveling on the road between Deal and Gravesend, catching the yokels right and left to carry heavy loads for them, I fancy every farm and cottage thereabouts would get empty very soon. Only here the dwellings were gone, too. Still I passed through several abandoned villages. There's something pathetically childish in the ruins of grass walls. Day after day, with the stamp and shuffle of sixty pair of bare feet behind me, each pair under a sixty-lb. load. Camp, cook, sleep, strike camp, march. Now and then a carrier dead in harness, at rest in the long grass near the path, with an empty water gourd and his long staff lying by his side. A great silence around and above. Perhaps on some quiet night the tremor of far-off drums, sinking, swelling, a tremor vast, faint; a sound weird, appealing, suggestive, and wild—and perhaps with as profound a meaning as the sound of bells in a Christian country. Once a white man in an unbuttoned uniform, camping on the path with an armed escort of lank Zanzibaris, very hospitable and festive—not to say drunk. Was looking after the upkeep of the road he declared. Can't say I saw any road or any upkeep, unless the body of a middle-aged Negro, with a bullethole in the forehead, upon which I absolutely stumbled three miles farther on, may be considered as a permanent improvement.

I had a white companion, too, not a bad chap, but rather too fleshy and with the exasperating habit of fainting on the hot hillsides, miles away from the least bit of shade and water. Annoying, you know, to hold your own coat like a parasol over a man's head while he is coming to. I couldn't help asking him once what he meant by coming there at all. 'To make money, of course. What do you think?' he said, scornfully. Then he got fever, and had to be carried in a hammock slung under a pole. As he weighed 224 pounds I had no end of rows with the carriers. They jibbed, ran away, sneaked off with their loads in the night—quite a mutiny. So, one evening, I made a speech in English with gestures, not one of which was lost to the sixty pairs of eyes before me, and the next morning I started the hammock off in front all right. An hour afterwards I came upon the whole concern wrecked in a bush—man, hammock, groans, blankets, horrors. The heavy pole had skinned his poor nose. He was very anxious for me to kill somebody, but there wasn't the shadow of a carrier near. I remember the old doctor, 'It would be interesting for science to watch the mental changes of individuals, on the spot.' I felt I was becoming scientifically interesting. However, all that is to no purpose. On the fifteenth day I came in sight of the big river again, and hobbled into the Central Station. It was on a back water surrounded by scrub and forest, with a pretty border of smelly mud on one side, and on the three others enclosed by a crazy fence of rushes. A neglected gap was all the gate it had, and the first glance at the place was enough to let you see the flabby devil was running that show. White men with long staves in their hands appeared languidly from amongst the buildings, strolling up to take a look at me, and then retired out of sight somewhere. One of them, a stout, excitable chap with black mustaches, informed

me with great volubility and many digressions, as soon
as I told him who I was, that my steamer was at the
bottom of the river. I was thunderstruck. What, how,
why? Oh, it was 'all right.' The 'manager himself' was
there. All quite correct. 'Everybody had behaved splendidly! splendidly!'—'you must,' he said in agitation, 'go
and see the general manager at once. He is waiting!'

"I did not see the real significance of that wreck at
once. I fancy I see it now, but I am not sure—not at
all. Certainly the affair was too stupid—when I think
of it—to be altogether natural. Still . . . But at the
moment it presented itself simply as a confounded nuisance. The steamer was sunk. They had started two days
before in a sudden hurry up the river with the manager
on board, in charge of some volunteer skipper, and before they had been out three hours they tore the bottom
out of her on stones, and she sank near the south bank.
I asked myself what I was to do there, now my boat was
lost. As a matter of fact, I had plenty to do in fishing
my command out of the river. I had to set about it the
very next day. That, and the repairs when I brought the
pieces to the station, took some months.

"My first interview with the manager was curious.
He did not ask me to sit down after my twenty-mile
walk that morning. He was commonplace in complexion, in feature, in manners, and in voice. He was of
middle size and of ordinary build. His eyes, of the usual
blue, were perhaps remarkably cold, and he certainly
could make his glance fall on one as trenchant and
heavy as an axe. But even at these times the rest of
his person seemed to disclaim the intention. Otherwise
there was only an indefinable, faint expression of his
lips, something stealthy—a smile—not a smile—I remember it, but I can't explain. It was unconscious, this
smile was, though just after he had said something it

got intensified for an instant. It came at the end of his speeches like a seal applied on the words to make the meaning of the commonest phrase appear absolutely inscrutable. He was a common trader, from his youth up employed in these parts—nothing more. He was obeyed, yet he inspired neither love nor fear, nor even respect. He inspired uneasiness. That was it! Uneasiness. Not a definite mistrust—just uneasiness—nothing more. You have no idea how effective such a . . . a . . . faculty can be. He had no genius for organizing, for initiative, or for order even. That was evident in such things as the deplorable state of the station. He had no learning, and no intelligence. His position had come to him— why? Perhaps because he was never ill . . . He had served three terms of three years out there. . . . Because triumphant health in the general rout of constitutions is a kind of power in itself. When he went home on leave he rioted on a large scale—pompously. Jack ashore—with a difference—in externals only. This one could gather from his casual talk. He originated nothing, he could keep the routine going—that's all. But he was great. He was great by this little thing that it was impossible to tell what could control such a man. He never gave that secret away. Perhaps there was nothing within him. Such a suspicion made one pause—for out there there were no external checks. Once when various tropical diseases had laid low almost every 'agent' in the station, he was heard to say, 'Men who come out here should have no entrails.' He sealed the utterance with that smile of his, as though it had been a door opening into a darkness he had in his keeping. You fancied you had seen things—but the seal was on. When annoyed at mealtimes by the constant quarrels of the white men about precedence, he ordered an immense round table to be made, for which a special house had to be

built. This was the station's messroom. Where he sat
was the first place—the rest were nowhere. One felt
this to be his unalterable conviction. He was neither
civil nor uncivil. He was quiet. He allowed his 'boy'—
an overfed young Negro from the coast—to treat the
white men, under his very eyes, with provoking insolence.

"He began to speak as soon as he saw me. I had been
very long on the road. He could not wait. Had to start
without me. The up-river stations had to be relieved.
There had been so many delays already that he did not
know who was dead and who was alive, and how they
got on—and so on, and so on. He paid no attention to
my explanations, and, playing with a stick of sealing
wax, repeated several times that the situation was 'very
grave, very grave.' There were rumors that a very important station was in jeopardy, and its chief, Mr. Kurtz,
was ill. Hoped it was not true. Mr. Kurtz was . . . I
felt weary and irritable. Hang Kurtz, I thought. I interrupted him by saying I had heard of Mr. Kurtz on
the coast. 'Ah! So they talk of him down there,' he murmured to himself. Then he began again, assuring me
Mr. Kurtz was the best agent he had, an exceptional
man, of the greatest importance to the company; therefore I could understand his anxiety. He was, he said,
'very, very uneasy.' Certainly he fidgeted on his chair
a good deal, exclaimed, 'Ah, Mr. Kurtz!' broke the stick
of sealing wax and seemed dumfounded by the accident. Next thing he wanted to know 'how long it would
take to' . . . I interrupted him again. Being hungry,
you know, and kept on my feet, too, I was getting savage. 'How could I tell?' I said. 'I hadn't even seen the
wreck yet—some months, no doubt.' All this talk seemed
to me so futile. 'Some months,' he said. 'Well, let us say
three months before we can make a start. Yes. That

ought to do the affair.' I flung out of his hut (he lived all alone in a clay hut with a sort of veranda) muttering to myself my opinion of him. He was a chattering idiot. Afterwards I took it back when it was borne in upon me startlingly with what extreme nicety he had estimated the time requisite for the 'affair.'

"I went to work the next day, turning, so to speak, my back on that station. In that way only it seemed to me I could keep my hold on the redeeming facts of life. Still, one must look about sometimes; and then I saw this station, these men strolling aimlessly about in the sunshine of the yard. I asked myself sometimes what it all meant. They wandered here and there with their absurd long staves in their hands, like a lot of faithless pilgrims bewitched inside a rotten fence. The word 'ivory' rang in the air, was whispered, was sighed. You would think they were praying to it. A taint of imbecile rapacity blew through it all, like a whiff from some corpse. By Jove! I've never seen anything so unreal in my life. And outside, the silent wilderness surrounding this cleared speck on the earth struck me as something great and invincible, like evil or truth, waiting patiently for the passing away of this fantastic invasion.

"Oh, these months! Well, never mind. Various things happened. One evening a grass shed full of calico, cotton prints, beads, and I don't know what else, burst into a blaze so suddenly that you would have thought the earth had opened to let an avenging fire consume all that trash. I was smoking my pipe quietly by my dismantled steamer, and saw them all cutting capers in the light, with their arms lifted high, 'when the stout man with mustaches came tearing down to the river, a tin pail in his hand, assured me that everybody was 'behaving splendidly, splendidly,' dipped about a quart of water and tore back again. I noticed there was a hole in the bottom of his pail.

"I strolled up. There was no hurry. You see the thing had gone off like a box of matches. It had been hopeless from the very first. The flame had leaped high, driven everybody back, lighted up everything—and collapsed. The shed was already a heap of embers glowing fiercely. A nigger was being beaten near by. They said he had caused the fire in some way; be that as it may, he was screeching most horribly. I saw him, later, for several days, sitting in a bit of shade looking very sick and trying to recover himself: afterwards he arose and went out—and the wilderness without a sound took him into its bosom again. As I approached the glow from the dark I found myself at the back of two men, talking. I heard the name of Kurtz pronounced, then the words, 'take advantage of this unfortunate accident.' One of the men was the manager. I wished him a good evening. 'Did you ever see anything like it—eh? It is incredible,' he said, and walked off. The other man remained. He was a first-class agent, young, gentlemanly, a bit reserved, with a forked little beard and a hooked nose. He was standoffish with the other agents, and they on their side said he was the manager's spy upon them. As to me, I had hardly ever spoken to him before. We got into talk, and by and by we strolled away from the hissing ruins. Then he asked me to his room, which was in the main building of the station. He struck a match, and I perceived that this young aristocrat had not only a silver-mounted dressing case but also a whole candle all to himself. Just at that time the manager was the only man supposed to have any right to candles. Native mats covered the clay walls; a collection of spears, assagais, shields, knives was hung up in trophies. The business intrusted to this fellow was the making of bricks—so I had been informed; but there wasn't a fragment of a brick anywhere in the station, and he had been there more than a year—waiting. It seems he could not make bricks without something, I don't know what—straw maybe. Anyways, it could not be found there, and as it was not likely to be sent from Europe, it did not appear clear to me what he was waiting for. An act of special creation perhaps. However, they were all waiting—all the sixteen or twenty pilgrims of them—for something; and upon my word it did not seem an uncongenial occupation, from the way they took it, though the only thing that ever came to them was disease—as far as I could see. They beguiled the time by backbiting and intriguing against each other in a foolish kind of way. There was an air of plotting about that station, but nothing came of it, of course. It was as unreal as everything else—as the philanthropic pretense of the whole concern, as their talk, as their government, as their show of work. The only real feeling was a desire to get appointed to a trading post where ivory was to be had, so that they could earn percentages. They intrigued and slandered and hated each other only on that account, but as to effectually lifting a little finger—oh, no. By heavens! There is something after all in the world allowing one man to steal a horse while another must not look at a halter. Steal a horse straight out. Very well. He has done it. Perhaps he can ride. But there is a way of looking at a halter that would provoke the most charitable of saints into a kick.

"I had no idea why he wanted to be sociable, but as we chatted in there it suddenly occurred to me the fellow was trying to get at something—in fact, pumping me. He alluded constantly to Europe, to the people I was supposed to know there—putting leading questions as to my acquaintances in the sepulchral city, and so on. His little eyes glittered like mica discs—with curiosity —though he tried to keep up a bit of superciliousness. At first I was astonished, but very soon I became awfully curious to see what he would find out from me. I couldn't possibly imagine what I had in me to make it worth his while. It was very pretty to see how he baffled himself, for in truth my body was full only of chills, and my head had nothing in it but that wretched steamboat business. It was evident he took me for a perfectly shameless prevaricator. At last he got angry, and, to conceal a movement of furious annoyance, he yawned. I rose. Then I noticed a small sketch in oils, on a panel, representing a woman, draped and blindfolded, carrying a lighted torch. The background was somber—almost black. The movement of the woman was stately, and the effect of the torchlight on the face was sinister.

"It arrested me, and he stood by civilly, holding an empty half-pint champagne bottle (medical comforts) with the candle stuck in it. To my question he said Mr. Kurtz had painted this—in this very station more than a year ago—while waiting for means to go to his trading post. 'Tell me, pray,' said I, 'who is this Mr. Kurtz?'

" 'The chief of the Inner Station,' he answered in a short tone, looking away. 'Much obliged,' I said, laughing. 'And you are the brickmaker of the Central Station. Everyone knows that.' He was silent for a while. 'He is a prodigy,' he said at last. 'He is an emissary of pity, and science, and progress, and devil knows what else. We want,' he began to declaim suddenly, 'for the guidance of the cause intrusted to us by Europe, so to speak, higher intelligence, wide sympathies, a singleness of purpose.' 'Who says that?' I asked. 'Lots of them,' he replied. 'Some even write that; and so *he* comes here, a special being, as you ought to know.' 'Why ought I to know?' I interrupted, really surprised. He paid no attention. 'Yes. Today he is chief of the best station, next year he will be assistant manager, two years more and . . . but I daresay you know what he will be in two years' time. You are of the new gang—the gang of virtue. The same people who sent him specially also recommended you. Oh, don't say no. I've my own eyes to trust.' Light dawned upon me. My dear aunt's influential acquaintances were producing an unexpected effect upon that young man. I nearly burst into a laugh. 'Do you read the company's confidential correspondence?' I asked. He hadn't a word to say. It was great fun. 'When Mr. Kurtz,' I continued, severely, 'is general manager, you won't have the opportunity.'

"He blew the candle out suddenly, and we went outside. The moon had risen. Black figures strolled about listlessly, pouring water on the glow, whence proceeded a sound of hissing; steam ascended in the moonlight, the beaten nigger groaned somewhere. 'What a row the brute makes!' said the indefatigable man with the mustaches, appearing near us. 'Serve him right. Transgression—punishment—bang! Pitiless, pitiless. That's the only way. This will prevent all conflagrations for the future. I was just telling the manager . . .' He noticed my companion, and became crestfallen all at once. 'Not in bed yet,' he said, with a kind of servile heartiness; 'it's so natural. Ha! Danger—agitation.' He vanished. I went on to the river side, and the other followed me. I heard a scathing murmur at my ear, 'Heap of muffs—go to.' The pilgrims could be seen in knots gesticulating, discussing. Several had still their staves in their hands. I truly believe they took these sticks to bed with them. Beyond the fence the forest stood up spectrally in the moonlight, and through the dim stir, through the faint sounds of that lamentable courtyard,

the silence of the land went home to one's very heart—
its mystery, its greatness, the amazing reality of its concealed life. The hurt nigger moaned feebly somewhere
near by, and then fetched a deep sigh that made me
mend my pace away from there. I felt a hand introducing itself under my arm. 'My dear sir,' said the fellow,
'I don't want to be misunderstood, and especially by
you, who will see Mr. Kurtz long before I can have that
pleasure. I wouldn't like him to get a false idea of my
disposition. . . .'

"I let him run on, this papier-mâché Mephistopheles,
and it seemed to me that if I tried I could poke my forefinger through him, and would find nothing inside but a
little loose dirt, maybe. He, don't you see, had been
planning to be assistant manager by and by under the
present man, and I could see that the coming of that
Kurtz had upset them both not a little. He talked pre-
cipitately, and I did not try to stop him. I had my shoulders against the wreck of my steamer, hauled up on the
slope like a carcass of some big river animal. The smell
of mud, of primeval mud, by Jove! was in my nostrils,
the high stillness of primeval forest was before my eyes;
there were shiny patches on the black creek. The moon
had spread over everything a thin layer of silver—over
the rank grass, over the mud, upon the wall of matted
vegetation standing higher than the wall of a temple,
over the great river I could see through a somber gap
glittering, glittering, as it flowed broadly by without a
murmur. All this was great, expectant, mute, while the
man jabbered about himself. I wondered whether the
stillness on the face of the immensity looking at us two
were meant as an appeal or as a menace. What were we
who had strayed in here? Could we handle that dumb
thing, or would it handle us? I felt how big, how confoundedly big, was that thing that couldn't talk, and

perhaps was deaf as well. What was in there? I could see a little ivory coming out from there, and I had heard Mr. Kurtz was in there. I had heard enough about it, too—God knows! Yet somehow it didn't bring any image with it—no more than if I had been told an angel or a fiend was in there. I believed it in the same way one of you might believe there are inhabitants in the planet Mars. I knew once a Scotch sailmaker who was certain, dead sure, there were people in Mars. If you asked him for some idea how they looked and behaved, he would get shy and mutter something about 'walking on all fours.' If you as much as smiled, he would—though a man of sixty—offer to fight you. I would not have gone so far as to fight for Kurtz, but I went for him near enough to a lie. You know I hate, detest, and can't bear a lie, not because I am straighter than the rest of us, but simply because it appalls me. There is a taint of death, a flavor of mortality in lies—which is exactly what I hate and detest in the world—what I want to forget. It makes me miserable and sick, like biting something rotten would do. Temperament, I suppose. Well, I went near enough to it by letting the young fool there believe anything he liked to imagine as to my influence in Europe. I became in an instant as much of a pretense as the rest of the bewitched pilgrims. This simply because I had a notion it somehow would be of help to that Kurtz whom at the time I did not see—you understand. He was just a word for me. I did not see the man in the name any more than you do. Do you see him? Do you see the story? Do you see anything? It seems to me I am trying to tell you a dream—making a vain attempt, because no relation of a dream can convey the dream-sensation, that commingling of absurdity, surprise, and bewilderment in a tremor of struggling revolt, that notion of being captured by the incredible which is of the very essence of dreams. . . ."

He was silent for a while.

". . . No, it is impossible; it is impossible to convey the life-sensation of any given epoch of one's existence —that which makes its truth, its meaning—its subtle and penetrating essence. It is impossible. We live, as we dream—alone. . . ."

He paused again as if reflecting, then added:

"Of course in this you fellows see more than I could then. You see me, whom you know. . . ."

It had become so pitch dark that we listeners could hardly see one another. For a long time already he, sitting apart, had been no more to us than a voice. There was not a word from anybody. The others might have been asleep, but I was awake. I listened, I listened on the watch for the sentence, for the word, that would give me the clue to the faint uneasiness inspired by this narrative that seemed to shape itself without human lips in the heavy night air of the river.

". . . Yes—I let him run on," Marlow began again, "and think what he pleased about the powers that were behind me. I did! And there was nothing behind me! There was nothing but that wretched, old, mangled steamboat I was leaning against, while he talked fluently about 'the necessity for every man to get on.' 'And when one comes out here, you conceive, it is not to gaze at the moon.' Mr. Kurtz was a 'universal genius,' but even a genius would find it easier to work with 'adequate tools—intelligent men.' He did not make bricks—why, there was a physical impossibility in the way—as I was well aware; and if he did secretarial work for the manager, it was because 'no sensible man rejects wantonly the confidence of his superiors.' Did I see it? I saw it.

What more did I want? What I really wanted was rivets, by heaven! Rivets. To get on with the work—to stop the hole. Rivets I wanted. There were cases of them down at the coast—cases—piled up—burst—split! You kicked a loose rivet at every second step in that station yard on the hillside. Rivets had rolled into the grove of death. You could fill your pockets with rivets for the trouble of stooping down—and there wasn't one rivet to be found where it was wanted. We had plates that would do, but nothing to fasten them with. And every week the messenger, a lone Negro, letter bag on shoulder and staff in hand, left our station for the coast. And several times a week a coast caravan came in with trade goods—ghastly glazed calico that made you shudder only to look at it, glass beads, value about a penny a quart, confounded spotted cotton handkerchiefs. And no rivets. Three carriers could have brought all that was wanted to set that steamboat afloat.

"He was becoming confidential now, but I fancy my unresponsive attitude must have exasperated him at last, for he judged it necessary to inform me he feared neither God nor devil, let alone any mere man. I said I could 'see that very well, but what I wanted was a certain quantity of rivets—and rivets were what really Mr. Kurtz wanted, if he had only known it. Now letters went to the coast every week. . . . 'My dear sir,' he cried, 'I write from dictation.' I demanded rivets. There was a way—for an intelligent man. He changed his manner; became very cold, and suddenly began to talk about a hippopotamus; wondered whether sleeping on board the steamer (I stuck to my salvage night and day) I wasn't disturbed. There was an old hippo that had the bad habit of getting out on the bank and roaming at night over the station grounds. The pilgrims used to turn out in a body and empty every rifle they could lay hands on at him. Some even had sat up o' nights for him. All this energy was wasted, though. 'That animal has a charmed life,' he said; 'but you can say this only of brutes in this country. No man—you apprehend me? —no man here bears a charmed life.' He stood there for a moment in the moonlight with his delicate hooked nose set a little askew, and his mica eyes glittering without a wink, then, with a curt good night, he strode off. I could see he was disturbed and considerably puzzled, which made me feel more hopeful than I had been for days. It was a great comfort to turn from that chap to my influential friend, the battered, twisted, ruined, tin-pot steamboat. I clambered on board. She rang under my feet like an empty Huntley and Palmer biscuit tin kicked along a gutter; she was nothing so solid in make, and rather less pretty in shape, but I had expended enough hard work on her to make me love her. No influential friend would have served me better. She had given me a chance to come out a bit—to find out what I could do. No, I don't like work. I had rather laze about and think of all the fine things that can be done. I don't like work—no man does—but I like what is in the work, the chance to find yourself. Your own reality —for yourself, not for others—what no other man can ever know. They can only see the mere show, and never can tell what it really means.

"I was not surprised to see somebody sitting aft, on the deck, with his legs dangling over the mud. You see I rather chummed with the few mechanics there were in that station, whom the other pilgrims naturally despised—on account of their imperfect manners, I suppose. This was the foreman—a boilermaker by trade— a good worker. He was a lank, bony, yellow-faced man, with big intense eyes. His aspect was worried, and his head was as bald as the palm of my hand; but his hair in falling seemed to have stuck to his chin, and had prospered in the new locality, for his beard hung down to his waist. He was a widower with six young children (he had left them in charge of a sister of his to come out there), and the passion of his life was pigeon flying. He was an enthusiast and a connoisseur. He would rave about pigeons. After work hours he used sometimes to come over from his hut for a talk about his children and his pigeons; at work, when he had to crawl in the mud under the bottom of the steamboat, he would tie up that beard of his in a kind of white serviette he brought for the purpose. It had loops to go over his ears. In the evening he could be seen squatted on the bank rinsing that wrapper in the creek with great care, then spreading it solemnly on a bush to dry.

"I slapped him on the back and shouted 'We shall have rivets!' He scrambled to his feet exclaiming 'No! Rivets!' as though he couldn't believe his ears. Then in a low voice, 'You . . . eh?' I don't know why we behaved like lunatics. I put my finger to the side of my nose and nodded mysteriously. 'Good for you!' he cried, snapped his fingers above his head, lifting one foot. I tried a jig. We capered on the iron deck. A frightful clatter came out of that hulk, and the virgin forest on the other bank of the creek sent it back in a thundering roll upon the sleeping station. It must have made some of the pilgrims sit up in their hovels. A dark figure obscured the lighted doorway of the manager's hut, vanished, then, a second or so after, the doorway itself vanished, too. We stopped, and the silence driven away by the stamping of our feet flowed back again from the recesses of the land. The great wall of vegetation, an exuberant and entangled mass of trunks, branches, leaves, boughs, festoons, motionless in the moonlight, was like a rioting invasion of soundless life, a rolling wave of plants, piled up, crested, ready to topple over the creek, to sweep every little man of us out of his little existence. And it moved not. A deadened burst of mighty splashes and snorts reached us from afar, as though an ichthyosaurus had been taking a bath of glitter in the great river. 'After all,' said the boilermaker in a reasonable tone, 'why shouldn't we get the rivets?' Why not, indeed! I did not know of any reason why we shouldn't. 'They'll come in three weeks,' I said, confidently.

"But they didn't. Instead of rivets there came an invasion, an infliction, a visitation. It came in sections during the next three weeks, each section headed by a donkey carrying a white man in new clothes and tan shoes, bowing from that elevation right and left to the impressed pilgrims. A quarrelsome band of footsore sulky niggers trod on the heels of the donkey; a lot of tents, campstools, tin boxes, white cases, brown bales would be shot down in the courtyard, and the air of mystery would deepen a little over the muddle of the station. Five such instalments came, with their absurd air of disorderly flight with the loot of innumerable outfit shops and provision stores, that, one would think, they were lugging, after a raid, into the wilderness for equitable division. It was an inextricable mess of things decent in themselves but that human folly made look like spoils of thieving.

"This devoted band called itself the Eldorado Exploring Expedition, and I believe they were sworn to secrecy. Their talk, however, was the talk of sordid buccaneers: it was reckless without hardihood, greedy without audacity, and cruel without courage; there was not an atom of foresight or of serious intention in the whole batch of them, and they did not seem aware these things are wanted for the work of the world. To tear treasure out of the bowels of the land was their desire, with no more moral purpose at the back of it than there is in burglars breaking into a safe. Who paid the expenses of the noble enterprise I don't know; but the uncle of our manager was leader of that lot.

"In exterior he resembled a butcher in a poor neighborhood, and his eyes had a look of sleepy cunning. He carried his fat paunch with ostentation on his short legs, and during the time his gang infested the station spoke to no one but his nephew. You could see these two roaming about all day long with their heads close together in an everlasting confab.

"I had given up worrying myself about the rivets. One's capacity for that kind of folly is more limited than you would suppose. I said Hang!—and let things slide. I had plenty of time for meditation, and now and then I would give some thought to Kurtz. I wasn't very interested in him. No. Still, I was curious to see whether this man, who had come out equipped with moral ideas of some sort, would climb to the top after all and how he would set about his work when there."

## II

"One evening as I was lying flat on the deck of my steamboat, I heard voices approaching—and there were the nephew and the uncle strolling along the bank. I laid my head on my arm again, and had nearly lost myself in a doze, when somebody said in my ear, as it were: 'I am as harmless as a little child, but I don't like to be dictated to. Am I the manager—or am I not? I was ordered to send him there. It's incredible.' . . . I became aware that the two were standing on the shore alongside the forepart of the steamboat, just below my head. I did not move; it did not occur to me to move: I was sleepy. 'It *is* unpleasant,' grunted the uncle. 'He has asked the administration to be sent there,' said the other, 'with the idea of showing what he could do; and I was instructed accordingly. Look at the influence that man must have. Is it not frightful?' They both agreed it was frightful, then made several bizarre remarks: 'Make rain and fine weather—one man—the council— by the nose'—bits of absurd sentences that got the better of my drowsiness, so that I had pretty near the whole of my wits about me when the uncle said, 'The climate may do away with this difficulty for you. Is he alone there?' 'Yes,' answered the manager; 'he sent his as- sistant down the river with a note to me in these terms: "Clear this poor devil out of the country, and don't bother sending more of that sort. I had rather be alone than have the kind of men you can dispose of with me." It was more than a year ago. Can you imagine such impudence!' 'Anything since then?' asked the other, hoarsely. 'Ivory,' jerked the nephew; 'lots of it—prime sort—lots—most annoying, from him.' 'And with that?' questioned the heavy rumble. 'Invoice,' was the reply fired out, so to speak. Then silence. They had been talk- ing about Kurtz.

"I was broad awake by this time, but, lying perfectly at ease, remained still, having no inducement to change my position. 'How did that ivory come all this way?' growled the elder man, who seemed very vexed. The other explained that it had come with a fleet of canoes in charge of an English half-caste clerk Kurtz had with him; that Kurtz had apparently intended to return him- self, the station being by that time bare of goods and stores, but after coming three hundred miles, had sud- denly decided to go back, which he started to do alone in a small dugout with four paddlers, leaving the half- caste to continue down the river with the ivory. The two fellows there seemed astounded at anybody at-

tempting such a thing. They were at a loss for an adequate motive. As to me, I seemed to see Kurtz for the
first time. It was a distinct glimpse: the dugout, four
paddling savages, and the lone white man turning his
back suddenly on the headquarters, on relief, on
thoughts of home—perhaps; setting his face towards the
depths of the wilderness, towards his empty and desolate station. I did not know the motive. Perhaps he was
just simply a fine fellow who stuck to his work for its
own sake. His name, you understand, had not been pronounced once. He was 'that man.' The half-caste, who,
as far as I could see, had conducted a difficult trip with
great prudence and pluck, was invariably alluded to as
'that scoundrel.' The 'scoundrel' had reported that the
'man' had been very ill—had recovered imperfectly.
. . . The two below me moved away then a few paces,
and strolled back and forth at some little distance. I
heard: 'Military post—doctor—two hundred miles—
quite alone now—unavoidable delays—nine months—
no news—strange rumors.' They approached again, just
as the manager was saying, 'No one, as far as I know,
unless a species of wandering trader—a pestilential fellow, snapping ivory from the natives.' Who was it they
were talking about now? I gathered in snatches that this
was some man supposed to be in Kurtz's district, and of
whom the manager did not approve. 'We will not be
free from unfair competition till one of these fellows is
hanged for an example,' he said. 'Certainly,' grunted
the other; 'get him hanged! Why not? Anything—anything can be done in this country. That's what I say;
nobody here, you understand, *here*, can endanger your
position. And why? You stand the climate—you outlast
them all. The danger is in Europe; but there before I
left I took care to—' They moved off and whispered,
then their voices rose again. 'The extraordinary series

of delays is not my fault. I did my best.' The fat man
sighed. 'Very sad.' 'And the pestiferous absurdity of his
talk,' continued the other; 'he bothered me enough
when he was here. "Each station should be like a beacon
on the road towards better things, a center for trade of
course, but also for humanizing, improving, instruct-
ing." Conceive you—that ass! And he wants to be manager! No, it's—' Here he got choked by excessive indignation, and I lifted my head the least bit. I was
surprised to see how near they were—right under me.
I could have spat upon their hats. They were looking on
the ground, absorbed in thought. The manager was
switching his leg with a slender twig; his sagacious
relative lifted his head. 'You have been well since you
came out this time?' he asked. The other gave a start.
'Who? I? Oh! Like a charm—like a charm. But the rest
—oh, my goodness! All sick. They die so quick, too,
that I haven't the time to send them out of the country
—it's incredible!' 'H'm. Just so,' grunted the uncle. 'Ah!
my boy, trust to this—I say, trust to this.' I saw him
extend his short flipper of an arm for a gesture that took
in the forest, the creek, the mud, the river—seemed to
beckon with a dishonoring flourish before the sunlit face
of the land a treacherous appeal to the lurking death, to
the hidden evil, to the profound darkness of its heart.
It was so startling that I leaped to my feet and looked
back at the edge of the forest, as though I had expected
an answer of some sort to that black display of confidence. You know the foolish notions that come to one
sometimes. The high stillness confronted these two figures with its ominous patience, waiting for the passing
away of a fantastic invasion.

"They swore aloud together—out of sheer fright, I
believe—then pretending not to know anything of my
existence, turned back to the station. The sun was low;

and leaning forward side by side, they seemed to be tugging painfully uphill their two ridiculous shadows of unequal length, that trailed behind them slowly over the tall grass without bending a single blade.

"In a few days the Eldorado Expedition went into the patient wilderness, that closed upon it as the sea closes over a diver. Long afterwards the news came that all the donkeys were dead. I know nothing as to the fate of the less valuable animals. They, no doubt, like the rest of us, found what they deserved. I did not inquire. I was then rather excited at the prospect of meeting Kurtz very soon. When I say very soon I mean it comparatively. It was just two months from the day we left the creek when we came to the bank below Kurtz's station.

"Going up that river was like traveling back to the earliest beginnings of the world, when vegetation rioted on the earth and the big trees were kings. An empty stream, a great silence, an impenetrable forest. The air was warm, thick, heavy, sluggish. There was no joy in the brilliance of sunshine. The long stretches of the waterway ran on, deserted, into the gloom of over-shadowed distances. On silvery sandbanks hippos and alligators sunned themselves side by side. The broadening waters flowed through a mob of wooded islands; you lost your way on that river as you would in a desert, and butted all day long against shoals, trying to find the channel, till you thought yourself bewitched and cut off forever from everything you had known once—some-where—far away—in another existence perhaps. There were moments when one's past came back to one, as it will sometimes when you have not a moment to spare to yourself; but it came in the shape of an unrestful and noisy dream, remembered with wonder amongst the overwhelming realities of this strange world of plants, and water, and silence. And this stillness of life did not in the least resemble a peace. It was the stillness of an implacable force brooding over an inscrutable intention. It looked at you with a vengeful aspect. I got used to it afterwards; I did not see it any more; I had no time. I had to keep guessing at the channel; I had to discern, mostly by inspiration, the signs of hidden banks; I watched for sunken stones; I was learning to clap my teeth smartly before my heart flew out, when I shaved by a fluke some infernal sly old snag that would have ripped the life out of the tin-pot steamboat and drowned all the pilgrims; I had to keep a lookout for the signs of dead wood we could cut up in the night for next day's steaming. When you have to attend to things of that sort, to the mere incidents of the surface, the reality— the reality, I tell you—fades. The inner truth is hidden —luckily, luckily. But I felt it all the same; I felt often its mysterious stillness watching me at my monkey tricks, just as it watches you fellows performing on your respective tightropes for—what is it? a half crown a tumble—"

"Try to be civil, Marlow," growled a voice, and I knew there was at least one listener awake besides myself.

"I beg your pardon. I forgot the heartache which makes up the rest of the price. And indeed what does the price matter, if the trick be well done? You do your tricks very well. And I didn't do badly either, since I managed not to sink that steamboat on my first trip. It's a wonder to me yet. Imagine a blindfolded man set to drive a van over a bad road. I sweated and shivered over that business considerably, I can tell you. After all, for a seaman, to scrape the bottom of the thing that's supposed to float all the time under his care is the unpardonable sin. No one may know of it, but you never forget the thump—eh? A blow on the very heart. You remember it, you dream of it, you wake up at night and think of it—years after—and go hot and cold all over. I don't pretend to say that steamboat floated all the time. More than once she had to wade for a bit, with twenty cannibals splashing around and pushing. We had enlisted some of these chaps on the way for a crew. Fine fellows—cannibals—in their place. They were men one could work with, and I am grateful to them. And, after all, they did not eat each other before my face: they had brought along a provision of hippo meat which went rotten, and made the mystery of the wilderness stink in my nostrils. Phoo! I can sniff it now. I had the manager on board and three or four pilgrims with their staves—all complete. Sometimes we came upon a station close by the bank, clinging to the skirts of the unknown, and the white men rushing out of a tumbledown hovel, with great gestures of joy and surprise and welcome, seemed very strange—had the appearance of being held there captive by a spell. The word ivory would ring in the air for a while—and on we went again into the silence, along empty reaches, round the still bends, between the high walls of our winding way, reverberating in hollow claps the ponderous beat of the stern wheel. Trees, trees, millions of trees, massive, immense, running up high; and at their foot, hugging the bank against the stream, crept the little begrimed steamboat, like a sluggish beetle crawling on the floor of a lofty portico. It made you feel very small, very lost, and yet it was not altogether depressing, that feeling. After all, if you were small, the grimy beetle crawled on—which was just what you wanted it to do. Where the pilgrims imagined it crawled to I don't know. To some place where they expected to get something, I bet! For me it crawled towards Kurtz—exclusively; but when the steam pipes started leaking we crawled very slow. The reaches opened before us and closed behind, as if the forest had stepped leisurely across the water to bar the way for our return. We penetrated deeper and deeper into the heart of darkness. It was very quiet there. At night sometimes the roll of drums behind the curtain of trees would run up the river and remain sustained faintly, as if hovering in the air high over our heads, till the first break of day. Whether it meant war, peace, or prayer we could not tell. The dawns were heralded by the descent of a chill stillness; the woodcutters slept, their fires burned low; the snapping of a twig would make you start. We were wanderers on prehistoric earth, on an earth that wore the aspect of an unknown planet. We could have fancied ourselves the first of men taking possession of an accursed inheritance, to be subdued at the cost of profound anguish and of excessive toil. But suddenly, as we struggled round a bend, there would be a glimpse of rush walls, of peaked grass roofs, a burst of yells, a whirl of black limbs, a mass of hands clapping, of feet stamping, of bodies swaying, of eyes rolling, under the droop of heavy and motionless foliage. The steamer toiled along slowly on the edge of a black and incomprehensible frenzy. The prehistoric man was cursing us, praying to us, welcoming us—who could tell? We were cut off from the comprehension of our surroundings; we glided past like phantoms, wondering and secretly appalled, as sane men would be before an enthusiastic outbreak in a madhouse. We could not understand because we were too far and could not remember, because we were traveling in the night of first ages, of those ages that are gone, leaving hardly a sign—and no memories.

"The earth seemed unearthly. We are accustomed to look upon the shackled form of a conquered monster, but there—there you could look at a thing monstrous and free. It was unearthly, and the men were— No, they were not inhuman. Well, you know, that was the worst of it—this suspicion of their not being inhuman. It would come slowly to one. They howled and leaped, and spun, and made horrid faces; but what thrilled you was just the thought of their humanity—like yours—the thought of your remote kinship with this wild and passionate uproar. Ugly. Yes, it was ugly enough; but if you were man enough you would admit to yourself that there was in you just the faintest trace of a response to the terrible frankness of that noise, a dim suspicion of there being a meaning in it which you—you so remote from the night of first ages—could comprehend. And why not? The mind of man is capable of anything —because everything is in it, all the past as well as all the future. What was there after all? Joy, fear, sorrow, devotion, valor, rage—who can tell?—but truth—truth stripped of its cloak of time. Let the fool gape and shudder—the man knows, and can look on without a wink. But he must at least be as much of a man as these on the shore. He must meet that truth with his own true stuff—with his own inborn strength. Principles won't do. Acquisitions, clothes, pretty rags—rags that would fly off at the first good shake. No; you want a deliberate belief. An appeal to me in this fiendish row—is there? Very well; I hear; I admit, but I have a voice, too, and for good or evil mine is the speech that cannot be silenced. Of course, a fool, what with sheer fright and fine sentiments, is always safe. Who's that grunting? You wonder I didn't go ashore for a howl and a dance? Well, no—I didn't. Fine sentiments, you say? Fine sentiments, be hanged! I had no time. I had to mess about with white lead and strips of woolen blanket helping to put bandages on those leaky steam pipes—I tell you. I had to watch the steering, and circumvent those snags, and get the tin-pot along by hook or by crook. There was surface truth enough in these things to save a wiser man. And between whiles I had to look after the savage who was fireman. He was an improved specimen; he could fire up a vertical boiler. He was there below me, and, upon my word, to look at him was as edifying as seeing a dog in a parody of breeches and a feather hat, walking on his hind legs. A few months of training had done for that really fine chap. He squinted at the steam gauge and at the water gauge with an evident effort of intrepidity—and he had filed teeth, too, the poor devil, and the wool of his pate shaved into queer patterns, and three ornamental scars on each of his cheeks. He ought to have been clapping his hands and stamping his feet on the bank, instead of which he was hard at work, a thrall to strange witchcraft, full of improving knowledge. He was useful because he had been instructed; and what he knew was this—that should the water in that transparent thing disappear, the evil spirit inside the boiler would get angry through the greatness of his thirst, and take a terrible vengeance. So he sweated and fired up and watched the glass fearfully (with an impromptu charm, made of rags, tied to his arm, and a piece of polished bone, as big as a watch, stuck flatways through his lower lip), while the wooded banks slipped past us slowly, the short noise was left behind, the interminable miles of silence—and we crept on, towards Kurtz. But the snags were thick, the water was treacherous and shallow, the boiler seemed indeed to have a sulky devil in it, and thus neither that fireman nor I had any time to peer into our creepy thoughts.

"Some fifty miles below the Inner Station we came upon a hut of reeds, an inclined and melancholy pole, with the unrecognizable tatters of what had been a flag of some sort flying from it, and a neatly stacked wood pile. This was unexpected. We came to the bank, and on the stack of firewood found a flat piece of board with some faded pencil writing on it. When deciphered it said: 'Wood for you. Hurry up. Approach cautiously.' There was a signature, but it was illegible—not Kurtz—a much longer word. Hurry up. Where? Up the river? 'Approach cautiously.' We had not done so. But the warning could not have been meant for the place where it could be only found after approach. Something was wrong above. But what—and how much? That was the question. We commented adversely upon the imbecility of that telegraphic style. The bush around said nothing, and would not let us look very far, either. A torn curtain of red twill hung in the doorway of the hut, and flapped sadly in our faces. The dwelling was dismantled; but we could see a white man had lived there not very long ago. There remained a rude table—a plank on two posts; a heap of rubbish reposed in a dark corner, and by the door I picked up a book. It had lost its covers, and the pages had been thumbed into a state of extremely dirty softness; but the back had been lovingly stitched afresh with white cotton thread, which looked clean yet. It was an extraordinary find. Its title was, *An Inquiry into Some Points of Seamanship*, by a man Tower, Towson—some such name—Master in his Majesty's Navy. The matter looked dreary reading enough, with illustrative diagrams and repulsive tables of figures, and the copy was sixty years old. I handled this amazing antiquity with the greatest possible tenderness, lest it should dissolve in my hands. Within, Towson or Towser was inquiring earnestly into the breaking strain of ships' chains and tackle, and other such matters. Not a very enthralling book; but at the first glance you could see there a singleness of intention, an

honest concern for the right way of going to work,
which made these humble pages, thought out so many
years ago, luminous with another than a professional
light. The simple old sailor, with his talk of chains and
purchases, made me forget the jungle and the pilgrims
in a delicious sensation of having come upon something
unmistakably real. Such a book being there was wonderful enough; but still more astounding were the notes
penciled in the margin, and plainly referring to the text.
I couldn't believe my eyes! They were in cipher! Yes, it
looked like cipher. Fancy a man lugging with him a
book of that description into this nowhere and studying
it—and making notes—in cipher at that! It was an extravagant mystery.

"I had been dimly aware for some time of a worrying
noise, and when I lifted my eyes I saw the wood pile
was gone, and the manager, aided by all the pilgrims,
was shouting at me from the river side. I slipped the
book into my pocket. I assure you to leave off reading
was like tearing myself away from the shelter of an old
and solid friendship.

"I started the lame engine ahead. 'It must be this
miserable trader—this intruder,' exclaimed the manager, looking back malevolently at the place we had left.
'He must be English,' I said. 'It will not save him from
getting into trouble if he is not careful,' muttered the
manager darkly. I observed with assumed innocence
that no man was safe from trouble in this world.

"The current was more rapid now, the steamer seemed
at her last gasp, the stern wheel flopped languidly, and
I caught myself listening on tiptoe for the next beat of
the boat, for in sober truth I expected the wretched
thing to give up every moment. It was like watching the
last flickers of a life. But still we crawled. Sometimes I
would pick out a tree a little way ahead to measure our

progress towards Kurtz by, but I lost it invariably before we got abreast. To keep the eyes so long on one thing was too much for human patience. The manager displayed a beautiful resignation. I fretted and fumed and took to arguing with myself whether or no I would talk openly with Kurtz; but before I could come to any conclusion it occurred to me that my speech or my silence, indeed any action of mine, would be a mere futility. What did it matter what anyone knew or ignored? What did it matter who was manager? One gets sometimes such a flash of insight. The essentials of this affair lay deep under the surface, beyond my reach, and beyond my power of meddling.

"Towards the evening of the second day we judged ourselves about eight miles from Kurtz's station. I wanted to push on; but the manager looked grave, and told me the navigation up there was so dangerous that it would be advisable, the sun being very low already, to wait where we were till next morning. Moreover, he pointed out that if the warning to approach cautiously were to be follcwed, we must approach in daylight—not at dusk, or in the dark. This was sensible enough. Eight miles meant nearly three hours' steaming for us, and I could also see suspicious ripples at the upper end of the reach. Nevertheless, I was annoyed beyond expression at the delay, and most unreasonably, too, since one night more could not matter much after so many months. As we had plenty of wood, and caution was the word, I brought up in the middle of the stream. The reach was narrow, straight, with high sides like a railway cutting. The dusk came gliding into it long before the sun had set. The current ran smooth and swift, but a dumb immobility sat on the banks. The living trees, lashed together by the creepers and every living bush of the undergrowth, might have been changed into stone,

even to the slenderest twig, to the lightest leaf. It was
not sleep—it seemed unnatural, like a state of trance.
Not the faintest sound of any kind could be heard. You
looked on amazed, and began to suspect yourself of being deaf—then the night came suddenly, and struck you
blind as well. About three in the morning some large fish
leaped, and the loud splash made me jump as though
a gun had been fired. When the sun rose there was a
white fog, very warm and clammy, and more blinding
than the night. It did not shift or drive; it was just there,
standing all round you like something solid. At eight
or nine, perhaps, it lifted as a shutter lifts. We had a
glimpse of the towering multitude of trees, of the immense matted jungle, with the blazing little ball of the
sun hanging over it—all perfectly still—and then the
white shutter came down again, smoothly, as if sliding
in greased grooves. I ordered the chain, which we had
begun to heave in, to be paid out again. Before it
stopped running with a muffled rattle, a cry, a very loud
cry, as of infinite desolation, soared slowly in the opaque
air. It ceased. A complaining clamor, modulated in savage discords, filled our ears. The sheer unexpectedness
of it made my hair stir under my cap. I don't know how
it struck the others: to me it seemed as though the mist
itself had screamed, so suddenly, and apparently from
all sides at once, did this tumultuous and mournful uproar arise. It culminated in a hurried outbreak of almost
intolerably excessive shrieking, which stopped short,
leaving us stiffened in a variety of silly attitudes, and
obstinately listening to the nearly as appalling and excessive silence. 'Good God! What is the meaning—'
stammered at my elbow one of the pilgrims, a little fat
man, with sandy hair and red whiskers, who wore side-
spring boots, and pink pajamas tucked into his socks.
Two others remained openmouthed a whole minute,

then dashed into the little cabin, to rush out incontinently and stand darting scared glances, with Winchesters at 'ready' in their hands. What we could see was
just the steamer we were on, her outlines blurred as
though she had been on the point of dissolving, and a
misty strip of water, perhaps two feet broad, around
her—and that was all. The rest of the world was nowhere, as far as our eyes and ears were concerned. Just
nowhere. Gone, disappeared; swept off without leaving
a whisper or a shadow behind.

"I went forward, and ordered the chain to be hauled
in short, so as to be ready to trip the anchor and move
the steamboat at once if necessary. 'Will they attack?'
whispered an awed voice. 'We will be all butchered in
this fog,' murmured another. The faces twitched with
the strain, the hands trembled slightly, the eyes forgot
to wink. It was very curious to see the contrast of expressions of the white men and of the black fellows of
our crew, who were as much strangers to that part of
the river as we, though their homes were only eight
hundred miles away. The whites, of course greatly discomposed, had besides a curious look of being painfully
shocked by such an outrageous row. The others had an
alert, naturally interested expression; but their faces
were essentially quiet, even those of the one or two who
grinned as they hauled at the chain. Several exchanged
short, grunting phrases, which seemed to settle the matter to their satisfaction. Their headman, a young, broad-
chested black, severely draped in dark-blue fringed
cloths, with fierce nostrils and his hair all done up art-
fully in oily ringlets, stood near me. 'Aha!' I said, just for
good fellowship's sake. 'Catch 'im,' he snapped, with a
bloodshot widening of his eyes and a flash of sharp
teeth—'catch 'im. Give 'im to us.' 'To you, eh?' I asked;
'what would you do with them?' 'Eat 'im!' he said,

curtly, and, leaning his elbow on the rail, looked out
into the fog in a dignified and profoundly pensive attitude. I would no doubt have been properly horrified,
had it not occurred to me that he and his chaps must be
very hungry: that they must have been growing increas-
ingly hungry for at least this month past. They had
been engaged for six months (I don't think a single one
of them had any clear idea of time, as we at the end of
countless ages have. They still belonged to the beginnings of time—had no inherited experience to teach
them as it were), and of course, as long as there was a
piece of paper written over in accordance with some
farcical law or other made down the river, it didn't
enter anybody's head to trouble how they would live.
Certainly they had brought with them some rotten
hippo meat, which couldn't have lasted very long, anyway, even if the pilgrims hadn't, in the midst of a shocking hullabaloo, thrown a considerable quantity of it
overboard. It looked like a high-handed proceeding;
but it was really a case of legitimate self-defense. You
can't breathe dead hippo waking, sleeping, and eating,
and at the same time keep your precarious grip on existence. Besides that, they had given them every week
three pieces of brass wire, each about nine inches long;
and the theory was they were to buy their provisions
with that currency in river-side villages. You can see
how *that* worked. There were either no villages, or the
people were hostile, or the director, who like the rest of
us fed out of tins, with an occasional old he-goat thrown
in, didn't want to stop the steamer for some more or less
recondite reasons. So, unless they swallowed the wire
itself, or made loops of it to snare the fishes with, I don't
see what good their extravagant salary could be to them.
I must say it was paid with a regularity worthy of a
large and honorable trading company. For the rest,

the only thing to eat—though it didn't look eatable in the least—I saw in their possession was a few lumps of some stuff like half-cooked dough, of a dirty lavender color, they kept wrapped in leaves, and now and then swallowed a piece of, but so small that it seemed done more for the looks of the thing than for any serious purpose of sustenance. Why in the name of all the gnawing devils of hunger they didn't go for us—they were thirty to five—and have a good tuck in for once, amazes me now when I think of it. They were big powerful men, with not much capacity to weigh the consequences, with courage, with strength, even yet, though their skins were no longer glossy and their muscles no longer hard. And I saw that something restraining, one of those human secrets that baffle probability, had come into play there. I looked at them with a swift quickening of interest—not because it occurred to me I might be eaten by them before very long, though I own to you that just then I perceived—in a new light, as it were—how unwholesome the pilgrims looked, and I hoped, yes, I positively hoped, that my aspect was not so—what shall I say?—so—unappetizing: a touch of fantastic vanity which fitted well with the dream-sensation that pervaded all my days at that time. Perhaps I had a little fever, too. One can't live with one's finger everlastingly on one's pulse. I had often 'a little fever,' or a little touch of other things—the playful paw-strokes of the wilderness, the preliminary trifling before the more serious onslaught which came in due course. Yes; I looked at them as you would on any human being, with a curiosity of their impulses, motives, capacities, weaknesses, when brought to the test of an inexorable physical necessity. Restraint! What possible restraint? Was it superstition, disgust, patience, fear—or some kind of primitive honor? No fear can stand up to hunger, no patience can wear it out, disgust simply does not exist where hunger is; and as to superstition, beliefs, and what you may call principles, they are less than chaff in a breeze. Don't you know the devilry of lingering starvation, its exasperating torment, its black thoughts, its somber and brooding ferocity? Well, I do. It takes a man all his inborn strength to fight hunger properly. It's really easier to face bereavement, dishonor, and the perdition of one's soul—than this kind of prolonged hunger. Sad, but true. And these chaps, too, had no earthly reason for any kind of scruple. Restraint! I would just as soon have expected restraint from a hyena prowling amongst the corpses of a battlefield. But there was the fact facing me—the fact dazzling, to be seen, like the foam on the depths of the sea, like a ripple on an unfathomable enigma, a mystery greater—when I thought of it—than the curious, inexplicable note of desperate grief in this savage clamor that had swept by us on the river bank, behind the blind whiteness of the fog.

"Two pilgrims were quarreling in hurried whispers as to which bank. 'Left.' 'No, no; how can you? Right, right, of course.' 'It is very serious,' said the manager's voice behind me; 'I would be desolated if anything should happen to Mr. Kurtz before we came up.' I looked at him, and had not the slightest doubt he was sincere. He was just the kind of man who would wish to preserve appearances. That was his restraint. But when he muttered something about going on at once, I did not even take the trouble to answer him. I knew, and he knew, that it was impossible. Were we to let go our hold of the bottom, we would be absolutely in the air—in space. We wouldn't be able to tell where we were going to—whether up- or down-stream, or across—till we fetched against one bank or the other, and then we wouldn't know at first which it was. Of course I made no move. I had no mind for a smashup. You couldn't imagine a more deadly place for a shipwreck. Whether drowned at once or not, we were sure to perish speedily in one way or another. 'I authorize you to take all the risks,' he said, after a short silence. 'I refuse to take any,' I said, shortly; which was just the answer he expected, though its tone might have surprised him. 'Well, I must defer to your judgment. You are captain,' he said, with marked civility. I turned my shoulder to him in sign of my appreciation, and looked into the fog. How long would it last? It was the most hopeless lookout. The approach to this Kurtz grubbing for ivory in the wretched bush was beset by as many dangers as though he had been an enchanted princess sleeping in a fabulous castle. 'Will they attack, do you think?' asked the manager, in a confidential tone.

"I did not think they would attack, for several obvious reasons. The thick fog was one. If they left the bank in their canoes they would get lost in it, as we would be if we attempted to move. Still, I had also judged the jungle of both banks quite impenetrable—and yet eyes were in it, eyes that had seen us. The riverside bushes were certainly very thick; but the undergrowth behind was evidently penetrable. However, during the short lift I had seen no canoes anywhere in the reach—certainly not abreast of the steamer. But what made the idea of attack inconceivable to me was the nature of the noise—of the cries we had heard. They had not the fierce character boding of immediate hostile intention. Unexpected, wild, and violent as they had been, they had given me an irresistible impression of sorrow. The glimpse of the steamboat had for some reason filled those savages with unrestrained grief. The danger, if any, I expounded, was from our proximity to a great human passion let loose. Even extreme grief may ultimately vent itself in violence—but more generally takes the form of apathy. . . .

"You should have seen the pilgrims stare! They had no heart to grin, or even to revile me: but I believe they thought me gone mad—with fright, maybe. I delivered a regular lecture. My dear boys, it was no good bothering. Keep a lookout? Well, you may guess I watched the fog for the signs of lifting as a cat watches a mouse; but for anything else our eyes were of no more use to us than if we had been buried miles deep in a heap of cotton-wool. It felt like it, too—choking, warm, stifling. Besides, all I said, though it sounded extravagant, was absolutely true to fact. What we afterwards alluded to as an attack was really an attempt at repulse. The action was very far from being aggressive—it was not even defensive, in the usual sense: it was undertaken under the stress of desperation, and in its essence was purely protective.

"It developed itself, I should say, two hours after the fog lifted, and its commencement was at a spot, roughly speaking, about a mile and a half below Kurtz's station. We had just floundered and flopped round a bend, when I saw an islet, a mere grassy hummock of bright green, in the middle of the stream. It was the only thing of the kind; but as we opened the reach more, I perceived it was the head of a long sandbank, or rather of a chain of shallow patches stretching down the middle of the river. They were discolored, just awash, and the whole lot was seen just under the water, exactly as a man's backbone is seen running down the middle of his back under the skin. Now, as far as I did see, I could go to the right or to the left of this. I didn't know either channel, of course. The banks looked pretty well alike, the depth appeared the same; but as I had been informed the station was on the west side, I naturally headed for the western passage.

"No sooner had we fairly entered it than I became aware it was much narrower than I had supposed. To the left of us there was the long uninterrupted shoal, and to the right a high, steep bank heavily overgrown with bushes. Above the bush the trees stood in serried ranks. The twigs overhung the current thickly, and from distance to distance a large limb of some tree projected rigidly over the stream. It was then well on in the afternoon, the face of the forest was gloomy, and a broad strip of shadow had already fallen on the water. In this shadow we steamed up—very slowly, as you may imagine. I sheered her well inshore—the water being deepest near the bank, as the sounding pole informed me.

"One of my hungry and forbearing friends was sounding in the bows just below me. This steamboat was exactly like a decked scow. On the deck, there were two little teakwood houses, with doors and windows. The boiler was in the fore-end, and the machinery right astern. Over the whole there was a light roof, supported on stanchions. The funnel projected through that roof, and in front of the funnel a small cabin built of light planks served for a pilot house. It contained a couch, two campstools, a loaded Martini-Henry leaning in one corner, a tiny table, and the steering wheel. It had a wide door in front and a broad shutter at each side. All these were always thrown open, of course. I spent my days perched up there on the extreme fore-end of that roof, before the door. At night I slept, or tried to, on the couch. An athletic black belonging to some coast tribe, and educated by my poor predecessor, was the helmsman. He sported a pair of brass earrings, wore a blue cloth wrapper from the waist to the ankles, and thought all the world of himself. He was the most unstable kind of fool I had ever seen. He steered with no end of a swagger while you were by; but if he lost sight of you, he became instantly the prey of an abject funk, and would let that cripple of a steamboat get the upper hand of him in a minute.

"I was looking down at the sounding pole, and feeling much annoyed to see at each try a little more of it stick out of that river, when I saw my poleman give up the business suddenly, and stretch himself flat on the deck, without even taking the trouble to haul his pole in. He kept hold on it though, and it trailed in the water. At the same time the fireman, whom I could also see below me, sat down abruptly before his furnace and ducked his head. I was amazed. Then I had to look at the river mighty quick, because there was a snag in the fairway. Sticks, little sticks, were flying about—thick: they were whizzing before my nose, dropping below me, striking behind me against my pilot house. All this time the river, the shore, the woods, were very quiet—perfectly quiet. I could only hear the heavy splashing thump of the stern wheel and the patter of these things. We cleared the snag clumsily. Arrows, by Jove! We were being shot at! I stepped in quickly to close the shutter on the land side. That fool helmsman, his hands on the spokes, was lifting his knees high, stamping his feet, champing his mouth, like a reined-in horse. Confound him! And we were staggering within ten feet of the bank. I had to lean right out to swing the heavy shutter, and I saw a face amongst the leaves on the level with my own, looking at me very fierce and steady; and then suddenly, as though a veil had been removed from my eyes, I made out, deep in the tangled gloom, naked breasts, arms, legs, glaring eyes—the bush was swarming with human limbs in movement, glistening, of bronze color. The twigs shook, swayed, and rustled, the arrows flew out of them, and then the shutter came to. 'Steer her straight,' I said to the helmsman. He held his head rigid, face forward; but his eyes rolled, he kept on, lifting and setting down his feet gently, his mouth foamed a little. 'Keep quiet!' I said in a fury. I might just as well have ordered a tree not to sway in the wind. I darted out. Below me there was a great scuffle of feet on the iron deck; confused exclamations; a voice screamed, 'Can you turn back?' I caught sight of a V-shaped ripple on the water ahead. What? Another snag! A fusillade burst out under my feet. The pilgrims had opened with their Winchesters, and were simply squirting lead into that bush. A deuce of a lot of smoke came up and drove slowly forward. I swore at it. Now I couldn't see the ripple or the snag either. I stood in the doorway, peering, and the arrows came in swarms. They might have been poisoned, but they looked as though they wouldn't kill a cat. The bush began to howl. Our woodcutters raised a warlike whoop; the report of a rifle just at my back deafened me. I glanced over my shoulder, and the pilot house was yet full of noise and smoke when I made a dash at the wheel. The fool nigger had dropped everything, to throw the shutter open and let off that Martini-Henry. He stood before the wide opening, glaring, and I yelled at him to come back, while I straightened the sudden twist out of that steamboat. There was no room to turn even if I had wanted to, the snag was somewhere very near ahead in that confounded smoke, there was no time to lose, so I just crowded her into the bank— right into the bank, where I knew the water was deep.

"We tore slowly along the overhanging bushes in a whirl of broken twigs and flying leaves. The fusillade below stopped short, as I had foreseen it would when

the squirts got empty. I threw my head back to a glinting whizz that traversed the pilot house, in at one
shutter-hole and out at the other. Looking past that mad
helmsman, who was shaking the empty rifle and yelling
at the shore, I saw vague forms of men running bent
double, leaping, gliding, distinct, incomplete, evanescent. Something big appeared in the air before the shutter, the rifle went overboard, and the man stepped back
swiftly, looked at me over his shoulder in an extraordinary, profound, familiar manner, and fell upon my
feet. The side of his head hit the wheel twice, and the
end of what appeared a long cane clattered round and
knocked over a little campstool. It looked as though
after wrenching that thing from somebody ashore he
had lost his balance in the effort. The thin smoke had
blown away, we were clear of the snag, and looking
ahead I could see that in another hundred yards or so I
would be free to sheer off, away from the bank; but my
feet felt so very warm and wet that I had to look down.
The man had rolled on his back and stared straight up at
me; both his hands clutched that cane. It was the shaft
of a spear that, either thrown or lunged through the
opening, had caught him in the side just below the ribs;
the blade had gone in out of sight, after making a frightful gash; my shoes were full; a pool of blood lay very
still, gleaming dark-red under the wheel; his eyes shone
with an amazing luster. The fusillade burst out again.
He looked at me anxiously, gripping the spear like something precious, with an air of being afraid I would try to
take it away from him. I had to make an effort to free
my eyes from his gaze and attend to the steering. With
one hand I felt above my head for the line of the steam
whistle, and jerked out screech after screech hurriedly.
The tumult of angry and warlike yells was checked instantly, and then from the depths of the woods went

out such a tremulous and prolonged wail of mournful fear and utter despair as may be imagined to follow the flight of the last hope from the earth. There was a great commotion in the bush; the shower of arrows stopped, a few dropping shots rang out sharply—then silence, in which the languid beat of the stern wheel came plainly to my ears. I put the helm hard a-starboard at the moment when the pilgrim in pink pajamas, very hot and agitated, appeared in the doorway. 'The manager sends me—' he began in an official tone, and stopped short. 'Good God!' he said, glaring at the wounded man.

"We two whites stood over him, and his lustrous and inquiring glance enveloped us both. I declare it looked as though he would presently put to us some question in an understandable language; but he died without uttering a sound, without moving a limb, without twitching a muscle. Only in the very last moment, as though in response to some sign we could not see, to some whisper we could not hear, he frowned heavily, and that frown gave to his black death mask an inconceivably somber, brooding, and menacing expression. The luster of inquiring glance faded swiftly into vacant glassiness. 'Can you steer?' I asked the agent eagerly. He looked very dubious; but I made a grab at his arm, and he understood at once I meant him to steer whether or no. To tell you the truth, I was morbidly anxious to change my shoes and socks. 'He is dead,' murmured the fellow, immensely impressed. 'No doubt about it,' said I, tugging like mad at the shoelaces. 'And by the way, I suppose Mr. Kurtz is dead as well by this time.'

"For the moment that was the dominant thought. There was a sense of extreme disappointment, as though I had found out I had been striving after something altogether without a substance. I couldn't have been more disgusted if I had traveled all this way for the sole purpose of talking with Mr. Kurtz. Talking with . . . I flung one shoe overboard, and became aware that that was exactly what I had been looking forward to—a talk with Kurtz. I made the strange discovery that I had never imagined him as doing, you know, but as discoursing. I didn't say to myself, 'Now I will never see him,' or 'Now I will never shake him by the hand,' but, 'now I will never hear him.' The man presented himself as a voice. Not of course that I did not connect him with some sort of action. Hadn't I been told in all the tones of jealousy and admiration that he had collected, bartered, swindled, or stolen more ivory than all the other agents together? That was not the point. The point was in his being a gifted creature, and that of all his gifts the one that stood out pre-eminently, that carried with it a sense of real presence, was his ability to talk, his words—the gift of expression, the bewildering, the illuminating, the most exalted and the most contemptible, the pulsating stream of light, or the deceitful flow from the heart of an impenetrable darkness.

"The other shoe went flying unto the devil-god of that river. I thought, by Jove! it's all over. We are too late; he has vanished—the gift has vanished, by means of some spear, arrow, or club. I will never hear that chap speak after all, and my sorrow had a startling extravagance of emotion, even such as I had noticed in the howling sorrow of these savages in the bush. I couldn't have felt more of lonely desolation somehow, had I been robbed of a belief or had missed my destiny in life. . . . Why do you sigh in this beastly way, somebody? Absurd? Well, absurd. Good Lord! mustn't a man ever— Here, give me some tobacco." . . .

There was a pause of profound stillness, then a match flared, and Marlow's lean face appeared, worn, hollow, with downward folds and dropped eyelids, with an aspect of concentrated attention; and as he took vigorous draws at his pipe, it seemed to retreat and advance out of the night in the regular flicker of the tiny flame. The match went out.

"Absurd!" he cried. "This is the worst of trying to tell. . . . Here you all are, each moored with two good addresses, like a hulk with two anchors, a butcher round one corner, a policeman round another, excellent appetites, and temperature normal—you hear—normal from year's end to year's end. And you say, Absurd! Absurd be—exploded! Absurd! My dear boys, what can you expect from a man who out of sheer nervousness had just flung overboard a pair of new shoes! Now I think of it, it is amazing I did not shed tears. I am, upon the whole, proud of my fortitude. I was cut to the quick at the idea of having lost the inestimable privilege of listening to the gifted Kurtz. Of course I was wrong. The privilege was waiting for me. Oh, yes, I heard more than enough. And I was right, too. A voice. He was very little more than a voice. And I heard—him—it—this voice—other voices—all of them were so little more than voices—and the memory of that time itself lingers around me, impalpable, like a dying vibration of one immense jabber, silly, atrocious, sordid, savage, or simply mean, without any kind of sense. Voices, voices—even the girl herself—now—"

He was silent for a long time.

"I laid the ghost of his gifts at last with a lie," he began, suddenly. "Girl! What? Did I mention a girl? Oh, she is out of it—completely. They—the women I mean —are out of it—should be out of it. We must help them to stay in that beautiful world of their own, lest ours gets worse. Oh, she had to be out of it. You should have heard the disinterred body of Mr. Kurtz saying, 'My Intended.' You would have perceived directly then how

completely she was out of it. And the lofty frontal bone
of Mr. Kurtz! They say the hair goes on growing sometimes, but this—ah—specimen, was impressively bald.
The wilderness had patted him on the head, and, behold,
it was like a ball—an ivory ball; it had caressed him,
and—lo!—he had withered; it had taken him, loved
him, embraced him, got into his veins, consumed his
flesh, and sealed his soul to its own by the inconceivable
ceremonies of some devilish initiation. He was its spoiled
and pampered favorite. Ivory? I should think so. Heaps
of it, stacks of it. The old mud shanty was bursting with
it. You would think there was not a single tusk left
either above or below the ground in the whole country.
'Mostly fossil,' the manager had remarked, disparag-
ingly. It was no more fossil than I am; but they call
it fossil when it is dug up. It appears these niggers do
bury the tusks sometimes—but evidently they couldn't
bury this parcel deep enough to save the gifted Mr.
Kurtz from his fate. We filled the steamboat with it,
and had to pile a lot on the deck. Thus he could see and
enjoy as long as he could see, because the appreciation
of his favor had remained with him to the last. You
should have heard him say, 'My ivory.' Oh yes, I heard
him. 'My Intended, my ivory, my station, my river,
my—' everything belonged to him. It made me hold
my breath in expectation of hearing the wilderness burst
into a prodigious peal of laughter that would shake the
fixed stars in their places. Everything belonged to him—
but that was a trifle. The thing was to know what he
belonged to, how many powers of darkness claimed him
for their own. That was the reflection that made you
creepy all over. It was impossible—it was not good for
one either—trying to imagine. He had taken a high seat
amongst the devils of the land—I mean literally. You
can't understand. How could you?—with solid pave-

ment under your feet, surrounded by kind neighbors ready to cheer you or to fall on you, stepping delicately between the butcher and the policeman, in the holy terror of scandal and gallows and lunatic asylums—how can you imagine what particular region of the first ages a man's untrammeled feet may take him into by the way of solitude—utter solitude without a policeman—by the way of silence—utter silence, where no warning voice of a kind neighbor can be heard whispering of public opinion? These little things make all the great differ- ence. When they are gone you must fall back upon your own innate strength, upon your own capacity for faith- fulness. Of course you may be too much of a fool to go wrong—too dull even to know you are being assaulted by the powers of darkness. I take it, no fool ever made a bargain for his soul with the devil: the fool is too much of a fool, or the devil too much of a devil—I don't know which. Or you may be such a thunderingly exalted crea- ture as to be altogether deaf and blind to anything but heavenly sights and sounds. Then the earth for you is only a standing place—and whether to be like this is your loss or your gain I won't pretend to say. But most of us are neither one nor the other. The earth for us is a place to live in, where we must put up with sights, with sounds, with smells, too, by Jove!—breathe dead hippo, so to speak, and not be contaminated. And there, don't you see? Your strength comes in, the faith in your ability for the digging of unostentatious holes to bury the stuff in—your power of devotion, not to yourself, but to an obscure, back-breaking business. And that's difficult enough. Mind, I am not trying to excuse or even explain —I am trying to account to myself for—for—Mr. Kurtz —for the shade of Mr. Kurtz. This initiated wraith from the back of Nowhere honored me with its amazing con- fidence before it vanished altogether. This was because

it could speak English to me. The original Kurtz had
been educated partly in England, and—as he was good
enough to say himself—his sympathies were in the right
place. His mother was half-English, his father was half-
French. All Europe contributed to the making of Kurtz;
and by and by I learned that, most appropriately, the
International Society for the Suppression of Savage Customs had intrusted him with the making of a report, for
its future guidance. And he had written.it, too. I've seen
it. I've read it. It was eloquent, vibrating with eloquence, but too high-strung, I think. Seventeen pages of
close writing he had found time for! But this must have
been before his—let us say—nerves, went wrong, and
caused him to preside at certain midnight dances ending
with unspeakable rites, which—as far as I reluctantly
gathered from what I heard at various times—were
offered up to him—do you understand?—to Mr. Kurtz
himself. But it was a beautiful piece of writing. The
opening paragraph, however, in the light of later information, strikes me now as ominous. He began with
the argument that we whites, from the point of development we had arrived at, 'must necessarily appear to
them [savages] in the nature of supernatural beings—
we approach them with the might as of a deity,' and so
on, and so on. 'By the simple exercise of our will we can
exert a power for good practically unbounded,' etc., etc.
From that point he soared and took me with him. The
peroration was magnificent, though difficult to remember, you know. It gave me the notion of an exotic Immensity ruled by an august Benevolence. It made me
tingle with enthusiasm. This was the unbounded power
of eloquence—of words—of burning noble words. There
were no practical hints to interrupt the magic current
of phrases, unless a kind of note at the foot of the last
page, scrawled evidently much later, in an unsteady

hand, may be regarded as the exposition of a method. It was very simple, and at the end of that moving appeal to every altruistic sentiment it blazed at you, luminous and terrifying, like a flash of lightning in a serene sky: 'Exterminate all the brutes!' The curious part was that he had apparently forgotten all about that valuable post-scriptum, because, later on, when he in a sense came to himself, he repeatedly entreated me to take good care of 'my pamphlet' (he called it), as it was sure to have in the future a good influence upon his career. I had full information about all these things, and, besides, as it turned out, I was to have the care of his memory. I've done enough for it to give me the indisputable right to lay it, if I choose, for an everlasting rest in the dust bin of progress, amongst all the sweepings and, figuratively speaking, all the dead cats of civilization. But then, you see, I can't choose. He won't be forgotten. Whatever he was, he was not common. He had the power to charm or frighten rudimentary souls into an aggravated witch dance in his honor; he could also fill the small souls of the pilgrims with bitter misgivings: he had one devoted friend at least, and he had conquered one soul in the world that was neither rudimentary nor tainted with self-seeking. No; I can't forget him, though I am not prepared to affirm the fellow was exactly worth the life we lost in getting to him. I missed my late helmsman awfully—I missed him even while his body was still lying in the pilot house. Perhaps you will think it passing strange this regret for a savage who was no more account than a grain of sand in a black Sahara. Well, don't you see, he had done something, he had steered; for months I had him at my back—a help—an instrument. It was a kind of partnership. He steered for me—I had to look after him, I worried about his deficiencies, and thus a subtle bond had been created, of which I only became aware when it was suddenly broken. And the intimate profundity of that look he gave me when he received his hurt remains to this day in my memory—like a claim of distant kinship affirmed in a supreme moment.

"Poor fool! If he had only left that shutter alone. He had no restraint, no restraint—just like Kurtz—a tree swayed by the wind. As soon as I had put on a dry pair of slippers, I dragged him out, after first jerking the spear out of his side, which operation I confess I performed with my eyes shut tight. His heels leaped together over the little doorstep; his shoulders were pressed to my breast; I hugged him from behind desperately. Oh! he was heavy, heavy; heavier than any man on earth, I should imagine. Then without more ado I tipped him overboard. The current snatched him as though he had been a wisp of grass, and I saw the body roll over twice before I lost sight of it forever. All the pilgrims and the manager were then congregated on the awning deck about the pilot house, chattering at each other like a flock of excited magpies, and there was a scandalized murmur at my heartless promptitude. What they wanted to keep that body hanging about for I can't guess. Embalm it, maybe. But I had also heard another, and a very ominous, murmur on the deck below. My friends the woodcutters were likewise scandalized, and with a better show of reason—though I admit that the reason itself was quite inadmissible. Oh, quite! I had made up my mind that if my late helmsman was to be eaten, the fishes alone should have him. He had been a very second-rate helmsman while alive, but now he was dead he might have become a first-class temptation, and possibly cause some startling trouble. Besides, I was anxious to take the wheel, the man in pink pajamas showing himself a hopeless duffer at the business.

"This I did directly the simple funeral was over. We were going half-speed, keeping right in the middle of the stream, and I listened to the talk about me. They had given up Kurtz, they had given up the station; Kurtz was dead, and the station had been burnt—and so on—and so on. The red-haired pilgrim was beside himself with the thought that at least this poor Kurtz had been properly avenged. 'Say! We must have made a glorious slaughter of them in the bush. Eh? What do you think? Say?' He positively danced, the bloodthirsty little gingery beggar. And he had nearly fainted when he saw the wounded man! I could not help saying, 'You made a glorious lot of smoke, anyhow.' I had seen, from the way the tops of the bushes rustled and flew, that almost all the shots had gone too high. You can't hit anything unless you take aim and fire from the shoulder; but these chaps fired from the hip with their eyes shut. The retreat, I maintained—and I was right—was caused by the screeching of the steam whistle. Upon this they forgot Kurtz, and began to howl at me with indignant protests.

"The manager stood by the wheel murmuring confidentially about the necessity of getting well away down the river before dark at all events, when I saw in the distance a clearing on the river side and the outlines of some sort of building. 'What's this?' I asked. He clapped his hands in wonder. 'That station!' he cried. I edged in at once, still going half-speed.

"Through my glasses I saw the slope of a hill interspersed with rare trees and perfectly free from undergrowth. A long decaying building on the summit was half buried in the high grass; the large holes in the peaked roof gaped black from afar; the jungle and the woods made a background. There was no enclosure or fence of any kind; but there had been one apparently,

for near the house half-a-dozen slim posts remained in a
row, roughly trimmed, and with their upper ends ornamented with round carved balls. The rails, or whatever there had been between, had disappeared. Of
course the forest surrounded all that. The river bank
was clear, and on the water side I saw a white man under a hat like a cart wheel beckoning persistently with
his whole arm. Examining the edge of the forest above
and below, I was almost certain I could see movements
—human forms gliding here and there. I steamed past
prudently, then stopped the engines and let her drift
down. The man on the shore began to shout, urging us
to land. 'We have been attacked,' screamed the manager. 'I know—I know. It's all right,' yelled back the
other, as cheerful as you please. 'Come along. It's all
right. I am glad.'

"His aspect reminded me of something I had seen—
something funny I had seen somewhere. As I maneu-
vered to get alongside, I was asking myself, 'What does
this fellow look like?' Suddenly I got it. He looked like
a harlequin. His clothes had been made of some stuff
that was brown holland probably, but it was covered
with patches all over, with bright patches, blue, red,
and yellow—patches on the back, patches on the front,
patches on elbows, on knees; colored binding around
his jacket, scarlet edging at the bottom of his trousers;
and the sunshine made him look extremely gay and
wonderfully neat withal, because you could see how
beautifully all this patching had been done. A beardless,
boyish face, very fair, no features to speak of, nose peel
ing, little blue eyes, smiles and frowns chasing each
other over that open countenance like sunshine and
shadow on a wind-swept plain. 'Look out, captain!' he
cried; 'there's a snag lodged in here last night.' What!
Another snag? I confess I swore shamefully. I had nearly

holed my cripple, to finish off that charming trip. The harlequin on the bank turned his little pug nose up to me. 'You English?' he asked, all smiles. 'Are you?' I shouted from the wheel. The smiles vanished, and he shook his head as if sorry for my disappointment. Then he brightened up. 'Never mind!' he cried, encouragingly. 'Are we in time?' I asked. 'He is up there,' he replied, with a toss of the head up the hill, and becoming gloomy all of a sudden. His face was like the autumn sky, overcast one moment and bright the next.

"When the manager, escorted by the pilgrims, all of them armed to the teeth, had gone to the house this chap came on board. 'I say, I don't like this. These natives are in the bush,' I said. He assured me earnestly it was all right. 'They are simple people,' he added; 'well, I am glad you came. It took me all my time to keep them off.' 'But you said it was all right,' I cried. 'Oh, they meant no harm,' he said; and as I stared he corrected himself, 'Not exactly.' Then vivaciously, 'My faith, your pilot house wants a clean-up!' In the next breath he advised me to keep enough steam on the boiler to blow the whistle in case of any trouble. 'One good screech will do more for you than all your rifles. They are simple people,' he repeated. He rattled away at such a rate he quite overwhelmed me. He seemed to be trying to make up for lots of silence, and actually hinted, laughing, that such was the case. 'Don't you talk with Mr. Kurtz?' I said. 'You don't talk with that man—you listen to him,' he exclaimed with severe exaltation. 'But now—' He waved his arm, and in the twinkling of an eye was in the uttermost depths of despondency. In a moment he came up again with a jump, possessed himself of both my hands, shook them continuously, while he gabbled: 'Brother sailor . . . honor . . . pleasure . . . delight . . . introduce myself . . .

Russian . . . son of an arch-priest . . . Government
of Tambov. . . . What? Tobacco! English tobacco; the
excellent English tobacco! Now, that's brotherly. Smoke?
Where's a sailor that does not smoke?'

"The pipe soothed him, and gradually I made out he
had run away from school, had gone to sea in a Russian
ship; ran away again; served some time in English ships;
was now reconciled with the arch-priest. He made a
point of that. 'But when one is young one must see
things, gather experience, ideas; enlarge the mind.'
'Here!' I interrupted. 'You can never tell! Here I met
Mr. Kurtz,' he said, youthfully solemn and reproachful.
I held my tongue after that. It appears he had persuaded a Dutch trading house on the coast to fit him
out with stores and goods, and had started for the interior with a light heart, and no more idea of what
would happen to him than a baby. He had been wandering about that river for nearly two years alone, cut
off from everybody and everything. 'I am not so young
as I look. I am twenty-five,' he said. 'At first old Van
Shuyten would tell me to go to the devil,' he narrated
with keen enjoyment; 'but I stuck to him, and talked
and talked, till at last he got afraid I would talk the
hind leg off his favorite dog, so he gave me some cheap
things and a few guns, and told me he hoped he would
never see my face again. Good old Dutchman, Van
Shuyten. I've sent him one small lot of ivory a year ago,
so that he can't call me a little thief when I get back.
I hope he got it. And for the rest I don't care. I had
some wood stacked for you. That was my old house.
Did you see?'

"I gave him Towson's book. He made as though he
would kiss me, but restrained himself. 'The only book
I had left, and I thought I had lost it,' he said, looking
at it ecstatically. 'So many accidents happen to a man

going about alone, you know. Canoes get upset sometimes—and sometimes you've got to clear out so quick
when the people get angry.' He thumbed the pages.
'You made notes in Russian?' I asked. He nodded. 'I
thought they were written in cipher,' I said. He laughed,
then became serious. 'I had lots of trouble to keep these
people off,' he said. 'Did they want to kill you?' I asked.
'Oh, no!' he cried, and checked himself. 'Why did they
attack us?' I pursued. He hesitated, then said shamefacedly, 'They don't want him to go.' 'Don't they?' I
said, curiously. He nodded a nod full of mystery and
wisdom. 'I tell you,' he cried, 'this man has enlarged my
mind.' He opened his arms wide, staring at me with his
little blue eyes that were perfectly round."

### III

"I looked at him, lost in astonishment. There he was
before me, in motley, as though he had absconded from
a troupe of mimes, enthusiastic, fabulous. His very existence was improbable, inexplicable, and altogether bewildering. He was an insoluble problem. It was inconceivable how he had existed, how he had succeeded in
getting so far, how he had managed to remain—why he
did not instantly disappear. 'I went a little farther,' he
said, 'then still a little farther—till I had gone so far
that I don't know how I'll ever get back. Never mind.
Plenty time. I can manage. You take Kurtz away quick
—quick—I tell you.' The glamor of youth enveloped
his parti-colored rags, his destitution, his loneliness, the
essential desolation of his futile wanderings. For months
—for years—his life hadn't been worth a day's pur-
chase; and there he was gallantly, thoughtlessly alive,
to all appearance indestructible solely by the virtue of
his few years and of his unreflecting audacity. I was se-

duced into something like admiration—like envy. Glamor urged him on, glamor kept him unscathed. He surely wanted nothing from the wilderness but space to breathe in and to push on through. His need was to exist, and to move onwards at the greatest possible risk, and with a maximum of privation. If the absolutely pure, uncalculating, unpractical spirit of adventure had ever ruled a human being, it ruled this bepatched youth. I almost envied him the possession of this modest and clear flame. It seemed to have consumed all thought of self so completely, that even while he was talking to you, you forgot that it was he—the man before your eyes— who had gone through these things. I did not envy him his devotion to Kurtz, though. He had not meditated over it. It came to him, and he accepted it with a sort of eager fatalism. I must say that to me it appeared about the most dangerous thing in every way he had come upon so far.

"They had come together unavoidably, like two ships becalmed near each other, and lay rubbing sides at last. I suppose Kurtz wanted an audience, because on a certain occasion, when encamped in the forest, they had talked all night, or more probably Kurtz had talked. 'We talked of everything,' he said, quite transported at the recollection. 'I forgot there was such a thing as sleep. The night did not seem to last an hour. Everything! Everything! . . . Of love, too.' 'Ah, he talked to you of love!' I said, much amused. 'It isn't what you think,' he cried, almost passionately. 'It was in general. He made me see things—things.'

"He threw his arms up. We were on deck at the time, and the headman of my woodcutters, lounging near by, turned upon him his heavy and glittering eyes. I looked around, and I don't know why, but I assure you that never, never before, did this land, this river, this jungle, the very arch of this blazing sky, appear to me so hopeless and so dark, so impenetrable to human thought, so pitiless to human weakness. 'And, ever since, you have been with him, of course?' I said.

"On the contrary. It appears their intercourse had been very much broken by various causes. He had, as he informed me proudly, managed to nurse Kurtz through two illnesses (he alluded to it as you would to some risky feat), but as a rule Kurtz wandered alone, far in the depths of the forest. 'Very often coming to this station, I had to wait days and days before he would turn up,' he said. 'Ah, it was worth waiting for!—sometimes.' 'What was he doing? Exploring or what?' I asked. 'Oh, yes, of course'; he had discovered lots of villages, a lake, too—he did not know exactly in what direction; it was dangerous to inquire too much—but mostly his expeditions had been for ivory. 'But he had no goods to trade with by that time,' I objected. 'There's a good lot of cartridges left even yet,' he answered, looking away. 'To speak plainly, he raided the country,' I said. He nodded. 'Not alone, surely!' He muttered something about the villages round that lake. 'Kurtz got the tribe to follow him, did he?' I suggested. He fidgeted a little. 'They adored him,' he said. The tone of these words was so extraordinary that I looked at him searchingly. It was curious to see his mingled eagerness and reluctance to speak of Kurtz. The man filled his life, occupied his thoughts, swayed his emotions. 'What can you expect?' he burst out; 'he came to them with thunder and lightning, you know—and they had never seen anything like it—and very terrible. He could be very terrible. You can't judge Mr. Kurtz as you would an ordinary man. No, no, no! Now—just to give you an idea—I don't mind telling you, he wanted to shoot me, too, one day—but I don't judge him.' 'Shoot you!' I cried. 'What

for?' 'Well, I had a small lot of ivory the chief of that
village near my house gave me. You see I used to shoot
game for them. Well, he wanted it, and wouldn't hear
reason. He declared he would shoot me unless I gave
him the ivory and then cleared out of the country, because he could do so, and had a fancy for it, and there
was nothing on earth to prevent him killing whom he
jolly well pleased. And it was true, too. I gave him the
ivory. What did I care! But I didn't clear out. No, no.
I couldn't leave him. I had to be careful, of course, till
we got friendly again for a time. He had his second
illness then. Afterwards I had to keep out of the way;
but I didn't mind. He was living for the most part in
those villages on the lake. When he came down to the
river, sometimes he would take to me, and sometimes
it was better for me to be careful. This man suffered
too much. He hated all this, and somehow he couldn't
get away. When I had a chance I begged him to try
and leave while there was time; I offered to go back
with him. And he would say yes, and then he would
remain; go off on another ivory hunt; disappear for
weeks; forget himself amongst these people—forget himself—you know.' 'Why! he's mad,' I said. He protested
indignantly. Mr. Kurtz couldn't be mad. If I had heard
him talk, only two days ago, I wouldn't dare hint at
such a thing. . . . I had taken up my binoculars while
we talked, and was looking at the shore, sweeping the
limit of the forest at each side and at the back of the
house. The consciousness of there being people in that
bush, so silent, so quiet—as silent and quiet as the
ruined house on the hill—made me uneasy. There was
no sign on the face of nature of this amazing tale
that was not so much told as suggested to me in desolate exclamations, completed by shrugs, in interrupted
phrases, in hints ending in deep sighs. The woods were

unmoved, like a mask—heavy, like the closed door of a prison—they looked with their air of hidden knowledge, of patient expectation, of unapproachable silence. The Russian was explaining to me that it was only lately that Mr. Kurtz had come down to the river, bringing along with him all the fighting men of that lake tribe. He had been absent for several months—getting himself adored, I suppose—and had come down unexpectedly, with the intention to all appearances of making a raid either across the river or downstream. Evidently the appetite for more ivory had got the better of the—what shall I say?—less material aspirations. However he had got much worse suddenly. 'I heard he was lying helpless, and so I came up—took my chance,' said the Russian. 'Oh, he is bad, very bad.' I directed my glass to the house. There were no signs of life, but there was the ruined roof, the long mud wall peeping above the grass, with three little square window holes, no two of the same size; all this brought within reach of my hand, as it were. And then I made a brusque movement, and one of the remaining posts of that vanished fence leaped up in the field of my glass. You remember I told you I had been struck at the distance by certain attempts at ornamentation, rather remarkable in the ruinous aspect of the place. Now I had suddenly a nearer view, and its first result was to make me throw my head back as if before a blow. Then I went carefully from post to post with my glass, and I saw my mistake. These round knobs were not ornamental but symbolic; they were expressive and puzzling, striking and disturbing—food for thought and also for the vultures if there had been any looking down from the sky; but at all events for such ants as were industrious enough to ascend the pole. They would have been even more impressive, those heads on the stakes, if their faces had not been turned to the house. Only one, the first I had made out, was facing my way. I was not so shocked as you may think. The start back I had given was really nothing but a movement of surprise. I had expected to see a knob of wood there, you know. I returned deliberately to the first I had seen—and there it was, black, dried, sunken, with closed eyelids, a head that seemed to sleep at the top of that pole, and, with the shrunken dry lips showing a narrow white line of the teeth, was smiling, too, smiling continuously at some endless and jocose dream of that eternal slumber.

"I am not disclosing any trade secrets. In fact, the manager said afterwards that Mr. Kurtz's methods had ruined the district. I have no opinion on that point, but I want you clearly to understand that there was nothing exactly profitable in these heads being there. They only showed that Mr. Kurtz lacked restraint in the gratification of his various lusts, that there was something wanting in him—some small matter which, when the pressing need arose, could not be found under his magnificent eloquence. Whether he knew of this deficiency himself I can't say. I think the knowledge came to him at last—only at the very last. But the wilderness had found him out early, and had taken on him a terrible vengeance for the fantastic invasion. I think it had whispered to him things about himself which he did not know, things of which he had no conception till he took counsel with this great solitude—and the whisper had proved irresistibly fascinating. It echoed loudly within him because he was hollow at the core       . I put down the glass, and the head that had appeared near enough to be spoken to seemed at once to have leaped away from me into inaccessible distance.

"The admirer of Mr. Kurtz was a bit crestfallen. In a hurried, indistinct voice he began to assure me he had not dared to take these—say, symbols—down. He was not afraid of the natives; they would not stir till Mr. Kurtz gave the word. His ascendancy was extraordinary. The camps of these people surrounded the place, and the chiefs came every day to see him. They would crawl. . . . 'I don't want to know anything of the ceremonies used when approaching Mr. Kurtz,' I shouted. Curious, this feeling that came over me that such details would be more intolerable than those heads drying on the stakes under Mr. Kurtz's windows. After all, that was only a savage sight, while I seemed at one bound to have been transported into some lightless region of subtle horrors, where pure, uncomplicated savagery was a positive relief, being something that had a right to exist —obviously—in the sunshine. The young man looked at me with surprise. I suppose it did not occur to him that Mr. Kurtz was no idol of mine. He forgot I hadn't heard any of these splendid monologues on, what was it? On love, justice, conduct of life—or whatnot. If it had come to crawling before Mr. Kurtz, he crawled as much as the veriest savage of them all. I had no idea of the conditions, he said: these heads were the heads of rebels. I shocked him excessively by laughing. Rebels! What would be the next definition I was to hear? There had been enemies, criminals, workers—and these were rebels. Those rebellious heads looked very subdued to me on their sticks. 'You don't know how such a life tries a man like Kurtz,' cried Kurtz's last disciple. 'Well, and you?' I said. 'I! I! I am a simple man. I have no great thoughts. I want nothing from anybody. How can you compare me to? . . .' His feelings were too much for speech, and suddenly he broke down. 'I don't understand,' he groaned. 'I've been doing my best to keep him alive, and that's enough. I had no hand in all this. I have no abilities. There hasn't been a drop of medicine or a mouthful of invalid food for months here. He was shamefully abandoned. A man like this, with such ideas. Shamefully! Shamefully! I—I—haven't slept for the last ten nights. . . .'

"His voice lost itself in the calm of the evening. The long shadows of the forest had slipped downhill while we talked, had gone far beyond the ruined hovel, beyond the symbolic row of stakes. All this was in the gloom, while we down there were yet in the sunshine, and the stretch of the river abreast of the clearing glittered in a still and dazzling splendor, with a murky and overshadowed bend above and below. Not a living soul was seen on the shore. The bushes did not rustle.

"Suddenly round the corner of the house a group of men appeared, as though they had come up from the ground. They waded waist-deep in the grass, in a compact body, bearing an improvised stretcher in their midst. Instantly, in the emptiness of the landscape, a cry arose whose shrillness pierced the still air like a sharp arrow flying straight to the very heart of the land; and, as if by enchantment, streams of human beings— of naked human beings—with spears in their hands, with bows, with shields, with wild glances and savage movements, were poured into the clearing by the dark-faced and pensive forest. The bushes shook, the grass swayed for a time, and then everything stood still in attentive immobility.

" 'Now, if he does not say the right thing to them we are all done for,' said the Russian at my elbow. The knot of men with the stretcher had stopped, too, half-way to the steamer, as if petrified. I saw the man on the stretcher sit up, lank and with an uplifted arm, above the shoulders of the bearers. 'Let us hope that the man who can talk so well of love in general will find some particular reason to spare us this time,' I said. I resented bitterly the absurd danger of our situation, as if to be at the mercy of that atrocious phantom had been a dishonoring necessity. I could not hear a sound, but through my glasses I saw the thin arm extended commandingly, the lower jaw moving, the eyes of that apparition shining darkly far in its bony head that nodded with grotesque jerks. Kurtz—Kurtz—that means short in German—don't it? Well, the name was as true as everything else in his life—and death. He looked at least seven feet long. His covering had fallen off, and his body emerged from it pitiful and appalling as from a winding sheet. I could see the cage of his ribs all astir, the bones of his arm waving. It was as though an animated image of death carved out of old ivory had been shaking its hand with menaces at a motionless crowd of men made of dark and glittering bronze. I saw him open his mouth wide—it gave him a weirdly voracious aspect, as though he had wanted to swallow all the air, all the earth, all the men before him. A deep voice reached me faintly. He must have been shouting. He fell back suddenly. The stretcher shook as the bearers staggered forward again, and almost at the same time I noticed that the crowd of savages was vanishing without any perceptible movement of retreat, as if the forest that had ejected these beings so suddenly had drawn them in again as the breath is drawn in a long aspiration.

"Some of the pilgrims behind the stretcher carried his arms—two shotguns, a heavy rifle, and a light revolver carbine—the thunderbolts of that pitiful Jupiter. The manager bent over him murmuring as he walked beside his head. They laid him down in one of the little cabins—just a room for a bedplace and a campstool or two, you know. We had brought his belated correspondence, and a lot of torn envelopes and open letters littered his bed. His hand roamed feebly amongst these papers. I was struck by the fire of his eyes and the composed languor of his expression. It was not so much the exhaustion of disease. He did not seem in pain. This shadow looked satiated and calm, as though for the moment it had had its fill of all the emotions.

"He rustled one of the letters, and looking straight in my face said, 'I am glad.' Somebody had been writing to him about me. These special recommendations were turning up again. The volume of tone he emitted without effort, almost without the trouble of moving his lips, amazed me. A voice! a voice! It was grave, profound, vibrating, while the man did not seem capable of a whisper. However, he had enough strength in him—factitious no doubt—to very nearly make an end of us, as you shall hear directly.

"The manager appeared silently in the doorway; I stepped out at once and he drew the curtain after me. The Russian, eyed curiously by the pilgrims, was staring at the shore. I followed the direction of his glance.

"Dark human shapes could be made out in the distance, flitting indistinctly against the gloomy border of the forest, and near the river two bronze figures, leaning on tall spears, stood in the sunlight under fantastic headdresses of spotted skins, warlike and still in statuesque repose. And from right to left along the lighted shore moved a wild and gorgeous apparition of a woman.

"She walked with measured steps, draped in striped and fringed cloths, treading the earth proudly, with a slight jingle and flash of barbarous ornaments. She carried her head high; her hair was done in the shape of a helmet; she had brass leggings to the knee, brass wire gauntlets to the elbow, a crimson spot on her tawny cheek, innumerable necklaces of glass beads on her neck; bizarre things, charms, gifts of witch men, that hung about her, glittered and trembled at every step.

She must have had the value of several elephant tusks upon her. She was savage and superb, wild-eyed and magnificent; there was something ominous and stately in her deliberate progress. And in the hush that had fallen suddenly upon the whole sorrowful land, the immense wilderness, the colossal body of the fecund and mysterious life seemed to look at her, pensive, as though it had been looking at the image of its own tenebrous and passionate soul.

"She came abreast of the steamer, stood still, and faced us. Her long shadow fell to the water's edge. Her face had a tragic and fierce aspect of wild sorrow and of dumb pain mingled with the fear of some struggling, half-shaped resolve. She stood looking at us without a stir, and like the wilderness itself, with an air of brooding over an inscrutable purpose. A whole minute passed, and then she made a step forward. There was a low jingle, a glint of yellow metal, a sway of fringed draperies, and she stopped as if her heart had failed her. The young fellow by my side growled. The pilgrims murmured at my back. She looked at us all as if her life had depended upon the unswerving steadiness of her glance. Suddenly she opened her bared arms and threw them up rigid above her head, as though in an uncontrollable desire to touch the sky, and at the same time the swift shadows darted out on the earth, swept around on the river, gathering the steamer into a shadowy embrace. A formidable silence hung over the scene.

"She turned away slowly, walked on, following the bank, and passed into the bushes to the left. Once only her eyes gleamed back at us in the dusk of the thickets before she disappeared.

" 'If she had offered to come aboard I really think I would have tried to shoot her,' said the man of patches, nervously. 'I had been risking my life every day for the last fortnight to keep her out of the house. She got in one day and kicked up a row about those miserable rags I picked up in the storeroom to mend my clothes with. I wasn't decent. At least it must have been that, for she talked like a fury to Kurtz for an hour, pointing at me now and then. I don't understand the dialect of this tribe. Luckily for me, I fancy Kurtz felt too ill that day to care, or there would have been mischief. I don't understand. . . . No—it's too much for me. Ah, well, it's all over now.'

"At this moment I heard Kurtz's deep voice behind the curtain: 'Save me!—save the ivory, you mean. Don't tell me. Save *me!* Why, I've had to save you. You are interrupting my plans now. Sick! Sick! Not so sick as you would like to believe. Never mind. I'll carry my ideas out yet—I will return. I'll show you what can be done. You with your little peddling notions—you are interfering with me. I will return. I . . .'

"The manager came out. He did me the honor to take me under the arm and lead me aside. 'He is very low, very low,' he said. He considered it necessary to sigh, but neglected to be consistently sorrowful. 'We have done all we could for him—haven't we? But there is no disguising the fact, Mr. Kurtz has done more harm than good to the Company. He did not see the time was not ripe for vigorous action. Cautiously, cautiously—that's my principle. We must be cautious yet. The district is closed to us for a time. Deplorable! Upon the whole, the trade will suffer. I don't deny there is a remarkable quantity of ivory—mostly fossil. We must save it, at all events—but look how precarious the position is—and why? Because the method is unsound.' 'Do you,' said I, looking at the shore, 'call it "unsound method?"' 'Without doubt,' he exclaimed, hotly. 'Don't you?' . . .

" 'No method at all,' I murmured after a while. 'Ex-

actly,' he exulted. 'I anticipated this. Shows a complete
want of judgment. It is my duty to point it out in the
proper quarter.' 'Oh,' said I, 'that fellow—what's his
name?—the brickmaker, will make a readable report for
you.' He appeared confounded for a moment. It seemed
to me I had never breathed an atmosphere so vile, and
I turned mentally to Kurtz for relief—positively for relief. 'Nevertheless I think Mr. Kurtz is a ·remarkable
man,' I said with emphasis. He started, dropped on me
a cold heavy glance, said very quietly, 'he *was*,' and
turned his back on me. My hour of favor was over; I
found myself lumped along with Kurtz as a partisan
of methods for which the time was not ripe: I was unsound! Ah! but it was something to have at least a choice
of nightmares.

"I had turned to the wilderness really, not to Mr.
Kurtz, who, I was ready to admit, was as good as
buried. And for a moment it seemed to me as if I also
were buried in a vast grave full of unspeakable secrets.
I felt an intolerable weight oppressing my breast, the
smell of the damp earth, the unseen presence of vic-
torious corruption, the darkness of an impenetrable
night. . . . The Russian tapped me on the shoulder.
I heard him mumbling and stammering something about
'brother seaman—couldn't conceal—knowledge of matters that would affect Mr. Kurtz's reputation.' I waited.
For him evidently Mr. Kurtz was not in his grave; I
suspect that for him Mr. Kurtz was one of the immortals.
'Well!' said I at last, 'speak out. As it happens, I am Mr.
Kurtz's friend—in a way.'

"He stated with a good deal of formality that had
we not been 'of the same profession,' he would have
kept the matter to himself without regard to consequences. 'He suspected there was an active ill will towards him on the part of these white men that—' 'You

are right,' I said, remembering a certain conversation I had overheard. 'The manager thinks you ought to be hanged.' He showed a concern at this intelligence which amused me at first. 'I had better get out of the way quietly,' he said, earnestly. 'I can do no more for Kurtz now, and they would soon find some excuse. What's to stop them? There's a military post three hundred miles from here.' 'Well, upon my word,' said I, 'perhaps you had better go if you have any friends amongst the savages near by.' 'Plenty,' he said. 'They are simple people—and I want nothing, you know.' He stood biting his lip, then: 'I don't want any harm to happen to these whites here, but of course I was thinking of Mr. Kurtz's reputation—but you are a brother seaman and—' 'All right,' said I, after a time. 'Mr. Kurtz's reputation is safe with me.' I did not know how truly I spoke.

"He informed me, lowering his voice, that it was Kurtz who had ordered the attack to be made on the steamer. 'He hated sometimes the idea of being taken away—and then again . . . But I don't understand these matters. I am a simple man. He thought it would scare you away—that you would give it up, thinking him dead. I could not stop him. Oh, I had an awful time of it this last month.' 'Very well,' I said. He is all right now.' 'Ye-e-es,' he muttered, not very convinced apparently. 'Thanks,' said I; 'I shall keep my eyes open.' 'But quiet—eh?' he urged, anxiously. 'It would be awful for his reputation if anybody here—' I promised a complete discretion with great gravity. 'I have a canoe and three black fellows waiting not very far. I am off. Could you give me a few Martini-Henry cartridges? I could, and did, with proper secrecy. He helped himself, with a wink at me, to a handful of my tobacco. 'Between sailors—you know—good English tobacco.' At the door of the pilot house he turned round—'I say, haven't you a pair of shoes you could spare?' He raised one leg. 'Look.' The soles were tied with knotted strings sandal-wise under his bare feet. I rooted out an old pair, at which he looked with admiration before tucking it under his left arm. One of his pockets (bright red) was bulging with cartridges, from the other (dark blue) peeped 'Towson's Inquiry,' etc., etc. He seemed to think himself excellently well equipped for a renewed encounter with the wilderness. 'Ah! I'll never, never meet such a man again. You ought to have heard him recite poetry—his own, too, it was, he told me. Poetry!' He rolled his eyes at the recollection of these delights. 'Oh, he enlarged my mind!' 'Good-by,' said I. He shook hands and vanished in the night. Sometimes I ask myself whether I had ever really seen him—whether it was possible to meet such a phenomenon! . . .

"When I woke up shortly after midnight his warning came to my mind with its hint of danger that seemed, in the starred darkness, real enough to make me get up for the purpose of having a look round. On the hill a big fire burned, illuminating fitfully a crooked corner of the station house. One of the agents with a picket of a few of our blacks, armed for the purpose, was keeping guard over the ivory; but deep within the forest, red gleams that wavered, that seemed to sink and rise from the ground amongst confused columnar shapes of intense blackness, showed the exact position of the camp where Mr. Kurtz's adorers were keeping their uneasy vigil. The monotonous beating of a big drum filled the air with muffled shocks and a lingering vibration. A steady droning sound of many men chanting each to himself some weird incantation came out from the black, flat wall of the woods as the humming of bees comes out of a hive, and had a strange narcotic effect upon my half-awake senses. I believe I dozed off leaning over the rail, till an abrupt burst of yells, an overwhelming outbreak of a pent-up and mysterious frenzy, woke me up in a bewildered wonder. It was cut short all at once, and the low droning went on with an effect of audible and soothing silence. I glanced casually into the little cabin. A light was burning within, but Mr. Kurtz was not there.

"I think I would have raised an outcry if I had believed my eyes. But I didn't believe them at first—the thing seemed so impossible. The fact is I was completely unnerved by a sheer blank fright, pure abstract terror, unconnected with any distinct shape of physical danger. What made this emotion so overpowering was—how shall I define it?—the moral shock I received, as if something altogether monstrous, intolerable to thought and odious to the soul, had been thrust upon me unexpectedly. This lasted of course the merest fraction of a second, and then the usual sense of commonplace, deadly danger, the possibility of a sudden onslaught and massacre, or something of the kind, which I saw impending, was positively welcome and composing. It pacified me, in fact, so much, that I did not raise an alarm.

"There was an agent buttoned up inside an ulster and sleeping on a chair on deck within three feet of me. The yells had not awakened him; he snored very slightly; I left him to his slumbers and leaped ashore. I did not betray Mr. Kurtz—it was ordered I should never betray him—it was written I should be loyal to the nightmare of my choice. I was anxious to deal with this shadow by myself alone—and to this day I don't know why I was so jealous of sharing with anyone the peculiar blackness of that experience.

"As soon as I got on the bank I saw a trail—a broad trail through the grass. I remember the exultation with which I said to myself, 'He can't walk—he is crawling on all fours—I've got him.' The grass was wet with dew. I strode rapidly with clenched fists. I fancy I had some vague notion of falling upon him and giving him a drubbing. I don't know. I had some imbecile thoughts. The knitting old woman with the cat obtruded herself upon my memory as a most improper person to be sitting at the other end of such an affair. I saw a row of pilgrims squirting lead in the air out of Winchesters held to the hip. I thought I would never get back to the steamer, and imagined myself living alone and unarmed in the woods to an advanced age. Such silly things—you know. And I remember I confounded the beat of the drum with the beating of my heart, and was pleased at its calm regularity.

"I kept to the track though—then stopped to listen. The night was very clear; a dark blue space, sparkling with dew and starlight, in which black things stood very still. I thought I could see a kind of motion ahead of me. I was strangely cocksure of everything that night. I actually left the track and ran in a wide semicircle (I truly believe chuckling to myself) so as to get in front of that stir, of that motion I had seen—if indeed I had seen anything. I was circumventing Kurtz as though it had been a boyish game.

"I came upon him, and, if he had not heard me coming, I would have fallen over him, too, but he got up in time. He rose, unsteady, long, pale, indistinct, like a vapc  exhaled by the earth, and swayed slightly, misty anc  ilent before me; while at my back the fires loomed between the trees, and the murmur of many voices issued from the forest. I had cut him off cleverly; but when actually confronting him I seemed to come to my senses, I saw the danger in its right proportion. It was by no means over yet. Suppose he began to shout?

Though he could hardly stand, there was still plenty of vigor in his voice. 'Go away—hide yourself,' he said, in that profound tone. It was very awful. I glanced back. We were within thirty yards from the nearest fire. A black figure stood up, strode on long black legs, waving long black arms, across the glow. It had horns—antelope horns, I think—on its head. Some sorcerer, some witch man, no doubt: it looked fiend-like enough. 'Do you know what you are doing?' I whispered. 'Perfectly,' he answered, raising his voice for that single word: it sounded to me far off and yet loud, like a hail through a speaking trumpet. If he makes a row we are lost, I thought to myself. This clearly was not a case for fisticuffs, even apart from the very natural aversion I had to beat that Shadow—this wandering and tormented thing. 'You will be lost,' I said—'utterly lost.' One gets sometimes such a flash of inspiration, you know. I did say the right thing, though indeed he could not have been more irretrievably lost than he was at this very moment, when the foundations of our intimacy were being laid—to endure—to endure—even to the end—even beyond.

"'I had immense plans,' he muttered irresolutely. 'Yes,' said I; 'but if you try to shout I'll smash your head with—' There was not a stick or a stone near. 'I will throttle you for good,' I corrected myself. 'I was on the threshold of great things,' he pleaded, in a voice of longing, with a wistfulness of tone that made my blood run cold. 'And now for this stupid scoundrel—' 'Your success in Europe is assured in any case,' I affirmed, steadily. I did not want to have the throttling of him, you understand—and indeed it would have been very little use for any practical purpose. I tried to break the spell—the heavy, mute spell of the wilderness —that seemed to draw him to its pitiless breast by the awakening of forgotten and brutal instincts, by the memory of gratified and monstrous passions. This alone, I was convinced, had driven him out to the edge of the forest, to the bush, towards the gleam of fires, the throb of drums, the drone of weird incantations; this alone had beguiled his unlawful soul beyond the bounds of permitted aspirations. And, don't you see, the terror of the position was not in being knocked on the head— though I had a very lively sense of that danger, too— but in this, that I had to deal with a being to whom I could not appeal in the name of anything high or low. I had, even like the niggers, to invoke him—himself— his own exalted and incredible degradation. There was nothing either above or below him, and I knew it. He had kicked himself loose of the earth. Confound the man! he had kicked the very earth to pieces. He was alone, and I before him did not know whether I stood on the ground or floated in the air. I've been telling you what we said—repeating the phrases we pronounced— but what's the good? They were common everyday words—the familiar, vague sounds exchanged on every waking day of life. But what of that? They had behind them, to my mind, the terrific suggestiveness of words heard in dreams, of phrases spoken in nightmares. Soul! If anybody had ever struggled with a soul, I am the man. And I wasn't arguing with a lunatic either. Believe me or not, his intelligence was perfectly clear—concentrated, it is true, upon himself with horrible intensity, yet clear; and therein was my only chance—barring, of course, the killing him there and then, which wasn't so good, on account of unavoidable noise. But his soul was mad. Being alone in the wilderness, it had looked within itself, and, by heavens! I tell you, it had gone mad. I had—for my sins, I suppose—to go through the ordeal of looking into it myself. No eloquence could have been so withering to one's belief in mankind as his final burst of sincerity. He struggled with himself, too. I saw it, I heard it. I saw the inconceivable mystery of a soul that knew no restraint, no faith, and no fear, yet struggling blindly with itself. I kept my head pretty well; but when I had him at last stretched on the couch, I wiped my forehead, while my legs shook under me as though I had carried half a ton on my back down that hill. And yet I had only supported him, his bony arm clasped round my neck—and he was not much heavier than a child.

"When next day we left at noon, the crowd, of whose presence behind the curtain of trees I had been acutely conscious all the time, flowed out of the woods again, filled the clearing, covered the slope with a mass of naked, breathing, quivering, bronze bodies. I steamed up a bit, then swung downstream, and two thousand eyes followed the evolutions of the splashing, thumping, fierce river-demon beating the water with its terrible tail and breathing black smoke into the air. In front of the first rank, along the river, three men, plastered with bright red earth from head to foot, strutted to and fro restlessly. When we came abreast again, they faced the river, stamped their feet, nodded their horned heads, swayed their scarlet bodies; they shook towards the fierce river-demon a bunch of black feathers, a mangy skin with a pendent tail—something that looked like a dried gourd; they shouted periodically together strings of amazing words that resembled no sounds of human language; and the deep murmurs of the crowd, interrupted suddenly, were like the responses of some satanic litany.

"We had carried Kurtz into the pilot house: there was more air there. Lying on the couch, he stared through the open shutter. There was an eddy in the mass of human bodies, and the woman with helmeted head and tawny cheeks rushed out to the very brink of the stream. She put out her hands, shouted something, and all that wild mob took up the shout in a roaring chorus of articulated, rapid, breathless utterance.

" 'Do you understand this?' I asked.

"He kept on looking out past me with fiery, longing eyes, with a mingled expression of wistfulness and hate. He made no answer, but I saw a smile, a smile of indefinable meaning, appear on his colorless lips that a moment after twitched convulsively. 'Do I not?' he said slowly, gasping, as if the words had been torn out of him by a supernatural power.

"I pulled the string of the whistle, and I did this because I saw the pilgrims on deck getting out their rifles with an air of anticipating a jolly lark. At the sudden screech there was a movement of abject terror through that wedged mass of bodies. 'Don't! Don't you frighten them away,' cried someone on deck disconsolately. I pulled the string time after time. They broke and ran, they leaped, they crouched, they swerved, they dodged the flying terror of the sound. The three red chaps had fallen flat, face down on the shore, as though they had been shot dead. Only the barbarous and superb woman did not so much as flinch, and stretched tragically her bare arms after us over the somber and glittering river.

"And then that imbecile crowd down on the deck started their little fun, and I could see nothing more for smoke.

"The brown current ran swiftly out of the heart of darkness, bearing us down towards the sea with twice the speed of our upward progress; and Kurtz's life was running swiftly, too, ebbing, ebbing out of his heart into the sea of inexorable time. The manager was very placid, he had no vital anxieties now, he took us both in with a comprehensive and satisfied glance: the 'affair' had come off as well as could be wished. I saw the time approaching when I would be left alone of the party of 'unsound method.' The pilgrims looked upon me with disfavor. I was, so to speak, numbered with the dead. It is strange how I accepted this unforeseen partnership, this choice of nightmares forced upon me in the tenebrous land invaded by these mean and greedy phantoms.

"Kurtz discoursed. A voice! a voice! It rang deep to the very last. It survived his strength to hide in the magnificent folds of eloquence the barren darkness of his heart. Oh, he struggled! he struggled! The wastes of his weary brain were haunted by shadowy images now —images of wealth and fame revolving obsequiously round his unextinguishable gift of noble and lofty expression. My Intended, my station, my career, my ideas —these were the subjects for the occasional utterances of elevated sentiments. The shade of the original Kurtz frequented the bedside of the hollow sham, whose fate it was to be buried presently in the mold of primeval earth. But both the diabolic love and the unearthly hate of the mysteries it had penetrated fought for the possession of that soul satiated with primitive emotions, avid of lying fame, of sham distinction, of all the appearances of success and power.

"Sometimes he was contemptibly childish. He desired to have kings meet him at railway stations on his return from some ghastly Nowhere, where he intended to accomplish great things. 'You show them you have in you something that is really profitable, and then there will be no limits to the recognition of your ability,' he

would say. 'Of course you must take care of the motives
—right motives—always.' The long reaches that were
like one and the same reach, monotonous bends that
were exactly alike, slipped past the steamer with their
multitude of secular trees looking patiently after this
grimy fragment of another world, the forerunner of
change, of conquest, of trade, of massacres, of blessings.
I looked ahead—piloting. 'Close the shutter,' said Kurtz
suddenly one day; 'I can't bear to look at this.' I did so.
There was a silence. 'Oh, but I will wring your heart
yet!' he cried at the invisible wilderness.

"We broke down—as I had expected—and had to
lie-up for repairs at the head of an island. This delay
was the first thing that shook Kurtz's confidence. One
morning he gave me a packet of papers and a photo-
graph—the lot tied together with a shoestring. 'Keep
this for me,' he said. 'This noxious fool' (meaning the
manager) 'is capable of prying into my boxes when I
am not looking.' In the afternoon I saw him. He was
lying on his back with closed eyes, and I withdrew
quietly, but I heard him mutter, 'Live rightly, die, die.
. . .' I listened. There was nothing more. Was he re-
hearsing some speech in his sleep, or was it a fragment
of a phrase from some newspaper article? He had been
writing for the papers and meant to do so again, 'for
the furthering of my ideas. It's a duty.'

"His was an impenetrable darkness. I looked at him
as you peer down at a man who is lying at the bottom
of a precipice where the sun never shines. But I had
not much time to give him, because I was helping the
engine driver to take to pieces the leaky cylinders, to
straighten a bent connecting rod, and in other such
matters. I lived in an infernal mess of rust, filings, nuts,
bolts, spanners, hammers, ratchet drills—things I abomi-
nate, because I don't get on with them. I tended the

little forge we fortunately had aboard; I toiled wearily in a wretched scrapheap—unless I had the shakes too bad to stand.

"One evening coming in with a candle I was startled to hear him say a little tremulously, 'I am lying here in the dark waiting for death.' The light was within a foot of his eyes. I forced myself to murmur, 'Oh, nonsense!' and stood over him as if transfixed.

"Anything approaching the change that came over his features I have never seen before, and hope never to see again. Oh, I wasn't touched. I was fascinated. It was as though a veil had been rent. I saw on that ivory face the expression of somber pride, of ruthless power, of craven terror—of an intense and hopeless despair. Did he live his life again in every detail of desire, temptation, and surrender during that supreme moment of complete knowledge? He cried in a whisper at some image, at some vision—he cried out twice, a cry that was no more than a breath: 'The horror! The horror!'

"I blew the candle out and left the cabin. The pilgrims were dining in the messroom, and I took my place opposite the manager, who lifted his eyes to give me a questioning glance, which I successfully ignored. He leaned back, serene, with that peculiar smile of his sealing the unexpressed depths of his meanness. A continuous shower of small flies streamed upon the lamp, upon the cloth, upon our hands and faces. Suddenly the manager's boy put his insolent black head in the doorway, and said in a tone of scathing contempt—

" 'Mistah Kurtz—he dead.'

"All the pilgrims rushed out to see. I remained, and went on with my dinner. I believe I was considered brutally callous. However, I did not eat much. There was a lamp in there—light, don't you know—and outside it was so beastly, beastly dark. I went no more near the remarkable man who had pronounced a judgment upon the adventures of his soul on this earth. The voice was gone. What else had been there? But I am of course aware that next day the pilgrims buried something in a muddy hole.

"And then they very nearly buried me.

"However, as you see, I did not go to join Kurtz there and then. I did not. I remained to dream the nightmare out to the end, and to show my loyalty to Kurtz once more. Destiny. My destiny! Droll thing life is—that mysterious arrangement of merciless logic for a futile purpose. The most you can hope from it is some knowledge of yourself—that comes too late—a crop of unextinguishable regrets. I have wrestled with death. It is the most unexciting contest you can imagine. It takes place in an impalpable grayness, with nothing underfoot, with nothing around, without spectators, without clamor, without glory, without the great desire of victory, without the great fear of defeat, in a sickly atmosphere of tepid skepticism, without much belief in your own right, and still less in that of your adversary. If such is the form of ultimate wisdom, then life is a greater riddle than some of us think it to be. I was within a hair's-breadth of the last opportunity for pronouncement, and I found with humiliation that probably I would have nothing to say. This is the reason why I affirm that Kurtz was a remarkable man. He had something to say. He said it. Since I had peeped over the edge myself, I understand better the meaning of his stare, that could not see the flame of the candle, but was wide enough to embrace the whole universe, piercing enough to penetrate all the hearts that beat in the darkness. He had summed up—he had judged. 'The horror!' He was a remarkable man. After all, this was the expression of some sort of belief; it had candor, it had conviction, it had a vibrating note of revolt in its whis-per, it had the appalling face of a glimpsed truth—the strange commingling of desire and hate. And it is not my own extremity I remember best—a vision of grayness without form filled with physical pain, and a careless contempt for the evanescence of all things—even of this pain itself. No! It is his extremity that I seem to have lived through. True, he had made that last stride, he had stepped over the edge, while I had been permitted to draw back my hesitating foot. And perhaps in this is the whole difference; perhaps all the wisdom, and all truth, and all sincerity, are just com-pressed into that inappreciable moment of time in which we step over the threshold of the invisible. Perhaps! I like to think my summing-up would not have been a word of careless contempt. Better his cry—much better. It was an affirmation, a moral victory paid for by in-numerable defeats, by abominable terrors, by abomi-nable satisfactions. But it was a victory! That is why I have remained loyal to Kurtz to the last, and even be-yond, when a long time after I heard once more, not his own voice, but the echo of his magnificent eloquence thrown to me from a soul as translucently pure as a cliff of crystal.

"No, they did not bury me, though there is a period of time which I remember mistily, with a shuddering wonder, like a passage through some inconceivable world that had no hope in it and no desire. I found myself back in the sepulchral city resenting the sight of people hurrying through the streets to filch a little money from each other, to devour their infamous cook-ery, to gulp their unwholesome beer, to dream their in-significant and silly dreams. They trespassed upon my thoughts. They were intruders whose knowledge of life was to me an irritating pretense, because I felt so sure they could not possibly know the things I knew. Their bearing, which was simply the bearing of commonplace individuals going about their business in the assurance of perfect safety, was offensive to me like the outrageous flauntings of folly in the face of a danger it is unable to comprehend. I had no particular desire to enlighten them, but I had some difficulty in restraining myself from laughing in their faces, so full of stupid importance. I daresay I was not very well at that time. I tottered about the streets—there were various affairs to settle—grinning bitterly at perfectly respectable persons. I admit my behavior was inexcusable, but then my temperature was seldom normal in these days. My dear aunt's endeavors to 'nurse up my strength' seemed altogether beside the mark. It was not my strength that wanted nursing, it was my imagination that wanted soothing. I kept the bundle of papers given me by Kurtz, not knowing exactly what to do with it. His mother had died lately, watched over, as I was told, by his Intended. A clean-shaved man, with an official manner and wearing gold-rimmed spectacles, called on me one day and made inquiries, at first circuitous, afterwards suavely pressing, about what he was pleased to denominate certain 'documents.' I was not surprised, because I had had two rows with the manager on the subject out there. I had refused to give up the smallest scrap out of that package, and I took the same attitude with the spectacled man. He became darkly menacing at last, and with much heat argued that the company had the right to every bit of information about its 'territories.' And said he, 'Mr. Kurtz's knowledge of unexplored regions must have been necessarily extensive and peculiar—owing to his great abilities and to the deplorable circumstances in which he had been placed: therefore—' I assured him Mr. Kurtz's knowledge, however extensive, did not bear upon the problems of commerce or administration. He invoked then the name of science. 'It would be an incalculable loss if,' etc., etc. I offered him the report on the 'Suppression of Savage Customs,' with the postscriptum torn off. He took it up eagerly, but ended by sniffing at it with an air of contempt. 'This is not what we had a right to expect,' he remarked. 'Expect nothing else,' I said. 'There are only private letters.' He withdrew upon some threat of legal proceedings, and I saw him no more; but another fellow, calling himself Kurtz's cousin, appeared two days later, and was anxious to hear all the details about his dear relative's last moments. Incidentally he gave me to understand that Kurtz had been essentially a great musician. 'There was the making of an immense success,' said the man, who was an organist, I believe, with lank gray hair flowing over a greasy coat collar. I had no reason to doubt his statement; and to this day I am unable to say what was Kurtz's profession, whether he ever had any—which was the greatest of his talents. I had taken him for a painter who wrote for the papers, or else for a journalist who could paint—but even the cousin (who took snuff during the interview) could not tell me what he had been—exactly. He was a universal genius—on that point I agreed with the old chap, who thereupon blew his nose noisily into a large cotton handkerchief and withdrew in senile agitation, bearing off some family letters and memoranda without importance. Ultimately a journalist anxious to know something of the fate of his 'dear colleague' turned up. This visitor informed me Kurtz's proper sphere ought to have been politics 'on the popular side.' He had furry straight eyebrows, bristly hair cropped short, an eyeglass on a broad ribbon, and, becoming expansive, confessed his opinion that Kurtz really couldn't write a bit—'but heavens! how that man could talk. He electrified large meetings. He had faith—don't you see?—he had the faith. He could get himself to believe anything—anything. He would have been a splendid leader of an extreme party.' 'What party?' I asked. 'Any party,' answered the other. 'He was an—an—extremist.' Did I not think so? I assented. Did I know, he asked, with a sudden flash of curiosity, 'what it was that had induced him to go out there?' 'Yes,' said I, and forthwith handed him the famous report for publication, if he thought fit. He glanced through it hurriedly, mumbling all the time, judged 'it would do,' and took himself off with this plunder.

"Thus I was left at last with a slim packet of letters and the girl's portrait. She struck me as beautiful—I mean she had a beautiful expression. I know that the sunlight can be made to lie, too, yet one felt that no manipulation of light and pose could have conveyed the delicate shade of truthfulness upon those features. She seemed ready to listen without mental reservation, without suspicion, without a thought for herself. I concluded I would go and give her back her portrait and those letters myself. Curiosity? Yes; and also some other feeling perhaps. All that had been Kurtz's had passed out of my hands: his soul, his body, his station, his plans, his ivory, his career. There remained only his memory and his Intended—and I wanted to give that up, too, to the past, in a way—to surrender personally all that remained of him with me to that oblivion which is the last word of our common fate. I don't defend myself. I had no clear perception of what it was I really wanted. Perhaps it was an impulse of unconscious loyalty, or the fulfilment of one of these ironic necessities that lurk in the facts of human existence. I don't know. I can't tell. But I went.

"I thought his memory was like the other memories of the dead that accumulate in every man's life—a vague impress on the brain of shadows that had fallen on it in their swift and final passage; but before the high and ponderous door, between the tall houses of a street as still and decorous as a well-kept alley in a cemetery, I had a vision of him on the stretcher, opening his mouth voraciously, as if to devour all the earth with all its mankind. He lived then before me; he lived as much as he had ever lived—a shadow insatiable of splendid appearances, of frightful realities; a shadow darker than the shadow of the night, and draped nobly in the folds of a gorgeous eloquence. The vision seemed to enter the house with me—the stretcher, the phantom-bearers, the wild crowd of obedient worshipers, the gloom of the forests, the glitter of the reach between the murky bends, the beat of the drum, regular and muffled like the beating of a heart—the heart of a conquering darkness. It was a moment of triumph for the wilderness, an invading and vengeful rush which, it seemed to me, I would have to keep back alone for the salvation of another soul. And the memory of what I had heard him say afar there, with the horned shapes stirring at my back, in the glow of fires, within the patient woods, those broken phrases came back to me, were heard again in their ominous and terrifying simplicity. I remembered his abject pleading, his abject threats, the colossal scale of his vile desires, the meanness, the torment, the tempestuous anguish of his soul. And later on I seemed to see his collected languid manner, when he said one day, 'This lot of ivory now is really mine. The company did not pay for it. I collected it myself at a very great personal risk. I am afraid they will try to claim it as theirs though. H'm. It is a difficult case. What do you think I ought to do—resist? Eh? I want no more

than justice. . . . He wanted no more than justice—
no more than justice. I rang the bell before a mahogany
door on the first floor, and while I waited he seemed to
stare at me out of the glassy panel—stare with that wide
and immense stare embracing, condemning, loathing all
the universe. I seemed to hear the whispered cry, 'The
horror! The horror!'

"The dusk was falling. I had to wait in a lofty drawing room with three long windows from floor to ceiling
that were like three luminous and bedraped columns.
The bent gilt legs and backs of the furniture shone in
indistinct curves. The tall marble fireplace had a cold
and monumental whiteness. A grand piano stood mas-
sively in a corner; with dark gleams on the flat surfaces
like a somber and polished sarcophagus. A high door
opened—closed. I rose.

"She came forward, all in black, with a pale head,
floating towards me in the dusk. She was in mourning.
It was more than a year since his death, more than a
year since the news came; she seemed as though she
would remember and mourn forever. She took both my
hands in hers and murmured, 'I had heard you were
coming.' I noticed she was not very young—I mean not
girlish. She had a mature capacity for fidelity, for belief,
for suffering. The room seemed to have grown darker, as
if all the sad light of the cloudy evening had taken
refuge on her forehead. This fair hair, this pale visage,
this pure brow, seemed surrounded by an ashy halo
from which the dark eyes looked out at me. Their glance
was guileless, profound, confident, and trustful. She
carried her sorrowful head as though she were proud of
that sorrow, as though she would say, I—I alone know
how to mourn for him as he deserves. But while we were
still shaking hands, such a look of awful desolation came
upon her face that I perceived she was one of those

creatures that are not the playthings of Time. For her he
had died only yesterday. And, by Jove! the impression
was so powerful that for me, too, he seemed to have
died only yesterday—nay, this very minute. I saw her
and him in the same instant of time—his death and her
sorrow—I saw her sorrow in the very moment of his
death. Do you understand? I saw them together—I
heard them together. She had said, with a deep catch of
the breath, 'I have survived' while my strained ears
seemed to hear distinctly, mingled with her tone of despairing regret, the summing-up whisper of his eternal
condemnation. I asked myself what I was doing there,
with a sensation of panic in my heart as though I had
blundered into a place of cruel and absurd mysteries not
fit for a human being to behold. She motioned me to a
chair. We sat down. I laid the packet gently on the little
table, and she put her hand over it. . . . 'You knew
him well,' she murmured, after a moment of mourning
silence.

" 'Intimacy grows quickly out there,' I said. 'I knew
him as well as it is possible for one man to know another.'

" 'And you admired him,' she said. 'It was impossible
to know him and not to admire him. Was it?'

" 'He was a remarkable man,' I said, unsteadily. Then
before the appealing fixity of her gaze, that seemed to
watch for more words on my lips, I went on, 'It was
impossible not to—'

" 'Love him,' she finished eagerly, silencing me into
an appalled dumbness. 'How true! how true! But when
you think that no one knew him so well as I! I had all
his noble confidence. I knew him best.'

" 'You knew him best,' I repeated. And perhaps she
did. But with every word spoken the room was growing
darker, and only her forehead, smooth and white, re-

mained illumined by the unextinguishable light of belief
and love.

"'You were his friend,' she went on. 'His friend,' she
repeated, a little louder. 'You must have been, if he had
given you this, and sent you to me. I feel I can speak to
you—and oh! I must speak. I want you—you who have
heard his last words—to know I have been worthy of
him. . . . It is not pride. . . . Yes! I am proud to
know I understood him better than anyone on earth—he
told me so himself. And since his mother died I have
had no one—no one—to—to—'

"I listened. The darkness deepened. I was not even
sure whether he had given me the right bundle. I rather
suspect he wanted me to take care of another batch of
his papers which, after his death, I saw the manager
examining under the lamp. And the girl talked, easing
her pain in the certitude of my sympathy; she talked as
thirsty men drink. I had heard that her engagement
with Kurtz had been disapproved by her people. He
wasn't rich enough or something. And indeed I don't
know whether he had not been a pauper all his life. He
had given me some reason to infer that it was his impatience of comparative poverty that drove him out
there.

"'. . . Who was not his friend who had heard him
speak once?' she was saying. 'He drew men towards him
by what was best in them.' She looked at me with intensity. 'It is the gift of the great,' she went on, and the
sound of her low voice seemed to have the accompaniment of all the other sounds, full of mystery, desolation,
and sorrow, I had ever heard—the ripple of the river,
the soughing of the trees swayed by the wind, the murmurs of the crowds, the faint ring of incomprehensible
words cried from afar, the whisper of a voice speaking

from beyond the threshold of an eternal darkness. 'But you have heard him! You know!' she cried.

"'Yes, I know,' I said with something like despair in my heart, but bowing my head before the faith that was in her, before that great and saving illusion that shone with an unearthly glow in the darkness, in the triumphant darkness from which I could not have defended her—from which I could not even defend myself.

"'What a loss to me—to us!'—she corrected herself with beautiful generosity; then added in a murmur, 'To the world.' By the last gleams of twilight I could see the glitter of her eyes, full of tears—of tears that would not fall.

"'I have been very happy—very fortunate—very proud,' she went on. 'Too fortunate. Too happy for a little while. And now I am unhappy for—for life."

"She stood up; her fair hair seemed to catch all the remaining light in a glimmer of gold. I rose, too.

"'And of all this,' she went on, mournfully, 'of all his promise, and of all his greatness, of his generous mind, of his noble heart, nothing remains—nothing but a memory. You and I—'

"'We shall always remember him,' I said, hastily.

"'No!' she cried. 'It is impossible that all this should be lost—that such a life should be sacrificed to leave nothing—but sorrow. You know what vast plans he had. I knew of them, too—I could not perhaps understand—but others knew of them. Something must remain. His words, at least, have not died.'

"'His words will remain,' I said.

"'And his example,' she whispered to herself. 'Men looked up to him—his goodness shone in every act. His example—'

"'True,' I said; 'his example, too. Yes, his example. I forgot that.'

"'But I do not. I cannot—I cannot believe—not yet. I cannot believe that I shall never see him again, that nobody will see him again, never, never, never.'

"She put out her arms as if after a retreating figure, stretching them black and with clasped pale hands across the fading and narrow sheen of the window. Never see him! I saw him clearly enough then. I shall see this eloquent phantom as long as I live, and I shall see her, too, a tragic and familiar Shade, resembling in this gesture another one, tragic also, and bedecked with powerless charms, stretching bare brown arms over the glitter of the infernal stream, the stream of darkness. She said suddenly very low, 'He died as he lived.'

"'His end,' said I, with dull anger stirring in me, 'was in every way worthy of his life.'

"'And I was not with him,' she murmured. My anger subsided before a feeling of infinite pity.

"'Everything that could be done—' I mumbled.

"'Ah, but I believed in him more than anyone on earth—more than his own mother, more than—himself. He needed me! Me! I would have treasured every sigh, every word, every sign, every glance.'

"I felt like a chill grip on my chest. 'Don't,' I said, in a muffled voice.

"'Forgive me. I—I—have mourned so long in silence—in silence. . . . You were with him—to the last? I think of his loneliness. Nobody near to understand him as I would have understood. Perhaps no one to hear. . . .'

"'To the very end,' I said, shakily. 'I heard his very last words. . . .' I stopped in a fright.

"'Repeat them,' she murmured in a heartbroken tone.

'I want—I want—something—something—to—to live with.'

"I was on the point of crying at her, 'Don't you hear them?' The dusk was repeating them in a persistent whisper all around us, in a whisper that seemed to swell menacingly like the first whisper of a rising wind. 'The horror! the horror!'

" 'His last word—to live with,' she insisted. 'Don't you understand I loved him—I loved him—I loved him!'

"I pulled myself together and spoke slowly.

" 'The last word he pronounced was—your name.'

"I heard a light sigh and then my heart stood still, stopped dead short by an exulting and terrible cry, by the cry of inconceivable triumph and of unspeakable pain. 'I knew it—I was sure!' . . . She knew. She was sure. I heard her weeping; she had hidden her face in her hands. It seemed to me that the house would collapse before I could escape, that the heavens would fall upon my head. But nothing happened. The heavens do not fall for such a trifle. Would they have fallen, I wonder, if I had rendered Kurtz that justice which was his due? Hadn't he said he wanted only justice? But I couldn't. I could not tell her. It would have been too dark—too dark altogether. . . ."

Marlow ceased, and sat apart, indistinct and silent, in the pose of a meditating Buddha. Nobody moved for a time. "We have lost the first of the ebb," said the director, suddenly. I raised my head. The offing was barred by a black bank of clouds, and the tranquil waterway leading to the uttermost ends of the earth flowed somber under an overcast sky—seemed to lead into the heart of an immense darkness.

# *Europe, Asia, and the East*

~~~~~~~~~~~~~~~~~~~~~~~~~~~~~~~~~~~~~~~~~~~~~~~~~~~

## IL CONDE

## THE LAGOON

## THE SECRET SHARER

. . . for this miracle or this wonder troubleth me right gretly.
—Boethius de Con: Phil: B. iv, Prose vi
[on the title-page of *The Mirror of the Sea*]

Calling shapes and beckoning shadows dire
And airy tongues that syllable men's names
On sands and shores and desert wildernesses.
—Milton: *Comus* [on the title-page of *Victory*]

The world of the living contains enough marvels and mysteries
as it is; marvels and mysteries acting upon our emotions and
intelligence in ways so inexplicable that it would almost justify the conception of life as an enchanted state.
—Conrad: Note to *The Shadow Line*

"Perhaps life is just like that . . . a dream and a fear."
—Razumov in *Under Western Eyes*

"All a man can betray is his conscience."
—Razumov in *Under Western Eyes*

Conrad caught his first sight of the East in the early months of 1883. The old barque *Palestine,* on which he sailed as second mate from London in September 1881, was delayed by needed repairs for a year before she left Falmouth in September 1882, and headed toward Bangkok. Crossing the Indian Ocean in March, she caught fire, exploded, and was abandoned, the crew saving themselves in open boats. "The portals of the East" were now open to Conrad, and before he took passage in a steamer from Singapore back to London, he saw the coasts of Java and had his first vision of the shores and islands which he held in memory the rest of his life. His earlier sailings to Australia had not touched the Orient, but from now on, the ports of India, Singapore, Java, Celebes, Borneo, Siam, Indo-China, and the China Seas were to figure repeatedly in his voyages. The *Palestine* herself became the *Judea* when he wrote her story in "Youth" in 1898, and the closing pages of that tale summon up the splendor and mystery with which the East fixed itself in Conrad's imagination: ". . . the first sight of the East on my face. That I can never forget. It was impalpable and enslaving like a charm, like a whispered promise of mysterious delight . . . for me all the East is contained in that vision of my youth." From *Almayer's Folly* in 1895 to *The Rescue* in 1920 it remained a recurring presence in his fiction, a world that responded alike to his secret fears and romantic fancies, always able to call his most evocative phrases from his pen: "The islands are very quiet. One sees them lying about, clothed in their dark garments of leaves, in a great hush of silver and azure, where the sea without murmurs meets the sky in a ring of magic stillness. A sort of smiling somnolence broods over them; the very voices of their people are soft and subdued, as if afraid to break some protecting spell."

The East that Conrad brought into the English novel has its points of kinship with the exoticism which other writers —Morier, Kipling, Stevenson, Haggard, and Maugham— brought into modern fiction. It always carries overtones of the fabulous and inscrutable, and frequently it lays Conrad open to the criticism of specialists like his friend Sir Hugh Clifford, who accused him of idealizing and romanticizing his Malays and their world. The Orient of Almayer, of Willems (*An Outcast of the Islands*), of Heyst (*Victory*), and of Lingard and Mrs. Travers (*The Rescue*) is a cognate of the sea, a world of more elemental nature, elusive influences, impalpable forces, in which the conscious personality of Western man dissolves and encounters a play of instinct and passions unbroken to the reason and the assertive wills of civilized life. But at its best, it becomes the medium for an authentic allegory of psychic and moral conflict, where the aggressive egoisms of Europe meet the challenge of powers they have forgotten or denied, and where life resumes the terms of a primary hostility and danger. That Conrad was able to engage those terms in a drama wholly western is testified to by books in which the sea and the East figure slightly or not at all—*Nostromo, The Secret Agent, Under Western Eyes,* and *Chance;* but when the more elusive psychic and subconscious elements of mankind taxed his imagination, it was toward the East that he turned—toward the spectral atmosphere evoked for "Il Conde" in Naples, toward the remoter shores of Borneo or Indo-China or the Malay states, or toward the ultimate island which gave him the setting of his most intense and sustained allegorical drama in *Victory.* "Il Conde" leads us in that direction, and in "The Secret Sharer" we enter fully the "destructive element" of human error and guilt, where the sea and the East combine to create one of Conrad's most powerful fables of the mystery man must know and master before he can, in Stein's words in *Lord Jim,* save himself from himself.

An English critic, V. S. Pritchett, has recently guessed that "Conrad seems to have turned the Polish exile's natural preoccupation with nationality, history, defeat and unavailing struggle from his own country to these Eastern islands. The natives are a defeated people. They remember massacre. They live under Dutch and English overlords, swindled by Arab traders, with eyes and hearts in the past. . . . They are really transplantations from Polish history. They are an exile's interpretation of the bloody history of the islands, and of the historical situation at the time he was writing. And knowing the situation, he knows the intrigue—how it is something which goes far deeper than human idiosyncrasy and private jealousy or ambition, but is the ferment of a defeated society itself." And Conrad does go further: "this gift of his is turned from society to psychology, that is to say, to a man's intrigue with himself." That intrigue, already dramatized in *Lord Jim*, receives its perfected version in "The Secret Sharer," wherein Leggatt, the murderer, "a fugitive and a vagabond on the earth, with no brand of the curse on his sane forehead to stay a slaying hand," becomes the double of the ship captain who saves him from the sea and hides him ("I wondered how far I should turn out faithful to that ideal conception of one's own personality every man sets up for himself secretly"). The fugitive comes out of the sea under cover of darkness; he wears, as Miss M. C. Bradbrook has noted, a sleeping suit, the garb of the unconscious life; and when he finally leaves the ship again with the captain's connivance, he slips back again into the sea at night. But he has left the captain with a knowledge of himself he never had before. He has shared the secret of the guilt all men carry behind their pride and courage.

"Il Conde" (whose title, as Conrad admitted, was misspelled, *il* being Italian, *conde* Spanish: it presumably should be "Il Conte"—"The Count" in Italian) was written in 1907 and included in *A Set of Six* in 1908. "The Lagoon," one of his first short stories, was written in 1896, and included in *Tales of Unrest* in 1898. "The Secret Sharer" was written in November 1909 and published in *'Twixt Land and Sea* in 1912.

# Il Conde

*"Vedi Napoli e poi mori."*

~~~~~~~~~~~~~~~~~~~~~~~~~~~~~~~~~~~~~~~~~~~

THE first time we got into conversation was in the National Museum in Naples, in the rooms on the ground floor containing the famous collection of bronzes from Herculaneum and Pompeii: that marvelous legacy of antique art whose delicate perfection has been preserved for us by the catastrophic fury of a volcano.

He addressed me first, over the celebrated Resting Hermes which we had been looking at side by side. He said the right things about that wholly admirable piece. Nothing profound. His taste was natural rather than cultivated. He had obviously seen many fine things in his life and appreciated them; but he had no jargon of a dilettante or the connoisseur. A hateful tribe. He spoke like a fairly intelligent man of the world, a perfectly unaffected gentleman.

We had known each other by sight for some few days past. Staying in the same hotel—good, but not extravagantly up to date—I had noticed him in the vestibule going in and out. I judged he was an old and valued client. The bow of the hotelkeeper was cordial in its deference, and he acknowledged it with familiar courtesy. For the servants he was *Il Conde*. There was some squabble over a man's parasol—yellow silk with white lining sort of thing—the waiters had discovered abandoned outside the dining-room door. Our gold-laced

609

doorkeeper recognized it and I heard him directing one of the lift boys to run after *Il Conde* with it. Perhaps he was the only count staying in the hotel, or perhaps he had the distinction of being *the* Count *par excellence,* conferred upon him because of his tried fidelity to the house.

Having conversed at the Museo—(and by the by he had expressed his dislike of the busts and statues of Roman emperors in the gallery of marbles: their faces were too vigorous, too pronounced for him)—having conversed already in the morning I did not think I was intruding when in the evening, finding the dining room very full, I proposed to share his little table. Judging by the quiet urbanity of his consent he did not think so either. His smile was very attractive.

He dined in an evening waistcoat and a "smoking" (he called it so) with a black tie. All this of very good cut, not new—just as these things should be. He was, morning or evening, very correct in his dress. I have no doubt that his whole existence had been correct, well ordered and conventional, undisturbed by startling events. His white hair brushed upwards off a lofty forehead gave him the air of an idealist, of an imaginative man. His white mustache, heavy but carefully trimmed and arranged, was not unpleasantly tinted a golden yellow in the middle. The faint scent of some very good perfume, and of good cigars (that last an odor quite remarkable to come upon in Italy) reached me across the table. It was in his eyes that his age showed most. They were a little weary with creased eyelids. He must have been sixty or a couple of years more. And he was communicative. I would not go so far as to call it garrulous —but distinctly communicative.

He had tried various climates, of Abbazia, of the Riviera, of other places, too, he told me, but the only

one which suited him was the climate of the Gulf of
Naples. The ancient Romans, who, he pointed out to
me, were men expert in the art of living, knew very well
what they were doing when they built their villas on
these shores, in Baiæ, in Vico, in Capri. They came
down to this seaside in search of health, bringing with
them their trains of mimes and flute-players to amuse
their leisure. He thought it extremely probable that the
Romans of the higher classes were specially predisposed
to painful rheumatic affections.

This was the only personal opinion I heard him express. It was based on no special erudition. He knew no
more of the Romans than an average informed man of
the world is expected to know. He argued from personal
experience. He had suffered himself from a painful and
dangerous rheumatic affection till he found relief in this
particular spot of Southern Europe.

This was three years ago, and ever since he had taken
up his quarters on the shores of the gulf, either in one
of the hotels in Sorrento or hiring a small villa in Capri.
He had a piano, a few books; picked up transient acquaintances of a day, week, or month in the stream of
travelers from all Europe. One can imagine him going
out for his walks in the streets and lanes, becoming
known to beggars, shopkeepers, children, country people; talking amiably over the walls to the *contadini*—
and coming back to his rooms or his villa to sit before
the piano, with his white hair brushed up and his thick
orderly mustache, "to make a little music for myself."
And, of course, for a change there was Naples near by
—life, movement, animation, opera. A little amusement,
as he said, is necessary for health. Mimes and flute-
players, in fact. Only unlike the magnates of ancient
Rome, he had no affairs of the city to call him away
from these moderate delights. He had no affairs at all.

Probably he had never had any grave affairs to attend to in his life. It was a kindly existence, with its joys and sorrows regulated by the course of Nature—marriages, births, deaths—ruled by the prescribed usages of good society and protected by the State.

He was a widower; but in the months of July and August he ventured to cross the Alps for six weeks on a visit to his married daughter. He told me her name. It was that of a very aristocratic family. She had a castle —in Bohemia, I think. This is as near as I ever came to ascertaining his nationality. His own name, strangely enough, he never mentioned. Perhaps he thought I had seen it on the published list. Truth to say, I never looked. At any rate, he was a good European—he spoke four languages to my certain knowledge—and a man of fortune. Not of great fortune evidently and appropriately. I imagine that to be extremely rich would have appeared to him improper, *outré*—too blatant altogether. And obviously, too, the fortune was not of his making. The making of a fortune cannot be achieved without some roughness. It is a matter of temperament. His nature was too kindly for strife. In the course of conversation he mentioned his estate quite by the way, in reference to that painful and alarming rheumatic affection. One year, staying incautiously beyond the Alps as late as the middle of September, he had been laid up for three months in that lonely country house with no one but his valet and the caretaking couple to attend to him. Because, as he expressed it, he "kept no establishment there." He had only gone for a couple of days to confer with his land agent. He promised himself never to be so imprudent in the future. The first weeks of September would find him on the shores of his beloved gulf.

Sometimes in traveling one comes upon such lonely

men, whose only business is to wait for the unavoidable. Deaths and marriages have made a solitude round them, and one really cannot blame their endeavors to make the waiting as easy as possible. As he remarked to me, "At my time of life freedom from physical pain is a very important matter."

It must not be imagined that he was a wearisome hypochondriac. He was really much too well bred to be a nuisance. He had an eye for the small weaknesses of humanity. But it was a good-natured eye. He made a restful, easy, pleasant companion for the hours between dinner and bedtime. We spent three evenings together, and then I had to leave Naples in a hurry to look after a friend who had fallen seriously ill in Taormina. Having nothing to do, *Il Conde* came to see me off at the station. I was somewhat upset, and his idleness was always ready to take a kindly form. He was by no means an indolent man.

He went along the train peering into the carriages for a good seat for me, and then remained talking cheerily from below. He declared he would miss me that evening very much and announced his intention of going after dinner to listen to the band in the public garden, the Villa Nazionale. He would amuse himself by hearing excellent music and looking at the best society. There would be a lot of people, as usual.

I seem to see him yet—his raised face with a friendly smile under the thick mustaches, and his kind, fatigued eyes. As the train began to move, he addressed me in two languages: first in French, saying, *"Bon voyage"*; then, in his very good, somewhat emphatic English, encouragingly, because he could see my concern: "All will—be—well—yet!"

My friend's illness having taken a decidedly favorable turn, I returned to Naples on the tenth day. I cannot say

I had given much thought to *Il Conde* during my absence, but entering the dining room I looked for him in his habitual place. I had an idea he might have gone back to Sorrento to his piano and his books and his fishing. He was great friends with all the boatmen, and fished a good deal with lines from a boat. But I made out his white head in the crowd of heads, and even from a distance noticed something unusual in his attitude. Instead of sitting erect, gazing all round with alert urbanity, he drooped over his plate. I stood opposite him for some time before he looked up, a little wildly, if such a strong word can be used in connection with his correct appearance.

"Ah, my dear sir! Is it you?" he greeted me. "I hope all is well."

He was very nice about my friend. Indeed, he was always nice, with the niceness of people whose hearts are genuinely humane. But this time it cost him an effort. His attempts at general conversation broke down into dullness. It occurred to me he might have been indisposed. But before I could frame the inquiry he muttered:

"You find me here very sad."

"I am sorry for that," I said. "You haven't had bad news, I hope?"

It was very kind of me to take an interest. No. It was not that. No bad news, thank God. And he became very still as if holding his breath. Then, leaning forward a little, and in an odd tone of awed embarrassment, he took me into his confidence.

"The truth is that I have had a very—a very—how shall I say?—abominable adventure happen to me."

The energy of the epithet was sufficiently startling in that man of moderate feelings and toned-down vocabulary. The word unpleasant I should have thought would have fitted amply the worst experience likely to befall a man of his stamp. And an adventure, too. Incredible! But it is in human nature to believe the worst; and I confess I eyed him stealthily, wondering what he had been up to. In a moment, however, my unworthy suspicions vanished. There was a fundamental refinement of nature about the man which made me dismiss all idea of some more or less disreputable scrape.

"It is very serious. Very serious." He went on, nervously. "I will tell you after dinner, if you will allow me."

I expressed my perfect acquiescence by a little bow, nothing more. I wished him to understand that I was not likely to hold him to that offer, if he thought better of it later on. We talked of indifferent things, but with a sense of difficulty quite unlike our former easy, gossipy intercourse. The hand raising a piece of bread to his lips, I noticed, trembled slightly. This symptom, in regard to my reading of the man, was no less than startling.

In the smoking room he did not hang back at all. Directly we had taken our usual seats he leaned sideways over the arm of his chair and looked straight into my eyes earnestly.

"You remember," he began, "that day you went away? I told you then I would go to the Villa Nazionale to hear some music in the evening."

I remembered. His handsome old face, so fresh for his age, unmarked by any trying experience, appeared haggard for an instant. It was like the passing of a shadow. Returning his steadfast gaze, I took a sip of my black coffee. He was systematically minute in his narrative, simply in order, I think, not to let his excitement get the better of him.

After leaving the railway station, he had an ice, and read the paper in a café. Then he went back to the hotel, dressed for dinner, and dined with a good appetite. After dinner he lingered in the hall (there were chairs and tables there) smoking his cigar; talked to the little girl of the Primo Tenore of the San Carlo Theater, and exchanged a few words with that "amiable lady," the wife of the Primo Tenore. There was no performance that evening, and these people were going to the Villa also. They went out of the hotel. Very well.

At the moment of following their example—it was half-past nine already—he remembered he had a rather large sum of money in his pocketbook. He entered, therefore, the office and deposited the greater part of it with the bookkeeper of the hotel. This done, he took a *carozella* and drove to the seashore. He got out of the cab and entered the Villa on foot from the Largo di Vittoria end.

He stared at me very hard. And I understood then how really impressionable he was. Every small fact and event of that evening stood out in his memory as if endowed with mystic significance. If he did not mention to me the color of the pony which drew the *carozella*, and the aspect of the man who drove, it was a mere oversight arising from his agitation, which he repressed manfully.

He had then entered the Villa Nazionale from the Largo di Vittoria end. The Villa Nazionale is a public pleasure-ground laid out in grass plots, bushes, and flowerbeds between the houses of the Riviera di Chiaja and the waters of the bay. Alleys of trees, more or less parallel, stretch its whole length—which is considerable. On the Riviera di Chiaja side the electric tramcars run close to the railings. Between the garden and the sea is the fashionable drive, a broad road bordered by a low wall, beyond which the Mediterranean splashes with gentle murmurs when the weather is fine.

As life goes on late at night in Naples, the broad drive was all astir with a brilliant swarm of carriage lamps moving in pairs, some creeping slowly, others running rapidly under the thin, motionless line of electric lamps defining the shore. And a brilliant swarm of stars hung above the land humming with voices, piled up with houses, glittering with lights—and over the silent flat shadows of the sea.

The gardens themselves are not very well lit. Our friend went forward in the warm gloom, his eyes fixed upon a distant luminous region extending nearly across the whole width of the Villa, as if the air had glowed there with its own cold, bluish, and dazzling light. This magic spot, behind the black trunks of trees and masses of inky foliage, breathed out sweet sounds mingled with bursts of brassy roar, sudden clashes of metal, and grave, vibrating thuds.

As he walked on, all these noises combined together into a piece of elaborate music whose harmonious phrases came persuasively through a great disorderly murmur of voices and shuffling of feet on the gravel of that open space. An enormous crowd immersed in the electric light, as if in a bath of some radiant and tenuous fluid shed upon their heads by luminous globes, drifted in hundreds round the band. Hundreds more sat on chairs in more or less concentric circles, receiving unflinchingly the great waves of sonority that ebbed out into the darkness. The Count penetrated the throng, drifted with it in tranquil enjoyment, listening and looking at the faces. All people of good society. mothers with their daughters, parents and children, young men and young women all talking, smiling, nodding to each other. Very many pretty faces, and very many pretty toilettes. There was, of course, a quantity of diverse types: showy old fellows with white mustaches, fat men, thin men, officers in uniform; but what predominated, he told me, was the South Italian type of young man, with a colorless, clear complexion, red lips, jet-black little mustache and liquid black eyes so wonderfully effective in leering or scowling.

Withdrawing from the throng, the Count shared a little table in front of the café with a young man of just such a type. Our friend had some lemonade. The young man was sitting moodily before an empty glass. He looked up once, and then looked down again. He also tilted his hat forward. Like this—

The Count made the gesture of a man pulling his hat down over his brow, and went on:

"I think to myself: he is sad; something is wrong with him; young men have their troubles. I take no notice of him, of course. I pay for my lemonade, and go away."

Strolling about in the neighborhood of the band, the Count thinks he saw twice that young man wandering alone in the crowd. Once their eyes met. It must have been the same young man, but there were so many there of that type that he could not be certain. Moreover, he was not very much concerned except in so far that he had been struck by the marked, peevish discontent of that face.

Presently, tired of the feeling of confinement one experiences in a crowd, the Count edged away from the band. An alley, very somber by contrast, presented itself invitingly with its promise of solitude and coolness. He entered it, walking slowly on till the sound of the orchestra became distinctly deadened. Then he walked back and turned about once more. He did this several times before he noticed that there was somebody occupying one of the benches.

The spot being midway between two lampposts the light was faint.

The man lolled back in the corner of the seat, his legs stretched out, his arms folded and his head drooping on his breast. He never stirred, as though he had fallen asleep there, but when the Count passed by next time he had changed his attitude. He sat leaning forward. His elbows were propped on his knees, and his hands were rolling a cigarette. He never looked up from that occupation.

The Count continued his stroll away from the band. He returned slowly, he said. I can imagine him enjoying to the full, but with his usual tranquility, the balminess of this southern night and the sounds of music softened delightfully by the distance.

Presently, he approached for the third time the man on the garden seat, still leaning forward with his elbows on his knees. It was a dejected pose. In the semiobscurity of the alley his high shirt collar and his cuffs made small patches of vivid whiteness. The Count said that he had noticed him getting up brusquely as if to walk away, but almost before he was aware of it the man stood before him asking in a low, gentle tone whether the signore would have the kindness to oblige him with a light.

The Count answered this request by a polite "Certainly," and dropped his hands with the intention of exploring both pockets of his trousers for the matches.

"I dropped my hands," he said, "but I never put them in my pockets. I felt a pressure there—"

He put the tip of his finger on a spot close under his breastbone, the very spot of the human body where a Japanese gentleman begins the operations of the hara-kiri, which is a form of suicide following upon dishonor, upon an intolerable outrage to the delicacy of one's feelings.

"I glance down," the Count continued in an awestruck voice, "and what do I see? A knife! A long knife—"

"You don't mean to say, I exclaimed, amazed, "that you have been held up like this in the Villa at half-past ten o'clock, within a stone's throw of a thousand people!"

He nodded several times, staring at me with all his might.

"The clarinet," he declared, solemnly, "was finishing its solo, and I assure you I could hear every note. Then the band crashed *fortissimo*, and that creature rolled its eyes and gnashed its teeth hissing at me with the greatest ferocity, 'Be silent! No noise or—' "

I could not get over my astonishment.

"What sort of knife was it?" I asked, stupidly.

"A long blade. A stiletto—perhaps a kitchen knife. A long narrow blade. It gleamed. And his eyes gleamed. His white teeth, too. I could see them. He was very ferocious. I thought to myself: 'If I hit him he will kill me.' How could I fight with him? He had the knife and I had nothing. I am nearly seventy, you know, and that was a young man. I seemed even to recognize him. The moody young man of the café. The young man I met in the crowd. But I could not tell. There are so many like him in this country."

The distress of that moment was reflected in his face. I should think that physically he must have been paralyzed by surprise. His thoughts, however, remained extremely active. They ranged over every alarming possibility. The idea of setting up a vigorous shouting for help occurred to him, too. But he did nothing of the kind, and the reason why he refrained gave me a good opinion of his mental self-possession. He saw in a flash that nothing prevented the other from shouting, too.

"That young man might in an instant have thrown away his knife and pretended I was the aggressor. Why not? He might have said I attacked him. Why not? It was one incredible story against another! He might have said anything—bring some dishonoring charge against me—what do I know? By his dress he was no common robber. He seemed to belong to the better classes. What could I say? He was an Italian—I am a foreigner. Of course, I have my passport, and there is our consul—but to be arrested, dragged at night to the police office like a criminal!"

He shuddered. It was in his character to shrink from scandal, much more than from mere death. And certainly for many people this would have always remained —considering certain peculiarities of Neapolitan manners—a deucedly queer story. The Count was no fool. His belief in the respectable placidity of life having received this rude shock, he thought that now anything might happen. But also a notion came into his head that this young man was perhaps merely an infuriated lunatic.

This was for me the first hint of his attitude towards this adventure. In his exaggerated delicacy of sentiment he felt that nobody's self-esteem need be affected by what a madman may choose to do to one. It became apparent, however, that the Count was to be denied that consolation. He enlarged upon the abominably savage way in which that young man rolled his glistening eyes and gnashed his white teeth. The band was going now through a slow movement of solemn braying by all the trombones, with deliberately repeated bangs of the big drum.

"But what did you do?" I asked, greatly excited.

"Nothing," answered the Count. "I let my hands hang

down very still. I told him quietly I did not intend making a noise. He snarled like a dog, then said in an ordinary voice:

"'Vostro portofolio.'"

"So I naturally," continued the Count—and from this
point acted the whole thing in pantomime. Holding me
with his eyes, he went through all the motions of reaching into his inside breast pocket, taking out a pocket-
book, and handing it over. But that young man, still
bearing steadily on the knife, refused to touch it.

He directed the Count to take the money out himself, received it into his left hand, motioned the pocket-
book to be returned to the pocket, all this being done to
the sweet trilling of flutes and clarinets sustained by
the emotional drone of the hautboys. And the "young
man," as the Count called him, said: "This seems very
little."

"It was, indeed, only 340 or 360 lire," the Count
pursued. "I had left my money in the hotel, as you
know. I told him this was all I had on me. He shook his
head impatiently and said:

"'Vostro orologio.'"

The Count gave me the dumb show of pulling out
his watch, detaching it. But, as it happened, the valuable gold half-chronometer he possessed had been left
at a watchmaker's for cleaning. He wore that evening
(on a leather guard) the Waterbury fifty-franc thing he
used to take with him on his fishing expeditions. Perceiving the nature of this booty, the well-dressed robber
made a contemptuous clicking sound with his tongue
like this, "Tse-Ah!" and waved it away hastily. Then,
as the Count was returning the disdained object to his
pocket, he demanded with a threateningly increased
pressure of the knife on the epigastrium, by way of reminder:

*"Vostri anelli."*

"One of the rings," went on the Count, "was given me many years ago by my wife; the other is the signet ring of my father. I said, 'No. *That* you shall not have!'"

Here the Count reproduced the gesture corresponding to that declaration by clapping one hand upon the other, and pressing both thus against his chest. It was touching in its resignation. "That you shall not have," he repea ed, firmly, and closed his eyes, fully expecting —I don't know whether I am right in recording that such an unpleasant word had passed his lips—fully expecting to feel himself being—I really hesitate to say— being disemboweled by the push of the long, sharp blade resting murderously against the pit of his stomach —the very seat, in all human beings, of anguishing sensations.

Great waves of harmony went on flowing from the band.

Suddenly the Count felt the nightmarish pressure removed from the sensitive spot. He opened his eyes. He was alone. He had heard nothing. It is probable that "the young man" had departed, with light steps, some time before, but the sense of the horrid pressure had lingered even after the knife had gone. A feeling of weakness came over him. He had just time to stagger to the garden seat. He felt as though he had held his breath for a long time. He sat all in a heap, panting with the shock of the reaction.

The band was executing, with immense bravura, the complicated finale. It ended with a tremendous crash. He heard it, unreal and remote, as if his ears had been stopped, and then the hard clapping of a thousand, more or less, pairs of hands, like a sudden hail shower passing away. The profound silence which succeeded recalled him to himself.

A tramcar resembling a long glass box wherein people sat with their heads strongly lighted, ran along swiftly within sixty yards of the spot where he had been robbed. Then another rustled by, and yet another going the other way The audience about the band had broken up, and were entering the alley in small conversing groups. The Count sat up straight and tried to think calmly of what had happened to him. The vileness of it took his breath away again. As far as I can make it out he was disgusted with himself. I do not mean to say with his behavior. Indeed, if his pantomimic rendering of it for my information was to be trusted, it was simply perfect. No, it was not that. He was not ashamed. He was shocked at being the selected victim, not of robbery so much as of contempt. His tranquillity had been wantonly desecrated. His lifelong, kindly nicety of outlook had been defaced.

Nevertheless, at that stage, before the iron had time to sink deep, he was able to argue himself into comparative equanimity. As his agitation calmed down somewhat, he became aware that he was frightfully hungry. Yes, hungry. The sheer emotion had made him simply ravenous. He left the seat and, after walking for some time, found himself outside the gardens and before an arrested tramcar, without knowing very well how he came there. He got in as if in a dream, by a sort of instinct. Fortunately he found in his trouser pocket a copper to satisfy the conductor. Then the car stopped, and as everybody was getting out he got out, too. He recognized the Piazza San Ferdinando, but apparently it did not occur to him to take a cab and drive to the hotel. He remained in distress on the Piazza like a lost dog, thinking vaguely of the best way of getting something to eat at once.

Suddenly he remembered his twenty-franc piece. He explained to me that he had that piece of French gold for something like three years. He used to carry it about with him as a sort of reserve in case of accident. Anybody is liable to have his pocket picked—a quite different thing from a brazen and insulting robbery.

The monumental arch of the Galleria Umberto faced him at the top of a noble flight of stairs. He climbed these without loss of time, and directed his steps towards the Café Umberto. All the tables outside were occupied by a lot of people who were drinking. But as he wanted something to eat, he went inside into the café, which is divided into aisles by square pillars set all round with long looking glasses. The Count sat down on a red plush bench against one of these pillars, waiting for his *risotto*. And his mind reverted to his abominable adventure.

He thought of the moody, well-dressed young man, with whom he had exchanged glances in the crowd around the bandstand, and who, he felt confident, was the robber. Would he recognize him again? Doubtless. But he did not want ever to see him again. The best thing was to forget this humiliating episode.

The Count looked round anxiously for the coming of his *risotto*, and, behold! to the left against the wall—there sat the young man. He was alone at a table, with a bottle of some sort of wine or syrup and a carafe of iced water before him. The smooth olive cheeks, the red lips, the little jet-black mustache turned up gallantly, the fine black eyes a little heavy and shaded by long eyelashes, that peculiar expression of cruel discontent to be seen only in the busts of some Roman emperors—it was he, no doubt at all. But that was a type. The Count looked away hastily. The young officer over there reading a paper was like that, too. Same type. Two young men farther away playing checkers also resembled—

The Count lowered his head with the fear in his heart of being everlastingly haunted by the vision of that young man. He began to eat his *risotto*. Presently he heard the young man on his left call the waiter in a bad-tempered tone.

At the call, not only his own waiter, but two other idle waiters belonging to a quite different row of tables, rushed towards him with obsequious alacrity, which is not the general characteristic of the waiters in the Café Umberto. The young man muttered something and one of the waiters walking rapidly to the nearest door called out into the Galleria: "Pasquale! O! Pasquale!"

Everybody knows Pasquale, the shabby old fellow who, shuffling between the tables, offers for sale cigars, cigarettes, picture postcards, and matches to the clients of the café. He is in many respects an engaging scoundrel. The Count saw the gray-haired, unshaven ruffian enter the café, the glass case hanging from his neck by a leather strap, and, at a word from the waiter, make his shuffling way with a sudden spurt to the young man's table. The young man was in need of a cigar with which Pasquale served him fawningly. The old peddler was going out, when the Count, on a sudden impulse, beckoned to him.

Pasquale approached, the smile of deferential recognition combining oddly with the cynical searching expression of his eyes. Leaning his case on the table, he lifted the glass lid without a word. The Count took a box of cigarettes and urged by a fearful curiosity, asked as casually as he could—

"Tell me, Pasquale, who is that young signore sitting over there?"

The other bent over his box confidentially.

"That, *Signor Conde*," he said, beginning to rearrange his wares busily and without looking up, "that is a young *Cavaliere* of a very good family from Bari. He studies in the University here, and is the chief, *capo*, of an association of young men—of very nice young men."

He paused, and then, with mingled discretion and pride of knowledge, murmured the explanatory word "*Camorra*" and shut down the lid. "A very powerful *Camorra*," he breathed out. "The professors themselves respect it greatly . . . *una lira e cinquanti centesimi, Signor Conde.*"

Our friend paid with the gold piece. While Pasquale was making up the change, he observed that the young man, of whom he had heard so much in a few words, was watching the transaction covertly. After the old vagabond had withdrawn with a bow, the Count settled with the waiter and sat still. A numbness, he told me, had come over him.

The young man paid, too, got up, and crossed over, apparently for the purpose of looking at himself in the mirror set in the pillar nearest to the Count's seat. He was dressed all in black with a dark green bow tie. The Count looked round, and was startled by meeting a vicious glance out of the corners of the other's eyes. The young *Cavaliere* from Bari (according to Pasquale; but Pasquale is, of course, an accomplished liar) went on arranging his tie, settling his hat before the glass, and meantime he spoke just loud enough to be heard by the Count. He spoke through his teeth with the most insulting venom of contempt and gazing straight into the mirror.

"Ah! So you had some gold on you—you old liar— you old *birba*—you *furfante!* But you are not done with me yet."

The fiendishness of his expression vanished like lightning, and he lounged out of the café with a moody, impassive face.

The poor Count, after telling me this last episode, fell back trembling in his chair. His forehead broke into perspiration. There was a wanton insolence in the spirit of this outrage which appalled even me. What it was to the Count's delicacy I won't attempt to guess. I am sure that if he had been not too refined to do such a blatantly vulgar thing as dying from apoplexy in a café, he would have had a fatal stroke there and then. All irony apart, my difficulty was to keep him from seeing the full extent of my commiseration. He shrank from every excessive sentiment, and my commiseration was practically unbounded. It did not surprise me to hear that he had been in bed a week. He had got up to make his arrangements for leaving Southern Italy for good and all.

And the man was convinced that he could not live through a whole year in any other climate!

No argument of mine had any effect. It was not timidity, though he did say to me once: "You do not know what a *Camorra* is, my dear sir. I am a marked man." He was not afraid of what could be done to him. His delicate conception of his dignity was defiled by a degrading experience. He couldn't stand that. No Japanese gentleman, outraged in his exaggerated sense of honor, could have gone about his preparations for hara-kiri with greater resolution. To go home really amounted to suicide for the poor Count.

There is a saying of Neapolitan patriotism, intended for the information of foreigners, I presume: "See Naples and then die." *Vedi Napoli e poi mori*. It is a saying of excessive vanity, and everything excessive was abhorrent to the nice moderation of the poor Count. Yet, as I was seeing him off at the railway station, I thought he was behaving with singular fidelity to its conceited spirit. *Vedi Napoli!* . . . He had seen it! He had seen it with startling thoroughness—and now he was going to his grave  He was going to it by the *train de luxe* of the International Sleeping Car Company, via Trieste and Vienna. As the four long, somber coaches pulled out of the station I raised my hat with the solemn feeling of paying the last tribute of respect to a funeral cortège. *Il Conde's* profile, much aged already, glided away from me in stony immobility, behind the lighted pane of glass —*Vedi Napoli e poi mori!*

# The Lagoon

THE white man, leaning with both arms over the roof of the little house in the stern of the boat, said to the steersman:

"We will pass the night in Arsat's clearing. It is late."

The Malay only grunted, and went on looking fixedly at the river. The white man rested his chin on his crossed arms and gazed at the wake of the boat. At the end of the straight avenue of forests cut by the intense glitter of the river, the sun appeared unclouded and dazzling, poised low over the water that shone smoothly like a band of metal. The forests, somber and dull, stood motionless and silent on each side of the broad stream. At the foot of big, towering trees, trunkless nipa palms rose from the mud of the bank, in bunches of leaves enormous and heavy, that hung unstirring over the brown swirl of eddies. In the stillness of the air every tree, every leaf, every bough, every tendril of creeper and every petal of minute blossoms seemed to have been bewitched into an immobility perfect and final. Nothing moved on the river but the eight paddles that rose flashing regularly, dipped together with a single splash; while the steersman swept right and left with a periodic and sudden flourish of his blade describing a glinting semicircle above his head. The churned-up water frothed alongside with a confused murmur. And the white man's canoe, advancing upstream in the short-lived disturbance of its own making, seemed to enter the portals of a land from which the very memory of motion had forever departed.

The white man, turning his back upon the setting sun, looked along the empty and broad expanse of the sea-reach. For the last three miles of its course the wandering, hesitating river, as if enticed irresistibly by the freedom of an open horizon, flows straight into the sea, flows straight to the east—to the east that harbors both light and darkness. Astern of the boat the repeated call of some bird, a cry discordant and feeble, skipped along over the smooth water and lost itself, before it could reach the other shore, in the breathless silence of the world.

The steersman dug his paddle into the stream, and held hard with stiffened arms, his body thrown forward. The water gurgled aloud; and suddenly the long straight reach seemed to pivot on its center, the forests swung in a semicircle, and the slanting beams of sunset touched the broadside of the canoe with a fiery glow, throwing the slender and distorted shadows of its crew upon the streaked glitter of the river. The white man turned to look ahead. The course of the boat had been altered at right angles to the stream, and the carved dragon head of its prow was pointing now at a gap in the fringing bushes of the bank. It glided through, brushing the overhanging twigs, and disappeared from the river like some slim and amphibious creature leaving the water for its lair in the forests.

The narrow creek was like a ditch: tortuous, fabulously deep; filled with gloom under the thin strip of pure and shining blue of the heaven. Immense trees soared up, invisible behind the festooned draperies of creepers. Here and there, near the glistening blackness of the water, a twisted root of some tall tree showed amongst the tracery of small ferns, black and dull, writhing and motionless, like an arrested snake. The short words of the paddlers reverberated loudly between the thick and somber walls of vegetation. Darkness oozed out from between the trees, through the tangled maze of the creepers, from behind the great fantastic and unstirring leaves; the darkness, mysterious and invincible; the darkness scented and poisonous of impenetrable forests.

The men poled in the shoaling water. The creek broadened, opening out into a wide sweep of a stagnant lagoon. The forests receded from the marshy bank, leaving a level strip of bright green, reedy grass to frame the reflected blueness of the sky. A fleecy pink cloud drifted high above, trailing the delicate coloring of its image under the floating leaves and the silvery blossoms of the lotus. A little house, perched on high piles, appeared black in the distance. Near it, two tall nibong palms, that seemed to have come out of the forests in the background, leaned slightly over the ragged roof, with a suggestion of sad tenderness and care in the droop of their leafy and soaring heads.

The steersman, pointing with his paddle, said, "Arsat is there. I see his canoe fast between the piles."

The polers ran along the sides of the boat glancing over their shoulders at the end of the day's journey. They would have preferred to spend the night somewhere else than on this lagoon of weird aspect and ghostly reputation. Moreover, they disliked Arsat, first as a stranger, and also because he who repairs a ruined house, and dwells in it, proclaims that he is not afraid to live amongst the spirits that haunt the places abandoned by mankind. Such a man can disturb the course of fate by glances or words; while his familiar ghosts are not easy to propitiate by casual wayfarers upon whom they long to wreak the malice of their human master. White men care not for such things, being unbelievers and in league with the Father of Evil, who leads them unharmed through the invisible dangers of this world. To the warnings of the righteous they oppose an offensive pretense of disbelief. What is there to be done?

So they thought, throwing their weight on the end of their long poles. The big canoe glided on swiftly, noiselessly, and smoothly, towards Arsat's clearing, till, in a great rattling of poles thrown down, and the loud murmurs of "Allah be praised!" it came with a gentle knock against the crooked piles below the house.

The boatmen with uplifted faces shouted discordantly, "Arsat! O Arsat!" Nobody came. The white man began to climb the rude ladder giving access to the bamboo platform before the house. The juragan of the boat said sulkily, "We will cook in the sampan, and sleep on the water."

"Pass my blankets and the basket," said the white man, curtly.

He knelt on the edge of the platform to receive the bundle. Then the boat shoved off, and the white man, standing up, confronted Arsat, who had come out through the low door of his hut. He was a man young, powerful, with broad chest and muscular arms. He had nothing on but his sarong. His head was bare. His big, soft eyes stared eagerly at the white man, but his voice and demeanor were composed as he asked, without any words of greeting:

"Have you medicine, Tuan?"

"No," said the visitor in a startled tone. "No. Why? Is there sickness in the house?"

"Enter and see," replied Arsat, in the same calm manner, and turning short round, passed again through the small doorway. The white man, dropping his bundles, followed.

In the dim light of the dwelling he made out on a couch of bamboos a woman stretched on her back under a broad sheet of red cotton cloth. She lay still, as if dead; but her big eyes, wide open, glittered in the gloom, staring upwards at the slender rafters, motionless and unseeing. She was in a high fever, and evidently unconscious. Her cheeks were sunk slightly, her lips were partly open, and on the young face there was the ominous and fixed expression—the absorbed, contemplating expression of the unconscious who are going to die. The two men stood looking down at her in silence.

"Has she been long ill?" asked the traveler.

"I have not slept for five nights," answered the Malay, in a deliberate tone. "At first she heard voices calling her from the water and struggled against me who held her. But since the sun of today rose she hears nothing—she hears not me. She sees nothing. She sees not me—me!"

He remained silent for a minute, then asked softly:

"Tuan, will she die?"

"I fear so," said the white man, sorrowfully. He had known Arsat years ago, in a far country in times of trouble and danger, when no friendship is to be despised. And since his Malay friend had come unexpectedly to dwell in the hut on the lagoon with a strange woman, he had slept many times there, in his journeys up and down the river. He liked the man who knew how to keep faith in council and how to fight without fear by the side of his white friend. He liked him—not so much perhaps as a man likes his favorite dog—but still he liked him well enough to help and ask no questions, to think sometimes vaguely and hazily in the midst of his own pursuits, about the lonely man and the long-haired woman with audacious face and triumphant eyes, who lived together hidden by the forests—alone and feared.

The white man came out of the hut in time to see the enormous conflagration of sunset put out by the swift and stealthy shadows that, rising like a black and impalpable vapor above the treetops, spread over the heaven, extinguishing the crimson glow of floating clouds and the red brilliance of departing daylight. In a few moments all the stars came out above the intense blackness of the earth and the great lagoon gleaming suddenly with reflected lights resembled an oval patch of night sky flung down into the hopeless and abysmal night of the wilderness. The white man had some supper out of the basket, then collecting a few sticks that lay about the platform, made up a small fire, not for warmth, but for the sake of the smoke, which would keep off the mosquitoes. He wrapped himself in the blankets and sat with his back against the reed wall of the house, smoking thoughtfully.

Arsat came through the doorway with noiseless steps and squatted down by the fire. The white man moved his outstretched legs a little.

"She breathes," said Arsat in a low voice, anticipating the expected question. "She breathes and burns as if with a great fire. She speaks not; she hears not—and burns!"

He paused for a moment, then asked in a quiet, incurious tone:

"Tuan . . . will she die?"

The white man moved his shoulders uneasily and muttered in a hesitating manner:

"If such is her fate."

"No, Tuan," said Arsat, calmly. "If such is my fate. I hear, I see, I wait. I remember. . . . Tuan, do you remember the old days? Do you remember my brother?"

"Yes," said the white man. The Malay rose suddenly and went in. The other, sitting still outside, could hear the voice in the hut. Arsat said: "Hear me! Speak!" His words were succeeded by a complete silence. "O Diamelen!" he cried, suddenly. After that cry there was a deep sigh. Arsat came out and sank down again in his old place.

They sat in silence before the fire. There was no sound within the house, there was no sound near them; but far away on the lagoon they could hear the voices of the boatmen ringing fitful and distinct on the calm water. The fire in the bows of the sampan shone faintly in the distance with a hazy red glow. Then it died out. The voices ceased. The land and the water slept invisible, unstirring and mute. It was as though there had been nothing left in the world but the glitter of stars streaming, ceaseless and vain, through the black stillness of the night.

The white man gazed straight before him into the darkness with wide-open eyes. The fear and fascination, the inspiration and the wonder of death—of death near, unavoidable, and unseen, soothed the unrest of his race and stirred the most indistinct, the most intimate of his thoughts. The ever-ready suspicion of evil, the gnawing suspicion that lurks in our hearts, flowed out into the stillness round him—into the stillness profound and dumb, and made it appear untrustworthy and infamous, like the placid and impenetrable mask of an unjustifiable violence. In that fleeting and powerful disturbance of his being the earth enfolded in the starlight peace became a shadowy country of inhuman strife, a battlefield of phantoms terrible and charming, august or ignoble, struggling ardently for the possession of our helpless hearts. An unquiet and mysterious country of inextinguishable desires and fears.

A plaintive murmur rose in the night; a murmur saddening and startling, as if the great solitudes of surrounding woods had tried to whisper into his car the wisdom of their immense and lofty indifference. Sounds hesitating and vague floated in the air round him, shaped themselves slowly into words; and at last flowed on gently in a murmuring stream of soft and monotonous sentences. He stirred like a man waking up and changed his position slightly. Arsat, motionless and shadowy, sitting with bowed head under the stars, was speaking in a low and dreamy tone:

". . . for where can we lay down the heaviness of our trouble but in a friend's heart? A man must speak of war and of love. You, Tuan, know what war is, and you have seen me in time of danger seek death as other men seek life! A writing may be lost; a lie may be written; but what the eye has seen is truth and remains in the mind!"

"I remember," said the white man, quietly. Arsat went on with mournful composure:

"Therefore I shall speak to you of love. Speak in the night. Speak before both night and love are gone—and the eye of day looks upon my sorrow and my shame; upon my blackened face; upon my burnt-up heart."

A sigh, short and faint, marked an almost imperceptible pause, and then his words flowed on, without a stir, without a gesture.

"After the time of trouble and war was over and you went away from my country in the pursuit of your desires, which we, men of the Islands, cannot understand, I and my brother became again, as we had been before, the sword bearers of the Ruler. You know we were men of family, belonging to a ruling race, and more fit than any to carry on our right shoulder the emblem of power. And in the time of prosperity Si Dendring showed us favor, as we, in time of sorrow, had showed to him the faithfulness of our courage. It was a time of peace. A time of deer hunts and cock fights; of idle talks and foolish squabbles between men whose bellies are full and weapons are rusty. But the sower watched the young rice shoots grow up without fear, and the traders came and went, departed lean and returned fat into the river of peace. They brought news, too. Brought lies and truth mixed together, so that no man knew when to rejoice and when to be sorry. We heard from them about you also. They had seen you here and had seen you there. And I was glad to hear, for I remembered the stirring times, and I always remembered you, Tuan, till the time came when my eyes could see nothing in the past, because they had looked upon the one who is dying there—in the house."

He stopped to exclaim in an intense whisper, "O Mara bahia! O Calamity!" then went on speaking a little louder:

"There's no worse enemy and no better friend than a brother, Tuan, for one brother knows another, and in perfect knowledge is strength for good or evil. I loved my brother. I went to him and told him that I could see nothing but one face, hear nothing but one voice. He told me: 'Open your heart so that she can see what is in it—and wait. Patience is wisdom. Inchi Midah may die or our Ruler may throw off his fear of a woman!' . . . I waited! . . . You remember the lady with the veiled face, Tuan, and the fear of our Ruler before her cunning and temper. And if she wanted her servant, what could I do? But I fed the hunger of my heart on short glances and stealthy words. I loitered on the path to the bathhouses in the daytime, and when the sun had fallen behind the forest I crept along the jasmine hedges of the women's courtyard. Unseeing, we spoke to one another through the scent of flowers, through the veil of leaves, through the blades of long grass that stood still before our lips; so great was our prudence, so faint was the murmur of our great longing. The time passed swiftly . . . and there were whispers amongst women —and our enemies watched—my brother was gloomy, and I began to think of killing and of a fierce death. . . . We are of a people who take what they want—like you whites. There is a time when a man should forget loyalty and respect. Might and authority are given to rulers, but to all men is given love and strength and courage. My brother said, 'You shall take her from their midst. We are two who are like one.' And I answered, 'Let it be soon, for I find no warmth in sunlight that does not shine upon her.' Our time came when the Ruler and all the great people went to the mouth of the river to fish by torchlight. There were hundreds of boats, and on the white sand, between the water and the forests, dwellings of leaves were built for the households of the Rajahs. The smoke of cooking fires was like a blue mist of the evening, and many voices rang in it joyfully. While they were making the boats ready to beat up the fish, my brother came to me and said, 'Tonight!' I looked to my weapons, and when the time came our canoe took its place in the circle of boats carrying the torches. The lights blazed on the water, but behind the boats there was darkness. When the shouting began and the excitement made them like mad we dropped out. The water swallowed our fire, and we floated back to the shore that was dark with only here and there the glim mer of embers. We could hear the talk of slave girls amongst the sheds. Then we found a place deserted and silent. We waited there. She came. She came running along the shore, rapid and leaving no trace, like a leaf driven by the wind into the sea. My brother said

gloomily, 'Go and take her; carry her into our boat.' I
lifted her in my arms. She panted. Her heart was beating against my breast. I said, 'I take you from those people. You came to the cry of my heart, but my arms take
you into my boat against the will of the great!' 'It is
right,' said my brother. 'We are men who take what we
want and can hold it against many. We should have
taken her in daylight.' I said, 'Let us be off'; for since
she was in my boat I began to think of our Ruler's many
men. 'Yes. Let us be off,' said my brother. 'We are cast
out and this boat is our country now—and the sea is our
refuge.' He lingered with his foot on the shore, and I entreated him to hasten, for I remembered the strokes of
her heart against my breast and thought that two men
cannot withstand a hundred. We left, paddling down-
stream close to the bank; and as we passed by the creek
where they were fishing, the great shouting had ceased,
but the murmur of voices was loud like the humming of
insects flying at noonday. The boats floated, clustered
together, in the red light of torches, under a black roof
of smoke; and men talked of their sport. Men that
boasted, and praised, and jeered—men that would have
been our friends in the morning, but on that night were
already our enemies. We paddled swiftly past. We had
no more friends in the country of our birth. She sat in
the middle of the canoe with covered face; silent as she
is now; unseeing as she is now—and I had no regret at
what I was leaving because I could hear her breathing
close to me—as I can hear her now."

He paused, listened with his ear turned to the doorway, then shook his head and went on:

"My brother wanted to shout the cry of challenge—
one cry only—to let the people know we were freeborn
robbers who trusted our arms and the great sea. And
again I begged him in the name of our love to be silent.

Could I not hear her breathing close to me? I knew the
pursuit would come quick enough. My brother loved
me. He dipped his paddle without a splash. He only
said, 'There is half a man in you now—the other half is
in that woman. I can wait. When you are a whole man
again, you will come back with me here to shout defiance. We are sons of the same mother.' I made no answer. All my strength and all my spirit were in my hands
that held the paddle—for I longed to be with her in a
safe place beyond the reach of men's anger and of
women's spite. My love was so great, that I thought it
could guide me to a country where death was unknown,
if I could only escape from Inchi Midah's fury and from
our Ruler's sword. We paddled with haste, breathing
through our teeth. The blades bit deep into the smooth
water. We passed out of the river; we flew in clear channels amongst the shallows. We skirted the black coast;
we skirted the sand beaches where the sea speaks in
whispers to the land; and the gleam of white sand
flashed back past our boat, so swiftly she ran upon the
water. We spoke not. Only once I said, 'Sleep, Diamelen, for soon you may want all your strength.' I
heard the sweetness of her voice, but I never turned my
head. The sun rose and still we went on. Water fell from
my face like rain from a cloud. We flew in the light and
heat. I never looked back, but I knew that my brother's
eyes, behind me, were looking steadily ahead, for the
boat went as straight as a bushman's dart, when it leaves
the end of the sumpitan. There was no better paddler,
no better steersman than my brother. Many times, together, we had won races in that canoe. But we never
had put out our strength as we did then—then, when
for the last time we paddled together! There was no
braver or stronger man in our country than my brother.
I could not spare the strength to turn my head and look

at him, but every moment I heard the hiss of his breath getting louder behind me. Still he did not speak. The sun was high. The heat clung to my back like a flame of fire. My ribs were ready to burst, but I could no longer get enough air into my chest. And then I felt I must cry out with my last breath, 'Let us rest!' . . . 'Good!' he answered; and his voice was firm. He was strong. He was brave. He knew not fear and no fatigue . . . My brother!"

A murmur powerful and gentle, a murmur vast and faint; the murmur of trembling leaves, of stirring boughs, ran through the tangled depths of the forests, ran over the starry smoothness of the lagoon, and the water between the piles lapped the slimy timber once with a sudden splash. A breath of warm air touched the two men's faces and passed on with a mournful sound— a breath loud and short like an uneasy sigh of the dreaming earth.

Arsat went on in an even, low voice.

"We ran our canoe on the white beach of a little bay close to a long tongue of land that seemed to bar our road; a long wooded cape going far into the sea. My brother knew that place. Beyond the cape a river has its entrance, and through the jungle of that land there is a narrow path. We made a fire and cooked rice. Then we lay down to sleep on the soft sand in the shade of our canoe, while she watched. No sooner had I closed my eyes than I heard her cry of alarm. We leaped up. The sun was halfway down the sky already, and coming in sight in the opening of the bay we saw a prau manned by many paddlers. We knew it at once; it was one of our Rajah's praus. They were watching the shore, and saw us. They beat the gong, and turned the head of the prau into the bay. I felt my heart become weak within my breast. Diamelen sat on the sand and covered her face.

There was no escape by sea. My brother laughed. He had the gun you had given him, Tuan, before you went away, but there was only a handful of powder. He spoke to me quickly: 'Run with her along the path. I shall keep them back, for they have no firearms, and landing in the face of a man with a gun is certain death for some. Run with her. On the other side of that wood there is a fisherman's house—and a canoe. When I have fired all the shots I will follow. I am a great runner, and before they can come up we shall be gone. I will hold out as long as I can, for she is but a woman—that can neither run nor fight, but she has your heart in her weak hands.' He dropped behind the canoe. The prau was coming. She and I ran, and as we rushed along the path I heard shots. My brother fired—once—twice—and the booming of the gong ceased. There was silence behind us. That neck of land is narrow. Before I heard my brother fire the third shot I saw the shelving shore, and I saw the water again; the mouth of a broad river. We crossed a grassy glade. We ran down to the water. I saw a low hut above the black mud, and a small canoe hauled up. I heard another shot behind me. I thought, 'That is his last charge.' We rushed down to the canoe; a man came running from the hut, but I leaped on him, and we rolled together in the mud. Then I got up, and he lay still at my feet. I don't know whether I had killed him or not. I and Diamelen pushed the canoe afloat. I heard yells behind me, and I saw my brother run across the glade. Many men were bounding after him. I took her in my arms and threw her into the boat, then leaped in myself. When I looked back I saw that my brother had fallen. He fell and was up again, but the men were closing round him. He shouted, 'I am coming!' The men were close to him. I looked. Many men. Then I looked at her. Tuan, I pushed the canoe! I pushed it into deep water. She was kneeling forward looking at me, and I said, 'Take your paddle,' while I struck the water with mine. Tuan, I heard him cry. I heard him cry my name twice; and I heard voices shouting, 'Kill! Strike!' I never turned back. I heard him calling my name again with a great shriek, as when life is going out together with the voice—and I never turned my head. My own name! . . . My brother! Three times he called—but I was not afraid of life. Was she not there in that canoe? And could I not with her find a country where death is forgotten—where death is unknown!"

The white man sat up. Arsat rose and stood, an indistinct and silent figure above the dying embers of the fire. Over the lagoon a mist drifting and low had crept, erasing slowly the glittering images of the stars. And now a great expanse of white vapor covered the land: it flowed cold and gray in the darkness, eddied in noiseless whirls round the tree trunks and about the platform of the house, which seemed to float upon a restless and impalpable illusion of a sea. Only far away the tops of the trees stood outlined on the twinkle of heaven, like a somber and forbidding shore—a coast deceptive, pitiless and black.

Arsat's voice vibrated loudly in the profound peace. "I had her there! I had her! To get her I would have faced all mankind. But I had her—and—"

His words went out ringing into the empty distances. He paused, and seemed to listen to them dying away very far—beyond help and beyond recall. Then he said quietly:

"Tuan, I loved my brother."

A breath of wind made him shiver. High above his head, high above the silent sea of mist the drooping leaves of the palms rattled together with a mournful and expiring sound. The white man stretched his legs. His chin rested on his chest, and he murmured sadly without lifting his head:

"We all love our brothers."

Arsat burst out with an intense whispering violence:

"What did I care who died? I wanted peace in my own heart."

He seemed to hear a stir in the house—listened—then stepped in noiselessly. The white man stood up. A breeze was coming in fitful puffs. The stars shone paler as if they had retreated into the frozen depths of immense space. After a chill gust of wind there were a few seconds of perfect calm and absolute silence. Then from behind the black and wavy line of the forests a column of golden light shot up into the heavens and spread over the semicircle of the eastern horizon. The sun had risen. The mist lifted, broke into drifting patches, vanished into thin flying wreaths; and the unveiled lagoon lay, polished and black, in the heavy shadows at the foot of the wall of trees. A white eagle rose over it with a slanting and ponderous flight, reached the clear sunshine and appeared dazzlingly brilliant for a moment, then soaring higher, became a dark and motionless speck before it vanished into the blue as if it had left the earth forever. The white man, standing gazing upwards before the doorway, heard in the hut a confused and broken murmur of distracted words ending with a loud groan. Suddenly Arsat stumbled out with outstretched hands, shivered, and stood still for some time with fixed eyes. Then he said:

"She burns no more."

Before his face the sun showed its edge above the treetops rising steadily. The breeze freshened; a great brilliance burst upon the lagoon, sparkled on the rippling water. The forests came out of the clear shadows of the morning, became distinct, as if they had rushed nearer—to stop short in a great stir of leaves, of nodding boughs, of swaying branches. In the merciless sunshine the whisper of unconscious life grew louder, speaking in an incomprehensible voice round the dumb darkness of that human sorrow. Arsat's eyes wandered slowly, then stared at the rising sun.

"I can see nothing," he said half aloud to himself.

"There is nothing," said the white man, moving to the edge of the platform and waving his hand to his boat. A shout came faintly over the lagoon and the sampan began to glide towards the abode of the friend of ghosts.

"If you want to come with me, I will wait all the morning," said the white man, looking away upon the water.

"No, Tuan," said Arsat, softly. "I shall not eat or sleep in this house, but I must first see my road. Now I can see nothing—see nothing! There is no light and no peace in the world; but there is death—death for many. We are sons of the same mother—and I left him in the midst of enemies; but I am going back now."

He drew a long breath and went on in a dreamy tone:

"In a little while I shall see clear enough to strike—to strike. But she has died, and . . . now . . . darkness."

He flung his arms wide open, let them fall along his body, then stood still with unmoved face and stony eyes, staring at the sun. The white man got down into his canoe. The polers ran smartly along the sides of the boat, looking over their shoulders at the beginning of a weary journey. High in the stern, his head muffled up in white rags, the juragan sat moody, letting his paddle trail in the water. The white man, leaning with both arms over the grass roof of the little cabin, looked back at the shining ripple of the boat's wake. Before the sampan passed out of the lagoon into the creek he lifted his eyes. Arsat had not moved. He stood lonely in the searching sunshine; and he looked beyond the great light of a cloudless day into the darkness of a world of illusions.

# The Secret Sharer

ON MY right hand there were lines of fishing
stakes resembling a mysterious system of half-
submerged bamboo fences, incomprehensible in its division of the domain of tropical fishes, and crazy of
aspect as if abandoned forever by some nomad tribe of
fishermen now gone to the other end of the ocean; for
there was no sign of human habitation as far as the eye
could reach. To the left a group of barren islets, suggest-
ing ruins of stone walls, towers, and blockhouses, had its
foundations set in a blue sea that itself looked solid, so
still and stable did it lie below my feet; even the track
of light from the westering sun shone smoothly, without
that animated glitter which tells of an imperceptible
ripple. And when I turned my head to take a parting
glance at the tug which had just left us anchored outside the bar, I saw the straight line of the flat shore
joined to the stable sea, edge to edge, with a perfect and
unmarked closeness, in one leveled floor half brown, half
blue under the enormous dome of the sky. Corresponding in their insignificance to the islets of the sea, two
small clumps of trees, one on each side of the only fault
in the impeccable joint, marked the mouth of the river
Meinam we had just left on the first preparatory stage of
our homeward journey; and, far back on the inland
level, a larger and loftier mass, the grove surrounding
the great Paknam pagoda, was the only thing on which

the eye could rest from the vain task of exploring the monotonous sweep of the horizon. Here and there gleams as of a few scattered pieces of silver marked the windings of the great river; and on the nearest of them, just within the bar, the tug steaming right into the land became lost to my sight, hull and funnel and masts, as though the impassive earth had swallowed her up without an effort, without a tremor. My eye followed the light cloud of her smoke, now here, now there, above the plain, according to the devious curves of the stream, but always fainter and farther away, till I lost it at last behind the miter-shaped hill of the great pagoda. And then I was left alone with my ship, anchored at the head of the Gulf of Siam.

She floated at the starting point of a long journey, very still in an immense stillness, the shadows of her spars flung far to the eastward by the setting sun. At that moment I was alone on her decks. There was not a sound in her—and around us nothing moved, nothing lived, not a canoe on the water, not a bird in the air, not a cloud in the sky. In this breathless pause at the threshold of a long passage we seemed to be measuring our fitness for a long and arduous enterprise, the appointed task of both our existences to be carried out, far from all human eyes, with only sky and sea for spectators and for judges.

There must have been some glare in the air to interfere with one's sight, because it was only just before the sun left us that my roaming eyes made out beyond the highest ridge of the principal islet of the group something which did away with the solemnity of perfect solitude. The tide of darkness flowed on swiftly; and with tropical suddenness a swarm of stars came out above the shadowy earth, while I lingered yet, my hand resting lightly on my ship's rail as if on the shoulder of a trusted friend. But, with all that multitude of celestial bodies staring down at one, the comfort of quiet communion with her was gone for good. And there were also disturbing sounds by this time—voices, footsteps forward; the steward flitted along the main deck, a busily ministering spirit; a hand bell tinkled urgently under the poop deck. . . .

I found my two officers waiting for me near the supper table, in the lighted cuddy. We sat down at once, and as I helped the chief mate, I said:

"Are you aware that there is a ship anchored inside the islands? I saw her mastheads above the ridge as the sun went down."

He raised sharply his simple face, overcharged by a terrible growth of whisker, and emitted his usual ejaculations: "Bless my soul, sir! You don't say so!"

My second mate was a round-cheeked, silent young man, grave beyond his years, I thought; but as our eyes happened to meet I detected a slight quiver on his lips. I looked down at once. It was not my part to encourage sneering on board my ship. It must be said, too, that I knew very little of my officers. In consequence of certain events of no particular significance, except to myself, I had been appointed to the command only a fortnight before. Neither did I know much of the hands forward. All these people had been together for eighteen months or so, and my position was that of the only stranger on board. I mention this because it has some bearing on what is to follow. But what I felt most was my being a stranger to the ship; and if all the truth must be told, I was somewhat of a stranger to myself. The youngest man on board (barring the second mate), and untried as yet by a position of the fullest responsibility, I was willing to take the adequacy of the others for granted. They had simply to be equal to their tasks; but

I wondered how far I should turn out faithful to that ideal conception of one's own personality every man sets up for himself secretly.

Meantime the chief mate, with an almost visible effect of collaboration on the part of his round eyes and frightful whiskers, was trying to evolve a theory of the anchored ship. His dominant trait was to take all things into earnest consideration. He was of a painstaking turn of mind. As he used to say, he "liked to account to himself" for practically everything that came in his way, down to a miserable scorpion he had found in his cabin a week before. The why and the wherefore of that scorpion—how it got on board and came to select his room rather than the pantry (which was a dark place and more what a scorpion would be partial to), and how on earth it managed to drown itself in the inkwell of his writing desk—had exercised him infinitely. The ship within the islands was much more easily accounted for; and just as we were about to rise from the table he made his pronouncement. She was, he doubted not, a ship from home lately arrived. Probably she drew too much water to cross the bar except at the top of spring tides. Therefore she went into that natural harbor to wait for a few days in preference to remaining in an open roadstead.

"That's so," confirmed the second mate, suddenly, in his slightly hoarse voice. "She draws over twenty feet. She's the Liverpool ship *Sephora* with a cargo of coal. Hundred and twenty-three days from Cardiff."

We looked at him in surprise.

"The tugboat skipper told me when he came on board for your letters, sir," explained the young man. "He expects to take her up the river the day after tomorrow."

After thus overwhelming us with the extent of his

information he slipped out of the cabin. The mate observed regretfully that he "could not account for that young fellow's whims." What prevented him telling us all about it at once, he wanted to know.

I detained him as he was making a move. For the last two days the crew had had plenty of hard work, and the night before they had very little sleep. I felt painfully that I—a stranger—was doing something unusual when I directed him to let all hands turn in without setting an anchor watch. I proposed to keep on deck myself till one o'clock or thereabouts. I would get the second mate to relieve me at that hour.

"He will turn out the cook and the steward at four," I concluded, "and then give you a call. Of course at the slightest sign of any sort of wind we'll have the hands up and make a start at once."

He concealed his astonishment. "Very well, sir." Outside the cuddy he put his head in the second mate's door to inform him of my unheard-of caprice to take a five hours' anchor watch on myself. I heard the other raise his voice incredulously: "What? The captain himself?" Then a few more murmurs, a door closed, then another. A few moments later I went on deck.

My strangeness, which had made me sleepless, had prompted that unconventional arrangement, as if I had expected in those solitary hours of the night to get on terms with the ship of which I knew nothing, manned by men of whom I knew very little more. Fast alongside a wharf, littered like any ship in port with a tangle of unrelated things, invaded by unrelated shore people, I had hardly seen her yet properly. Now, as she lay cleared for sea, the stretch of her main deck seemed to me very fine under the stars. Very fine, very roomy for her size, and very inviting. I descended the poop and paced the waist, my mind picturing to myself the coming passage through the Malay Archipelago, down the Indian Ocean, and up the Atlantic. All its phases were familiar enough to me, every characteristic, all the alternatives which were likely to face me on the high seas —everything! . . . except the novel responsibility of command. But I took heart from the reasonable thought that the ship was like other ships, the men like other men, and that the sea was not likely to keep any special surprises expressly for my discomfiture.

Arrived at that comforting conclusion, I bethought myself of a cigar and went below to get it. All was still down there. Everybody at the after end of the ship was sleeping profoundly. I came out again on the quarter-deck, agreeably at ease in my sleeping suit on that warm breathless night, barefooted, a glowing cigar in my teeth, and, going forward, I was met by the profound silence of the fore end of the ship. Only as I passed the door of the forecastle I heard a deep, quiet, trustful sigh of some sleeper inside. And suddenly I rejoiced in the great security of the sea as compared with the unrest of the land, in my choice of that untempted life presenting no disquieting problems, invested with an elementary moral beauty by the absolute straightforwardness of its appeal and by the singleness of its purpose.

The riding light in the fore-rigging burned with a clear, untroubled, as if symbolic, flame, confident and bright in the mysterious shades of the night. Passing on my way aft along the other side of the ship, I observed that the rope side ladder, put over, no doubt, for the master of the tug when he came to fetch away our letters, had not been hauled in as it should have been. I became annoyed at this, for exactitude in small matters is the very soul of discipline. Then I reflected that I had myself peremptorily dismissed my officers from duty, and by my own act had prevented the anchor watch being formally set and things properly attended to. I asked myself whether it was wise ever to interfere with the established routine of duties even from the kindest of motives. My action might have made me appear eccentric. Goodness only knew how that absurdly whiskered mate would "account" for my conduct, and what the whole ship thought of that informality of their new captain. I was vexed with myself.

Not from compunction certainly, but, as it were mechanically, I proceeded to get the ladder in myself. Now a side ladder of that sort is a light affair and comes in easily, yet my vigorous tug, which should have brought it flying on board, merely recoiled upon my body in a totally unexpected jerk. What the devil! . . . I was so astounded by the immovableness of that ladder that I remained stock-still, trying to account for it to myself like that imbecile mate of mine. In the end, of course, I put my head over the rail.

The side of the ship made an opaque belt of shadow on the darkling glassy shimmer of the sea. But I saw at once something elongated and pale floating very close to the ladder. Before I could form a guess a faint flash of phosphorescent light, which seemed to issue suddenly from the naked body of a man, flickered in the sleeping water with the elusive, silent play of summer lightning in a night sky. With a gasp I saw revealed to my stare a pair of feet, the long legs, a broad livid back immersed right up to the neck in a greenish cadaverous glow. One hand, awash, clutched the bottom rung of the ladder. He was complete but for the head. A headless corpse! The cigar dropped out of my gaping mouth with a tiny plop and a short hiss quite audible in the absolute stillness of all things under heaven. At that I suppose he raised up his face, a dimly pale oval in the shadow of the ship's side. But even then I could only barely make out down there the shape of his black-haired head. However, it was enough for the horrid, frost-bound sensation which had gripped me about the chest to pass off. The moment of vain exclamations was past, too. I only climbed on the spare spar and leaned over the rail as far as I could, to bring my eyes nearer to that mystery floating alongside.

As he hung by the ladder, like a resting swimmer, the sea lightning played about his limbs at every stir; and he appeared in it ghastly, silvery, fishlike. He remained as mute as a fish, too. He made no motion to get out of the water, either. It was inconceivable that he should not attempt to come on board, and strangely troubling to suspect that perhaps he did not want to. And my first words were prompted by just that troubled incertitude.

"What's the matter?" I asked in my ordinary tone, speaking down to the face upturned exactly under mine.

"Cramp," it answered, no louder. Then slightly anxious, "I say, no need to call anyone."

"I was not going to," I said.

"Are you alone on deck?"

"Yes."

I had somehow the impression that he was on the point of letting go the ladder to swim away beyond my ken—mysterious as he came. But, for the moment, this being appearing as if he had risen from the bottom of the sea (it was certainly the nearest land to the ship) wanted only to know the time. I told him. And he, down there, tentatively:

"I suppose your captain's turned in?"

"I am sure he isn't," I said.

He seemed to struggle with himself, for I heard something like the low, bitter murmur of doubt. "What's the good?" His next words came out with a hesitating effort.

"Look here, my man. Could you call him out quietly?"

I thought the time had come to declare myself.

"*I* am the captain."

I heard a "By Jove!" whispered at the level of the water. The phosphorescence flashed in the swirl of the water all about his limbs, his other hand seized the ladder.

"My name's Leggatt."

The voice was calm and resolute. A good voice. The self-possession of that man had somehow induced a corresponding state in myself. It was very quietly that I remarked:

"You must be a good swimmer."

"Yes. I've been in the water practically since nine o'clock. The question for me now is whether I am to let go this ladder and go on swimming till I sink from exhaustion, or—to come on board here."

I felt this was no mere formula of desperate speech, but a real alternative in the view of a strong soul. I should have gathered from this that he was young; indeed, it is only the young who are ever confronted by such clear issues. But at the time it was pure intuition on my part. A mysterious communication was established already between us two—in the face of that silent, darkened tropical sea. I was young, too; young enough to make no comment. The man in the water began suddenly to climb up the ladder, and I hastened away from the rail to fetch some clothes.

Before entering the cabin I stood still, listening in the lobby at the foot of the stairs. A faint snore came through the closed door of the chief mate's room. The second mate's door was on the hook, but the darkness in there was absolutely soundless. He, too, was young and could sleep like a stone. Remained the steward, but he was not likely to wake up before he was called. I got a sleeping suit out of my room and, coming back on deck, saw the naked man from the sea sitting on the main hatch, glimmering white in the darkness, his elbows on his knees and his head in his hands. In a moment he had concealed his damp body in a sleeping suit of the same gray-stripe pattern as the one I was wearing and followed me like my double on the poop. Together we moved right aft, barefooted, silent.

"What is it?" I asked in a deadened voice, taking the lighted lamp out of the binnacle, and raising it to his face.

"An ugly business."

He had rather regular features; a good mouth; light eyes under somewhat heavy, dark eyebrows; a smooth, square forehead; no growth on his cheeks; a small, brown mustache, and a well-shaped, round chin. His expression was concentrated, meditative, under the inspecting light of the lamp I held up to his face; such as a man thinking hard in solitude might wear. My sleeping suit was just right for his size. A well-knit young fellow of twenty-five at most. He caught his lower lip with the edge of white, even teeth.

"Yes," I said, replacing the lamp in the binnacle. The warm, heavy tropical night closed upon his head again.

"There's a ship over there," he murmured.

"Yes, I know. The *Sephora*. Did you know of us?"

"Hadn't the slightest idea. I am the mate of her—" He paused and corrected himself. "I should say I *was*."

"Aha! Something wrong?"

"Yes. Very wrong indeed. I've killed a man."

"What do you mean? Just now?"

"No, on the passage. Weeks ago. Thirty-nine south. When I say a man—"

"Fit of temper," I suggested, confidently.

The shadowy, dark head, like mine, seemed to nod

imperceptibly above the ghostly gray of my sleeping suit. It was, in the night, as though I had been faced by my own reflection in the depths of a somber and immense mirror.

"A pretty thing to have to own up to for a Conway boy," murmured my double, distinctly.

"You're a Conway boy?"

"I am," he said, as if startled. Then, slowly . . . "Perhaps you too—"

It was so; but being a couple of years older I had left before he joined. After a quick interchange of dates a silence fell; and I thought suddenly of my absurd mate with his terrific whiskers and the "Bless my soul—you don't say so" type of intellect. My double gave me an inkling of his thoughts by saying:

"My father's a parson in Norfolk. Do you see me before a judge and jury on that charge? For myself I can't see the necessity. There are fellows that an angel from heaven—— And I am not that. He was one of those creatures that are just simmering all the time with a silly sort of wickedness. Miserable devils that have no business to live at all. He wouldn't do his duty and wouldn't let anybody else do theirs. But what's the good of talking! You know well enough the sort of ill-conditioned snarling cur—"

He appealed to me as if our experiences had been as identical as our clothes. And I knew well enough the pestiferous danger of such a character where there are no means of legal repression. And I knew well enough also that my double there was no homicidal ruffian. I did not think of asking him for details, and he told me the story roughly in brusque, disconnected sentences. I needed no more. I saw it all going on as though I were myself inside that other sleeping suit.

"It happened while we were setting a reefed fore-

sail, at dusk. Reefed foresail! You understand the sort
of weather. The only sail we had left to keep the ship
running; so you may guess what it had been like for
days. Anxious sort of job, that. He gave me some of his
cursed insolence at the sheet. I tell you I was overdone
with this terrific weather that seemed to have no end
to it. Terrific, I tell you—and a deep ship. I believe the
fellow himself was half crazed with funk. It was no time
for gentlemanly reproof, so I turned round and felled
him like an ox. He up and at me. We closed just as an
awful sea made for the ship. All hands saw it coming
and took to the rigging, but I had him by the throat,
and went on shaking him like a rat, the men above us
yelling, 'Look out! look out!' Then a crash as if the sky
had fallen on my head. They say that for over ten
minutes hardly anything was to be seen of the ship—
just the three masts and a bit of the forecastle head
and of the poop all awash driving along in a smother
of foam. It was a miracle that they found us, jammed
together behind the forebits. It's clear that I meant business, because I was holding him by the throat still when
they picked us up. He was black in the face. It was too
much for them. It seems they rushed us aft together,
gripped as we were, screaming 'Murder!' like a lot of
lunatics, and broke into the cuddy. And the ship running for her life, touch and go all the time, any minute
her last in a sea fit to turn your hair gray only a-looking
at it. I understand that the skipper, too, started raving
like the rest of them. The man had been deprived of
sleep for more than a week, and to have this sprung on
him at the height of a furious gale nearly drove him out
of his mind. I wonder they didn't fling me overboard
after getting the carcass of their precious shipmate out
of my fingers. They had rather a job to separate us, I've
been told. A sufficiently fierce story to make an old

judge and a respectable jury sit up a bit. The first thing I heard when I came to myself was the maddening howling of that endless gale, and on that the voice of the old man. He was hanging on to my bunk, staring into my face out of his sou'wester.

"'Mr. Leggatt, you have killed a man. You can act no longer as chief mate of this ship.'"

His care to subdue his voice made it sound monotonous. He rested a hand on the end of the skylight to steady himself with, and all that time did not stir a limb, so far as I could see. "Nice little tale for a quiet tea party," he concluded in the same tone.

One of my hands, too, rested on the end of the skylight; neither did I stir a limb, so far as I knew. We stood less than a foot from each other. It occurred to me that if old "Bless my soul—you don't say so" were to put his head up the companion and catch sight of us, he would think he was seeing double, or imagine himself come upon a scene of weird witchcraft; the strange captain having a quiet confabulation by the wheel with his own gray ghost. I became very much concerned to prevent anything of the sort. I heard the other's soothing undertone.

"My father's a parson in Norfolk," it said. Evidently he had forgotten he had told me this important fact before. Truly a nice little tale.

"You had better slip down into my stateroom now," I said, moving off stealthily. My double followed my movements; our bare feet made no sound; I let him in, closed the door with care, and, after giving a call to the second mate, returned on deck for my relief.

"Not much sign of any wind yet," I remarked when he approached.

"No, sir. Not much," he assented, sleepily, in his

hoarse voice, with just enough deference, no more, and barely suppressing a yawn.

"Well, that's all you have to look out for. You have got your orders."

"Yes, sir."

I paced a turn or two on the poop and saw him take up his position face forward with his elbow in the rat-lines of the mizzen-rigging before I went below. The mate's faint snoring was still going on peacefully. The cuddy lamp was burning over the table on which stood a vase with flowers, a polite attention from the ships' provision merchant—the last flowers we should see for the next three months at the very least. Two bunches of bananas hung from the beam symmetrically, one on each side of the rudder casing. Everything was as before in the ship—except that two of her captain's sleeping suits were simultaneously in use, one motionless in the cuddy, the other keeping very still in the captain's stateroom.

It must be explained here that my cabin had the form of the capital letter L, the door being within the angle and opening into the short part of the letter. A couch was to the left, the bed-place to the right; my writing desk and the chronometers' table faced the door. But anyone opening it, unless he stepped right inside, had no view of what I call the long (or vertical) part of the letter. It contained some lockers surmounted by a book-case; and a few clothes, a thick jacket or two, caps, oilskin coat, and such like, hung on hooks. There was at the bottom of that part a door opening into my bath-room, which could be entered also directly from the saloon. But that way was never used.

The mysterious arrival had discovered the advantage of this particular shape. Entering my room, lighted strongly by a big bulkhead lamp swung on gimbals above my writing desk, I did not see him anywhere till he stepped out quietly from behind the coats hung in the recessed part.

"I heard somebody moving about, and went in there at once," he whispered.

I, too, spoke under my breath.

"Nobody is likely to come in here without knocking and getting permission."

He nodded. His face was thin and the sunburn faded, as though he had been ill. And no wonder. He had been, I heard presently, kept under arrest in his cabin for nearly seven weeks. But there was nothing sickly in his eyes or in his expression. He was not a bit like me, really; yet, as we stood leaning over my bed-place, whispering side by side, with our dark heads together and our backs to the door, anybody bold enough to open it stealthily would have been treated to the uncanny sight of a double captain busy talking in whispers with his other self.

"But all this doesn't tell me how you came to hang on to our side ladder," I inquired, in the hardly audible murmurs we used, after he had told me something more of the proceedings on board the *Sephora* once the bad weather was over.

"When we sighted Java Head I had had time to think all those matters out several times over. I had six weeks of doing nothing else, and with only an hour or so every evening for a tramp on the quarter-deck."

He whispered, his arms folded on the side of my bed-place, staring through the open port. And I could imagine perfectly the manner of this thinking out—a stubborn if not a steadfast operation; something of which I should have been perfectly incapable.

"I reckoned it would be dark before we closed with

the land," he continued, so low that I had to strain my hearing, near as we were to each other, shoulder touching shoulder almost. "So I asked to speak to the old man. He always seemed very sick when he came to see me—as if he could not look me in the face. You know, that foresail saved the ship. She was too deep to have run long under bare poles. And it was I that managed to set it for him. Anyway, he came. When I had him in my cabin—he stood by the door looking at me as if I had the halter around my neck already—I asked him right away to leave my cabin door unlocked at night while the ship was going through Sunda Straits. There would be the Java coast within two or three miles, off Angier Point. I wanted nothing more. I've had a prize for swimming my second year in the Conway."

"I can believe it," I breathed out.

"God only knows why they locked me in every night. To see some of their faces you'd have thought they were afraid I'd go about at night strangling people. Am I a murdering brute? Do I look it? By Jove! if I had been he wouldn't have trusted himself like that into my room. You'll say I might have chucked him aside and bolted out, there and then—it was dark already. Well, no. And for the same reason I wouldn't think of trying to smash the door. There would have been a rush to stop me at the noise, and I did not mean to get into a confounded scrimmage. Somebody else might have got killed—for I would not have broken out only to get chucked back, and I did not want any more of that work. He refused, looking more sick than ever. He was afraid of the men, and also of that old second mate of his who had been sailing with him for years—a gray-headed old humbug; and his steward, too, had been with him devil knows how long—seventeen years or more—a dogmatic sort of loafer who hated me like poison, just because I was the chief mate. No chief mate ever made more than one voyage in the *Sephora,* you know. Those two old chaps ran the ship. Devil only knows what the skipper wasn't afraid of (all his nerve went to pieces altogether in that hellish spell of bad weather we had)—of what the law would do to him—of his wife, perhaps. Oh, yes! she's on board. Though I don't think she would have meddled. She would have been only too glad to have me out of the ship in any way. The 'brand of Cain' business, don't you see. That's all right. I was ready enough to go off wandering on the face of the earth—and that was price enough to pay for an Abel of that sort. Anyhow, he wouldn't listen to me. 'This thing must take its course. I represent the law here.' He was shaking like a leaf. 'So you won't?' 'No!' 'Then I hope you will be able to sleep on that,' I said, and turned my back on him. 'I wonder that *you* can,' cries he, and locks the door.

"Well, after that, I couldn't. Not very well. That was three weeks ago. We have had a slow passage through the Java Sea; drifted about Carimata for ten days. When we anchored here they thought, I suppose, it was all right. The nearest land (and that's five miles) is the ship's destination; the consul would soon set about catching me; and there would have been no object in bolting to these islets there. I don't suppose there's a drop of water on them. I don't know how it was, but tonight that steward, after bringing me my supper, went out to let me eat it, and left the door unlocked. And I ate it—all there was, too. After I had finished I strolled out on the quarter-deck. I don't know that I meant to do anything. A breath of fresh air was all I wanted, I believe. Then a sudden temptation came over me. I kicked off my slippers and was in the water before I had made up my mind fairly. Somebody heard the splash and they raised an awful hullabaloo. 'He's gone! Lower the boats! He's committed suicide! No, he's swimming.' Certainly I was swimming. It's not so easy for a swimmer like me to commit suicide by drowning. I landed on the nearest islet before the boat left the ship's side. I heard them pulling about in the dark, hailing, and so on, but after a bit they gave up. Everything quieted down and the anchorage became as still as death. I sat down on a stone and began to think. I felt certain they would start searching for me at daylight. There was no place to hide on those stony things—and if there had been, what would have been the good? But now I was clear of that ship, I was not going back. So after a while I took off all my clothes, tied them up in a bundle with a stone inside, and dropped them in the deep water on the outer side of that islet. That was suicide enough for me. Let them think what they liked, but I didn't mean to drown myself. I meant to swim till I sank—but that's not the same thing. I struck out for another of these little islands, and it was from that one that I first saw your riding light. Something to swim for. I went on easily, and on the way I came upon a flat rock a foot or two above water. In the daytime, I dare say, you might make it out with a glass from your poop. I scrambled up on it and rested myself for a bit. Then I made another start. That last spell must have been over a mile."

His whisper was getting fainter and fainter, and all the time he stared straight out through the porthole, in which there was not even a star to be seen. I had not interrupted him. There was something that made comment impossible in his narrative, or perhaps in himself; a sort of feeling, a quality, which I can't find a name for. And when he ceased, all I found was a futile whisper: "So you swam for our light?"

"Yes—straight for it. It was something to swim for.

I couldn't see any stars low down because the coast was in the way, and I couldn't see the land, either. The water was like glass. One might have been swimming in a confounded thousand-feet deep cistern with no place for scrambling out anywhere; but what I didn't like was the notion of swimming round and round like a crazed bullock before I gave out; and as I didn't mean to go back . . . No. Do you see me being hauled back, stark naked, off one of these little islands by the scruff of the neck and fighting like a wild beast? Somebody would have got killed for certain, and I did not want any of that. So I went on. Then your ladder—"

"Why didn't you hail the ship?" I asked, a little louder.

He touched my shoulder lightly. Lazy footsteps came right over our heads and stopped. The second mate had crossed from the other side of the poop and might have been hanging over the rail, for all we knew.

"He couldn't hear us talking—could he?" My double breathed into my very ear, anxiously.

His anxiety was an answer, a sufficient answer, to the question I had put to him. An answer containing all the difficulty of that situation. I closed the porthole quietly, to make sure. A louder word might have been overheard.

"Who's that?" he whispered then.

"My second mate. But I don't know much more of the fellow than you do."

And I told him a little about myself. I had been appointed to take charge while I least expected anything of the sort, not quite a fortnight ago. I didn't know either the ship or the people. Hadn't had the time in port to look about me or size anybody up. And as to the crew, all they knew was that I was appointed to take the ship home. For the rest, I was almost as much of a stranger on board as himself, I said. And at the moment I felt it most acutely. I felt that it would take very little to make me a suspect person in the eyes of the ship's company.

He had turned about meantime; and we, the two strangers in the ship, faced each other in identical attitudes.

"Your ladder—" he murmured, after a silence. "Who'd have thought of finding a ladder hanging over at night in a ship anchored out here! I felt just then a very unpleasant faintness. After the life I've been leading for nine weeks, anybody would have got out of condition. I wasn't capable of swimming round as far as your rudder chains. And, lo and behold! there was a ladder to get hold of. After I gripped it I said to myself, 'What's the good?' When I saw a man's head looking over I thought I would swim away presently and leave him shouting—in whatever language it was. I didn't mind being looked at. I—I liked it. And then you speaking to me so quietly—as if you had expected me—made me hold on a little longer. It had been a confounded lonely time—I don't mean while swimming. I was glad to talk a little to somebody that didn't belong to the *Sephora*. As to asking for the captain, that was a mere impulse. It could have been no use, with all the ship knowing about me and the other people pretty certain to be round here in the morning. I don't know—I wanted to be seen, to talk with somebody, before I went on. I don't know what I would have said. . . . 'Fine night, isn't it?' or something of the sort."

"Do you think they will be round here presently?" I asked with some incredulity.

"Quite likely," he said, faintly.

He looked extremely haggard all of a sudden. His head rolled on his shoulders.

"H'm. We shall see then. Meantime get into that bed," I whispered. "Want help? There."

It was a rather high bed-place with a set of drawers underneath. This amazing swimmer really needed the lift I gave him by seizing his leg. He tumbled in, rolled over on his back, and flung one arm across his eyes. And then, with his face nearly hidden, he must have looked exactly as I used to look in that bed. I gazed upon my other self for a while before drawing across carefully the two green serge curtains which ran on a brass rod. I thought for a moment of pinning them together for greater safety, but I sat down on the couch, and once there I felt unwilling to rise and hunt for a pin. I would do it in a moment. I was extremely tired, in a peculiarly intimate way, by the strain of stealthiness, by the effort of whispering and the general secrecy of this excitement. It was three o'clock by now and I had been on my feet since nine, but I was not sleepy; I could not have gone to sleep. I sat there, fagged out, looking at the curtains, trying to clear my mind of the confused sensation of being in two places at once, and greatly bothered by an exasperating knocking in my head. It was a relief to discover suddenly that it was not in my head at all, but on the outside of the door. Before I could collect myself the words "Come in" were out of my mouth, and the steward entered with a tray, bringing in my morning coffee. I had slept, after all, and I was so frightened that I shouted, "This way! I am here, steward," as though he had been miles away. He put down the tray on the table next the couch and only then said, very quietly, "I can see you are here, sir." I felt him give me a keen look, but I dared not meet his eyes just then. He must have wondered why I had drawn the curtains of my bed before going to sleep on the couch. He went out, hooking the door open as usual.

I heard the crew washing decks above me. I know I would have been told at once if there had been any wind. Calm, I thought, and I was doubly vexed. Indeed, I felt dual more than ever. The steward reappeared suddenly in the doorway. I jumped up from the couch so quickly that he gave a start.

"What do you want here?"

"Close your port, sir—they are washing decks."

"It is closed," I said, reddening.

"Very well, sir." But he did not move from the doorway and returned my stare in an extraordinary, equivocal manner for a time. Then his eyes wavered, all his expression changed, and in a voice unusually gentle, almost coaxingly:

"May I come in to take the empty cup away, sir?"

"Of course!" I turned my back on him while he popped in and out. Then I unhooked and closed the door and even pushed the bolt. This sort of thing could not go on very long. The cabin was as hot as an oven, too. I took a peep at my double, and discovered that he had not moved, his arm was still over his eyes; but his chest heaved; his hair was wet; his chin glistened with perspiration. I reached over him and opened the port.

"I must show myself on deck," I reflected.

Of course, theoretically, I could do what I liked, with no one to say nay to me within the whole circle of the horizon; but to lock my cabin door and take the key away I did not dare. Directly I put my head out of the companion I saw the group of my two officers, the second mate barefooted, the chief mate in long india-rubber boots, near the break of the poop, and the steward halfway down the poop ladder talking to them eagerly. He happened to catch sight of me and dived, the second ran down on the main deck shouting some order or other, and the chief mate came to meet me, touching his cap.

There was a sort of curiosity in his eye that I did not like. I don't know whether the steward had told them that I was "queer" only, or downright drunk, but I know the man meant to have a good look at me. I watched him coming with a smile which, as he got into point-blank range, took effect and froze his very whiskers. I did not give him time to open his lips.

"Square the yards by lifts and braces before the hands go to breakfast."

It was the first particular order I had given on board that ship; and I stayed on deck to see it executed, too. I had felt the need of asserting myself without loss of time. That sneering young cub got taken down a peg or two on that occasion, and I also seized the opportunity of having a good look at the face of every foremast man as they filed past me to go to the after braces. At breakfast time, eating nothing myself, I presided with such frigid dignity that the two mates were only too glad to escape from the cabin as soon as decency permitted; and all the time the dual working of my mind distracted me almost to the point of insanity. I was constantly watching myself, my secret self, as dependent on my actions as my own personality, sleeping in that bed, behind that door which faced me as I sat at the head of the table. It was very much like being mad, only it was worse because one was aware of it.

I had to shake him for a solid minute, but when at last he opened his eyes it was in the full possession of his senses, with an inquiring look.

"All's well so far," I whispered. "Now you must vanish into the bathroom."

He did so, as noiseless as a ghost, and I then rang for the steward, and facing him boldly, directed him to tidy up my stateroom while I was having my bath—"and be quick about it." As my tone admitted of no excuses, he said, "Yes, sir," and ran off to fetch his dustpan and brushes. I took a bath and did most of my dressing, splashing, and whistling softly for the steward's edification, while the secret sharer of my life stood drawn up bolt upright in that little space, his face looking very sunken in daylight, his eyelids lowered under the stern, dark line of his eyebrows drawn together by a slight frown.

When I left him there to go back to my room the steward was finishing dusting. I sent for the mate and engaged him in some insignificant conversation. It was, as it were, trifling with the terrific character of his whiskers; but my object was to give him an opportunity for a good look at my cabin. And then I could at last shut, with a clear conscience, the door of my stateroom and get my double back into the recessed part. There was nothing else for it. He had to sit still on a small folding stool, half smothered by the heavy coats hanging there. We listened to the steward going into the bathroom out of the saloon, filling the water bottles there, scrubbing the bath, setting things to rights, whisk, bang, clatter—out again into the saloon—turn the key —click. Such was my scheme for keeping my second self invisible. Nothing better could be contrived under the circumstances. And there we sat; I at my writing desk ready to appear busy with some papers, he behind me, out of sight of the door. It would not have been prudent to talk in daytime; and I could not have stood the excitement of that queer sense of whispering to myself. Now and then, glancing over my shoulder, I saw him far back there, sitting rigidly on the low stool, his bare feet close together, his arms folded, his head hanging on his breast—and perfectly still. Anybody would have taken him for me.

I was fascinated by it myself. Every moment I had to glance over my shoulder. I was looking at him when a voice outside the door said:

"Beg pardon, sir."

"Well!" . . . I kept my eyes on him, and so, when the voice outside the door announced, "There's a ship's boat coming our way, sir," I saw him give a start—the first movement he had made for hours. But he did not raise his bowed head.

"All right. Get the ladder over."

I hesitated. Should I whisper something to him? But what? His immobility seemed to have been never disturbed. What could I tell him he did not know already? . . . Finally I went on deck.

II

The skipper of the *Sephora* had a thin red whisker all round his face, and the sort of complexion that goes with hair of that color; also the particular, rather smeary shade of blue in the eyes. He was not exactly a showy figure; his shoulders were high, his stature but middling —one leg slightly more bandy than the other. He shook hands, looking vaguely around. A spiritless tenacity was his main characteristic, I judged. I behaved with a politeness which seemed to disconcert him. Perhaps he was shy. He mumbled to me as if he were ashamed of what he was saying; gave his name (it was something like Archbold—but at this distance of years I hardly am sure), his ship's name, and a few other particulars of that sort, in the manner of a criminal making a re- luctant and doleful confession. He had had terrible weather on the passage out—terrible—terrible—wife aboard, too.

By this time we were seated in the cabin and the steward brought in a tray with a bottle and glasses. "Thanks! No." Never took liquor. Would have some water, though. He drank two tumblerfuls. Terrible thirsty work. Ever since daylight had been exploring the islands round his ship.

"What was that for—fun?" I asked, with an appear- ance of polite interest.

"No!" He sighed. "Painful duty."

As he persisted in his mumbling and I wanted my double to hear every word, I hit upon the notion of informing him that I regretted to say I was hard of hearing.

"Such a young man, too!" he nodded, keeping his smeary blue, unintelligent eyes fastened upon me. What was the cause of it—some disease? he inquired, without the least sympathy and as if he thought that, if so, I'd got no more than I deserved.

"Yes; disease," I admitted in a cheerful tone which seemed to shock him. But my point was gained, because he had to raise his voice to give me his tale. It is not worth while to record that version. It was just over two months since all this had happened, and he had thought so much about it that he seemed completely muddled as to its bearings, but still immensely impressed.

"What would you think of such a thing happening on board your own ship? I've had the *Sephora* for these fifteen years. I am a well-known shipmaster."

He was densely distressed—and perhaps I should have sympathized with him if I had been able to detach my mental vision from the unsuspected sharer of my cabin as though he were my second self. There he was on the other side of the bulkhead, four or five feet from us, no more, as we sat in the saloon. I looked politely at Captain Archbold (if that was his name), but it was the other I saw, in a gray sleeping suit, seated on a low stool, his bare feet close together, his arms folded, and every word said between us falling into the ears of his dark head bowed on his chest.

"I have been at sea now, man and boy, for seven-and-thirty years, and I've never heard of such a thing happening in an English ship. And that it should be my ship. Wife on board, too."

I was hardly listening to him.

"Don't you think," I said, "that the heavy sea which, you told me, came aboard just then might have killed the man? I have seen the sheer weight of a sea kill a man very neatly, by simply breaking his neck."

"Good God!" he uttered, impressively, fixing his smeary blue eyes on me. "The sea! No man killed by the sea ever looked like that." He seemed positively scandalized at my suggestion. And as I gazed at him, certainly not prepared for anything original on his part, he advanced his head close to mine and thrust his tongue out at me so suddenly that I couldn't help starting back.

After scoring over my calmness in this graphic way he nodded wisely. If I had seen the sight, he assured me, I would never forget it as long as I lived. The weather was too bad to give the corpse a proper sea burial. So next day at dawn they took it up on the poop, covering its face with a bit of bunting; he read a short prayer, and then, just as it was, in its oilskins and long boots, they launched it amongst those mountainous seas that seemed ready every moment to swallow up the ship herself and the terrified lives on board of her.

"That reefed foresail saved you," I threw in.

"Under God—it did," he exclaimed fervently. "It was by a special mercy, I firmly believe, that it stood some of those hurricane squalls."

"It was the setting of that sail which—" I began.

"God's own hand in it," he interrupted me. "Nothing less could have done it. I don't mind telling you that I hardly dared give the order. It seemed impossible that we could touch anything without losing it, and then our last hope would have been gone."

The terror of that gale was on him yet. I let him go on for a bit, then said, casually—as if returning to a minor subject:

"You were very anxious to give up your mate to the shore people, I believe?"

He was. To the law. His obscure tenacity on that point had in it something incomprehensible and a little awful; something, as it were, mystical, quite apart from his anxiety that he should not be suspected of "countenancing any doings of that sort." Seven-and-thirty virtuous years at sea, of which over twenty of immaculate command, and the last fifteen in the *Sephora*, seemed to have laid him under some pitiless obligation.

"And you know," he went on, groping shamefacedly amongst his feelings, "I did not engage that young fellow. His people had some interest with my owners. I was in a way forced to take him on. He looked very smart, very gentlemanly, and all that. But do you know—I never liked him, somehow. I am a plain man. You see, he wasn't exactly the sort for the chief mate of a ship like the *Sephora*."

I had become so connected in thoughts and impres-

sions with the secret sharer of my cabin that I felt as
if I, personally, were being given to understand that I,
too, was not the sort that would have done for the chief
mate of a ship like the *Sephora*. I had no doubt of it in
my mind.

"Not at all the style of man. You understand," he
insisted, superfluously, looking hard at me.

I smiled urbanely. He seemed at a loss for a while.

"I suppose I must report a suicide."

"Beg pardon?"

"Sui-cide! That's what I'll have to write to my owners
directly I get in."

"Unless you manage to recover him before tomorrow," I assented, dispassionately. . . . "I mean, alive."

He mumbled something which I really did not catch,
and I turned my ear to him in a puzzled manner. He
fairly bawled:

"The land—I say, the mainland is at least seven miles
off my anchorage."

"About that."

My lack of excitement, of curiosity, of surprise, of
any sort of pronounced interest, began to arouse his
distrust. But except for the felicitous pretense of deaf-
ness I had not tried to pretend anything. I had felt
utterly incapable of playing the part of ignorance properly, and therefore was afraid to try. It is also certain
that he had brought some ready-made suspicions with
him, and that he viewed my politeness as a strange and
unnatural phenomenon. And yet how else could I have
received him? Not heartily! That was impossible for
psychological reasons, which I need not state here. My
only object was to keep off his inquiries. Surlily? Yes,
but surliness might have provoked a point-blank question. From its novelty to him and from its nature, punc-

tilious courtesy was the manner best calculated to restrain the man. But there was the danger of his breaking through my defense bluntly. I could not, I think, have met him by a direct lie, also for psychological (not moral) reasons. If he had only known how afraid I was of his putting my feeling of identity with the other to the test! But, strangely enough—(I thought of it only afterward)—I believe that he was not a little disconcerted by the reverse side of that weird situation, by something in me that reminded him of the man he was seeking—suggested a mysterious similitude to the young fellow he had distrusted and disliked from the first.

However that might have been, the silence was not very prolonged. He took another oblique step.

"I reckon I had no more than a two-mile pull to your ship. Not a bit more."

"And quite enough, too, in this awful heat," I said.

Another pause full of mistrust followed. Necessity, they say, is mother of invention, but fear, too, is not barren of ingenious suggestions. And I was afraid he would ask me point-blank for news of my other self.

"Nice little saloon, isn't it?" I remarked, as if noticing for the first time the way his eyes roamed from one closed door to the other. "And very well fitted out, too. Here, for instance," I continued, reaching over the back of my seat negligently and flinging the door open, "is my bathroom."

He made an eager movement, but hardly gave it a glance. I got up, shut the door of the bathroom, and invited him to have a look round, as if I were very proud of my accommodation. He had to rise and be shown round, but he went through the business without any raptures whatever.

"And now we'll have a look at my stateroom," I de-

clared, in a voice as loud as I dared to make it, crossing
the cabin to the starboard side with purposely heavy
steps.

He followed me in and gazed around. My intelligent double had vanished. I played my part.

"Very convenient—isn't it?"

"Very nice. Very comf . . ." He didn't finish, and
went out brusquely as if to escape from some unright-
eous wiles of mine. But it was not to be. I had been too
frightened not to feel vengeful; I felt I had him on the
run, and I meant to keep him on the run. My polite
insistence must have had something menacing in it, because he gave in suddenly. And I did not let him off a
single item; mate's room, pantry, storerooms, the very
sail locker which was also under the poop—he had to
look into them all. When at last I showed him out on the
quarter-deck he drew a long, spiritless sigh, and mumbled dismally that he must really be going back to his
ship now. I desired my mate, who had joined us, to see
to the captain's boat.

The man of whiskers gave a blast on the whistle
which he used to wear hanging round his neck, and
yelled, "*Sephoras* away!" My double down there in my
cabin must have heard, and certainly could not feel
more relieved than I. Four fellows came running out
from somewhere forward and went over the side, while
my own men, appearing on deck too, lined the rail. I
escorted my visitor to the gangway ceremoniously, and
nearly overdid it. He was a tenacious beast. On the very
ladder he lingered, and in that unique, guiltily conscientious manner of sticking to the point:

"I say . . . you . . . you don't think that—"

I covered his voice loudly:

"Certainly not. . . . I am delighted. Good-by."

I had an idea of what he meant to say, and just saved

myself by the privilege of defective hearing. He was too shaken generally to insist, but my mate, close witness of that parting, looked mystified and his face took on a thoughtful cast. As I did not want to appear as if I wished to avoid all communication with my officers, he had the opportunity to address me.

"Seems a very nice man. His boat's crew told our chaps a very extraordinary story, if what I am told by the steward is true. I suppose you had it from the captain, sir?"

"Yes. I had a story from the captain."

"A very horrible affair—isn't it, sir?"

"It is."

"Beats all these tales we hear about murders in Yankee ships."

"I don't think it beats them. I don't think it resembles them in the least."

"Bless my soul—you don't say so! But of course I've no acquaintance whatever with American ships, not I, so I couldn't go against your knowledge. It's horrible enough for me. . . . But the queerest part is that those fellows seemed to have some idea the man was hidden aboard here. They had really. Did you ever hear of such a thing?"

"Preposterous—isn't it?"

We were walking to and fro athwart the quarter-deck. No one of the crew forward could be seen (the day was Sunday), and the mate pursued:

"There was some little dispute about it. Our chaps took offense. 'As if we would harbor a thing like that,' they said. 'Wouldn't you like to look for him in our coal hole?' Quite a tiff. But they made it up in the end. I suppose he did drown himself. Don't you, sir?"

"I don't suppose anything."

"You have no doubt in the matter, sir?"

"None whatever."

I left him suddenly. I felt I was producing a bad impression, but with my double down there it was most trying to be on deck. And it was almost as trying to be below. Altogether a nerve-trying situation. But on the whole I felt less torn in two when I was with him. There was no one in the whole ship whom I dared take into my confidence. Since the hands had got to know his story, it would have been impossible to pass him off for anyone else, and an accidental discovery was to be dreaded now more than ever. . . .

The steward being engaged in laying the table for dinner, we could talk only with our eyes when I first went down. Later in the afternoon we had a cautious try at whispering. The Sunday quietness of the ship was against us; the stillness of air and water around her was against us; the elements, the men were against us— everything was against us in our secret partnership; time itself—for this could not go on forever. The very trust in Providence was, I suppose, denied to his guilt. Shall I confess that this thought cast me down very much? And as to the chapter of accidents which counts for so much in the book of success, I could only hope that it was closed. For what favorable accident could be expected?

"Did you hear everything?" were my first words as soon as we took up our position side by side, leaning over my bed-place.

He had. And the proof of it was his earnest whisper, "The man told you he hardly dared to give the order."

I understood the reference to be to that saving foresail.

"Yes. He was afraid of it being lost in the setting."

"I assure you he never gave the order. He may think he did, but he never gave it. He stood there with me on the break of the poop after the maintopsail blew away, and whimpered about our last hope—positively whimpered about it and nothing else—and the night coming on! To hear one's skipper go on like that in such weather was enough to drive any fellow out of his mind. It worked me up into a sort of desperation. I just took it into my own hands and went away from him, boiling, and—. But what's the use telling you? *You* know! . . . Do you think that if I had not been pretty fierce with them I should have got the men to do anything? Not it! The bosun perhaps? Perhaps! It wasn't a heavy sea— it was a sea gone mad! I suppose the end of the world will be something like that; and a man may have the heart to see it coming once and be done with it—but to have to face it day after day— I don't blame anybody. I was precious little better than the rest. Only—I was an officer of that old coal-wagon, anyhow—"

"I quite understand," I conveyed that sincere assurance into his ear. He was out of breath with whispering; I could hear him pant slightly. It was all very simple. The same strung-up force which had given twenty-four men a chance, at least, for their lives, had, in a sort of recoil, crushed an unworthy mutinous existence.

But I had no leisure to weigh the merits of the matter—footsteps in the saloon, a heavy knock. "There's enough wind to get under way with, sir." Here was the call of a new claim upon my thoughts and even upon my feelings.

"Turn the hands up," I cried through the door. "I'll be on deck directly."

I was going out to make the acquaintance of my ship. Before I left the cabin our eyes met—the eyes of the only two strangers on board. I pointed to the recessed part where the little campstool awaited him and laid

my finger on my lips. He made a gesture—somewhat
vague—a little mysterious, accompanied by a faint smile,
as if of regret.

This is not the place to enlarge upon the sensations
of a man who feels for the first time a ship move under
his feet to his own independent word. In my case they
were not unalloyed. I was not wholly alone with my
command; for there was that stranger in my cabin. Or
rather, I was not completely and wholly with her. Part
of me was absent. That mental feeling of being in two
places at once affected me physically as if the mood of
secrecy had penetrated my very soul. Before an hour
had elapsed since the ship had begun to move, having
occasion to ask the mate (he stood by my side) to take
a compass bearing of the Pagoda, I caught myself reaching up to his ear in whispers. I say I caught myself,
but enough had escaped to startle the man. I can't de-
scribe it otherwise than by saying that he shied. A grave,
preoccupied manner, as though he were in possession
of some perplexing intelligence, did not leave him
henceforth. A little later I moved away from the rail to
look at the compass with such a stealthy gait that the
helmsman noticed it—and I could not help noticing the
unusual roundness of his eyes. These are trifling instances, though it's to no commander's advantage to be
suspected of ludicrous eccentricities. But I was also
more seriously affected. There are to a seaman certain
words, gestures, that should in given conditions come
as naturally, as instinctively as the winking of a menaced
eye. A certain order should spring on to his lips without
thinking; a certain sign should get itself made, so to
speak, without reflection. But all unconscious alertness
had abandoned me. I had to make an effort of will to
recall myself back (from the cabin) to the conditions of
the moment. I felt that I was appearing an irresolute

commander to those people who were watching me more or less critically.

And, besides, there were the scares. On the second day out, for instance, coming off the deck in the afternoon (I had straw slippers on my bare feet) I stopped at the open pantry door and spoke to the steward. He was doing something there with his back to me. At the sound of my voice he nearly jumped out of his skin, as the saying is, and incidentally broke a cup.

"What on earth's the matter with you?" I asked, astonished.

He was extremely confused. "Beg your pardon, sir. I made sure you were in your cabin."

"You see I wasn't."

"No, sir. I could have sworn I had heard you moving in there not a moment ago. It's most extraordinary . . . very sorry, sir."

I passed on with an inward shudder. I was so identified with my secret double that I did not even mention the fact in those scanty, fearful whispers we exchanged. I suppose he had made some slight noise of some kind or other. It would have been miraculous if he hadn't at one time or another. And yet, haggard as he appeared, he looked always perfectly self-controlled, more than calm—almost invulnerable. On my suggestion he remained almost entirely in the bathroom, which, upon the whole, was the safest place. There could be really no shadow of an excuse for anyone ever wanting to go in there, once the steward had done with it. It was a very tiny place. Sometimes he reclined on the floor, his legs bent, his head sustained on one elbow. At others I would find him on the campstool, sitting in his gray sleeping suit and with his cropped dark hair like a patient, unmoved convict. At night I would smuggle him into my bed-place, and we would whisper together, with the regular footfalls of the officer of the watch passing and repassing over our heads. It was an infinitely miserable time. It was lucky that some tins of fine preserves were stowed in a locker in my stateroom; hard bread I could always get hold of; and so he lived on stewed chicken, paté de foie gras, asparagus, cooked oysters, sardines—on all sorts of abominable sham delicacies out of tins. My early morning coffee he always drank; and it was all I dared do for him in that respect.

Every day there was the horrible maneuvering to go through so that my room and then the bathroom should be done in the usual way. I came to hate the sight of the steward, to abhor the voice of that harmless man. I felt that it was he who would bring on the disaster of discovery. It hung like a sword over our heads.

The fourth day out, I think (we were then working down the east side of the Gulf of Siam, tack for tack, in light winds and smooth water)—the fourth day, I say, of this miserable juggling with the unavoidable, as we sat at our evening meal, that man, whose slightest movement I dreaded, after putting down the dishes ran up on deck busily. This could not be dangerous. Presently he came down again; and then it appeared that he had remembered a coat of mine which I had thrown over a rail to dry after having been wetted in a shower which had passed over the ship in the afternoon. Sitting stolidly at the head of the table I became terrified at the sight of the garment on his arm. Of course he made for my door. There was no time to lose.

"Steward," I thundered. My nerves were so shaken that I could not govern my voice and conceal my agitation. This was the sort of thing that made my terrifically whiskered mate tap his forehead with his forefinger. I had detected him using that gesture while talking on deck with a confidential air to the carpenter. It was too far to hear a word, but I had no doubt that this panto-mime could only refer to the strange new captain.

"Yes, sir," the pale-faced steward turned resignedly to me. It was this maddening course of being shouted at, checked without rhyme or reason, arbitrarily chased out of my cabin, suddenly called into it, sent flying out of his pantry on incomprehensible errands, that ac-counted for the growing wretchedness of his expression.

"Where are you going with that coat?"

"To your room, sir."

"Is there another shower coming?"

"I'm sure I don't know, sir. Shall I go up again and see, sir?"

"No! never mind."

My object was attained, as of course my other self in there would have heard everything that passed. During this interlude my two officers never raised their eyes off their respective plates; but the lip of that confounded cub, the second mate, quivered visibly.

I expected the steward to hook my coat on and come out at once. He was very slow about it; but I dominated my nervousness sufficiently not to shout after him. Sud-denly I became aware (it could be heard plainly enough) that the fellow for some reason or other was opening the door of the bathroom. It was the end. The place was literally not big enough to swing a cat in. My voice died in my throat and I went stony all over. I expected to hear a yell of surprise and terror, and made a movement, but had not the strength to get on my legs. Everything remained still. Had my second self taken the poor wretch by the throat? I don't know what I would have done next moment if I had not seen the steward come out of my room, close the door, and then stand quietly by the sideboard.

Saved, I thought. But, no! Lost! Gone! He was gone!

I laid my knife and fork down and leaned back in my chair. My head swam. After a while, when sufficiently recovered to speak in a steady voice, I instructed my mate to put the ship round at eight o'clock himself.

"I won't come on deck," I went on. "I think I'll turn in, and unless the wind shifts I don't want to be disturbed before midnight. I feel a bit seedy."

"You did look middling bad a little while ago," the chief mate remarked without showing any great concern.

They both went out, and I stared at the steward clearing the table. There was nothing to be read on that wretched man's face. But why did he avoid my eyes I asked myself. Then I thought I should like to hear the sound of his voice.

"Steward!"

"Sir!" Startled as usual.

"Where did you hang up that coat?"

"In the bathroom, sir." The usual anxious tone. "It's not quite dry yet, sir."

For some time longer I sat in the cuddy. Had my double vanished as he had come? But of his coming there was an explanation, whereas his disappearance would be inexplicable. . . . I went slowly into my dark room, shut the door, lighted the lamp, and for a time dared not turn round. When at last I did I saw him standing bolt upright in the narrow recessed part. It would not be true to say I had a shock, but an irresistible doubt of his bodily existence flitted through my mind. Can it be, I asked myself, that he is not visible to other eyes than mine? It was like being haunted. Motionless, with a grave face, he raised his hands slightly at me in a gesture which meant clearly, "Heavens! what a narrow escape!" Narrow indeed. I think I had come creeping quietly as near insanity as any man who has not actually gone over the border. That gesture restrained me, so to speak.

The mate with the terrific whiskers was now putting the ship on the other tack. In the moment of profound silence which follows upon the hands going to their stations I heard on the poop his raised voice: "Hard alee!" and the distant shout of the order repeated on the main-deck. The sails, in that light breeze, made but a faint fluttering noise. It ceased. The ship was coming round slowly; I held my breath in the renewed stillness of expectation; one wouldn't have thought that there was a single living soul on her decks. A sudden brisk shout, "Mainsail haul!" broke the spell, and in the noisy cries and rush overhead of the men running away with the main brace we two, down in my cabin, came together in our usual position by the bed-place.

He did not wait for my question. "I heard him fumbling here and just managed to squat myself down in the bath," he whispered to me. "The fellow only opened the door and put his arm in to hang the coat up. All the same—"

"I never thought of that," I whispered back, even more appalled than before at the closeness of the shave, and marveling at that something unyielding in his character which was carrying him through so finely. There was no agitation in his whisper. Whoever was being driven distracted, it was not he. He was sane. And the proof of his sanity was continued when he took up the whispering again.

"It would never do for me to come to life again."

It was something that a ghost might have said. But what he was alluding to was his old captain's reluctant admission of the theory of suicide. It would obviously serve his turn—if I had understood at all the view which seemed to govern the unalterable purpose of his action.

"You must maroon me as soon as ever you can get amongst these islands off the Cambodje shore," he went on.

"Maroon you! We are not living in a boy's adventure tale," I protested. His scornful whispering took me up.

"We aren't indeed! There's nothing of a boy's tale in this. But there's nothing else for it. I want no more. You don't suppose I am afraid of what can be done to me? Prison or gallows or whatever they may please. But you don't see me coming back to explain such things to an old fellow in a wig and twelve respectable tradesmen, do you? What can they know whether I am guilty or not—or of *what* I am guilty, either? That's my affair. What does the Bible say? 'Driven off the face of the earth.' Very well. I am off the face of the earth now. As I came at night so I shall go."

"Impossible!" I murmured. "You can't."

"Can't? . . . Not naked like a soul on the Day of Judgment. I shall freeze on to this sleeping suit. The Last Day is not yet—and . . . you have understood thoroughly. Didn't you?"

I felt suddenly ashamed of myself. I may say truly that I understood—and my hesitation in letting that man swim away from my ship's side had been a mere sham sentiment, a sort of cowardice.

"It can't be done now till next night," I breathed out. "The ship is on the offshore tack and the wind may fail us."

"As long as I know that you understand," he whispered. "But of course you do. It's a great satisfaction to have got somebody to understand. You seem to have been there on purpose." And in the same whisper, as if we two whenever we talked had to say things to each other which were not fit for the world to hear, he added, "It's very wonderful."

We remained side by side talking in our secret way
—but sometimes silent or just exchanging a whispered
word or two at long intervals. And as usual he stared
through the port. A breath of wind came now and again
into our faces. The ship might have been moored
in dock, so gently and on an even keel she slipped
through the water, that did not murmur even at our passage, shadowy and silent like a phantom sea.

At midnight I went on deck, and to my mate's great
surprise put the ship round on the other tack. His terrible whiskers flitted round me in silent criticism. I
certainly should not have done it if it had been only a
question of getting out of that sleepy gulf as quickly as
possible. I believe he told the second mate, who relieved
him, that it was a great want of judgment. The other
only yawned. That intolerable cub shuffled about so
sleepily and lolled against the rails in such a slack, improper fashion that I came down on him sharply.

"Aren't you properly awake yet?"

"Yes, sir! I am awake."

"Well, then, be good enough to hold yourself as if
you were. And keep a lookout. If there's any current
we'll be closing with some islands before daylight."

The east side of the gulf is fringed with islands, some
solitary, others in groups. On the blue background of
the high coast they seem to float on silvery patches of
calm water, arid and gray, or dark green and rounded
like clumps of evergreen bushes, with the larger ones,
a mile or two long, showing the outlines of ridges, ribs
of gray rock under the dark mantle of matted leafage.
Unknown to trade, to travel, almost to geography, the
manner of life they harbor is an unsolved secret. There
must be villages—settlements of fishermen at least—on
the largest of them, and some communication with the
world is probably kept up by native craft. But all that

forenoon, as we headed for them, fanned along by the faintest of breezes, I saw no sign of man or canoe in the field of the telescope I kept on pointing at the scattered group.

At noon I gave no orders for a change of course, and the mate's whiskers became much concerned and seemed to be offering themselves unduly to my notice. At last I said:

"I am going to stand right in. Quite in—as far as I can take her."

The stare of extreme surprise·imparted an air of ferocity also to his eyes, and he looked truly terrific for a moment.

"We're not doing well in the middle of the gulf," I continued, casually. "I am going to look for the land breezes tonight."

"Bless my soul! Do you mean, sir, in the dark amongst the lot of all them islands and reefs and shoals?"

"Well—if there are any regular land breezes at all on this coast one must get close inshore to find them, mustn't one?"

"Bless my soul!" he exclaimed again under his breath. All that afternoon he wore a dreamy, contemplative appearance which in him was a mark of perplexity. After dinner I went into my stateroom as if I meant to take some rest. There we two bent our dark heads over a half-unrolled chart lying on my bed.

"There," I said. "It's got to be Koh-ring. I've been looking at it ever since sunrise. It has got two hills and a low point. It must be inhabited. And on the coast opposite there is what looks like the mouth of a biggish river—with some town, no doubt, not far up. It's the best chance for you that I can see."

"Anything. Koh-ring let it be."

He looked thoughtfully at the chart as if surveying

chances and distances from a lofty height—and following with his eyes his own figure wandering on the blank land of Cochin-China, and then passing off that piece of paper clean out of sight into uncharted regions. And it was as if the ship had two captains to plan her course for her. I had been so worried and restless running up and down that I had not had the patience to dress that day. I had remained in my sleeping suit, with straw slippers and a soft floppy hat. The closeness of the heat in the gulf had been most oppressive, and the crew were used to see me wandering in that airy attire.

"She will clear the south point as she heads now," I whispered into his ear. "Goodness only knows when, though, but certainly after dark. I'll edge her in to half a mile, as far as I may be able to judge in the dark—"

"Be careful," he murmured, warningly—and I realized suddenly that all my future, the only future for which I was fit, would perhaps go irretrievably to pieces in any mishap to my first command.

I could not stop a moment longer in the room. I motioned him to get out of sight and made my way on the poop. That unplayful cub had the watch. I walked up and down for a while thinking things out, then beckoned him over.

"Send a couple of hands to open the two quarter-deck ports," I said, mildly.

He actually had the impudence, or else so forgot himself in his wonder at such an incomprehensible order, as to repeat:

"Open the quarter-deck ports! What for, sir?"

"The only reason you need concern yourself about is because I tell you to do so. Have them open wide and fastened properly."

He reddened and went off, but I believe made some jeering remark to the carpenter as to the sensible practice of ventilating a ship's quarter-deck. I know he popped into the mate's cabin to impart the fact to him because the whiskers came on deck, as it were by chance, and stole glances at me from below—for signs of lunacy or drunkenness, I suppose.

A little before supper, feeling more restless than ever, I rejoined, for a moment, my second self. And to find him sitting so quietly was surprising, like something against nature, inhuman.

I developed my plan in a hurried whisper.

"I shall stand in as close as I dare and then put her round. I shall presently find means to smuggle you out of here into the sail locker, which communicates with the lobby. But there is an opening, a sort of square for hauling the sails out, which gives straight on the quarter-deck and which is never closed in fine weather, so as to give air to the sails. When the ship's way is deadened in stays and all the hands are aft at the main braces you shall have a clear road to slip out and get overboard through the open quarter-deck port. I've had them both fastened up. Use a rope's end to lower yourself into the water so as to avoid a splash—you know. It could be heard and cause some beastly complication."

He kept silent for a while, then whispered, "I understand."

"I won't be there to see you go," I began with an effort. "The rest . . . I only hope I have understood, too."

"You have. From first to last," and for the first time there seemed to be a faltering, something strained in his whisper. He caught hold of my arm, but the ringing of the supper bell made me start. He didn't, though; he only released his grip.

After supper I didn't come below again till well past eight o'clock. The faint, steady breeze was loaded with dew; and the wet, darkened sails held all there was of propelling power in it. The night, clear and starry, sparkled darkly, and the opaque, lightless patches shifting slowly against the low stars were the drifting islets. On the port bow there was a big one more distant and shadowily imposing by the great space of sky it eclipsed.

On opening the door I had a back view of my very own self looking at a chart. He had come out of the recess and was standing near the table.

"Quite dark enough," I whispered.

He stepped back and leaned against my bed with a level, quiet glance. I sat on the couch. We had nothing to say to each other. Over our heads the officer of the watch moved here and there. Then I heard him move quickly. I knew what that meant. He was making for the companion; and presently his voice was outside my door.

"We are drawing in pretty fast, sir. Land looks rather close."

"Very well," I answered. "I am coming on deck directly."

I waited till he was gone out of the cuddy, then rose. My double moved too. The time had come to exchange our last whispers, for neither of us was ever to hear each other's natural voice.

"Look here!" I opened a drawer and took out three sovereigns. "Take this, anyhow. I've got six and I'd give you the lot, only I must keep a little money to buy some fruit and vegetables for the crew from native boats as we go through Sunda Straits."

He shook his head.

"Take it," I urged him, whispering desperately. "No one can tell what—"

He smiled and slapped meaningly the only pocket of the sleeping jacket. It was not safe, certainly. But I produced a large old silk handkerchief of mine, and tying the three pieces of gold in a corner, pressed it on him. He was touched, I suppose, because he took it at last and tied it quickly round his waist under the jacket, on his bare skin.

Our eyes met; several seconds elapsed, till, our glances still mingled, I extended my hand and turned the lamp out. Then I passed through the cuddy, leaving the door of my room wide open. . . . "Steward!"

He was still lingering in the pantry in the greatness of his zeal, giving a rub-up to a plated cruet stand the last thing before going to bed. Being careful not to wake up the mate, whose room was opposite, I spoke in an undertone.

He looked round anxiously. "Sir!"

"Can you get me a little hot water from the galley?"

"I am afraid, sir, the galley fire's been out for some time now."

"Go and see."

He fled up the stairs.

"Now," I whispered, loudly, into the saloon—too loudly, perhaps, but I was afraid I couldn't make a sound. He was by my side in an instant—the double captain slipped past the stairs—through the tiny dark passage . . . a sliding door. We were in the sail locker, scrambling on our knees over the sails. A sudden thought struck me. I saw myself wandering barefooted, bareheaded, the sun beating on my dark poll. I snatched off my floppy hat and tried hurriedly in the dark to ram it on my other self. He dodged and fended off silently. I wonder what he thought had come to me before he understood and suddenly desisted. Our hands met gropingly, lingered united in a steady, motionless clasp for a second. . . . No word was breathed by either of us when they separated.

I was standing quietly by the pantry door when the
steward returned.

"Sorry, sir. Kettle barely warm. Shall I light the spirit
lamp?"

"Never mind."

I came out on deck slowly. It was now a matter of
conscience to shave the land as close as possible—for
now he must go overboard whenever the ship was put
in stays. Must! There could be no going back for him.
After a moment I walked over to leeward and my heart
flew into my mouth at the nearness of the land on the
bow. Under any other circumstances I would not have
held on a minute longer. The second mate had followed
me anxiously.

I looked on till I felt I could command my voice.

"She will weather," I said then in a quiet tone.

"Are you going to try that, sir?" he stammered out
incredulously.

I took no notice of him and raised my tone just enough
to be heard by the helmsman.

"Keep her good full."

"Good full, sir."

The wind fanned my cheek, the sails slept, the world
was silent. The strain of watching the dark loom of the
land grow bigger and denser was too much for me. I had
shut my eyes—because the ship must go closer. She
must! The stillness was intolerable. Were we standing
still?

When I opened my eyes the second view started my
heart with a thump. The black southern hill of Koh ring
seemed to hang right over the ship like a towering fragment of the everlasting night. On that enormous mass of
blackness there was not a gleam to be seen, not a sound
to be heard. It was gliding irresistibly toward us and yet
seemed already within reach of the hand. I saw the

vague figures of the watch grouped in the waist, gazing in awed silence.

"Are you going on, sir?" inquired an unsteady voice at my elbow.

I ignored it. I had to go on.

"Keep her full. Don't check her way. That won't do now," I said warningly.

"I can't see the sails very well," the helmsman answered me, in strange, quavering tones.

Was she close enough? Already she was, I won't say in the shadow of the land, but in the very blackness of it, already swallowed up as it were, gone too close to be recalled, gone from me altogether.

"Give the mate a call," I said to the young man who stood at my elbow as still as death. "And turn all hands up."

My tone had a borrowed loudness reverberated from the height of the land. Several voices cried out together: "We are all on deck, sir."

Then stillness again, with the great shadow gliding closer, towering higher, without a light, without a sound. Such a hush had fallen on the ship that she might have been a bark of the dead floating in slowly under the very gate of Erebus.

"My God! Where are we?"

It was the mate moaning at my elbow. He was thunderstruck, and as it were deprived of the moral support of his whiskers. He clapped his hands and absolutely cried out, "Lost!"

"Be quiet," I said sternly.

He lowered his tone, but I saw the shadowy gesture of his despair. "What are we doing here?"

"Looking for the land wind."

He made as if to tear his hair, and addressed me recklessly.

"She will never get out. You have done it, sir. I knew it'd end in something like this. She will never weather, and you are too close now to stay. She'll drift ashore before she's round. O my God!"

I caught his arm as he was raising it to batter his poor devoted head, and shook it violently.

"She's ashore already," he wailed, trying to tear himself away.

"Is she? . . . Keep good full there!"

"Good full, sir," cried the helmsman in a frightened, thin, childlike voice.

I hadn't let go the mate's arm and went on shaking it. "Ready about, do you hear? You go forward"—shake—"and stop there"—shake—"and hold your noise"—shake—"and see these head sheets properly overhauled"—shake, shake—shake.

And all the time I dared not look toward the land lest my heart should fail me. I released my grip at last and he ran forward as if fleeing for dear life.

I wondered what my double there in the sail locker thought of this commotion. He was able to hear everything—and perhaps he was able to understand why, on my conscience, it had to be thus close—no less. My first order "Hard alee!" re-echoed ominously under the towering shadow of Koh-ring as if I had shouted in a mountain gorge. And then I watched the land intently. In that smooth water and light wind it was impossible to feel the ship coming-to. No! I could not feel her. And my second self was making now ready to slip out and lower himself overboard. Perhaps he was gone already . . . ?

The great black mass brooding over our very mastheads began to pivot away from the ship's side silently. And now I forgot the secret stranger ready to depart, and remembered only that I was a total stranger to the ship. I did not know her. Would she do it? How was she to be handled?

I swung the mainyard and waited helplessly. She was perhaps stopped, and her very fate hung in the balance, with the black mass of Koh-ring like the gate of the everlasting night towering over her taffrail. What would she do now? Had she way on her yet? I stepped to the side swiftly, and on the shadowy water I could see nothing except a faint phosphorescent flash revealing the glassy smoothness of the sleeping surface. It was impossible to tell—and I had not learned yet the feel of my ship. Was she moving? What I needed was something easily seen, a piece of paper, which I could throw overboard and watch. I had nothing on me. To run down for it I didn't dare. There was no time. All at once my strained, yearning stare distinguished a white object floating within a yard of the ship's side. White on the black water. A phosphorescent flash passed under it. What was that thing? . . . I recognized my own floppy hat. It must have fallen off his head . . . and he didn't bother. Now I had what I wanted—the saving mark for my eyes. But I hardly thought of my other self, now gone from the ship, to be hidden forever from all friendly faces, to be a fugitive and a vagabond on the earth, with no brand of the curse on his sane forehead to stay a slaying hand . . . too proud to explain.

And I watched the hat—the expression of my sudden pity for his mere flesh. It had been meant to save his homeless head from the dangers of the sun. And now—behold—it was saving the ship, by serving me for a mark to help out the ignorance of my strangeness. Ha! It was drifting forward, warning me just in time that the ship had gathered sternway.

"Shift the helm," I said in a low voice to the seaman standing still like a statue.

The man's eyes glistened wildly in the binnacle light as he jumped round to the other side and spun round the wheel.

I walked to the break of the poop. On the overshadowed deck all hands stood by the forebraces waiting for my order. The stars ahead seemed to be gliding from right to left. And all was so still in the world that I heard the quiet remark "She's round," passed in a tone of intense relief between two seamen.

"Let go and haul."

The foreyards ran round with a great noise, amidst cheery cries. And now the frightful whiskers made themselves heard giving various orders. Already the ship was drawing ahead. And I was alone with her. Nothing! no one in the world should stand now between us, throwing a shadow on the way of silent knowledge and mute affection, the perfect communion of a seaman with his first command.

Walking to the taffrail, I was in time to make out, on the very edge of a darkness thrown by a towering black mass like the very gateway of Erebus—yes, I was in time to catch an evanescent glimpse of my white hat left behind to mark the spot where the secret sharer of my cabin and of my thoughts, as though he were my second self, had lowered himself into the water to take his punishment: a free man, a proud swimmer striking out for a new destiny.

# On Life and Letters

THE CONDITION OF ART

THE CONDITION OF LIFE

LETTERS

Conrad's genius was imaginative and dramatic, but it was also moral in impulse and philosophical in direction, like that of all great narrative artists, and his books are rich in passages of commentary. He had, also, from the beginning, a strong sense of the exactions of the art he practiced. If he had literary masters, they were the men of the nineteenth century—Flaubert, Turgenev, Henry James—who had imposed a new discipline on the art of the novel, making of it a finer instrument of expression and sensibility, seeking to bring to it the "quality of mind" which James required as the ultimate test of literature. Conrad formulated the laws of his craft early in his career in the "Preface" which he published at the end of *The Nigger of the "Narcissus"* when Henley serialized it in *The New Review,* August-December 1897. This "Preface," defining the "condition of art" as Conrad conceived it, was after 1914 printed as a foreword to all subsequent editions of that novel, and it is printed here at the head of a small section of passages from Conrad's books which give, in concise form, the literary ideals he envisaged and the standards of craftsmanship and intention he practiced.

"The condition of life" is a no less insistent theme of his books, appearing continuously in the observations and marginal comments that accompany his narratives, and that find more explicit, if less spontaneous or assured, expression in the essays collected in *Notes on Life and Letters* (1921) and the posthumous *Last Essays* (1926). A brief selection of such passages is given here (none repeating passages which will be found in the stories included in this volume). It is only in the passages on literature and life included in this section (and occasionally in the letters that follow) that

Conrad's texts in the present book are printed in partial form. Conrad himself on one occasion approved the excerpting of illustrative passages from his work when he permitted his friend, Miss M. Harriet M. Capes, to compile her book of selections called *Wisdom and Beauty from Conrad,* and this has encouraged the present editor to make his own selection of passages which may constitute at least a partial self-portrait of Conrad's mind and sensibility.

Conrad was a voluminous letter-writer, and his letters form the most intimate and revealing personal document he ever wrote, exceeding *The Mirror of the Sea* and *A Personal Record* in their revelation of his personality and labors. When G. Jean-Aubry compiled his *Life and Letters* of Conrad (1927), he made a choice from over 2000 letters at his disposal, and further collections have been made from the letters Conrad wrote—in Polish, French, and English—to such correspondents as Richard Curle, Edward Garnett, his French friends, and his "aunt" in Brussels (actually the wife of his maternal grandmother's first cousin), Mme. Marguerite Poradowska. Still others await publication. The following short selection has been made from the letters included in M. Jean-Aubry's *Life and Letters* (New York: Doubleday, Doran and Co., 1927), with the exception of three short passages from *Letters of Joseph Conrad to Marguerite Poradowska,* as translated from the French and edited by John A. Gee and Paul J. Sturm (New Haven: Yale University Press, 1940), included here by kind permission of the Yale University Press. This important volume contains the best evidence on Conrad's life between 1890 and 1895, when he was making a hazardous transition from his maritime career to a career in authorship.

His other correspondents in the letters printed here are among the friends of his lifetime: Edward Noble, whose efforts at authorship Conrad encouraged in the nineties; Edward Garnett, editor and critic, who in 1895, as reader for T. Fisher Unwin, brought about the publication of *Almayer's Folly;* R. B. Cunninghame Graham, the Scottish writer, one of Conrad's first and staunchest literary friends; John Galsworthy, whom Conrad first met in 1893 as a passenger on his ship, the *Torrens;* Edward Lancelot Sanderson, another passenger on that voyage, later headmaster at Elstree school, who became a lifelong friend; Edmund Gosse, who in 1905 was instrumental, with William Rothenstein, in securing for Conrad a Civil List pension; Henry James, the American novelist, who in 1908 sent Conrad the first six volumes of the Collected Edition of his works; Barrett H. Clark, the American critic of drama; George T. Keating, the American collector of Conrad, whose great collection is now housed at Yale University; and Richard Curle, whose book on Conrad in 1914 was the first extended study of his work and who in 1923 wrote an article in the London *Times Literary Supplement* on J. M. Dent and Sons' Uniform Edition of Conrad's works.

Some elisions, indicated by running periods, have been made in the letters as printed here, and their texts follow the authorized editions. The complete texts will be found in the collections edited by G. Jean-Aubry and Messrs. Gee and Sturm.

# The Condition of Art

A WORK that aspires, however humbly, to the condition of art should carry its justification in every line. And art itself may be defined as a single-minded attempt to render the highest kind of justice to the visible universe, by bringing to light the truth, manifold and one, underlying its every aspect. It is an attempt to find in its forms, in its colors, in its light, in its shadows, in the aspects of matter and in the facts of life, what of each is fundamental, what is enduring and essential— their one illuminating and convincing quality—the very truth of their existence. The artist, then, like the thinker or the scientist, seeks the truth and makes his appeal. Impressed by the aspect of the world the thinker plunges into ideas, the scientist into facts—whence, presently, emerging they make their appeal to those qualities of our being that fit us best for the hazardous enterprise of living. They speak authoritatively to our common sense, to our intelligence, to our desire of peace or to our desire of unrest; not seldom to our prejudices, sometimes to our fears, often to our egoism—but always to our credulity. And their words are heard with reverence, for their concern is with weighty matters: with the cultivation of our minds and the proper care of our bodies, with the attainment of our ambitions, with the perfection of the means and the glorification of our precious aims.

It is otherwise with the artist.

Confronted by the same enigmatical spectacle the artist descends within himself, and in that lonely region of stress and strife, if he be deserving and fortunate, he finds the terms of his appeal. His appeal is made to our less obvious capacities: to that part of our nature which, because of the warlike conditions of existence, is necessarily kept out of sight within the more resisting and hard qualities—like the vulnerable body within a steel armor. His appeal is less loud, more profound, less distinct, more stirring—and sooner forgotten. Yet its effect endures forever. The changing wisdom of successive generations discards ideas, questions facts, demolishes theories. But the artist appeals to that part of our being which is not dependent on wisdom: to that in us which is a gift and not an acquisition—and, therefore, more permanently enduring. He speaks to our capacity for delight and wonder, to the sense of mystery surrounding our lives; to our sense of pity, and beauty, and pain; to the latent feeling of fellowship with all creation—to the subtle but invincible conviction of solidarity that knits together the loneliness of innumerable hearts, to the solidarity in dreams, in joy, in sorrow, in aspirations, in illusions, in hope, in fear, which binds men to each other, which binds together all humanity—the dead to the living and the living to the unborn.

It is only some such train of thought, or rather of feeling, that can in a measure explain the aim of the attempt, made in the tale which follows, to present an unrestful episode in the obscure lives of a few individuals out of all the disregarded multitude of the bewildered, the simple, and the voiceless. For, if any part of truth dwells in the belief confessed above, it becomes evident that there is not a place of splendor or a dark corner of the earth that does not deserve if only a passing glance of wonder and pity. The motive, then, may be held to justify the matter of the work; but this preface, which is simply an avowal of endeavor, cannot end here—for the avowal is not yet complete.

Fiction—if it at all aspires to be art—appeals to temperament. And in truth it must be, like painting, like music, like all art, the appeal of one temperament to all the other innumerable temperaments whose subtle and resistless power endows passing events with their true meaning, and creates the moral, the emotional atmosphere of the place and time. Such an appeal, to be effective, must be an impression conveyed through the senses; and, in fact, it cannot be made in any other way, because temperament, whether individual or collective, is not amenable to persuasion. All art, therefore, appeals primarily to the senses, and the artistic aim when expressing itself in written words must also make its appeal through the senses, if its high desire is to reach the secret spring of responsive emotions. It must strenuously aspire to the plasticity of sculpture, to the color of painting, and to the magic suggestiveness of music— which is the art of arts. And it is only through complete, unswerving devotion to the perfect blending of form and substance; it is only through an unremitting, never-discouraged care for the shape and ring of sentences that an approach can be made to plasticity, to color, and that the light of magic suggestiveness may be brought to play for an evanescent instant over the commonplace surface of words: of the old, old words, worn thin, defaced by ages of careless usage.

The sincere endeavor to accomplish that creative task, to go as far on that road as his strength will carry him, to go undeterred by faltering, weariness, or reproach, is the only valid justification for the worker in prose. And if his conscience is clear, his answer to those who in the fullness of a wisdom which looks for immediate profit, demand specifically to be edified, consoled, amused; who demand to be promptly improved, or encouraged, or frightened, or shocked, or charmed, must run thus:—My task which I am trying to achieve is, by the power of the written word, to make you hear, to make you feel—it is, before all, to make you *see*. That—and no more, and it is everything. If I succeed, you shall find there, according to your deserts, encouragement, consolation, fear, charm, all you demand—and, perhaps, also that glimpse of truth for which you have forgotten to ask.

To snatch, in a moment of courage, from the remorseless rush of time a passing phase of life, is only the beginning of the task. The task approached in tenderness and faith is to hold up unquestioningly, without choice and without fear, the rescued fragment before all eyes in the light of a sincere mood. It is to show its vibration, its color, its form; and through its movement, its form, and its color, reveal the substance of its truth—disclose its inspiring secret: the stress and passion within the core of each convincing moment. In a single-minded attempt of that kind, if one be deserving and fortunate, one may perchance attain to such clearness of sincerity that at last the presented vision of regret or pity, of terror or mirth, shall awaken in the hearts of the beholders that feeling of unavoidable solidarity; of the solidarity in mysterious origin, in toil, in joy, in hope, in uncertain fate, which binds men to each other and all mankind to the visible world.

It is evident that he who, rightly or wrongly, holds by the convictions expressed above cannot be faithful to any one of the temporary formulas of his craft. The enduring part of them—the truth which each only imperfectly veils—should abide with him as the most precious of his possessions, but they all—Realism, Romanticism, Naturalism, even the unofficial Sentimentalism (which, like the poor, is exceedingly difficult to get rid of)—all these gods must, after a short period of fellowship, abandon him—even on the very threshold of the temple—to the stammerings of his conscience and to the outspoken consciousness of the difficulties of his work. In that uneasy solitude the supreme cry of Art for Art itself loses the exciting ring of its apparent immorality. It sounds far off. It has ceased to be a cry, and is heard only as a whisper, often incomprehensible, but at times and faintly encouraging.

Sometimes, stretched at ease in the shade of a roadside tree, we watch the motions of a laborer in a distant field, and after a time, begin to wonder languidly as to what the fellow may be at. We watch the movements of his body, the waving of his arms; we see him bend down, stand up, hesitate, begin again. It may add to the charm of an idle hour to be told the purpose of his exertions. If we know he is trying to lift a stone, to dig a ditch, to uproot a stump, we look with a more real interest at his efforts; we are disposed to condone the jar of his agitation upon the restfulness of the landscape; and even, if in a brotherly frame of mind, we may bring ourselves to forgive his failure. We understand his object, and, after all, the fellow has tried, and perhaps he had not the strength—and perhaps he had not the knowledge. We forgive, go on our way—and forget.

And so it is with the workman of art. Art is long and life is short, and success is very far off. And thus, doubtful of strength to travel so far, we talk a little about the aim—the aim of art, which, like life itself, is inspiring, difficult—obscured by mists. It is not in the clear logic of a triumphant conclusion; it is not in the unveiling of one of those heartless secrets which are called the Laws of Nature. It is not less great, but only more difficult.

To arrest, for the space of a breath, the hands busy about the work of the earth, and compel men entranced by the sight of distant goals to glance for a moment at the surrounding vision of form and color, of sunshine and shadows; to make them pause for a look, for a sigh, for a smile—such is the aim, difficult and evanescent, and reserved only for a very few to achieve. But sometimes, by the deserving and the fortunate, even that task is accomplished. And when it is accomplished—behold! —all the truth of life is there: a moment of vision, a sigh, a smile—and the return to an eternal rest.

—Preface to *The Nigger of the "Narcissus"*

A reviewer observed that I liked to write of men who go to sea or live on lonely islands untrammeled by the pressure of worldly circumstances because such characters allowed freer play to my imagination, which in their case was only bounded by natural laws and the universal human conventions. There is a certain truth in this remark, no doubt. It is only the suggestion of deliberate choice that misses its mark. I have not sought for special imaginative freedom or a larger play of fancy in my choice of characters and subjects. The nature of the knowledge, suggestions, or hints used in my imaginative work has depended directly on the conditions of my active life. It depended more on contacts, and very slight contacts at that, than on actual experience; because my life as a matter of fact is far from being adventurous in itself. Even now when I look back on it with a certain regret (who would not regret his youth?) and positive affection, its coloring wears the sober hue of hard work and exacting calls of duty; things which in themselves are not much charged with a feeling of romance. If these things appeal strongly to me even in retrospect, it is, I suppose, because the romantic feeling of reality was in me an inborn faculty. This in itself may be a curse, but, when disciplined by a sense of personal responsibility and a recognition of the hard facts of existence shared with the rest of mankind, becomes but a point of view from which the very shadows of life appear endowed with an internal glow. And such romanticism is not a sin. It is none the worse for the knowledge of truth. It only tries to make the best of it, hard as it may be; and in this hardness discovers a certain aspect of beauty.

I am speaking here of romanticism in relation to life, not of romanticism in relation to imaginative literature, which, in its early days, was associated simply with medieval subjects, or, at any rate, with subjects sought for in a remote past. My subjects are not medieval, and I have a natural right to them because my past is very much my own. If their course lie out of the beaten path of organized social life, it is, perhaps, because I myself did in a sort break away from it early in obedience to an impulse which must have been very genuine since it has sustained me through all the dangers of disillusion. But that origin of my literary work was very far from giving a larger scope to my imagination. On the contrary, the mere fact of dealing with matters outside the general run of everyday experience laid me under the obligation of a more scrupulous fidelity to the truth of my own sensations. The problem was to make unfamiliar things credible. To do that I had to create for them, to reproduce for them, to envelop them in their proper atmosphere of actuality. This was the hardest task of all and the most important, in view of that conscientious rendering of truth in thought and fact which has always been my aim.

—*Author's Note to Within the Tides*

As in political, so in literary action, a man wins friends for himself mostly by the passion of his prejudices and by the consistent narrowness of his outlook. But I have never been able to love what was not lovable or hate what was not hateful out of deference for some general principle. Whether there be any courage in making this admission, I know not. After the middle turn of life's way we consider dangers and joys with a tranquil mind. So I proceed in peace to declare that I have always suspected, in the effort to bring into play the extremities of emotions, the debasing touch of insincerity. In order to move others deeply we must deliberately allow ourselves to be carried away beyond the bounds of our normal sensibility—innocently enough, perhaps, and of necessity, like an actor who raises his voice on the stage above the pitch of natural conversation—but still we have to do that. And surely this is no great sin. But the danger lies in the writer becoming the victim of his own exaggeration, losing the exact notion of sincerity, and in the end coming to despise truth itself as something too cold, too blunt for his purpose—as, in fact, not good enough for his insistent emotion. From laughter and tears the descent is easy to snivelling and giggles.

—*A Personal Record*

The ethical view of the universe involves us at last in so many cruel and absurd contradictions, where the last vestiges of faith, hope, charity, and even of reason

itself, seem ready to perish, that I have come to suspect
that the aim of creation cannot be ethical at all. I would
fondly believe that its object is purely spectacular; a
spectacle for awe, love, adoration, or hate, if you like,
but in this view—and in this view alone—never for
despair! Those visions, delicious or poignant, are a moral
end in themselves. The rest is our affair—the laughter,
the tears, the tenderness, the indignation, the high
tranquillity of a steeled heart, the detached curiosity
of a subtle mind—that's our affair! And the unwearied
self-forgetful attention to every phase of the living universe reflected in our consciousness may be our appointed task on this earth—a task in which fate has
perhaps engaged nothing of us except our conscience,
gifted with a voice in order to bear true testimony to
the visible wonder, the haunting terror, the infinite passion, and the illimitable serenity; to the supreme law
and the abiding mystery of the sublime spectacle.

—*A Personal Record*


   It has been said a long time ago that books have
their fate. They have, and it is very much like the
destiny of man. They share with us the great incertitude of ignominy or glory—of severe justice and senseless persecution—of calumny and misunderstanding—
the shame of undeserved success. Of all the inanimate
objects, of all men's creations, books are the nearest to
us, for they contain our very thought, our ambitions,
our indignations, our illusions, our fidelity to truth, and
our persistent leaning towards error. But most of all
they resemble us in their precarious hold on life. . . .
No secret of eternal life for our books can be found
amongst the formulas of art, any more than for our
bodies in a prescribed combination of drugs. This is not

because some books are not worthy of enduring life, but because the formulas of art are dependent on things variable, unstable, and untrustworthy; on human sympathies, on prejudices, on likes and dislikes, on the sense of virtue and the sense of propriety, on beliefs and theories that, indestructible in themselves, always change their form—often in the lifetime of one fleeting generation.

—"Books," *Notes on Life and Letters*

Of all books, novels, which the Muses should love, make a serious claim on our compassion. The art of the novelist is simple. At the same time it is the most elusive of all creative arts, the most liable to be obscured by the scruples of its servants and votaries, the one pre-eminently destined to bring trouble to the mind and the heart of the artist. After all, the creation of a world is not a small undertaking except perhaps to the divinely gifted. In truth every novelist must begin by creating for himself a world, great or little, in which he can honestly believe. This world cannot be made otherwise than in his own image: it is fated to remain individual and a little mysterious, and yet it must resemble something already familiar to the experience, the thoughts and the sensations of his readers.

—"Books," *Notes on Life and Letters*

The good artist should expect no recognition of his toil and no admiration of his genius, because his toil can with difficulty be appraised and his genius cannot possibly mean anything to the illiterate who, even from the dreadful wisdom of their evoked dead, have, so far, culled nothing but inanities and platitudes. I would

wish him to enlarge his sympathies by patient and loving observation while he grows in mental power. It is in
the impartial practice of life, if anywhere, that the
promise of perfection for his art can be found, rather
than in the absurd formulas trying to prescribe this or
that particular method of technique or conception. Let
him mature the strength of his imagination amongst the
things of this earth, which it is his business to cherish
and know, and refrain from calling down his inspiration
ready-made from some heaven of perfections of which
he knows nothing. And I would not grudge him the
proud illusion that will come sometimes to a writer: the
illusion that his achievement has almost equaled the
greatness of his dream.

> —"Books," *Notes on Life and Letters*

Neither his fellows, nor his gods, nor his passions
will leave a man alone. In virtue of these allies and
enemies, he holds his precarious dominion, he possesses
his fleeting significance; and it is this relation in all its
manifestations, great and little, superficial and profound, and this relation alone, that is commented upon,
interpreted, demonstrated by the art of the novelist in
the only possible way in which the task can be performed: by the independent creation of circumstance
and character, achieved against all the difficulties of
expression, in an imaginative effort finding its inspiration from the reality of forms and sensations. That a
sacrifice must be made, that something has to be given
up, is the truth engraved in the innermost recesses of
the fair temple built for our edification by the masters
of fiction. There is no other secret behind the curtain.
All adventure, all love, every success is resumed in the
supreme energy of an act of renunciation. It is the

uttermost limit of our power; it is the most potent and effective force at our disposal on which rest the labors of a solitary man in his study, the rock on which have been built commonwealths whose might casts a dwarfing shadow upon two oceans. Like a natural force which is obscured as much as illuminated by the multiplicity of phenomena, the power of renunciation is obscured by the mass of weaknesses, vacillations, secondary motives and false steps and compromises which make up the sum of our activity. But no man or woman worthy of the name can pretend to anything more, to anything greater.

—"Henry James," *Notes on Life and Letters*

# The Condition of Life

### THE SHADOW LINE

ONLY the young have such moments. I don't mean the very young. No. The very young have, properly speaking, no moments. It is the privilege of early youth to live in advance of its days in all the beautiful continuity of hope which knows no pauses and no introspection.

One closes behind one the little gate of mere boyishness—and enters an enchanted garden. Its very shades glow with promise. Every turn of the path has its seduction. And it isn't because it is an undiscovered country. One knows well enough that all mankind had streamed that way. It is the charm of universal experience from which one expects an uncommon or personal sensation—a bit of one's own.

One goes on recognizing the landmarks of the predecessors, excited, amused, taking the hard luck and the good luck together—the kicks and the halfpence, as the saying is—the picturesque common lot that holds so many possibilities for the deserving or perhaps for the lucky. Yes. One goes on. And the time, too, goes on—till one perceives ahead a shadow line warning one that the region of early youth, too, must be left behind.

This is the period of life in which such moments of

which I have spoken are likely to come. What moments?
Why, the moments of boredom, of weariness, of dis-
satisfaction. Rash moments. I mean moments when the
still young are inclined to commit rash actions, such as
getting married suddenly or else throwing up a job for
no reason.

*—The Shadow Line*


### THE DESTRUCTIVE ELEMENT

STEIN TO MARLOW:

He lifted up a long forefinger.

"There is only one remedy! One thing alone can us
from being ourselves cure!" The finger came down on
the desk with a smart rap. The case which he had made
to look so simple before became if possible still simpler
—and altogether hopeless. There was a pause. "Yes,"
said I, "strictly speaking, the question is not how to
get cured, but how to live."

He approved with his head, a little sadly as it seemed.
"*Ja! ja!* In general, adapting the words of your great
poet: That is the question. . . ." He went on nodding
sympathetically. . . . "How to be! *Ach!* How to be!"

He stood up with the tips of his fingers resting on the
desk. "We want in so many different ways to be," he
began again. "This magnificent butterfly finds a little
heap of dirt and sits still on it; but man he will never
on his heap of mud keep still. He want to be so, and
again he want to be so. . . ." He moved his hand up,
then down. . . . "He wants to be a saint, and he wants
to be a devil—and every time he shuts his eyes he sees
himself as a very fine fellow—so fine as he can never be.
. . . In a dream. . . ." ". . . And because you not always can keep your eyes shut there comes the real
trouble—the heart pain—the world pain. I tell you, my

friend, it is not good for you to find you cannot make your dream come true, for the reason that you not strong enough are, or not clever enough. *Ja!* . . . And all the time you are such a fine fellow, too! *Wie? Was? Gott in Himmel!* How can that be? Ha! ha! ha!"

The shadow prowling amongst the graves of butter-flies laughed boisterously.

"Yes! Very funny this terrible thing is. A man that is born falls into a dream like a man who falls into the sea. If he tries to climb out into the air as inexperienced people endeavor to do, he drowns—*nicht wahr?* . . . No! I tell you! The way is to the destructive element submit yourself, and with the exertions of your hands and feet in the water make the deep, deep sea keep you up. So if you ask me—how to be?"

His voice leaped up extraordinarily strong, as though away there in the dusk he had been inspired by some whisper of knowledge. "I will tell you! For that, too, there is only one way."

With a hasty swish-swish of his slippers he loomed up in the ring of faint light, and suddenly appeared in the bright circle of the lamp. His extended hand aimed at my breast like a pistol; his deep-set eyes seemed to pierce through me, but his twitching lips uttered no word, and the austere exaltation of a certitude seen in the dusk vanished from his face. The hand that had been pointing at my breast fell, and by and by, coming a step nearer, he laid it gently on my shoulder. There were things, he said mournfully, that perhaps could never be told, only he had lived so much alone that sometimes he forgot—he forgot. The light had destroyed the assurance which had inspired him in the distant shadows. He sat down and, with both elbows on the desk, rubbed his forehead. "And yet it is true—it is true. In the destructive element immerse." . . .

He spoke in a subdued tone, without looking at me, one hand on each side of his face. "That was the way. To follow the dream, and again to follow the dream—and so—*ewig—usque ad finem.* . . ." The whisper of his conviction seemed to open before me a vast and uncertain expanse, as of a crepuscular horizon on a plain at dawn—or was it, perchance, at the coming of the night? One had not the courage to decide. . . .

—Lord Jim

A man's real life is that accorded to him in the thoughts of other men by reason of respect or natural love.

—*Under Western Eyes*

Men, I mean really masculine men, those whose generations have evolved an ideal woman, are often very timid. Who wouldn't be before the ideal? It's your sentimental trifler who has just missed being nothing at all, who is enterprising, simply because it is easy to appear enterprising when one does not mean to put one's belief to the test.

—Chance

The dead can live only with the exact intensity and quality of the life imparted to them by the living.

—*Under Western Eyes*

No man succeeds in everything he undertakes. In that sense we are all failures. The great point is not to fail in ordering and sustaining the effort of our life. In this matter vanity is what leads us astray. It hurries us into situations from which we must come out damaged; whereas pride is our safeguard, by the reserve it im-

poses on the choice of our endeavor as much as by the
virtue of its sustaining power.

—"The Duel" in *A Set of Six*

Are not our lives too short for that full utterance
which through all our stammerings is, of course, our
only and abiding intention? I have given up expecting
those last words whose ring, if they could only be pronounced, would shake both heaven and earth. There is
never time to say our last word—the last word of our
love, of our desire, faith, remorse, submission, revolt.

—*Lord Jim*

There are none so ignorant as not to know suffering,
none so simple as not to feel and suffer from the shock
of warring impulses. The ignorant must feel and suffer
from their complexity as well as the wisest; but to them
the pain of struggle and defeat appears strange, mysterious, remediable and unjust.

—*An Outcast of the Islands*

A man who has had his way is seldom happy, for
generally he finds that the way does not lead very far
on this earth of desires which can never be fully satisfied.

—*Chance*

One aspect of conventions which people who declaim
against them lose sight of is that conventions make both
joy and suffering easier to bear in a becoming manner.

—*Chance*

It is respectable to have no illusions—and safe—and
profitable—and dull. Yet you too in your time must
have known the intensity of life, that light of glamour

created in the shock of trifles, as amazing as the glow of sparks struck from a cold stone—and as short-lived, alas!

—*Lord Jim*

Action is consolatory. It is the enemy of thought and the friend of flattering illusions. Only in the conduct of our action can we find the sense of mastery over the Fates.

—*Nostromo*

To be busy with material affairs is the best preservative against reflection, fears, doubts—all these things which stand in the way of achievement. I suppose a fellow proposing to cut his throat would experience a sort of relief while occupied in stropping his razor carefully.

—*Chance*

Nothing more awful to watch than a man who has been found out, not in a crime but in a more than criminal weakness. The commonest sort of fortitude prevents us from becoming criminals in a legal sense; it is from weakness unknown, but perhaps suspected, as in some parts of the world you suspect a deadly snake in every bush—from weakness that may lie hidden, watched or unwatched, prayed against or manfully scorned, repressed or maybe ignored more than half a lifetime, not one of us is safe. We are snared into doing things for which we get called names, and things for which we get hanged, and yet the spirit may well survive—survive the condemnation, survive the halter, by Jove! And there are things—they look small enough sometimes too—by which some of us are totally and completely undone.

—*Lord Jim*

We live at the mercy of a malevolent word. A sound, a mere disturbance of the air, sinks into our very soul sometimes.

—Chance

And a word carries far—very far—deals destruction through time as the bullets go flying through space.

—Lord Jim

It can't be denied that our wits are much more alert when engaged in wrong-doing (in which one mustn't be found out) than in a righteous occupation.

—Chance

Being a woman is a terribly difficult trade, since it consists principally of dealings with men.

—Chance

There is hardly a woman in the world, no matter how hard, depraved or frantic, in whom something of the maternal instinct does not survive, unconsumed like a salamander, in the fires of the most abandoned passion.

—Chance

In every, even terrestrial, mystery there is as it were a sacred core. A sustained commentary on love is not fit for every eye. A universal experience is exactly the sort of thing which is most difficult to appraise justly in a particular instance.

—The Arrow of Gold

A woman may be a fool, a sleepy fool, an agitated fool, a too awfully noxious fool, and she may even be simply stupid. But she is never dense. She's never made of wood through and through as some men are. There is in woman always, somewhere, a spring. Whatever men don't know about women (and it may be a lot, or it may be very little), men and even fathers do know that much. And that is why so many men are afraid of them.

—*Chance*

"It's always so difficult to know what to do for the best," Fyne assured me. It is. Good intentions stand in their own way so much. Whereas if you want to do harm to any one you needn't hesitate. You have only to go on. No one will reproach you with your mistakes or call you a confounded, clumsy meddler.

—*Chance*

Razumov stood on the point of conversion. He was fascinated by its approach, by its overpowering logic. For a train of thought is never false. The falsehood lies deep in the necessities of existence, in secret fears and half-formed ambitions, in the secret confidence combined with a secret mistrust of ourselves, in the love of hope and the dread of uncertain days.

—*Under Western Eyes*

Razumov longed desperately for a word of advice, for moral support. Who knows what true loneliness is —not the conventional word, but the naked terror? To the lonely themselves it wears a mask. The most miserable outcast hugs some memory or some illusion. Now and then a fatal conjunction of events may lift the veil for an instant. For an instant only. No human being could bear a steady view of moral solitude without going mad.

—*Under Western Eyes*

Razumov: "Betray. A great word. What is betrayed? They talk of a man betraying his country, his friends, his sweetheart. There must be a moral bond first. All a man can betray is his conscience. And how is my conscience engaged here; by what bond of common faith, of common conviction, am I obliged to let that fanatical idiot drag me down with him? On the contrary—every obligation of true courage is the other way."

—*Under Western Eyes*

Of Mrs. Travers: After a time this absolute silence which she almost could feel pressing upon her on all sides induced a state of hallucination. She saw herself standing alone, at the end of time, on the brink of days. All was unmoving as if the dawn would never come, the stars would never fade, the sun would never rise any more; all was mute, still, dead—as if the shadow of the outer darkness, the shadow of the uninterrupted, of the everlasting night that fills the universe, the shadow of the night so profound and so vast that the blazing suns lost in it are only like sparks, like pinpoints of fire, the restless shadow that like a suspicion of an evil truth darkens everything upon the earth on its passage, had enveloped her, had stood arrested as if to remain with her forever.

And there was such a finality in that illusion, such an accord with the trend of her thought, that when she murmured into the darkness a faint "so be it" she seemed to have spoken one of those sentences that resume and close a tale.

As a young girl, often reproved for her romantic ideas, she had dreams where the sincerity of a great passion appeared like the ideal fulfillment and the only truth of life. Entering the world she discovered that ideal to be unattainable because the world is too prudent to be sincere. Then she hoped that she could find the truth of life in ambition which she understood as a life-long devotion to some unselfish idea. Mr. Travers' name was on men's lips; he seemed capable of enthusiasm and of devotion; he impressed her imagination by his impenetrability. She married him, found him enthusiastically devoted to the nursing of his own career, and had nothing to hope for now.

—*The Rescue*

Solitude from mere outward condition of existence becomes very swiftly a state of soul in which the affectations of irony and skepticism have no place. It takes possession of the mind, and drives forth the thought into the exile of utter unbelief.

—*Nostromo*

Of Mrs. Gould: It had come into her mind that for life to be large and full, it must contain the care of the past and of the future in every passing moment of the present.

—*Nostromo*

Forty-five is the age of recklessness for many men, as if in defiance of the decay and death waiting with open arms in the sinister valley at the bottom of the inevitable hill. For every age is fed on illusions, lest men should renounce life early and the human race come to an end.

—*Victory*

We all seem a little mad to each other; an excellent arrangement for the bulk of humanity which finds in it an easy motive of forgiveness.

—*Chance*

The wisdom of the heart, having no concern with the erection or demolition of theories any more than with the defense of prejudices, has no random words at its command. The words it pronounces have the value of acts of integrity, tolerance, and compassion. A woman's true tenderness, like the true virility of man, is expressed in action of a conquering kind.

—Nostromo

A transgression, a crime, entering a man's existence, eats it up like a malignant growth, consumes it like a fever.

—Nostromo

It is when we try to grapple with another man's infinite need that we perceive how incomprehensible, wavering, and misty are the beings that share with us the sight of the stars and the warmth of the sun. It is as if loneliness were a hard and absolute condition of existence; the envelop of flesh and blood on which our eyes are fixed melts before the outstretched hand, and there remains only the capricious, unconsolable, and elusive spirit that no eye can follow, no hand can grasp.

—Lord Jim

Love, though in a sense it may be admitted to be stronger than death, is by no means so universal and so sure. In fact, love is rare—the love of men, of things, of ideas, the love of perfected skill. For love is the enemy of haste; it takes count of passing days, of men who pass away, of a fine art matured slowly in the course of years and doomed in a short time to pass away too, and be no more. Love and regret go hand in hand in this world of changes swifter than the shifting of the clouds reflected in the mirror of the sea.

*—The Mirror of the Sea*

"Ah, Davidson, woe to the man whose heart has not learned while young to hope, to love—and to put its trust in life!"

*—Victory*

OF SINGLETON: He steered with care.

*—The Nigger of the "Narcissus"*

# Letters

TO MME. MARGUERITE PORADOWSKA, BRUSSELS

[Barr, Moering & Co., Dyer's Hall Wharf,
95 Upper Thames Street, London, E.C.]
26 Aug., [189]1.

MY DEAREST AUNT,

Thanks for your kind letter, which I received the day before yesterday.

My health is not exactly radiant, but on the whole I don't feel badly, despite an occasional touch of fever. I am writing to you here in the vast (and dusty) solitude of this warehouse, as I have a free moment about the middle of the day. In the evening, back home again, I feel so lazy that I look upon pens with horror; and as for the inkwell, I have banished it from my room long since.

After all, I am not so happy to be working as you seem to think. There is nothing very exhilarating in doing disagreeable work. It is too much like penal servitude, with the difference that while rolling the stone of Sisyphus you lack the consolation of thinking of what pleasure you had in committing the crime. It is here that convicts have the advantage over your humble servant. . . .

Thursday. London. 17 Gillingham St., S. W.
[29 March or 5 April (?), 1894].

MY DEAREST AUNT,

Forgive me for not having written sooner, but I am
in the midst of struggling with Chap. XI [of *Almayer's
Folly*]; a struggle to the death, you know! If I let up,
I am lost! I am writing you just before going out. I must
go out sometimes, alas! I begrudge each minute I spend
away from paper. I do not say "from pen" because I
write very little, but inspiration comes to me in looking
at the paper. Then there are soaring flights; my thought
goes wandering through vast spaces filled with shadowy
forms. All is yet chaos, but, slowly, the apparitions
change into living flesh, the shimmering mists take
shape, and—who knows?—something may be born of
the clash of nebulous ideas.

I send you the first page (of which I have made a
copy) to give you an idea of the appearance of my manuscript. I owe you this since I have seen yours. I like, so
I do, to conform to the rules of etiquette.

I embrace you heartily. Ever yours. . . .

[London, 20 July (?), 1894].
Friday.

MY DEAR, GOOD AUNT,

I received your letter this morning. As you wrote me
you were leaving Paris for some time, I refrained from
writing until further word came.

So you are in a period of "dark gloom"! I well understand this regret for the past as it slips away little by

little, leaving traces of its passage in tombs and regrets. It is only this that is eternal.

Remember, though, that one is never entirely alone. Why are you afraid? And of what? Is it of solitude or of death? O strange fear! The only two things that make life bearable! But cast fear aside. Solitude never comes —and death must often be waited for during long years of bitterness and anger. Do you prefer that?

But you are afraid of yourself; of the inseparable being forever at your side—master and slave, victim and executioner—who suffers and causes suffering. That's how it is! One must drag the ball and chain of one's selfhood to the end. It is the [price] one pays for the devilish and divine privilege of thought; so that in this life it is only the elect who are convicts—a glorious band which comprehends and groans but which treads the earth amidst a multitude of phantoms with maniacal gestures, with idiotic grimaces. Which would you be: idiot or convict?

I embrace you with all my heart.

TO EDWARD NOBLE

17, Gillingham Street, S. W. [London]
28 Oct. '95

MY DEAR NOBLE,

I received your discouraged letter this morning and can assure you I felt very sorry for your disappointment ending the long-drawn hope. . . .

You have any amount of stuff in you, but you (I think) have not found your way yet. Remember that death is not the most pathetic,—the most poignant thing,—and you must treat events only as illustrative of human sensation,—as the outward sign of inward feelings,—of live feelings,—which alone are truly pathetic and interesting. You have much imagination: much more than I ever will have if I live to be a hundred years old. That much is clear to me. Well, that imagination (I wish I had it) should be used to create human souls: to disclose human hearts,—and not to create events that are properly speaking *accidents* only. To accomplish it you must cultivate your poetic faculty,—you must give yourself every sensation, every thought, every image,—mercilessly, without reserve and without remorse: you must search the darkest corners of your heart, the most remote recesses of your brain,—you must search them for the image, for the glamour, for the right expression. And you must do it sincerely, at any cost: you must do it so that at the end of your day's work you should feel exhausted, emptied of every sensation and every thought, with a blank mind and an aching heart, with the notion that there is nothing,—nothing left in you. To me it seems that it is the only way to achieve true distinction—even to go some way towards it.

It took me 3 years to finish the *Folly*. There was not a day I did not think of it. Not a day. And after all I consider it honestly a miserable failure. Every critic (but two or three) overrated the book. It took me a year to tear the *Outcast* out of myself and upon my word of honour,—I look on it (now it's finished) with bitter disappointment. Judge from that whether my opinion is worth having. I may be on the wrong tack altogether. I say what I think and from a sincere desire to see you succeed,—but I may be hopelessly astray in my opinions . . .

Monday [London]
[March 23, 1896.]

DEAR GARNETT,

I am very glad you wrote to me the few lines I have just received. If you spoke as a friend I listened in the same manner,—listened and was only a little, a very little, dismayed. If one looks at life in its true aspect then everything loses much of its unpleasant importance and the atmosphere becomes cleared of what are only unimportant mists that drift past in imposing shapes. When once the truth is grasped that one's own personality is only a ridiculous and aimless masquerade of something hopelessly unknown, the attainment of serenity is not very far off. Then there remains nothing but the surrender to one's impulses, the fidelity to passing emotions which is perhaps a nearer approach to truth than any other philosophy of life. And why not? If we are "ever becoming—never being," then I would be a fool if I tried to become this thing rather than that; for I know I never will be anything. I would rather grasp the solid satisfaction of my wrong-headedness and shake my fist at the idiotic mystery of Heaven . . .

10 P.M. 14 Jan. '98.
Stanford-le-Hope,
Essex.

CHER AMI:

. . . . . Nothing would be more delightful to me than to read a review of the *Nigger* by you. I never dreamed you would care to do this thing! I do not know who, when and how it is to be reviewed. But is the *N.* worthy of your pen and especially of your thought? Is it too late? Do you really mean it? There will be a vol. of short stories appearing in March. One of them "The Outpost." Now if you are really anxious to give me a good slating . . .

"Put the tongue out," why not? One ought to really. And the machine will run on all the same. The question is whether the fatigue of the muscular exertion is worth the transient pleasure of indulged scorn. On the other hand one may ask whether scorn, love, or hate are justified in the face of such shadowy illusions.

The machine is thinner than air and as evanescent as a flash of lightning. The attitude of cold unconcern is the only reasonable one. Of course reason is hateful,— but why? Because it demonstrates (to those who have the courage) that we, living, are out of life,—utterly out of it. The mysteries of a universe made of drops of fire and clods of mud do not concern us in the least. The fate of a humanity condemned ultimately to perish from cold is not worth troubling about. If you take it to heart it becomes, an unendurable tragedy. If you believe in improvement you must weep, for the attained perfection must end. in cold, darkness and silence. In a dispassionate view the ardour for reform, improvement, for virtue, for knowledge and even for beauty is only a vain sticking up for appearances, as though one were anxious about the cut of one's clothes in a community of blind men.

Life knows us not and we do not know life,—we don't know even our own thoughts. Half the words we use have no meaning whatever and of the other half each man understands each word after the fashion of his own folly and conceit. Faith is a myth and beliefs shift like mists on the shore: thoughts vanish: words, once pronounced, die: and the memory of yesterday is as shadowy as the hope of tomorrow,—only the string of my platitude seems to have no end. As our peasants say: "Pray, brother, forgive me for the love of God." And we don't know what forgiveness is, nor what is love, nor where God is. *Assez!* . . .

TO JOHN GALSWORTHY

Pent Farm.
Sunday evening [Feb. 11, 1899].

Dearest Jack,

Yes, it is good criticism. Only I think that to say Henry James does not write from the heart is maybe hasty. He is cosmopolitan, civilized, very much *homme du monde* and the acquired (educated if you like) side of his temperament,—that is,—restraints, the instinctive, the nurtured, fostered, cherished side is always presented to the reader first. To me even the R. T. [*The Real Thing*] seems to flow from the heart because and only because the work, approaching so near perfection, yet does not strike cold. Technical perfection, unless there is some real glow to illumine and warm it from within, must necessarily be cold. I argue that in H. J. there is such a glow and not a dim one either, but to us used, absolutely accustomed, to unartistic expression of fine, headlong, honest (or dishonest) sentiments the art of H. J. does appear heartless. The outlines are so clear, the figures so finished, chiselled, carved and brought out that we exclaim,—we, used to the shades of the contemporary fiction, to the more or less malformed shades, —we exclaim,—stone! Not at all. I say flesh and blood, —very perfectly presented,—perhaps with too much perfection of *method*.

The volume of short stories entitled, I think, *The Les-*

*son of the Master* contains a tale called "The Pupil," if I remember rightly, where the underlying feeling of the man,—his really wide sympathy,—is seen nearer the surface. Of course he does not deal in primitive emotions. I maintain he is the most civilized of modern writers. He is also an idealizer. His heart shows itself in the delicacy of his handling. Things like "The Middle Years" and "The Altar of the Dead" in the vol. entitled *Terminations* would illustrate my meaning. Moreover, your cousin admits the element of pathos. Mere technique won't give the elements of pathos. I admit he is not *forcible,*—or let us say, the only forcible thing in his work is his technique. Now a literary intelligence would be naturally struck by the wonderful technique, and that is so wonderful in its way that it dominates the bare expression. The more so that the expression is only of delicate shades. He is never in deep gloom or in violent sunshine. But he feels deeply and vividly every delicate shade. We cannot ask for more. Not everyone is a Turgeniev. Moreover Turgeniev is not civilized (therein much of his charm for us) in the sense H. J. is civilized. *Satis.* Please convey my defence of the *Master* with my compliments. My kindest and grateful regards to Mrs. Sauter and love to the boy. The finishing of "H. of D" took a lot out of me. I haven't been able to do much since.

TO E. L. SANDERSON

Pent Farm.
12 Oct. '99.

My Dear Ted,

Were you to come with a horsewhip you would be still welcome. It's the only kind of visit I can imagine myself as deserving from you. Only the other day Jessie asked me whether I had written to you and over- whelmed me with reproaches. Why wait another day? But I am incorrigible; I will always look to another day to bring something good, something one would like to share with a friend,—something,—if only a fortunate thought. But the days bring nothing at all,—and thus they go by empty-handed,—till the last day of all.

I am always looking forward to some date, to some event, when I finish this: before I begin that other thing, —and there never seems to be any breathing time, not because I do much but because the toil is great. I try at times to persuade myself that it is my honesty that makes the burden so heavy, but, alas! the suspicion will force itself upon one that, may be, it is only lack of strength, of power, of an uplifting belief in oneself. Whatever the cause, the struggle is hard, and this may be no more than justice.

I haven't been in town since last March, I haven't been to see you, I have not gone to visit other people. My dear Ted, you have much to forgive me: but try to imagine yourself trying your hardest to save the School from downfall, annihilation, and disaster: and the thing going on and on endlessly. That's exactly how I am situ- ated: and the worst is that the menace (in my case) does not seem to come from outside but from within: that the menace and danger or weakness are in me, in myself alone. I fear I have not the capacity and the power to go on,—to satisfy the just expectations of those who are dependent on my exertions. I fear! I fear! And sometimes I hope. But it is the fear that abides.

But even were I wrong in my fear the very fact that such a fear exists would argue that everything is not right,—would in itself be a danger and a menace. So I turn in this vicious circle and the work itself becomes like the work in a treadmill,—a thing without joy,—a punishing task.

You can see now why I am so often remiss in my correspondence. There is nothing one would gladly write under that shadow. This is the sort of thing that one writes, and the more one loves his friends, the more belief one has in their affection, the less one is disposed to cast upon them the gloom of one's intimate thoughts. My silence is seldom selfish and never forgetful. It is often a kind of reserve, *pudor*, something in the nature of instinctive decency. One expects to fall every instant and one would like to fall with a covered face, with a decorous arrangement of draperies, with no more words than greatest men have used. One would! And when one sits down, it is to write eight pages without coming to the end of one's groans.

I am ashamed, bitterly ashamed, to make the same eternal answer, the same eternal wail of incertitude, to your hospitable voice. I am now trying to finish a story which began in the Oct. No. of *Blackwood*. I am at it day after day, and I want all day, every minute of a day, to produce a beggarly tale of words or perhaps to produce nothing at all. And when that is finished (I thought it would be so on the first of this month,—but no fear!) I must go on, even go on at once and drag out of myself another 20,000 words, if the boy is to have his milk and I my beer (this is a figure of speech,—I don't drink beer, I drink weak tea, yearn after dry champagne) and if the world is not absolutely to come to an end. And after I have written and have been paid, I shall have the satisfaction of knowing that I can't allow myself the relaxation of being ill more than three days under the penalty of starvation: nor the luxury of going off the hooks altogether without playing the part of a thief regarding various confiding persons, whose desire to serve me was greater than their wisdom. Do you take me, sir? *Verb: sap:* that is, circumlocution is clear to the wise.

And yet,—one hopes, as I had the honour to remark above.

A book of mine (Joseph Conrad's last) is to come out in March. Three stories in one volume. If only five thousand copies of that *could* be sold! If only! But why dream of the wealth of the Indies? I am not the man for whom Pactolus flows and the mines of Golconda distill priceless jewels (What an absurd style. Don't *you* think I am deteriorating?). Style or no style,—I am not the man. And oh! dear Ted, it is a fool's business to write fiction for a living. It is indeed.

It is strange. The unreality of it seems to enter one's real life, penetrate into the bones, make the very heartbeats pulsate illusions through the arteries. One's will becomes the slave of hallucinations, responds only to shadowy impulses, waits on imagination alone. A strange state, a trying experience, a kind of fiery trial of untruthfulness. And one goes through it with an exaltation as false as all the rest of it. One goes through it,—and there's nothing to show at the end. Nothing! Nothing! Nothing! . . . .

TO JOHN GALSWORTHY

Pent Farm
Friday [ab. 20th July 1900].

DEAREST JACK,
. . . The end of [*Lord Jim*] has been pulled off with a steady drag of 21 hours. I sent wife and child out of the house (to London) and sat down at 9 A.M. with a desperate resolve to be done with it. Now and then I took a walk round the house, out at one door in at the

other. Ten-minute meals. A great hush. Cigarette ends growing into a mound similar to a cairn over a dead hero. Moon rose over the barn, looked in at the window and climbed out of sight. Dawn broke, brightened. I put the lamp out and went on, with the morning breeze blowing the sheets of MS. all over the room. Sun rose. I wrote the last word and went into the dining-room. Six o'clock I shared a piece of cold chicken with Escamillo (who was very miserable and in want of sympathy, having missed the child dreadfully all day). Felt very well, only sleepy: had a bath at seven and at 1.30 was on my way to London . . .

TO (SIR) EDMUND GOSSE

> Villa di Maria
> Capri, Italy.
> 23rd Mch. 1905.

DEAR MR. GOSSE,

I have received to-day a communication from W. Rothenstein, the answer to which is due to you directly and without delay. Acutely conscious of being neither the interpreter in any profound sense of my own epoch nor a magician evoker of the past either in its spirit or its form, I have often suffered in connection with my work from a sense of unreality, from intellectual doubt of the ground I stood upon. This has occurred especially in the periods of difficult production. I had just emerged from such a period of utter mistrust when Rothenstein's letter came to hand revealing to me the whole extent of *your* belief and the length to which you have taken the trouble to go to prove it—even to the length of making another mind share in your conviction. I accept this revelation with eagerness. I need not tell you that this moral support of belief is the greatest help a writer can receive in those difficult moments which Baudelaire has defined happily as *"les stérilités des écrivains nerveux."* Quincey too, I believe, has known that anguished suspension of all power of thought that comes to one often in the midst of a very revel of production, like the slave with his *memento mori* at a feast.

For that kind of support my gratitude is due to you in the first instance. It can, properly speaking, hardly equal the obligation. The material outcome of your active belief, I accept *sans phrases*, which I am sure you do not desire either for yourself or the Prime Minister [Balfour]. I know too that you will be good enough to express the perfect sincerity of my sentiments in the proper quarters with greater tact and juster measure than I, in my inexperience, could command.

The feeling of pride is not perhaps one to entertain in this connection. It is the one however that comes to the surface at the end of this letter. It cannot be but a matter of pride for me that two minds like yours and the Prime Minister's, which it has never entered into the compass of my hopes to reach, have been moved by an acquaintance with my work to a friendly interest in my mere personality.

TO JOHN GALSWORTHY

Someries
6th Jan. of the New Year 1908

DEAREST JACK,

. . . *"Et le misérable écrivait toujours."*

He is writing now a story the title of which is *Razumov*. Isn't it expressive? I think that I am trying to capture the very soul of things Russian,—*Cosas de Russia*. It is not an easy work but it may be rather good when it's done. It may also be worth a hundred pounds if the good Pinker flies round with it actively enough to become crimson. . . . But there's no heart in my jokes.

Listen to the theme. The Student Razumov (a natural son of a Prince K.) gives up secretly to the police his fellow student, Haldin, who seeks refuge in his rooms after committing a political crime (supposed to be the murder of de Plehve). First movement in St. Petersburg. (Haldin is hanged of course.)

2d in Genève. The student Razumov meeting abroad the mother and sister of Haldin falls in love with that last, marries her and, after a time, confesses to her the part he played in the arrest of her brother.

The psychological developments leading to Razumov's betrayal of Haldin, to his confession of the fact to his wife and to the death of these people (brought about mainly by the resemblance of their child to the late Haldin), form the real subject of the story.

And perhaps no magazine will touch it. *Blackwood's,* since the Old Man has retired, do not care much to have my work. I think of trying the *Fortnightly.* Ah! my dear, you don't know what an inspiration-killing anxiety it is to think: "Is it salable?" There's nothing more cruel than to be caught between one's impulse, one's act, and that question, which for me simply is a question of life and death. There are moments when the mere fear sweeps my head clean of every thought. It is agonizing, —no less. And,—you know,—that pressure grows from day to day instead of getting less.

But I had to write it. I had to get away from *Chance,* with which I was making no serious progress.

Otherwise things are not well with me. The *Secret Agent* may be pronounced by now an honourable failure. It brought me neither love nor promise of literary success. I own that I am cast down. I suppose I am a fool to have expected anything else. I suppose there is something in me that is unsympathetic to the general public,—because the novels of Hardy, for instance, are generally tragic enough and gloomily written too,—and yet they have sold in their time and are selling to the present day.

Foreignness, I suppose.

All this is matter for anxious thought. Will the long novel serialize? If it does not! I shouldn't wonder if P[inker] were not anxious about that too. He does not hurry me up, but is very expectant. It must be confessed that the work of the last three months makes a miserable show,—as to the quantity. And I have sat and sat days and days. It is an impossible existence. I am a vegetarian now. I eat very little too on purpose. The head is very clear just now, but there are moments when I think against my will that I must give up. It's fatal for an imaginative man,—this ill-omened suggestion coming like that from outside, as it were. I fight it down,— of course,—while I can . . .

TO ARTHUR SYMONS

Someries
Monday. [Aug., 1908.]

My dear Sir,

Thanks for communicating to me your study of my work—this "rejected address" to the public on behalf of my art. I can be nothing but grateful for the warm, living sincerity of your impression and of your analysis. You may imagine with what curiosity I went on from page to page.

You say things which touch me deeply. Reading certain passages I feel that 14 years of honest work are not gone for nothing. A big slice of life that, which thanks to you I may say, is not altogether lost. There has been in all that time not 10 minutes of amateurishness. That is the truth. For the rest I may say that there are certain passages which have surprised me. I did not know that I had "a heart of darkness" and an "unlawful" soul. Mr. Kur[t]z had, and I have not treated him with the easy nonchalance of an amateur. Believe me, no man paid more for his lines than I have. By that I possess an inalienable right to the use of all my epithets. I did not know that I delighted in cruelty and that the shedding of blood was my obsession.

The fact is that I am really a much simpler person. Death is a fact, and violent death is a fact too. In the simplicity of my heart, I tried to realize these facts when they came in. Do you really think that old Flaubert gloated over the deathbed of Emma, or the death march of Matho, or the last moments of Félicie [Félicité]? And for the other things you say, things splendid and laudatory, particularizing and generalizing your generous appreciation, I will simply say, I don't know. I've never asked myself, or looked into myself or thought of myself. There was no time in these years to turn my head away from the table. There are whole days when I did not know whether the sun shone or not. And, after all, the books are there! Also a sense of disillusioned weariness. You may be sure that the Editor who rejected your article has never known such faithful service nor yet what it costs one. But the writing of novels, as a charming lady who disturbed me cruelly on a certain afternoon said, "is such a delightful occupation."

Delightful or not, I have always approached my task in the spirit of love for mankind. And I've rather taken it seriously, an attitude I should say impossible for the Editor of a serious Review, perhaps of an august Quarterly.

It seems almost indecent to thank you. But I stand

outside and feel grateful to you for the recognition of
the work, not the man. Once the last page is written the
man does not count. He is nowhere.

F. Cooper is a rare artist. He has been one of my
masters. He is my constant companion. That dismal
"bajazzo" with his debased jargon of niggers and "mean"
whites smirches whatever he touches. He's a "mean
white" himself, about the meanest that ever stole the
gift of words from a nodding god.

*Là-dessus une poignée de main bien attendrie.*

TO ARTHUR SYMONS

29 Aug., 1908.

DEAR MR. SYMONS,

I doubt whether I have expressed sufficiently that
sort of special pleasure the recognition of my work by a
man like you was certain to give me. That feeling partaking of shyness and delight is difficult to express. And
the characteristic generosity of the recognition has almost frightened me. Meditating the trouble you have
taken over my pages I feel remorseful also—as though
I had cheated you—not your intelligence; that would
be impossible, but your benevolence and perhaps your
hopes a little—just a little. A reader like you puts so
much of his own high quality into a work he is reading,
directly the writer has been lucky enough to awaken his
sympathy! I am afraid that you have given without
counting, and yet I would be glad to believe that I deserve this profusion; for indeed what you give is em-
inently worth holding.

One thing that I am certain of is that I have approached the object of my task, things human, in a spirit
of piety. The earth is a temple where there is going on a
mystery play, childish and poignant, ridiculous and aw-

ful enough, in all conscience. Once in I've tried to behave decently. I have not degraded any quasi-religious
sentiment by tears and groans; and if I have been
amused or indignant, I've neither grinned nor gnashed
my teeth. In other words, I've tried to write with dignity, not out of regard for myself, but for the sake of the
spectacle, the play with an obscure beginning and an
unfathomable *dénouement*.

I don't think that this has been noticed. It is your
penitent beating the floor with his forehead and the
ecstatic worshipper at the rails that are obvious to the
public eye. The man standing quietly in the shadow of
the pillar, if noticed at all, runs the risk of being suspected of sinister designs. Thus I've been called a heartless wretch, a man without ideals and a *poseur* of brutality. But I will confess to you under seal of secrecy
that *I don't believe* I am such as I appear to mediocre
minds.

But enough. You have, unexpected, like a burglar,
forced the lock of the safe where I keep my stock of
megalomania, so I don't apologize for these worthless
outpourings. It's your fault clearly, but you shall be no
longer punished. As I wrote to a friend lately, I have
been quarrying my English out of a black night, working like a coal miner in his pit. For fourteen years now I
have been living as if in a cave without echoes.—If you
come shouting gloriously at the mouth of the same you
can't really expect from me to pretend I am not there.

I am profoundly touched by your letter, but that I am
sure you understand already . . .

Someries, Luton.
12 Dec., 1908

Très Cher Maître,

They have arrived,—the six of them: I have felt them all in turn and all at one time as it were, and to celebrate the event I have given myself a holiday for the morning, not to read any one of them—I could not settle to that—but to commune with them all, and gloat over the promise of the prefaces. But of these last I have read one already, the preface to *The American*, the first of your long novels I ever read—in '91. This is quite a thrill to be taken thus into your confidence; a strong emotion it is a privilege to be made to feel—*à cinquante ans!* Afterwards I could not resist the temptation of reading the beautiful and touching last ten pages of the story. There is in them a perfection of tone which calmed me, and I sat for a long while with the closed volume in my hand going over the preface in my mind and thinking—that is how it began, that's how it was done!

I thank you for the gift, I thank you before all for the opportunity to breathe in the assurance of your good-will, the fortifying atmosphere of your serene achievement.

Yours most affectionately and gratefully.

Aldington,
23 Dec., 1909.

Dear Douglas,

I don't know what you think of me. You can be no more disgusted than I am. I simply couldn't write to you

—tho' God knows—I wanted to very badly. There is nothing to say. We have barely existed. As for myself, all I can say is that I wonder at it . . .

The novel [*Under Western Eyes*] hangs on the last 12,000 words, but there's neither inspiration nor hope in my work. It's mere hard labour for life—with this difference, that the life convict is at any rate out of harm's way—and may consider the account with his conscience closed; and this is not the case with me. I envy the serene fate and the comparative honesty of the gentlemen in gray who live in Dartmoor. I do really, I am not half as decent or half as useful. Health is better. My wife is as usual. The kids, too. And nothing is any good! It's a horrible feeling and I can't shake it off for more than a day or two at a time.

All the same, don't give me up in your thoughts entirely. In the light of a "tormented spirit" I am not to be altogether despised. What are you doing? Are you ever coming back?

TO BARRETT H. CLARK

Capel House.<br>May 4th, 1918.

DEAR MR. CLARK,

No. I am not continually besieged by the sort of correspondence you have in mind. I will admit that what there is of it is for the most part fatuous and not at all like your communication, which, by its matter and still more by its friendly tone, has given me great pleasure. You must not mind me answering it on a typewriter, as on account of the state of my wrist the handling of the pen just now is a matter of difficulty.

You are right in thinking that I would be gratified by the appreciation of a mind younger than my own. But in truth I don't consider myself an Ancient. My writing life extends but only over twenty-three years, and I need not point out to an intelligence as alert as yours that all that time has been a time of evolution, in which some critics have detected three marked periods—and that the process is still going on. Some critics have found fault with me for not being constantly' myself. But they are wrong. I am always myself. I am a man of formed character. Certain conclusions remain immovably fixed in my mind, but I am no slave to prejudices and formulas, and I shall never be. My attitude to subjects and expressions, the angles of vision, my methods of composition will, within limits, be always changing—not because I am unstable or unprincipled but because I am free. Or perhaps it may be more exact to say, because I am always trying for freedom—within my limits.

Coming now to the subject of your inquiry, I wish at first to put before you a general proposition: that a work of art is very seldom limited to one exclusive meaning and not necessarily tending to a definite conclusion. And this for the reason that the nearer it approaches art, the more it acquires a symbolic character. This statement may surprise you, who may imagine that I am alluding to the Symbolist School of poets or prose writers. Theirs, however, is only a literary proceeding against which I have nothing to say. I am concerned here with something much larger. But no doubt you have meditated on this and kindred questions yourself.

So I will only call your attention to the fact that the symbolic conception of a work of art has this advantage, that it makes a triple appeal covering the whole field of life. All the great creations of literature have been symbolic, and in that way have gained in complexity, in power, in depth and in beauty.

I don't think you will quarrel with me on the ground

of lack of precision; for as to precision of images and analysis my artistic conscience is at rest. I have given there all the truth that is in me; and all that the critics may say can make my honesty neither more nor less. But as to "final effect" my conscience has nothing to do with that. It is the critic's affair to bring to its contemplation his own honesty, his sensibility and intelligence. The matter for his conscience is just his judgment. If his conscience is busy with petty scruples and trammelled by superficial formulas then his judgment will be superficial and petty. But an artist has no right to quarrel with the inspirations, either lofty or base, of another soul.

Of course, your interpretation of *Victory's* final aim, of its artistic secret as it were, is correct; and indeed I must say that I did not wrap it up in very mysterious processes of art. I made my appeal to feelings in as clear a language as I can command; and I don't think there is a critic in England or France who was in any doubt about it. In one or two instances the book was attacked on grounds which I simply cannot understand. Other criticisms struck me by their acuteness in the analysis of method and language. Some readers frankly did not like the book; but not on the ground of irony. And yet irony is not altogether absent from those pages, which, I am glad to think, have not failed to move your feelings and imagination. Pray accept this long screed as a warm acknowledgment of your sympathy with my work. With my best wishes for your success in the life of your choice.

Oswalds.
December 14th, 1922.

My Dear Mr. Keating,

Our warmest and most sincere wishes for health, success, and all that's good for you both and all yours for this festive season and all the years to come. And may they be many!

Thank you for your friendly and interesting letter. How good of you to give me so much of your time and so much of your thought. Your appreciation and your interest in my work are very precious to me. I wish I were a better letter writer, both as to quantity and quality, and then perhaps I could convince you of my gratitude. But when it comes to truth of that sort words fail me as a rule. It's the concoction of artistic lies that is my strong point, as twenty-four volumes of pure fiction testify. However, as you and a few other men I care for seem to like them I will try to continue for a little while longer on my reprehensible course.

Mencken's vigour is astonishing. It is like an electric current. In all he writes there is a crackle of blue sparks like those one sees in a dynamo house amongst revolving masses of metal that give you a sense of enormous hidden power. For that is what he has. Dynamic power. When he takes up a man he snatches him away and fashions him into something that (in my case) he is pleased with—luckily for me, because had I not pleased him he would have torn me limb from limb. Whereas as it is he exalts me almost above the stars. It makes me giddy. But who could quarrel with such generosity, such vibrating sympathy and with a mind so intensely alive? What, however, surprises me is that a personality

so genuine in its sensations, so independent in judgment, should now and then condescend to mere parrot
talk; for his harping on my Slavonism is only that. I
wonder what meaning he attaches to the word? Does he
mean by it primitive natures fashioned by a Byzantine
theological conception of life, with an inclination to
perverted mysticism? Then it cannot possibly apply to
me. Racially I belong to a culture derived at first from
Italy and then from France; and a rather Southern
temperament; an outpost of Westernism with a Roman
tradition, situated between Slavo-Tartar Byzantine barbarism on one side and the German tribes on the other;
resisting both influences desperately and still remaining
true to itself to this very day. I went out into the world
before I was seventeen, to France and England, and in
neither country did I feel myself a stranger for a moment: neither as regards ideas, sentiments, nor institutions. If he means that I have been influenced by so-
called Slavonic literature then he is utterly wrong. I
suppose he means Russian; but as a matter of fact I
never knew Russian. The few novels I have read I have
read in translation. Their mentality and their emotional-
ism have been always repugnant to me, hereditarily and
individually. Apart from Polish my youth has been fed
on French and English literature. While I was a boy in
a great public school we were steeped in classicism to
the lips, and, though our historical studies were naturally tinted with Germanism, I know that all we boys,
the six hundred of us, resisted that influence with all
our might, while accepting the results of German re-
search and thoroughness. And that was only natural. I
am a child, not of a savage but of a chivalrous tradition, and if my mind took a tinge from anything it was
from French romanticism perhaps. It was fed on ideas,
not of revolt but of liberalism of a perfectly disinter-

ested kind, and on severe moral lessons of national misfortune. Of course I broke away early. Excess of individualism perhaps? But that, and other things, I have settled a long time ago with my conscience. I admit I was never an average, able boy. As a matter of fact, I was not able at all. In whatever I have achieved afterwards I have simply followed my instinct: the voice from inside. Mencken might have given me the credit of being just an individual somewhat out of the common, instead of ramming me into a category, which proceeding, anyhow, is an exploded superstition.

This outburst is provoked, of course, by dear Mencken's amazing article about me, so many-sided, so brilliant and so warm-hearted. For that man of a really ruthless mind, pitiless to all shams and common formulas, has a great generosity. My debt of gratitude to him has been growing for years, and I am glad I have lived long enough to read the latest contribution. It's enough to scare anyone into the most self-searching mood. It is difficult to believe that one has deserved all that. So that is how I appear to Mencken! Well, so be it.

What more could anyone expect! . . .

TO MRS. JOSEPH CONRAD

New York. 11 May, 1923

DARLING OWN JESS,

Thank you for your letters, which are arriving regularly. The news of the offer to direct the cooking dept. of a magazine has excited me greatly. I don't see why it should come to nothing if you feel like accepting it. I am sure you would do it very well.

I am writing you on this card because there is nothing else in this flat where we slept last night: and if I waited till we get back to Oyster Bay I would miss tomorrow's packet. And besides, dearest girl, I feel at this moment (10.30 A.M.) perfectly flat, effect of re-action after last evening,—which ended only after mid-night,—at Mrs. Curtiss James's. I may tell you at once that it was a most brilliant affair, and I would have given anything for you to have been there and seen all that crowd and all that splendour, the very top of the basket of the fashionable and literary circles. All last week there was desperate fighting and plotting in the N. York society to get invitations. I had the lucky in-spiration to refuse to accept any payment; and, my dear, I had a perfect success. I gave a talk and pieces of reading out of *Victory*. After the applause from the audience, which stood up when I appeared, had ceased· I had a moment of positive anguish. Then I took out the watch you had given me and laid it on the table, made one mighty effort and began to speak. That watch was the greatest comfort to me. Something of you. I timed myself by it all along. I began at 9.45 and ended ex-actly at 11. There was a most attentive silence, some laughs and at the end, when I read the chapter of Lena's death, audible snuffling. Then handshaking with 200 people. It was a great experience. On Tuesday we start for a tour towards Boston. They are calling me to go and see Vance. I must end. Love to you, best of darlings.

TO RICHARD CURLE

Oswalds.
July 14th, 1923.

MY DEAREST DICK,

I am returning you the article with two corrections as to matters of fact and one of style.

As it stands I can have nothing against it. As to my

feelings that is a different matter; and I think that, looking at the intimate character of our friendship and trusting to the indulgence of your affection, I may disclose them to you without reserve.

My point of view is that this is an opportunity, if not unique then not likely to occur again in my lifetime. I was in hopes that on a general survey it could also be made an opportunity for me to get freed from that infernal tail of ships and that obsession of my sea life, which has about as much bearing on my literary existence, on my quality as a writer, as the enumeration of drawing rooms which Thackeray frequented could have had on his gift as a great novelist. After all, I may have been a seaman, but I am a writer of prose. Indeed, the nature of my writing runs the risk of being obscured by the nature of my material. I admit it is natural; but only the appreciation of a special personal intelligence can counteract the superficial appreciation of the inferior intelligence of the mass of readers and critics. Even Doubleday was considerably disturbed by that characteristic as evidenced in press notices in America, where such headings as "Spinner of sea yarns—master mariner—seaman writer," and so forth, predominated. I must admit that the letter-press had less emphasis than the headings; but that was simply because they didn't know the facts. That the connection of my ships with my writings stands, with my concurrence I admit, recorded in your book is of course a fact. But that was biographical matter, not literary..And where it stands it can do no harm. Undue prominence has been given to it since, and yet you know yourself very well that in the body of my work barely one tenth is what may be called sea stuff, and even of that, the bulk, that is *Nigger* and *Mirror,* has a very special purpose which I emphasize myself in my Prefaces.

Of course there are seamen in a good many of my books. That doesn't make them sea stories any more than the existence of de Barral in *Chance* (and he occupies there as much space as Captain Anthony) makes that novel a story about the financial world. I do wish that all those ships of mine were given a rest, but I am afraid that when the Americans get hold of them they will never, never, never get a rest.

The summarizing of Prefaces, though you do it extremely well, has got this disadvantage, that it doesn't give their atmosphere, and indeed it cannot give their atmosphere, simply because those pages are an intensely personal expression, much more so than all the rest of my writing, with the exception of the *Personal Record*, perhaps. A question of policy arises there; whether it is a good thing to give people the bones, as it were. It may destroy their curiosity for the dish. I am aware, my dear Richard, that while talking over with you the forthcoming article, I used the word historical in connection with my fiction, or with my method, or something of the sort. I expressed myself badly, for I certainly had not in my mind the history of the books. What I was thinking at the time was a phrase in a long article in the *Seccolo*. The critic remarked that there was no difference in method or character between my fiction and my professedly autobiographical matter, as evidenced in the *Personal Record*. He concluded that my fiction was not historical of course but had an authentic quality of development and style which in its ultimate effect resembled historical perspective.

My own impression is that what he really meant was that my manner of telling, perfectly devoid of familiarity as between author and reader, aimed essentially at the intimacy of a personal communication, without any thought for other effects. As a matter of fact, the thought for effects is there all the same (often at the cost of mere directness of narrative), and can be detected in my unconventional grouping and perspective, which are purely temperamental and wherein almost all my "art" consists. This, I suspect, has been the difficulty the critics felt in classifying it as romantic or realistic. Whereas, as a matter of fact, it is fluid, depending on grouping (sequence) which shifts, and on the changing lights giving varied effects of perspective.

It is in those matters gradually, but never completely, mastered that the history of my books really consists. Of course the plastic matter of this grouping and of those lights has its importance, since without it the actuality of that grouping and that lighting could not be made evident, any more than Marconi's electric waves could be made evident without the sending-out and receiving instruments. In other words, without mankind my art, an infinitesimal thing, could not exist . . . .

# Bibliographical Note

REVISED, 1968, BY FREDERICK R. KARL

The works of Joseph Conrad are published in collected editions by J. M. Dent and Company in London and by Doubleday and Company in New York. It is from the editions published and copyrighted by the latter that the texts reproduced in this volume have been drawn.

The chief biographical authorities on Conrad are *Joseph Conrad: A Critical Biography*, by Jocelyn Baines (London: Weidenfeld & Nicolson, New York: McGraw-Hill, 1960); *The Sea Years of Joseph Conrad* (New York: Doubleday, 1965; London: Methuen, 1967) and *The Thunder and the Sunshine* (New York: Putnam's, 1958), both by Jerry Allen; and *Conrad's Polish Background: Letters to and from Polish Friends*, by Zdzisław Najder (London: Oxford University Press, 1964). Of secondary importance are *Joseph Conrad: Life and Letters*, by G. Jean-Aubry (New York: Doubleday, Page & Co., London: Heinemann, 1927, in 2 vols.); also *Vie de Conrad*, by G. Jean-Aubry (Paris: Gallimard, 1947), translated by Helen Sebba as *The Sea Dreamer: A Definitive Biography of Joseph Conrad* (New York: Doubleday & Co., London: Allen & Unwin, 1957), incorporating Jean-Aubry's *Joseph Conrad in the Congo* (London: Bookman's Journal Office, 1926); *The Last Twelve Years of Joseph Conrad*, by Richard Curle (London: Sampson Low, New York: Doubleday, Doran & Co., 1928); and Mrs. Jessie Conrad's two books, *Joseph Conrad as I Knew Him* (London: Heinemann, 1926; New York: Doubleday, Page & Co., 1928) and *Joseph Conrad and His Circle* (London: Jarrold,

758

New York: Dutton, 1935). *Conrad's Prefaces to His Works*, with a long introduction by Edward Garnett (London: Dent & Co., 1937), is also of biographical interest.

Further letters appear in *Joseph Conrad's Letters to His Wife* (London: Bookman's Journal, 1927); in *Conrad to a Friend*, edited by Richard Curle (London: Sampson Low, New York: Doubleday, Page & Co., 1928); in *Letters from Joseph Conrad: 1895-1924*, edited by Edward Garnett (London: Nonesuch Press, Indianapolis: Bobbs-Merrill, 1928); in Conrad's *Lettres françaises*, edited by G. Jean-Aubry (Paris: Gallimard, 1929); in *Letters of Joseph Conrad to Marguerite Poradowska*, translated and edited by John A. Gee and Paul J. Sturm (New Haven: Yale University Press, 1940; London: Oxford University Press, 1941); and in *Joseph Conrad: Letters to William Blackwood and David S. Meldrum*, edited by William Blackburn (Durham, N.C.: Duke University Press, 1958; London: Cambridge University Press, 1959). In the early 1970s, the first volumes of the *Collected Letters of Joseph Conrad*, edited by Frederick R. Karl (Stanford University Press), will begin to appear.

An authoritative study of Conrad's first six years of authorship and of the informative influences of his Polish youth and maritime experiences is John Dozier Gordan's *Joseph Conrad: The Making of a Novelist* (Cambridge, Mass.: Harvard University Press, 1940; London: Oxford University Press, 1941). Another study, speculating boldly on the part played in Conrad's thought and art by his Polish origins, is *The Polish Heritage of Joseph Conrad*, by Gustav Morf (London, Sampson Low, 1930; New York: Richard R. Smith, 1931).

BIBLIOGRAPHY. The first comprehensive bibliography of Conrad is *Joseph Conrad at Mid-Century: Editions and Studies 1859-1955* by Kenneth A. Lohf and Eugene P. Sheehy (Minneapolis: University of Minnesota Press, London: Oxford University Press, 1957). Less comprehensive but perhaps of greater practical use is "Criticism of Joseph Conrad: A Selected Checklist," by Maurice Beebe (*Modern*

*Fiction Studies*, I, Feb. 1955, 30-45), brought up to date in *Modern Fiction Studies*, X, Spring 1964, 81-106, by Maurice Beebe.

Two additional guides are *A Conrad Library: A Catalogue of Printed Books, Manuscripts and Autograph Letters* by Thomas James Wise (London: privately printed, 1928) and *A Conrad Memorial Library: The Collection of George T. Keating* (New York: Doubleday, Doran, 1929), to which many additions have been made in *The Library Gazette* of Yale University, where the Keating collection is now installed.

For a checklist of Polish items, see *Joseph Conrad: Centennial Essays,* edited by Ludwick Krzyzanowski (New York: The Polish Institute of Arts and Sciences in America, 1960).

For current scholarship, see the annual bibliography in PMLA.

SELECTED CRITICISM. The following list, chiefly of books on Conrad, is selective. It does not aim to cover all the studies that have appeared in periodicals or books on fiction. Titles listed in the original edition are included.

Bancroft, W. W. *Joseph Conrad: His Philosophy of Life* (Boston: Stratford Co., 1933).

Beach, Joseph Warren. "Impressionism: Conrad," *The Twentieth Century Novel: Studies in Technique* (New York and London: Appleton Century Crofts, 1932).

Bradbrook, M. C. *Joseph Conrad: Poland's English Genius* (London: Cambridge University Press, New York: Macmillan, 1941).

Crankshaw, Edward. *Joseph Conrad: Some Aspects of the Art of the Novel* (London: John Lane, The Bodley Head, 1936).

Curle, Richard. *Joseph Conrad: A Study* (London: Kegan Paul, New York: Doubleday, Page & Co., 1914).

Fleishman, Avrom. *Conrad's Politics: Community and Anarchy in the Fiction of Joseph Conrad* (Baltimore: Johns Hopkins Press, 1967).

Ford, Ford Madox (Hueffer). *Joseph Conrad: A Personal*

*Remembrance* (London: Duckworth, Boston: Little, Brown & Co., 1924); *Return to Yesterday* (London: Gollancz, 1931; Phila.: Lippincott, 1932); *Portraits from Life* (Boston: Houghton Mifflin Co., 1937; London: George Allen & Unwin, Ltd., 1938 [British title: *Mightier Than the Sword*]).

Gillon, Adam. *The Eternal Solitary: A Study of Joseph Conrad* (New York: Bookman Associates, 1960).

Guerard, Albert, Jr. *Conrad the Novelist* (Cambridge, Mass.: Harvard University Press, London: Oxford University Press, 1958).

Haugh, Robert. *Joseph Conrad: Discovery in Design* (Norman, Okla.: University of Oklahoma Press, 1957).

Hay, Eloise Knapp. *The Political Novels of Joseph Conrad* (Chicago and London: University of Chicago Press, 1963).

Hewitt, Douglas. *Conrad: A Reassessment.* (Cambridge, Eng.: Bowes & Bowes, 1952).

Howe, Irving. "Conrad: Order and Anarchy," *Politics and the Novel* (New York: Horizon, 1957; London: Mayflower, 1958).

James, Henry. "The New Novel," *Notes on Novelists* (London: Dent, New York: Scribner's, 1914).

Karl, Frederick R. *A Reader's Guide to Joseph Conrad* (New York: Noonday, London: Thames & Hudson, 1960).

Leavis, F. R. *The Great Tradition* (London: Chatto & Windus, 1948; New York: Stewart, 1950).

Mégroz, R. L. *Joseph Conrad's Mind and Method* (London: Faber, 1931).

Meyer, Bernard, M. D. *Joseph Conrad: A Psychoanalytic Biography* (Princeton: Princeton University Press, London: Oxford University Press, 1967).

Moser, Thomas. *Conrad: Achievement and Decline* (Cambridge, Mass.: Harvard University Press, London: Oxford University Press, 1957).

Mudrick, Marvin, ed. *Conrad: A Collection of Critical Essays* (Englewood Cliffs, N.J., and London: Prentice-Hall, Inc., 1966).

Said, Edward W. *Joseph Conrad and the Fiction of Auto-biography* (Cambridge, Mass.: Harvard University Press, London: Oxford University Press, 1966).

Sherry, Norman. *Conrad's Eastern World* (London: Cambridge University Press, 1966).

Stallman, R. W., ed. *The Art of Joseph Conrad: A Critical Symposium* (East Lansing, Mich.: Michigan State University Press, London & Sydney: Angus & Robertson, 1960).

Visiak, E. H. *The Mirror of Conrad* (London: W. Laurie, 1955).

Warren, R. P. "Introduction" to *Nostromo* (New York: Random House, 1951).

Wiley, Paul L. *Conrad's Measure of Man* (Madison: University of Wisconsin Press, 1954).

Wright, Walter F. *Romance and Tragedy in Joseph Conrad* (Lincoln: University of Nebraska Press, 1949).

Zabel, Morton Dauwen. "Conrad: Nel Mezzo del Cammin," *The New Republic,* December 23, 1940; "Conrad: The Secret Sharer," *The New Republic,* April 21, 1941; "Conrad in His Age," *The New Republic,* November 16, 1942; "Joseph Conrad: Chance and Recognition," *The Sewanee Review,* January–March, 1945.

———. "Introduction" to *The Nigger of the "Narcissus"* (New York: Harper & Bros., 1950).

———. "Introduction" to *Under Western Eyes* (New York: New Directions, 1951).

———. "Conrad: Chance and Recognition," "The East and the Sea," "The Threat to the West," "Conrad in His Age," in *Craft and Character in Modern Fiction* (New York: The Viking Press, London: Gollancz, 1957).